T. J. GREEN

TOM'S

Young Adult Arthurian Fantasy

ARTHURIAN

LEGACY

BOOKS 1 – 3

Tom's Arthurian Legacy
Published by Mountolive Publishing
Copyright 2018 © TJ Green
ISBN 978-0-473-44955-1

"Or how should England dreaming of *his* sons
Hope more for these than some inheritance
Of such a life, a heart, a mind as thine"

– Alfred, Lord Tennyson (1809–92)

Idylls of the King

For Jason

Invite from the author -

If you'd like to read more about the characters from Tom's Arthurian Legacy, you can get free short stories by subscribing to my newsletter.

By staying on my mailing list you'll receive free excerpts of my new books, as well as new short stories and news of giveaways. I'll also be sharing information about other books in this genre you might enjoy.

To get your FREE short stories please visit my website -
http://tjgreen.nz/
I look forward to you joining my readers' group.

Tom's Arthurian Legacy
Contents

T. J. GREEN

YOUNG ADULT ARTHURIAN FANTASY

TOM'S INHERITANCE

TOM'S ARTHURIAN LEGACY BOOK ONE

Prologue

One evening towards the end of summer, Jack strolled down the path to the bottom of his garden, pushing through the thick vegetation that crowded on either side. The air was thick with pollen and heat, and bees buzzed drunkenly around him. He rested his elbows on the gate and leant his weight against it, feeling his pruning clippers push into his hip. He lit his pipe, narrowing his eyes against the smoke, which he blew around him in an effort to drive off the midges that now appeared in the twilight.

Beyond the gate a stream trickled by, and here the air was cooler. It smelt earthy and damp; he could feel its sharpness on the back of his throat.

Jack's knees and lower back ached. He'd spent too long in the garden and he was too old to cope with it as he used to. He rubbed his cheek and felt the stubble. He could almost feel the grey in it, as if it were coarser than in his youth.

The silence was disturbed only by the stream, and the wind easing through the trees. He breathed deeply, savouring the cool and the smoke. Shadows slanting through the trees cast the banks into deep shadow, so that he could no longer distinguish between the trees, the banks, the rocks or the stream.

He started singing an old folk tune, and as he did, saw something stir at the foot of the gnarled yew tree across the stream. Were his eyes playing tricks on him? It looked as if a figure was moving, as if someone was stirring from a long deep sleep. Maybe what looked like long limbs were in fact tree roots thrown into relief by the shadows, and what looked like a face was a knot in the trunk. But then the figure moved again, and legs and arms became distinct. With a jolt, he realised he was looking into two unblinking eyes, fixed upon him with an unexpected intensity.

Jack's singing faltered and he blinked rapidly, several times. The figure moved its head as if it were a snake, its eyes glittering, before blinking languorously. It rose in one swift movement and became a man. No, not a man, but something that looked like a man; tall and slim with the grace of wind through tall grass, or water over stones. He was dressed in shades of green and a long cloak fell from his shoulders, almost to his feet, shimmering like a low mist.

And Jack knew what it must be, and that all the stories from his childhood were true.

1 The Visitors

A flicker of movement in the wood caught Tom's attention. Normally he would take no notice; people often walked in the wood. But this time something was different. The dark shapes flitting around the trees seemed to be hiding, and for the briefest of seconds he saw a tall figure stepping back between the trees before it vanished.

He stood in his grandfather's kitchen, looking through the broad window that framed the garden, down to the wood beyond. What if this strange activity in the wood was to do with Granddad?

More than a year ago, when Tom was fourteen, his grandfather, Jack, had mysteriously disappeared. He'd walked out of his house one evening and never came back. There was no sign of a struggle, only a note left for the family, explaining that he was going on trip with a new friend and that he would send a "sign" that he was all right.

Impatient after months of waiting, Tom grabbed his jacket and headed into the garden. He jogged down the path, through the gate and across the stream, cursing under his breath as he plunged into an icy pool. He thrust onwards, pushing aside the overhanging branches of a yew before pausing to look around.

The wood was still and silent. Tom edged forward, peering behind tree trunks and up into the bare branches high overhead. A prickle of unease travelled up his spine and he spun around, convinced he was being watched. Frustrated, he yelled, "Who's there? I know someone's there. I saw you!"

The wood remained silent, frozen in watchfulness, and he stepped back nervously, a branch cracking loudly beneath his feet like a gunshot.

Swallowing his fear he shouted again. "I know you can hear me! Come out!"

His prickle of unease grew stronger, and feeling suddenly alone and defenceless, he became sharply aware of the biting cold and his freezing feet. Time to go. Unwilling to turn his back on whatever was out there, he walked slowly backwards, scanning left and right until he reached the stream.

Someone or something was out there; he knew it, but there was nothing more he could do. Reluctantly, he returned to the cottage.

The heating was turned up high, but the kitchen still felt cold. Tom sank into the comfortable overstuffed armchair next to the big stone fireplace and pulled off his boots and socks, placing them on the hearth. He lit the fire, and as the flames caught and raced along the wood, he stood warming himself, absentmindedly running his hands through his dark blond hair. Although the prickle along his spine had gone, the after-effects remained and he felt strangely unsettled, as if his privacy had been invaded.

Tom glanced around the kitchen, reassuring himself with its solid familiarity. A few months ago, he and his father had moved into the cottage, which had stood empty since Granddad's disappearance. A terrible fight between his parents had prompted the move. Dad had walked out, saying he was going to "look after" the cottage. Tom had come with him, while his little sister had stayed with Mum. But the house felt different without Granddad in it, and Tom missed him. Dad was distracted and working long hours, and every now and again there were more arguments between his parents over the phone.

Tom's gaze drifted to one end of the mantelpiece, to a blue stripy bowl filled with old keys, nails and screws. Beneath it was Granddad's last letter. He picked it up and read it again, musing that he had never known Granddad go on a trip – he'd always been here at the cottage, tending his garden and smoking his pipe. But Dad said he used to travel a lot when he was younger. Maybe he'd got bored and wanted a change.

As he stood reading and warming his feet, he heard the front door open and a voice called out, "Hiya, it's me. Where are you?"

"I'm in the kitchen."

The door pushed open and a small slim girl came in, strawberry blond hair swinging behind her. It was his fourteen-year-old cousin, Rebecca, also known as Beansprout on account of her lean and lanky frame. "What you up to?"

"Not much, just looking at Granddad's letter again. What *you* up to?"

She rolled her eyes. "Mum's driving me mad, fussing about food and stuff for Christmas. I'm heading to the shop to pick up some extras and thought I'd drop in." She noticed his wet boots. "Where have you been?"

He paused, wondering how much to say, then grinned. "Hunting!"

She frowned, "Hunting what?"

"Watchers in the woods."

"Have you gone mad? What are you on about?" She moved to the window and looked out. "There's no-one there."

He joined her, still carrying his granddad's letter. "But there was. Someone was over there, watching this house."

She noticed the letter in Tom's hand. "Why are you reading Granddad's letter again? Do you know where he's gone?"

Tom sighed. "No, I've told you before. I have no idea."

"So why are you looking at his letter again?"

"Because I think that whoever's watching, knows something about Granddad."

"That seems a bit of a leap Tom!" she said, looking doubtful. "Did you find anyone?"

"No." He gazed out of the window, desperately hoping he'd see something again. "But I swear someone was there, watching me. I could feel it."

Suddenly excited she said, "Let's go again. Two of us may have more luck."

Tom shook his head. "What's the point? What would we say? 'Have you kidnapped my granddad?' They'd laugh at us."

"But if we find them, we can follow them and see where they go."

"Now who's being mad? We'd be spotted!"

She grabbed the letter off him, "Maybe they're here to leave the sign!"

Beansprout's excitement was catching and he grinned. "Maybe. We might solve the mystery!"

Beansprout leaned against the counter and looked around the kitchen. "It's weird, isn't it? Why would he just leave and not tell us where he was going?"

"OK," he said, "it's too late today, but we'll go out there again tomorrow and have another look. We'll go a bit further, maybe up to the folly, see if we can see anything. If you want to come?"

"Of course I want to come. Anything to get out of Christmas prep," she said with a huff. "I'll bring food too. What time?"

"About nine?" Tom thought the earlier they went, the more time they'd have. Dad would be at work, so no one would worry about where they were.

"Great, I'll be here. Anyway I better get on. Need anything?"

"Nah, I'm good," he said, with a shrug. "See you tomorrow. And don't be late."

2 A Sign

The next morning was bright and clear, and Tom woke early, jolting out of an unsatisfactory night's sleep. Ever since Granddad had disappeared he'd been having strange dreams about a woman with long white hair. She whispered his name to him. "Tom," she called, "it is time." But she never said anything else, and when he tried to answer she would fade away and the dream would evaporate.

Sometimes other images would come. He would see water, and the glint of something shining deep down beneath the shifting waves where he couldn't see it clearly. Sometimes he saw a bright blaze of firelight, and heard a low murmured chanting that became louder and louder until it roared in his ears before receding like a tide. And sometimes when he woke up, it felt like someone had punched him on the birthmark at the top of his arm.

Shrugging off the dreams which he had long since decided to ignore, he lay in bed, looking forward to the day that stretched before him, wondering what it might hold. He had no idea what he might find, or even what to look for, but it would be good to have company. He'd already packed his backpack with spare socks, a jumper and bottles of water, and the sandwiches he'd made the night before were in the fridge.

He jumped out of bed and went to look at an old map on the bedroom wall. It showed the surrounding land as it had been over a hundred years ago. The cottages along the stream, including Granddad's, were marked, but the fields and farmland behind them were now covered in houses. The large woods across the narrow stream remained unchanged and were still surrounded by fields, and just visible at the top edge of the map was the small village of Downtree, also virtually unchanged since the map had been made.

Marked on the map, in the centre of the wood, was the strange, tumbledown stone tower that he and Beansprout would walk to today. Mishap Folly had been built more than a hundred years ago by the owner of the manor house. It was so-called because of the series of unfortunate events that had overtaken the owner: the manor had been damaged by fire, crops had failed, and the owner's son had died after been thrown from a horse. Then the owner himself had disappeared and was never seen again.

The tower had stood empty over the years, beginning to crumble as the woods encroached on all sides.

Tom estimated it would take an hour or so to walk there. It was probably unlikely that Granddad had passed that way, but it had always annoyed Tom that so far, no one had checked it out.

He dragged on his jeans, pulled on a T-shirt and jumper, and ran down the stairs. After putting some bread in the toaster he opened the back door and took a deep breath as the cold crisp air came flooding in. As he stepped outside he noticed an odd-shaped package on the doorstep. How had that got there?

He grabbed the parcel as if it might suddenly disappear, and turned back into the kitchen to examine it. The outer wrapping was a lightweight piece of bark, and as he lifted the edges a gauzy material shimmered beneath it. He unfolded it to find his grandfather's watch and a note. Tom gasped. Who had brought this?

Behind him the toaster popped loudly and in shock he dropped everything onto the table. Cross with himself for being so jumpy, he frowned at the toaster as he pulled the note from under the watch. It was Granddad's writing.

Sorry for the delay, but I've been very busy!

I've sent you my watch as it doesn't really work here, but I wanted you to know that I'm all right.

I probably won't be coming home so I hope someone's looking after the house and garden.

I miss you all, but I know you'll be fine.

Don't try to find me!

Love, Granddad xxx

Tom felt hugely relieved to know Granddad was fine. And then he felt really cross. What did he mean, "Don't try to find me"? How ridiculous. Where on Earth was he?

The letter was written on thick parchment-like paper. He wondered if there was some sort of secret message in it, but after reading the note several times, was sure there wasn't.

He kicked the table in frustration and buttered his now cold toast. Beansprout had better be on time. Whoever had delivered the note might still be around, and Tom intended to find them.

Beansprout was as mystified as Tom. She propped her bulging backpack against the table and examined the package while Tom finished his breakfast.

"Who brings a watch wrapped in bark, Tom? That's just odd. Perhaps he's run out of money and is living off the land, like Robinson Crusoe?"

"And his Man Friday has brought us a present? I doubt it. Besides, he said he doesn't need his watch where he is, so he must be somewhere *else*!"

"Where *else*? That doesn't make sense either."

"*None* of this makes sense Beansprout!"

Beansprout glared at him, but changed the subject. "So are we going to leave your dad a message?"

"What did you tell your mum?"

"Just that we're going out for the day and I'd see her this evening."

"Cool, I'll do the same."

He scribbled a note and left it on the kitchen table, then put the contents of the package in his backpack.

The wood was a tangled mass of bare tree limbs, its floor carpeted in dead leaves. Branches sprang at them, catching their hair and scratching their faces. They slipped and slid on the damp ground, stubbing their toes against roots that lay hidden under layers of slimy leaves.

Spooked by the stillness around them, which seemed to mock their attempts at conversation, they fell silent; the only sound was their ragged breathing and the occasional crack of a twig.

It wasn't until he spotted the roof of the folly through the trees that Tom broke the silence. "I can see it, we're nearly there!"

They emerged into a clearing. The round tower loomed above them, its stone walls cracked and crumbling, its roof jagged. The ground was littered with broken stones. Moss had spread like patchwork, and ivy snaked up the walls until there was barely an inch of grey stone to see.

"Wow!" said Beansprout, "I didn't know it was so big!"

"You check the inside and I'll look round the back," Tom said. "Be careful!" he added as he tripped over a snaking branch of ivy.

"Yeah, yeah," he heard her mutter as she made her way to the entrance. "I'm not a child!"

Tom reached the far side of the tower. He peered around him at the trees, the tower, and the debris on the floor, and all at once felt stupid. What was he thinking? That he could find Granddad, or the person who had brought the package? He huffed, and thumped back against the wall before sliding to the floor, his backpack squashed behind him.

Without a whisper of noise, a tall figure emerged from the wood and walked towards him, stopping a few feet away. It was a young man, just a few years older than Tom, with long dark hair and pale skin. There was something different about him that Tom couldn't quite put his finger on. He wore a loose pale-grey shirt and black cotton trousers tucked into leather boots. A long, thick, grey cloak hung from his shoulders, almost reaching the ground. But what was unnerving was the sword at his side, and the longbow and arrows visible over his shoulder.

For a while they assessed each other, before the man dropped to the ground and sat cross-legged.

"Greetings," he said. "My name is Woodsmoke." His voice was soft and low with a strange accent.

Surprised, Tom said, "Hi."

"And you are?"

After debating whether telling this stranger anything was a good idea, he said, "Tom."

Woodsmoke nodded, as if that was the answer he'd been expecting. "I know your grandfather," he said.

Tom's head shot forward, his mouth open wide. "How? Have you seen him recently? Is he all right?"

Woodsmoke laughed, so gently it sounded like rain on the roof. "So many questions, Tom. You remind me of him. He's fine. He doesn't want you to worry about him. That's why I brought his watch for you."

"It was you? And you were in the wood yesterday! But where is he? I want to see him. So much has happened since he left, he could help – I know he could."

"He's too far away to help, Tom. As he said in his letter, he won't be coming back. Whatever it is, you'll have to manage. You aren't alone, are you?" Woodsmoke looked concerned, as if he'd misunderstood.

"No, I live with my dad. But ..." He shrugged.

Woodsmoke sighed. "I don't know if he could help, Tom."

"Well, I want to see him anyway!"

"I'm sorry, that's not possible. I shouldn't be speaking to you, I should have just gone." Woodsmoke looked cross with himself. "I must go now, I have a long way to travel, and you must go home too. Stop worrying, your grandfather is fine." He rose swiftly to his feet, but as he turned to go, a woman came running around the side of the tower.

"Woodsmoke, quickly – the girl has gone into the tunnel."

"You said you'd sealed it!"

By now Tom was on his feet and looking at both of them. "What girl? Do you mean Beansprout?" But Woodsmoke and the woman were already running back round the tower.

3 Into the Other

Tom hurtled after them, trying not to fall and break his neck, and saw Woodsmoke and the woman disappear into a hole in the ground he was sure hadn't been there before. Looking around the clearing he saw no sign of Beansprout, so he threw himself into the hole after them.

For several seconds he slid and coughed as dust rose in waves around him. Then he stopped with a thump, and looked up to find himself in a tunnel. Woodsmoke was looking at him in exasperation.

"You should not be here!"

"I'm coming with you if Beansprout's down here. She's my cousin; I'm not leaving without her." All thoughts of his grandfather were temporarily forgotten.

Before Woodsmoke could answer, the woman shouted, "Come on!"

Woodsmoke pulled Tom to his feet, saying, "Stay close." He looked above Tom's head, murmuring something under his breath that Tom couldn't understand, then a door slid shut across the opening. Tom experienced a moment of panic as he realised he was trapped, but before he could say anything, Woodsmoke set off after the woman.

Tom followed. The tunnel was narrow and dark, lit by occasional burning torches attached to the wall, their flames giving off an acrid smoke that made Tom's eyes smart. The roof was low and the walls rough, tree roots spearing in from all directions.

Woodsmoke moved ahead with ease, gliding through the gaps. They reached an archway made of smooth, close-fitting stone, across the top of which words were carved in a strange language.

Woodsmoke shouted, "Brenna, wait!"

The woman called back, her voice flattened by the earth above them. "Hurry up!"

On the other side of the arch, the tunnel walls were made of the same smooth grey stone, the ceiling rising higher and higher as the walls moved further apart. The path sloped downwards, deeper and deeper into the earth.

Tom couldn't understand how the woman had got ahead of them so quickly, but as they rounded the corner he saw her standing in the middle of a high domed space. Brenna had the whitest skin he'd ever seen, but her hair, falling long and straight to the base of her back, was so black that it had glints of blue in it. In contrast to her skin, her eyes were dark, the whites barely visible. Like Woodsmoke, she carried a sword at her belt. She looked completely at home in this space. It seemed to fold around her.

The floor was laid with intricately carved stones forming patterns of diamonds, circles, and interlocking squares, while the walls were decorated with patterns of leaves and animals – fierce-looking winged creatures with hooves and fangs. Tom thought he could hear murmurings and rustlings.

Around the edge of the semi-circular cavern were four wide-arched entranceways. Beyond each was a black void; it was as if the floor just dropped away. Beansprout was nowhere in sight.

"Where is she? Did you see where she went?"

Tom was worried by the urgency in Woodsmoke's voice. However, Brenna looked calm.

"She went into the Realm of Water," she replied.

Woodsmoke turned to Tom. "You must wait here; you cannot come with us."

Tom looked around at this strange place so far beneath the earth, and knew he must go too. They didn't know Beansprout – they would need his help to find her. And besides, what if something came out of those arches? What if Woodsmoke and Brenna never came back? He would die down here, entombed.

"No," he said. "I'm coming. You can bring us both back." In those seconds Tom felt the weight of the backpack on his shoulders and tasted the decay in the air around him, and knew he was watched by all those hundreds of eyes in the carvings as they waited with him in the long-abandoned tunnel.

Woodsmoke swore under his breath and then extended one hand to Tom and the other to Brenna. She turned and quickly pulled them into one of the archways.

For several seconds Tom felt completely weightless, and couldn't tell if he was falling or flying, or simply suspended in the dark, a speck in an ocean of blackness. He heard a murmur, like waves lapping a beach, and a whispered "Welcome," then felt a wrenching pull in the centre of his body. All at once there was light and ground beneath his feet. He felt himself cry out as air was forced from his body, and his hands instinctively reached out to protect himself as he pitched forward onto a mixture of hard grey rock and moss.

Taking a deep breath he pushed back onto his haunches and looked around. They were on a broad stone path in the centre of a large horseshoe-shaped curve of rock and water. Granite cliffs stretched high into the air, and waterfalls streamed down from the misty heights into an enormous lake in front of them, frothing and churning where they hit the water. The cliffs were pitted with caves and crevasses, some small, others cathedral-like in their enormity. Ferns grew everywhere, anchored to the rock with clinging roots. A broad stone bridge crossed to the far side of the lake, and beyond that the cliffs extended in a straight line, a deep gorge disappearing into the distance.

And it was hot and humid. Despite the fact that the sun was sinking in a cloudless pale blue sky, the oppressive heat lay across them like a blanket, and sweat was already beading on Tom's brow.

Woodsmoke and Brenna seemed nervous. "It brought us here? To the Eye? Of all the places ..." Woodsmoke whispered.

Brenna's pallor was almost luminous in this light, which made her eyes appear even darker. "Well we must be quick then – and quiet!" she said.

Tom wanted to ask where they were, and what the Eye was, and who had whispered in his head so quietly it was as if he'd imagined it, but Brenna's words stilled his tongue.

They hurried across the bridge. It wasn't until he was halfway across that Tom thought to look below him, into the clear green water, and he stopped, astonished. Beneath the waves was a huge castle with turrets, parapets, courtyards and towers. It was completely intact; it wasn't a ruin that had been swallowed by the lake. Far below he saw lights flashing in the darkness on the floor of the lake, and wondered who lived there. He ran to catch up to Woodsmoke, pulling at his arm. Woodsmoke hissed, "Wait".

The bridge ended with a low parapet, and they gazed over its edge. Water from the lake thundered to the base of the gorge to form a fast-flowing river. He saw a figure down there, much further along on the right.

"Look – out there. Is that Beansprout? Why is she down there?" he asked, bewildered.

"The doorways open onto different spaces, depending on the time you enter," said Brenna. "The closer you are in time when you cross, the closer in distance you will be. That's why we had to come here quickly,"

"We have to get down there. She must be terrified!"

Brenna looked at Woodsmoke. "I'll go first, I can wait with her. We'll walk back this way." Then, in front of Tom's eyes, she turned into a big black bird and plunged over the parapet, heading towards Beansprout.

Astonished, Tom turned to Woodsmoke. "What is this place? Where am I?"

"You're in the Eye, which is the centre of The Realm of Water. It can be dangerous, so we need to leave. Stay quiet."

Woodsmoke led the way down a wide stone ramp that dropped to the floor of the gorge. The cliffs either side were so high that Tom felt the size of an ant. It seemed to take forever to cross a small distance, as if they were crawling. It didn't help that he kept slowing down to look around him. He wanted to see everything, to imprint it on his mind forever.

On the far side of the gorge was an identical ramp; the gorge was in symmetry. He wondered who had designed it all. It was peaceful and beautiful.

"We haven't got all day, Tom. Hurry up." Woodsmoke's strides were long and fluid, and Tom almost had to jog to keep up with him.

"Is this where you live?"

"No, I live in the Realm of Earth, which is where your granddad is." Woodsmoke kept his voice low and Tom struggled to hear him.

"Is that close? Are we going there next?"

"No. You are going home next. And keep close to the cliff side; we'll be less visible there."

Tom decided to ignore the "going home" warning and asked, "Why is it sometimes dangerous here?"

"The water spirits who live here are not always friendly, and there are other things lurking in the rocks and the water that are even more frightening. It is not good that it's so late in the day." He looked thoughtfully at Tom and asked, "Why is it that a girl would go into a tunnel she doesn't know, and then enter an archway that is black and appears to lead nowhere? Is she stupid?"

It was a good question. Tom wasn't sure how to answer, but he thought he should defend Beansprout because he was actually pleased to be here.

"She's quite inquisitive," was all he could think of.

"Really?"

Tom thought he detected sarcasm. "I suppose she thought she was helping. She probably thought our grandfather was living in the tunnel beneath the folly."

"Really?" Woodsmoke said again.

"Well, *I* would have thought so if I'd seen the tunnel; I'd have done the same thing. Anyway, it's your fault. You left the tunnel open."

Woodsmoke's eyes narrowed as he stared at Tom. "Actually, Brenna did."

Tom realised he'd better not be cheeky, or Woodsmoke might leave him here.

It was nearly dark when they reached the others. Brenna and Beansprout were waiting inside a small cleft in the rock face.

"Tom!" Beansprout said nervously. "Sorry to have caused so much trouble." She looked as if she was going to hug him, but thought better of it.

"Are you OK?" he asked.

"I am now." She smiled at Brenna. "I was a bit panic-stricken at first."

"Well, this is Woodsmoke and he's annoyed! Woodsmoke, my cousin Beansprout."

Woodsmoke nodded briefly, and then said, "We need to get out of here." He turned to Brenna. "I think we should go higher, find a cave and get out of sight."

"I've already found one." Brenna pointed to a small black hole in the rock wall, several metres above the path. "It's small, but there are no other caves leading off it. It's the best we can do for now."

Woodsmoke sighed. "All right. Lead the way."

4 The Eye

Excitement and nervousness fought inside Tom's head. He wanted to see more of the Eye and the Realm of Water, but he didn't want to come across the weird and dangerous creatures that lurked beneath the waters. Well, actually he *did* want to see them, but from a safe distance.

The four of them were at the back of a shallow cave looking out over the gorge. It was hot and airless, and Tom was uncomfortably sweaty. He could just see Woodsmoke and Brenna in the darkness as they leaned back against the walls, seemingly deep in thought.

"So what's the plan?" he asked.

"We need to find another portal, Tom," said Woodsmoke, "so we can take you back home. The portals between the four worlds are rarely used now. We certainly don't know where to find one here, so we'll need to search, but we can't do that at night." He groaned and rubbed his hands across his face. "It could take us days. And if we can't find a portal it will be a long journey back to our realm."

Beansprout spoke, her voice quiet. "I'm sorry. It's my fault we're here. I didn't mean to …" Her voice trailed off with a sigh.

Tom asked, "What happened? How …?"

"I was eating and I saw this hole in the ground, so I thought I should check it out – you know, just in case. So I stuck my head in and then ended up sliding in. Once I was in I thought I'd see where it went."

"But why didn't you call me when you saw it?"

Beansprout shrugged. "In case it was nothing. I followed that tunnel, which was really amazing, and then I sort of stuck my hand in that black hole and it pulled me right in!" She sounded sheepish and delighted with herself all at the same time. "I freaked out initially, kind of froze, then decided I should sit tight and hope someone came for me – and here you are!"

Woodsmoke sounded cross. "Well, you are very lucky we found you intact. In fact you are lucky we found you at all."

The word "intact" seemed to hang in the air.

"Well I'm starved," said Beansprout. "Let's eat."

"Great idea," Tom answered. "And while we eat you can tell us about this place, and how you know our granddad."

Beansprout and Tom rummaged through their backpacks, handing out food and drinks.

"Very well," said Woodsmoke. He paused, as if wondering how much to tell them. "First you need to know we are no longer in your world. I'm sure that's obvious. We are in the Otherworld, which lies alongside yours. There are four realms here – Earth, Air, Water and Fire – and different spirits and beings live in each. This, as you know, is the Realm of Water, and we have arrived in the Eye, the absolute centre of the realm, where the Emperor lives. Brenna and I are from the Realm of Earth. Years ago we passed between the four realms all the time, but for years now we have remained separate. It's the same with your world – we no longer come and go from there as we used to. In your world we have different names – faeries, elves, fauns, nymphs, or even Sidhe."

"Faeries!" gasped Beansprout. "Like in the old stories – the ones where people would disappear and never be seen again?"

"That's right. At certain times of day – dawn and dusk – and in certain places, the edges of our worlds would dissolve and humans could pass from their world to ours, usually by accident. Now, for most people, only the portals will enable passage, but they are well hidden."

"Hidden how? By magic?" asked Tom.

"Of a sort. And they are usually built underground, or in remote places, with concealed entrances. My grandfather, Fahey, was trapped in your world for many years. When he was released from the spell, he managed to find the portals in the wood. He said he could hear our realm singing to him, as if to call him home, and he followed the music."

"Where was he trapped?" asked Beansprout.

"In that old yew tree at the edge of the wood beyond your grandfather's garden. He was trying to travel to Avalon but triggered a spell. For years we had no idea what had happened to him, although we searched and searched." He shook his head. "And then he returned a few months ago, with your grandfather, Jack. He was the first person Fahey saw after he was released from the spell."

"Wow!" Tom exclaimed, "So why is Granddad here?"

"My grandfather liked him and so he invited him. I don't know why he said yes, Tom. I know how much I missed my grandfather – that's why I agreed to bring you that package, so you wouldn't worry."

"Then you must know why we want to see him, Woodsmoke."

"I do, but it's not that easy. Our world is dangerous, full of magic, strange places and even stranger creatures; far more dangerous than your world is to us. I have heard rumours of the Emperor here. If they are true, he's someone we should keep away from."

"So if this is the Realm of Water, why are we on land?" Beansprout asked.

"A portion of it *is* land, although it's filled with rivers and waterways. Most of the realm is under the sea; whole cities are sprawled across the sea bed, or perched on underwater mountain ranges or deep within trenches far from light. From what I have heard there are different groups who all fight for control, and petty skirmishes are constantly breaking out. The Emperor must be a busy man," Woodsmoke said thoughtfully.

"Do people fight in the Realm of Earth too?" Tom asked.

"Sometimes. There are disturbing rumours coming out of Aeriken Forest in our realm. The Queen of the Aerikeen is strange, and rarely seen. Her people have disappeared from the villages." He exchanged a worried glance with Brenna. "We fear something terrible is happening there."

"Do you know Jack too, Brenna?" Beansprout asked.

"Yes," she answered from the darkness. "At the moment I live with Woodsmoke and his family. We're friends. I said I would travel to your world with him, for safety. And I was curious too. After meeting Jack, I wanted to know what your world was like."

"If Granddad's safe, then it must be all right here," Tom said.

"Your grandfather is with Fahey, in a safe area," Woodsmoke replied. "We are a long way from there."

While they were talking, faint sounds of strange music and singing started to fill the gorge. Then there was an almighty roaring sound and the clatter of what sounded like hooves racing along the path.

Woodsmoke jumped to his feet and peered from the entrance of the cave. "I think we've been found," he said over his shoulder.

Tom's heart beat faster, as if it would leap out of his chest. Beansprout waited motionless beside him. The rumbling and clattering became louder, accompanied by wild singing and laughing. A huge towering water spout erupted from the river, filling the cave with spray, before collapsing and leaving a murky green light to illuminate the night.

Woodsmoke stepped back as a large figure appeared in the cave entrance, a black shadow against the eerie green glow. A booming voice declared, "Welcome to the Eye, travellers." It didn't sound welcoming.

Woodsmoke replied with a bow, "Greetings, we thank you for your welcome."

The voice answered, "The Emperor is waiting to see you." He stepped aside, gesturing for them to leave.

As they made their way out of the cave, they saw below them dozens of horses, carrying men and women armed with swords and spears. The middle of the river was a boiling mass of giant tentacles, waving in the strange green light.

They scrambled down, and were each hustled on to a horse with another rider. The animals stamped impatiently until the four of them were seated, then wheeled round, heading back to the lake. Tom gripped his rider. He'd never been on a horse before and was convinced he was going to be thrown off.

The castle that had been beneath the water was now above it, hundreds of lights shining from the windows, bright against the black night. They rushed up the broad ramp, along the parapet, and swept onto the bridge that had previously crossed the lake, but which now led to huge gates and a courtyard beyond. The sheer black granite walls were slick with running water which cascaded down and through grates in the floor.

The riders shouted to each other as they dismounted. Tossing the reins to others who emerged from the shadows, they headed towards a broad entrance on the left of the courtyard.

Tom, Beansprout, Woodsmoke and Brenna stood uncertainly watching the movements around the courtyard, wondering where they were expected to go. Tom imagined deep dark dungeons, dank and cold. However, the man with the booming voice shepherded them into a large dining hall crowded with people eating and drinking at long tables. Servants milled around, replenishing enormous plates and dishes as the sound of music came from a group in the corner of the room.

Slowly, as everyone turned to look at them, the room fell silent.

A voice came from the far end of the room. "So, our visitors *finally* arrive in my hall."

Craning his neck, Tom saw a man, his dark hair streaked with grey, sitting at a table raised on a dais. He leaned forward on his ornate chair, looking at them intently. This must be the Emperor.

Woodsmoke and Brenna immediately bowed, a sweeping gesture

reaching down to their feet, before Woodsmoke strode forward.

"I would like to apologise for our unannounced presence in the Eye," he said. "It was completely unplanned, and we were aiming to be out before disturbing Your Majesty."

"Were you indeed?" The Emperor's voice boomed out across the hall. "And what did you hope to achieve by visiting the Eye? Are you spies?"

"No! We are not spies. We came to rescue the human child who passed through the portal. It was an accident."

Tom felt all eyes fall on him and his cousin. He opened his mouth to take the blame, but before he could speak, Beansprout said in a shaky voice, "I'm sorry, Your Majesty. It was my fault. I didn't realise what would happen."

"So, human child, it is you that brings visitors to my hall." The Emperor peered closely at them both. "How did you find the doorway? It has surely been closed for many years."

"I saw a hole in the ground and found it that way."

"It was our fault," interrupted Woodsmoke. "We left the passage open. But I would like to reassure you that it is now closed, and with Your Majesty's permission we will leave tomorrow to return the visitors to their home. If you could direct us to a portal that would be most helpful."

"And what," said the Emperor, "are two of the fey from the Realm of Earth doing with humans? Didn't we stop passing to their world many hundreds of years ago?"

"I had to deliver a message. A guest came to our realm of late. He wanted to send a message to his family, telling them that he was safe."

The Emperor paused, his face stern as he stared at Woodsmoke. He spoke softly. "It has also been a very long time since anyone from the Realm of Earth came to the Eye."

Woodsmoke smiled a thin smile. "Too long. But you are not who we expected to see, Your Majesty."

After another long pause, during which there was only a breathless silence, the Emperor said, "No, I would not be. There have been many changes here." He gazed into the middle distance for a moment and then, suddenly relaxing, said, "Well, I would be a poor host if I did not offer you food. Come, sit, all of you, and you can tell me what is happening in your realm."

With that the general hum of noise started again. The people sitting around the Emperor moved aside to make room, and Tom and Beansprout sat on the Emperor's left, while Woodsmoke and Brenna sat to his right. The Emperor started talking to Woodsmoke and Brenna, leaving Tom and Beansprout to eat and think.

Servants put plates in front of them, and they helped themselves from platters in the centre of the table. There were whole baked fish the length of a man's arm; piles of mussels and oysters, and steaming bowls of fish stew. Tom took a bite of something green that was probably fried seaweed, and discretely spat the salty mouthful into a table napkin. Beansprout was merrily tucking into a huge bowl of trifle.

Looking around the room, Tom realised the other guests weren't really "people", in the usual sense of the word. Neither were Woodsmoke and Brenna. The Emperor had called them "fey".

Tom couldn't quite explain what made them different, other than a peculiar awareness they seemed to have. It was quite unnerving. When they looked at you, it was as if they could see right into your mind; could tell exactly what you were thinking. Even though he had no evidence of this, Tom felt he should try and hide his thoughts.

And Brenna could turn into a bird! He wondered if the people in the Eye could turn into animals too. They looked a little different to Woodsmoke and Brenna. Their skin was slightly shimmery, as if dusted with silver, and their eyes were a bright shiny blue. And the castle – what an amazing place! The hall was similar to the old English halls he'd seen in books, but instead of having fireplaces, there were fountains in alcoves along the wall. The water cooled the hall – a welcome change from the sticky heat outside.

Tom tried to look at the Emperor without being too obvious about it, watching him out of the corner of his eye. He was much younger than Tom had thought an Emperor would be. His hair was pulled up into a knot on his head, his face was sharp, his eyebrows high and quizzical, and he wore long loose robes of dark blue, which pooled like water at his feet. His chair looked as if it were made from polished coral.

Tom suddenly felt a long way from home. It was hard to believe that only this morning they were in the wood by his house. It was then that Tom realised his father would have no idea where he was, or Beansprout's mother, but there was nothing he could do now. He knew though that he still wanted to see his granddad before going back.

He was incredibly tired, and he noticed Beansprout's eyes beginning to close, her head nodding gently before she snapped it up, trying to stay awake. He turned to her. "You OK?"

"Exhausted, Tom. But I don't want to go to bed – there's too much to see. This is all so weird." She shook her head as she gazed around the room.

"Do you still want to find Granddad?" Tom asked.

"Yes. Absolutely! We're so close it would be mad not to. Woodsmoke will take us. We'll make him!"

"Good. Because I'm not ready to go home yet. This place was under water earlier, can you believe that? And nothing's wet. Well, not like you'd expect."

"Really? How does that happen? We have to stay. I don't want to go home yet, Tom."

The Emperor turned their way, saw Beansprout yawning, and immediately summoned a servant. "Give our guests a room each in the East Tower." Turning back to them he said, "You two are tired. You do not keep such late hours as we do. Sleep now and we will talk tomorrow."

It seemed they had little choice. Tom caught Woodsmoke's attention, and he nodded, so they followed the servant out of the hall.

He led them along winding corridors and up stairs grand and sweeping and small and spiralling, until they were completely disorientated. They ended up on a short corridor and were shown rooms next to each other. Tom lay on his bed thinking he'd be awake all night, but in minutes he was fast asleep.

5 The Cavern of the Four Portals

Several hours later, Tom woke feeling groggy and disorientated, and for a few seconds couldn't work out where he was. He struggled to open his eyes – his eyelids felt as heavy as lead.

Events from the previous day began to filter into his thoughts, and he sat up in bed, looking wildly around the room. Then he remembered – he was in the bedroom in the tower. Flopping back down, he wondered if this was what jetlag felt like.

His dreams started to return to him. Again the white-haired woman had appeared, but this time the image had been sharper, clearer. She'd looked impatient, saying, "Come, Tom, you are nearly here. Hurry! There are things you must do." Again firelight had filled his vision and he'd felt its heat; chanting had filled his ears.

With a shock he realised it had been her voice in his head when they'd crossed the portal. Who was she? What things must he do?

He brushed off the dream and looked round the room, which was filled with a dull green light. Why was the room green? Were there leaves over the window? Then he had another thought. Were they back under the water? He jumped out of bed and ran to the window. That was definitely water.

The lake floor was of smooth rock and sand. Large tree-like plants waved about in the current, their thick knotted roots anchored into the rock. Fish of all sizes swam past the window, and horses grazed on the lake floor. Looking up, he saw a pale yellow disc, and the surface of the lake glinting like a mirror far above. Shafts of sunlight pierced the gloom.

The urge to explore woke him fully. On a table in the corner of his room was a bowl of steaming water, a bar of soap, and towels. He had a quick wash and raked his fingers through his hair. Wondering if Beansprout was awake he stepped into the empty corridor and knocked on her door. "Come in," he heard her call.

She was at the window, staring into the water. "Tom! You're right, we're under the water. How is this possible?"

"Magic, I guess."

"But how do we get out of here? We're trapped."

"I'm more worried about how we find breakfast! Fancy a wander?"

"Should we? What if we get lost?"

"Oh we'll definitely get lost, but we're lost anyway, aren't we?" He shrugged and smiled.

Grabbing their packs, they headed down the corridor, attempting to retrace their steps from the night before. They met no one, and the castle was eerily silent. Before long it was clear they were lost – these ornate hallways were different to those they had walked along the night before. The walls were hung with tapestries of underwater scenes, and decorated with the skeletal remains of unfamiliar creatures. Rills of water trickled down the edges of the corridors, and there were small pools filled with lily pads, and plants that they didn't recognise.

"I think we're in the main part of the castle, Tom," Beansprout whispered. They had come to a large circular space with a grand staircase leading down to an atrium. Huge windows let in the green glow of the water, and large purple fronds of aquatic plants tapped against the panes.

As they reached the atrium, a door opened and a woman stepped out. She looked surprised for the briefest of seconds, and then smiled. "You must be our human visitors. Follow me."

On the far side of the atrium, a wooden arched doorway led to a courtyard. Above them, water was suspended from its downward rush by some mysterious force.

"Don't worry," the Emperor called. "It's quite safe." He was seated at a stone table laden with food and what looked like a pot of tea. "Come and join me, I have lots to ask you."

They sat while he poured tea – which was most definitely not normal tea – and offered them fish for breakfast. Tom took a sip of the green liquid; it was an odd-tasting salty brew.

"Woodsmoke has been telling me how you came to be here. I trust you are enjoying yourselves?"

Tom answered, trying to swallow his food quickly. "Yes. It's ... different."

"Years ago," said the Emperor, thoughtfully, "many people from your world visited here – accidentally, of course – but it was easier then. The doorways were simpler to find and the walls between our worlds came and went. Only those who know where to look visit now, and few have this knowledge. Those who do come are not always friendly." He looked regretful.

"It has also been a long time since we saw anyone from the Realm of Earth," he continued. "As I explained to your friends last night, I have been Emperor since my father died, and things have been difficult." Tom and Beansprout carried on eating and nodding. "My father was suspicious and treated visitors badly – I understand why your friends were worried about being here. He would probably have fed you to the Mantis."

Beansprout's face grew pale.

"We have tried to keep my father's death a secret. This has allowed me to make changes and defeat certain groups, particularly the swamp goblins."

Noticing Beansprout's discomfort, he changed the subject. "Tell me all about you. I once visited your world, when the forests ran thick, tangled and unbroken right to the shores of your seas. What is it like now?"

Between them they attempted to answer his question, and were on to their third pot of "tea", when Woodsmoke and Brenna appeared, looking more relaxed than the day before, and not in the slightest concerned at the water suspended high above their heads.

"Last night," the Emperor nodded at Woodsmoke, "I agreed to escort you to our closest portal to the Realm of Earth. Unfortunately my father destroyed many portals, particularly those to your world," he said, looking at Tom and Beansprout, "so I cannot send you home. But I think you are not displeased with that?" He looked amused at their excited faces.

"We still want to find our grandfather," said Tom, glaring at Woodsmoke, who rolled his eyes.

"Yes, yes. All right," said Woodsmoke. "We'll see where we end up. But I'm not promising anything!"

"Obviously my father didn't succeed in completely destroying the portals," said the Emperor, "otherwise you wouldn't be here. But I would instead suggest that we escort you up the river that runs to the border. It will be a difficult journey, passing through swamps and then the mangrove forests, which, at this time of year, are full of flesh flies, and it could take many weeks–"

"No," said Woodsmoke. "It would take far too long. We have to attempt the portal."

"Very well then. We shall leave tonight."

After the sun had set, and the water around them had become black and impenetrable, the castle rose majestically to the surface of the lake. It was a discomforting experience to find themselves shooting upwards, the floor rocking beneath them as if there was an earthquake. The roar of water filled the castle and Tom felt his ears become thick with pressure, all sound becoming muffled, before they popped and everything returned to normal.

The castle doors were thrown open and fresh air began to circulate, getting rid of the stuffiness that had built up during the day.

Accompanied by the Emperor and a dozen men carrying lanterns, they exited the castle through the rear gate. Passing over the stone bridge, they paused at the rocky ledge.

"We'll just summon the hippocamps," said the Emperor.

"Sea horses," said Woodsmoke, in response to Tom's baffled expression.

One of the Emperor's men pulled a flute out of his pocket and blew into it.

"I can't hear anything," Beansprout said.

"I expect it's too high-pitched for our ears," Tom answered.

Moments later, four horses broke the surface, whinnying softly as they swam towards the shore. They had normal horse heads, but the manes trailing down their backs were webbed and transparent. Small wings sprouted from their sides, and large fishtails propelled them through the water.

"They're so beautiful," Beansprout said, leaning forward to pat them.

"Oh yes, and quite tame," the Emperor said. He turned and led the way to one side of the waterfall, pushing through lush ferns into a partially hidden cleft in the rock. Tom followed the Emperor down a passageway that opened into a wider tunnel, through which rushed a fast-flowing river. In one direction the river emptied into the lake; in the other it ran along the tunnel into darkness.

The hippocamps were waiting for them beside a small ship. There were no sails; instead Tom saw neatly stacked oars alongside rows of seats.

The men harnessed the animals to the front before boarding the vessel, hanging their lanterns along the sides and on the prow. Tom, Beansprout, Woodsmoke and Brenna made their way to the stern with the Emperor. When everyone was seated, they gently pushed out.

The air in the tunnel was damp and the walls trickled with water. Beyond the ship the darkness was absolute. Their progress was slow but steady.

The Emperor turned to them. "We have had much rain lately so the river should be deep enough to take us all the way to the portal. In places the current is swift and strong, so don't fall in."

"How far does the river go?" asked Tom.

"Oh, miles and miles – far beyond our destination. But it becomes narrower, and then you have to climb. There are many waterfalls, and places where the water completely fills the caverns. The traveller must take great care to avoid those. And the river often branches in two. It is easy to become lost. People have entered here and never been seen again." He paused, then added, "You're lucky the portal didn't bring you here when you arrived." His words hung in the air and seemed to echo in the enclosed space.

Tom felt a cold shudder run down his spine as he realised they could have emerged anywhere. "Could we have ended up in the sea?"

"Oh yes, the portals can be quite hazardous."

Understatement of the year. Tom turned to Woodsmoke and Brenna. "Could we come out somewhere really bad in your realm?"

Brenna nodded. "Yes, but we know our world well, so hopefully we will be fine. We may still have further to travel than we would want, though."

Woodsmoke added a word of warning. "This place is not for the unprepared traveller, Tom. Like your own world, ours has areas that are hostile to outsiders."

"Blimey," said Beansprout, "I wish I'd known that before I stuck my hand in."

"This reminds me of the Greek ships I've seen in history books," said Tom.

"Ah, how clever of you Tom! It is in fact a version of the trireme, one of the ships we introduced to the Greeks. We were very influential in the Mediterranean many years ago. We are a seafaring people–"

"Really?" interrupted Tom, disbelief in his voice. "You helped the Greeks?"

"Oh, only slightly," the Emperor answered, modestly. "Not me personally – I was far too young. Unfortunately we are also responsible for the presence of the giant squid and sea serpents in your seas. An accidental crossing from our world."

Tom now had so many questions whizzing around his head, he didn't know which to ask first. "Sea serpents? But they're a myth. And how old are you? That was over two thousand years ago!"

The Emperor looked at the floor and scratched his chin. "Well, I am older than I look. We are a race that lives for many years. Woodsmoke and Brenna are much older than you imagine."

Beansprout, who had been following the conversation with some interest, butted in. "So how old *are* you two?"

Woodsmoke laughed. "I am four hundred and twenty-three years old – quite young, really. What about you, Brenna?"

"Oh, three hundred and seventy, or thereabouts," she said with a wry smile.

"If you're interested in sea creatures, Tom," the Emperor said, "we may see one later. Or perhaps you're not *that* interested," he added, noting Tom's expression.

"Where might we see one?" Tom asked nervously.

"We are going to the Cavern of the Four Portals – although there are of course only three now. It's a huge cave, and the river there forms a deep lake connected by a passageway to the sea. One of our greatest explorers found it. Unfortunately, on occasions a giant dectopus swims up the passageway and takes up residence in the lake. If it's there, we must try not to disturb it." He looked at their worried faces and added, "I'm sure we won't."

"What's a dectopus?" Tom asked.

"It is a ten-tentacled sea creature. Haven't you heard of them?"

"I've only heard of an octopus."

"Well, there you are then. Much the same, just a bit bigger."

For a while they fell silent, listening to the sound of the hippocamps splashing in the inky black river. At least, Tom hoped it was the hippocamps.

A while later the river started to curl to the left and the passageway became bigger. The walls were slick with moisture, the torchlight slipping off the walls and up to the roof or down to the water, where it was swallowed by the unrelenting blackness.

"Water is leaking through the rock," the Emperor said. "This section of the tunnel is quite porous." Stalactites hung from the roof, and streaks of pink and yellow glimmered like underground rainbows.

It seemed as if they had been in the tunnel for hours, and Tom became more and more aware of the huge amount of rock over their heads as they moved still further underground. Tributaries opened up on either side, and water poured down from the suffocating blackness. Tom peered up the tunnels, seeing nothing, but hearing strange gurgles and splashes. Every now and again the Emperor would impart some bit of knowledge about the warren of tunnels and mysterious whirlpools they were passing, but their worried faces eventually drove him to silence.

Just as Tom was beginning to think the journey would never end, the passage opened up, and the light from the ship was swallowed up by the bigger space. The Emperor touched the wick from his lantern to the wall, and a band of bright orange flame raced along the rock face. He did the same on the other side of the passage, and the cavern became brighter as the flames spread in a circle beneath a domed roof. Craning his neck, Tom saw huge, elaborate carvings on the walls towering above him, depicting fights between enormous sea creatures. They seemed to move in the flickering light.

They headed to a pier jutting out into the far side of the lake, beyond which was a broad stone floor on which boxes and ropes were coiled. Behind the boxes, steps led to a dark shadowy recess like the one through which Tom and Beansprout had passed. They had reached the portals.

He turned to the Emperor. "What are all the boxes for?"

"This is where we built the ship. And we store other things here, for journeying further inland." He nodded to the rear of the cavern where the river exited into another tunnel.

As they passed the centre of the pool, bubbles appeared on the surface. The hippocamps became nervous, snorting wildly and straining towards the shore. Seeing the commotion, the men raised their short sharp tridents, and stood peering into the water.

"Is it the dectopus?" said Beansprout.

No one answered. Woodsmoke raised his longbow, keeping his eyes on the water, and Brenna pulled her sword free from its scabbard.

The Emperor touched Tom and Beansprout gently on the arm, pulling them back from the side of the ship. "Stay in the middle."

The hippocamps pulled furiously towards the shore. Then, in front of them, a sleek and scaly tentacle uncoiled on the surface before plunging into the depths again. For a few seconds the water fell still, then several more tentacles appeared, followed by the enormous bulbous body of the dectopus. It reared into the air, water streaming over it. Its skin was wrinkled and thick like elephant's, and two enormous eyes blinked slowly. It flicked several tentacles towards them, and Tom saw its suckers raised and ready to grasp the ship.

Beansprout screamed; Woodsmoke released several arrows at its head. Some found their target, but most bounced off into the water. Before Woodsmoke could fire again, the dectopus plunged back beneath the surface, making the boat rock wildly.

"He wasn't kidding when he said giant dectopus!" Tom exclaimed.

The hippocamps raced forward, but the dectopus rose again, this time on the starboard side of the ship. Shadows from the flames writhed across its mottled deep-purple skin. Another volley of arrows left Woodsmoke's bow, but again the dectopus's tentacles whipped across the surface of the pool. One grabbed a hippocamp, lifting it as if it were a toy, ripping it free of its harness and dropping it into its gaping mouth. Other tentacles latched onto the ship, causing it to lurch wildly. Everyone grabbed for something fixed; Tom slid across the deck and hit the side, hurting his elbow. Brenna rolled and quickly regained her feet, slashing at the closest tentacle. The dectopus roared in pain, the noise echoing around the cave, but the ship tipped further. Woodsmoke and the Emperor joined Brenna, and the three slashed at the tentacles as the men released a volley of tridents. With another roar the tentacles finally released the ship, which shot upright, waves rolling across the deck.

The remaining hippocamps had broken free and were racing away with deafening shrieks that echoed around the cave. Then they disappeared beneath the surface of the water.

"Start rowing!" the Emperor yelled. They were within reach of the pier when the dectopus rose again, directly ahead. It towered above them, and this time its tentacles grabbed both sides of the boat, pulling it towards its open mouth. A tentacle whipped across their heads, its huge suckers flexing like white mouths. It grabbed one of the Emperor's men. With a scream he was dropped into its waiting mouth.

"Abandon ship!" commanded the Emperor, as they were dragged ever closer to the dectopus's waiting mouth.

Tom grabbed Beansprout and pushed her forward. "Go!" he shouted. "I'll follow."

Beansprout leapt into the mass of frothing churning water. Tom followed, gasping as he hit the icy lake. It was so cold it felt like a fist was squeezing his lungs. The water blinded and deafened him, and he flailed around, desperately trying to reach the surface, his clothes heavy and billowing around him. His head emerged and he gasped for air.

He was surrounded by seething water and thrashing tentacles. Did it only have ten tentacles? It seemed like so many more. He heard an enormous splintering crash, and watched as a chunk of the boat was ripped off and sent flying overhead.

As he started swimming for the shore, a hippocamp appeared beneath him and he grasped its webbed mane. It raced through the water, tipping him off in the shallows. Once clear of the water he turned, then quickly ducked and rolled as a tentacle whipped towards him. It slapped the ground, it suckers slurping.

He saw Beansprout lying exhausted nearby and dragged himself to her side. "Run!" he yelled, grabbing her arm. Together they raced for the back of the cave, their wet clothes flapping around them.

Woodsmoke and Brenna had also managed to jump free of the boat and were pulled swiftly to shore by the hippocamps. The water was still a churning mass of men and tentacles. Some made it to the shore, while others disappeared beneath the surface.

Woodsmoke took up position at the shattered end of the pier, firing a blur of arrows. Brenna began helping the men who'd made it out of the water gather a pile of silvery-looking ropes. At the bow of his shattered ship, the Emperor looked towards the shore before diving into the water.

The dectopus pursued those still in the lake. Although the men were fast, some weren't fast enough. Those who made it to the shore climbed up to where several large pieces of machinery hung high on the rock walls. Thick silvery ropes ran from these to a giant web suspended over the pool.

The Emperor emerged in the middle of the churning lake before dipping out of sight again. The dectopus darted towards him. For several seconds nothing happened, and the water became smooth and still. Just as Tom began to worry that the Emperor had drowned, he surfaced right under the web and shouted, "Now!"

The dectopus rose above the surface as the Emperor disappeared, and before it could follow him, the giant web dropped, along with several hundredweight of stone it had supported. An enormous boom rang out as the weight crashed down onto the creature, which sank below the surface. A large wave rose and raced to the shore and with it came the Emperor, who landed on the rocky edge.

"Quickly," he shouted. "Secure him with the ropes!" His remaining men dived back into the water, dragging the ropes behind them. This time they were submerged for a long time.

"How can they stay under water for so long?" asked Beansprout.

Woodsmoke answered, joining them from the pier. "They're water spirits. That's why their skin is silvery looking, almost as if they are half fish. They can swim under water for hours. They just don't live in it."

"And what was the web thing under the roof?"

"Giant water spiders make very strong webs!"

Beansprout looked a little sick. "I hope we don't meet one of those too."

6 In the Greenwood

While the Emperor and his men finished their tasks under water, Woodsmoke lit a fire from the woodpile he found in a dry corner and they warmed themselves by the bright flames. They were still shocked by their violent encounter.

"That was too close for comfort," Woodsmoke said.

"Too close for some of the men," Brenna said sadly.

"And the hippocamp," Beansprout added.

"I take it you've seen the portals?" Woodsmoke gestured to the shadowy recess above them.

Tom nodded. "I suppose we'll leave when the Emperor gets back?"

"Yes. We're lucky he was feeling generous. We would never have found this place without him."

"Who built the portals?"

"They were built thousands of years ago, by the powerful magic of the ancient gods."

"Oh." That wasn't the answer Tom had expected. "What gods?"

"That tale's for another time, Tom," Woodsmoke said.

"And will you take us to our grandfather? Please, Woodsmoke. We're so close."

"I suppose so. And anyway, I don't know of any other portal to take you to your world, apart from the one we used. We don't have a choice."

Beansprout gave Woodsmoke a beaming smile.

The Emperor and his men finally emerged from the deep cold waters and shook the water off their skin like otters.

"All done," said the Emperor with a faint smile. "We have wrapped it up so tightly it will take weeks to break free, if it ever does. And now I'm starved. Fish, anyone?"

His men brought a dozen large rainbow-scaled fish from the half-ruined boat, lit a second fire and spread the fish on flat grills to cook. Water and wine were handed out, and they sat talking while the smell of cooking fish filled the air.

"I'm sorry you've lost men," said Woodsmoke. "I feel it's our fault. It wouldn't have happened if you hadn't brought us here. We owe you a huge debt."

"Not at all. It's happened before and will no doubt happen again. We risk these encounters all the time when we travel, and although it's sad to lose men, we accept it. I'm tempted to pass through the portal with you, but the realm remains unsettled and I still have much to do here. Another time."

He paused to rummage in his pockets, and pulled out a curious spiral shell inlaid with silver and jade. Muttering a few words, he passed his hand across it.

"A present," he said, "to remember your time in the Eye. Any time you need help and there's water nearby, just throw it in. I won't tell you what will happen. It will be a surprise. Which of you would like to look after it?"

"Thank you. Tom should," Beansprout said immediately.

"Thanks," said Tom, hoping he wouldn't lose it as he slipped it into his pocket.

After eating, they gathered their things and walked up the stone steps to the portals high above the lake. Carvings of beasts marched beside the path, as if accompanying them.

They stood before the three doorways. At the far end was a mass of rubble where once a fourth had stood. Tom wouldn't have thought it possible to destroy these doorways; they looked as if they would stand forever.

The portal to the Realm of Earth was in the middle, surrounded by carvings of trees, mountains, and strange hoof-footed half-men. Directly over the arch were carvings of a woman with a serene face, and a man with enormous antlers rising from his head.

"Time to go," said Woodsmoke. Holding hands, they stepped through the archway and passed out of the Realm of Water.

With a rush and a swooping, falling motion, Tom felt the blackness slide by and heard fluttering, just for a moment, until they landed with a thump. This time he felt soft earth, a loamy richness beneath his hands.

It was quiet, the eerie silence before dawn, with the barest suggestion of light. There was a faint pulsing of wind, as if something was breathing, and the air was crisp and sharp, carrying the smell of snow and pine.

They waited in silence for the light to grow, and as it did, birds started to sing. Before long the air was thick with birdsong, long looping notes smothering the silence. The sunrise revealed a pine forest, the trunks pressed close, the branches knotted together just above their heads. A thick mist silvered the ground.

"We're on the mountain," Brenna murmured, "on the lower slopes. Can you smell the snow?"

Woodsmoke nodded. "Come."

The ground sloped away in front of them, and despite the rising sun, the light remained dim. The birds fell silent. Beneath their feet, the thick carpet of pine needles swallowed their footsteps. Mist swirled around their legs in whispery tendrils, rising almost unnoticed, until the others had disappeared from Tom's view. Distracted by his new surroundings, he wandered down a tunnel that hollowed out in the mist before him. Passing through it, he found himself in a clearing. The sweet pungent scent of honeysuckle perfumed the air.

There was no sign of the others. A woman sat cross-legged in the centre of the clearing. She was beautiful, with long white hair framing her pale face. She seemed both very young and very old. Her eyes were pale green, and she wore a long grey dress trimmed with fur. With a shock, Tom realised she was the woman he had seen in his dreams.

She gazed at him, and without seeming to speak, said, "Tom, at last you have arrived. Come and sit so we can talk."

Trapped within the circle of mist, he warily moved closer.

She smiled. "So, Tom, I have called you here because there is something you must do."

"I think you're confusing me with someone else," he said crossly. "I came here to find my grandfather and take him home. Who *are* you? How do you know my name, and how did you get into my dreams?"

"But Tom," she said, ignoring his questions. "What if he doesn't want to return home?"

"Of course he will, why wouldn't he?" Tom felt a slight panic as he answered; a sense of unease as other possibilities suggested themselves.

Ignoring his question again, she said, "There is something else I want you to do while you are here."

"What could you possibly want *me* to do?" he asked, increasingly confused by the conversation.

"I need you to wake the King who lies sleeping on the Isle of Avalon. Your grandfather's friend Fahey once tried to wake the King, many years ago, but it wasn't time and I sent him far from here. However, Queen Gavina has become dangerous; she hunts her own people, the Aerikeen. *This* is the time to wake the King, and you are the one who must wake him."

Tom sat there dumbfounded. "What king? On where? How can I wake him if this Fahey, or whatever his name is, couldn't?"

"Because you have something Fahey didn't."

The woman held out a supple, fresh, living twig, ripe with spring growth.

"This will enable you to wake the King. Only with the bough can you do this."

Tom felt panic building in him again. "But how? I don't know where this place is. What king? Why me? And who are *you*?"

"Ask Woodsmoke. He can show you the way. It is important Tom. The Queen's people need your help. You are linked to the King by your blood, and only someone of his blood can wake him. And you must hurry. You have taken far too long to get here." There was a hint of impatience in her tone.

Too long? What was she talking about? Just as he was about to ask, Tom felt a weight in his lap and, looking down, saw that the twig had magically appeared there, and had turned from a living branch to solid silver. He picked it up, wondering how she had managed such a clever trick.

As he held it, a ball of light grew within the woman until it was so bright that Tom had to close his eyes and cover them with his hands. When the light faded, she had gone, and he was sitting alone in bright sunshine.

Tom sat dazed. The distant shouts of his friends finally disturbed his trance, and he stumbled to his feet. "I'm here, over here!" he called.

A large, black, glossy-plumed bird burst into the clearing and, spotting him, swooped off again. Brenna, gone to guide the others.

When they finally found him, Beansprout was exasperated. "Tom, where have you been? We've been calling for hours!"

Brenna turned to Woodsmoke. "I swear I flew over here earlier, but I couldn't see him!"

Woodsmoke said, "Are you OK, Tom? You look odd."

"I've had a weird encounter."

"What do you mean? With whom?"

"A really old woman with long white hair, dressed in grey. Except she didn't seem old. Not really."

Brenna and Woodsmoke stood gaping at Tom. Brenna gathered herself first. "You met the Lady of the Lake?"

"I don't know. Did I?" Tom shrugged.

"What did she want, Tom?"

"She said I have to wake the King."

Woodsmoke groaned and sat suddenly on the ground, as if his legs had given way. Brenna patted his shoulder in sympathy and sat next to him. For a while they sat silently, deep in thought, while Tom wondered where he'd heard the woman's name before.

Beansprout broke the silence. "Will someone please tell me what's going on? Who's the King that Tom has to wake? Why is he asleep?"

"Years ago," Woodsmoke said, "there was a famous king. He was much loved, and saved the ancient Britons from attack many times. He was given a magical sword, and he had the help of a powerful wizard. Does this ring any bells for you?"

"It sounds like King Arthur," Tom said.

"That's exactly who it is. He has been asleep for centuries, and now it seems you must wake him."

Tom stared at Woodsmoke. "But he died. At least fifteen hundred years ago – if he ever existed at all."

"Oh, he was real, Tom. It is said he will reappear when he's most needed. Our stories say he will awaken here."

"But he's dead."

Woodsmoke shook his head. "No, he's asleep – a deep enchanted sleep, in a tomb on the Isle of Avalon. In exchange for the sword, Excalibur, Merlin made a deal with the fey, and therefore so did Arthur, and close to death he was brought here to rest until he was needed again. The island can only be reached by summoning the Lady of the Lake who will take you across on a boat. It's old magic, Tom."

"How do you know all this?"

"Because my grandfather is a bard, a teller of stories, and that was his favourite. Arthur was the king my grandfather tried to wake."

"The woman told me that, but she said it was the wrong time and he was the wrong person. So why did he try to wake him?"

"He was trying to help a friend. And it seemed like fun."

Tom looked at him suspiciously. "Really?"

"You'll see when you meet him." He rolled his eyes. "But I don't understand why we need the King now."

"She said something about Queen Gavina 'hunting her own.' What does that mean?"

Woodsmoke looked with alarm at Brenna. She went pale and stuttered, "I suppose that means she's hunting her own people. But why would she do that?" She stared at Tom. "How are you to wake him? She must have said."

"She told me to use this." Tom produced the silver twig with a flourish. "And she said you would show me the way, Woodsmoke. And that we should hurry."

"Did she now?" Woodsmoke took the silver twig off him, examining it closely. "I have no idea what this is, but Fahey might. We need to get back home as soon as possible. Come on, let's go." And with that he stood up and gestured down through the forest and to the west. "We know where we are, and that's where we need to go."

Tom stood, putting the silver twig in his pack. He extended a hand to Beansprout, pulling her to her feet.

"I don't understand," she said, frowning. "Why do *you* have to do this?"

Tom laughed. "Something about me being his blood."

"What?" she exclaimed. "So you're related to King Arthur?"

"Mmm, I suppose so."

"So I am too?"

"I don't know. She didn't say. Maybe it's on my mum's side?"

With a shrug he strolled off after the others, leaving Beansprout open-mouthed behind him.

The pines thinned out, and became mixed with oak, birch and beech trees. Spring flowers grew underfoot, and the scent of blossom filled the air. The powerful feeling of magic had gone, but Tom could still feel a tingle, like static. Woodsmoke strode ahead, while Brenna flew most of the time.

Woodsmoke explained that when they left the wood, they would enter the orchard terraces that ran above the river, adding that he'd heard rumours about attacks from the wood sprites that had left Aeriken Forest to hunt further afield.

Tom laughed. "What? Tiny little wood sprites with bells on their hats? How can they be dangerous?"

"Because they are *not* small," said Brenna, "and they have vicious sharp teeth. In fact, they are deadly hunters."

"Oh," was all Tom could think of to reply.

Beansprout smirked. "Idiot."

They had been walking for hours and the sun was sinking into the west. The woodland was now behind them, on the slopes of the mountain. The pines straggled upwards to meet the snow, which glowed in the fading light. The peak was lost in clouds. Beyond the mountain was a series of ridges retreating into a misty blueness.

They snaked down the slopes and across broad sprawling terraces, filled with unruly trees covered in blossom. Mouldy fruit was rotting on the ground. Between the trees the grass grew tall, and they stumbled over fallen branches and abandoned tools.

"What happened here?" Beansprout asked.

"The wood sprites have been busy," said Woodsmoke. "Everyone's abandoned this place. Be careful – we don't know if the sprites are still close."

They progressed steadily through the deserted terraces. About halfway down they heard the river roaring in the distance, and saw a collection of stone buildings which looked abandoned.

"Perfect," said Woodsmoke, "we can stay here for the night."

Cautiously he entered the closest one. Inside, baskets were strewn across the floor, and wooden tables had been overturned, suggesting a fight.

In the corner was a ladder leading to the upper floor. Brenna pulled her sword free and climbed up, peering slowly over the edge. "It's empty," she called down.

Woodsmoke looked at Tom. "Come with me, we'll check the other buildings." Tom was glad to help. He'd felt useless in the cavern when the dectopus attacked, and now he'd been told he had to wake the King he felt he should prove his worth. As they entered the other buildings he stood watch at the door while Woodsmoke checked inside.

Once satisfied there was no one else there, they strolled to the far edge of the terraces and Woodsmoke pulled out his longbow, saying, "I'll see if I can get us some dinner."

Tom watched him for a few moments and then asked, "Is waking the King dangerous?"

Woodsmoke kept his gaze ahead. "I have no idea, Tom. I'm sure it won't be easy."

"But you will help me get there?"

"Of course. We'll take you to the lakeshore, but I don't know what to expect any more than you do. I wonder what the Queen is up to?" He quickly released three arrows, which disappeared in the long grass. "Dinner," he said, strolling over to pick up the limp rabbits.

7 Beneath the Hill

The evening was uneventful. They were all tired and hungry, and thankful for Woodsmoke's rabbit stew. After collecting sacking from the floor to use as blankets, they were soon asleep.

The next morning the four carried on towards the river, a ribbon of light in the distance. Tom was distracted by thoughts of the silver twig and waking the King. He didn't know how he was going to do it, but couldn't help feeling excited. He had read so many stories about King Arthur and his knights; he tried to imagine what he would be like. Occasionally he glanced back to where Beansprout lagged behind, stopping often to gaze across the landscape. Exasperated, he shouted, "Beansprout, keep up!"

She ignored him, giving an occasional wave to keep him happy, and eventually he gave up, figuring she'd catch up when they stopped.

The sun burned hot and the day was still, without a breath of wind. Tom was also distracted, by strange sounds around him. Every now and then he heard singing, and sometimes whispering, but he couldn't work out where the sound was coming from. It was always just out of reach, and when he thought it was getting louder, it disappeared completely.

At last they reached the river, which meandered across the base of the terraces, separating them from the broad flower-filled meadows beyond. Out of the meadows rose a large mound that glowed a fierce green, vigorous with life, drawing their gaze.

The river was too wide and deep to cross, so they headed for a stone bridge they could see in the distance. It was a high, single-spanned arch, and as they got closer they saw that big chunks of stone had fallen, tumbling into the river below. Woodsmoke went across first, saying, "Tread carefully, and let's keep some distance between us."

Brenna flew ahead while Woodsmoke kept to the edge by the low stone wall, avoiding gaping holes beneath which the water passed lazily.

The large mound, a perfect half-sphere and covered with smooth cropped grass, was now over to their left. They followed the road from the bridge, and as they drew level with the mound they heard a deep rumbling sound, which travelled up through Tom's feet and into his chest. He stopped and looked around with alarm. A large dark opening appeared in the side of the hill, and out of it came bloodcurdling cries. A crowd of what Tom assumed to be wood sprites came pouring from the open doorway, heading across the meadows towards them. They were tall, their limbs sinewy with muscle, and there was a faint greenish tinge to their skin.

Woodsmoke yelled, "Wood sprites! Tom, Beansprout, get behind me!" Ahead of them, Brenna swooped down to earth, turned back into her humanlike form and pulled her sword from its scabbard.

Turning, Tom saw that Beansprout was still some way behind them. He couldn't tell if she'd seen what was happening, but hoped she would stay where she was – it would be safer.

Woodsmoke and Tom raced across the meadows to Brenna's side. She relentlessly attacked the sprites, ploughing through the middle of them, her sword flashing in the sunlight. Some of the sprites fell at her feet, covered in blood. Arrows from Woodsmoke's bow hissed through the air, thudding into the sprites. They stumbled and fell and were trampled by others close behind them.

As Tom grew closer he could see their lips pulled back as they whooped, their sharp teeth gleaming, but it seemed they were only after Brenna. She ran backwards, towards Tom and Woodsmoke, but there were too many sprites. A large net was thrown over her, knocking her to the ground, and she disappeared from view.

Tom and Woodsmoke were trapped. Some of the sprites had separated from the pack and blocked them from Brenna. Tom rolled to the ground, trying to fight his way through legs and spears, but the butts jammed repeatedly into him. He frantically scrabbled around and finally fought his way clear, staggering to his feet, bloodied and bruised, only to see the main pack dragging Brenna behind them through the dark doorway. He raced towards them and then, hearing thundering footsteps behind him, dived into the long grass. In seconds the last few sprites passed him, and he heard the groan of the doorway starting to close. With one final effort, Tom threw himself into the narrowing entrance before it clanged shut behind him.

He lay breathless, his face against the floor, for precious seconds, hoping he would go undetected. As the sprites' shouts faded down a corridor to his left, he sat up, his back pressed against the doorway.

If he had given any thought to what was inside the mound, he would have imagined a warren of corridors made from earth and rock. But it was far from that. He was in an ornate, richly carved passageway stretching to his left and right. The roof was high overhead, arched and glinting with a silver inlay, while the floor beneath him was shiny black marble. Directly ahead was a broad set of stairs climbing steeply upwards into blackness.

The sprites had headed left, so that was the way he must go. He took a few deep breaths to steady himself and started creeping down the passageway. Before long the light became brighter and he heard voices and laughter. Peering cautiously around a bend, he saw a small group of wood sprites talking, and no way of going around them. He'd have to turn back and find Brenna another way. She should be safe for now; he had the feeling that if they'd wanted to kill her, she'd be dead already. He decided to try to understand the layout of the mound so that when he found her, he'd know how to get out.

He retraced his steps and then followed the path to the right. It ran in a gentle curve, following the contours of the hill. Veins of gold and silver illuminated the walls and floors with a dim light, and clusters of glowing jewel-like stones hung like tempting fruit from the high ceiling. Steps ran off the path to lower levels, but he ignored them, and soon came to an antechamber lit by three torches that flamed and flickered on the walls. He cautiously opened one of the three doors leading off the chamber. The room beyond glowed with the same faint light. There was no one in sight.

The room was magnificent. There were shelves full of books, and more were stacked on the floor, on desks and on chairs. He ran his hands along their covers and wondered what the strange curled writing meant. On the walls were carved wood panels and large, richly embroidered tapestries. But the room had no other doorways – it was a dead end.

The second room was equally magnificent. It was like a reception room, with sofas and well-padded chairs. The third door led to another corridor, but this became so winding and twisted, and there were so many turnings off it, that Tom became afraid he would get lost, so he carefully retraced his steps.

Back in the antechamber he followed the original corridor back to the entrance, and then climbed up the staircase. There was no sign of the wood sprites, and Tom was so intrigued at what appeared to be a palace under the hill that he forgot to be afraid. At the top of the stairs was another antechamber and an ornate double doorway. Passing through it he found himself in a huge mirrored ballroom barely lit by the pale silvery light. He pulled a torch out of his backpack and shone the beam around the room, angling it quickly downwards when shattered light sparkled at him from all directions.

Piles of clothing were strewn across the ballroom floor. He picked his way through, and then, stooping to take a closer look, nearly dropped his torch in shock. He leapt backwards, his heart pounding.

These weren't just clothes. There were people inside them.

At first Tom thought they were dead, but as he looked closer he realised they were sleeping. Hundreds of them – not people, he saw, but faeries, with high arched eyebrows and a slight point to their ears, lying where they must have fallen, in a deep enchanted sleep.

Dust lay across their clothes and faces, and flew up from the floor as he walked. He tried not to sneeze. This was the creepiest thing he'd ever seen. With every step he took, he thought one of them would awake and grab his foot, but he kept moving. He could see doorways leading off to other rooms, also filled with enchanted faeries. They had fallen asleep upon chairs and tables, their faces landing on plates of food, their drinks abandoned.

His ears were playing tricks on him – he thought he heard whispers as soft, violet-scented breezes caressed his face. He repeated to himself, "They're asleep, they're asleep, keep going."

He crossed to doors on the far side of the room and found they opened onto a long broad balcony with stairs at either end. The balcony was also filled with sleepers, and it was here that Tom nearly gave himself away.

Below him was a vast hall, dominated by a cavernous fireplace in which blazed a huge fire. And there were more sleeping faeries. And wood sprites – dozens of them. Quickly turning off his torch, Tom dropped down next to the sleepers and wriggled forward to peer through the carved railings.

They seemed to be celebrating, probably because they'd captured Brenna. They passed round drinks, shouting and singing, while a smaller group clustered together, their heads close, their voices hushed. Tom could smell roasting meat, and his stomach rumbled.

One of the wood sprites stood and banged on a long table that ran the length of the room. When he had the others' attention he shouted, "At last we have someone to offer the Queen. We will leave at dark to meet the others and take her subject to her, then we will be assured of her help!"

At this there was a roar of pleasure from the crowd. "Are you pleased, Duke?" He looked to a faerie standing in their midst, dressed in black and with an unpleasant smile on his lips.

"I am, although it is unfortunate it has taken so long. To change!" he said, raising his glass in a toast, and everyone roared again.

Tom needed to find Brenna and get her out of there fast. He could see only one door in the room, to the right of the fireplace. He hoped this would lead to Brenna, but to remain unseen he needed the sprites to stay clustered around the Duke in the middle of the room. He crawled, belly low to the floor, sniffing dust and grime, down the staircase, then weaved his way between the sleepers until he reached the far side of the hall, which was in deep shadow. While the planning and cheering continued, Tom crawled between the bodies which had been unceremoniously pushed up against the wall. He could feel their limbs squashing beneath him, and he tried to push them out of the way, feeling for the hard floor. Every now and again he paused and flopped, feigning sleep. Finally he was close enough to stand and slip through the doorway.

Making sure there was no one on the other side, Tom followed a corridor until he came to steps leading downwards. At the foot of the steps he stopped and looked around. The corridor was poorly lit; shadows thrown by the occasional torch snaked across the floor. The ornate decoration of the upper corridors had gone, and through half-open doors he saw storerooms housing boxes, bags of flour, jars and bottles. Eventually he came to a closed door. Trying the handle he found it was locked, but fortunately the key was still in the hole.

He pressed his ear to the door, but it was silent within. "Brenna, are you there?" he called softly.

"Yes, yes, it's me! Tom?"

He unlocked the door.

"Tom! How did you find me?" Brenna joined him in the corridor, looking rumpled and slightly grubby, but otherwise unharmed. Her sword had gone, and she looked vulnerable without it.

"Ssh, not now. We have to get out of here." He locked the door behind them so it looked undisturbed.

"No, we can't go yet."

"What? Why not?"

"There's another prisoner, right next door. I heard them speak to him."

"Brenna, we haven't got time!"

"We can't leave him. You know we can't."

He sighed with exasperation. "But we could be caught any second!"

"We are not leaving without him. Here," she said, removing the key from the door, "I think they used the same key."

They slid the key into the lock. It turned easily.

Inside was a sleeping faerie. He was tied to a chair placed against the far wall, his body secured by coils of pale smoke that had solidified around his arms, legs and torso. He had long white-blond hair that shone with a pale light, and wore clothes that had been fine once, but which were now dirty and torn. Tom shook him gently.

The faerie's head shot up and he shouted, "Get away! How dare you touch me!" His eyes were a deep midnight blue.

Tom jumped back. "I'm here to help!" He looked anxiously at the door where Brenna waited.

"Who are you? What are you doing here?" said the faerie.

"I am *trying* to rescue you."

He shook himself awake, his eyes bright and eager. "Really? At last!" Then he looked down at the smoke wrapped solidly about him. "But I can't leave unless we can remove this restraint."

"Well we need to go now, so unless we can do this quickly we'll have to leave you here."

"These coils have to be unlocked, but I know where the key is. I have just enough power left to disguise you so you can get it for me." He looked pleadingly at Tom.

Tom glanced at the smoky restraints and wondered where a key would fit, but only asked, "Where is the key?"

"Around the neck of my treacherous rat of a brother, the Duke of Craven."

"He's your brother? I've just seen him in the hall, surrounded by murderous wood sprites! It would be impossible to get close enough."

Panic shot across the faerie's face. "I can disguise you, I promise! Please. If I don't get out of here soon he'll find out how to use the Starlight Jewel, and then he'll be too powerful for me to stop! And he'll kill me."

Tom felt his heart sinking. He just wanted to get out of here, but felt he didn't really have a choice. He looked at Brenna and she nodded. "Tom, we have to!" He grunted, not entirely seeing the "we" in this.

"If I do this I'm going to have to lock you back in the room," he said to her.

"I understand." Her face was pale but determined, and he recognised that look – it was a look that Beansprout used far too often.

8 Starfall

Tom sighed. "All right. What do I have to do?"

"As I said, the Duke has my key around his neck. It's a small key that looks like glass. It fits here." He pointed to the centre of his chest. "This binding has reduced my magic, but I can cast a spell that will draw some of this smoke to you and allow you to pass unseen into the hall. The enchantment won't last for long, but you can take the key and bring it back to me. Once I'm free I promise to get you out of here."

"How long's not long?"

"Half an hour or so?"

Tom hoped the Duke was still in the hall or he would never find him, and then he'd be captured too. "OK. Do it now."

"Come here – kneel beside me so I can reach you."

Tom knelt and the faerie pressed his index finger to Tom's forehead. He felt a strange sensation pass through him. As he looked down, he saw his body shimmering,

"What on earth …?"

"Go, quickly!"

They ran out of the door, Brenna locking it carefully behind them.

"Tom, he's right," she said, going back into the room she'd been held in. "You're barely visible. Just stick to the shadows and you'll be fine. Good luck!"

"Barely visible" wasn't reassuring, but as Brenna handed him the key he was relieved to find he could still grip things properly.

After locking Brenna in, he ran back up the corridor. It felt twice as long as before. A sprite appeared and Tom froze, but it disappeared into a store room, reappearing moments later with an armful of bottles. As the sprite went back up the stairs, Tom followed, treading softly, his heart hammering in his chest.

He edged into the hall, trying to get his breathing under control. The sprites continued to shout and sing, some aiming their spears at the far wall where several figures had been drawn. There was a rhythmical thump and cheer as the spears found their mark.

Tom saw the Duke sitting on a chair deep in the shadows cast by the balcony above. He was examining a map spread out on the table before him, in a pool of light cast by a single candle.

Tom again hugged the walls and the shadows, but nobody was even looking in his direction. He couldn't even see himself. He crept closer and closer to the Duke until he was standing behind him. It was uncanny – the Duke of Craven looked like a photographic negative of his brother. His eyes were dark and his hair was black, but with a faint dusty sheen to it, like diamond dust. He had sharper features, but they were otherwise identical.

The Duke's attention was completely on the map. Tom could see the glass key on a chain around his neck, chinking next to other, bigger keys. He flexed his fingers and tried not to breathe heavily. The Duke leaned back in his chair, closed his eyes and rubbed his face wearily with his hands. As he dropped his hands to his sides, Tom edged closer, reaching over the Duke's shoulder towards the key. The Duke's hand shot up and went to grab Tom's arm, but Tom snatched his hand back and pressed against the wall. The Duke opened his eyes and patted his shoulder, confused, then sat up and looked round, scanning the space behind him. Tom stood motionless, holding his breath.

Distracted by an approaching sprite, the Duke turned away.

"Duke, we need to go soon," said the sprite.

"Yes, all right, just give me a few more minutes. Are the horses ready?"

"I'll send someone down, they can get the girl on their way back." He strode off, shouting to one of the others.

The Duke pulled a large jewel out of his pocket. It was the size of a duck egg, and its centre glowed. He lifted it level with his eyes and gazed into it. Tom leaned forward too, peering into its depths. He thought he saw swirling stars, and leaned in closer and closer, halting abruptly as the Duke sighed, re-pocketed the jewel, and then leaned back and closed his eyes again.

Tom's stomach churned – he had to get the key now or it would all be over. He reached forward and pulled the key gently between his thumb and forefinger. The key melted off the chain and into his hands; the key recognised him.

Without hesitation he ran back across the hall, down the stairs and along the corridor. He could tell the spell was wearing off – he reckoned he had five or ten minutes' invisibility left. He heard footsteps behind him, but the sprite entered a doorway without noticing Tom.

He made it back to Brenna's room without encountering any more sprites.

"I have it," called Tom, as he and Brenna unlocked the faerie's door.

He placed the key over the spot the faerie had indicated. Magically a keyhole appeared, and the key slotted in and disappeared. There was a strange hissing sound and the smoke began to thin and disappear.

"You have no idea how good that feels!" the faerie said. Colour returned to his cheeks and he stood up gingerly. "Oh, I am so stiff!" he groaned, limping to the door, where he went to turn left.

"Not that way," Tom said. "There are hundreds of them in the hall, and some are coming any minute now to get Brenna. Is there a back way out?"

The faerie looked thoughtful. "All right, follow me. And by the way, who are you? How did a human child and another faerie arrive here?" He turned to Brenna, looking at her curiously. "Why do they want you?"

"Not now!" said Tom, giving him a gentle push. "Keep going."

The faerie frowned at him, but did as Tom suggested. They continued down passageway after passageway, twisting and turning until Tom was completely disorientated, before finally entering a larger space. In front of them was a large wooden door.

Tom tried pushing and pulling, but it wouldn't budge.

"My dear boy," said the faerie, "this is a faerie palace. It won't open just like that. Now, who are you?"

"Can't this wait?" Tom asked. "They'll discover we've gone any minute." Tom was sure he could hear voices getting louder.

The faerie smiled. "I'm not going anywhere. This is my palace and I shall have my revenge. No one knows this place better than me. They caught me by surprise last time, but not again."

"But there are *hundreds* of them. And we can't help any more. Our friends will be worried."

The faerie grimaced and lowered his voice to a whisper. "Don't worry, you have done more than enough. I can manage now. If I so choose, there will be endless staircases that lead nowhere; corridors that shrink to the size of a mouse hole; rooms that seal as soft and moist as a hungry mouth; doorways that lead to a howling abyss; mirrors that show your reflection then steal it and swallow you whole. They will regret ever attacking us. And he will regret ever betraying me."

As he finished, Tom saw over his shoulder two wood sprites running towards them, spears raised. Tom opened his mouth to shout a warning, but the faerie was already turning, and with a flick of his hand and a mutter of something unintelligible, the floor beneath the sprites vanished, replaced by a gaping mouth full of teeth and blood-red gums. The sprites fell in and with soft sucking noises, the mouth closed.

The faerie smiled smugly and asked, "You didn't happen to see my subjects, did you?"

"Well yes, actually," Tom said, struggling to concentrate. "They're asleep all over the floor, on the steps, in the ballroom …"

The faerie looked thoughtful. "Good. And your name?"

"Tom, and this is Brenna."

"And your friends?"

"Woodsmoke and Beansprout," Tom said impatiently, wondering why on earth that mattered.

The man bowed majestically and kissed Brenna's hand. "Madam, Sir. I am indebted. But you haven't answered my earlier question. How are you here?"

Brenna answered. "I was kidnapped by the wood sprites – I was to be given to the Queen of Aeriken."

"Some sort of exchange for her power, from what I overheard," added Tom.

"Really. She doesn't normally share her power. I wonder what's in it for her? And why you?" he mused, looking at Brenna, "and not Tom or the others?"

Brenna flushed. "I have no idea," she answered quickly. "And your name?" she asked, changing the subject.

"I am Prince Finnlugh, Bringer of Starfall and Chaos, Head of the House of Evernight. Now go, quickly. Avoid the edge of Aeriken Forest; if there's any more of them, that's where they'll be waiting."

He muttered and waved his hands, just as Woodsmoke had done under the tower, and the door opened.

Outside it was night. Tom hadn't realised they had been in the mound for so long.

The Prince added under his breath, "If ever there was a time for the King, perhaps it is now."

Tom and Brenna stopped and looked at him. "What did you say?" asked Tom.

He looked at them warily. "Nothing, ignore me."

Tom persisted. "You mentioned a king."

"I am merely thinking aloud. Forget I ever said anything."

"Well," Tom said, considering his words carefully, "we're travelling to the lake if you wish to see us again."

The Prince stared at him and then gave a slow smile. "By the way, don't worry about being followed. I will make sure they never leave."

They stepped through the door and with a crack it shut behind them, leaving them halfway up the hill.

Tom looked at Brenna. "Thank God we're out of there. That has to be the freakiest place ever. I hope Woodsmoke doesn't live in one of those things. Are you OK?"

"Yes, apart from my shoulder. It's really sore. I fell on it when they threw that wretched net on me."

"So the Prince asked a good question. Why you? They didn't bother with the rest of us. What did they mean when they called you her 'subject'?"

Brenna glanced away, reluctant to meet Tom's eye. "I have no idea. They probably confused me with someone else. It's nothing, Tom. Just an exchange for power."

Again she changed the conversation. "Didn't you take a bit of a risk just then? The whole King thing?"

He shrugged. "It felt right."

The grass on the hill was smooth and velvety, clipped short, unlike the meadows below which were luxuriant with waist-high grasses. Once they reached the bottom, there was no sign of the main entrance. The grasses tangled around their calves and smelt fragrant and fresh. They searched for the spot where they had been attacked, hoping to pick up Woodsmoke's and Beansprout's tracks.

Keeping the river on their right, they eventually stumbled into an area of flattened grass – and the dead bodies of wood sprites. There was a moment of panic, of wondering if Woodsmoke or Beansprout lay among them, but there was no sign of either.

Tom took out his torch, holding it low over the ground, and eventually found a faint track leading away from the mound. It was too risky to shout out, so they called in low voices: "Woodsmoke, Beansprout."

They hadn't gone far when they came across another dead sprite. They called again, and this time relief swept through Tom as Woodsmoke answered, "Tom, Brenna, is that you?" They saw a tall figure, black against the pale silver of the grass.

"Woodsmoke?" Tom shone his torch, lighting up Woodsmoke's face. "Are you OK?"

"I am, but Beansprout's not so good. How are you two?"

"We're okay. It's been … eventful," Tom answered.

They followed Woodsmoke to a ring of flattened grass. Beansprout was curled on a blanket, sleeping heavily.

"What happened?" Brenna dropped to her knees next to Beansprout, her face worried.

"She was hit in the arm by a spear. Fortunately it's only grazed, but the spear took a good chunk of skin with it. I've bound the wound, but it bled a lot and was very painful. I've given her herbs to ease the pain and help her sleep. She should be better by tomorrow, I hope."

Woodsmoke sat and Tom dropped next to him.

"How did you get out?" said Woodsmoke. "I'm sorry, I tried to get in but the magic was too strong. I thought you must be dead."

Tom related everything that happened, while Brenna curled up on the blanket next to Beansprout.

"So the Queen wants her subjects back." He looked across at Brenna, but she was silent, her eyes glinting in the starlight.

"You don't live in one of those hills, do you?" Tom asked.

"Oh no, they are used only by the old royal tribes."

"Good, because it was really creepy. And the Prince was … odd."

Woodsmoke laughed. "Odd and powerful; I have heard many stories. Not least from my grandfather."

"Like what?"

"Another time, I think."

"Who are the other royal tribes?"

"There are quite a few, but locally there's the Duchess of Cloy's tribe, and Prince Ironroot's. Their palaces are over there." He gestured over the river. "We don't really see them any more; they hole up in their under-palaces dancing and feasting their long lives away." He stopped, lost in thought.

"And how are we getting back tomorrow, to your home?"

"We'll try to make it to the river, find a boat. It will be quicker and certainly easier. And then we go to the Isle of Avalon."

9 Vanishing Hall

The sky started to lighten, a green wash spreading across the eastern horizon. Tom had barely slept. He was cold and stiff, and was torn between going back to sleep – for days – and wanting to get moving, just to be warm. And he was very hungry. It had been hours since he'd eaten and he had only a few biscuits left.

He rummaged in his pack as Brenna stirred. Woodsmoke was gently shaking Beansprout. She woke, her face ashen in the early morning light, and struggled to sit up.

"My arm's so sore," she said, wincing as she wriggled it.

"Are you able to walk today, or do you need more rest?" said Woodsmoke.

"I'll be OK to walk, but I may not be very fast."

"I can't fly, either," said Brenna. "I hurt my shoulder yesterday. I don't want to risk it."

"We'll walk to the river, see if there's a boat we can get on. I know we're all hungry, but we should press on."

Beansprout looked over at Tom and Brenna. "I was worried we'd never see you again. How did you get out?"

Brenna laughed. "It's quite a story, we'll tell you as we walk," she said.

At about midday they reached the Little Endevorr River, a tributary of the main river they had crossed the day before. It ran slowly, its waters clear, the riverbed visible in the shallows.

They had been following it for a short time when a boat appeared, heading downstream. A man called out, "Is that you, Brenna?" Haven't seen you for a while."

Brenna waved. "Fews! How are you? I don't suppose you're taking passengers?"

"Well I don't normally, but I can make an exception for you."

He steered his boat over to the bank. It was long, like a barge, and filled with sacks and barrels. Fews was grey haired with a wrinkled brown face like an old apple. When he smiled, his eyes almost disappeared into his wrinkles, and Tom saw he'd lost most of his teeth.

"You must know Woodsmoke?" said Brenna.

"I reckon I know your face," he answered, looking Woodsmoke up and down. "You're Fahey's grandchild?"

"I am," said Woodsmoke, smiling.

"So who are these two? They don't look like they're from round here."

"They're humans, come to visit their grandfather, Jack," Brenna answered.

Tom and Beansprout said hello as they clambered into the centre of the boat and settled themselves in the gaps between the sacks.

"Oh, I see, we're having some cross-cultural relations are we? Well welcome to my boat, and don't squash anything!"

He made sure they were all settled before setting off again. "What you done to your shoulder, Brenna?"

"Had a run-in with some wood sprites by the Starfall Under-Palace."

Fews' smile disappeared. "They're getting closer, then. I hope you got rid of a few?"

"Of course. They came off worse."

"Good. There's far too many around for my liking. Don't know what's bringing them out of the forest really. Usually don't like the open."

Tom dozed in the warmth of the sun, the sacks comfortable beneath him. But every time he closed his eyes, images from the previous day raced through his mind. He could see the Prince's malevolent smile, and hear him describing what the palace could do. Once again he realised how far he was from home and how strange this place was.

His stomach rumbled, but even hunger couldn't keep him awake. Finally, he slept deeply.

He woke up when the boat changed direction and bumped the riverbank. A murmur of voices prodded his consciousness and his eyes flickered open. It was dusk and the birds called loudly, swooping over the water, black against a pale-grey sky.

He sat up and found they were surrounded by other boats, moored up and down the river around them, nudging each other in the current. They were mostly deserted, with just the odd light shining from masts and bows. On either side, high banks blocked his view beyond the river, but overhead he could see bridges crisscrossing back and forth.

Brenna and Woodsmoke stood on the riverbank talking to a short squat man who looked like a toad. He nodded a few times before hopping from view in one bound.

Tom nudged Beansprout. "Wake up madam. We're here, wherever that is."

She roused and stretched, stopping short when her injured arm hurt. "God I'm so exhausted. I want a proper bed."

"Well, we might get one tonight, and we might find Granddad too."

She sat up quickly. "Of course, I forgot. He's going to be surprised to see us. Have you any idea where we're going now?"

"Nope, I'm just doing as I'm told."

"Well, that makes a change."

They made their way to the top of the bank where they could see their surroundings more clearly.

On either side of the river was a sprawling village, its edges melting into the twilight. There was a jumble of buildings and market stalls, several running alongside the river. Walkways and bridges linked the buildings and spanned the river, some high above the ground. Lights twinkled in the dusk. Strange-looking people were milling around, and music and singing drifted through the air. Tempting scents mingled and beckoned; Tom could smell food. His mouth watered.

Woodsmoke called them over to where he stood at the crossroads of the road and a bridge. "I'm borrowing a horse and cart to take us home; we should be there by midnight." He looked tired but pleased, and ran his hand through his long hair. He had unslung his bow and it rested at his feet while he flexed his shoulders up and down. Brenna stood next to him, deep in thought as she gazed across the village and the surrounding countryside.

"So where are we?" Beansprout asked.

"Endevorr Village. And that," Woodsmoke pointed across the river, "is Vanishing Wood, where we live."

"That's great. I'm starving. Can we get some food?" Tom asked.

Beansprout nodded. "Me too! Please don't make me wait."

"All right," said Woodsmoke. "I'm pretty hungry myself. We have a while before the cart arrives."

They strolled across to the nearest stalls and gazed at the displays of food. There was a big roast pig turning on a spit, the fat hissing as it dripped onto the fire; plates full of pies and pastries, and dishes of fruit that looked sweet and juicy.

"I want it all," Tom said, drooling.

"I'll get you some pies," said Woodsmoke. "Trust me, they're good!" He handed over some money and received a tray of thick crust pies in return. They tucked in, groaning with pleasure.

Distracted by the rumbling of wheels, Tom looked around and saw a horse and cart being driven by the short toad-like man he'd seen before. He hopped down and threw the reins at Woodsmoke, saying in a gruff voice, "See you sometime tomorrow then, Woodsmoke. Safe journey."

He took little interest in the rest of them and headed off over the bridge, the strange lollop in his walk making the curve of his upper spine more noticeable.

They bought some more food for the journey, then Woodsmoke jumped up onto the front of the cart and grabbed the reins. The others climbed into the back, snuggling under blankets.

They trundled along the road next to the river, but while Brenna slept, Tom and Beansprout were wide awake, staring at everything around them. Small lanes tunnelled between the buildings, burrowing into the heart of the village. They were full of strange beings hurrying about their business. The people – or rather faeries, Tom corrected himself – looked like something out of a story book. Some were tall and stately, and glided along without appearing to walk. Most of them had long hair, which the women wore elaborately braided and piled on top of their heads.

There were also little people that looked like pixies, olive skinned and sharp featured, as well as creatures that were half-animal, half-human. A man with the enormous ears of a hare walked past, and Tom thought he saw a satyr down by the river.

Eventually they passed out of the village and into woodland, where the twilight thickened and midges rose in clouds. The crowds thinned, and before long all they could hear was the jingle of the reins and the clomp of hooves.

They travelled for several hours before turning off on to a road that led into thicker woodland. It was now deep night, and the starlight was blocked by the canopy of leaves. Occasionally Tom saw flickering lights in the distance, but they quickly disappeared before he could work out what they were. Then, at last, a mass of golden lights appeared through the trees.

They entered a clearing containing a well, and a grassy area on which several horses were grazing. Lanterns hung from the trees, illuminating a rambling building of wood and stone that spread in a semi-circle around them. Assorted towers sprouted out of it, some short and squat, others tall and spindly, piercing the canopy high overhead. Vast tree trunks lay at angles to form part of the buildings, and rooms seemed suspended in the branches. It was the oddest collection of buildings Tom had ever seen, and they looked as if they would topple down at any minute.

Woodsmoke directed the horse through an archway into a courtyard, and jumped down, the rest of them following. A door at the base of one of the corkscrew towers flew open and a figure strode out saying, "Who's there? We're not expecting guests."

"Well we're not guests! It's me, Woodsmoke, with Brenna and a couple of friends."

"Oh the Gods – you're back! We were wondering what was taking you so long." The figure strode into view and Tom saw an older faerie with feathered eyebrows and a shock of white hair shot through with red. He trailed sparks, and thick black smoke billowed out of the doorway behind him.

"Are you burning the place down, Father?" Woodsmoke asked.

"No, just experimenting. Have a little faith," he said. "My my my, so you've brought Jack's grandchildren. How very pleased I am to meet you." He shook their hands and reached to kiss Brenna on both cheeks. His hand was firm and dry and he smelt of gunpowder. His clothes were patched and ripped and speckled with burns and singed edges, and across his cheek was a smear of a grey glittery substance. There was a wild distraction in his eyes; he looked as if he wasn't quite all there.

"Well, I'm glad you're back. Your grandfather's somewhere in the main house," he said, striding back towards the tower. "I'll leave you to it!"

"Typical," muttered Woodsmoke. "He's more interested in his experiments than in what's happening anywhere else. You go ahead, I'll sort the horse and see you in a minute."

They followed Brenna into the house and across a huge high-ceilinged kitchen lit only by a smouldering fire. They wound their way through room after room and up several stairways inside tree trunks, before coming out into a big square room dimly lit by candles.

Tom saw two figures in front of the fire. One was standing with his arms outstretched, as if performing to an audience. The other sat watching and listening. They were both so absorbed that Tom hesitated to interrupt;

instead the three of them listened at the door as the man who was standing said, "And he flung his club so far and so high that he knocked a star from the sky. The star skittered across the night sky leaving a blazing trail of light behind it until, gathering speed, it fell to earth."

And then they were spotted, and the man sitting in the chair jumped to his feet and shouted, "Tom! Beansprout! What are you doing here?" He was already trotting across the room, arms outstretched and a big grin on his face. "I thought I'd never see you again!"

Tom and Beansprout ran across the room to meet him, and he crushed them in bear hugs. Tom felt himself become shaky, and had an urge to sit down. He could hardly believe that Granddad was actually here.

"Hello Fahey," said Brenna, greeting the other man with a half-hug, betraying the injury to her shoulder.

Tom's grandfather turned to Fahey, his eyes bright and his voice slightly breathless. "My grandchildren, they're here!"

"Well I can see that, Jack. I'm not blind! What are we all standing for? Come on, sit down and tell us why you're here. Longfoot!" he yelled. "Bring us drinks and snacks."

After a bustle of moving chairs they sat around the fire and looked at each other, a silence falling momentarily as they all wondered where to start. Jack spoke first. "So why – and how – are you here?"

"Perhaps we shouldn't start there." Beansprout winced slightly. "It's sort of an accident. But how are *you*? And how did *you* get here?" He looked so well that she added, "You look great!"

"I am, I am! But you've grown since I last saw you, and it's only been a few months."

"Longer than that, Granddad," she said. "It's been over a year!"

Jack looked open-mouthed at Fahey who shrugged and said, "I told you so."

Tom hadn't wanted to criticise, but seeing his grandfather all warm and happy in front of the fire made him suddenly cross. "We've been really worried about you! How could you just go?"

Jack looked stricken. "I'm sorry, Tom. I realise it seems thoughtless, but at the time it felt like the right thing to do."

"But how? Why? Didn't you think we'd be worried?"

"That's why I left the note." Panic crossed his face. "You did see the note, didn't you?"

"Yes we did, but it was still odd!"

Beansprout interrupted. "Tom, maybe we should talk about this later?" She turned to Jack and smiled. "It's so good to see you! I swear you look younger!"

Tom was still fuming, but he bit his tongue. He realised Beansprout was right – Granddad did look younger, almost fresher.

"It's the air in this place, it does marvellous things to you. I've learnt to ride a horse!"

"Have you? That's so exciting! And you live here?" said Beansprout.

"He certainly does," said Fahey. "He helps me with my storytelling."

Tom looked at Fahey with dislike. He was about to say something to him when he saw Beansprout glaring, so he continued to sit in silence.

Beansprout turned to Fahey and asked, "So is that what you do, tell stories?"

"I do. I am a bard, and a very good one," he said proudly. He had a noble face with silver hair that was combed and shining and tied back in a ponytail secured by a black ribbon.

"Oh he is – and what stories!" said Jack. "Tom, you'd love them." He smiled nervously, as if fearing another outburst. Tom looked at him in stony silence.

While the others talked, Tom fumed. This wasn't the reunion he'd hoped for. He'd expected his grandfather to be worn out and tired, desperate to return home – but he didn't look desperate at all.

Longfoot arrived, a plump faerie in a long frock coat, with a face that was a little mouse-like. His nose twitched ever so slightly, and he had long quivering whiskers arching over a small pink mouth. He carried a large tray on which were crowded glasses of wine and pots of tea, and a pile of toast and butter, which they all tucked into with relish – even Tom who, although grumpy, was still starving.

When Woodsmoke arrived they told Jack and Fahey about their journey. It was a chaotic, much-interrupted story, but before they could tell them about the Lady of the Lake, Woodsmoke said, "Enough. It's late. Everyone's tired, and two of us are injured, so we should go to bed. We can continue this tomorrow." He said this with such finality and authority that no one argued.

Longfoot was summoned, and Tom and Beansprout were escorted to bedrooms, somewhere in the cavernous house.

10 Old Tales

The house was old and ramshackle with warmth that seemed to ooze out of the walls. It creaked and moaned unexpectedly, and seemed to mutter to itself, which gave Tom a restless night full of vivid dreams that chased themselves around and around in his head.

His grumpiness was still apparent the next morning. He brooded and scowled as Longfoot escorted them through the confusion of rooms to the first-floor breakfast room, perched in the leafy branches of a large oak.

"Stop it, Tom," hissed Beansprout. "You're behaving like a child."

He ignored her and picked up a plate, loading it with a large breakfast from the selection laid out on the sideboard.

It wasn't long before Fahey and Jack arrived. Beansprout gave her grandfather a kiss on the cheek, but Tom just grumbled a greeting under his breath. No one else seemed to notice his bad mood; they started chatting without him, Beansprout asking about the house and why they lived in the middle of the wood.

Fahey took a last bite of scrambled egg and buttery toast, sighed contentedly and said, "Can I tell you The Tale of Vanishing Hall?"

Tom rolled his eyes, but Beansprout, remembering how mesmerising his story had been the previous night, said, "Yes please!"

Fahey began. "Once upon a time there lived a count – Count Slipple – one of the fey who lived in the under-palace of the House of Evernight. The under-palace was a warren of vast halls, twisted corridors and shadowy rooms, hidden under the earth in a great grassy mound. Time moved differently in this place, slipping quickly like ghosts through walls, and all of its inhabitants were as old as the earth that buried them, although by a quirk of their race their skin looked as smooth and fresh as thick cream.

"One day, Count Slipple had a terrible argument with Prince Vastness, the head of the House of Evernight. Prince Vastness was powerful and vengeful, and his words carried great power, but Count Slipple was stronger than the Prince realised. Years of resentment rose between them and their words spat back and forth like fireworks. The air steamed and hissed, and fiery barbs and stings snatched at their skin and scorched their hair, until their clothes hung from them in tatters. Grand faerie noblemen, ladies and courtiers ran shrieking into dark hollows and hidden corners as the air crackled with harmful intent. Eventually the evil in their words manifested into a great black tornado before which Count Slipple ran for his life.

"He fled to the stables deep below the under-palace and, flinging himself upon his horse, he whispered the magic words. The hillside rumbled opened above him, starlight pouring through. He raced across the plains and into the tangled woods, pursued by black stallions carrying Prince Vastness and his royal guard. Branches whipped his face and grabbed at his clothes until, in the middle of the woods, he fell from his horse. Exhausted and injured he lay face down in the oil-dark earth, the slime of autumn leaves crushed beneath him, the scent of decay heavy in his nostrils. The ground thundered with the hooves of the pursuing horses and he realised if they found him, he would die.

"Inches from his eyes he saw an acorn resting on the forest floor, and he imagined how warm and safe he would feel in such a small tidy space. As the wild screams of the stallions grew closer he reached for the acorn, and holding it in his hand, whispered, 'I wish, I wish, I wish.'

"The next thing he knew, he was cushioned in a cocoon of velvety blackness. He could still feel the thudding of the black stallions and the ground shook beneath him, but he was warm and content. The thundering hooves fell silent, replaced by the taunts and threats of the riders, which carried menacingly across the still glade. He lay there for what seemed like hours, maybe days, exhausted and weak, sometimes sleeping, other times thinking and regretting.

"Eventually, when he felt better, and when the percussion of hooves and voices had ceased, replaced by the murmur of wind and rain and the creep of roots beneath him, he decided it was time to leave his cocoon. He thought he would wish himself out of it as he had wished himself in, but however hard he tried, nothing happened. Frustrated, he shouted and cursed and uttered magical incantations, but his howls were swallowed by his prison.

"He tried another way, pushing against his boundaries with his fingers, toes, hands, feet, elbows, knees, shoulders and head, and as he pushed he grew and grew, and the acorn grew with him. It was exhausting work, but slowly a crack appeared in the shell of the acorn and light glinted in the Count's eyes; a gleam of gold in the velvety blackness that dazzled his light-bewildered gaze.

"Eventually there came a time when he stopped growing, but the acorn didn't. It grew around him until it was the size of a room, and the crack in the acorn was the size of his arm; a slice of silver pierced the space, cutting the floor in two.

"The Count lay and gathered his strength, admiring the rippled walls that looked like the surface of water. He thought that, as he had no place to live, it would make a fine house and would hide him from those seeking to find him. But he was hungry and needed food, so he made the crack wider and wider until he could step out, and found himself where he had fallen earlier.

"He stood under the glow of the moon. Seeing soft green foliage all around, he realised he had lain in the acorn for months. He heard an insistent splash and, walking a small distance, saw a spring bubbling up from the ground. In the distance, deer were grazing. His horse had long since disappeared.

"Smiling, he looked back at the now giant acorn and saw that it was continuing to grow, roots pushing beneath the ground with blind urgency. Its roof was arched and branches grew from its rounded sides, contorting and twisting into towers that shot vertically upwards, reaching to the stars. The walls were as shiny as a polished apple and slivers of light slid across its curved walls like a smile.

"The Count slipped through the shadows of the tangled wood, his footfall soft on the ground. He looked for signs that the Prince or his men might still be watching, and he was wary of traps in the undergrowth. But apart from the hoots of owls, the wood was silent. He walked as far as the edge of the wood, and gazing across the plains saw the grassy mound in the distance; an absence against the dark night sky. He sighed, knowing he could never return there.

"He walked back across the forest as the ground mist rose and the trees announced themselves in the pale dawn light; beeches and oaks that locked branches against intruders but which, recognising him as their own, let him pass with an unravelling whisper before knotting themselves thickly in his wake. Bird calls rose in a mass, and soon he walked through an ever-increasing crescendo of noise back to the acorn that had sheltered him.

So Count Slipple turned his back on the under-palace and became Lord Vanishing, and the acorn became Vanishing Hall. In time he took a wife and had many children, grandchildren and great-grandchildren, and it wasn't until he was on his deathbed that he told them who he really was, and what lay beneath the great green mound in the distance.

"And all of his descendants lived to an uncanny old age. Their skin had a creamy whiteness, their eyes a vivid greenness that captured the fruitfulness of the forest, and their tempers were as vicious as the summer storms that lit the landscape with the unexpected flash and sizzle of lightening."

By the time Fahey had finished his tale he was standing, waving his arms around, his face animated and excited.

"So this house is from that acorn?" said Beansprout. "That's so amazing!"

Even Tom had to admit that was interesting.

Woodsmoke, who had walked in unnoticed, so engrossed were they in the story, said, "Are you telling tall tales again, Grandfather?"

Fahey looked slightly put out. "It's not a tall tale, and I shall show you the original room later." He turned to Beansprout and Tom. "It's slightly damp now so we don't use it much anymore. Obviously it's been built on over the years, bits added by different generations, but it's essentially the same place, and every now and then a new tower will sprout or an old one will collapse. It's a wonderful place to live. In fact, when I was away the old spindle tower completely disappeared." He sighed and a shadow briefly fell across his face. "I missed this place when I was away."

Jack patted his shoulder. "Don't think of that time, Fahey. You're back now."

"Talking of old tales," said Woodsmoke, "we have something to tell you. Tom met the Lady of the Lake, and she gave him a job to do."

Fahey slapped the table and looked at Woodsmoke with ill-concealed hunger, and a touch of wariness. "He met who? What did she want?"

"He has to wake the King."

"No!" Jack interrupted immediately. "He will not. I won't have him put in danger. He shouldn't even be here, Woodsmoke. It's your fault he's here."

Tom was shocked at his grandfather's outburst. What did he know that made him think it was dangerous? He looked at Woodsmoke, wondering what he would say, but Woodsmoke nodded saying, "Tell them what happened, Tom."

There was an air of expectancy, as if they knew something that he didn't, but he told them of his encounter in the Greenwood and what the wood sprites were threatening in the House of Evernight. He ended by saying, "I don't think I have much choice. And besides, Prince Finnlugh, Bringer of Starfall and Chaos might be able to help."

"Well well well." There was a fire burning in Fahey's eyes now. "You can't rely on the old Royal Houses, Tom. They have their own interests. But show me the silver twig."

Tom still felt a bit resentful of Fahey's friendship with his grandfather, and now of his interference with his task, so he shrugged and said, "I haven't got it now. It's in my room."

Fahey looked at him thoughtfully. "All right, I'll have a look later. But Tom, don't underestimate how hard this will be, even with this silver twig – which, by the way, is probably a powerful charm giving you some protection as you travel through this realm."

"How do you know it's a dangerous task?" Tom snapped.

"Because I tried to wake him myself, and was imprisoned for decades for my efforts!" Fahey looked annoyed.

"But that's because it wasn't meant to happen then. Now it is. She imprisoned you, but she told me it was time."

Jack intervened. "I still don't want you doing this. This isn't your fight."

"Actually," said Woodsmoke, "it is now. You don't refuse the Lady of the Lake. And besides, apparently he's related."

"To whom?" asked Fahey.

"The King."

"How can he possibly be related to King Arthur?" Jack spluttered.

"Because she said so! And I don't know how!" Tom yelled.

"I don't care if you are. You are not doing this," persisted Jack.

Fahey smiled grimly. "It isn't a case of what we want, Jack. The best thing we can do is to help. It will take a few days' riding to get to the Isle, and we can go too. In fact, the sooner we go the better. I presume you'll come?"

Jack looked across at Beansprout. "I suppose you'll go too? Even though I don't want you to."

"Sorry, Granddad, but yes." She looked sheepish as she added, "You came here without asking anyone!"

Tom glared at him. "Yes, you did."

Jack pushed away from the table and paced around the room, running his hands through his hair just as Tom did when he was thinking. He muttered to himself, "Well it's a fine example I gave, I suppose."

"You did say you wanted adventure, Jack," said Fahey.

Jack turned to Tom, now very annoyed. "Tom, this wouldn't have happened if you hadn't come. I told you I was fine. Why doesn't anybody ever listen to me?"

"Well, you can be sure I won't bother again!" Tom yelled as he marched out of the door.

Jack yelled after him. "Well you're stuck with me for now, because I'm coming too!"

Tom retrieved the charm from his room and left the house.

"So what are you so grumpy about?"

Tom turned to see Woodsmoke following him. He shrugged. "Nothing, I'm fine."

"You are not fine, you're sulking like a child."

Tom glared at him. "Well you're not the one who's travelled here to find his grandfather, only to find he's not even been missed!"

"Oh, so that's what this is all about!" Woodsmoke looked at Tom in puzzlement.

Tom ignored him and headed towards what he presumed were the stables. He could hear the horses snickering and he smelt sweet hay and manure. In the far corner was the twisted tower where Woodsmoke's father lived. It was a beautiful day; cool in the shade but hot in the sun. The sky was blue and the trees were flush with bright green leaves. It was difficult to believe they were somewhere other than the world he was so familiar with. He looked at the silver bough in his hands and felt the world tilt slightly. This was not familiar. He was in a strange place being asked to do things he didn't quite understand. It was supposed to be simple – find Granddad and go home. His resentment grew – he was having to do something for people he didn't really know, and for a place that wasn't his home.

He wheeled round and shouted to Woodsmoke. "Actually, I don't see why I should have to do this." He waved the bough in the air. "We've found Granddad, and he doesn't seem that bothered to see us. I may as well go home. All this," he gestured wildly at everything, "is not my problem."

"I thought you wanted to help? She asked you – specifically you!"

"I did, but now I don't." Tom stared fiercely at Woodsmoke, his anger now obvious. "I've changed my mind, and I'm sick of being here. Just leave me alone – I don't want to talk about it any more." He turned his back and strode off. He had no idea where he was going and he didn't care.

Tom's angry thoughts led him out beyond the stables, where he meandered through the trees. Here they were well-spaced, like trees in a park. He found a large flat rock, beyond which was a tangled thicket of trees. This must be the boundary of Woodsmoke's land. He lay on the rock sunning himself, mulling over the disaster of finally being reunited with Granddad.

His thoughts were interrupted by a voice calling some way behind him. It was Beansprout, sounding forlorn.

"Tom, where are you? It's me."

He ignored her, hoping she wouldn't see him and would go away.

She shouted again. She was getting closer. He lay still, hoping the silver twig gave him powers of invisibility, when suddenly she spoke right next to him, making him jump.

"Tom, stop ignoring me. I've come to see if you're okay. Are you?"

"As you can see, I'm fine," he said, refusing to look at her.

She shuffled herself into a spot next to him on the rock, and he reluctantly gave way.

"What do you want?"

"Oh, aren't you gracious? Like I said, I've come to see if you're all right. Woodsmoke said you'd marched off in a strop. He thinks you're crazy. I explained this is normal for you. What's the matter?"

"Nothing. I've just had enough and it's time to go." He looked anywhere but at her.

"But you've been given a task–"

"Who cares about the task?" Tom interrupted. "Why should you care, why should I? This isn't our world or our problem. It's theirs."

"Well, that will make Granddad happy, at least. He didn't want you to do it."

Tom snorted with impatience. "Like that's supposed to make it so much better? He doesn't care that we're here anyway."

"That's not true and you know it!" Beansprout shot back. "Although it would help if you'd actually speak to him. We've travelled all this way and you've barely looked at him!"

"Well it hardly looks like he's missed us. Look where he's living!"

"Isn't that a good thing? What kind of people would we be if we wanted him to be miserable?"

Tom glared into the distance, saying nothing.

"Seriously, Tom, what did you think would happen?"

Tom remained silent.

"I don't think he'll be coming back with us. You know that, right? If he's going to stay here, shouldn't we make sure it's safe for him? If we can?"

"No!" Tom replied, finally. "If he decides to stay he'll have to cope with whatever happens, wood sprites or not! That's his choice, just like it was his choice to come here."

Beansprout sighed. "Why do you always get like this?"

"Get like what?" he snapped.

"Get sulky when what happens in your head doesn't happen in real life."

"I do not get sulky."

"You do it all the time."

Tom didn't reply, trying to ignore the little voice inside telling him it was true.

Beansprout sat looking at the side of Tom's head. "I'd do it, using your twig thingy, but she didn't ask me," she said, a note of regret in her voice.

Tom pulled the little silver twig out of his pocket. He'd put it there meaning to show Jack and Fahey. He turned it slowly in his hands.

For the first time since Beansprout had sat down, Tom turned and looked at her properly. He scratched absently at the sole of his trainer as he spoke. "I don't know what I want to do – or anything, really."

For a few minutes they sat in silence, then Beansprout pushed her hair back behind her ears, saying, "So what's the plan? Are we going home?"

He continued to pick at his shoe and sighed. "No, I suppose we'll stay."

"And are you going to speak to Granddad – properly?"

He narrowed his eyes at her. "Don't nag, it's unattractive."

"Well don't wait too long then, or *I* will!" And with that she slipped off the rock and started walking back, a smile of triumph on her face.

Tom didn't yet feel ready to return to the hall. He lay on the rock feeling its warmth beneath him and the sun on his face, and wondered what he really *had* expected once he got here. He hadn't thought beyond finding Jack. He'd assumed Jack must be in trouble, even though his note said he wasn't, because Tom couldn't imagine why he'd want to leave. He groaned inwardly. Why didn't he think about things more? Oh well, too late now. He was here and he had a sort of job to do, and he had no idea why he'd been asked to do it. Why hadn't he asked more questions at the time? Instead he'd sat there blankly, just nodding, without a clue what it was all about. In fact, the only one who seemed to know anything was Fahey, and Tom had been so rude to him. He groaned again. Now he was going to have to go back and be pleasant and apologise for behaving like an ass.

But he wanted to put that moment off for a while, so he continued to lie on the rock, eyes closed against the sun, holding the bough loosely in his hands.

Hearing noises, he sat up and looked around, thinking there was someone there … but he was alone. After another cautious scan of his surroundings, he lay down and closed his eyes again. He could hear the wind in the treetops; it sounded like voices, a soft muttering of encouragement to the leaves to grow. He could hear the movement of small creatures in the earth below him, and something that felt like a pulse, like hearing his own blood moving through his body. He could feel the bough, warm beneath his fingers. A sudden image shot into his mind, of an island: fields of fruit trees, golden wheat, flowers and bees, and in the centre a large, dark, deep cave. He felt dread in the pit of his stomach, like a nightmare, and opened his eyes again quickly to chase away the image. He hoped it wasn't what he thought it was.

11 The Hidden Isle

The shadows around them lengthened and the air grew cool as the day drew to a close. A chill wind blew, carrying the smell of rain and wet earth across the tufts of springy grass and purple and yellow heathers that covered the moor. Huge rocks, blunt and misshapen, rose from the ground, some big enough to offer shelter. Ahead of them was the massive granite formation of Fell Tor.

They had been travelling for well over a week, climbing to the higher ground of the moor. Vanishing Wood, and the neighbouring Fret Woods, were far behind them and the summery weather had also gone. Tom was aching, cold and saddle-sore. No matter how many layers he wore, the wind seemed to find its way through them, and it wasn't until they sheltered at night he could even begin to get warm.

Night brought its own problems. The wind carried howls, whispers and threats. The fire they huddled around gave off only a meagre amount of light, as if the surrounding darkness was sucking it up. After nightfall, the ground mist rose and ghostly figures appeared, standing just beyond the edge of the firelight, watching and listening. When they emerged, Tom felt the hair on the back of his neck prickle, and goosebumps rise along his skin. Woodsmoke, Brenna and Fahey took little notice of the watchers, but Tom, Beansprout and Jack were nervous and slept badly, even though they had a night watch.

Beansprout had asked if the watchers were real.

"Of course they are," Fahey had said, "although they can't touch you – they're not real in the sense that we are. They are–" he'd leaned forward for emphasis, raising his feathered eyebrows, "your guilty thoughts, brought to life by the dark night."

"They're what?" Beansprout had asked, her face alarmed and confused.

"Every little lie, harsh word or unfair judgement," Fahey had said, shaking his head. "They're out there, watching."

For a moment they had all looked beyond the light of the fire, wondering what they had done that caused a figure to be standing there, watching, before quickly dropping their eyes to the fire again.

However, today Tom was so tired he knew he'd sleep well tonight, regardless of who or what the figures were. The party aimed for the foot of the tor where there was a cave offering proper shelter. From there it was another half a day's ride to the lake.

Tom adjusted his position behind Brenna. A horse had to be the most uncomfortable method of transport. There were four horses and six riders; he was sharing a ride, as was Beansprout behind Woodsmoke. His grandfather, however, looked very comfortable on his horse.

Tom tried to adjust his movements to the horse's, but failed miserably. He gave up and bumped along painfully.

They dismounted at the base of Fell Tor and, lighting torches, inspected the interior of the cave. It was large and dry with plenty of room for them to spread out. After satisfying himself that there were no hidden exits, Woodsmoke unpacked the food and Tom built the fire. When it was burning steadily he called to Woodsmoke, "I'm going to walk up the tor to join the others."

The wind blew fiercely as he rounded the rough path that circled the tor, and he pulled his clothes tightly around him. About halfway up he found the others sheltering in a hollow. They were looking at the silver shine of the lake in the distance, a shine that stopped abruptly as it met the mist dividing the lake.

"That mist never goes," Fahey said. "No matter how hot the day, it's always impossible to see the island in the centre."

"Are you sure it has an island?" Jack asked.

"Well, so the old tales say."

"Has anyone tried to land on it?"

"It's impossible to sail anywhere on that lake. You think you're making headway and then the shore's back in front of you again. I tried for hours, only to end up back where I started. Until of course … Boom! I was suddenly trapped in a tree." He didn't look at them, his attention wrapped up in the lake and the past.

"Are you feeling OK?" Beansprout asked.

"Strange memories, that's all."

The moor below them was desolate, its wide expanses of wind-flattened greenery relieved only by blunt-headed rocks rising like whales from the earth.

Down by the lake edge Tom saw a circle of standing stones. They must be huge, he thought, because even from here they were an impressive sight. The circle reminded him of Stonehenge.

Perhaps it was something to do with the tor, but that night, the watchers seemed to Tom to be stronger, more visible, as if they insisted on being acknowledged. They had built the fire as close to the cave entrance as they could without smoking themselves out. The flames flickered and obscured the view of the moor beyond them, but still Tom could see the watchers.

While they ate, they sat close to the fire, piling on wood so that the flames climbed steadily higher. But as they settled down to sleep, they all crept to the back of the cave and sheltered behind bags and blankets. Woodsmoke had said they wouldn't see the watchers after tonight, as they wouldn't venture close to the lake. Tom could hear the horses snuffling and shuffling unconcerned outside, and wished he could ignore the visitors too.

They came upon the circle at midday, when the stones' shadows were at their shortest. The stones looked as if they had stood there for centuries, solid and unyielding to the weather and the passage of time. Carvings jostled for space on every stone, reminding Tom of the carvings under Mishap Folly at home. In the centre of the ring was a smooth floor of white stone.

They walked around and between the stones, their fingers tracing the carvings, the stone cold beneath their touch. The shoreline of the lake was a short distance away, fringed by a narrow beach of sand sculpted by wind and waves. Now they were closer to the lake they could see that the mist rose up like a wall across the water.

Tom walked to the water's edge. The others joined him, forming a straggling line along the beach. As they gazed across the water Tom turned to them. "What now?"

Fahey pointed to the mist. "Someone's coming."

A long, narrow boat slipped out of the mist, gliding through the water without a ripple. The curved bronze peak of its prow rose high above them, topped by a roaring dragon figurehead, its fierce eyes glaring across the water. A huge square sail stretched across the middle of the boat, filled with wind, even though there wasn't so much as a breeze blowing. Eventually the boat stopped a short distance from the shore.

Tom felt a thrill of anticipation. No one spoke. They stood rapt, as silent and still as statues.

The Lady of the Lake stepped into view on the bow. She looked regal and imposing with her long silver hair flowing around her shoulders and across her vivid green dress. She raised her arm and pointed at them.

Tom felt his head tighten as if there was a band around it, and a soft voice spoke directly in his head. He stumbled and fell to his knees, his hands clutching his head.

Beansprout rushed to his side. "Tom, are you all right?"

"I can hear her, *right in here*. Can't you? Damn! It didn't hurt like this the other day."

"No, I can't hear anything. What's she saying?" Beansprout turned to glare at the woman who stood pointing at Tom. "Stop it!" she yelled at her. "You're hurting him!"

The others remained motionless, gazing towards the boat.

"I don't think she meant to hurt me, it's OK." Tom's face eased and he straightened up. "She wants me to go with her."

"Go where?"

"Where do you think? The island in the lake!"

"On your own? What about me? Ow!" Beansprout clutched her head too.

"What did she say?" Tom asked, guessing what had caused the pain.

"She told me to wait."

"Well then, I'd better go." He smiled nervously at Beansprout and added, "Wish me luck."

He walked across the narrow beach and into the water, every step taking him deeper, until the water lapped his thighs. When he reached the boat he grabbed the side and hauled himself over. As soon as Tom's feet touched the deck the boat started to move, back towards the mist. The sail flapped and turned, and the shoreline disappeared.

The mist pressed into his skin, eyes and hair. Every time he breathed in, moisture rushed into his mouth and lungs, until he felt saturated. Beads of water formed on the hairs on the back of his hands. His jeans were already soaked through and he shivered in the cold. The ends of the ship were invisible, and he couldn't even see the water.

The Lady of the Lake had gone and he stood alone. Seeking shelter, he looked for a hatch in the deck, but saw nothing except wet planks of wood. It was very un-boat-like. There were no stores or ropes, no helm or anchor.

He shrugged off his backpack and took out a fleece. He didn't change his wet jeans, thinking he may have to wade into the water again when they reached the next shore – if there was one.

He couldn't even detect movement. There was no wind, no sign of rippling water, no noise of any kind that might indicate where land was. For all he knew he was motionless, stranded in the middle of the lake, freezing to death.

At least his head felt better now her voice was out of it. He tried to remember her exact words, but struggled, as if he had heard them a long time ago. Well he knew *what* he had to do, just not *how*.

He decided it was pointless to keep standing. No matter how hard he looked, the mist was impenetrable, so he sat with his back against the mast, his pack in the small of his back, closed his eyes and tried to rest.

Tom was awoken by the boat scraping across the ground. He had no idea how long he'd been asleep for. He was cold and stiff, and it was only with difficulty that he pushed himself up off the deck to see where he was.

The mist had cleared to reveal a pale blue sky, although tendrils still ribboned through the air and wrapped themselves about the rocks on the shore in front of him. Gnarled trees lined the beach, and beyond were steep hills thickly clad in tangled trees and bushes. On the summit of the highest hill was a stand of trees, light trickling through the gaps. To the right, a narrow crevasse punctured the smooth line of the hills.

He was utterly alone. The only sound was of an unseen bird calling high above, its cry eerie and forlorn, emphasising his solitude. The waves hushed insistently against the shingle, and Tom realised he was going to have to get wet again.

He slid over the side of the boat and waded to the shore, then tried to squeeze the water out of his jeans, telling himself, "It's not cold, you're just imagining it." He debated building a fire, but curiosity drew him onwards, away from the shore towards the break in the hills.

The shingle slid beneath his feet, making his movements awkward, but once he entered the crevasse the ground flattened and hardened. The shadowed sides were cushioned with moss and dripping with slime and trickling water. The sky was a narrow band of blue high above him, and his footsteps echoed as he walked further in.

After a while the path climbed and curled around the hill. The undergrowth was dense and crowded the path, and he began to sweat with the effort of the climb. Finally he emerged into a clearing and saw a broad vale below, filled with fertile fields, green meadows and trees. It was the scene from the dream he'd had on the flat rock, and although it was beautiful, his stomach tightened with dread. On the far side of the vale he made out a long low building of golden stone, glowing in the sunlight, while in the centre was a rocky hill and the dark mouth of a cave. Tom sank on to the sandy path, drank from a bottle of water and wondered what to do.

The light was falling, the sun sinking rapidly, the sky turning from pale blue to smoky violet. Stars appeared, brighter and closer to him than they had ever been before.

Below him in the vale the woman appeared beneath the trees. She gazed up at him and he felt a gentle push inside his head, before she turned and walked towards the cave.

"OK, so you want me to follow you? I get it," Tom muttered, and he scrambled to his feet and down the path.

The valley was silent. Odd shapes appeared at the edges of his vision, and although he turned quickly, he saw only shadows of an uncertain size and shape. The woman flitted like a ghost, always just ahead of him, through the soft twilight. No matter how he hurried, he couldn't seem to get closer. Arriving at the cave, she stepped in and disappeared.

Tom jogged to keep up with her and arrived breathing heavily. He stopped at the threshold and peered into the murky gloom. She waited in the shadows beyond a small fire burning in the centre. To the left was a cavernous hole, and Tom could see the start of a narrow staircase descending into the blackness.

He took a few steps. "What is this place?"

For the first time she actually spoke, and her voice was odd, like wind chimes. "It's the place where things end, rest, wait, and watch."

"And why am I here?"

"Tom, you know why! You have to wake the King."

"Why? What for?"

"He has to stop the Queen. She is destroying everything. He must go to the old forest."

She had the most maddening way of talking, as if he should know this.

"But why me? Why blood? And how do you know? You might be making it up!"

"Merlin insisted that whoever woke Arthur must be related by blood. It was one of his conditions during our negotiations, and so it was woven into the spell."

Before he could speak, images appeared in Tom's mind. An old man and a young woman, sitting around a fire at the edge of the lake, under a star-filled sky. Between them a long silver sword, flashing with firelight and shadow. The old man shouting, "Vivian! I insist. If he must awake here, he must not be alone. One of his kin must wake him."

"You are a sentimental old fool. He will not be alone!"

"If you deny this request, I deny you him!"

"And I keep the sword."

He softens. "Please, he is like my son."

She hesitates and eventually nods. "Then his descendants will be marked, and I shall follow them all." She reaches into a bag at her side and pulls out herbs and a small cauldron, and together they start to chant.

Tom shook his head and blinked. "Was that you? You're Vivian?"

"A very young me."

"But you aren't one of them. The fey. What are you?"

"I am human, like you. I dedicated my life to magic and decided to stay here, a very long time ago. I helped negotiate the sword."

"But why me?" he insisted.

"I followed all of you. Some of you are too old, some too young, some too weak. Who sent Fahey to your world, Tom? Who did he bring here? Who followed? Was it chance? Luck? Design? And you have the mark, do you not? A dark sword-shaped birthmark across your arm."

Again he had a feeling of being out of his depth; a pawn in someone else's game. His hand moved subconsciously over the top of his right arm, over the long birthmark, and he remembered his mother's mark and wondered if either of her parents had had one too. "How do you know that?"

"I put it there."

He had a sudden rush of dizziness at the implications of her words. Feeling a little sick, he asked, "So what now?"

She pointed to the stairway. "Down there. Follow the steps to the bottom, and then go along the passageway. Remember to use the bough I gave you. It will help you speak to Arthur, too."

"Oh great," he said sarcastically. "I seem to spend my time in dark underground tunnels. I suppose it would be too much to expect his tomb to be somewhere light and pleasant. And how do I find my way in the dark?" He had visions of his torch battery failing and leaving him in the blackness.

She leaned forward and pulled a flaming branch from the fire, muttering a few words over it. She handed it to Tom wordlessly.

Tom grabbed the torch and headed towards the steps, wondering why he'd allowed himself to become involved.

As he started down the steps she shouted, "Do not turn off the main path!"

Tom had been descending for hours, slithering on the steps that widened and narrowed, switching between earth and stone, sometimes crumbling beneath his feet. The torch spluttered and flared as he encountered unexpected breezes carrying damp rotten smells. Crumbling side passages led off into blackness. The air grew stale, and several times he considered turning back, before realising he might not get off the island if he didn't fulfil this quest. His limbs ached and he was hungry and thirsty. He sat down occasionally to rest his legs and drink some water, but the steps were so uncomfortable that he didn't stop for long.

Eventually he came to a wider space – a break in the stairs where he could wedge his light upright and rest properly. He was so tired he could barely think, so although this was probably the worst place in which he would ever attempt to sleep, he decided he had to get some rest. The silence that settled around him was unnerving, but he convinced himself he was safe. He rolled his pack under his head, trying to get comfortable, wondering as he settled down what the others were doing, out there in the sunlight. And what of Finnlugh? Would he come?

12 The Lakeside

For a few minutes Beansprout stood watching as Tom disappeared behind the mist, heading to some distant place she would never know.

A chill swept through her. The boat was clearly ancient; it reminded her of images she had seen of similar boats from the past. Its familiarity scared her – it was as if the past had crossed an invisible barrier and was suddenly right next to her. It challenged everything she had ever known.

Trying to shake off the feeling, and realising there was nothing she could do now to help Tom, she hurried across to where the others stood, still motionless. She stopped in front of her grandfather. His eyes were filled with tears and he gazed beyond her into the distance. She hesitated, wondering if it would be dangerous to disturb him and the others, but decided she couldn't just leave them standing there.

She reached out her hand and laid it gently on his arm. "Granddad, wake up." He remained motionless, so she shook him, watching his eyes carefully. "Granddad, can you hear me? It's me, Beansprout." She thought she detected a flicker of movement in his eyes, but then it was gone.

She sighed and moved to Woodsmoke. He was much taller than her, so she couldn't see his eyes properly. Feeling self-conscious, she touched his sleeve and then his hand, shaking it. "Woodsmoke, wake up."

He didn't stir and she sighed again. With her back to the wide expanse of grey water, she looked at the desolate moor, the windswept grass, the trees, knotted and bent, and the tall standing stones, mysterious and indifferent to her needs. She felt overwhelmingly lonely.

She panicked. "Woodsmoke, I'm scared. Don't leave me here alone!" She shook him more aggressively, and felt a pressure on her hand as he squeezed back. He shook his head as if emerging from a deep sleep, blinked a few times, and then looked down at her. She suddenly became aware that she was still holding his hand, and released it quickly, asking, "Are you OK?"

"I think so. I had the weirdest dream." He looked around. "What's going on? Where's Tom?"

"Gone. With her. And you've been bewitched. All of you." She nodded at the others. "I couldn't wake Granddad."

"And what are we supposed to do?" He moved in front of Jack, Fahey and Brenna, looking at their patient faces.

"We have to wait. Shall we try and wake them? And then we can set up camp."

Brenna and Jack roused more quickly than Fahey, who seemed to be in the deepest sleep. Smiles played across his dreaming face, and it was with the greatest reluctance that he finally woke up, annoyed to leave a perfectly good dream.

It seemed wrong to set up camp within the standing stones, so they found a spot to the side of them, behind the narrow beach. They rigged up a waterproof shelter and built a fire of dry brushwood collected from along the shore. It was mid-afternoon by the time they had finished, and they sat around the fire, warming their hands and drinking a strange herbal tea that Beansprout didn't really like, but had managed to get used to.

They talked about what they had seen while they were bewitched. Each had had a different kind of dream. Brenna's seemed to be the worst; she had dreamt her wings had been clipped and her powers of flight taken. On waking she'd been pale and panic-stricken, and had turned into a bird, flying in wide arcs across the moor. Now she sat shrugging her shoulders, as if she could feel her wings, even though they weren't there. Beansprout wondered if she was always aware of them, as if they had a presence on her human form.

Fahey described visions of the old tales that he told, rolling like a film before his closed eyes, while Jack had floated over the Realm of Earth, which was full of sights he now wanted to see. Woodsmoke had hunted deep within the old forest, chasing spectres and wolves in rich green twilight.

Retelling their magical visions made them uneasy, and they shivered, drawing closer to the fire.

"So how long do you think this will take?" Beansprout asked.

Fahey still seemed caught in the tendrils of his dreamlike trance, gazing out at the mist as if hoping to penetrate its secrets. He murmured, "It could take weeks. We have no idea of what he has to do or where he must go. I wish I was with him."

Woodsmoke frowned. "Or it could take just hours. He might be back here before nightfall."

Brenna shrugged. "I'm sure it will take longer than one night, Woodsmoke. We may as well make ourselves comfortable." She stood up and rolled her shoulders. "I'm going to see what else is happening out there." She nodded across the moor. "I'll see you later." In a blink she had gone, soaring upwards until she was only a black speck.

Beansprout was fascinated by the standing stones. She walked around them, her fingers tracing the carvings, feeling the warmth of the stone against her palm. How long had they stood here, unchanged by the wind, rain and burning sun? Who had made them? It must have taken a long time to carve these beautiful shapes and figures, with their detailed expressions of fear, wonder and horror. She recognised some of the creatures from the carvings they had seen on the gateways, and in the great cavern in the Realm of Water, but others were strange and unnerving – creatures with tentacles, multiple limbs, large eyes, pointed teeth, snarling expressions and sharp claws. She should have felt frightened, but instead felt wonder at being in such a place; that such a place could exist. Beansprout felt suspended at the edge of the world, hovering between the known of her past and the unknown of her future. She had moved from one set of expectations to another, and should have been scared at this uncertainty, but felt only excitement.

She looked over to where her grandfather stood talking to Fahey, gestures filling the space between them, and understood why he would want to stay here. The limits of his life had shifted dramatically. His best friend was a bard, a dreamer and spinner of magic. His words conjured worlds and images, desires and hopes; they chased away the old normal, replacing it with breath-taking strangeness and wonder. In fact, this whole place was a breath-taking wonder.

Beansprout realised she didn't care how long they had to wait. It didn't seem to matter anymore. The important thing was being here, to witness whatever happened. She wondered if this was the spell the Lady of the Lake had cast upon her, but then admitted to herself that this feeling had been growing for some time, it had just taken until now to recognise it.

She had been here only a matter of days, but already it felt like a lifetime. She had no idea what was happening at home, and wasn't sure that she really cared. Hopefully no one was frantic with worry – perhaps their absence hadn't been noticed; maybe some mysterious magic had taken care of that. She nodded to herself. Yes, that would be for the best.

Brenna loved flying. The currents were like silk against her skin, and she felt her feathers ruffling and settling as she adjusted her flight. She angled herself so that she coasted comfortably on cushions of air, and for a while just enjoyed being. She watched the others far below, curious as to the turn of events that had brought them here, with two humans she barely knew. She hoped Tom and Beansprout could help, but wondered how that was possible – they knew nothing of this place, and had no powers.

A sudden faraway movement on the edge of her vision caught her attention, and she stopped her musing and turned. She could see a patch of darkness on the land. She dropped, searching for other currents and headed towards it.

Woodsmoke lay on his back and gazed at Brenna flying high above him, a small speck against the blue. He felt lazy, glad to rest after days of travel. The sun was setting and the horizon was edged with an orange glow. The silence here was deep and endless, and it lulled his senses.

Just as he was drifting to sleep, his attention snapped to Brenna, plunging quickly earthwards. Catching another air current she soared away to his left, heading to where the edge of the moor hit the woods. He rolled on his side and, propped on his arms, gazed after her, wondering what had caught her attention. Feeling uneasy, he jumped to his feet and checked the saddlebags for his weapons. If there was an attack, they were horribly exposed. There was nowhere to shelter, and nowhere to run.

Brenna wheeled on the air currents, landing softly next to the beach where the others were gathered around the fire. The dusk was thickening, the grass turning inky blue in the hollows across the moor. The flames flickered and the wood spat, the only sound on the otherwise silent moor.

"Others are coming." She looked at Woodsmoke with concern.

"What others?"

"The Royal Houses seem to have left their under-palaces. Prince Finnlugh leads them, and I saw the Duchess of Cloy. There were about twenty guards with them."

"Damn! What does he want? This can only mean trouble."

"Not necessarily," said Fahey, "they may be here to help. Historically they're not fans of the Queen."

"I don't trust them, but there's really not much we can do against so many of them, is there?" He turned to Brenna. "How long until they're here?"

"They are far away, on the edge of the moor, but even so they travel much quicker than we do. Maybe two days?"

"That gives us a little time. Well, I don't think Tom will be back tonight. Let's get some sleep. We need to be ready for whatever happens. I'll take first watch, and I'll wake you in a few hours." Brenna nodded in agreement.

Prince Finnlugh, Bringer of Starfall and Chaos, sat on his horse and waited impatiently for the rest of the group to catch up. His horse fretted beneath him, as anxious as he was to continue. He had reached the edge of the woodlands, and the moor stretched out in front of him. He was annoyed. It had taken too long to persuade the others to act.

After Tom and Beansprout had freed him, he had strode about his palace unleashing his fury on the unsuspecting wood sprites who lounged around, drunk on his wine and beer, fattened by his food and lazy with arrogance. He had blasted them into various parts of the known and unknown universe. The lucky ones were dead; the others would be left to an uncertain fate in whatever place they ended up in.

The fight with his brother had been unsatisfactory. He had tried to shrivel him to the size of a walnut, sending a spell that would suck every inch of moisture out of him. But his brother was wily and clever, and the Prince narrowly avoided being splintered into a million pieces by a well-aimed curse. The Duke had managed to escape, leaving behind him a trail of destruction and a large hole in the rounded walls of his palace. The Prince had no doubt he had fled to Aeriken Forest, to recover. But the worst news was that he had escaped with the Starlight Jewel. The Prince had to get it back before the Duke learnt to master it.

He had sealed the palace, creating new spells to protect it, and then went to work waking the members of the Royal Houses strewn across his ballroom floor. His brother's attack had been perfectly timed. The other members of the under-palaces had been visiting for a ball, so not only was his own household there, but all of the others too.

His brother had put a strong sleeping spell on them that took some time to break, and when they did wake they were groggy and confused. Old Prince Featherfoot would probably never be the same again. As outraged as they were by the attack, they hadn't wanted to retaliate, preferring to hole up in their palaces as they had done for centuries, trying to avoid trouble. It was the Duchess of Cloy who finally saw sense.

"My dear Cloy," the Prince had sneered. "If it has happened here, it could happen to you! Do you think this will just go away? That they will not attack again? This is not over."

"I shall seal my Palace of Scents so that no one will ever get in again," she had raged. "Do you think I'm weak?"

"I am the strongest of all of us, and I was still attacked."

"You were betrayed by your greedy infantile brother. No one will betray me."

"We are weaker if we remain isolated and alone, my dear stupid Madame!" he had said, raising an arched eyebrow. "Don't you think he covets your treacherous scents that beguile and bewitch? He may already have raided your palace. He might well be selling your secrets right now! Now we know he is not to be trusted, he is free to act openly. And he won't stop there. We don't know what he will do! I have no idea what he will do! No one will be safe unless we capture him."

He knew she couldn't bear to think of her secrets escaping. Her creamy skin was flushed with rose, and her ruby red hair, which looked like flower petals, quivered in a mound high on her head. Rich earthy scents with a hint of sulphur rose from her skin as her rage increased. "He wouldn't dare."

"There is no one to stop him, apart from us. Unless we count the Queen; she is the only one as powerful as me. However, it seems she has made some sort of alliance with him, and is on his side. I fear she wants the Starlight Jewel."

Now he had her attention.

"And how do you suggest we stop them?" she asked icily.

"With help. And I think I know where we can get it."

Eventually she agreed to accompany him, along with a small company of the Royal Guard. The rest returned to the under-palaces to protect them, and Prince Ironroot was placed in charge. And now they were heading to the lake. If Tom was waking the King, he wanted to be there.

13 Arthur's Icy Tomb

Tom awoke with a start. The torch was still burning strongly and he had no idea what time it was. He stretched, drank some water and ate some dry biscuits. He was so hungry his stomach growled. Other than the flickering torchlight, he was surrounded by a musty blackness. The path ahead was shrouded in darkness, and his pool of light billowed from small draughts. Heaviness settled on him; the weighty expectation of his strange inheritance. He pulled his sleeve up to look at his birthmark.

It seemed to move in the torchlight, and he ran his fingers over it as if he might feel its edges raised and different from his normal skin. But it felt the same as usual. He hadn't really taken notice of it before, and to him its darker tone didn't even look like a sword.

Suddenly fearful of remaining where he was a second longer, he gathered his things and started down the path.

He could hear voices – whisperings and murmurs. He came across a tiny warm yellow light in a passage off to his right, the entrance marked by a metal gate on rusty hinges. As he paused before it, the gate swung wide in welcome. The yellow light flared brightly at the end of the passage, and scented air raced out to envelop him. It looked so welcoming and warm, and he was so cold that he decided to investigate. He stepped closer and the light flared even brighter, but as he laid his hand on the gate his own torch flickered and nearly went out, causing him to halt sharply. He stepped back warily as Vivian's warning came to him – stay on the path. A shriek pierced the silence and the light at the end of the passage flared white and then disappeared. As the breeze carried the smell of rotten flesh towards him, and the shriek faded away, Tom fled. He felt sick with fear. Taking some deep breaths he noticed the torchlight was once again burning strong and bright. He wouldn't forget Vivian's instructions a second time.

As Tom plunged deeper underground it became colder and colder, until by the time he reached the bottom of the steps his breath appeared as icy clouds. There was now only one route to follow – a passageway thick with frost that disappeared into intense darkness. Feeling he was nearing his goal, he set off quickly, his torchlight reflecting on the walls as a dull spark of orange. He began to imagine he could see things emerging out of the blackness, and then thought he heard something pattering behind him. Instead of slowing to listen, he started to walk even quicker until he was almost jogging. Then he had a horrible thought, that he might plunge into a hole in the floor or miss a turning, so he slowed down again. His hands and nose were freezing and he started to shiver.

Finally he saw dim light ahead, and emerged into a long cavern. Murky green light was filtering through a low transparent roof, and a flash of movement overhead made him realise he was under the lake. There were fish and ... other things. Things that seemed very big.

It was like being in an aquarium. But he couldn't work out what the roof was made of. Maybe crystal or thickened glass. Or ice. The floor was made of huge flat slabs of stone, and in the centre was a rectangular tomb made of thick ice. Deep within it he could see the shadowy shape of a man.

Tom sighed with relief. He'd made it. Now he just needed to work out what to do. If Arthur wasn't dead, why was he in a tomb?

He tried to push the lid off, but it was heavy and sealed shut.

The cavern walls were covered in thick frozen vines. Some had spread across the roof, and a small tangle of vines had grown across the tomb. He remembered the silver branch. Did he need to use it here?

He pulled it from his backpack, his cold fingers fumbling. Its silvery brightness glowed in the dim green light. He walked around the cavern peering at the vines, hoping the branch in his hand would fit somewhere. Nothing.

He plonked his backpack on the ground and sat beside the tomb, staring at the sleeping man below the ice. Something glinted in the figure's hands, something which ran the length of his body. Excalibur. Made by faeries as a gift for Merlin. How weird was this? He put the silver branch down on the tomb and pulled the water from his pack. There was hardly any left, and he might need to share it, assuming he could somehow wake the King. They would have to climb all the way out again. What if the King was old and decrepit? Or weak from sleeping for hundreds of years?

Contact with the tomb seemed to be doing something to the silver branch. Its brightness was decreasing – it was turning back into wood, as it had been when Vivian gave it to him. Now shoots were sprouting rapidly, and tendrils spread across the tomb. As they touched the old frozen vines, these started thawing and growing too.

Tom leapt backwards, away from the tomb as the vines spread and the walls started moving with green wriggling growth. The tomb was soon invisible under a mass of vines, and the bough returned to silver, glinting under the fresh growth. How on earth was he supposed to get into the tomb now?

He glanced back towards the entrance and saw with a shock that it was completely smothered in vines, and with a rumble the weight of them pulled the earth down. He was trapped.

Thick shoots were now punching their way through the tomb's weakening ice. The cavern walls began to drip with moisture as the temperature warmed. Chunks of the icy tomb fell to the floor, and puddles formed beneath his feet. Tom pocketed the silver bough, put his backpack on, and began to pull chunks of ice away in an effort to speed things up.

A movement in the wall opposite stopped him momentarily. He felt a breeze and heard a dull roar. What now? He stood looking warily at the wall and felt a splash of cold water on his head. Then he saw drops hitting the floor across the cavern. He looked up with horror. The roof was melting. He would drown if he didn't get out of here quickly.

Tom grabbed the torch, ran to the wall and pushed aside the vines. Thrusting the torch forward he saw another long passageway, and he could hear running water.

Something slid and crashed behind him, and he heard a groan. His heart in his mouth, he span round and saw Arthur roll free of the ice. The King rose onto his hands and knees, breathing deeply, and then stood slowly, as if it were a great effort. Excalibur lay at his feet.

He was younger than Tom had expected, and tall with a powerful build. For a few seconds he looked dazed, then he focused on Tom, saying something that Tom couldn't understand.

Tom shook his head. "What? I'm sorry, I can't understand you. Look, we're under the lake and we have to go. Now!" Tom grabbed Arthur by the arm and pulled him towards the vines.

Arthur resisted, again saying something Tom couldn't understand.

Tom pointed upwards at the dripping roof, trying to show the urgency of their situation. "We have to go – now!" He pulled on Arthur's arm again.

Arthur looked up and around the cavern, and then understanding dawned. He sheathed his sword and staggered after Tom, who pushed through the vines and set off quickly along the tunnel.

Every few metres Tom glanced behind him, but Arthur kept up. The passageway led to an underground river running alongside the path. The floor was slick beneath them, glinting in the flickering light, and the roar of water became louder as they began to climb upwards. Then, abruptly, they reached a steep crumbling rock face. To their right, a waterfall tumbled over the rocks, spray filling the air around them.

Tom peered upwards into the darkness, and wondered how high they would have to climb. He gripped the torch tightly. If he dropped it they would be in total blackness. With his other hand he sought hand-holds as he clambered up the treacherous path. Arthur slipped and muttered behind him.

Tom had the horrible feeling the entire journey back to the surface was going to be this difficult. He wanted the stairs back. If the cavern roof cracked it would flood, as would the path they were on. He did not want to drown. Don't think of anything, he thought, but climbing and keep climbing. Hand over hand, upwards and upwards. His limbs burned and his fingers were sore and bruised. His chest ached with every breath he took. Beyond his laboured breathing and the roar of the waterfall, he heard and felt a deeper rumble. Was that the roof collapsing?

Just when he thought he couldn't climb any longer, the path started to level out and the roof came into view not far above his head. He collapsed onto the ground, gasping for breath, closely followed by Arthur who lay next to him, chest heaving.

Tom wondered why Arthur couldn't understand him; this would make life tricky. And then it struck him – Vivian had said to use the branch. He pulled it out of his pocket and, nudging Arthur with his foot, handed it to him. Arthur sat up, looking puzzled. "Why are you giving me this?"

"Yes! I can understand you! It worked."

Arthur looked shocked and then smiled. "What an interesting trick!" He turned the bough over and over in his hands, as if it would reveal its secrets, then handed it back to Tom, looking at him intently. "To whom do I owe my life?"

"My name is Tom, and I was sent by Vivian to wake you. I didn't really plan on it, you know." And because he was still feeling annoyed, he added, "It wasn't my choice. I had to do it. And I'm not very happy about it."

"Well, Tom, my reluctant rescuer, I am Arthur, and I'm not sure I'm very happy about it either."

"I do know who I'm rescuing!"

Arthur laughed and gazed beyond Tom. "Well, Tom, I can see a boat, so let us use that, because I don't think I can walk much further. I find I am weak, but hope I will regain my strength soon."

Tom saw Arthur was right. They were on the edge of water – not a river, something bigger. He could feel a change in the air and in the sounds around them. The far side was hidden in blackness, but there was a small boat pulled up onto the shore. On his right the water churned and raced before pouring over the edge.

They pushed the boat into the water and clambered in, bobbing unevenly as they sat on narrow benches. Tom propped the torch in the prow as they looked for ways to move the boat, but within seconds the boat started to move on its own.

Arthur murmured, "The Lady of the Lake is always resourceful."

Tom just grunted in reply. There were other things he'd have said about her.

"And where are we, Tom? Other than underground."

"Well, we're not in England any more. We are in The Other, The Land of the Fey, or something of the sort."

Arthur nodded slowly. "Ah! Merlin's deal. I didn't really believe that. I should have known better."

The boat moved silently across the inky blackness of the lake, the roof low and uneven over their heads. They had come such a long way that Tom guessed they were travelling back to the lakeshore, not the Isle of Avalon. He glanced up, unsettled that there was water above them and below, with the possibility of more water arriving. If the cavern flooded, the water level would start to rise, and there wasn't much room for that.

Arthur lay down, eyes closed, his head on the edge of the boat, his feet under the bench. Tom guessed he was in his thirties. His hair was long and dark, and he had a short beard. His sword lay sheathed at his side, and the hilt's strange engravings flashed in the light. Had he only been this old when he'd died? Or had he been put into a magical sleep? Or had faerie magic made him younger?

Tom looked again at his birthmark, comparing it with the sword next to Arthur. Was it his imagination or did his birthmark look sharper than before, like the real Excalibur? Were there shapes coiling in the centre? Shaking his head as if to free himself from a trance, he covered his arm and shivered.

Without warning they plunged into mist. Mist underground? Faerie magic again. Tom was exhausted. He lay down in the bottom of the boat and gazed at the roof passing overhead, trusting that Vivian would protect them.

14 Waiting and Watching

The group at the lakeside slept later than usual, but it was still earlier than Beansprout would ever rise at home. The first thing she did after waking was feel her arm, where the spear had punctured it. It was healing quickly now, and it had begun to itch. It would leave a scar. She smiled; she had a battle wound.

As she rolled on to her back she saw the blue sky above her, pale like a duck egg. She sat up, clutching the blanket around her shoulders, and faced the wall of mist stretched across the lake. Her grandfather and Fahey were still dozing, but someone had added wood to the fire and it blazed brightly. A kettle hung above it, steam seeping from its spout.

She smiled with contentment. She could get used to this. It felt so freeing to be lying on the lakeshore beside a fire. She felt she could do anything, go anywhere. Anything she needed she had with her.

Before they'd gone to sleep last night, Fahey had insisted on telling one of his tales – to help them relax, he'd said. He told a tale about an ancient king who outwitted a forest goblin. It was very funny, particularly as he paced around the fire acting out the parts. Beansprout presumed he was trying to make them feel brave, and it sort of worked.

She grabbed her dirty cup from beside her and walked over to the lake to swill it, before refilling it with sweet herb tea. Sitting down again she looked around for Brenna and Woodsmoke. She presumed Brenna was flying, but where was Woodsmoke? She swivelled to look back over the moor. Grasses and heathers rippled all the way to the horizon, a blackish-green line where the wood began. To the north was the old forest – Aeriken Forest. She rolled it around her tongue, and tried to imagine what mysteries it contained. Woodsmoke had told her it was the home and hunting grounds of the Aerikeen, and that some of the Realm of the Earth's stranger creatures lived there.

She looked for signs that Prince Finnlugh was approaching, but saw only unbroken grass and scrub. A figure bobbed over to the left.

Woodsmoke, emerging from one of the hollows.

"I think we should move," he said as he sat down next to her. "The hollow over there is broad and deep, sheltered from the wind, and more importantly will give us cover from unwelcome attention."

"Do you really think we're in danger?"

"I don't know, but I'd rather we at least try and hide."

"Wouldn't we be better heading back to the Tor? At least we'd be high, and able to defend ourselves."

"It would take too long. And what if Tom arrives back here and finds himself alone, without help?"

"He'd better not be on his own!"

"Even if he's with the King, we can't leave him here."

"No, I know. It was just a suggestion. What if they surround us – around the hollow?"

"They're more likely to head for the shore, then we can retreat back across the moor."

"Without Tom?"

"He might be here by then. Stop being awkward."

"Sorry." She looked sheepish. "Just trying to help. OK, let's pack up and hide in the hollow."

"If you two have finished bickering, I would like to agree," said Jack, stirring from his blankets. "Let's head for the hollow. I feel a bit exposed here."

Brenna returned at midday. She had ranged over the moor and woods, but not over the thick canopy of Aeriken.

"The Prince and his company are nearly halfway across the moor," she said.

Beansprout gasped. "But they move so quickly. It took us days to travel that far."

"They have a far greater magic than we ever will," said Woodsmoke, "and their horses are swifter and more powerful. They're bred from an ancient line of magical beasts."

"It is said that one of the royal line came with his followers to the lakeshore, millennia ago, to raise a new house," said Fahey. "He wanted to solve the mystery of the lake and reach the Isle of Avalon. But not even he was strong enough to do that." He sighed regretfully.

"Why, what happened to him?"

"He disappeared and was never seen again. His cries echoed through the halls day and night, and many perished trying to find him. They abandoned the place in the end. No one could stand it there."

"Where was it?"

He nodded downwards. "Somewhere beneath our feet!"

Beansprout looked uncomfortably at the ground below them.

"I'm going to remain out there, as a bird," said Brenna, "perched on the standing stones. I can keep watch for them – and for Tom." She flitted out of the hollow.

"I've changed my mind" grumbled Fahey. "I don't like hiding here, it makes me feel like a coward. And I can't see what's going on."

Woodsmoke gave him a long impatient look, filled with distaste. "We are not hiding like cowards, we are trying to protect ourselves from attack, old man. Are you going to produce a sword from under that cloak?"

"That's unfair and you know it."

"Apart from your skill with words, have you anything that could protect us?"

"I might know a few charms that could make us invisible, a protection from unwanted eyes." He looked sly, as if he was doing things he shouldn't.

"Good, do it."

The light was falling and long shadows were stretching over the ground when Brenna returned. They sat at the base of the hollow, a bright fire burning merrily, eating a supper of stewed rabbit that filled the air with a rich warm smell.

Beansprout was relieved they had moved camp. It was so much warmer out of the moorland wind, and it felt safer somehow.

Woodsmoke sighed. "I don't think Tom will appear tonight. I had hoped we'd be out of here before Finnlugh arrived, but now ..."

Beansprout adjusted the blanket across her shoulders and, turning to Fahey, said, "Maybe to pass the time you should tell us another tale."

"I have many. Any particular one?"

"Yes. I would like to know more about Arthur."

"There are many such tales. Arthur's knights, Arthur's battles, Arthur and Merlin ..."

"I'd just like to know a little bit about him."

"Then I shall keep it simple. Centuries ago, Britain was in turmoil. There were many kings, fighting for power and land, and then outsiders came who fought them all. One king, Uther, was more powerful than most, and he had a very clever man as his advisor. He was called Merlin.

"There were rumours that Merlin was a wizard. They said he could control the elements — earth, water, air and fire; that he could turn night to day, control animals and cross to the Otherworld. At that time the paths between both worlds were easier to walk, if you knew where to look. Many fey and humans passed to and fro, and Merlin crossed many times.

"Uther had a son, called Arthur. He was born in Tintagel, Uther's castle by the sea. Merlin spent much time with him, teaching him many things. The things he couldn't teach, he made sure Arthur learnt from other skilled men.

"Uther's son grew strong, and yet he was a gentle man, keen to talk with his enemies rather than fight. But when he did fight, everyone marvelled at his strong hands and quick feet. Warriors admired his skill and pledged him allegiance.

"When Uther died, Arthur became king, but the time was fraught with danger. In spite of the invading outsiders the kings still fought each other ferociously. Merlin wanted to give Arthur a weapon with magical powers to protect him in battle, and which would unite the people. He crossed through the mists to the Otherworld to bargain for such a weapon.

"His friend Vivian had magical powers, and great influence amongst the fey. She was wise and gentle and lived upon the Isle of Avalon that straddled both worlds. She spoke to the Forger of Light, who agreed to make a sword – Excalibur. But in exchange for this magical weapon, Arthur had to come to the Otherworld when his life was all but over, to rest until he was needed. Merlin felt he had little choice and agreed to the bargain, though he never forgave Vivian for it.

"So Merlin performed one of his greatest feats of magic. In order to prove the sword's powers, and Arthur's power to rule over all, he set the sword in a great stone, telling the kings that whoever could withdraw the sword would be the one and only true King of Britain. Many tried and many failed, all except Arthur. He withdrew the sword from the stone as if he were pulling it from butter. And he held it aloft, and the sun struck it and dazzled those watching, and they fell at his feet acknowledging he was the one true King.

"These warriors became his knights, and to promote fairness and equality Arthur had them sit at a round table, and the land of Britain united to fight and repel the newcomers. His court was at Camelot and it dazzled beneath the sun and moon like a shining jewel. Arthur ruled for years and years. His knights fought, quested, feasted and held tournaments; his people loved him and the land was at peace.

"But in the land of light, some still sought the shadows.

"Arthur had an older half-sister, called Morgan le Fay. She resented the time that Merlin gave to Arthur, and she begrudged Arthur's success. Morgan was half-fey and half-human, and a powerful sorceress. Merlin didn't trust her. She conspired against Arthur, seeking to destroy him. Using her magic arts, she lured Arthur's nephew, Mordred, with promises of power and wealth. She filled his head with lies and trained him to kill Arthur. She was patient, waiting and watching until Arthur was distracted. And finally the time came.

"Arthur was betrayed by his wife, Guinevere. She was beautiful but weak, and desired Sir Lancelot, one of Arthur's greatest knights. And Lancelot desired her. When Arthur found out, Guinevere was banished and Lancelot fled the kingdom, swiftly pursued by Arthur who chased Lancelot far and wide, full of anger and vengeance.

"Morgan seized her chance. By the time Arthur returned, Mordred had taken the land. They fought in the great Battle of Camlann, and Arthur was mortally wounded. As required by the bargain, Arthur's body was carried to the lakeshore from whence he could be taken to Avalon. Excalibur was thrown into the lake as a signal to Vivian, and she emerged from the mists with her eight sister priestesses to escort Arthur to the Other.

"And Britain fell into darkness."

That night, Beansprout dreamt of Vivian and the large bronze boat with the dragon-headed prow coming to take Arthur to Avalon, in the same way as Vivian had taken Tom to wake the King.

15 Strange Alliances

Tom sensed that the lake had narrowed – something in the air seemed to have changed. He daydreamed as the unreality of his situation nagged at his brain, lying on his back and gazing up at the thick tendrils of mist obscuring his view.

Again he had the feeling of not moving, of being suspended in time and place, caught forever in a pocket of air between two lakes.

Arthur was motionless beside him. Tom couldn't understand how a man who had slept for hundreds of years could want to sleep again. Feeling charitable, he put it down to physical exhaustion. It had been an abrupt awakening. Finding yourself on the floor of an underground cavern after being asleep, in ice, for hundreds of years, would be very odd. He wondered if Arthur could remember dying? He would ask him when he woke up.

He wanted to sit up and look around, but the mist continued to hide the low roof and he didn't want to hit his head, so he remained lying down. He was bored, and felt as if he had been in the dark forever.

Tom lost track of time. He heard a strange distant shout and thought his ears were playing tricks, but then he heard it again, coming closer. His skin prickled with goosebumps and he froze. Something was coming towards them. Again, a moan and a splash. He rolled onto his stomach and peered over the edge of the boat, dreading that he might see something there, but all was darkness except for the small sphere of torchlight on mist and water. He hurriedly lay down again and the sound stopped. He wanted to see the sky again and feel a warm breeze. When he got out of here, it was time to go home.

Eventually a soft grey light banished the darkness and the mist disappeared, revealing a high, vaulted natural roof. Tom sat up and peered into the gloom. They were again on a river, but to their right was a large, seemingly unending cavern, like an underground cathedral. Huge columns reached up to a carved stone roof.

Tom nudged Arthur. "Wake up, look at this."

Arthur barely stirred, but Tom kept prodding him with his foot, unable to take his eyes from the cavern. He wanted to get out of the boat. They must be near the lakeshore now.

As if the boat had read his thoughts, it steered to the riverbank and stopped.

Arthur sat up, bleary-eyed. He looked as amazed as Tom. "Where are we?"

"I've no idea, but I think we might find a way out."

They clambered out onto shallow stone steps and entered the silent halls that glowed with pale light. Their footsteps echoed as they walked past soaring columns, stairways that crumbled halfway up walls, and doorways that stood empty and dark. There was no obvious source of the light, except perhaps from the stone itself.

Arthur carried his sword in readiness, although there were no signs of life. Tom carried the torch – just in case darkness fell once more. He thought this was possibly the weirdest place he'd been so far. It was creepy because it was so obviously deserted. But someone had lived here, someone had built this. Who?

A long wailing cry echoed in the air, and Tom halted in alarm. "What the hell was that?"

They turned quickly, looking in all directions, but the hall was empty.

"I heard that earlier, on the lake," said Tom. "This place is freaky. Let's find an exit, quickly!"

Another wail punctuated the silence.

"Tom."

"Yes," he answered impatiently.

"Look down."

Tom did so, and saw water lapping gently across the floor.

"The cave roof must have collapsed. The cavern's flooding."

"Vivian doesn't like to make life too easy, does she?" Arthur muttered angrily.

They ran along corridors and sloshed through rooms while the water continued to rise, until eventually they came to a broad set of stone stairs ascending to another level.

"This will buy us some time," Tom said, relieved.

On the next level they saw rooms stretching away on either side, but the stairs continued to climb. Carrying on upwards, they came to a sealed circular space.

"There are no doors here," Arthur said.

"There has to be some way out," Tom said. "Start looking."

They examined the walls closely, feeling along the cracks, hoping to find a hidden opening or some sort of mechanism, but with no success.

"Let's try the floor, Tom," said Arthur. "Look, there's an interesting pattern right in the middle, and maybe ..." He broke off as he pressed a small depression in one of the centre stones.

With a rumble and a grating sound that set Tom's teeth on edge, stones started to shoot up around them.

Arthur looked at him and grinned. "Exactly as I thought."

The floor formed itself into a series of steps that joined up with steps descending from above. Blue sky winked through an opening in the roof, and Tom sighed with relief. Neither of them could get up the stairs fast enough.

They emerged in the centre of the standing stones. The sun was dropping towards the horizon and the stones' shadows fell long and dark across the moor.

Brenna stood at the edge of the circle, grinning broadly, while Woodsmoke, Beansprout, Fahey and Jack raced over the moor, almost colliding with Brenna. Woodsmoke looked relieved and Beansprout rushed over to hug Tom, but Fahey, although pleased, looked far more interested in the gaping hole beneath them.

"Tom, you're back! You did it!" whooped Jack, grabbing Tom in a bear hug.

Tom grinned broadly at them. "I guess I did. Let me introduce you to Arthur."

Arthur stepped forward, greeting them each in turn. Beansprout blushed as Arthur took her hand and kissed it. The myth had become a man.

As they stood shaking hands, Tom glanced beyond them puzzled, "Who's that?"

They all turned and groaned, except for Beansprout, who was extremely curious to meet the much talked of and mysterious Royal Houses. The setting sun fell on the approaching Prince and his group; their silver armour flashed, the horses' black coats gleamed, and their pennants fluttered in the wind as they raced across the moor towards them.

"Prince Finnlugh, Bringer of Starfall and Chaos, and a few friends ..." Brenna explained, her eyebrows raised and a smile playing across her lips.

"He came?" Tom asked.

"So much for trying to hide," Woodsmoke groaned.

Fahey looked at the hole, then at Tom. "So where did you come from, Tom?"

"You won't believe what's down there," he said.

"I bet I will," said Fahey, smirking.

Woodsmoke ignored them all and walked to the edge of the standing stones, Brenna at his side, watching the approaching riders. The Prince and his party drew closer in a swirl of wind and thundering hooves. Coming to a stop, the Prince jumped down and strode quickly towards Tom and Arthur. Before he could get close, however, Woodsmoke stopped him, stepping directly into his path.

"What do you want here, Prince Finnlugh?"

"I was invited," he replied, looking past Woodsmoke towards Brenna and Tom, his eyes finally coming to rest on Arthur. "I wanted to know if it was true." He looked at Woodsmoke. "I'm not here to cause trouble."

"Then you are welcome," said Brenna, and she led the way to the others.

It was a strange company that gathered that night on the edge of the moor, the brooding wall of mist on the lake marking the edge of the visible world. Several camp fires had been lit, and the Prince and the Duchess had magically erected enormous pavilions for shelter, grown from the heathers and small bushes that lay thickly around them.

Before darkness had fallen, Fahey and several of the Prince's party had been unable to resist descending the great stone steps leading to the underground palace. Not that they could explore far – the water continued to rise and the lower floor was now completely submerged.

Tom lounged on a couch, revelling in his moment of glory. He tried to work out how deep he had been and how far he'd travelled, but time and distance had lost all meaning. He was amazed to find that only two days had passed – it felt more like a week. He looked across to where Arthur sat by the fire, surrounded by people pressing him with questions. Fahey was gazing at him gleefully, unable to get enough of this unexpected figure from the past. Tom felt he should be more awed than he actually was, but he was so exhausted from the pace of the previous days that he couldn't properly take anything in. It was too unreal.

He was more curious about the oddities of the Prince's party. The Duchess of Cloy had a towering mass of hair like an enormous wedding cake piled on her head. At least, he thought it was hair, but it looked like petals. She wore a pendant around her neck, on which hung a large green stone mounted on gold – but the stone rested at the back of her neck rather than at her throat. He was unnerved when it blinked like an eye, and even more unnerved when the Duchess turned around and gazed at him for long seconds. He could smell violets, sweet and overpowering, and then as she turned away the smell vanished, leaving him feeling giddy and sick.

They were all odder than Woodsmoke, Brenna and Fahey. He hadn't realised how much he'd grown used to his friends' otherness. But the people, or rather the fey, from the Royal Houses were very strange. Some had peach-like skin, soft and furry; others had skin as smooth as cream, or skin covered with whiskers. Their hair was like silk, or balls of cotton candy, coloured like rainbows or as white as snow. They were draped in magic; it crackled over them like static electricity.

Beansprout sat next to him. "You all right? You're very quiet."

"I'm exhausted. The rescuing business is hard work."

She laughed. Tom had related how he'd woken Arthur, and the mad dash through the tunnel and onto the underground lake.

"I think Woodsmoke is feeling happier about the Prince." They looked to where Woodsmoke and the Prince sat next to the fire, speaking earnestly. "I wonder what happens now?"

"Back home I guess," Tom said.

Beansprout took a deep breath. "I don't want to go back, Tom."

"What? Are you kidding me?"

"No. I love it here. I have room to think. I'm not going, and you can't make me."

"You can't not go home. What would your mum say? She'd freak out."

Beansprout shrugged. "It's just the way I feel."

"You might feel it now, but you won't forever. What will you do? You're being crazy. This isn't real," he said, gesturing at everything around them.

"Of course it's real. It's just a different real."

"But you don't belong here."

"But I could," she said stubbornly. Getting up, she left him and walked back towards Woodsmoke. Sighing, and getting to his feet with difficulty, Tom followed.

The Prince was gazing at Arthur's sword. It glinted in the firelight, which illuminated the rich and fantastical engravings along its polished blade and hilt. "Merlin was a powerful man to negotiate that for you, Arthur," he said admiringly.

Arthur laughed. "Merlin liked to get his own way, and generally did. Until his luck ran out." He sighed deeply, his laughter gone, and he gazed back to the fire. "It's because of that sword that I'm here, honouring his bargain, when I should be dust by now."

"You have a purpose, Arthur."

"It seems so. The Lady has decided I must stop the Queen."

"And I must stop my brother. We can help each other."

"How?"

"Travel together, into Aeriken. I think they are working together; why shouldn't we?"

"You don't need me. I don't have powerful magic."

"Neither do I at the moment. I am weakened by the loss of my jewel. But you have Excalibur; it is a talisman, forged by faeries and full of protection. And besides, Vivian seems to think differently. She woke you especially for this reason. And I can help you!"

Woodsmoke and Brenna were watching this exchange with interest. And no wonder, thought Tom. A Prince who had isolated himself and his retinue in his under-palace for years, and an ancient King of Britain, far from home, brought back from the dead.

The Prince turned to them. "I'd like your help, too."

"How could I possibly help you?" asked Woodsmoke. "I have less magic than you, and I don't have an all-powerful sword."

"But you are a hunter and a tracker. If anyone can help find my brother, it should be you! And I bet you know Aeriken better than anyone here, except for perhaps … you my dear," he said, turning to Brenna. "You can fly, and therefore must be of the Aerikeen, ruled by our beloved murderous Queen Gavina. Therefore you can help us in other ways."

Brenna's face drained of colour and she turned away abruptly.

"Oh come now, Brenna. You must want to stop her. She's hurting your people! Here's your chance," Finnlugh said in his most persuasive tones.

16 Aeriken Forest

The trees of Aeriken Forest grew closely together, as if trying to repel newcomers. The thick green canopy was suffocating, the branches forming a tight tangled knot overhead, and the forest interior was dim and soupy.

The track was narrow, forcing the band of travellers into a strung out, winding line.

They had been in the forest for several days now, but there was still no sign of the Duke of Craven. Woodsmoke had led them to an area the sprites had lived in, but it had obviously been deserted for some time. He told them he hadn't hunted there for years, and much had changed, but said the deeper they moved into the forest, the more dangerous it would become. They would start seeing wolves and satyrs soon. Already the wolves' howls echoed through the night, sending prickles up their necks. The horses were becoming spooked, skittering nervously in the darkness, and everyone was jumpy, thinking they were seeing things in the murky gloom.

Beansprout was by now quite at home on horseback. "I think we're being watched," she said, riding beside Tom.

"Why do you think that?"

"Can't you feel it? It's like there's a million eyes on us."

"It's just this place, the Otherworld. I feel like that all the time."

"No, this forest is different. It's brooding, wondering what we're doing here."

Occasionally a figure would materialise out of a tree trunk and stand watching from a distance, barely visible, dark eyed and green skinned, before melting back into the shadows. Fahey whispered that they were dryads – spirits of the trees and guardians of the forest.

By nightfall they had changed their plan. Brenna would lead them to the Aerie, a palace built into the crags of a steep cliff deep in the forest. It seemed inevitable that the Duke would head there – if he dared risk it.

"Of course my brother will risk it. He's desperate to use the Jewel." Prince Finnlugh looked as if he was beginning to regret this march into the forest. "And we have to find him quickly, before he learns to harness its destructive powers."

"So," said Arthur, "you have brought us into the forest, but we seem to have moved no further forward. May I ask your plan? We will not succeed without one. Travelling to the palace on a whim is foolhardy."

"Good question," Woodsmoke said. "Steal back the jewel? Kill the Queen? Save her subjects and restore order to the forest?"

"I don't need sarcasm, thank you." Finnlugh turned to Arthur. "Do you have a better idea, Sir?"

"Not really." The King shook his head thoughtfully. "I feel a little unprepared. Vivian seems to think that I shall know what to do, but frankly I have no idea. I know nothing of this Queen, or what she is accused of. As you know, I have been in an enchanted sleep for a very long time. Perhaps someone can explain to me what it is she has done. Who *is* she?"

"She walked out of the forest and into our palace hundreds of years ago," Brenna said. "She was lost, hungry, exhausted, and needed help. I wasn't born then, but we all know the tale. She looked fragile and seemed kind, and quickly our King fell in love. His wife had died and he was lonely.

"She wasn't one of us, but he didn't care, and neither did we. They were happy, and had children and then grandchildren. But as the years went on we began to see a different side to her. She was quick-tempered, manipulative and sly. But the King couldn't see it. And then the King died and we mourned. And although his firstborn son should have become King, the Queen continued to rule.

"Slowly but surely things started to change for the worse, and when she was challenged, those who had dared to question started to disappear, particularly the heirs to the throne. And so we left, drifting away to hidden parts of Aeriken where we could not be found. Some left the forest altogether, as I did.

"And it seems she is now worse; that she has turned on even those whom she trusted."

"But how did she gain so much control?" Arthur asked.

"She tricked us with her magic, until it was too late to stop her. This had never happened to us before; we were innocent and trusting. And if we couldn't stop her then, I'm not sure we can now. She seems to have gone mad."

"Her whole court may be dead, if she has been 'hunting her own'," Woodsmoke said. "I'm just not sure what she wants with your brother,

Finnlugh, or what your brother wants from her."

They were crouched around a small fire, the horses snickering quietly, tethered to the trees. Tonight the Prince and Duchess had raised elaborate three-sided tents, protecting their backs from the cold dark eyes of the forest. Their lack of progress was beginning to annoy everyone, and the forest's atmosphere twisted their thoughts.

"And," Brenna added, "the forest has changed. There's no one here. It's as if all the forest creatures are hiding. Something is very wrong."

"I think she wants the Starlight Jewel," Finnlugh said thoughtfully. "It could greatly increase her power. Why else would the Duke be coming here?"

"Well, in that case," Arthur said quietly, "we must head to the palace."

Towering above them was the steep wall of the cliff. The top was hidden from view, shielded by clouds and mist. Despite its height, it had been impossible to see from the forest as the trees were so dense and the canopy so thick. It felt like it had taken weeks to reach it.

Mosses covered the floor, disguising fallen trees, and they stumbled along making slow progress. It didn't help that the paths to the Aerie were hidden from outsiders, and Brenna had difficulty finding them again.

The feeling of gloom had grown ever stronger, until they were barely sleeping, their dreams filled with strange images. They had taken their mind off things by sword-fighting with each other. Beansprout and Tom were given swords suitable for learning with, and Arthur taught them, saying he needed to practise too.

For the past few nights, wolves had surrounded the camp. It had taken several volleys of arrows before they'd retreated, their teeth flashing in the firelight, their eyes glinting yellow.

And then a group of dryads had appeared out of the shadows, silent and solemn, barely visible in the fire's glow. Those sitting round the fire had leapt to their feet, wondering how the dryads could have passed the guards. A dryad stepped forward asking, "What do you want here?"

Finnlugh answered, "The Queen and my brother. Nothing else."

"She will kill you. We hide from her now; everyone hides from her now. Beware your fire." And then they had vanished.

Finnlugh had put out the fire, and they had fallen silent in the dark.

At the base of the crag, they searched for hours before finding the narrow stony path to the top. They decided to leave the horses at the bottom with some of Finnlugh's Royal Guard.

There had been another argument. "You should stay here, help protect the horses," Finnlugh said to the Duchess. "I can feel very strong strange magic. Something is very wrong here."

"I did not journey all this way to look after horses," she hissed in reply.

"If and when we escape from the palace, we'll need the horses to return. And I don't want anyone following us up that hill. I have no wish to be trapped."

Jack joined in. "Actually, there's no way I can get up there without a horse. I'll stay, and so should you," he said to Tom and Beansprout.

"Not a chance," they answered at the same time.

"You have no idea how dangerous it may be!" argued Jack.

"And that's why I'm going," answered Tom. Despite weeks of moaning, he now realised he had no wish to be left out of anything.

"And don't think you'll change my mind!" Beansprout said.

Fahey looked at Jack. "I'll stay. My knees will never manage that climb, unfortunately. And they're right. They should go. I feel they're part of this."

Jack looked as if he was going to protest, but then sighed and fell silent.

"See!" Finnlugh said to the Duchess. "You need to protect them too."

She stared at him, frowning.

"You know I'm right, dear Duchess. You can feel it too."

The eye in her pendant blinked slowly, and she stroked the necklace absentmindedly, as if listening to something. "All right. But if you're not back in three days, I leave you here."

"A deal then. We start at first light."

Before they set off, the Prince and the Duchess magically built a tall fence of thick thorny wood to protect the camp. It was set back under the trees, the horses secured inside and the remaining guards positioned around the edge.

The Duchess settled herself in front of the small bright fire. Rummaging in her bags, she brought out a variety of herbs which she cast into the fire, muttering quietly. With a sizzle, the flames changed colour to smoky blues and greens, and she sat for some time in a trance, gazing into their changing shapes. Eventually she roused herself. "We shall manage without a fire again tonight."

"But the wolves – we need to keep them away!" Fahey said.

"We must rely on the boundary. There are worse things than wolves out there. We must become invisible, we must appear dead."

"What? What's out there? And how can we appear dead?"

"We will smell dead, which will attract the wolves but keep away other things. Trust me on this, Fahey. You heard the dryads. We do not want the Queen finding us."

She moved off to prepare her magic, and Tom wondered yet again what he'd got himself into.

17 The Rotten Heart

The stony shale slid under Tom's feet and he cursed as he climbed. In places he needed to bend double against the steepness of the path. He was grumpily aware of Brenna ahead of him, stepping lightly and effortlessly.

"Brenna, why aren't you flying?" he called.

She paused and looked back at him. "I can't".

He stopped in surprise, catching his breath and stretching out his aching back. "Why not?"

"Something's stopping me."

"Like what?"

"The magic Finnlugh mentioned. It's making the air feel syrupy, so I can't fly."

"It feels fine to me," Tom replied, puzzled.

"Trust me, it's not." She turned and kept on climbing.

Tom gazed out over the forest. He'd passed clefts and hollows, and forced his way through thick vegetation. They were above the canopy now and Aeriken stretched to the horizon. His muscles burned with the effort and he was sweaty and tired. The rest of the party toiled above him, some out of view. He sighed as Brenna disappeared ahead of him, then with a great effort pushed on, muttering to himself about stupid quests.

A scream interrupted his thoughts and he looked up, pushing his hair out of his eyes. Was that Beansprout? The scream was followed by shouts and yells. Damn! He ran, cursing his aching muscles. Rounding a corner, he stumbled into Brenna and the others.

He found himself on the edge of a wide cleft reaching deep into the cliff face. At its furthest corner were the palace gates, hanging open, the entrance dark. Carved out of the rock was the Aerie. The cleft was filled with dead birds – hundreds of them. Their bodies lay thick upon the ground, bloodied, their feathers torn. The smell of decay was strong and Tom's stomach turned.

But that wasn't what had caused the shouts and screams. Spread on the cliffs above them were scores more birds, and other creatures, half-human, half-bird, their huge wings spread behind them, shackled to the rock. They were all dead. Many had rotted, leaving skeletons to bleach in the sun.

Tears poured down Brenna's face, and the rest of them stood in shock.

"Who could have done this?" said Arthur.

Nobody answered.

Arthur pulled Excalibur from its sheath. "Allow me." He pushed ahead, and the rest of them followed, peering nervously upwards. Their footsteps echoed on the rock, bounding around them. Shale slipped and slithered down, landing at Tom's feet. Woodsmoke halted briefly, his bow angled steeply upwards. Apart from wind-ruffled feathers, nothing moved. He lowered his bow and walked on.

Beyond the shattered gates of the palace was a broad hall, illuminated by beams of light slanting in from above. The roof was high overhead – if it could be called a roof.

Most of the walls were solid rock pitted with openings, out of which scrubby bushes and trees grew haphazardly, but closer to the top the walls became a lattice work of rock, open to the wind and sky. Bridges of stone arched above them, weaving backwards and forwards, higher and higher, like the spokes of a wheel.

"It's like an aviary," the Prince murmured.

"Well, we *are* birds. What did you expect?" Brenna answered abruptly. Her tears had dried and she looked pale and angry.

The floor was thick with feathers and droppings, with the odd paw print visible. "Wolves," said Woodsmoke.

Arthur scanned around. "Where to now?"

"I have no idea. I thought I'd see signs of my brother, but ..." Finnlugh trailed off.

"We should go to the throne room." Brenna said. "That's where the Queen's power is concentrated. We should see what's there."

An eerie cry punctuated the air and arrows thudded into the ground around them. Some of Finnlugh's guard's were hit and fell awkwardly to the floor, arrows jutting from their bodies.

Everyone ran for shelter. Woodsmoke fired arrows above them, but their enemies were out of sight.

Brenna shouted, "This way!" and ran, zigzagging towards a dark recess in the far wall.

A body almost fell on Tom, and he stumbled as he ran round it. Next to him, Beansprout sprinted, her hair streaming behind her. The guards who had already reached the recess fired arrows back into the hall. Tom threw himself through the arch as Finnlugh shouted, "Keep behind me!" The Prince muttered something unintelligible and thrust out his hand, from which a ball of white light flew into the hall. A boom echoed off the walls, hurting their ears. Several wood sprites thudded to the floor, dead, their limbs splayed.

"My brother! He's here!" Finnlugh said. He turned with a wolfish grin. "Lead on, Madame!"

"The throne room's up there," Brenna said, pointing upwards.

"Up there?" Tom repeated, feeling his legs protesting already.

"There are steps cut into the rock on either side of the bridges," explained Brenna, "and rooms leading back into the hillside. But we have to cross the bridges to make our way up."

"I'm sure there will be more sprites up there too," Finnlugh added.

Tripping on each other's heels, they followed Brenna up the stone staircase until they reached the first bridge. Finnlugh's guards made their way quickly across, and the rest jogged after them, weapons drawn. Thankfully the way was clear, and they were able to move upwards across the first few tiered bridges, zigzagging their way across the palace.

Tom took deep breaths and tried not look down as he ran across the bridges, which were far too high and narrow for his liking. As they reached the end of each one, they paused to search for signs of life on the bridges above them and in the rooms on each level.

"Who lived here?" Beansprout asked.

"Members of the court – anyone who slept in human form rather than in bird form. It varies; depends on your mood or your duties."

"What do you mean, duties?" Arthur asked.

"The Queen demanded that most retained their human form, and we each had to serve her if we lived here. I decided to leave. It wasn't forbidden, but …" she paused. "I made myself an outcast, and I wasn't the only one. She could be very demanding. And I had other things to fear too."

The rooms were abandoned and dirty, but there were no more bodies. "It's as if they fled and were caught outside," Brenna said.

As they stepped out onto the next bridge, another volley of arrows and spears rained down from above and they retreated quickly – except for Arthur and Tom, who were too far ahead. They ducked and dodged, managing to reach the other side unscathed. Tom had just drawn his sword when a small group of sprites thundered down the steps towards them. While Arthur leapt into action, Tom could barely think how to swing his sword and he stabbed wildly, feeling his sword sink into flesh and bone. A sprite swung at his head and, as Tom ducked, the sprite fell dead at his feet. Arthur stood behind having barely raised a sweat.

"Are you all right, Tom?"

"I'll let you know later."

Arthur and Tom ran to the top of the stairs and saw several more sprites halfway across the bridge, unaware of Tom and Arthur as they fired on the bridge below. Tom had forgotten how big they were, their bodies solid muscle, their flesh a dull greenish brown, their faces sharp and angular. Some had horns spiralling out of their skulls, around which their matted hair was wrapped.

Arthur ran silently, his sword held before him. Tom followed hesitantly, his sword also drawn. If he was honest, he didn't feel he was needed. Arthur fought with an effortless grace and strength, and his sword looked as if it was an extension of him. He was surefooted and well balanced, and Tom realised clearly, as he hadn't done before, that he was watching Arthur, King of the Britons. He felt a jolt, a sense of unreality that was stronger than anything he'd felt before on this strange journey. The feeling jolted him into the present. He saw everything with an icy clarity: the vast spanning bridges, the high-walled palace of pitted rock, and the cries and shrieks of sprites in the sharp icy air.

Tom ran to Arthur's side and helped distract the sprites, attacking one from behind, unbalancing him so that he fell from the bridge. Tom's heart was pumping, but he didn't have time to feel afraid. When the last sprite was killed, they rolled the bodies off the bridge.

The others joined them and they scanned the upper levels again, but the bridges once more appeared empty, the dark entrances in the rock devoid of life, the spindly trees motionless. After hushed reassurances they pressed on, higher and higher.

There were now eight of them: Arthur, Brenna, Woodsmoke, Finnlugh, Beansprout, and two of the Royal Guard – not many at all, considering what they may find at the top, particularly as Tom and Beansprout had next to no fighting skills. Tom held the sword he had been given, thinking how awkward it felt. He gripped it tighter, wishing his hands didn't feel so sweaty.

Just before they reached the top, Arthur suggested they shared some food to keep them going. He had assumed charge of their small group, and no one thought to question his natural command, not even Finnlugh.

When they had rested, they pressed on to the final bridge and then stopped to assess their position.

They were dizzyingly high. Above them was open sky. The solid walls had gone, and perches lined the latticed walls, beyond which they could see patches of mist that drifted through and hung in the air around them. The wind moaned ceaselessly, carrying the smell of ice and snow. It was freezing, and night was falling. Faint stars began to spark, and a full moon edged above the forest canopy. Below them the bridges criss-crossed back and forth, the floor disappearing into the inky blackness like the bottom of a well. The bridge ahead glowed in the dusk like a ghost road.

Several armed wood sprites stood looking out over the bridge from the opposite side, their dark silhouettes misshapen and deformed.

"They're guarding the throne room," said Brenna.

From the shelter of the doorway, Woodsmoke and the guards exchanged a volley of arrows with the attacking sprites. Eventually the return fire stopped and Arthur led the way across the bridge. The anteroom was empty except for their lifeless bodies.

"Useless brutes," Finnlugh said, kicking one as he strode past.

Arthur paid them greater attention, checking to ensure they were all dead.

Beansprout gingerly stepped over them. "It's so eerie here."

Woodsmoke nodded. "I have heard much about this place, but still, this is not what I was expecting."

"Are they all dead? The court, I mean."

"I don't know." He shrugged, looking a little lost.

Finnlugh coughed impatiently. "Finished?"

Woodsmoke bristled with annoyance, but Tom answered, "What now?"

"Now we find my brother and regain the jewel that is rightfully mine."

"Are you prepared for what we'll find in there, Finnlugh?" Arthur asked.

"No. Are you?" Finnlugh asked pointedly.

Arthur ignored him and turned to Brenna. "Do you think the Queen is in there?"

"No. She would have made her presence felt," she said grimly.

"Well then, Finnlugh, the show is yours. Just ensure you do not put anyone here in danger. Or you'll answer to me."

The throne room was guarded by huge double doors of burnished rock and wood. They stood listening for a few seconds, but it was deathly quiet. Arthur turned the handle and pushed open the door.

The throne room was a large square wilderness of cold stone. It was surrounded on three sides by high sheer rocks, and above, it was open to the sky. The fourth side, directly opposite the doors, was edged with a low balustrade, beyond which the sky stretched pitilessly. The floor was of smooth stone, and tall square pillars ran like sentries down either side, creating a ceremonial path to the throne at the far side of the room.

The throne was carved from black granite, and it seemed to suck what little light was left into itself. Crouched in the seat, looking small and insignificant, was the Duke of Craven.

He was focused entirely on a small glowing object in his hands. It gave off a cold blue light, flashing occasionally as he turned it. Before the others could even think, Finnlugh swept his hand to the right and the jewel flew from the Duke's grasp, clattering into the wall and then to the floor.

"Tom, get the jewel!" ordered Finnlugh.

The Duke jerked upright, but before he could react, Finnlugh made a pulling gesture. There was an enormous crack, which echoed off the sheer walls, and the throne began to grate across the floor towards them, the grinding of rock against rock sounding like a wounded animal.

The Duke looked up and smirked, extending his own hands as he did so. The floor rocked with what felt like a wave, knocking the others onto their knees. Only Finnlugh remained standing, his gaze fixed intently on his brother, muttering under his breath, his arm outstretched and his hand palm up.

The noise of the grating stone was almost unbearable. Tom pressed his hands to his ears, but unlike the others, who were edging back beyond the entrance, Tom ran towards the jewel, glowing faintly in the distance.

Finnlugh and the Duke were locked together with fierce intensity. Shards of rock began to fly off the throne, shattering against the surrounding walls and cutting and scratching the others as they retreated. Tom tried to protect his head and eyes and focused only on the jewel. The floor continued to jolt, and Tom ran and fell, and ran and fell.

The others ran back through the open doorway, diving for cover either side of the entrance.

Just as Tom was closing on the jewel, the floor's motion changed. For a moment he thought the floor was dissolving, then he realised it was a shallow pool of water – the violent jolting had caused the water in the pool to slosh across the stone floor. He skidded in the wetness until he finally fell in front of the glowing jewel, and clasped it within his hands.

Tom looked back towards the Prince, but saw only monstrous shadows within a whirling cloud of rocky flints. Moonlight fell on the hall, casting slanting shadows from the pillars, turning the hall into a prison of barred light. The floor continued to buck, and shale started to slip and slither down the walls, forming rivers of rock.

Tom staggered back towards the Prince, wondering how he was going to get the jewel to him as his attention was so fully focused on the Duke. Tom's feet snagged on rock and he stumbled; shale stung his face and he felt blood trickle down his cheeks. Finnlugh saw him and extended his right hand. The wind that now whirled around them meant that Tom could get no closer, so he threw the jewel towards Finnlugh's outstretched hand, hoping it would find a way through the tornado of rock. Finnlugh's break in concentration caused the Duke to push back and Finnlugh staggered, giving the Duke time to turn to Tom, sending a pulse of energy so strong that it threw him back against the wall in the centre of the hall. He dropped like a rag doll into the shale at its base. But it was as if the jewel had been summoned to Finnlugh, and it snapped into his hand with a sound like a thunderclap.

The Duke howled, "No!"

"I told you I would find you and take back my jewel!" Finnlugh shouted. "Surrender while you can."

"Never – you waste your power. It is pointless you having it!"

As the jewel connected to the Prince, it started to swell with light until it encompassed Finnlugh and blinded his brother. An enormous pulse of energy hit the Duke and he rose high into the air before slamming to the floor, motionless.

Finnlugh seemed to shrink, and the jewel pulsed in his hand like a purring cat. He stumbled over to where the Duke lay and stood looking at him in silence, before sinking on to the floor next to his brother's broken but still moving body.

Tom sat rubbing the back of his head. There was a large lump on it, and bits of flint were lodged in his hair. And he ached all over. The wind had dropped, and now all that disturbed the silence was the trickle of shale.

Arthur stepped through the doorway, followed by the others. He stood next to Finnlugh and said, "You couldn't kill him, then?"

But Finnlugh didn't answer. Arthur continued to watch the twitching form of the Duke.

18 The Old Enemy

Tom sat gazing numbly into the shallow pool of water in front of him. He was too tired to lift his head and instead gazed at the moon's reflection, glittering in the water. The stars were brilliant with diamond light and the sky was thick with them, bathing the hall in a cold white glow.

As Tom sat, half-aware of Arthur's muted footfalls pacing the hall, he saw a gathering patch of darkness in the night sky. The stars started to wink out in ever-increasing numbers, until it seemed something was swallowing them. An arch of shadow cut into the moon, growing bigger. What the hell? It looked like wings, but …

A screech pierced his ears and he looked up to see a vast winged figure fly over the hall. He heard the panic in Brenna's voice as she cried out, "The Queen!"

The black shape wheeled overhead in ever-decreasing circles, until the Queen landed with a shake of her immense wings.

The moonlight cast the Queen's features into sharp lines. Her long oval face was framed by straight black hair that swept past her shoulders and down her back. She was semi-human in form, her legs ending in talons that clattered on the floor, her arms at her side, a cruel jagged knife in one hand. Wings spread from either shoulder, spanning at least five metres, raising and flexing as she strode forward towards her shattered throne. Her eyes were dark black beads that glittered in the half light.

"Brenna," her voice rasped, "it's been too long. I'm so glad you're back. I've been searching for you, and the others. They think they can hide from me, but they can't hide forever. Come into the light, I want to see you."

Brenna moved forward, as if under a spell. Her feet dragged and she clenched her fists, but she was drawn irresistibly onwards until she stepped out of the shadows of the pillars and into a bright patch of moonlight.

"Did you really think you could come here, and that I would allow you to leave?" asked the Queen.

"What did you do to them?" Brenna said, her voice hoarse. "Did you do all this? Did you kill your own people? Your family?"

"They betrayed me! They refused to do as I asked and then tried to depose me. How could I tolerate that?" Her voice rose higher as her anger increased. "Then they abandoned me and the palace. They left me. Me! Fled into the forest. They all left me!" She paused, and stepped forward into the light, her voice now low and dangerous, "And you. You left me years ago, without asking permission."

"You betrayed me, remember? You killed my parents."

"It was a fit punishment for the crime. Treason is an ugly thing."

Arthur remained in the shadows, but his voice rang out. "And you know all about treason, don't you?"

The Queen turned abruptly, trying to find the source of the voice. "Who is that?"

"But I'm so upset. You don't recognise me? I know you. I would recognise that voice anywhere."

She paused, bewildered. "I know who you sound like, but you can't possibly be ..."

Arthur had circled behind her, and he called out, "Oh, but I can."

She whirled round in an effort to see him. "But you are dead. You fell in battle."

"As should you be, Morgan. You live well beyond your lifespan."

She gave a cackling laugh. "This world offers many benefits. I could not stay in our world. Others came looking for me. So I made the crossing permanently, to my other home."

Arthur continued to hide in the blackest shadows, pacing silently out of view, leading her away from Brenna.

"So while I have been sleeping," he said, "you have been meddling and destroying – again."

Her claws clattered on the stone as she stepped towards his voice. "I was going to live quietly here in the forest, but ... you know me, Arthur."

"Yes I do."

Arthur remained stubbornly hidden from view, fighting for time.

"And you?" she asked. "How are you here?"

"Vivian wished it. But enough of me. You look different. What happened?"

She flexed her wings self-consciously, and for a second Tom sensed regret in her tone. "I had hoped my change in appearance would help me fit in, but things were not as I intended. Magic can be tricky." She tilted her head to one side and looked across to where Finnlugh was slumped with the jewel pulsing softly in his hands.

"I think you've done enough damage here." Arthur stepped out of the shadows, unexpectedly close to the Queen, and with a flash plunged Excalibur deep into her side.

She screeched and moved swiftly, hurling Arthur backwards with her wing. "You aren't stronger than me any more, Arthur," she said, laughing. "Although Vivian obviously thinks so."

With barely a pause, Arthur rolled forward, slashing Excalibur towards her legs. Taking advantage of the distraction, Woodsmoke released a volley of arrows and the guards rushed in with their swords raised. The arrows bounced off the Queen's wings and onto the floor, and as the guards stepped within her reach she slashed at one with her jagged knife and smashed the other with her powerful wings. The first guard collapsed in a pool of blood and the other was swept over the parapet into the void below. As if to taunt them, she then rose effortlessly out of reach. The wound in her side poured with blood, but it didn't seem to be holding her back.

She landed close to Brenna, calling out, "Try as hard as you like, you can't save Brenna!"

All this time Tom had remained stranded halfway down the throne room, unable to move, where the Duke's blast had thrown him. Beansprout had tried to help Brenna, but the Queen's magic was preventing Brenna from moving.

The Queen was not far from Tom now. He could make out her sharp cruel features and powerful form, and her evil seemed to fill the air.

At some unheard command, Brenna screamed and fell to her knees, her shoulders beginning to tear as wings forced their way out. The air became thick and sticky.

Tom was aware of movement beyond Brenna, and hoped Finnlugh was doing something. Arrows winged through the air, but fell short of the Queen. Brenna continued her terrifying screams as Arthur ran towards the Queen, his sword raised, but with a wave of her hand the air around him seemed to solidify and he stopped as if turned to stone.

The Queen turned back to Brenna. "I shall put you on these walls; a fine decoration for my hall. And then I shall put Arthur next to you."

Tom couldn't let this happen. But the Queen was so powerful – what could he possibly do? As water lapped gently in the pool in front of him, he remembered the small shell the Emperor had pressed on him before leaving.

He pulled it from his pocket and tried to remember what he was supposed do with it. Something about throwing it in water in times of trouble? That seemed too easy. But with Brenna now writhing on the floor and the Queen advancing, he needed to act, not think.

The Queen was standing close to the pool. He threw the shell, and it landed with a splash in the water, ripples spreading outwards. But instead of becoming weaker, the ripples grew stronger, gaining in height and intensity until they broke across the floor of the hall. The Queen hesitated as the water started to froth and boil, and as she paused, thick grasping tentacles whipped upwards out of the pool, followed by a large horny head covered in dozens of round flat eyes. The tentacles grabbed the Queen, enveloping her in their suckered grasp. She screeched and tried to pull free, but the beast had already crushed her wings.

Tom saw her knife rise and fall, but it slashed uselessly. He heard her wings tear as she struggled, and her screams filled the air.

Brenna had now collapsed, seemingly unconscious. Arthur, released from the spell, ran towards the Queen, slashing and parrying, but the tentacles lashing and whipping the air prevented him from reaching her.

Woodsmoke and Beansprout raced to Brenna's side and dragged her to safety.

Tom was too close to the Queen and the tentacled creature. He pushed backwards, hoping to bury himself in the shale. Incredibly, the wounded Queen seemed to be freeing herself. Arthur was caught by a flailing tentacle and thrown against the wall opposite Tom. They could only watch in horror as the Queen wrestled with increasing strength.

Finnlugh rose to his feet. He looked exhausted, but stepping over his brother he strode purposefully to the edge of the pool. He raised his hand and released the power of the jewel. Again its light grew and expanded, and this time Finnlugh grew with it until he was as tall as the pillars, blazing with an unearthly brilliance.

"Hold on tight!" Finnlugh shouted as lightning whipped from the jewel and across the hall.

With an immense crack, a huge rent opened in the sky above the throne room. Tom felt as if he'd been plunged into the centre of the universe. He could see galaxies and planets swirling in reds, greens and blues. They hung above him like fruit; it was as if he could pluck one and take a bite; as if he could step right off this planet and onto one of them. He could almost taste the cosmic dust that glittered in swathes in the vastness of space. Then, with a stab of fear, he realised he couldn't breathe. His lungs heaved and he started to rise into the air. He lunged at the closest pillar and gripped tightly, willing himself not to pass out. He saw Arthur do the same before he was blocked from view.

The tentacled creature was wrapped tightly around the Queen, and together they rose into the air. Still writhing, they were sucked into the immensity of the universe. Light seemed to be leaking from their every pore, and Tom's last glimpse of the Queen was of one wing breaking free, every tiny feather illuminated by the light beyond it. There was a roar and a shriek, and then silence. The night sky returned and Tom could breathe again.

Tom released the pillar and slumped back to the floor. Finnlugh shrank and collapsed. Tom looked beyond him and realised with a jolt that the Duke had disappeared. He sat up. "Finnlugh, your brother, he's …"

But before he could finish his sentence, Arthur interrupted. "Tom," he said, shaking his head and pointing upwards.

"You mean–" Tom couldn't finish the sentence.

"Yes."

Tom sighed and looked over at Finnlugh, lying where he'd fallen. After all that, his brother was gone.

He roused himself. What of Beansprout, Woodsmoke and Brenna? How were they? He was about to launch himself to his feet when he saw the doors to the throne room open and Woodsmoke peering through. "All right in there?"

"Just about," Tom said. But he really wasn't sure if any of them would be, ever again.

19 Legacies and Choices

It was a long night for Tom and the others, perched high above the forest. They crossed to the far side of the bridge and made themselves comfortable in the rooms around the stairway. Arthur gathered wood and made a fire at the start of each bridge, to keep away anything else that might have been lurking in the dark. The flames burned bright and high and took the chill off the air. They gathered blankets and sat round the lower fire, not wanting to peer across to the battered throne room.

There were large bleeding wounds on Brenna's shoulders, caused by the forced expansion of her wings, and an exhausted Finnlugh used the jewel to heal them. The scars were red and sore, but her pain was eased.

Nobody felt like talking, and they lay by the fire and fell into a light sleep, Tom haunted by dreams of death.

The next morning they walked out of the palace and down the ridged cliff face, pausing frequently to rest. The thick syrupy air of strong magic had gone, but the forest still seemed to bristle around them with a watchful intensity. Their mood was grim and they mostly walked in silence. When they entered the camp it was with an air of mourning.

"Well thank the Gods, you're all still alive! It's been a horrible night," Jack said, welcoming them with relief.

"You should thank Finnlugh, he was the one who saved us. It was nothing to do with Gods," Tom said.

Jack carried on regardless. "That smell caused by the Duchess's spell was so awful I thought I'd be sick. The wolves came and howled round us for hours, which really upset the horses, and then we saw the lightning shoot from the top of that rock and I nearly had a heart attack."

"I think we all nearly had a heart attack, Granddad," Tom sighed. "At least the smell's gone now," he added reassuringly.

Jack rolled his eyes. "She lifted it at sunrise," he said. "She's a funny old bird, Tom!"

"Not half as bad as the funny old bird we met," Tom grumbled.

Jack burst out laughing. "Good to see you still have your sense of humour."

Tom turned to Finnlugh. "I'm sorry about your brother."

Finnlugh sighed. "I was furious with him, but I didn't want that to happen."

Tom hesitated, wondering what else to say, but Beansprout interrupted. "Well, you shouldn't blame yourself. You did the only thing you could. You saved everyone else."

Finnlugh smiled and patted her arm. "Probably the most good I've done in a long time. However, I do seem to have deprived the forest of its Queen."

"I have the feeling they're not going to miss her much."

"But they need someone," he said.

Woodsmoke interrupted them. "You fancy the job, Finnlugh?"

"Why? Do you?"

"Always so funny," Woodsmoke muttered.

"But shouldn't it be a surviving member of the royal family? As in someone related to Queen Gavina, or Morgan, or whatever her name is? Was?" Beansprout asked.

Woodsmoke and Finnlugh looked at each other and then over at Brenna, who stood grooming her horse, her movements stiff and awkward.

"Is she related? I mean really related?" Finnlugh asked, the ghost of a smile crossing his face.

"You should probably ask her yourself," Woodsmoke said.

Tom sat facing the fire, staring into its roaring heart as if the answer to every question could be found there. Arthur sat next to him and started to polish his sword. "You look deep in thought, Tom."

"I'm wondering what will happen now."

"What do you want to happen?"

"I have no idea. I suppose I should go home, back to the real world."

"This is a real world."

"Now you sound like Beansprout."

"Really? I've always thought she talked a lot of sense."

Tom sighed. "So what are you going to do?"

"I have no idea. I might go travelling. I want to see more of this new world I'm living in."

"I forgot that you didn't come from here. You're such a legend it seems impossible that you ever really existed in our world. In fact there's nothing to prove you did. It's all just stories."

The light glinted along Excalibur as Arthur cleaned it. "Well I can assure you it was very real. I lived a whole lifetime. It was only yesterday to me, Tom. One day I died and then you woke me here, albeit a younger version of myself than when I died."

"Do you actually remember dying?" asked Tom. "Sorry, is that a gruesome question?" he added, stricken.

Fortunately, Arthur laughed. "No. I remember being injured and feeling this searing pain, like fire, through my side." He gripped his left side as if to remind himself. "I'd been fighting, and I knew it would probably be my last fight, but even so ..." He paused and his voice dropped. "There was smoke everywhere, thick and choking as if the camp were on fire, and beneath that was the smell of blood. Sweat was stinging my eyes so that I could hardly see, and I was absolutely bone weary and full of sorrow and regret. And there was a lot of shouting, and the horses were screaming; I remember the thudding of their hooves."

For a second Tom was lost in Arthur's memories, as if he could see it all unfolding around him. "And then?"

"Blackness. Nothingness. No – sometimes there were strange dreams, like being at the bottom of a pool looking up through the murky depths. But I think those came later. Oh, I don't know. Mostly nothing, until you woke me and I rolled out onto the floor of that cave, wondering where I was."

"Did you know about Merlin's deal? That you wouldn't die?"

"Not really. I knew there was something, but not what, and to be honest I didn't care. I had other worries. And I trusted Merlin."

"Do you wish I hadn't woken you?"

"And miss all this? Not many people get two lives, Tom. I should enjoy it while it lasts."

It was evening, and they were all seated around the fire talking quietly when there was a flurry of activity at the edge of the camp. Finnlugh's guards shouted, and they heard muffled responses. Finnlugh and Arthur leapt to their feet, but Brenna was quickest. She ran to the guards, and after a brief explanation they drew back to let a small group of men and women enter the camp. Brenna hugged them all, and after a few brief words they followed her to the fire.

"They are members of the court," she explained. "Old friends I feared were dead." She turned to them. "Come and join us, have some food."

They were an assortment of the young and old, and all looked weary, although they smiled with relief once they had sat and examined everyone – as closely as everyone looked at them.

"So tell me, are others alive?" asked Brenna, sitting close to them.

"Yes, we are not the only ones. We've been hiding in remote parts of Aeriken for months, some longer than others. But first, is it true? Is she dead?"

"Yes, Finnlugh came to the rescue," Brenna said, pointing him out. "He blasted her out into the universe."

"Indeed," Finnlugh said. "She's somewhere up there, wrestling with a giant sea creature until the end of time."

"That's quite some trick," said one of the younger women, looking worried.

"Don't worry, it exhausts me too much to do it often. But it is impressive," he smirked. The Starlight Jewel was now on a long silver chain around his neck, although buried beneath his clothes, out of sight.

Tom half listened as he gazed into the fire, hearing about others who had fled the Queen's wrath, and her increasing insanity. He was thinking of going to bed when a question grabbed his attention. "So will you stay, Brenna, and help us to bury our dead? And lead us?"

Everyone fell quiet, waiting for Brenna's response. She stared into the fire for a long time, and eventually Woodsmoke said softly, "Brenna?"

She looked at him and then at the others. "I'll stay to help bury our dead, but then I leave. I cannot stay here. It is a place of death. I'll rejoin Woodsmoke and live there. That's my home now."

The oldest man in the group spoke. "But the whole court should move. We would follow you."

"No! I don't want that." She shook her head. "I'm sorry, but that's the way I feel. And actually, I really don't think you need a king or a queen. But I will stay for a while."

"I'll stay too," Woodsmoke said. "I'll help however I can."

"No. It's our job, not yours. But thank you." Brenna gave him the ghost of a smile.

"So," Finnlugh said, "you are the heir?"

"I suppose I am. The Queen was my grandmother. And I hated her."

The last sentence fell awkwardly, and it was Beansprout who broke the silence. "I'm so sorry, Brenna. This is awful. We will all leave tomorrow to let you grieve." She rose and hugged a surprised Brenna. Tom marvelled at Beansprout – she always said the right thing.

The next morning they packed up the camp and said their goodbyes.

"You know you're welcome at any time," Fahey said to Brenna. "It's your home and I'll miss you."

"And you're the sweetest man and I'll miss you too," she said, tears in her eyes.

Brenna hugged Tom, Beansprout and Jack, and even Finnlugh. The Duchess merely nodded. "I wish you luck, my dear," was her only comment.

Woodsmoke was less sweet. "You'd better not stay here! This place smells of death. And the wood sprites, they'll be back!"

"We'll be fine! Now stop moaning and go. I'll see you in a few months."

Woodsmoke hesitated, but Brenna persisted. "Go! Please Woodsmoke!" He finally relented and got on his horse.

They nudged their horses and moved off into the forest, leaving Brenna and her friends in the clearing.

"So, what are we going to do?" Tom asked Beansprout.

"I've told you, I'm staying."

"To do what?"

"I don't know, Tom! Do I have to have a plan?"

This was an extension of a long argument that had started on their way back to Woodsmoke's home. They were now only days away, and it seemed as if they had been travelling forever. Aeriken was enormous and ancient, and they had only recently passed the huge stone hawk statues that marked the boundary between Aeriken and Vanishing Wood. Tom couldn't work out how long it had been since they first arrived.

Jack interrupted. "You should both go. You have your whole lives ahead of you. You belong in your own world."

"You have no right to deliver that speech!" said Tom, rounding on him angrily.

"I have every right – I'm your grandfather!"

"Don't you want us here?"

"I didn't think you wanted to be here. Do you know how contrary you are, Tom?" Jack stared angrily back at him. "And of course I want you to stay.

It's nice to have my family here. But I'm not going home," he added, preventing any further questions on that. "I'm an old man there, and here – well, I'm less old."

"Don't you care that Mum and Dad have split up?"

"Of course I care, Tom! But my going back wouldn't change anything. They'd still be split up, it's been inevitable for years. And you shouldn't let it affect you. It has nothing to do with you; what you have or haven't done. It's life, and you should get on with yours. Finish school, travel, enjoy yourself."

Jack paused, looking at Tom's mutinous expression. "Just think about the things you've done here. The things you've seen! You're not a child any more."

Arthur joined in. "If life is unsatisfactory, stay here. It sounds like you'd have as much family here as you did there – including me, in case you'd forgotten."

Finnlugh interrupted them all. "You speak as if there was only one choice. You could stay for as long as you wanted, and then go when you were ready."

Tom fell silent. What if he left and then realised he'd made a mistake, and found he could never come back. What then?

A peculiar mood had settled over them all. Although they'd known each other for only a short time, they were reluctant to part. Fahey had been badgering them for information, cheerful in the knowledge he had great tales to create and tell. He and Jack had already arranged to visit Finnlugh's under-palace. Arthur had accepted an invitation to stay at Vanishing Hall, but was planning to travel onwards after a short stay. Beansprout and Tom had also been invited, and Beansprout had accepted immediately.

Tom still wanted to leave. He couldn't explain this need to himself, other than that he somehow felt he should stick to his original intent, which had been to find his grandfather and return home. His questions had been answered, and he felt reassured, if annoyed. He and Jack had made their peace, and he understood Jack's reasons for staying. But he still felt abandoned, and therefore couldn't bring himself to stay too. Now he'd made up his mind, he wanted to leave as quickly as possible.

It was dawn on the outskirts of the wood around Vanishing Hall, and Finnlugh, the Duchess, and the remaining Royal Guard were leaving. Finnlugh shook Tom's hand. "Any time you need anything, just ask."

"That would be a bit difficult from so far away. But thanks. I may see you again."

"And you, dear lady, gentlemen, I shall see you soon." He kissed Beansprout on the cheek, shook hands with the others and then, with a flash of silver and a thudding of hooves, they were gone.

Jack's and Fahey's goodbyes were muted and sad. "I may never see you again, Tom," said Jack, smiling, "but I know you'll be OK." He was unable to hide the small tear that loitered in the corner of his eye. "I can't come to the tower, it will be too much," he said, his voice starting to thicken.

Tom nodded, feeling a little choked and squashing a slight sense of regret. As he shook hands with Fahey, he discovered that his resentment towards his grandfather's friend also seemed to have vanished.

Woodsmoke, Arthur and Beansprout accompanied Tom as they set off back to the doorways.

"I have never heard of these doorways, or seen them," Arthur said. "In my time we crossed by magic through mists and shadows, at dawn or dusk."

"It's only a few hours' ride," Woodsmoke said, "and you'll probably recognise the place."

"What do you mean?" asked Beansprout.

"You'll see."

Slowly emerging through the trees, they saw a large round tower. It was considerably more intact than Mishap Folly. The walls were solid, not crumbling, and it had a door, but the main difference was the long, low, stone building attached to it, with windows and a chimney.

Tom and Beansprout walked towards the tower, mystified.

"The man who built it somehow managed to cross here, and the tower he built on your side appeared here too."

"And where is he?" Tom asked. "Dead, I presume?"

"Oh no. He's around, somewhere. Probably hunting. Sometimes he goes to the village. Anyway, the doorways remain the same, but the entrance here isn't blocked."

Moving to the side of the tower they saw an entrance leading underground. They followed it downwards into a large cave, where four large, stone, arched doorways stood in the centre of the space. The entrances were identical to those they had crossed through, the spaces filled with darkness. They stood before them, and Tom recognised Earth's portal immediately.

There were no strange creatures etched in the stone, only images of men and women, a stag's head, and forests.

"Are you sure you want to go, Tom?" Beansprout searched his face carefully, as if he was hiding something.

Now he was here, he really wasn't sure, but he couldn't think of a good reason to stay.

"I must admit, Tom, as anxious as I was to get rid of you, I will miss you," Woodsmoke said.

"Well I'm tempted to come with you," said Arthur, "just to see what the place is like after all these years. But there are things I must see here first. And I've decided to visit Vivian. I think we have lots to talk about."

"Will you ever come back, Beansprout?" Tom asked.

"I'm not sure. Probably. What if we say we'll cross in a year from now?"

"Yes, we'll come, see how you are. See if you want to return," Woodsmoke said.

"See if I want to stay!" Beansprout added.

"Yes, OK." Tom nodded. "The time may be different there, but I'll be at the cottage or thereabouts."

"What will you tell my mother?"

"What do you want me to tell her?"

"Tell her I'm fine, and I'm safe, and I'm staying with Granddad. The rest is up to you."

"OK." Tom looked around for the last time, at his friends, at the cave, at the doorways, and took a deep breath. He gave them a brief hug. "No goodbyes!" Turning, he stood in front of Earth's doorway then stepped through.

He felt the weightlessness, the sensation of falling, and the now-familiar jolt, as the ground appeared beneath him. He felt warm earth and sunshine. Looking up he found himself on the bank opposite his grandfather's house. It was summer. The trees were thick with dark green leaves and the garden was choked with flowers.

He was home.

T. J. GREEN

YOUNG ADULT ARTHURIAN FANTASY

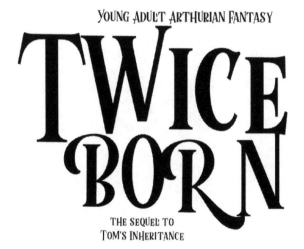

TWICE BORN

THE SEQUEL TO
TOM'S INHERITANCE

And every marge enclosing in the midst
A square of text that looks a little blot,
The text no larger than the limbs of fleas;
And every square of text an awful charm,
Writ in a language that has long gone by.

– Alfred, Lord Tennyson (1809–92)

1 Exile

Tom sat cross-legged on top of Glastonbury Tor wrapped in a blanket, gazing into the middle distance. The soft grey light of dawn revealed the mists that lay across the plains below, blurring the landscape.

According to the myths and legends he'd been avidly reading, Glastonbury Tor was Avalon. This was the third morning in a row he'd waited, holding the silver bough that Vivian had given to him when he first arrived in the Other; the bough that had allowed him to wake King Arthur. He held it tightly, hoping its magical properties would reveal Avalon to him.

He had also sat here at noon, dusk and midnight, the times when the walls between the worlds were at their most fragile, willing himself into a trance-like state as if that would help. But it was in vain. Glastonbury Tor and the surrounding plain remained unchanged. A couple of times he'd imagined he'd seen water lying across the green fields, but then the light shifted and the illusion vanished, along with any hope that he could make his own way to the Other. He might as well pack up his tent and return home.

His visits to the Tor had been born from frustration and boredom. It had been more than twelve months since his return from the Realm of Earth, and he'd heard nothing from Beansprout, Arthur, Woodsmoke or Brenna. And now he wondered with regret if he ever would.

A few days later he was back in the woods near home, and had returned to his old routine. The folly, which sat above the hidden entrance to the Otherworld portals, loomed out of the trees, jagged and black against the early evening sky. It was now cleared of debris. The ivy had been chopped back, the fallen rocks stacked into a pile, and the floor swept clean, revealing old cracked flagstones. In the centre of the half-collapsed building was Tom's tent, his occasional home of the last few months, ever since the weather had started to get warmer.

He poked his head through the tent flap and grabbed a towel, rubbing himself dry after his evening jog. He really needed a shower, but that could wait until tomorrow when he returned to the cottage to freshen up. Instead he splashed his face with cold water from a bucket next to the tent.

The evening was chill, and the light was fading quickly. Autumn was well advanced and he wouldn't be able to camp out for much longer. He lit a couple of lanterns he had secured to the wall and then lit a fire, putting a saucepan of sausages and beans on to heat.

He'd been so sure at the time that he didn't want to stay in the Otherworld, but within days of returning he knew he'd made a mistake. He and his cousin Beansprout had been there for six months, and their families had been panic-stricken. And to turn up without Beansprout had been insane.

He'd been about to tell them all about the Other, but they'd looked at him with such suspicion, and his aunt with such open hostility, that he'd known he couldn't. So he'd lied, saying they'd travelled around looking for his granddad. This excuse seemed lame, but his family were more prepared to believe that than anything else. His aunt had accused him of "doing something" to Beansprout, and he'd been genuinely terrified that he'd be arrested and charged. The police had interviewed him for hours, but a lack of evidence that he'd done anything wrong meant he'd had to be released. His father had calmed his aunt down, and he had told them all a half-truth – that they had found his granddad, who was living a new life with new friends and didn't want to come home. He'd told them Beansprout was staying with him.

It had been a nightmarish time. Even now he could see the doubt in their eyes, their lack of faith in him.

His entire family seemed to have aged. His dad looked cross with the inconvenience of it all, and although he seemed pleased that Tom had returned, he quickly returned to his own preoccupations and his new girlfriend, who now lived with them at the cottage.

Tom's mother looked drawn and anxious. She pleaded with him to live with her in Downtree village, but he refused, wanting to stay close to the folly, where he could be found by whoever came looking for him. The only thing he wanted from his mother was information about family birthmarks.

"Yes Tom, I have got one actually, very similar to yours and your sister's," she'd replied when he finally asked, and she showed him the long slim mark at the top of her arm.

"Must be genetics," he'd murmured, brooding on his strange legacy and family bloodlines.

If anybody did come for him, he had every intention of going back with them. He couldn't really understand why he'd left such an amazing place. The most frustrating part about the whole thing was that he had no one to talk to. He'd tried to get back into normal life; he'd sat exams, played football, and enrolled to go to college, but it all seemed pointless. His old friends looked at him with a sort of respect for his absence and curiosity about where he had been. Just when he thought he could tell one of his friends, he realised he didn't want to. He wanted to keep his secrets close.

Over the past few months he'd realised they might never come for him. He'd taken to visiting the folly once a week, examining it for signs of life and checking where the passageway opened, and then when it was warm enough he moved there for days at a time. He classed it as training. He went jogging, and used an old stick as a sword to practise with. He still wasn't very good, but he was improving.

It was now fully dark, and the moon was hidden behind thick, low clouds. He finished eating and scrubbed out his pans with water and leaves, and then threw some more logs on the fire and pulled a blanket round his shoulders. He tried to ignore what was worrying him most; that perhaps they hadn't come for him because something was wrong. The alternative, that it was because they had forgotten him, was too unbearable to think about.

He was woken in the middle of the night by howling winds and lashing rain. The tent flapped and snapped, but was sheltered from the worst of it by the tower, so he rolled over, plumped his pillow and tried to go back to sleep. As he closed his eyes a flash of bright white light illuminated the tent – lightning. He snuggled down further into his sleeping bag, trying to block out the noise and light. Then he heard a thud, low voices, and the clanking sound of a pan rolling across the ground. All of a sudden he was wide awake and sitting up, staring wildly into the dark. More talking, coming closer, into the tower. And then the sound of someone tripping.

"What the hell is all this stuff doing here?" someone muttered. "And what about this damn rain? Seriously, of all the times! I'm soaked."

"Sshhh." And then there was silence.

But he knew that voice. Leaping up, half tangled in his bag, he opened the zip and stuck his head out. And there in the entrance of the tower he saw two slight figures, barely visible in the dark. His heart leapt with huge relief. "Beansprout! It's me!"

"Tom? Oh thank God! I was *not* going to walk to the cottage in this weather!"

He grinned. "You'd better come in," he said, and he scooted back to make room.

Tom couldn't stop grinning. It was fixed on to his face like a mask. Now and again he tried to straighten his features into a normal expression, but then the grin just slid back into place and stayed there. It had been a long time since he'd been so happy.

He lit his lamp and the shadows sidled up their faces, making them look ghoulish. They sat cross legged – Tom, Beansprout and Brenna – knee to knee in a small tight circle.

"What are you doing in a tent, Tom?" Beansprout was almost breathless in her enthusiasm, and was grinning as much as Tom.

"Waiting for you! It took you long enough. Where have you been?"

"What do you mean? How long has it been?"

"Longer than a year!"

"I'm sorry, Tom, but you know it's impossible to judge time accurately in our world," Brenna apologised. "We have been delayed too, by certain events." She shrugged.

"What events? Is everyone all right?" He squinted at her and held up the lamp. "And what have you done to your hair?" There were feathers braided through her hair and along her hair line, adding to her otherworldly appearance.

She waved her hand as if to brush him off. "It's how it's supposed to look, now I don't have to hide."

"Oh, OK. So the others, they're all right?" he persisted.

"Yes, they're fine. I've been busy with certain duties in Aeriken, and Beansprout's been helping me. Jack's still with Fahey. But Vivian asked Arthur to do something for her and we thought we'd help. And we thought you'd like to come too?"

"Yes! Yes, yes, yes! You're not going back without me. What are we doing?"

"Vivian asked Arthur to search for one of the other priestesses from Avalon. She disappeared a short time ago. He's already started the search with Woodsmoke, and we're supposed to join them at Holloways Meet."

Tom had no idea where Holloways Meet was, but he nodded enthusiastically. "So when do we go?"

"Whenever you're ready," Beansprout said.

"I've been ready ever since I got back here! But …" Tom thought awkwardly of his aunt and her anguish. "You should see your mum before we go." He recounted the nightmare of his return without her.

"Crap. I had no idea it would be so bad. I'm sorry, Tom. But really, do I have to? It might make things worse."

"Yes, you have to. You *really* have no idea. She looks at me like I'm a murderer."

Guilt flickered across Beansprout's face. "Now I feel terrible, I've just been having so much fun! I didn't even think. All right. In the morning then. And until then you can tell us what you've been up to."

The next morning the wild weather had passed and Tom and Beansprout started the walk back to the cottage at dawn. Brenna remained at the tower; she looked far too odd with her feathers to go with them.

Tom glared at her, "Don't you dare leave without us."

"Don't worry, Tom. I'll be here," she said, full of her usual calm efficiency, and she stretched out in the entrance to the tower in the pale dawn light and closed her eyes.

They trudged back along the leafy paths, finally coming to the old yew and the stream. "I'll stay here to pack a few more things; you go on and meet me back here when you're done," Tom said.

"I think you should come with me."

"No chance. Call me if you need help."

"But I feel so nervous! What if she doesn't let me go?"

"Well, the good thing is that you look fine! Better than fine, actually." And it was true, Tom thought. Beansprout looked healthy and happy, as if she carried a residual glow from the Other. "Good luck!"

He watched her walk along the path towards her house, her shoulders slumped and her head lowered. He wished he could help, but knew this was something she had to do alone. And if he was honest, he didn't really like seeing his aunt any more.

He passed through the back garden into the kitchen. His dad and his girlfriend had already left for work, their breakfast things piled in the sink. Good. It would save awkward goodbyes. He put the kettle on and headed upstairs to his room, emptying his backpack onto the bed. He propped his folded tent in the corner of his room. He wouldn't need that again. But first he needed a shower.

Refreshed, he packed some clean clothes and a few other things he thought would be useful, and then wandered around the house, checking to see if there was anything else he wanted to take. It was strange, but he already felt distanced from the cottage. If he was honest, it wasn't a world he'd been fully engaged with for a long time.

In the kitchen he washed the pans he'd brought back from the folly, leaving them on the drainer. He even tidied his bedroom. He wanted to leave everything tidy, no loose ends. This was probably how his grandfather had felt. He laughed to himself. He'd been so mad at him, and here he was doing the same thing. Anyway, he had plenty of time, so he raided the fridge and cooked a huge breakfast while he waited for Beansprout.

An hour later Beansprout arrived, flushed and red-eyed with crying. "I never want to go through that again."

"I did warn you."

"No, you did not. That was awful. I'm on the missing persons list!"

"Are you sure you want to go?"

"Yes," she said, nodding distractedly. "Are you ready?"

He nodded towards the note he'd left on the table. "Deja vu."

He paused and took a long look round. He might never see this place again. Satisfied, he locked the door, pocketed the key and followed Beansprout up the path.

2 The Holloways

They stood beneath the folly in front of the portal to the Realm of Earth, and Tom looked around, recalling the first time he had stood here with the strange carvings of birds and beasts looking down at him. Then he'd been nervous at what lay before him; now he was excited to be going back.

Brenna pulled a flat disc the size of a small plate out of her pack.

"What's that?" Tom asked.

"A gift from Finnlugh," she said.

Tom remembered the prince from the ancient royal fey family who had helped them defeat the queen, Morgan Le Fey. "He found it in his library. It's a portal compass."

She passed it to Tom. It looked much like a regular compass, but on it was a map of the other Earth in tiny detail, and a marker that could be set to a specific place. "That's fantastic!" he said.

"I know, and it should save us a lot of time. We're going to Endevorr Village. We have horses there."

Tom passed the compass back and Brenna set the marker. "Ready?"

They nodded, held hands and stepped forward into blackness.

Again Tom experienced the falling weightless sensation, and the strange jolting and pulling feeling in the pit of his stomach. And then there was grass beneath him and light dazzling his eyes, bouncing off the water from the river in front of him. On the opposite bank he could see the village and the high bridges and walkways that spanned the buildings. Relief washed over him. He was back.

How could he have ever doubted that being here was the single greatest gift of his life? Everything seemed to have an intensity he hadn't noticed before. The air was perfumed with a delicate blossom and honey scent, and the colours seemed bright and sharp with a richness that his earth didn't seem to have. He could hear bees buzzing and birds singing, and the sounds of fey from the village drifted across the river with a clarity that startled him.

"You all right, Tom?" Beansprout asked, smiling.

"Absolutely," he said, unable to restrain a grin. And then he added quickly, before he became too embarrassed, "Thanks for coming back for me."

"S'all right," Beansprout said, punching him playfully on the arm. "I missed you. Sometimes."

They crossed the bridge and weaved through the maze of small alleyways and streets until they reached a large building with a sign reading "The Emperor's Tears" hanging above a double-fronted doorway. Passing through, they reached a courtyard with stables lining the left-hand side.

"I'll speak to the manager, you wait by the horses," Brenna said, heading to the far side of the courtyard.

They crossed to the dim warm interior of the stables. The pungent smell of straw and manure made Tom wrinkle his nose, but Beansprout seemed oblivious as she strolled to a chestnut-brown horse with its head over the gate of its enclosure, and patted its nose.

"Hello, Brownie," she murmured. "Have you missed me?"

The horse snickered softly in reply.

"You named your horse after cake?" Tom scoffed, but Beansprout shot him a withering glance and he moved swiftly on.

"So how long has it been for you since I left?" Tom asked.

"Nearly twelve months, I guess, it's hard to tell," she said. "And no winter!"

Tom looked at her thoughtfully. "It's weird. You look older, as if you've been here for ages. You're sort of … mature," he said awkwardly.

She shrugged, unperturbed. "Maybe it's the air. It makes granddad younger. Everything's odd in the Other."

"What have you been doing?"

"I've spent some time with Woodsmoke, some with Brenna. After you left I stayed at Vanishing Hall, just exploring being here, really. But then Woodsmoke announced he was going back to Aeriken – he was worried about Brenna. So I went with him. And when we got to the Aerie, Brenna and the Aerikeen were still cleaning the palace after mourning their dead." She shrugged. "I wanted to help, so I stayed on."

"Doing what?" he asked, wondering how much cleaning they needed to do.

"Just helping. The others who had fled the queen kept returning with their stories of what had happened. Really *awful* stories. And the dryads returned. A couple of satyrs turned up too. Wow, they are really odd." She shook her head in disbelief. "Such amazing things here! And then Arthur turned up. He had met with Vivian, and she asked him to help her find that priestess we mentioned. I think her name was Nimue."

"Who? Oh, wait. I think I know that name." He had been doing lots of reading about Arthur while he waited.

"She lives on Avalon too, apparently."

Tom nodded. "Yes, she had some sort of love affair with Merlin, I think." He could hardly believe that these people had really existed. That some *still* existed. "But I didn't see anyone else on Avalon."

"Apparently she remained in the temple buildings while you were there. Anyway, she's gone and could be in trouble, so Arthur has to find her. Woodsmoke went with him, and we're meeting them somewhere over there." She gestured vaguely over Tom's head.

"And granddad, how's he?"

"Just fine! Looking forward to seeing you. Not sure when, because we're going soon, but you'll see him at some point."

"Yes I will, because I'm staying here now," he said with determination.

Beansprout smiled. "Me too. I feel a little guilty, because I don't miss home at all. I'm glad you're back, though!"

They were interrupted by Brenna's return. "All settled. Tom, we brought a horse with us for you. Don't worry," she said, looking at his alarmed expression, "it's the horse you had last time, the calm one. Midnight." She pointed to a stall in which he saw a medium-sized black horse with a streak of grey down her nose.

"I don't remember her being that calm!"

"Oh don't start already!" Beansprout groaned.

"What do you mean, 'start already'?"

"Well honestly, Tom, you really can be such a grump."

After packing their saddle bags with supplies, they headed out of the village along a road that led in the opposite direction from Avalon, towards the rolling hills in the distance. Over to the right was the river Tom had travelled on in Few's boat on his first visit, and beyond that was Finnlugh's labyrinthine House of Evernight.

It was a road unlike any Tom had been on before. Before long it had burrowed into the surrounding fields, becoming rutted and worn. High banks topped by hedgerows shielded them from view, and trees arched above them, plunging them into a green and shadowy place. It smelt of pollen-soaked earthiness and it was quiet, the horses' hooves muffled by the dusty path.

"So why are we going to Holloways Meet?" Tom asked, shuffling uncomfortably on Midnight, trying to find his rhythm again.

Brenna, effortlessly graceful astride her horse next to him, said, "Because it's the last place Vivian knew Nimue had been, and it's where Arthur and Woodsmoke will be."

"What was she doing there?"

She shrugged. "I think it was just a place to stop on the way to Dragon's Hollow, where she was going to meet the sorcerer, Raghnall. It's a big place too; a popular meeting spot, and somewhere to get supplies."

"How long will it take us to get there?"

"A few days. We just keep following this road and we'll get there eventually. We're on one of the old Holloways now."

"I like to call them the hidden ways, Tom," Beansprout said, lit up by the pale rays of sunshine breaking through the leaf cover. "They run all across the Otherworld like warrens between places. It's like travelling in secret."

"Except they're not a secret," Brenna said. "They're used by all sorts of creatures. I'm sure we'll meet a few as we travel. These paths were mostly formed by the royal houses as they moved back and forth between the various Under-Palaces."

"So we'll pass other Under-Palaces?"

"We'll pass close by. But don't get too excited. We probably won't see anyone from them. And you would never know if we passed by an entrance, because they would be disguised as part of the landscape." She gestured at the bank, covered in grasses and flowers. "That could be one. How would we know? Anyway, we'd better pick up the pace," she said, urging her horse to a trot, and Tom and Beansprout hurried to keep up.

They travelled all day, breaking only for a brief rest at lunchtime, by a small stream where the horses could drink. Every now and again they passed small steep paths which led up to the fields around them, and eventually, as the sun began to set and the Holloway filled with billowing clouds of midges, Brenna led them up one of these paths and onto the meadows above them.

They gathered some dry wood and made a fire, preparing to camp for the night.

"So who's looking after the Aerikeen while you're with us?" Tom asked Brenna.

"They don't need me to look after them, Tom, they're not children."

"So you're really not going to be queen, even though you are?"

Brenna avoided his gaze for some time while Beansprout grimaced at him. He looked at her and mouthed, "What?"

"It's all right, Beansprout," Brenna said. "It's something I've avoided for too long." She turned to Tom. "Have you ever avoided something you know you should do, but really don't want to?"

"Loads."

"Well this is me avoiding being crowned queen. I feel very guilty for having left them in the first place to go into hiding, so I don't feel I deserve it."

"You were in fear of losing your life!" Beansprout said.

"So were many others."

"Not like you. Morgan killed your parents."

"She killed a lot more than that in the end," she said. "And I like travelling around with my friends, and I don't want to think I'll be shut up in the Aerie making boring decisions."

"But if you're queen, surely you can choose to rule however you want?" Tom said.

"There are responsibilities. Things I will be expected to do."

"It didn't seem to stop Arthur when he was king. I've been reading all about him. He travelled, led battles, went everywhere. Well, *if* what I've read is true. There are so many stories. It's hard to know what was real and what was made up. If anyone can give advice on leadership, it's Arthur. You should ask him."

3 The Hollow Bole

Tom and the others rode into Holloways Meet on a hot dusty afternoon. The road broadened and dipped until they reached a large archway formed by thick interlaced branches. Beyond that, a few small buildings began to appear, built into the high banks of the road. Within a short distance they could hear a steady hum of voices, shouts, laughter and music, and the banks fell back to form a large irregular square dominated by a central group of trees with other Holloways leading into it. It was filled with an assorted collection of beings, young and old, colourful and drab, and the smell of business.

Wooden buildings threaded through the meeting place, some of them perched precariously in branches, others jostling for position on the fields above them, casting deep shadows onto the activities in the centre.

"This place looks busier than ever," Brenna murmured.

"What do people do here?" Tom asked, looking around curiously.

"Many things. I have been told you can buy almost anything here, and travellers use it to stock up on supplies. Consequently, a lot of people pass through so it's particularly useful for finding out information."

"I love it!" Beansprout said, grinning.

"We'd better find Woodsmoke and Arthur. Woodsmoke said he would try to check into the Quarter Way House," said Brenna. She pointed to a big building with balconies on the far side of the square, built against the bank and onto the field at the top. "It's more expensive than most, but it guarantees a clean bed and good food."

They found Woodsmoke and Arthur sitting in a bar to the side of the main entrance. It was an oasis of calm after the bustle of the square, filled with an assortment of tables and chairs, and screened from the square by thick-limbed climbing plants covered with flowers and a coating of wind-blown dust.

"Well, don't you two look relaxed!" Brenna said, hands on hips.

"The rest of the deserving after a hard day's work!" Woodsmoke said with a smirk as he and Arthur stood to greet them. "Tom – you're here! And you've grown." He walked around the table and grabbed him in a bear hug. "I wasn't sure if I'd ever see you again."

"You have no idea how pleased I am to be back," Tom said, giving Woodsmoke an equally big hug in return.

Tom turned to Arthur, who gripped the top of his arms and stared at him. "You look well, Tom. It's good to have my great-great-great-something-relative here," and he gave him such a crushing hug that Tom struggled for breath.

Now he was reunited with all five of his closest friends in the Other (or anywhere else), he really felt he was back. Unlike Brenna and Beansprout, Arthur and Woodsmoke looked reassuringly the same. Although Tom had grown, they were both still taller than him, Woodsmoke lean and rangy, his longbow propped next to him at the table, and Arthur muscular, Excalibur in its scabbard at his side.

"Let's get more drinks to celebrate," Arthur said, and called to the barman. "Five pints of Red Earth Thunder Ale please!"

As they sat, Beansprout asked, "So how long have you been here?"

"We arrived this morning," Woodsmoke answered, "and thought we needed to recover after our long days on the road." He paused as their ale arrived, and took a long drink as if to emphasise his need to recuperate.

"But," said Arthur, "we think that Nimue stayed at the Hollow Bole – well, Vivian thought she did, apparently it's where she's stayed before. That's where I'll be going soon, to ask a few questions." He looked at Tom. "Do you want to come?"

"Yes," Tom said, spluttering his drink in an effort to answer. "But first tell me what happened with Vivian."

"Ah!" Arthur said gazing into his pint, "Vivian. It was very strange to meet her again, after so many years. I felt quite sick seeing that big, bronze, dragon-headed prow gliding out of the mist." He sighed, trying to organise his story. "I met her by the lake, at her request. I'd wanted to contact her, but didn't know how. I thought that standing at the lakeside, yelling into the mist probably wouldn't work," he said with a grin. "But then I had these images enter my dreams, about the standing stones and the lakeside."

"Oh, yes," Tom interrupted, "I've experienced those!"

"So I headed to the lake and within an hour the boat was there, and then almost instantly she was at my side. She looked so old, and yet so young." He looked up at the others as if trying to make them see what he had. "I couldn't believe her hair was white! It used to be a rich dark brown that glinted with red when it caught the sunlight. She had freckles then, all over her nose and cheeks." He shook himself out of his reverie as his friends watched him, fascinated by what he must be remembering. "She asked me if I remembered her sisters, the other priestesses, particularly Nimue, which I did. Nimue helped me rule when Merlin disappeared. Vivian explained that Nimue had vanished on her way to Dragon's Hollow to see Raghnall, the dragon enchanter – whoever he is. She was taking her time, visiting various people along the way. The last time Vivian heard from her was when she was here, at Holloways Meet. It takes about a week to travel to Dragon's Hollow from here, but she never arrived there."

"And how does Vivian know she hasn't arrived?" Beansprout asked.

"Because Raghnall contacted Vivian, by scrying, to find out where Nimue was. Apparently Vivian has been trying to contact her ever since, again by scrying, which is apparently how they communicate long distance. Now Vivian thinks she's being blocked, either by Nimue or someone else."

"What's Nimue like?" Tom asked.

"Oh, she's very different to Vivian. She's small and dark haired, liked a pixie, very pretty. Merlin was infatuated with her," Arthur said thoughtfully. "Vivian is worried that something is wrong, so we've spent the last few weeks trying to track her route, but we've found nothing of interest. It all seems a wild goose chase," he said, finishing his pint. "So, Tom, shall we go? Woodsmoke looks too comfortable to move." He frowned at Woodsmoke, who had his feet up on a chair looking very relaxed.

"It's been a busy few weeks," Woodsmoke said, indignant, "and I'm much older than you are, so I deserve to relax. Besides, I also have news to catch up on," he added, gesturing to Brenna and Beansprout. He waved them off. "Enjoy your afternoon."

Tom and Arthur set off on a slow circuitous route.

"I know I've been here a few months now, Tom, but I still can't get used to the place."

Tom nodded. "I know what you mean."

Strange creatures bustled across the square, some tall, some small, male and female, some part human, part animal. They passed a group of satyrs and felt small by comparison. The satyrs were over seven feet tall, with muscular bodies, the upper half bare-chested, the lower half with the hairy legs of goats. Their hair was thick and coarse, large curling rams' horns protruded from their heads, and their eyes were a disconcerting yellow that made them look belligerent. Tom and Arthur skirted past them, making their way to a row of buildings at the side of the square. These were a mixture of shops, semi-permanent markets, eating places and inns, ranging from the small and shabby to the large and less shabby. Smoke from braziers drifted through the still air. They looked at the wooden signs that hung from the entrances, trying to find the Hollow Bole.

They had been looking for nearly an hour, taking their time drifting through the warren of buildings, before they had any joy. Walking down the start of one of the Holloways, they saw a vast tree to their left, pressing against the bank at its back. There was a narrow cleft in its trunk, above which a small sign announced *The Hollow Bole*. Peering upwards through the leaves they saw small windows scattered along thick and misshapen branches. Ducking to avoid hitting their head on the low entrance, they stepped into a small hall hollowed out of the trunk and followed the narrow spiralling stairs upwards into the gloom. They emerged into a larger hall built into a broad branch overlooking the Holloway and the edge of the square. There were no straight edges anywhere. Instead, the chairs, tables and balcony were an organic swirl of living wood.

A dryad, green skinned and willowy, stepped out of the shadows and said, "Can I help you?"

Thinking they were alone, Tom jumped. Arthur remained a little more composed and said, "I'm looking for an old friend who passed through here, probably a few weeks ago now. Can you confirm if she stayed here?"

"And what do you want with this friend?" the dryad snapped.

"She hasn't arrived where she should have, and I want to find out if anything has happened to her," Arthur said, trying to keep the impatience out of his voice.

The dryad went silent for a moment. "It depends who it is. Her name?"

"Nimue. Our mutual friend Vivian asked me to find her. She's worried."

The dryad was startled. "Nimue? The witch?" She spat out "witch" viciously.

Now Arthur was startled. "Yes, Nimue, one of the priestesses of Avalon. Or *witch*, as you choose to call her."

"They are all witches on Avalon," the dryad replied disdainfully. "Yes, she stayed here for a few days. And then she left. I don't know where," she added, to avoid further questions.

Arthur groaned. "She gave no indication at all of where she might be going?"

"She stays here because we are discreet. We ask no questions of our clients."

"But you know her well? She stays here often I believe."

"Not often. She travels less frequently now. But yes, I believe she usually stays here. However, I do not know her well. I do not ask questions."

Tom was curious about the word "now", and clearly Arthur was too.

"But she used to travel here more frequently? In the past?" said Arthur.

The dryad was visibly annoyed at the constant questions. "Yes, many years ago. But, I do not see what that has to do with now – and I was not here then."

"So if you weren't here then, how do know she came here?" Arthur persisted.

"Her name appears in our old registers. We are an old establishment. And her reputation precedes her."

Now Arthur was clearly very curious, and he leaned in. "What reputation?"

"As a witch from another world. A meddler in the affairs of others."

"What affairs?"

"Witches meddle with the natural order of nature!" the dryad snapped, now furious. "As a dryad, I am a natural being, born of the earth and all her darkest mysteries. Witches plunder that knowledge! They have no respect for natural laws. How do *you* know her?"

Arthur looked uncomfortable and decided not to answer that. "I am just an old friend who cares for her safety. I am sorry to have taken so much of your time. If you're sure you don't remember anything else?"

"Nothing."

"Just one more question. Did she ever stay here with anyone else?"

"Yes. The greatest meddler of them all – Merlin." With that, she stepped back into the shadows and melted into the tree trunk, becoming invisible and unreachable.

"With Merlin?" Arthur turned to Tom dumbfounded, his face pale at this unexpected news.

Tom felt a thrill run through him at the mention of Merlin, but why was Arthur so upset? Before he could ask, Arthur turned and raced down the stairs. Tom raced after him. Maybe it was because Merlin had travelled here, to the Meet, which, Tom reflected, was probably unexpected.

Arthur was halfway back to the Quarter Way House before Tom caught up with him. "Arthur, what's the matter?"

"Everything!"

"What do you mean, 'everything'?" Tom asked, even more confused.

Arthur didn't answer and instead headed to their inn, ran up the stairs and banged on what Tom presumed was their shared room door.

"Yes, I'm here and I'm not deaf! Come in, the door's open."

But Arthur was already in, throwing the door wide and striding across the room.

"What's the matter with you?" Woodsmoke asked, alarmed. He was sitting on a chair on the small balcony overlooking the square.

Tom followed Arthur, closing the door behind him, while Arthur sat agitatedly beside Woodsmoke. "Nimue used to come here with Merlin."

Looking confused, Woodsmoke asked, "Is that good or bad?"

"I don't know," Arthur said. "Both? Neither? It's just odd. It's a shock, that's all."

"But this was a long time ago? She wasn't here with him recently?" Woodsmoke asked.

"No, no, of course not. He disappeared a long time ago. Well not so long ago for me, merely a few years. But even so, it's a shock."

"Why? You said they knew each other?"

"Yes, but to know that they were *here*! *Together*! I didn't think she liked him. She actively avoided him at first, I think." Arthur looked troubled as he tried to recall the nature of their relationship.

"So you're shocked because you didn't think they knew each other well?" Woodsmoke asked, trying to get to the root of Arthur's problem, and looking further confused in the process.

"Yes," Arthur said. "And now it seems they knew each other better than I realised. Merlin had a sort of obsession with Nimue, but she used to keep him at a distance. Of course he was much older than her at the time, an old man. A very grumpy, unkempt old man. Still powerful, of course. And she was young and very beautiful. I saw her more often than Vivian – she represented Vivian and Avalon at Camelot. It was there that Merlin first met her." Arthur gazed into the middle distance as he tried to remember the details. "But he could be charming. And he never stopped trying to impress her."

"So, maybe he finally managed to charm her into friendship."

"Maybe. I think she was impressed with his powers, if nothing else.

Perhaps that's what swayed her? Maybe they *did* become good friends?" he mused.

"What powers did Merlin have?" Tom asked. He sat on the floor of the balcony, leaning back against the railing, watching the exchange.

"He was a shapeshifter. He favoured fish and stags, but he could turn into anything he chose. And he had the power of prophecy. But he could perform other magic and spells. I gather he learnt much from travelling here. Obviously the dryad at the Hollow Bole did not approve of either Merlin or Nimue."

Woodsmoke looked puzzled. "Why not?"

"She said they meddled in the natural order. She seemed to prize her own natural magical abilities far more highly."

"Maybe because their magic is acquired. And of course, they are human."

"Perhaps. Although I believe Merlin was born with his powers of prophecy and shapeshifting. The rumours were that nobody knew who his father was." Arthur shrugged. "I don't know. Merlin always guarded his secrets closely. He didn't like to share where he was going or what he was doing."

"Perhaps he bewitched Nimue?" Woodsmoke asked.

Arthur looked up sharply. "No, I find that hard to believe. Although," he said thoughtfully, "he was not averse to doing things that would benefit him."

Arthur shot off his chair and paced up and down. "You cannot understand how odd this is for me! I have been dead, or asleep, whatever you choose to call it, for hundreds and hundreds of years, but for me that time was only months ago. And yet all of my friends are dead and buried, my kingdom has disappeared, my home is gone, and I am a myth! It's as if I never existed, as Beansprout and Tom told me." He gestured vaguely in Tom's direction. "No evidence that I ever existed at all! As if I am a shadow. But I find Vivian is still alive, that Morgan was alive, albeit in some other form, and now Nimue! Such unnatural life spans! And Merlin disappeared hundreds of years ago, but the dryad spoke as if he had just left the room." Deflated, he sat down again. "I don't think I will ever get used to this."

Woodsmoke seemed to take this outburst in his stride, as if he expected it. "I'm sorry Arthur. I can only imagine how confusing this must be for you. But I thought you liked your chance at another life?"

"I did, and I suppose I still do most of the time. But today has made me reconsider. However, there isn't much I can do about it. This is my fate and I must live with it."

4 Nimue's Secret

In the end, Tom had left Arthur with Woodsmoke, heading to the bathroom where he had a long cool bath, glad to wash off the dust from the road. Tom couldn't help but feel a little left out. Arthur and Woodsmoke had obviously become good friends, and Arthur trusted Woodsmoke's judgement.

They met Brenna and Beansprout back in the bar for their evening meal, Arthur still shaken by the news he had heard. "Did you find out anything on your way here?" he asked Brenna.

"Nothing," she answered. "Many of the people we asked had no idea who Nimue was, and no one had seen a woman travelling alone. Sorry."

"It's all right," Woodsmoke said, distributing the drinks the barman brought over. "We always knew this would be tricky."

"So what now?" Beansprout asked.

Arthur huffed. "Well, seeing as that dryad wouldn't tell me anything, we still have plenty to find out. I can't believe how unhelpful she was!"

"I think she was annoyed by your constant questions, Arthur," said Tom.

"How can I find out anything if I don't ask questions?" said Arthur. "Anyway, we haven't spoken to everyone here yet. Lots of people pass through, so it's worth us staying for another day or two."

"I'll fly over the surrounding area," Brenna said. "See if I can spot anyone who looks like Nimue."

"Thanks, I was hoping you'd offer," Arthur said. "In the meantime, we'll split up and cover the rest of the Meet, and hopefully we'll find out something. Woodsmoke and Beansprout, if you two can cover from the Hollow Bole to the Merry Satyr, Tom and I will do the rest."

"Sure," Woodsmoke said, "whatever you need."

"I'm looking forward to exploring this place," Beansprout said, studying the menu. "And maybe you should try to get some clothes while you're here, Tom? It would help you blend in more."

Tom looked down at his jeans and T-shirt and then at the others in their cotton trousers, shirts and leather boots. "I suppose you're right. I do stick out."

"Good idea, Beansprout," Arthur said. "It will be my treat, Tom. I am no longer a pauper; Vivian is paying me."

"I have a suggestion, Beansprout," Woodsmoke said quietly as Arthur was ordering some food. "Arthur managed to upset the dryad in The Hollow Bole, but I think we should try again. Perhaps a subtler approach by a pleading female friend would have more success."

"Sneaky!" exclaimed Beansprout, "Yes, let's. Nimue must have said something."

The next morning after breakfast they split up. Arthur set off to visit every inn and drinking place – the darker and more secretive-looking, the better.

"Do you think she was up to something?" Tom asked.

"Not originally, but I think she found out something that has spooked her. She's either gone into hiding, or she's gone to deal with whatever it is."

They had no luck in any of the dark dank inns. They were treated with suspicion and received nothing but grunting shakes of the head. It was only when they stopped at a stall in the village square that they began to get somewhere. Drawn by the smell of meat roasting over a smoky fire, they gazed at the char-grilled chunks of beef and lamb.

"Feeling hungry?" asked the stall owner, a small dwarf-like creature with the ears and muzzle of a dog. He stood on a large box behind his counter, beneath a flapping striped awning.

"Yes, I am!" Arthur declared. "Asking questions is hungry work. Lots of that, that and that," he said, pointing, "for two."

"So what you been asking that's worn you out so much?" said the owner as he sorted out their food.

"My good friend Nimue was meant to meet me here, but I'm very late and she has already gone, without leaving me a note or anything." Arthur shrugged dramatically. "I'm trying to find out where she could have gone so that I can catch up with her." Then for good measure he added, "Women!"

"I know Nimue," the stall owner answered, passing over plates of steaming meats and crusty bread. "She likes my food. She says it's the best in the Meet."

"Does she now!" Arthur said, his mouth full of food.

Tom stood next to him, also cramming in food as if they hadn't had a huge breakfast only a short time before.

"Oh yes, comes here most days when she's in the village. She likes the Bole for a bed, but always grabs snacks from here. Especially for the road. I bag it all up for her, special like, to keep. She'd got a long journey ahead of her last time."

Arthur almost choked in his excitement and Tom intervened, slapping him hard between his shoulder blades.

"It's good to know you're looking out for her," said Arthur. "We worry when she has so far to travel on her own. Did she mention where she was heading? We might still be able to catch up with her."

"Beyond Cervini land, I know that much. You know the Cervini?"

"Not really, we're new here."

"They're shifters. Part deer, part man, sort of. They change between the two."

"Like the Aerikeen?" Tom asked, confused.

"You know *them*? Yes, just like that! I was here when she met that man."

"What man's that?" Tom asked, trying to be calm.

"Just a traveller passing through. They were both here, getting food and having an idle chat. He was the scruffiest-looking man. Must have been on the road for weeks." He broke off, deep in thought.

Arthur was anxious to keep the story going. "So what were they chatting about?"

"Nimue noticed he had this big dirty dressing on his arm. She asked him about it, and he said he'd been caught in a rock fall up on Scar Face Fell, on the moors beyond White Woods. It's wild land up there, forever in the mists. There'd been a landslip after days of rain – he'd been trying to find shelter in one of the caves, when all of a sudden the rocks fell and he was nearly crushed. Then, lucky for him, this new cave opens up in the hillside behind him."

He paused to serve another customer, and Tom and Arthur bit back their impatience. Once he'd gone, Arthur asked, "So what then?"

"Nimue went dead white when he told his tale. I had to sit her down, looked like she might faint. Strange, she never struck me as the sensitive type before. She asked him if he went in the new cave, and he said yes, but it proved to be many caves and he was afraid of getting lost so he gave up, staying in the main one instead. As soon as the weather got better, he left."

"So is that where she went? Scar Face Fell?"

"I reckon so. She said his story reminded her of something from when she was younger, and it might be nice to go and see the place again. Long way to go if you ask me!"

"Are you sure she didn't mention anything else? Anywhere else?"

"No. Just said she'd need some more supplies, and asked me to prepare some food for her to take. She came to pick it up, and that was the last I saw of her."

Tom and Arthur arrived back at the inn an hour or two later. True to his word, Arthur had helped Tom buy more suitable clothing, and they now carried an assortment of packages. Tom was feeling more and more uncomfortable in his own clothing, and began to imagine people were staring at him. He itched to go and change, but he also wanted to tell the others what they had found out, and hear their news.

They found Woodsmoke and Beansprout sitting at a quiet corner table in the bar, well away from others, their heads together as they examined a map spread out in front of them. Their hands were cupped around half-empty glasses and the menus were pushed to the side of the table. Arthur and Tom bought drinks and joined them, Tom piling the chair next to him with his packages.

"Looks like you've been successful. Anything in particular you're looking for?" Arthur asked.

"Don't get too excited," Woodsmoke said. "All we know is that Nimue confirmed to the dryad at the Bole that she was changing her plans. She said she'd received news of an old friend and wanted to see if she could find him, and that she wanted to get there before the weather worsened." He gestured at the map. "We were trying to work out where she may have gone."

"An old friend? Interesting, considering what we have heard. And what do you mean, the dryad. She was damn unhelpful to me!"

"As suspected, you obviously didn't know how to ask properly," Beansprout said. "She was extremely lovely to me. And what have *you* found out?"

"Nimue heard about a rock fall up beyond the White Woods of the Cervini, and it seemed to shock her. Frighten her, even." Arthur related the story they'd heard from the stall owner.

"Why would that frighten her?" Woodsmoke asked.

"We don't know." Tom shrugged. "Maybe she knew something about those caves? She seemed keen to know if the traveller had explored them or found anything there."

"Or any*one* there? News of an old friend ..." Arthur looked thoughtful and then worried. "I wonder if this is to do with Merlin."

"Merlin!" Woodsmoke said. "I think you're becoming obsessed with him, Arthur."

"No, no. Hear me out. Merlin disappeared years ago. According to Nimue he walked into the Caledonian woods – in our world, not yours – and never came out. She said at the time that he'd needed some time to himself. But later, now I think about it, her story changed. She said he became threatening – that they'd argued and she had fled. But he never reappeared. Now that in itself is odd; he knew those woods well. He couldn't have got lost, so what happened to him?"

"Didn't you look for him?"

"I couldn't. For a while I didn't even think about it; Merlin was always disappearing for months at a time. Nimue stepped in as my advisor, and I was busy with court affairs, as usual. Not long after, I found out that my best friend had betrayed me, and so I had other things to worry about." He paused and stared at the table, as if to summon his courage. "He'd been having an affair with my wife. When he knew I'd found out, he fled the court, and in a mad rage I raced after him. When I came back, Mordred, my nephew, had seized control of the country and we went to war. And then I died, and you know the rest ..."

They fell into an awkward silence, Tom wondering what on earth to say after that. Then, a thought banished everything else from his mind. Slapping the table, he shouted, "I've been so stupid!"

The others jumped, and people sitting close by turned to stare. "Sorry," he said, lowering his voice again, "but I've just remembered. In some of the stories I've been reading about Arthur, it says that Nimue imprisoned Merlin!"

"What? And you've only just remembered?" Beansprout said, looking incredulous.

"There are hundreds, if not thousands, of stories about Arthur and his knights! And some of the names and characters double up just to add to confusion. Actually, I was reading them mostly to try and work out a way back here."

"What do mean, hundreds of stories about me? You said I was a myth. That no one knew if I ever really existed at all."

"That didn't stop the stories, or the fact that you're a national hero."

"I am?" Arthur asked, looking mollified and a little smug.

"Yes," Tom said, grinning. "But to go back to Nimue, there are several versions. Merlin was besotted with her. Completely obsessed. Finally, she had enough of his attentions, but before leaving she decided to learn as much magic as she could from him first. When he was no longer of use she either imprisoned him in a tomb in the middle of the forest, or in a cave, or in a crystal tower that she made, which then became invisible. Most stories say he was imprisoned alive, but then died. But obviously, who would ever know? None of the stories suggest he reappeared after you died, Arthur. I think." He shrugged. "When you died, that was the end of everyone's story."

The others looked dumbfounded. Woodsmoke stirred first. "So this *could* be about Merlin. What better way to ensure he was never found than by imprisoning him here?"

"… in the Scar Face Fell caves," Beansprout said. "And now they are exposed, she's worried he'll be found!"

"But surely he'd be dead?" Tom said.

"Nimue is not convinced, obviously. She's gone to find him. And we have to follow her," Arthur said, pulling the map towards him. "Let's order some food and plan our route. If there's a chance he's alive, I have to save him."

5 The Chase

They were gathered in Tom, Arthur and Woodsmoke's room. It was late evening and the sun was sinking below the horizon. Lights were springing up in the Meet and surrounding trees. Woodsmoke and Beansprout were in chairs on the balcony, and Arthur and Tom were sitting on the floor, hunched over the map spread between them. Supplies were strewn everywhere.

Their lively discussion of what to do next was interrupted by a knock on the door, and Brenna peered in. "Oh good, I've found you." She dropped into the nearest chair, looking tired.

"How did you get on?" Arthur asked.

"Badly. No sign of Nimue. There were no women travelling alone. But I flew close to every group I passed, to check who was travelling with them. No one matched Nimue's description." She wearily rubbed her hands across her face and through her hair. "What about you?"

"We found out a lot," Arthur answered. "I'm sorry you had a useless trip, though."

"No, it's fine. It was good to be able to fly all day." She starting laughing, "You look like you're going to burst, Arthur! What have you found out?"

"She's gone to find Merlin! In Scar Face Fells."

Brenna looked at the others, then back at Arthur. "Merlin. Your Merlin?"

"Yes. She's been the one responsible for his disappearance all along." Arthur was flushed and excited, glad to share his news.

"We think," cautioned Woodsmoke.

"Did you like Nimue, Arthur?" Brenna asked.

He looked surprised by the question. "Yes, of course. I had no reason to suspect her of anything until now. She was always very helpful."

She seemed reassured. "Good. I'm glad we've made progress. But I'm way too tired for this. I'm going to have a bath and then go to bed. Are we leaving in the morning?"

"Straight after breakfast."

"I'll see you then."

They left the Meet on the north-west Holloway that led out of the meadowlands and into the hills. This path continued on to the White Woods of the Cervini and then the fells. Woodsmoke had warned them the land would get rougher and the weather colder as they travelled higher. They had bought thick travelling cloaks and extra blankets, and for shelter, a large circular sheet of sewn-together tanned hides, and a thick wooden pole.

"Is that a tent?" Tom had asked when they bought it.

"Of a fashion," Woodsmoke said. "At least it will provide us with some protection when the weather worsens."

"I thought you always had good weather here. Isn't it called the summer country?"

"It is by some. But places still vary, and the higher we go, the colder it gets."

Woodsmoke had strapped the pole awkwardly behind him on his horse, along with the bulky mass of the tent. They were all similarly heavily laden, their saddlebags bulging with supplies of dried meats, fruits and extra clothing.

None of them were familiar with the places they were travelling to, but for Tom and Beansprout this was an exciting chance to learn more of the Other. They had pored over the map, reading the strange names, tracing their route.

"Who are the Cervini?" Beansprout asked as they trekked along.

"They are shapeshifters, like me," Brenna said, "but they turn into deer rather than birds. They live in the White Woods."

"Merlin was fond of turning into a stag," Arthur said. "It was his favourite animal form. That might explain why he would travel here with Nimue – they would have seemed like family."

"So some of them may know him?" Tom asked.

"I suppose so. But it was a long time ago since anyone last saw Merlin," Woodsmoke said.

"I wonder how they would feel if they knew he might still be alive?" Tom said thoughtfully. "And I wonder if some of them would know Nimue?" he added as an afterthought.

Tom woke up with a crick in his neck. Light was beginning to seep through the thick tanned hide, illuminating the flap that served as the tent entrance. He sat up slowly and quietly, unwilling to wake the others. He glanced round at the various-sized humps covered in blankets that snuffled and snored gently, cramped in the confined space, and wrinkled his nose at the musty smell that filled the air. Easing his legs from beneath his blankets, he made his way out of the tent.

The sky was low and heavy with thick grey clouds, and a brisk wind blew across the hills. Their surroundings were springing into shape as the light increased, revealing the flat sheltered area in the curve of a hillside where they had set up camp. The grass was shaggy and tufted, broken by small stones, and had been uncomfortable to sleep on. The meadowlands and Holloways were a lush green in the distance.

They had been travelling for over a week, making good time, and were now not far from the Cervini lands. Yesterday, Brenna had flown over the White Woods, and on towards Scar Face Fell. She returned with interesting news. Although she hadn't seen Nimue, a herd of stags had gathered at a point midway along the long stretch of pitted and pock-marked rock that rose out of the moor, exposed by centuries of wind and rain. Some of the cliff faces were tall and imposing, towering menacingly over the landscape, while others were low, barely twice the height of a man. They ran in a continuous ragged chain, scarring the lowlands for miles.

"I hadn't realised how big they are," she said on her return. "We would have been searching for weeks!"

"So you think the stags have found something? Merlin?" Arthur asked eagerly.

"They've found *something*. Some were in human form; they were heading in and out of a cave entrance. And there did look to have been a rock fall. I have no idea how recently, though."

"It must be Merlin. What else could they have found?"

"Who knows what they do there, Arthur," Woodsmoke said. "It could be where they bury their dead."

"No, I don't believe in coincidences." Arthur pulled the map out of his pack. "Are the Cervini aggressive?"

"Not that I'm aware. Not needlessly, anyway," Woodsmoke answered.

Arthur ran his finger over the map, tracing routes and muttering to himself. After a few minutes he looked up. "I think we should split up, but I'm going to think on it, and we'll discuss it in the morning."

Not long after that they had rolled into bed, and now, as Tom prodded the smouldering fire in the dawn stillness, he wondered what their strategy would be. He pulled his heavy cloak round his shoulders and smiled as he thought over the past few days. Ever since he'd arrived here, a huge weight had lifted off his shoulders, a weight he hadn't realised he'd been carrying. It felt so good to be back that he couldn't believe he'd ever left. He shook his head as he tried to dismiss any lingering doubts. He'd done what he thought was right.

Arthur had assumed a fatherly role that Tom found disconcerting, but also reassuring. He had continued teaching him how to sword fight, maintaining it was a skill Tom should learn. He'd bought Tom a sword from one of the stalls in the Meet – slightly smaller and lighter than Excalibur, and easier for him to handle – and they practised every evening.

After a clumsy start, some of the skills he'd learnt on the way to Aeriken started to return, but it was going to take time. "It's all right, Tom," Arthur had reassured him, "I started to learn as a child, but you'll get there."

Brenna and Woodsmoke would join in, but Beansprout practised using the longbow she usually wore slung behind her back. Woodsmoke had taught her to use it, and every now and again he would break off and watch her progress, adjusting her stance and her grip. It had taken Tom a while to get used to seeing her with a bow; it only reinforced how different things here were from at home.

A rustling sound disturbed his thoughts, and Arthur wriggled free of the tent to sit next to him. "Morning, Tom, you're up early," he said softly to avoid waking the others.

"I didn't sleep well, stiff neck," Tom said, rolling his shoulders.

Arthur laughed. "Ah, life on the road."

"So have you decided what we're going to do?"

"I've decided that we – me and you – should cross the Cervini land and head towards the fells. It's more direct and will get us there quicker, but we may be stopped and questioned. The others should go the longer way round and hang back to see what's happening. That way, if we get caught, we've got back up. Brenna can keep an eye on things."

"When you say 'caught', do you mean imprisoned?" Tom asked, alarmed.

"I hope not, but you never know."

"But why would they imprison us, if we're only passing through? Woodsmoke said it would be fine."

"It depends what they're up to. I'd actually like to run into them so we can ask them about Nimue." He thought for a moment, then said, "Unless of course we travel to the White Woods and seek them out, to ask if they've seen her passing through."

Tom watched as Arthur gazed into space, a furrow between his brows as he worked through his options. "No, it will take too long, and we know where she's going. Let's press on." He smiled at Tom. "We're getting close."

Woodsmoke wasn't impressed with the idea of splitting up. As they packed up he said, "There's strength in numbers, we should stay together. Or at least *we* should cross Cervini lands and *you* should go the long way round."

"No. I'd rather take the risks than you."

Tom could tell Arthur was excited at the thought of action, and had no intention of being relegated to a safe role.

"Besides, there's really no risk. You said they weren't dangerous."

"But I don't know that for sure!" Woodsmoke glared at Arthur. "Besides, it's not just you who's at risk."

"Tom will be fine, won't you Tom?" Arthur said, turning to him.

"Of course," Tom said, not willing to upset either Arthur or Woodsmoke.

Brenna interrupted. "The suggestion does make some sense, Woodsmoke. If for some reason one group is delayed, the other can continue the search."

"That's settled then," Arthur said. "I'm sure we'll meet up at the cave with no problems. And Brenna can keep on eye things, right Brenna?"

"Of course. But be careful, Arthur!"

Woodsmoke stood by his horse, adjusting his packs and brooding silently. When he couldn't contain himself any longer, he rounded on Arthur. "This is rash! We don't know where Nimue is. She could already be there. She could put a spell on you two, or all of us, and then what?"

"And this is why we're splitting up! Besides, she won't put a spell on us," Arthur said, rolling his eyes.

"She's hiding her actions from everyone, Arthur. She's obviously panicking; she's abandoned all her plans! We have no idea what she's capable of. Or what she's done. Everything we think we know is pure guesswork."

"It's good guesswork and you know it."

Arthur and Woodsmoke had stopped packing and stared at each other across the smoking remains of the fire.

"My point is, Arthur," said Woodsmoke, slowly and deliberately, "you seem to be in a rush to get to Merlin without considering anything else. If the Cervini have found Merlin, what are they doing there? What do they want with him? What if they are working with Nimue? We'll be outnumbered. We need to find out more before we go stumbling into this! Remember, we were only supposed to be finding Nimue."

Arthur answered, as slowly as Woodsmoke, "This is now about much more than just Nimue."

"For you."

"If Vivian knew–"

"She doesn't," Woodsmoke interrupted. "And you don't know what she'd think."

"I know her better than you do. This is not a discussion. We'll split up and meet at the rock face by the entrance to the cave. Or as close to it as we can get, depending on the Cervini. Brenna can liaise between us."

There was silence as Woodsmoke stared at Arthur. "I think the prospect of you possibly finding Merlin is skewing your judgement. When we get to the rock face, you'd better wait for us before doing anything." Woodsmoke strode to his horse and finished packing in silence.

For the next few hours of riding, no one spoke. Woodsmoke rode ahead, and when they eventually split up, his final words were, "Remember to wait, Arthur."

6 Scar Face Fell

Tom and Arthur travelled for the rest of the day without seeing anyone. The land rose higher and the heavy grey skies seemed to get lower and lower, until they felt squashed between them. A stiff breeze flattened the grass, and the chill made Tom pull his cloak closer around him.

In the distance, the White Woods appeared as a white haze of trees brooding over the windswept landscape. Arthur stopped for a minute to watch the tree line, but nothing moved and no one emerged, so they pressed on, Tom trying to ignore the woods and whatever they might contain.

At dusk they saw the craggy edge of the fells, breaking up the horizon into a jagged unwelcoming mass. Arthur pushed on despite the failing light, keen to find shelter from the unrelenting wind, as the others had the tent. The horses slowed to a weary trot, picking their way carefully over the broken ground, and eventually, as night fell, they stumbled into a rocky enclave marking the start of the fells.

The wind dropped immediately, replaced by an eerie silence. It was as if they had fallen into a dark pit. Tom could just make out Arthur's figure as he slid from his horse to the ground, calling, "Wait there, Tom."

Tom heard him scrabbling in his panniers, and then torchlight flared and the darkness scattered to reveal a small irregularly shaped space enclosed by rock and open to the night sky. The floor was covered with dry flattened grass. There were three other exits, opposite to where they had entered.

Tom dismounted and lit his own torch, waiting as Arthur investigated the other exits. It was unnerving, being on his own, and in the silence Tom became jumpy. He rummaged for some dried meats to chew on and patted Midnight, not sure who was more reassured by this comforting gesture.

After an interval of several interminable minutes, Arthur reappeared. "Two of them are just small passageways snaking through the rocks, but through this one," he gestured behind him, "there's a sheltered rocky hollow where we can light a fire."

"What's wrong with staying here?" Tom asked, thinking it was a good place to settle for the night.

"It's too close to the entrance. Follow me."

They led their horses down the passage, the harsh clop of hooves echoing off the stone. After a few minutes they came to a circular space protected on all sides by a rock wall. They secured the horses, then lit a fire beneath an overhanging rock. Arthur opened a bottle of dark ale from the inn, and after taking a drink passed it to Tom. He took a deep draught, feeling it warming and relaxing him.

Tom was shattered, aching from the long days of riding, the constant wind and uncomfortable sleeping. He rummaged in his pack and took out more dried meats, cheeses and bread, then settled his pack behind him and tried to get comfortable. Arthur sat staring into the fire, deep in thought. Tom nudged him, holding out some food. "Here, Arthur, you should eat."

He looked round startled. "Sorry, Tom. Miles away. I don't know about you, but I think we just rest tonight, no training."

"That's fine by me," Tom said, relieved. "What do you think will happen? Will we find Merlin?"

Arthur shook his head. "I don't know. Now we're so close, it feels unreal, especially considering how long it's been. The reality of us actually finding him seems unlikely."

"But the Cervini have found something."

"That could be anything. It's just wishful thinking on my behalf. Just like one of those old tales you've been reading."

Tom again rummaged in his pack, pulling out an old book. He gave it to Arthur. "I thought I'd bring this with me, in case you didn't believe me."

Arthur studied the book. "*Tales of King Arthur*. Is this about me?" he asked, shocked.

"Yes. And about your knights and your quests and your battles. And Merlin. And there are hundreds of these types of books. I told you – you're a legend."

Arthur looked at it as if it would burst into flames in his hands.

"You don't have to read it," Tom said. "I just wanted to show it to you. The others don't know I have it."

"There's a picture of a sword on the front."

"Of course. It's your symbol."

Arthur looked up and unexpectedly laughed. "This is ridiculous!"

Tom smiled. "It's pretty cool actually, Arthur. I'm sitting with a living legend. I'm actually related to you!" he said smugly.

Arthur laughed again. "Unbelievable."

"You should read it, if you can bear to, just to see what's true and what isn't. I'd like to know too! Just think," he mused, "if I ever went back to my Earth, I could write the *real* story of Arthur."

"But you're not going back," Arthur said, frowning.

"No, I'm not. It's just a thought." Tom took another swig of beer and wriggled into his cloak. "Do you miss your Earth?"

"Yes and no. I miss my friends, my home, but I don't miss war or bloodshed. Or endless decisions of policy and state. It's curious, though, not to have everyone hanging on your every word, looking to you to make every decision."

Tom wondered if he'd mention Woodsmoke and their argument earlier, but Arthur just sighed deeply. "It's actually quite liberating. I have a remarkable amount of freedom here, and anonymity. I like that."

"You're not bored, then?"

"Not yet." He said it evenly, but even so, Tom wondered how true that was. Surely it must be hard, going from being a King of Britain to a King of nothing.

During the night, despite his layers of clothing, cloak and blanket, the cold seeped into Tom's bones and he woke chilled. Mist had settled into the hollow, blurring the grey rock walls, and he could feel a faint slick of moisture on his face and hair. He sat up and prodded life back into the fire, then put some water on to boil for herb tea. Looking up, all he could see was white mist. A faint murmur of wind penetrated the unearthly silence. It was if they had passed out of this world and into another.

He felt groggy, as if he'd slept too long. He went to check the time, before remembering he'd taken off his watch and put it in his pack. It didn't work here.

Arthur still lay wrapped in his blankets, the book tucked under his cheek, looking so comfortable that Tom hesitated to wake him. But he was sure they'd slept later than normal, and that they needed to get moving. "Arthur," he said, shaking him, "wake up."

Tom stood up and stamped his feet to get warm, then wandered over to where the horses were feeding. At least they looked rested. Tom had a nagging doubt about today, and wished they were with the others … which then made him feel guilty about doubting Arthur.

After a quick breakfast and a hot drink, they set off. The mist remained thick and heavy, and a fine drizzle started to fall, further obstructing their view and muffling all sound. They kept the fells close to their right, the height of the massive stretch of rock lost in the mists. Huge chunks of stone, some the size of buildings, littered the floor, and they wound their way around them, listening carefully for any sign of the Cervini.

They had definitely overslept, and the thick mist delayed them further, so the day was growing steadily darker by the time they heard a low muffled shout. Arthur gestured to Tom to stop, whispering, "Did you hear that?"

Tom nodded. "Yes, but not what was said."

"Let's leave the horses here and proceed on foot." Arthur slipped to the ground and led them behind a large outcrop of fallen rock. They secured the horses and, staying close to the shelter of the rocks, edged their way forward.

They heard another voice, deep and gruff – much closer this time, and edged with amusement. "I think the witch actually looked scared."

"She should be," the first voice called from a short distance away. "Orlas is furious. She'll be lucky to keep her life."

"Well she'd better do what she's told, then," the second voice answered.

Arthur grabbed Tom's arm and pulled him back a few paces, whispering, "We'll be lucky if there's only two on guard. Stay here while I look."

Arthur disappeared into the mist, leaving Tom nervously peering around him at the fallen mounds of rock. The voices sounded like they were coming from just ahead and to the left, but the thick mist distorted everything, and he half-expected a Cervini to walk around the rocks and find him hiding.

Minutes later, Arthur reappeared.

"They're sitting a short distance away, at the top of the rise, with their backs to the cave entrance. There may well be more of them out on the slopes, but I can't see a damn thing in this mist." He grinned unpleasantly. "They obviously don't expect visitors from this direction, so we'll slip quietly behind them and into the caves. Ready?"

"No, not really," Tom said, surprised. "We're supposed to meet the others," he reminded Arthur. "Shouldn't we wait? Brenna will be looking for us."

"She'll never find us in this mist."

"But we promised Woodsmoke. And they could be very close. Especially as we overslept."

Arthur took a deep breath. "Plans change, Tom. We need to act before it's too late. And besides, if this mist has delayed us, it will definitely have delayed them. They could still be hours away."

"But Brenna definitely won't find us if we're in a cave."

"She'll see the horses and work it out. Then she can tell the others."

Tom's earlier uneasiness returned. "But Arthur, we don't know what to expect."

"Yes we do! The witch they referred to is Nimue. She's in there right now, with the Cervini, and not willingly by the sound of it. We cannot afford to wait if we're going to find Merlin."

"But then what? We haven't properly discussed this!"

"We are improvising."

Tom's uneasiness started to turn into panic. Arthur had no intention of waiting for the others, and Tom wondered if he was trying to prove a point to Woodsmoke. He stood implacable, clothed in a slight swagger, one hand on Excalibur, his other reaching to grasp Tom's forearm.

"Come on, Tom, no time for doubts. We'll be fine."

Tom nodded nervously, sensing that Arthur would go anyway, and he knew he'd rather go with Arthur than be alone. "All right," he answered eventually.

"Good, stay close."

Arthur led the way, weaving around the stones, making his way to the rock face. The grass was thick and damp, masking their footfalls, but they kept a hand to their swords just in case. As they rounded a large fallen rock, Tom saw the guards. Their backs were to them and they stood close together, laughing and talking, oblivious to their presence. Arthur gestured to his right, and Tom saw the cave entrance, high and narrow, with darkness beyond.

7 Blind Moor

Woodsmoke, Beansprout and Brenna stood tucked beneath the overhang of a large rock, Woodsmoke looking angry and worried.

Poor visibility had threatened to slow their progress, but they had raced recklessly over the uneven ground, Woodsmoke keen to maintain pace despite the mist and drizzle. Brenna had frequently corrected their progress as she flew to and fro, trying to orientate herself.

"I'm sorry, Woodsmoke," Brenna said, "but I cannot see through thick mist. I've flown very low and I still can't see them. But you'll be pleased to know we're close to the cave."

"I knew this would happen!" Woodsmoke said accusingly. "Splitting up was a stupid idea. And you encouraged it."

"I'm sorry, but it did seem a good idea. We had no idea this mist would come down so thickly for so long."

He glared at her and took a deep breath. "Where did you last see them?"

"At the edge of the rocks last night, a few hours' ride from the cave. But it was late and they looked fine, so I left them. I can't see them anywhere today. They should have arrived here hours ago."

"They must be somewhere."

"Of course they're somewhere," she spat.

"Have you seen the Cervini?"

"I can see two at the entrance to the cave, but most of them seem to have gone. The mist—"

"Yes, yes, yes. The mist," he echoed sarcastically. "So you don't know where the Cervini are, or where Tom and Arthur are?"

"No."

"I will go. Wait here." He tossed her his horse's reins and strode off without a backward glance.

Beansprout looked concerned. "He's very cross! I've never seen him like this before."

"I have," Brenna said. "He's like this when he's worried, and right now he's worried about Tom. And even though he's angry with Arthur, he's worried about him too. However, I would prefer he did not take it out on me."

They fell silent, the mist muffling sight and sound. Beansprout scanned what little she could see of the scrubby grass, heathers and curling ferns crowding together in a thick and luxuriant mass. The two of them waited an uncomfortably long time until Woodsmoke returned.

"They're already in the cave," he said, as he snatched his horse's reins back from Brenna. He was even more furious than before.

"What? How do you know?" Beansprout said.

"I found their horses tied up a short distance past the cave. And I could smell Tom and Arthur at the cave entrance."

"I can't believe they've gone in alone!" Beansprout said.

"I can. Arthur's doing, of course," Woodsmoke said. "And there's a smell of decay coming from those caves too, of something long buried and forgotten. There are torches inside the entrance, marking the route."

"Are there many Cervini?" Brenna asked.

"The two you saw at the entrance, and another dozen grazing on the moor. I made sure to pass upwind of them, so they couldn't smell me. We did well to circle so far around them," he added in consolation.

"So what do we do now?" Beansprout asked.

"We try to find them," Woodsmoke said grimly.

8 Nimue

Tom and Arthur followed the passageway upwards and inwards. The floor was uneven, and only a small amount of light was provided by the intermittent torches, so they stumbled along in near darkness, seeing only a faint orange glow up ahead.

Tom followed close on Arthur's heels, until eventually Arthur came to a sudden stop, and Tom thudded into him. Arthur gestured for silence, and Tom peered round him to see a large cave just ahead. A cluster of torches smoked and flickered in the centre, illuminating a small group of people. They were all male, except for a small woman Tom presumed was Nimue. Arthur and Tom stepped as close to the cave entrance as they dared, careful to remain in the shadows.

Nimue's voice rang out loudly. "How do I know I can trust you? If I release him, what will you do to me?"

"If you don't release him we shall leave you powerless, trapped within the binding spell. And then we will seal you in here. Forever." The man who spoke leaned over her aggressively.

"You should mind your threats, Orlas. In order for me to release Merlin, you must release me from the binding spell. I will have my powers restored."

"Temporarily. Until you prove yourself safe."

"You will have to do better than that. If I release him, you will allow me to leave, no repercussions, and no binding spell. You will have Merlin, and that is what you want, isn't it?"

"Will he be alive?"

She paused as she thought. "I don't know. I sealed him in here out of place and time. He should be alive, but I can't say for sure."

"Where is he?" Orlas turned slowly, looking at the walls and up into the impenetrable blackness of the roof.

Nimue smiled. "You'll see. You'd better release me, Nerian," she said to a tall lean man with a beard and long matted hair.

He turned to Orlas, who shook his head. "Not yet. You will get everything ready first."

Orlas then spoke to the other Cervini: "Set out the torches, and move back to the entrance."

Tom whispered to Arthur, "Should we leave?"

"Not a chance."

"But we'll be caught!"

Tom looked at the cave, wondering where in such a bare place they might be able to hide. As well as Orlas and Nerian, there were another three Cervini, who were now placing five torches in a rough circle around Nimue, who was rummaging in a bag.

Tom and Arthur were so transfixed by the activities in the cave that they failed to hear another Cervini creep up behind them. They were alerted by the hiss of a sword as he pulled it free from his scabbard to hover under Arthur's chin, the point nudging his neck.

Arthur's hand shot to Excalibur, but the Cervini's sword pushed more firmly into his neck and he dropped his hands. The gruff voice sounded unexpectedly loud. "I think not. One more twitch and I shall remove your head from your shoulders. Orlas!" he shouted. "You should pay better attention to your surroundings. You have visitors."

The others turned to watch as the Cervini, an older man of medium height with short grey hair, pushed Tom and Arthur into the cave, keeping his sword firmly pushed into Arthur's back. Tom edged his hand towards his own sword, but the Cervini just looked at him and tutted. "Now is not the time for heroics," he said softly.

At a nod from Orlas, two more Cervini withdrew their swords and flanked Tom and Arthur.

Orlas stood in front of them, a tall, imposing figure with broad shoulders and powerful arms. Dark hair fell to his shoulders, and in the torchlight they saw strange markings across his skin, and on the skin of the other Cervini – mottled browns, cream and tan, like camouflage. In fact, Tom thought, just like deer.

Orlas looked at Arthur. "Do I know you?"

"No," Arthur answered, "but I know Nimue."

She stepped closer to look at him. Orlas put a restraining hand on her arm, and she shook it off impatiently.

Tom watched, fascinated, as he saw her properly for the first time. She was so small and slender; she barely came up to his shoulders. Her dark hair tumbled across her shoulders and her skin was pale and creamy, but it was her eyes that held him. They were dark green, and utterly captivating.

But she wasn't looking at Tom; in fact, she barely glanced at him.

"Arthur," she said. "After all these years! How did you find me?"

"Vivian sent me. And as you should remember, Nimue, I am very persistent." His voice hardened as he added, "Especially when it comes to Merlin."

"Yes," she said. "Who'd have thought the old man would be so missed?"

Orlas interrupted. "Arthur? Merlin's Arthur? You look remarkably well preserved for a dead man."

"Don't I just?" Arthur answered dryly. "Preservation in a tomb of ice has beneficial consequences. Merlin's last gift."

Orlas nodded at Tom. "So who's this?"

"My rescuer, and also my descendant, Tom."

"I see. And you are here because?"

"Because Nimue disappeared and Vivian – our mutual friend – became worried about her safety. She asked me to find her. And eventually I suspected that Nimue had imprisoned Merlin and was making her way here to ensure he remained in the spell. However, Merlin was like a father to me, and I came here to rescue him and stop Nimue."

"An ally?" Orlas persisted. "You are not here to rescue the witch, then?"

"Definitely not," Arthur said, glaring at Nimue.

"And you're alone?" He looked beyond them to the entrance, as if others would suddenly emerge from the shadows.

"Absolutely," Arthur lied smoothly. Although in reality, Tom thought, he was telling the truth – they had no idea where Woodsmoke and the others were. "We have been tracking Nimue from Holloways Meet."

Orlas looked to the Cervini who had caught them. "Rek?"

"I've seen no one else," he confirmed.

Orlas nodded briefly at the others and they re-sheathed their swords. Tom relaxed; he hadn't realised he'd been standing so stiffly.

"May I ask how you come to be here with Nimue?" Arthur said.

"I found her," Rek answered. "She was cutting across our land, heading towards Scar Face Fell. Ever since Merlin disappeared, we have wondered what happened to him. Nimue was the last person we saw him with, so our laws say that if we ever saw Nimue again, she was to be escorted to the Great Hall for questioning. Fortunately, I have a good memory and I recognised her immediately." He must have seen Tom's startled expression. "I was a very young fawn in those days," he explained.

"So you confessed?" Arthur asked, looking at Nimue.

She remained stubbornly silent, leaving Orlas to explain. "No, she did not. In fact she tried to put a spell on those escorting her, but one of them spotted what she was up to and stopped her. Nerian, our shaman, has restricted her powers by using a binding spell. And due to her lack of co-operation ..." he smiled and gave a short bow to Nimue, "we have kept her locked in a cell as our guest for a week or so. Eventually our investigations led us here."

Arthur looked around the bare cave. "Are you sure this is the place? It could be a trick."

"It's no trick," Nerian said. "I used a spell tracer and it led us here. Merlin and Nimue entered, but only Nimue left."

"Well, this is all very entertaining," Nimue said, "but are we going to get on with it?" A small smiled played across her lips and Tom couldn't help but feel she had something planned.

"Yes we are. I have no idea how long you have been watching, but Nimue is about to lift the spell." Orlas turned back to her. "Continue, Nimue, we are all waiting."

Nimue moved back into the circle of torchlight and took a bundle of herbs from her bag. "This is all I need. You may wish to move back before I begin."

"No." Orlas shook his head. "Nerian and I will wait here. Everyone else should wait in the entrance. Arthur?"

"We remain here too."

Tom stood nervously beside Arthur, wondering what to expect, and not for the first time wished Arthur was a little less headstrong.

"All right then," Orlas said to the shaman. "Remove the binding spell."

Nerian's long matted hair seemed to writhe in the flickering torchlight as he pulled one of many necklaces free from his leather shirt. At the end was tied a small bound doll. Tom suppressed a gasp – it was an uncanny likeness of Nimue. Twisting the doll carefully in his hands, he unwound its leather binding, chanting slowly. He placed the leather strip carefully in his pocket, then snapped his fingers over the doll. A bright blue flame flashed along it and then disappeared.

Nimue took a long deep breath in and out, as if waking from a deep sleep. A ripple passed through her and she seemed to become more alert, more alive.

Orlas nodded at Nerian. "You too, back to the entrance. In case anything goes wrong."

"Wait. The doll." Nimue held out her hand expectantly. At Nerian's hesitation, she said, "Now."

Nerian reluctantly handed it over and retreated to the entrance.

Pocketing the doll, she turned away and started to separate the bundle of herbs. She stepped to the furthest of the torches and, muttering too quietly for anyone to hear, threw some of the herbs into the wavering flame. They burned instantly, and as she continued to mutter her incantations, the flame changed colour from a warm orange to a deep blood red. She thrust the rest of the bundle of herbs into the flames until it caught, and then withdrew it again. The herb bundle burnt steadily without being consumed, and she stepped beyond the circle of torchlight, carrying it around the outskirts of the cave, starting to the left of the entrance.

Tom stood watching her, holding his breath, wondering what would happen. Her movements were sure and steady, and she paced around the room until she had completed a full circle, coming to a stop at the entrance to the cave where she placed the still-burning bundle of herbs on the floor.

Those standing in the entrance looked uncertain. No one said a word. Glancing at Arthur, Tom saw that his eyes were bright with anticipation. But Tom started to have a very bad feeling; it seemed to him Nimue was blocking the entrance. Was she lifting the spell, or casting another?

She moved past them back into the circle of torchlight, and clapped her hands in a rapid staccato. The cave was suddenly plunged into almost complete darkness, as the torches burnt a deep blood red, painting everything with the colour of death. Then, as if a veil had been lifted from their eyes, the cave transformed into something else entirely.

9 The Silver Tower

The cave had vanished. They were standing in ancient woodland, the ground thick with moss. Ahead, on a rocky mound, stood a silver tower that shone in the sunlight, its door and windows flung open. The whole place had an air of desolation and decay.

Tom's skin prickled with unease, which soon turned to alarm as he realised he was standing next to a huge brown bear and a magnificent stag. The bear roared, and Tom backed off quickly, tripping and landing on the ground. But the bear ignored him and padded into the undergrowth. The stag gazed at Tom with liquid brown eyes and then moved off to graze in a patch of sunlight filtering down through the canopy. Tom realised the stag was Orlas, so the bear must be Arthur.

They were enchanted; he was alone.

Tom spun around, trying to orientate himself, but found it was impossible. He felt as if he'd been transported back hundreds of years; something in the air felt old and mysterious. And where were they? Had she transported them out of the cave, or were they still in it? And if he wasn't enchanted, how could he see the grove?

Panicking, Tom looked round for Nimue, and saw her entering the silver tower. He raced to catch up with her, clambering over the rocks to the entrance. Nimue didn't turn round. Ever since the binding spell had been lifted, she'd completely ignored them, as if they were irrelevant.

Tom paused on the threshold, looking up at the tower. He stroked the burnished walls; it really did look like silver. Close up, he could see curious engravings all around the doorway. The door itself was also silver, thick and solid, and beyond it was a sitting room in which a large chair sat next to a fireplace. Despite the sunshine outside, a small fire burned in the grate. Rugs were scattered across the floor, and the room was filled with sunlight reflecting off the silver walls. As the light danced around the room, he was reminded of being underwater in the Emperor's palace when he had visited the Eye.

Opposite him was a staircase, and before he had a chance to change his mind he crossed the room and started climbing the steps.

On the next level was a bedroom, luxuriously furnished with tapestries and rugs, and a bed piled high with pillows. This room was also empty, so he continued up the stairs. At the top was a small landing with a door that was partly closed. He could hear movement behind it, so he eased it open a little further, peering into the room beyond.

It was a workshop, filled with wooden benches, its walls crowded with shelves, and everything stacked high with books and papers, and hundreds of pots and jars of all sizes. Again a fire burned in the fireplace, and a large cauldron was suspended over it.

But this room wasn't empty. On the floor in front of the fire was the inert body of a man. He had long white hair and a thick white beard, and was wearing a long, grey, hooded robe. Crouched by his side was Nimue. Her back was to Tom, but he could see her hand stroking his face. Then her shoulders dropped and she sat back on the floor, her hands cradled in her lap.

Tom wondered what to do. He didn't want to disturb her, but equally he had to know what was happening. And Merlin – because that must be him lying on the floor – appeared to be dead.

He pushed the door open and stepped into the room. Immediately, Nimue leapt to her feet and turned, her hands raised.

"No!" Tom shouted, stepping back a pace. "I just want to talk to you."

She laughed and looked relieved. "Oh, it's you." Then her expression turned confused as she asked, "Why aren't you enchanted, like the others?"

He shrugged. "I have no idea."

"Curious," she said, suddenly interested in him. "You look normal enough. Ah!" she exclaimed. "You must possess a talisman."

Tom wondered what she was talking about. "I don't care. Why have you enchanted the others? Why is Arthur a bear?"

"A bear?" she said, laughing. "That's unexpected. That was his old name, Arturus, because of his bear-like qualities. In magic, we call it his animal spirit. This place, the spell, must have released it. Anyway, they are enchanted because I don't like being threatened."

"Maybe you shouldn't have imprisoned Merlin," Tom answered swiftly. "You've killed him, haven't you?"

She narrowed her eyes at him. "Watch your tongue, boy, or it will soon be mine, talisman or not."

"Is he dead?" he persisted.

"No. That is why the spell still exists. He is unconscious. Unrousable."

Despite the fact he'd never known Merlin, Tom was relieved to know he was still alive. "Where are we?" he asked, slightly mollified.

"Still in the cave, of course," she said, smirking.

"But how can that be? Where is all this coming from?" He gestured around him.

"My magic. Or should I say, Merlin's magic. I asked him to teach me the spell for how to imprison a man, and this is it." She leaned back against the bench, watching him.

"But why is it so … non-prison-like?" he asked, for want of a better word.

"Foolish boy. People are willing to imprison themselves in all sorts of things as long as it's comfortable enough."

"So, how long has he been lying there?"

"I have no idea. I used to visit him at first, but then I just got bored, and he never seemed to miss me, so …" Her voice trailed off.

Overcome with curiosity, Tom asked, "Can I see him?"

She shrugged. "If you wish," and she moved aside to let him pass.

He crossed the room and knelt next to Merlin, turning him over to see him properly. He looked as if he was sleeping; an old man who'd dozed off in front of the fire, creases lining his face, his mouth carrying the remnants of a smile. He certainly didn't look like a powerful wizard – not that he knew what one should look like. He felt inexplicably sad, and found himself worried about Arthur, who would be so upset.

Nimue interrupted his thoughts. "There's nothing else I can do, so I'm leaving."

He stood and faced her. "You can't leave us here, we've done nothing to you!" And then he realised that if he was to figure a way out of here, he needed to understand what had happened. "Why are we in the spell if you were releasing it?"

"You are so naïve. Because I didn't release it. I thought releasing it would definitely kill him, which would have been bad news for me, with Arthur and Orlas breathing down my neck. So I just decided to re-enter it, as I have done before, and you all came too. If I had decided to recast the spell you would all be in your own prisons."

"I don't understand."

"The spell imprisons a person in his own idea of pleasure. For Merlin that is nature. He is – was – a Druid, so nature is everything to him. Here he has trees, herbs, his workshop, everything he needs to make himself happy. I even gave him his sacred grove."

She crossed to the window. "Orlas and Arthur see Merlin's prison; it is not of their own choosing, but nevertheless, they are happy here. For now. I have no idea how long that will last, as to be quite honest I have never brought anyone with me before. I wasn't even sure it would work."

Tom joined her at the window and watched them amble through the trees and around the tower.

She gazed up at him. "What sort of man are *you*?" Her voice had dropped to a seductive murmur. "I would like to know what prison you would be in."

As he looked down into her green eyes, he could think of nothing except how pretty she was, and his gaze drifted across her face and down to her lips. "Why do you look so young, if you're as old as Vivian?"

She laughed. "Because Vivian's appearance is an affectation. She chooses to look that way. She says it is useful to remind herself of her great age." She stepped closer to Tom, almost whispering, causing him to lean in closer to her. "I think she does it because age suggests great wisdom." Smiling conspiratorially, she added, "I prefer to have people underestimate me."

And they'd certainly done that, he thought. Annoyed with himself, he stepped back to clear his head. "Release the spell now, and then go. I won't stop you. Arthur was your friend. And he's a fair man, you know that."

She stood for some moments thinking, and then shook her head. "I can't. If I release him then I release Orlas, that damn man who bound my powers and locked me up for days."

"But how long will the spell last?" Tom asked, desperately trying to find a way out of this.

"Forever. Probably."

"People will search for us! And you. We weren't the only ones looking for you and Merlin."

"They'll have a long search."

"You know Vivian sent us here. Once she knows we've disappeared, she'll come to find us. And she'll still be looking for you! She was worried about you. Don't you care about that?"

Nimue looked absently out of the window again. "She shouldn't have bothered. She knows I can take care of myself." Abruptly she turned. "What's your name again?"

"Tom."

"Well, Tom, it's been *very* nice to meet you, but you've distracted me enough. I need to cast another spell to get out of here, which is, to be quite honest, long winded and difficult, and one I avoid doing if at all possible. I'm going to put you to sleep for a while so I can cast uninterrupted."

"Wait! How do we break the spell? What if we wait until you've gone?" And then he realised what she'd said. "You're going to do *what* to me?"

She stepped even closer to him, making him edge backwards until his back was against the wall. Pressing her fingers to his forehead, she smirked. "Don't worry, I'll be gentle."

The last thing he remembered was a feeling of overwhelming tiredness and a rising wall of blackness as he slid to the floor, unconscious.

10 Without a Trace

Beansprout followed close behind Woodsmoke and Brenna, as Woodsmoke led the way to the cave entrance. The rain was a steady drizzle, the mist was getting thicker, and dusk was falling. She could see only a few feet in front of her.

Woodsmoke's movements were uncanny. He slipped like a ghost through the landscape; she could hardly see him. Brenna was easier to see, but silent, and Beansprout moved quickly to keep up, trying to keep her footing in the wet. For a few seconds they disappeared and she was alone, with just the shush of rain to keep her company. And then she was aware of noise – disembodied voices, shouting. She stopped, uncertain of what to do. And then Brenna and Woodsmoke reappeared, emerging wraith-like from the mist.

Woodsmoke spoke first. "Something's happened. I think I heard someone say that they've disappeared. There's a least half a dozen Cervini by the cave entrance. Wait here."

A cold feeling of dread crept through Beansprout. "Who's disappeared?"

But he'd gone.

Beansprout and Brenna looked at each other anxiously. They stood for a few minutes, listening to the muffled voices. Despite her heavy cloak, rain trickled down Beansprout's neck and caught on her eyelashes. She brushed the water away impatiently.

There was a break in the voices and she heard Woodsmoke speaking. Had they caught him? She stepped forward involuntarily, but Brenna caught her arm, gesturing at Beansprout to listen. The voices sounded calm, even reasonable. What was going on?

And then Woodsmoke appeared again. "Come on. It's all right."

He turned and led them a short distance around mounds of rock and ferns, until they emerged in front of the cave entrance where a group of Cervini stood talking. They fell silent as the three approached, and

Woodsmoke said, "These are the friends I was telling you about. It's just us, and our friends you saw in the cave. We want to help."

Despite the wet and the chill, the Cervini wore only sleeveless jackets and trousers made of animal skins, and their feet were bare. There were both men and women; some had long hair, some short, and they all had curious markings on their skin.

A tall grizzled man with grey hair stepped forward. He nodded at Brenna and Beansprout and said, "I gather you are friends of Arthur, the man I found in the caves." He studied Brenna for a few seconds longer and then smiled in recognition. "You are Aerikeen. Fellow shapeshifters are always welcome." Then his smile dropped. "I fear it's too late. They've disappeared and the cave is empty. They vanished before my eyes, and there was nothing I could do."

Beansprout's feeling of dread grew stronger. Surely they couldn't have just vanished? "Was Tom with him?"

"The young man? Yes, he's gone too."

"Can we see the cave?" Woodsmoke asked.

He shrugged. "If you want. Our shaman is there now."

Woodsmoke nodded.

The older man introduced himself. "I'm Rek, the one who first recognised Nimue. I wish now I had never laid eyes on her." He sighed as he turned. "Follow me and I'll tell you what happened. If I hadn't seen it with my own eyes, I'd swear someone had made it up."

As they followed the long winding passage, Rek told his story, and then Woodsmoke related how they had become involved.

At the cave entrance, Rek said, "This is where I was, watching it all."

The torches had now been relit, and the shaman stood examining something in his hands.

Rek pointed to the centre of the room. "They were standing within the circle of torches, where Nerian is now. And then in a second the torches burned blood red and they disappeared. Gone. And the torches went out."

Rek introduced them to Nerian, then asked him what he was looking at.

"The remains of those herbs Nimue left at the entrance."

"May I?" asked Woodsmoke, holding out his hands.

Nerian handed them over. "I recognise wormwood, sage and vervain, but there is something else in there I'm not familiar with."

Woodsmoke sniffed the bundle and wrinkled his nose. "It's bitter."

"Yes, I'll work it out," Nerian said.

"You didn't know the spell, I presume?"

"No. If I'd realised what was happening, I'd have stopped her." He looked around the cave. "There is nothing else here, except the herbs."

"Could you repeat the spell, if we had the herbs?" Brenna asked.

He shook his head, uncertain. "I don't think so. I couldn't hear what she was saying. She was very careful to remain quiet."

"Do you mind if we look around?"

"Go ahead."

Brenna changed form and flew up and around the cave. Beansprout joined Woodsmoke as he paced around, grim faced and irritable.

"What are we looking for?" she asked.

"I honestly have no idea. Something that looks like it doesn't belong here I suppose." He paused and then said, "I knew something like this would happen! Arthur should have waited."

"But even if we'd been here, we couldn't have stopped this, Woodsmoke. We'd have either disappeared with them, or watched them, like Rek did. At least we're able to help now."

Woodsmoke just grunted.

They continued their search, but the cave was empty and cold, the walls smooth; whatever was here had been hidden very well.

"This is hopeless," Beansprout said.

Brenna joined them and agreed. "I can't find anything."

They left the cave with Rek and Nerian. Beansprout had never felt so helpless, angry or frustrated. Or so impressed. It was at this point she decided she was going to learn magic.

At the entrance, Beansprout asked, "Can the spell be broken?"

"Usually only the witch who cast it can break it," said Nerian. "Unless death intervenes."

"Maybe we should ask Vivian?" Beansprout suggested.

"And how do we do that?" Woodsmoke asked.

"We've had an idea," Rek said. "Before you arrived, we decided to summon Herne."

"Who's Herne?" asked Beansprout.

"The God of the wilds, the moors, the forests, the ancient rocks; his magic is earthy and powerful. It is rumoured that Merlin was like a child to him. Surely he will release him."

"Surely he would have released Merlin a lot sooner than now?"

Woodsmoke said.

"We never knew what had really happened to Merlin before now. And besides," Nerian said, sounding slightly offended, "Gods do not usually intervene in our affairs."

"And we summon him how?" asked Brenna, ever practical.

"I will summon him," Nerian said. "Here, where the spell has been worked. But first I must return to the Great Hall, there are things I need to collect for the ritual. And we must tell the others what has happened." He looked beyond the cave entrance. It was dark and the rain was falling heavily. "I'll be back within a day."

Woodsmoke nodded his agreement. "I'll go and fetch the horses and we'll sleep here tonight. At least we'll be dry. Get a fire going ladies," he said with a wink on his way out.

11 Spells and Potions

When Tom woke up he had no idea how long he'd been unconscious for. The first things he became aware of were the cold, dusty floorboards pressed against his face, and the soreness of his right arm trapped beneath him. He rolled over onto his back, flexed his arm gently, and then sat up, wondering what had happened.

Nimue had gone, but other than that, the room looked the same. Had she really left them here? He struggled to his feet, shouting, "Nimue!" over and over again. But his calls were swallowed by the walls, and the silence quickly settled round him.

What was he going to do? If he did nothing he would be trapped here with the others, possibly forever, and he was in the unenviable position of being fully aware he was trapped in a spell. He'd go mad. There was no delirious enchantment to muffle his mind. He paused for a moment, weighing up his options. His unease doubled as he stood alone, feeling the weight of eons shifting around him. It was as if he was suffocating.

Suddenly it struck him – he knew what his talisman was. The silver bough, tucked in an inside pocket of his shirt. Fahey had said something about it protecting him. But from what? Madness? And then he had a moment of panic; had Nimue stolen it while he was unconscious? He patted his pocket and sighed with relief. It was still there. How come it didn't protect him from specific spells? He shrugged. He had enough to worry about.

He turned to Merlin. Perhaps if he could rouse him, Merlin might be able get them out. But then he realised – if Merlin could do that, surely he would have escaped years ago.

The advantage of not being enchanted, like the others, was that he had his sanity, and a talisman, and he was going to get them out of there.

First things first, he couldn't just leave Merlin lying on the floor. It was wrong. He ran downstairs and grabbed a pillow and blankets off the bed, putting the pillow under Merlin's head and wrapping the blankets around him. It was probably pointless, but it made Tom feel better.

Now it was time to see how Arthur and Orlas were. Outside the tower the air was mild, with hardly a breath of wind. It felt like spring or autumn, as if it was the beginning or the end of something, but some trees were in full leaf, while others were shedding leaves – rich reds and russets strewn across the ground, collecting in bundles against jumbles of rocks and in overgrown thickets. Daffodils poked out from hidden corners, and a tangle of roses was growing through the trees. Tom was sure all this wasn't meant to happen at the same time. If this place had no seasons, did it also mean it had no day or night? He would soon find out. But that also filled him with panic. How would he know how long they had been there? The Other already had a misplaced sense of time; with no markers at all he could be here centuries and never know. What if he'd been here months already?

But it felt almost beyond time, with a watchfulness that could wait, and had waited, for millennia. He was tempted to see if there was a boundary, and was about to set off in a straight line, keeping the tower behind him, when he decided against it. There was a very real chance he could get lost, or even forget what he was doing in the first place. Which was? Oh yes. Getting out of here. He shook himself. Was he drugged? He had to act. Now. Before he fell asleep, like Merlin.

He could see Arthur the bear, absently wandering through the trees. He made a beeline for him, jumping over streams and scrambling over boulders, before coming to a halt a short distance away. Feeling foolish, he shouted, "Arthur, can you hear me? See me? Hello! Are you in there?" But the bear simply shook himself like a gigantic dog and ignored him. And Orlas, grazing in the distance, continued to tear up huge chunks of grass. Whatever Tom decided to do, he was going to be doing it alone.

He raced back to Merlin's room. If Merlin had taught Nimue the spell, and if the tower was a representation of Merlin's workshop, then the spell must be here somewhere, maybe in a spell book. And if he found it, he might find a way to reverse it.

He was worried that something in the room might have changed, but he found it just as he had left it. The fire still burned, and candles still spluttered in dark nooks. He doubted Merlin's spell book would be on one of the shelves; surely it would be on a workbench if he used it frequently. He started looking on the bench furthest from the door. Papers were scattered across it haphazardly, and he rifled through them. What did a spell book look like? Old and leather-bound? He found letters, scrawled notes, books on animals, birds, and the properties of stones. But no spell book.

He moved on to the middle bench, working methodically from one end to the other, getting distracted by drawings of eyes, dissected hearts, and other grisly organs. And then, buried beneath a pile of papers and bags of herbs, he found it. A huge, black, leather-bound book of spells.

He cleared the space around it, and opened it carefully. It was very old, and worn with use. The front cover was marked and stained, and when he opened it he found the spine was broken, and the pages turned easily, some loose at the edges. The pages were well worn too, the edges grubby where they had been handled.

A quick glance was enough to show him there were hundreds of spells. Each started on a new page, and some were long, going on for pages, while others were only a few lines. There were notes and small drawings in the margins, and trapped within some pages were feathers, herbs or flowers, and what looked like fragments of animal skins. The writing was small and cramped, as if spiders had walked through ink and scrambled across the page.

Tom sighed. This could take a while. He pulled over a stool and settled in.

After what seemed like hours, during which he became distracted by several bizarre-sounding spells, Tom eventually reached the end of the book. There was no spell for imprisoning a person. That made sense – why would Merlin want to write that down?

A wave of despair washed over him and he realised he was very tired. How could he break a spell he couldn't even find? He rubbed his face and put his head in his hands. He had never felt so lonely. His eyes were closing with tiredness, and he rested his head on the spell book, his head spinning with questions.

Seconds later, he jerked upright. Nimue hadn't recast this spell, she had just taken them back into it. That was a different spell. He needed to reverse Nimue's spell, so *that* should be the spell he looked for. Now he groaned again. If he was to rescue Merlin, he would have to find the original spell and reverse that. But by reversing the spell and rescuing them, would he kill Merlin? Nimue had thought so.

His head hurt. Magic was complicated, and he had no idea what to do.

He dragged himself to his feet. He had to find the spell to imprison a person. It had to be here somewhere. Damn Nimue. And damn her green eyes.

12 Merlin's Cave

Beansprout sat in a circle with Brenna, Woodsmoke and about a dozen Cervini, in what they had now named Merlin's Cave.

Nerian had returned earlier that afternoon with small drums, herbs, and what looked like ceremonial clothing. He had arrived in stag form, with everything attached by a harness to his back. When he turned back to human form the harness hung from his shoulders and he was almost bowed beneath the weight of his pack. He had immediately summoned all of the Cervini, leaving only a few to guard the entrance as a precaution. Beansprout was sure no one else would venture this far across the fells in this weather.

She felt oddly claustrophobic. When she'd stepped onto the moor that morning, the rain had stopped, but with the granite walls rearing up behind her, and the mist pressing in thickly from all sides, the world seemed to have become very small and ominous. And now that so many of them were crowded into the cave, it felt much smaller than it had done when she'd first entered it yesterday.

Beansprout admitted to herself that she felt a little scared. She was about to participate in a ceremony to summon Herne. A God. Nerian had stressed that he needed as many people as possible, because it raised the energy levels. Part of her expected absolutely nothing to happen; that it would be a ceremony of words and gesticulations only. But the other part of her thought something *would* happen, because this was the Other, a place of magic and strange creatures, where the laws of reality were reversed. And she wanted to experience that more deeply than ever. And of course, she wanted Tom and Arthur to return.

It was cold on the bare stone floor, and she sat on a folded blanket, her cloak pulled around her. Woodsmoke was to her right, with Brenna next to him. A young female Cervini sat to her left. The Cervini seemed impervious to the cold, sitting cross-legged on the floor, patiently waiting for the ceremony to begin.

Beansprout turned to Woodsmoke and whispered, "Have you done this before?"

"No, but I've heard about such ceremonies. They can be quite long. Are you all right? You don't have to join in."

"Yes, I'm fine. Just curious. Do you think he'll come? That Nerian will actually summon a god?"

"Let's hope so. Gods are stubborn beings."

Nerian had lit a small fire in the centre of the cave, the smoke drifting up into the unseen heights. He sat next to it, bare-chested, wearing an elaborate headdress of antlers and a necklace of feathers and bones, his appearance grotesque in the flickering light. Next to him he'd arranged various items, and something bright glinted in the pale light. It had a familiar shape, and Beansprout squirmed in her seat trying to get a better view. It looked like Tom's silver branch, but a little bigger.

Satisfied the fire was burning as he needed it, Nerian gestured to the circle. When the steady beat of drums started, he dropped a bunch of herbs into the flames. Beating another rhythm on his own small skin drum, he began to chant. The effect was hypnotic. Very quickly, Beansprout lost all track of time and settled in, mesmerised.

13 Insidious Spells

Tom had found a shelf filled with very old books – and that was saying something, considering everything here looked ancient. They were high, out of reach, and tucked to the back of the shelf, so it was quite by chance that he saw them. Were they almost hidden for a reason? He pulled a stool over and stepped onto it, clutching the shelves for support.

One of the books drew his gaze immediately. It had a deep green leather cover and was unembellished, except for an image of bound hands. He reached for the book, and as soon as he touched it he felt a tingle in his fingers, so much so that he nearly dropped it. Did he just imagine that? It had felt like an electric shock.

He reached forward again, preparing himself for another jolt, but this time felt only a residual hum, as if it was vibrating in his hands. Breathing deeply to steady himself, he opened the book. Most of the pages were blank, but the half a dozen or so spells it did contain were spells of imprisonment. There were spells to lock the tongue, to bind the mind to a single moment, to bind within the form of an animal, to imprison within rocks or trees, to imprison within a nightmare, and … to imprison a person. Tom's heart raced and his mouth became dry as he realised he'd found it. But he still needed to know how to reverse it.

He put the book down and looked at the others it was shelved with. There was a book of poisons, one of blood rites and sacrifices which looked particularly gruesome, and then a thin ragged-edged book with a white cover, which had no markings on at all. Opening it, he found it contained one long spell: *The spell of reversal for all spells worked under the sun and moon, by fire or blood, and in which the will is bound by insidious means.* There was a warning next to it: *Only to be used in times of direst need as reversal of a spell cast by another involves the release of potent energies which can be fatal.*

Great. The spell that might release him could kill him. And Merlin. And maybe the others.

The spell of reversal stressed that specific ingredients from the original spell must be used. Scanning through both spells, he found a list of the things he needed, but both specified that it was important to cast the spell in a place of power, such as in a grove of sacred trees. Now that did sound familiar. Nimue had said there was one here. Looking out of the tower windows, he saw a small circle of trees, in the centre of which was a flat rock and blackened fire pit. That would do. Now he needed to find everything else.

Almost an hour later, Tom sat within the circle of trees, a small fire burning in front of him. There were bowls of herbs within easy reach, and in one there was also a cutting of Merlin's hair and a clipping of his nails. Tom reached into his pocket and took out his silver branch, resting it in his lap. His heart pounding, he double- and triple-checked everything, then started the spell. Whether he messed this up or got it right, he could easily die.

14 The Summoning

Beansprout felt disembodied as the smoke drifted through the cave, and the circle became indistinct. Nerian sat immobile by the fire, his drum on the floor in front of him. Strange shadows cast by the flames made his face appear to change shape, morphing into someone, or something else. Time had lost all meaning, and she was aware of only the drumming, her heartbeat, her breath, and the fire flickering in the centre of the room.

And then Nerian threw his head back and howled. The sound was so unearthly and unexpected that shivers rippled across her skin, the sound reaching into her very being until it seemed she was howling too. But she couldn't move and couldn't speak, and she couldn't take her eyes off Nerian.

Nerian wasn't Nerian any more. He seemed to have swelled in size, becoming huge and imposing, his chest strong and muscled, and the antlers large and many tined. His eyes were black, and he looked slowly around the room, his gaze raking through her. A scene imposed itself over the cave, flickering in and out of focus … a grove of tall trees, mossy grass, and lichen-covered boulders, and beyond them a glinting silver tower.

Beansprout saw Tom, sitting on the far side of the fire, looking small in such an ancient place. And whatever Nerian had become stood and gazed towards the silver tower and howled again and again, until she thought she would go mad or deaf. Then he strode across the fire and reached out to Tom, and there was an enormous booming sound as if the earth itself had shattered. The fire flared brilliantly into a column of flame, shooting high into the cave, and with another wild keening that seemed to come from all directions, a fierce wind carrying the dust of a thousand years ran through the cave, whipping Beansprout's hair around her face and into her mouth, and she covered her eyes. Then the fire shrank to the smallest pin-prick of light. The cave now felt as if it encompassed a universe, and the fire was the sun that burnt a galaxy away. Beansprout felt tiny, lost in the void, and she tipped forward, dizzy and terrified, having lost all sense of who and where she was; and then it was over.

The cave was just a cave again and the fire had returned to normal. There, sprawled unconscious in a heap by the fire, was Nerian, and next to him were the inert bodies of Tom, Arthur, Orlas, and an old man with a long white beard.

Beansprout wasn't quite sure of the order of what happened next, but after seconds in which everyone seemed to be in a state of immovable shock, Woodsmoke and two of the Cervini recovered and ran to the bodies in the centre of the room. Woodsmoke crouched beside Tom and then Arthur, and one of the Cervini checked Orlas, and with relief they shouted that they were still alive.

And then Rek spoke. "Merlin is dead."

A sigh swept around the room as the news sank in. Beansprout stood up on weak legs that protested beneath her – how long had she been sitting? – and made her way to the centre of the room. The Cervini crouched around Merlin, touching his hands and hair.

Beansprout was curious to see Merlin, but was more worried about Tom and Arthur. A chill seemed to have descended as the fire burned low. She threw some logs on and prodded it into life, then gathered some blankets and with Brenna and Woodsmoke's help, wrapped the unconscious bodies to keep them warm.

Arthur, Orlas and Tom were pale and clammy, their breathing shallow. The strange markings on Orlas's skin stood out against his pallor, making his otherness more apparent. It seemed they were only just clinging to life.

"Do you think they'll be OK?" she asked Brenna.

"I don't know. But they're strong. I'm sure it will just take a while," she answered absently.

A groan disturbed Beansprout's thoughts, and next to her Nerian stirred back to life.

Rek moved quickly to his side. "Nerian, it's Rek. Can you hear me?"

Nerian mumbled something and blinked rapidly, and in a few seconds his confusion cleared and he muttered hoarsely, "Did it work?"

Rek smiled thinly. "Well you summoned Herne and broke the spell."

Nerian groaned again. "I know I summoned Herne! That's why my head pounds!" He closed his eyes as if to shut out bad news. "And I know Merlin's dead. The others?"

"Alive. But only just."

Nerian opened his eyes again, looking more hopeful. "Good! Help me sit up."

Rek lifted him, putting an arm behind him to support his shoulders, and offered Nerian a warm smoky drink that smelt of peat fires.

After a few mouthfuls Nerian said, "That was a strong spell. It's a wonder they weren't all killed. I think Tom's attempt to break the spell helped."

"Tom did what?" Beansprout asked, confused.

"He was trying to break the spell. I saw him, through Herne, as we crossed between the real and the illusion."

"Really? Very enterprising," Woodsmoke said with a smile.

"Herne has given me instructions." Nerian paused and looked at Rek. "When we have recovered, we go to Ceridwen's Cauldron."

"We do what?" Rek spluttered.

Nerian looked bemused. "Surprising, yes?"

"But no one has been there for years!"

Beansprout interrupted. "Will someone please tell me what that is?" She turned to Woodsmoke and Brenna. "Have you heard of this cauldron place?"

They shook their heads, equally confused.

Nerian's eyes glittered in the firelight. "It is an ancient place. A place of rebirth. The place where we bring Merlin back to life."

They looked astounded, temporarily lost for words.

"It is forbidden ground," said Rek, sounding nervous.

"Forbidden by Herne. And now it is not. I told you he would do anything for Merlin."

Woodsmoke and Beansprout looked out across the moors. Dawn was breaking and a sliver of pale green light illuminated the horizon. The rain and heavy mist of the previous days had rolled away, revealing a sodden landscape pockmarked with pools and rivulets. And it was cold. Beansprout pulled her cloak close around her shoulders.

"Just when I think I'm getting use to this place, I find out something new, and it leaves me feeling weird again."

Woodsmoke smiled. "The trick is to never presume too much here."

"I suppose so," she sighed, "but I'm worried about this Cauldron place. It sounds dangerous."

"Well at least Tom and Arthur won't need it."

"But they're not awake yet."

"No. But they're not dead. And we'll be leaving for the Great Hall later. They'll be better cared for there. It will be warmer than a cave, at least."

"And what happens after Merlin's resurrection – if it works?"

Woodsmoke shrugged. "Maybe we look for Nimue. Maybe we go home."

Beansprout frowned. "What's the point in looking for Nimue? She'll be hiding somewhere. Or even if she's not, what could we do?"

"I guess it depends on how vengeful Arthur is."

"I thought you were annoyed with Arthur?"

Woodsmoke stared absently over the moors. "I am. But I'm not about to let him run off with Tom again."

"But Tom isn't a child. If he wants to go with Arthur we can't stop him. He might be feeling pretty vengeful himself."

The Cervini led them through the White Woods, named for the ghostly white trees that grew there. Their tall, spindly trunks stretched high above their heads, the leaves turning from a pale green to red in the autumn weather.

Some of the Cervini were harnessed to a large cart carrying Merlin and the unconscious bodies of the others. They pulled it along at a funereal pace.

A large group of Cervini in human form greeted them at the main door of the Great Hall, a solid single-storied building made from the pale wood that surrounded them. Half a dozen Cervini lifted the lifeless body of Merlin onto a pallet and carried him deep into the recesses of the hall, while Orlas was moved with equal ceremony to his chambers.

Beansprout, Brenna and Woodsmoke followed Tom and Arthur as they were carried to a room for the sick, then Rek led them to a series of interlinked rooms with simple beds and rugs. He left them to rest, promising to return later with news of the ceremony at the Cauldron.

15 The White Woods

As Tom drifted into consciousness he became aware of a pale light flickering beyond his closed eyes, and a splitting headache. The weight of blankets pressed against his stiff limbs. He opened his eyes and squinted against the light, edging himself to a sitting position. That was a mistake. His headache got worse and he was violently sick on the floor next to his bed. He collapsed back onto the bed and passed out.

Several hours later he woke up again. His headache had now subsided to a dull thump, his stomach felt horribly empty, and his mouth felt like sandpaper. He cautiously looked round the room, careful not to move too much. It was dim; a candle burned on the table next to him, beside a jug of water and a glass. Overhead he could make out the wooden beams of the low ceiling.

He really needed some water. Slowly he sat up and leaned back against the wall, taking a few steadying breaths. Where the hell was he? He remembered sitting next to a fire in a grove of trees and seeing a tall powerful man with huge antlers striding across the clearing towards him, and then nothing. Blackness.

He poured himself a glass of water and sipped slowly, his throat painfully dry. A fire burned in a stone fireplace, the only source of light other than the flickering candle. It showed a small room with half a dozen wooden-framed beds in it, and one long narrow window high in the wall opposite him. It was dark outside. Arthur lay in the bed next to him, still sleeping.

None of this explained where he was or how he had got here. But as he was wondering what to do, the door opened and a young male Cervini appeared. He smiled when he saw Tom sitting.

"You're awake. Good. I'll fetch Nerian. Do you need anything before I go?"

Tom shook his head, bewildered, and croaked, "No."

A few minutes later the dreadlocked shaman appeared.

"You survived then," Nerian said as he walked over to Tom.

"Remember me?"

Tom nodded. "Vaguely."

"How are you feeling?"

"Terrible. My head aches and my throat hurts. Where am I?"

Nerian sat on a chair next to the bed. "In the Great Hall of the Cervini. Your friends are here too. You're lucky you only have a bad head. Do you remember what happened?"

"I remember sitting by a fire in a grove of trees, but I don't know why I was there," Tom said.

"What's the last thing you remember?"

Tom realised he couldn't remember much of anything. "I remember the cave, and Nimue started the spell, and then nothing. Nothing at all until the antlered man."

"You remember Herne?" Nerian looked surprised. "Don't worry, hopefully your memories will return in time. The spell Nimue cast was powerful, and when it broke it nearly killed you all. It did kill Merlin."

"Oh, Merlin. I'd forgotten about him." Tom clutched his head again as the headache started to return.

"That's OK Tom, enough now. I'll bring you a drink that will help, and then I want to you to rest again."

When Tom next woke it was morning, and Arthur was awake in the bed next to him.

"About time, Tom! Get up lazy bones!"

Tom groaned as he sat up. "Funny aren't you, Arthur?"

Arthur's face was ashen, and his long dark hair looked wild and unkempt. He leaned back on a mound of pillows and gazed wearily at Tom. "I'm trying to find humour in our situation, Tom."

"Mmm. Keep trying. I feel half dead."

"I know that feeling. This is better than that. But from what Nerian said, we almost died. Merlin did, you know." Arthur gazed into space, his mind clearly elsewhere.

"I know. I'm sorry." Tom plumped up his pillows and leaned back. "Can you remember anything? I can remember flashes of things. Nimue, a silver tower, lots of trees."

"More than me. It seems like a dream. All I can see is trees, trees and more trees. I feel like I'm drunk just thinking about it. I didn't even see

Merlin. To be so close …" His voice was full of an aching regret.

"There was nothing you could have done, Arthur," Tom said, trying to console his friend. To distract him, he asked, "How long were we unconscious?" And then another thought struck him and he sat up straighter. "How long were we in the spell?"

"Not long, fortunately. These Cervini work quickly. About a day in the spell, and three days unconscious."

"Wow. Four days lost. Better than four years, I suppose. Or more." He paused, contemplating their possible fate and lucky escape. Memories now started to trickle back, of their time in the spell and their deliberate abandonment by Nimue. He looked at Arthur, horror spreading across his face. "What were we thinking, Arthur? We should have known better." He felt sick at the thought of how long they could have been trapped.

Arthur looked at him sharply and if anything, turned paler. "Tom, I should–"

The door opened, interrupting their conversation, and Beansprout entered. She smiled, relief evident on her face. "You're both awake! Nerian said you were OK."

"Just about," Arthur grumbled.

"Tell me everything!" she said, plonking herself on the end of Tom's bed.

"Only if you tell me what we're doing here."

"You're recovering!" Beansprout said. "We're preparing to go to Ceridwen's Cauldron to resurrect Merlin."

Arthur sat bolt upright. "Where? To that old hag? To do *what*?"

"Steady on, Arthur," Beansprout joked. "What old hag?"

"Ceridwen. How can she even still be alive?"

"I don't know what you're talking about," Beansprout said, looking at Arthur curiously. "I think you're still delirious. Ceridwen's Cauldron is a place, not a person. It's a hidden and forbidden place where someone can be resurrected from the dead."

"Well she was a hag when I was alive!" Arthur railed. "But – you said we're resurrecting Merlin?"

Tom, also confused, stared at Beansprout.

Beansprout looked surprised. "You didn't know? Nerian didn't tell you?"

"I can't believe it!" Arthur smiled softly. "I'll see Merlin again." He looked excitedly at the others. "You'll get to meet him." He flopped back down, looking flabbergasted and gazing at the ceiling above him. "I can't believe he was trapped for all those years …" Then he fell into a brooding silence.

Beansprout looked worriedly at him before turning to Tom, and then curled up at the end of the bed, making herself comfortable. "Spill then, Tom. What happened to you?"

Later that day, when Nerian was satisfied that Tom and Arthur were recovered, Beansprout showed them to their rooms.

Tom still felt tired and his limbs were weak, but after a long talk with everyone he was finally able to piece together the events of the past few days. His memories of their time inside the spell had now returned, but he found it difficult to believe how real it had all felt.

The one memory he couldn't shake was that of Nimue's green eyes. No matter how hard he tried to banish them from his mind, they kept returning, taunting him.

"You all right, Tom?" Woodsmoke asked. "You look miles away."

With a jerk Tom turned. "Yes, fine."

They were seated on thick cushions around a small low table, while Brenna updated them on the latest plans.

"Ceridwen's Cauldron is higher on the moors than Scar Face Fell. It's a lonely place, apparently, deserted now, and a few days' travel from here in a place called Enisled. Ceridwen was a real person, and her cauldron had the power of rebirth, inspiration and knowledge. When she died, the place was sealed. Access to the cauldron has been blocked for centuries."

Arthur interrupted. "There you go. I knew I recognised the name!"

"Why was it sealed?" Beansprout asked.

Woodsmoke answered. "It wouldn't do, would it, to keep resurrecting anyone who died?"

"No, I suppose not," she said. "It sort of makes a mockery of death."

Arthur squirmed uncomfortably in his seat. "Like me you mean?"

"No, of course not!" Beansprout said aghast. "Your rebirth was a deal, arranged by Merlin for Vivian. Neither he nor you had any choice."

"And yet you seem to treat it so lightly, Arthur," Woodsmoke said with a grim look, "and the lives of those around you."

A silence fell around the table as Arthur looked stonily back at him. "I do not treat it lightly. Or the lives of others. But I am sorry about what happened at the Fell. I said I'd wait and I didn't. I got carried away."

Woodsmoke glared at him. "Yes you did. You nearly killed both of you."

"Sometimes decisions have to be made in very little time," Arthur spat. "I was worried that if we didn't act quickly, we'd never know what had happened to Merlin. However, the consequences were greater than I thought." He turned to Tom. "I'm sorry, Tom. I put you in a difficult position."

Tom looked uncomfortable and stuttered, "It's OK Arthur."

Woodsmoke persisted. "No, it's not OK. Does Vivian know about any of this? She said she'd be in touch after the Meet."

"No, I haven't heard from her since before then."

"So Vivian doesn't know about Merlin and the spell, or Nimue's part in it?"

"Not from me." Arthur looked thoughtfully at Woodsmoke. "Unless she saw it all by scrying?"

"It seems strange she hasn't been in touch when she was so anxious to keep track of our progress."

They fell into an uneasy silence as they realised Woodsmoke was right. They had been so caught up in the chase they had almost forgotten about Vivian.

"Have we heard how Orlas is?" Woodsmoke asked Brenna.

"He's fine. He woke at the same time as Arthur and Tom. He'll be travelling with us. We're going to wait another day or two for him to fully recover, and then we leave."

"So we're all going?" Tom asked.

"Yes. Herne's instructions." At the look of astonishment on everyone's faces, she elaborated. "It's thanks to our involvement – particularly your efforts, Tom – that the spell was broken, so we are to join the resurrection."

"It was mainly self-preservation. I didn't want to be stuck in that spell forever. And frankly, Arthur," Tom joked, trying to lighten the atmosphere, "you weren't much help. You were a bear."

"A bear? And you've only just thought to tell me? No wonder all I can remember is trees!" he exclaimed.

"Sorry, I've had a lot on my mind. Nimue said it was your animal spirit."

Brenna laughed, "You'll be shapeshifting with me soon."

"You still have the silver branch, Tom?" Beansprout asked.

He patted his pocket. "It never leaves me."

"And what are we doing about Nimue?" Arthur asked.

"I don't give a damn about Nimue," Woodsmoke said. "We should leave her be."

Brenna and Beansprout agreed, Brenna adding, "She's dangerous, and the spell's broken. What's the point? She's lived quietly since she first put Merlin in the spell, and she's probably returned to Vivian, or carried on to Raghnall. Perhaps that's why Vivian hasn't been in touch."

Arthur didn't answer, nodding slowly and staring at the table again.

Brenna exchanged a glance with Woodsmoke and then added gently, almost persuasively, "We have Merlin. There is nothing else to gain, Arthur. And Vivian was worried about Nimue's welfare. Now that we know she was, and is, deliberately hiding, your obligation is over."

He gave a brief nod. "Well, I need to stretch my legs." And without further comment he left the room, leaving the others looking worriedly at each other.

"I don't think Arthur can leave this," Tom said. "He might feel guilty about almost getting us killed, but I think his need to find Nimue is greater."

Woodsmoke looked grim. "Revenge is not our problem, Tom. And it is most definitely not *your* problem."

And while Tom knew this, he also knew that it wasn't that simple.

16 Risky Business

The following morning, Tom stayed inside the Great Hall, which meant doing a lot of eating as well as sleeping. The others decided to explore the White Woods, apart from Arthur, who sat alone in the cellars with Merlin's body. He seemed mired in indecision and guilt, and Tom wasn't sure how to get him out of his strange mood.

Later, they were summoned to Orlas's private rooms, following a servant down the long corridors into the rear of the building. Arthur trailed behind, silent and morose.

The servant knocked on a door and ushered them through. Orlas stood in the middle of the room, leaning on a large wooden table. In front of him was a map, which he was studying with great concentration. Tom had almost forgotten what Orlas looked like, their first meeting had been so brief. His dark hair hung loosely around his shoulders, and his arms were bare, his stag markings looking like tattoos against his skin. Thick gold torcs were wrapped around the tops of both arms and his neck. A young woman stood next to him. She had long red hair, and her skin glowed with pale red Cervini markings. She too had a gold torc wrapped around each arm.

It took the pair a few seconds to register their arrival, then they strode across the room to greet them. Orlas shook their hands, his grip firm and reassuring.

"Arthur, Tom. It's good to see you again and a pleasure to meet the rest of you. Let me introduce you to Aislin, my wife."

She stepped forward. "Welcome to the Great Hall. I'm sorry I haven't met you sooner."

Orlas invited them to sit in the chairs grouped around the fire, and turning to Tom and Arthur said, "I trust you have recovered?"

Arthur nodded. "More or less. How are you?"

"The same, although I gather we're lucky to be alive."

"You helped break the spell," Aislin said to Tom.

"So everyone keeps saying," Tom said. "But I'm not sure I really helped. I wasn't sure anything in there was real enough to work."

"Nerian disagrees. Anyway, you're here – despite Nimue's best intentions." A flush of anger coloured Aislin's pale face.

"So even though the spell was a powerful illusion," said Beansprout, "the things in it were real? I mean, they could be used?"

"You are asking things that are beyond my knowledge," Orlas answered. "I reverted to my stag form, and was so completely in the spell I saw only endless woods. But Tom," Orlas leaned forward, "you spent time with Nimue. Where did she go?"

"I have no idea. She said she was going to cast another spell to escape, and made me unconscious so that I wouldn't interfere."

"She gave no clue? Think carefully, Tom."

Tom shook his head. He'd been racking his brains about it since waking. "Nothing."

"Do you think she has returned to Vivian, or Raghnall?"

"No. When I said Vivian would still be worried about her, she didn't care. She said she could look after herself."

Orlas looked frustrated and Arthur asked, "Do *you* want to find her?"

"Not really," he said. "But I want to know what she's up to. You knew her well, Arthur. What do you think she'll do?"

"No idea. But I know she's determined and confident. She stepped into Merlin's place in court as if she'd been there for years."

Woodsmoke intervened. "I really don't think finding her would achieve anything, Orlas," he said, repeating his earlier argument. Tom saw Arthur bristle, but he remained silent, looking only at Orlas.

Orlas sighed. "I agree. In fact I hope she's a long way from here. We should concentrate on the things we can fix. Like Merlin."

Arthur's shoulders drooped in disappointment and he stared into the fire.

Aislin spoke, her gaze falling on them one by one, weighing their response. "I disagree with Orlas about resurrecting Merlin. He was a friend to us, a great friend, but nevertheless I think we are interfering with things that should be left well alone." Orlas went to interrupt, but she stilled him with her hand. "I know it is Herne's will. It doesn't mean I like it. You have risked your life once for Merlin. I don't think you should risk it again." She looked towards the door at the rear of the room, from where they could hear children laughing.

Orlas rested his hand gently on hers. "We will be fine." To the others,

"Are you well enough to travel?"

They nodded.

"Good. We'll leave tomorrow for Enisled."

That night the Cervini held a banquet for those travelling with Merlin. The main meeting hall was decorated with cut branches, the green and red leaves bright against the pale wooden walls. Fresh rushes were strewn across the floor releasing their sweet scent into the air, and lanterns lined the walls and hung from the ceiling, casting a soft glow over the room. The tables were crowded with steaming bowls of food, and beer and wine were flowing. The Cervini were packed into the hall, and jostled together, elbow to elbow, good natured and excited at the prospect of Merlin's return.

Tom found himself seated next to an old frail Cervini who creaked when he moved. He looked as if once he sat down, he'd never be able to stand again. He proved, however, to have the most enormous appetite, and took the opportunity to fill his bowl and his cup many times. He introduced himself as Wulfsige, and he cocked a sly eye at Tom over his beer.

"So you got trapped by the beautiful Nimue, did you?"

Tom was about to protest, then laughed. "Yes. Unfortunately I did."

"Devious, isn't she?" he smirked, ripping bread with his fingers and mopping up his stew.

Tom turned, suddenly attentive. "You know her?"

"*Knew* her. I haven't seen her for a very long time. I thought the witch was going to kill me."

Tom looked at him and wondered if he was joking. "Why would she do that?"

Wulfsige smiled, his face dissolving into a thousand wrinkles. "I was a young man then. A hunter. One of the best. I tracked wolves. And I was tracking wolves that day …" He looked across the room as if he could still see them. "I caught her in the woods with Merlin. She was hypnotising him, or something like that. Beneath a withered tree." He became serious. "She turned on me with such fury I thought that was the end of me. Those eyes. They were glowing."

Immediately Nimue's green eyes were back again, filling Tom's vision. Wulfsige watched him. "They grab you, don't they, Tom? Fill your brain until you can see only them."

Tom blinked and nodded, his throat suddenly dry. He took a slug of beer.

"That might have been it for me, but for my hunting hound, Nyra. She'd been ranging ahead, but she suddenly burst in from the undergrowth, howling as if a great demon from the Fire Realm was chasing her. She completely distracted Nimue, and then Merlin stirred, and I grabbed her by the scruff of her neck and ran. I don't think we stopped running 'til we reached the moors." Wulfsige refilled his bowl and started eating again.

"What happened then? Did she ever find you?" Tom asked.

"I don't think she got a good look at me. And I extended my hunt for a few days, just to make sure I avoided her."

"So what do you think she was doing?"

"Nothing good." He looked up from his bowl. "You take care. She's had a quiet few years, but don't let that fool you."

"Surely it's only Merlin she had a problem with. She helped Arthur for ages after Merlin disappeared."

"It didn't stop her the other day though, did it?" he said wryly.

Tom took another long drink and wondered why Nimue hadn't taken his talisman when she had the chance. Was it because she couldn't, because Vivian had given it to him? Or was it something else? Did she want them to have a chance? He shook his head. Woodsmoke was right. They should keep well away from Nimue.

17 Enisled

Enisled appeared ahead of them, swathed in mist; a collection of eroded rock faces rising out of the wind-blown heather. Rek led their group along an old disused track that led across a land of windswept grass, small pools and tumbled rocks. He was followed by Orlas and Nerian, two Cervini pulling Merlin's body along in a covered cart, and another four Cervini who had come for support – huge beasts with broad shoulders and many tined antlers. All the Cervini travelled in stag form. Tom and the others were behind, travelling on horseback.

As they drew closer, it became clear that the eroded rocks were in fact a castle, ravaged by time and the elements. The track led them to a choked archway of stones and earth, on either side of which was a surprisingly solid perimeter wall.

The Cervini changed form, securing the cart containing Merlin's body, while Nerian examined the archway.

"What are you looking for?" Tom asked, puzzled.

"The key to the spell protecting the cauldron," Rek explained.

Nerian was too distracted to reply.

"Didn't Herne remove it?"

"No. But he told Nerian how to."

"Ha!" Nerian scoffed. "In theory."

Seeing them watching him, Nerian waved them away. "Give me space. This could take a while."

"Come on," Arthur said. His mood seemed to have improved now they were on the move again. "Let's check the perimeter while we wait." He led the way around the wall to the left.

"So you knew Ceridwen, Arthur?" Beansprout asked.

"Not really. I met her once. But she had quite the reputation."

"Why?"

"She was powerful and independent, and refused to be allied to anyone. But that was fine. As long as you didn't mess with her, she didn't mess with you."

"But she lived in England, not here?" Tom asked, confused.

"Like many people with magic powers, she straddled two worlds. Perhaps her castle still exists in Britain now."

"I don't think so," Tom said, wondering if it could be buried under something, or was tangled in a wood, or had been dismantled over the years.

Long grasses and scrubby bushes ran right up to the castle walls, where the stones were packed in tight, offering no chink of an entrance. Every now and again they caught a glimpse of crumbling towers screened by trees, and then the view would be obscured again. Brenna found she couldn't fly over the castle grounds, blocked by whatever sealed the entrance.

By the time they had made their way back to the archway, a fine drizzle had started to fall and the grey light of the afternoon was darkening to twilight. Orlas was debating with Rek whether to camp outside the walls when Nerian shouted, "Yes!"

They turned in alarm to see a white light rolling up from the ground to encompass the archway. The light then flashed away and across the walls, rippling around the entire castle. In seconds it was over and the archway stood in front of them, clear of debris. Beyond was a short tunnel through which they caught a glimpse of a courtyard.

Nerian didn't hesitate. He hurried up the tunnel and into the courtyard, where there was an unexpected sight – the castle blazed before them, every window glowing with candlelight.

Tom felt a prickle run up his spine. The spell that had sealed the entrance had also preserved it in time. He expected to see Ceridwen step out to greet them.

The courtyard was surrounded by stables, tack rooms, and other long low buildings. Ahead, the main doorway stood open, light falling on the stone steps, beckoning them forward.

"Is this real?" Beansprout asked.

"As real as we're standing here," Nerian answered.

"Did you know this would happen?" Orlas asked.

"Of course not. Herne reveals little or nothing."

"So where's the cauldron?" Orlas asked, still fixated on the castle.

"He did tell me that. It's in a courtyard, somewhere in the middle of that." Nerian gestured to the castle ahead. "Shall we?"

But they all seemed strangely reluctant to cross the courtyard.

"It feels like a trap," Woodsmoke said suspiciously.

Rek grunted his agreement. "I don't trust magic after the last time."

"Magic is a tool, nothing else. Besides, Herne would not send us to our deaths," Nerian said, although Tom thought he detected doubt in his tone.

"Well, we're here now," Orlas said. He turned to the Cervini waiting in the shadows behind him. "Bring Merlin in to the courtyard and secure the entrance."

"Let's check the main hall," Arthur said.

"You go ahead," Woodsmoke said, "I'll stable the horses."

"I think I'd rather camp outside," Beansprout muttered to Tom. But Arthur was already crossing to the light-filled entrance and they hurried after him.

Crossing the threshold, they found themselves in a huge reception hall with several doors leading off it. Many stood open, revealing glimpses of rooms and corridors beyond. Directly ahead was an enormous fireplace, filled with a roaring fire.

"Now that's what I call a fireplace!" Beansprout said.

The room was filled with a soft yellow glow from the hundreds of candles tucked into alcoves and corners. Rich tapestries lined the walls, and plump cushions filled the chairs. In the centre of the room was a table set for a meal, the plates and dishes filled with hot steaming food.

"It looks like we're expected," Orlas said.

"I'm telling you, it's a trap," Rek said, echoing Woodsmoke's opinion. He pulled his sword free as he paced the room.

"Do we really want to stay in here?" Brenna asked.

"At least it's dryer than outside," Tom said, putting his pack down on a chair.

"I'd like to take a look around," Brenna said. In a split second she changed form and flew across the room and up a staircase.

"Good idea," Rek agreed, standing by a door on the right of the hall. "I'm going to check out the rooms on this side."

"Wait," called Orlas, crossing the room to join him. "I'll come too."

They left, leaving Arthur to prowl round the main hall, poking into its nooks and crannies.

Tom headed to the table and picked up a hot chicken leg. He was about to take a bite when Nerian yelled, "No!"

Tom dropped it in shock. "What's wrong?"

"Sorry, but I don't think we should eat or drink anything."

"I thought this place was safe?"

"I'd rather take precautions."

Beansprout and Nerian joined Tom at the table, and Nerian examined the food with the aid of a small stick he produced from his pocket.

"Do you think it's poisoned?" she asked.

"I think it's enchanted, like everything else here. We could end up asleep, or forgetful, or dead."

"But why would Herne send us here if it was so dangerous?"

"Because of Merlin." Clearly troubled, he said, "I felt something when Herne took over my body." He paused as he remembered the moment. "He was relieved, overjoyed even at finding him, and then grief stricken when he knew he was dead. It was like the emotion of a parent, or a sibling. It was so powerful."

Tom looked shocked. "Are you saying that Herne is related to Merlin?"

"It felt that way. That would explain why he's lifted a centuries-old spell on this place."

"It would also explain Merlin's natural magic," Beansprout said, thinking of Merlin's powers. "Particularly that he's a shapeshifter; that he could become a stag, like you. Did you know him?"

"No, I'm too young. He was gone by the time I was born. But everyone remembers him. He's like a father of the tribe."

"Arthur describes him as being like a father." And then dropping her voice so Arthur wouldn't hear, "And he's behaved very rashly to find him too."

Tom laughed dryly. "And yet Nimue was desperate to keep him hidden. Strange isn't it, what some people are prepared to do for others."

Their conversation was interrupted by Woodsmoke coming in from the stables. He looked round and whistled. "It looks like we were expected. The stables are stocked with fresh hay and water too. Is that why you look so worried?"

"I think we're in over our heads, Woodsmoke," Beansprout said.

"I know that. Every single star out there has disappeared. The sky is black and the night is still. You could hear a pin drop. It's like everything is waiting for something to happen."

"Are the others all right?" Nerian asked, referring to the Cervini.

"They're fine, for now."

"By Herne's breath!" Nerian said, "I don't know whether it's safer for them to stay out or come in."

Woodsmoke looked around, thinking. "Bring them in, with Merlin of course. Better we should stick together, especially if a storm's coming. Shall I call them?"

Nerian nodded and Woodsmoke headed back out.

Beansprout looked pale. "I have a horrible feeling in the pit of my stomach, just like when you disappeared, Tom. Is the Cauldron the only reason this place was sealed?" she said to Nerian.

"Ceridwen was an enchantress whose Cauldron had the power of rebirth, inspiration and knowledge. Isn't that enough? Many would kill for just one of those things."

Arthur called Tom from where he stood by an open doorway to the left of the room. "There's nothing to see here. Do you want to join me, Tom? If Rek's checking that side, we should check this one." He unsheathed Excalibur.

"Yes, wait, I'm coming." Tom hurried across the room, his sword drawn too, leaving Nerian and Beansprout deep in conversation.

Beyond the door was a shadowy corridor. Immediately the sound of voices from the hall disappeared, and they stood in the silence waiting to see if anything moved in the shadows.

"This is too weird," Tom whispered.

Arthur turned, the pale light glinting in his eyes. "I think anything might happen tonight, Tom."

His words hung between them, and then he pressed on, Tom hard on his heels. They entered another room. Again candles cast a welcoming glow and a small fire burned in the grate. They looked through the window, which overlooked the courtyard. Outside they could see the cart had been pulled into a corner, and the Cervini were talking with Woodsmoke.

On the far side of the room a doorway led into another room. They passed from one room to another, and the doorways again led on and on, rectangles of welcoming light. And all was silent; waiting and watching.

18 Ceridwen's Cauldron

Tom and Arthur returned to the main hall and found everyone there. Merlin's body was laid in the corner of the room on a stretcher, still wrapped in fine-scented linens designed to preserve him until the ritual.

"I suppose you found nothing either?" Rek asked, lounging in a chair in front of the fire.

"No." Arthur turned to Brenna. "You?"

"Nothing and no one." She smiled, but it didn't quite reach her eyes. "It's all too easy."

"Nevertheless, it's what we're here for. Now you're back," Orlas said, "we may as well get on with it. Any objections?"

They all shook their heads.

"I'd rather do this thing and get out of here," Rek said, rising.

Orlas turned to the other Cervini. "You two, stay here and secure the door. And you," he said, indicating the other four, "bring Merlin."

He turned to Nerian. "Lead on."

Nerian led them along the ground floor corridors towards the centre of the castle.

"Are you sure you know where you're going, Nerian?" Rek asked. "We've been this way and found nothing."

They were walking down a long corridor, whole areas of which were in virtual darkness. Nerian paused next to a section of wood-panelled wall. "Patience, Rek." He quickly explored the panel with his fingers, then said, "Found it."

With a sigh the panel slid back, revealing a dark tunnel sloping downwards. Groping inside, Nerian found a lantern hooked on the wall. Lighting it, he set off.

For Tom, the light from Nerian's lantern seemed a long way ahead; a small bobbing glow showing glimpses of stone walls and a low roof. The tunnel led downwards for a short way and then levelled off, running mostly straight. They stumbled along behind until Nerian came to a sudden stop when the tunnel split into two. He hesitated briefly and then turned right. After only a short distance they came to a flight of steps leading steeply upwards. They followed them up and round several sharp bends, the Cervini behind struggling with Merlin's body, until Nerian stopped again.

For a few seconds nothing happened, and Tom had a horrible feeling they would be stuck in the tunnels forever. Beansprout jostled against him in the dark and he could hear her shallow breaths. Then he heard a grating sound, and fresh air flooded the passage.

They tumbled out one after another into an open air courtyard. The walls were high, and in the centre of the octagonal space was a large round pool filled with water. Pale blue lights eddied lazily beneath its surface, colouring the surroundings with an unearthly pallor. They provided the only light; the courtyard was otherwise in darkness.

For a second their shuffling stilled as they gazed at the pool.

"So that's the cauldron?" Orlas asked.

Nerian nodded and crouched next to it, peering into its depths.

As they looked at it more closely, they could see the metal curve of the pool edge glinting in the light.

"So what now?" Rek asked, as the Cervini carrying Merlin placed him at the edge of the pool. "Do we just drop him in?"

"He's not a fish," said Nerian, sitting next to Merlin. "The pool needs to be prepared, its energies activated."

"So why seal the palace if it doesn't work?" Tom asked.

"Because many here have magic, Tom, and therefore many are capable of activating the pool with the right knowledge. And those who lack knowledge will steal and kill and maim to get it. And then use it unscrupulously."

"OK," Tom said, finally getting why the cauldron had been sealed for years.

"I need three of you to help me."

"I will," Beansprout said immediately. "What should I do?"

"Sit opposite me; you are earth. Tom?"

"Yes?"

"Sit to my left; you are water. And Brenna," he turned to find her scanning the top of the walls.

"Yes?" she said distractedly.

He gestured to his right, "If you would be so kind as to be air."

"So you are ...?" Beansprout asked, as Brenna settled herself into position.

"Fire. We sit at the four points of the compass, and as such you will help me harness fire. I want you to touch the metal edges of the cauldron, like this," and he rested his hands on the lip of the pool. "We need to warm the pool and ignite its energies, and then," he looked at the others, "two of you need to carry Merlin's body into the water."

"I'll do it." Arthur's response was immediate.

"And I will," Orlas said.

"No. I will," Rek said. "You should watch. You've risked your life once already. I presume it's safe for us to enter the pool?" he asked Nerian.

"Relatively." Ignoring Rek's unfavourable response he pulled his small drum out of his pack and cradled it in his lap.

Tom watched these preparations with interest, especially as he hadn't been part of the last summoning. The four Cervini who had carried Merlin's body had positioned themselves around the courtyard and appeared relaxed, their hands resting on their sword hilts. Orlas stood next to one of them, and Woodsmoke stood leaning against the wall next to the only entrance and the stairs beyond, his keen eyes and ears missing nothing. Rek and Arthur stood behind Merlin. Tom looked uneasily at Merlin's covered body. He found it unnerving to travel with a dead man, no matter that he was wrapped in sweet-smelling linens.

The night remained still. Tom looked up at the inky blackness, where not a spark of starlight was visible. The sky seemed very low, as if it was only just above the castle ramparts. He shuddered and wondered if it was from the cold night air, or a premonition of something to come. His gaze followed the top of the high wall around the courtyard, but nothing moved.

His train of thought was broken by a noise to his right. Nerian's head had sagged downward, his chin against his chest, but his lips moved furiously; strange unintelligible mumblings that sounded guttural and threatening. A flash of light pulsed across his chest and then down to his fingers, where it turned into a flame. For a few seconds it flickered erratically and looked as if it was going out, and then it grew stronger and steadier.

Tom edged forward to make sure his hands remained touching the cauldron, and as he did the flame ran around the cauldron's rim. Tom was so shocked he almost pulled his fingers away. He gritted his teeth and prepared for the pain of the fire, but it passed over and through his fingers harmlessly, leaving a strange warm sensation where it had passed.

He looked across at the others, wondering if that was it, but they continued to grip the cauldron and Nerian continued to chant, his voice growing in strength. Although the flame had gone, Tom could feel the metal growing warmer beneath him, and deep within the pool he saw an orange glow.

The chanting stopped and Nerian looked up, and again Tom started, this time shocked to see that Nerian's eyes were white, his expression vacant. The water in front of him began to swirl and the pale blue lights glowed brighter, sparking and flashing until the pool was full of incandescent light which banished the dark from the far corners of the courtyard.

Tom started to feel the strangest sensation, as if water was running through him like he was conduit. Looking down he saw water trickling from his fingers and into the pool. Opposite him he saw Brenna's hair begin to lift in an imperceptible breeze, while Beansprout's lap filled with flowers until they tumbled around her on to the floor.

Small waves began to form, passing across the surface until they rebounded off the side, chasing each other round and round to form a frothing mass.

The silence was shattered when Nerian shouted, "Now!"

Arthur and Rek stepped into the pool. Reaching over they picked up Merlin, and in one swift movement lifted him over the rim and dipped him in the water.

The water was now warm; Tom could see steam rising off the surface, steadily getting thicker. The swirling current lifted Merlin and the linens peeled away from his body, revealing his pale face, his long white hair and beard, and the grey cloak eddying around him. Rek and Arthur no longer needed to support his body and he floated free of their grip, his body turning with the current. In unspoken agreement they swiftly left the pool and crouched dripping at the edge.

For a few seconds Merlin drifted with the current, and then he was swiftly pulled under. They all leaned forward. For a few seconds nothing happened. Merlin's body lay unmoving at the bottom of the pool, the blue lights sparking around him, nudging and prodding as if trying to wake him. Then the intensity of the light increased until it was almost blinding, the individual lights fusing into one bright mass obscuring Merlin's body.

Tom pulled away from the cauldron and covered his eyes. The energy that coursed through his body abruptly stopped, as did the water flowing through his hands. Then the light faded and Tom looked up.

Merlin rose from the depths in an explosion of water, his arms flailing as he gasped for breath.

"Merlin!" Arthur cried.

Merlin's eyes opened for the first time, his eyes as blue as the light that surrounded him. But they were wild and frightened, and he looked around at the gathered faces and uttered a string of unintelligible words.

Then he stared beyond Arthur, looking up towards the top of the wall. He fell silent and Tom heard someone laugh.

They all whirled around. But Tom knew who it was before he saw her. Nimue. She stood on the high stone wall, almost invisible against the night sky, laughing at the scene below her. How had she found them?

But before anyone could do anything, Merlin struggled upright and shouted again, his voice hoarse and rasping. It sounded as if he was calling someone, or something.

They all retreated now from the edges of the pool, scuttling back like crabs. Only Arthur remained close. Ignoring Nimue, he called, "Merlin, it's me, Arthur." Desperation was etched across his face.

And then several things happened at once.

Nimue raised her arm, pointing down to them. Woodsmoke swiftly raised his bow and released an arrow, which thudded into her outstretched arm. Nimue screamed and turned, outraged, towards him, her left hand supporting her injured arm.

Thunder rumbled loudly from above. Deep and resonant, it echoed through the castle and out across the moors. Lightning cracked the sky open and flashed down, jagged and hot, into the courtyard.

And then shooting white lights pitched down from above; white lights full of teeth and claws and a whirr of wings. Ethereal figures, translucent and barely visible, landed softly around the pool. Some flew directly at Nimue, and she fell into the courtyard, landing heavily against the far wall. The figures turned their backs to Merlin; bright silver daggers flashed in their hands, and they lowered long sharp spears to form a protective wall around him.

Immediately Tom and the others were on their feet, weapons drawn. The Cervini changed form, lowering their antlers and broad shoulders at the strange creatures that had suddenly arrived.

Tom felt cold fingers with sharp nails pulling at his arms, and turned to see a woman with a bird's body, her face close to his own, her breath cold. Shocked, he pulled his sword free and jabbed at the creature until it retreated, shrieking and cursing.

Before a word was spoken, a whirr of wings surrounded Merlin and he was hauled into the air and through a rent in the cloud, where he disappeared. As swiftly as they had arrived, the winged creatures withdrew.

Brenna streaked after them.

Thunder reverberated over the castle and lightning sizzled down, and they retreated against the walls for cover. One last searing lightning blast shattered the pool in an explosion of splintering metal. The water evaporated instantly, leaving a shining blue mist for a few seconds before it vanished completely, leaving them in near total darkness.

The Cervini became human again. One lit a torch, and the flare from the orange flames lit up the shocked group. Orlas shouted to Nerian, "Nimue!"

Nerian pulled a small female doll from his pocket, an exact replica of the one he had before, and started to utter the binding spell.

Arthur advanced on Nimue, Excalibur drawn, its blade flashing with torchlight, as if it were made of fire. He stood where she lay awkwardly, her breathing shallow, blood pouring from her arm where the shattered haft of the arrow still protruded. Arthur slid Excalibur against her pale white throat, and he didn't move until Nerian called, "It is done."

19 Vivian's Request

Sharp metal shards filled the courtyard, which was pockmarked and blackened from lightning blasts. The top of one of the walls had been blasted clean away, rubble strewn at its base. One of the Cervini had scorch marks down the side of his body and singed eyebrows from the intense heat.

"I don't think they were trying to kill us," Orlas said, after checking no one was seriously hurt. "I think they were just trying to frighten us. And protect Merlin."

Rek struggled to his feet, dusting off bits of rubble and debris. "Well they achieved that."

"Who were they?" asked Beansprout, rubbing a trickle of blood off her arm.

"Sylphs – Spirits of Air," Woodsmoke said, crouching beside her and examining her injured arm.

"But why were they here?" asked Tom. "How did they know to come?"

Nerian turned from where he was examining Nimue. "Merlin summoned them, didn't you hear?"

"He did?" Tom asked, baffled. "Why?"

"He was terrified," Arthur said. "He didn't know where he was, or who we were. Not even me. Although I think he recognised Nimue." He sat on the floor at Nimue's side, reluctant to leave her even though her powers were bound.

Tom looked at the ruined pool. "And look what they've done. Did they control the storm?"

"They manipulated it, especially the lightning," Nerian explained.

"Did you understand what Merlin was saying, Arthur?" Beansprout asked.

"Some of it. He was calling them to take him home."

"Home as in England?"

"Home as in his House of Smoke and Glass."

"What?" Tom asked.

"I have never been there, "Arthur said, "but he talked of it, every now and again. I never knew where it was, either, other than his 'other home' as he called it."

"It must be in the Realm of Air, then?" Tom said.

Rek answered. "I guess it must, or why would he call the Spirits of Air?"

"Well," Orlas said wearily, "I'm disappointed he's gone so soon."

"But at least he's alive," Nerian said. "And we have Nimue."

"But no Brenna," Beansprout said.

"She'll be fine," Woodsmoke said, casting a worried glance at the sky above.

Another rumble of thunder interrupted the silence and heavy rain started to fall.

They made their way back to the main hall, the Cervini this time carrying Nimue on the stretcher. But when they emerged from the hidden passageway they found the castle in darkness.

"What's happened?" Tom asked.

"The destruction of the cauldron has broken the spell that gave life to the castle," Nerian answered.

"So no lights, no fire, no food?"

"Exactly."

The eerie feeling from earlier had disappeared, and now it was just a dark, empty castle that smelt of damp. On entering the hall, Nerian headed for the fireplace while Tom lit all the candles he could find.

Now the glamour of the spell had gone they could see dust lying thick along the floor and the surfaces, and the detritus of rotten food lying mouldy on the table. But the building was still surprisingly intact, the floor and walls secure.

The only person who still seemed charmed by it was Arthur. "Who owns this, Orlas?"

"No one. Or me, I suppose. It lies on our land. Why?"

"I was thinking that I need a home, and this one's going spare. Would you like a tenant?" He smiled at Orlas hopefully.

Orlas laughed. "I can think of worse tenants. It's yours if you want it." He looked round, wrinkling his nose with distaste. "I certainly don't."

"Then we'll talk terms later," Arthur said, shaking hands with Orlas to secure the deal.

A small bang disturbed them and the fire roared into life under Nerian's skills, just as Brenna swooped into the hall. She collapsed on her knees in front of the fire. Water streamed from her, and she shook with cold. A slight smell of burnt feathers wafted around her.

Woodsmoke and Beansprout rushed to her side. Beansprout spoke first. "Are you all right?"

"I will be," Brenna said, shaking.

Woodsmoke untied his cloak and threw it around her. "What happened?"

"I was nearly incinerated several times. I do not recommend flying through a storm." She eased closer to the fire, drawing the cloak around her.

Arthur walked over. "But did you see where they went?"

She shook her head. "They headed to the sky meadows, as I expected. But they were too fast for me and I lost them over Dragon Skin Mountain. There was nothing else I could do."

Arthur sank to the floor next to her. "Damn it."

In the corner of the room a shadowy apparition slowly manifested. Shapes swirled within its heart, edges defined and features sharpened, and eventually Vivian appeared. Or rather, a projected image of her. She stood, regal and imperious, her hair bound in an elaborate style, wearing a blood red gown that draped softly to the floor. She looked very different to when Tom had seen her before.

It took a few seconds for the whole group to see her. Rek responded quickly, drawing his sword and advancing towards her.

Arthur stopped him, jumping to his feet. "No, Rek wait; she's not really here." He stood in front of her, as if they were really in the same room. "Vivian. We've been wondering where you've been."

"As I have you, Arthur. You've been tricky to find." She looked at him accusingly.

"I've been busy," he said impatiently.

"And to find you here ..." Her voice trailed off as she looked around the room and saw Nimue lying motionless, guarded by two Cervini. She looked startled, and turning to Arthur said, "What have you done to Nimue?"

"Nothing. She was attacked by sylphs. You should be asking what she has done to us."

Vivian ignored him and appeared to glide rather than walk across the room. She knelt at Nimue's side. Although she couldn't touch her, she examined her ashen face and injured arm, and then whirled round to face Arthur. "That injury on her arm was not caused by a sylph."

Woodsmoke stepped forward, his voice icy. "No. It was caused by me. And if she attempts to curse any one of us again, my arrow will go straight through her heart."

Arthur intervened. "Vivian, you have no idea what Nimue has done. I suggest you listen."

"Go on," she said, crossing her arms and transferring her glare from Woodsmoke to Arthur.

"Nimue is responsible for Merlin's disappearance. She imprisoned him in a spell, and when she thought that spell might be broken and her part in it revealed, she went to investigate."

Vivian's already pallid face paled even further at this, and the accusing glare slipped from her face to be replaced by anguish.

Arthur looked confused. "You don't seem surprised, Vivian."

"I suspected, all those years ago, but I didn't know. And–" she stilled Arthur before he could interrupt, "I did not know of this when I asked you to help."

"She nearly killed Tom, Orlas and me by imprisoning us in the same spell as Merlin."

"You found him?"

"You'd better get comfortable, it's a long story."

At Vivian's request, Nerian had reluctantly cleaned Nimue's arm and manufactured a small bandage out of strips of material to wrap round it. An examination of her other injuries suggested a broken arm and a head injury. But that was all he agreed to do. Her fate, good or ill, meant little to him.

Some of the group had curled up in the shadows and gone to sleep; faint snores came from Rek. Still awake were two Cervini guarding Nimue in a far corner of the room, Tom, who lay close to the fire, and Arthur and Vivian, who sat nearby talking quietly. Tom pretended to be asleep, but was eavesdropping, peeping at them between half-closed eyes.

Vivian was arguing with Arthur. "I accept that you won't return Nimue to Avalon. I accept that you want to find Merlin. But I can't help Nimue from here, and it's clear the Cervini won't. Will you at least take her to Dragon's Hollow? It's along your route – halfway up Dragon Skin Mountain."

"That sounds a long way to go with an unwelcome guest."

"Nerian's binding spell means she can do you no harm."

"And what do I do with her in Dragon's Hollow?"

"Take her to Raghnall, that's where she was going anyway. Healing is one of his many skills. And then," she paused, thinking, "he will ensure her return to Avalon. If that's what she wants."

"And her punishment for all of this?" Arthur gestured at the room. "Do I have to remind you of what she tried to do to us?"

"I will deal with it."

"No you won't. Don't lie." Arthur looked furious. "Merlin was my friend too."

"You used him for your own ends, Vivian, the same as you do me. You sent me to fight Morgan without telling me who she was!"

She had the grace to look sheepish. "Must I apologise again? I have already explained that I feared you wouldn't go if you knew. It's old news!"

"At least Merlin was honest in his wishes."

She laughed, a short sharp bark. "Ha! Really? He wanted you to succeed so badly he promised away your death."

"Because you made him."

"He didn't have to agree."

"You left him with little choice. He was trying to unite Britain."

"He was cementing his power," Vivian said cynically.

Arthur fell silent, his gaze falling to Excalibur sheathed at his side. The only thing Tom could hear was the crackle of the fire and the soft thump of the burning wood as it collapsed on itself.

Eventually Arthur spoke. "Being a pawn is not something I enjoy, Vivian. I will deliver Nimue to this sorcerer. And then I will find Merlin and satisfy myself he is well and safe. And then I will leave him in his tower and I will leave you on Avalon. And you will not call on me again."

Vivian narrowed her eyes questioningly.

"I mean it," he said. "I will do nothing else for you. This is my life and I will live it as I choose. Find someone else to fight your battles."

"It's thanks to me you sit here arguing."

"To deal with something you couldn't. I owe you nothing. So while I'm still feeling generous, you'd better tell me where I'm taking Nimue."

After this, Tom's tiredness overwhelmed him and he fell asleep.

They woke at dawn to find Vivian gone. Arthur had a purpose about him that Tom hadn't noticed the night before.

He announced his plans over breakfast. "I don't expect anyone to come with me, I'm going because I want to satisfy myself that Merlin's safe." He shrugged. "And then, as long as he is well, I'll leave him and return here, if I may, Orlas?"

"Of course. I will send a group from the Great Hall to make it habitable. But–" Orlas looked worried, "we can't come with you. I have duties I must attend to."

"Don't worry, Orlas," Woodsmoke said, "Arthur will have back-up."

Arthur looked quickly at Woodsmoke. "I said I'm happy to go alone."

"The dragon mountain is dangerous. I'll come with you."

"So will I," added Brenna.

Tom and Beansprout looked at each other in horror at the prospect of being left behind. "Obviously we're coming too."

Nerian looked as serious as Orlas. "Good. In that case you should take the poppet with you," he said, referring to the doll he'd used the binding spell on. "I have bound her powers again, but it's a simpler binding this time, one that does not require a spell to release it. Keep it safe, and well out of reach of Nimue. Do not underestimate the witch. Her powers may be bound, but she is not to be trusted."

20 Around the Campfire

At last they came to the edge of the Blind Moor. It was well named. Mist rolled across its surface and pooled in hollows, obscuring the thick tufted grasses that lay underfoot. The bronze tones of sedge appeared unexpectedly, glinting in the occasional ray of weak sunshine. They proceeded slowly so the horses wouldn't stumble into hidden holes and shallow streams. At unexpected moments the mist rose, swelling and thickening until only vague images were visible.

Enisled lay behind them, lost from view. There they had said their goodbyes to the Cervini, planning to see them again on their return.

Tom sat at the back of the line, which he'd decided was his favourite place. He could see what was happening ahead and have a good look around him as they travelled. He liked that he didn't have to set the pace, and as he had no idea where they were going anyway, he was able to sit and think.

He was sick of the cold damp air, but he liked the remote wilderness they were travelling through and the keening wind that sliced through its muffled silence. They no longer saw Cervini in the distance, or even the ordinary wild deer that roamed the lowlands. Every now and again hares, their ears raised and attentive, appeared on the horizon before melting back into the land like ghosts. And once they saw a large round mound covered with smooth green grass rearing up to their left. Tom had an overwhelming urge to race over and demand entry to the Under-Palace of the old royal tribes. It reminded him of Finnlugh, and he wondered what he was doing.

Ahead he could see Arthur, and he caught a glimpse of Nimue propped in front of him on his horse. She had regained consciousness, but remained drowsy. For long periods she slept, leaning back against Arthur where he could ensure her compliance. Beansprout rode at Arthur's side, wary of Nimue's every move.

Brenna and Woodsmoke led them, picking their way down paths that snaked alongside ice cold streams. Nymphs lived in these shallow inland waters. Tom and Beansprout craned round on their horses to see them better.

They were teasing and alluring, their slender forms shining in the light and their hair cascading in green ribbons down their backs. They mostly kept to themselves, giggling to each other in little groups, watching them pass with half-hearted interest. But one, overcome with curiosity, popped up suddenly from a stream at Tom's side. She was draped in silky clothes that barely covered her, and she gazed up at him with big round eyes, casting her gaze over him appreciatively, beckoning him with a smile. Tom was so shocked he nearly fell off his horse. It was only with the greatest concentration that he kept going in the right direction.

Nightfall brought them to the base of Dragon Skin Mountain. It was low, as mountains go, and long, as if it had been stretched out. In the middle were twin peaks looking like hunched shoulders, and between these was the pass through to the Sky Meadows.

They set up camp for the night with the ease of a well-oiled machine. They had fallen into a routine in which Tom and Beansprout raised the tent and collected wood for the fire, while Woodsmoke and Brenna hunted for food – if they hadn't already caught it during the day. Arthur watched Nimue and tended the horses; Nimue watched them silently, or pretended to sleep.

After finishing a bowl of hot rabbit stew, Tom asked, "So who is it we're going to visit in Dragon's Hollow?"

"I wouldn't really call it a visit," Arthur said. "It's not a social call."

"You know what I mean," Tom said, helping himself to more food.

"Raghnall, the dragon sorcerer."

A disdainful voice added, "My jailor."

They looked to where Nimue sat, barely visible on the edges of the firelight.

"He is not your jailor, he's your healer," Arthur said.

"I am healed," she retorted.

"No, you are not," Arthur bit back. "Your arm is broken, your shoulder is hunched, and you are still woozy from your head injury. And you were going to visit him anyway!"

"I could have made my own way."

Arthur's eyes were hard and pitiless. "Don't be ridiculous, you have been unconscious for most of the past few days. If you hadn't appeared at Ceridwen's you wouldn't be injured and we wouldn't be stuck with you."

Nimue remained silent, her face in shadow.

"Seeing as you're awake for the first time in days, tell me, how did you know where we were?" said Arthur.

Nimue hesitated, as if wondering how much to say, then shrugged. "Oh, what does it matter? When I left the spell I travelled only as far as the top of Scar Face Fell, right above the cave. I wanted to see what happened. I felt the spell break and I heard the Cervinis' plans. So I decided to go there too."

"And would you like to explain why you imprisoned Merlin all those years ago?"

"Not really," she said, looking up and holding Arthur's gaze. "You wouldn't understand anyway."

"We were friends once; why don't you try?"

"Because being endlessly pursued by an obsessed man is something you have never experienced. And therefore you have no idea how awful it was. Everywhere I went, he was there, like a malevolent shadow. I felt suffocated." Her small frame shuddered with the memory.

Arthur looked down, momentarily awkward, while the others watched, intrigued. "I know he became a little infatuated with you."

"A little?" Nimue laughed.

"All right, a lot. I did at one point suggest he should leave you alone."

"You did?" Her voice softened a little.

"Yes, but he denied it and said I was imagining things."

They again fell silent, looking at each other across the fire, and it seemed to those watching that the years had disappeared, and so had they, and that Nimue and Arthur were sitting alone around the fire.

"I'd had enough, so I used his own spell against him. And I was glad I did," she added, her eyes flashing again with malice. "I got my life back."

"So why go back to the cave?"

"Because when I heard the rock fall had revealed the caves, I feared that the spell had been broken and he would come after me, for revenge. Or that his obsession would start over again. The thought filled me with dread."

Arthur sighed. "I can understand that, but why trap us in the spell too?"

"You saw what was happening. The spell had held, but Orlas insisted on me releasing it, and then he would have dragged me back to that cell. I saw a way out and I took it. Trapping you in that spell was the only way I could get out. It wasn't personal."

"So you would have come and released us, eventually?" The question was laced with disbelief.

She squirmed. "I don't know. But I'm glad you are out. My fight is not with you, Arthur, it never has been. If it helps, I promise that I won't harm you or your friends."

"I hope you mean that, Nimue. Because getting out of that spell took the intervention of Herne, and it nearly killed us."

"I'm sorry. And sorry to you too, Tom." For the first time since waking she looked at him and smiled. He had no idea what to say, so he just stared at her, stupidly. She didn't seem to notice, instead saying, "I used to help you, Arthur. We made a good team. All those people coming and going from Camelot. I miss it." She hesitated before adding crossly, "I told you not to go chasing after that fool Lancelot. That's when it all went wrong. She wasn't worth it."

Tom knew why she'd hesitated and he looked at Arthur, wondering how he'd react, but he was calm.

"Please don't talk about Guinevere that way. I had to go. And the rest is history."

Nimue was now animated, her hostility gone, and she seemed keen to re-establish her old friendship with Arthur. "You won't know this, obviously, but I was one of the nine priestesses who carried you to Avalon. That was a sad day, Arthur. Very sad. I cried for a week. I only crossed back to Britain a few times after that."

"Why? What happened?" He leaned forward, eager to hear her response.

"It was as if the whole world had gone mad. It was chaotic, frightening; full of warmongering men and invading tribes. I hated it. And there was nothing I could do. Nothing." She sounded bitter and angry. "So I came here to live, as did some of the other priestesses. The old ways were failing there, but not here."

"That sounds similar to something Morgan said. So why didn't you stop her last year when she started killing the Aerikeen – Brenna's kin?" He indicated to where Brenna sat.

Nimue glanced at Brenna and her face changed as if suddenly realising who she was. "Sorry, that was slow of me. Of course you are Aerikeen. Morgan was half-fey and far stronger than me, than any of us, except the fey. So Vivian thought of you Arthur. You scared Morgan."

"Ha! She'd outgrown her fear of me. If it hadn't been for Finnlugh we'd all be dead."

"Well, she is gone and you are here. And it is *so* good to see you." And she flashed her brilliant smile again.

"I'd like to believe you, Nimue, but I'm not sure I can," Arthur said softly.

Silence fell and Nimue's smile faltered, and Tom realised they were all wondering how far they could trust Nimue.

Eventually Brenna spoke, changing the subject. "I hear Raghnall is a great man. He subdued the dragons and won the pass for the fey, allowing access to the Sky Meadows."

"And allowing himself access to the ancient dragon caves riddling the mountain," Nimue retorted.

"You disapprove of him then?" Brenna asked.

"I disapprove of him proclaiming to be a great man while all along he grubs for the bright gems of the dragons and makes deals with the sylphs."

"I suppose he felt he deserved some reward for his efforts."

"He certainly has that. He lives in splendour; they all do up there. Have you ever been to Dragon's Hollow?"

"Never."

She turned to Woodsmoke. "Have you?"

He shook his head. "No."

"Well, you'll soon see," Nimue said. "The place is dripping in gold and gems."

"Why are you going to see him?" Woodsmoke asked.

"Dragon's Hollow is the best source of gems and metals; there are some we need for spells which we cannot get from anywhere else. And we have known him a long time." Nimue didn't elaborate.

Tom had been following this conversation with interest, and he finally burst out, "Do you mean there are dragons on the mountain?"

"Yes," Brenna answered, "but they have been driven to the outer reaches, the far passes and the deepest caves. I have heard that the main path up the mountain is generally clear."

Tom's mouth fell open. Recovering quickly, he turned to Arthur. "Did you know?"

"Vivian warned me," he said, nodding.

And as if to validate their discussion, a long, low, rumbling roar rolled down the mountain. Tom felt his skin prickle and a shiver ran down his spine.

"Don't worry," Arthur said, "I killed a few back in my other life."

"In England?" Beansprout asked excitedly.

"In Britain," Arthur corrected.

"But I thought that was a myth," Tom said.

"And you used to think magic didn't exist, either," Arthur said, a trace of a smile on his lips.

"So will the dragons fly down here, off the mountain?"

Woodsmoke answered. "They are bound to the mountain; part of the great spell. Before that the land was burnt and the mountain was impassable. The path to the north led far round the mountain, and the Sky Meadows were inaccessible for all except those who could fly, and the air spirits themselves."

"And the Sky Meadows are …?"

"The way to the Realm of Air. Where we find Merlin."

21 The Attractions of Magic

The trail they followed the next day was well used and followed a gentle gradient, winding up through the folds of the mountain as it slowly climbed higher and higher. They travelled through low brush and shrubs and then through stands of trees, some ancient, some only a few years old, new growth following fires. And every now and again they saw the bleached white bones of dragons shining in the sunlight.

Beansprout had dropped back to speak to Tom. "What do you think of magic, Tom?"

He looked at her, puzzled. "I don't know. It's just there I suppose."

She rolled her eyes in frustration. "But aren't you fascinated by it? It exists. It's real. You tried to do some!"

"I thought I was going to die trapped in a spell forever. It was a motivating moment."

"But how did it feel?" At his blank look she elaborated. "You know, when you read the spell and assembled all the things you needed, and then started to read it. How did it feel? Did your fingers tingle? Did the air change? What happened?"

"I don't know. I had no idea what I was doing. I didn't even think it would work. In fact I don't think it did. Herne appeared and everything went *Boom*." He threw his hands wide to demonstrate.

"So you didn't feel anything?"

"No."

Beansprout took a deep breath. "OK. Well what did it feel like in the spell?"

This time he had no hesitation. "That *was* weird!"

"Weird how?"

"Everything felt so ancient, as if I was trapped in time – you know, like one of those mosquitoes trapped in amber in *Jurassic Park*."

"I'm not completely stupid, Tom. So it felt different?"

"Hugely different. Like time had no meaning. No–" he paused, considering. "More like I was outside time. Completely removed from it." He looked ahead to where Nimue sat with Arthur. "It was immense. And terrifying."

"Immense, that's the word," she said enthusiastically. "That's what I felt around the cauldron. Did you feel the energy then?"

He nodded, remembering. "Yes, it was like an electric current. You had flowers in your lap."

"It was the most amazing feeling. I felt connected to everything. I could feel this power surging up through me, like a spring. And I felt I was a small part of something really huge. I want to be able to do that."

Now she had Tom's full attention. "Do you?" he asked, alarmed.

"Yes. Don't you?"

"No. It's dangerous. It's too big."

"Well I'd have to learn. Properly. Nimue did, she's human and look what she can do."

"And she's dangerous," he said, as if that proved his point.

"Not really. It seems to me that Merlin was too persistent and she'd had enough. She had the ability to do something about it, so she did. Everything else was self-preservation."

Tom started to feel annoyed. "So it was OK to put me in a spell?"

"No, of course not, that's not what I'm saying. She misused her power and over-reacted. And has since apologised. But she obviously felt vulnerable."

Tom narrowed his eyes at her. "You're defending her? Because I can assure you she did not appear the slightest bit vulnerable at the time."

"She might not have appeared it, but I bet she felt it! It's a reasonable reaction under the circumstances."

"I can't believe you're taking her side!"

"Someone needs to. Didn't you listen last night? Can't you imagine what it must have felt like? To have to put up with that constant attention?"

They had stopped and were now shouting at each other, their horses fretful, sensing the tension.

"I'm sure Merlin didn't mean it."

"I'm sure he did. He didn't stop, did he? Selfish old bastard."

The others became aware of the noise and whirled round.

"Are you OK?" Arthur called.

"We're fine," they both yelled, glaring at each other.

Arthur looked relieved and then confused. "Are you sure?"

"Yes!"

"Well, keep up then," and he waved Woodsmoke and Brenna on, following them up the slope.

Beansprout's voice dropped and she hissed at Tom as they started moving again. "If it was me and I had Nimue's skills, I'd do the same thing. And I would like to think that as my friend and cousin, you would be on my side, instead of being overawed by the tales of some old man."

And she spurred her horse on, leaving Tom on his own.

They halted for lunch, turning off the trail and sheltering from the sun beneath the spreading branches of a grove of old trees. Close by, a narrow stream wound through the undergrowth.

"Why is it getting hotter?" Beansprout asked as she dismounted. "Shouldn't it be colder as we get higher up the mountain? Not that I'm complaining – it's great."

Nimue answered as she slid to the ground, holding her arm awkwardly and grimacing. "This place has a different climate to what you'd expect. It was designed that way because the fey in the Hollow like it hot. The unfortunate thing is, the dragons like it too."

"Oh." Beansprout's enthusiasm was slightly dimmed. "By the way, Nimue, when we have a chance later, I'd like to ask you a few questions."

Tom stopped halfway through getting his pack off his horse and looked over at Beansprout. She caught him staring, but ignored him and turned back to Nimue. Nimue was oblivious. "Of course, whatever I can help you with. You're Beansprout, is that right? I think that's what Arthur told me."

"Yes, Tom's cousin. I'm so glad he's back," she said, smiling in a sickly way at Tom. "He's so much fun to have around."

A distant roar rocked the ground beneath their feet, ending their conversation. Apart from Nimue, everyone withdrew their weapons.

"That sounded closer than I'd like," Woodsmoke said, scanning the sky.

They heard another roar, even closer.

"Is it coming for us?" Tom asked, alarmed.

"The dragons shouldn't be this close to the main path," Nimue answered, "but maybe something's attracting this one's attention."

She turned to Arthur. Excalibur gleamed in a ray of sun. "Your sword,

Arthur. It hears it. That's what draws it close."

"What do you mean, it hears it?" Arthur asked.

"It is made from the precious metals of the fey by the Forger of Light; it's imbued with spells for protection and strength. It sings of where it was and where it is, as do all fey weapons of this quality."

"But what about Woodsmoke's weapons, and Brenna's? They're obviously faerie made too."

"But they were not made with spells by the Forger of Light. Excalibur is a weapon of peculiar powers, Arthur. And dragons like such weapons. The singing comforts them."

"You might have mentioned this before, Nimue," Arthur said angrily, as the others warily eyed Excalibur.

"I honestly didn't think," she snapped.

"So if it comforts them," Tom said as another roar sounded, "why does it sound so annoyed?"

"I presume because it wants Excalibur but doesn't have it yet," Woodsmoke answered, as a large shadow fell across them.

They looked up to see the scaly underside, powerful legs and broad wings of a dragon passing overhead.

"You should go. Leave me here, I can fight it alone," Arthur said.

They watched as the dragon turned and flew back in their direction. It shimmered bright blue and green in the sunlight. As it grew closer they could see its long neck and head, and its narrow red eyes. Tom couldn't believe he was actually seeing a dragon, and from the pale look on Beansprout's face, neither could she.

"It's too late for that, Arthur," Woodsmoke said, stepping out from under the trees' cover and releasing an arrow at the dragon's vulnerable abdomen. He called back over his shoulder. "Someone protect the horses!"

Nimue and Beansprout quickly retreated into the trees beyond the stream with the horses, which were now starting to panic. Tom heard Nimue shout, "Further back Beansprout, much further! Arthur, this would be a good time to restore my powers."

Arthur shouted back, "Good try Nimue, but no thanks."

Woodsmoke continued to fire arrows with unerring accuracy, a handful sinking into the dragon's flesh, the others bouncing off its thick skin. It roared again, possibly in pain, but to Tom it sounded more like anger. It dropped onto the path in front of them, crushing the surrounding bushes, and they ran back to the trees, desperately seeking cover.

The dragon was easily as big as a house. Its long neck ended with a sharp angular head, its jaw filled with razor-sharp teeth. Red eyes blazed with anger. Thick scales like armour plating covered its body and neck, wrapping around its chest like a breastplate. Its broad wings flexed across its back and smoke steamed out of its long nose as it probed forward, its tail thumping and slithering along. Tom could feel the ground shaking.

For a brief second they froze as it raised its head, sniffing deeply. Arthur seized his moment and bounded out from the shadows, running with Excalibur extended before him. But the dragon immediately dropped its head and shot a long tongue of fire at Arthur, causing him to roll to his right. The dragon lunged after him.

Brenna, Woodsmoke and Tom rushed forward to distract it. With swords drawn, they rushed beneath its outspread wings and jabbed at any soft fleshy parts they could see.

The dragon roared and flames shot out, burning the dry grasses and shrubs in a wide semi-circle. Its huge muscular tail thrashed, and Tom rolled and scrambled out of the way, hacking awkwardly with his sword. One of the dragon's wings clipped Woodsmoke, sending him reeling backwards.

Tom weaved beneath the bulk of the dragon, avoiding its stamping feet as it trampled the baked earth. Uselessly he stabbed upwards at the dragon's soft underbelly, but he could barely reach it, and his sword only pricked its skin. He watched as the others ran to and fro, dodging around its flapping wings and streams of fire. The dragon brushed them aside like flies. Tom was so close to being squashed he couldn't keep track of what was happening, then just as he was planning to dive out from under the dragon, Arthur skidded to a halt next to him. Again Tom stabbed wildly upwards, but Arthur was far more accurate and he wielded Excalibur expertly. He drove the blade into the soft flesh and pulled the sword along its belly, the blade moving easily, as if through butter.

"Tom, move – now!" yelled Arthur, as hot blood and guts fell to the ground and the dragon's legs started to crumple.

They both dived outwards as its body hit the ground. The dragon was dying, but it continued to attack, spraying fire in all directions, grass and trees flaring into flames. But the bursts of fire became shorter and weaker as the dragon's head dropped lower and lower. Woodsmoke and Brenna hacked at its neck, their swords barely denting its thick scales.

Arthur raced across the smouldering grass and stood next to them. He raised Excalibur high above his head and then brought it down in one swift stroke. It sliced through the neck cleanly, severing the dragon's head from its body.

For a few seconds the dragon's long neck thrashed about, blood spurting from the open wound before pooling thickly on the ground, then it crashed to the floor.

Tom staggered to his feet, gasping for breath and coughing. A veil of smoke choked the air and he trampled down the flames where they licked the dry grass. His eyes stung and he blinked rapidly as he made his way over to the severed head, the dragon's eyes glazing over already.

Nimue's voice disturbed the silence. "You must cut out the heart."

She stood on the edge of the charred clearing, Beansprout next to her. They carried large bundles of bush they had been using to beat out the flames, and were singed and black with soot. Beansprout had a smear of blood across her cheek.

"Why?" Arthur leant against the dragon, breathing heavily.

"Here, in the Other, dragons have many special properties they do not have anywhere else. They live for gold, gems and precious metals, because part of them is made of those things. After death, parts of the body transform into jewels, except for the heart. It must be cut out immediately after death; only then will it transform into a gem that is highly prized here – dragonyx. And by cutting out its heart you claim the dragon as yours, which means you keep all profits from its body."

"That's crazy," Arthur said, looking confused.

"It's true," Woodsmoke agreed, "or at least, so I've heard."

Woodsmoke and Brenna were trying to stop the fire spreading, kicking dirt over patches of flames, and hacking off burning branches before whole trees could catch.

"I have no wish to butcher the creature any further," Arthur answered. "And besides, it's huge. It will take too long."

He was right. The dragon had brought down several trees and now completely blocked the path with its bulk. It had fallen forward onto its chest and stomach, and its enormous wings had wrapped around its front and sides as it had tried to protect itself from further attack.

"Arthur," Nimue sighed. "You have no money here, no prestige. This will give you security. And although this isn't the biggest dragon I've seen, it's big enough. And hardly anyone sees dragonyx any more."

Arthur hesitated, clearly tempted.

"As much as I hate to agree with Nimue," Woodsmoke said, "she's right."

"But the longer we stay here, the more at risk we are. We could be attacked again," Arthur reasoned.

"Then I suggest we're quick," Woodsmoke said decisively. "We'll take the heart, eat on the road, and get to Dragon's Hollow before dark. As fun as this was, I don't particularly want to be attacked again. And," he added, "it means you won't have to run errands for Vivian again." He looked pointedly at Nimue.

Ignoring Woodsmoke's jibe, Nimue walked over to Tom. "May I?" she asked, indicating his sword.

Tom handed it to her wordlessly, and they watched as Nimue pulled the wing aside with Woodsmoke's help and thrust the sword into the dragon's right chest. It barely pierced its horny skin.

"Right here," she said to Arthur.

Arthur started cutting into the dragon's side, around the spot Nimue had indicated. Hot, thick blood oozed out of the gaping wound, splashing him. He stripped off his shirt and removed his boots.

Woodsmoke pulled his hunting knife from his pack and helped Arthur slice through the layers of muscle and bone. "I'm afraid I'm not much help, Arthur. I haven't carved open many dragons."

"That's all right – I'm not planning on doing this again." Arthur hacked and carved and hacked and carved, stopping and starting until he could see what he was looking for. Thick muscles and wiry tendons glistened in the light.

"Is that gold?" Arthur asked, seeing a glint of yellow along a huge ropey tendon.

"Probably," Nimue said, trying to get a better look.

Arthur straightened up. "Is this another reason dragons are hunted?"

"You made this look easy, Arthur," Nimue said wryly. "Many perish trying to kill dragons. There are probably as many bones of fey here as bones of dragons. That's why the city needs Raghnall's spell."

"Well when I see this sorcerer," Arthur said, continuing his grizzly business, "I'll tell him his spells aren't working."

"Perhaps because Excalibur is stronger," Nimue said softly.

22 Blood and Bone

After a long bloody battle with sinew and tendon, Arthur finally extracted the dragon's heart. He was slick with blood, and Woodsmoke wasn't much cleaner. While Woodsmoke washed his arms at the edge of the stream, Arthur stood in the middle, sluicing water over himself and scrubbing his skin with grass to get rid of the blood that had hardened in the sun.

When he was clean, Arthur turned to the heart. It sat on the bank streaked with dried blood. "I suppose I'd better clean this," he said to the others, who had crowded round. "I thought we were going to eat on the road?" he added, noticing they were munching on dried meats and cheese.

"That was before we realised slicing out a dragon's heart was going to take half the afternoon," Tom said, through a mouthful of food.

"An hour is not half the afternoon."

Arthur had worked quickly, but extracting the heart without damaging it had taken longer than expected. He'd needed Woodsmoke's advice on slicing through arteries as thick as his arms, and the enormous muscles that anchored it.

The heart was big – the size of a cartwheel – and was an irregular round shape. At the moment it was covered in gunk. It looked like an ugly chunk of flesh, and it smelt rotten, like fungus-filled earth that had never seen the sun. But as Arthur scrubbed it clean it began to transform and shine in the sun. Slowly a pale ruby red stone was revealed. The surface was mostly pitted and cloudy, but clear lucent patches began to appear, allowing them a glimpse inside the stone, where they saw thick veins of gold, and a black star in the centre.

"That's clean enough for now," Arthur said.

"The gem workers of the Hollow will polish it up. You won't recognise it once they've finished with it," Nimue said.

Woodsmoke fetched a large blanket from his pack. "Here, use this."

They rolled the gem in the blanket and secured it to the tent poles strapped to one of the horses.

"What do I do with the rest of it?" Arthur looked at the dragon carcass. Its bright green and blue scales still shone in the sun, and from the path you couldn't see the wound in its side, or tell that its head had been separated from its neck. It looked like it was sleeping.

"The goblins will come and collect it soon enough," Nimue said.

"I can't believe I've seen a dragon! And then Arthur killed it," Beansprout said to Tom, a note of sadness in her voice, as they rode up the mountain. The two of them had spent some time examining the dragon while Arthur carved out the heart, feeling its hard skin and thick scales.

"Well yeah," Tom agreed. "But it would have killed us, so ..."

Beansprout had managed to free a scale from the dragon's body, and she turned it over in her hands, admiring the way it glistened in the sun. "Look at it!" she said. "It's so beautiful. What do you think they'll do with the rest of the body?"

"Break it down like an old car, by the sound of it. From what Brenna said, there's a whole industry built around dragons and their gold. You could have that made into something. Maybe a decoration for your bow, or your knife hilt."

"I suppose so, although it seems a bit grizzly," Beansprout said, re-pocketing the scale.

Woodsmoke had picked up the pace after their stop, and as the sun dipped to the horizon they neared Dragon's Hollow. They were high on the mountain and the two peaks rose ahead of them, the path leading to the natural depression between. The road widened and flattened, and as they rounded a bend the great walls of the town came into view. The gates were made of burnished rose gold, and on them, inlaid in silver and black metal, was an ornately carved roaring dragon, its wings spread in flight. The high city walls were solidly built of thick stone, extending on both sides to the edge of the peaks. Along the top, carved stone dragons glowered menacingly.

"Is this wall to keep dragons out?" Tom asked, thinking surely that was impossible.

"No," Nimue answered. "Nothing keeps dragons out – except the sorcerer's spell. The wall is to keep out those who would attack the Hollow. And that really would be foolish, so no one has tried for a long time."

"So why such enormous gates?" Beansprout asked.

"Because it looks good, and besides, you never know. Sometimes people do stupid things for gold." Nimue shrugged.

"And how do we get in?" Arthur asked.

"The sentries will let us in," said Nimue, pointing to the small figures on top of the wall.

As they approached, the gates began to swing slowly back, revealing a cavernous tunnel beyond. A booming trumpet call echoed out of the tunnel, and half a dozen fey on horseback came to meet them. They were richly dressed in bright silks, and their horses had elaborate bridles, their manes woven with silver and gold thread.

Instinctively, Woodsmoke, Arthur and Brenna reached for their weapons, but Nimue stopped them, saying in harsh whisper, "Wait!"

An imperious fey, dressed in rich scarlet, led the group. His hair was as red as his clothing, and he had a long beard plaited with silver thread. He bowed his head briefly before addressing Arthur. "Who do we have the honour of welcoming, mighty dragon slayer?"

Tom wondered how they could possibly know about the dragon, when Arthur answered smoothly and courteously. "I am Arthur, King of the ancient Britons, Boar of Cornwall, Twice Born, Wielder of Excalibur gift of the Forger of Light. To whom do I owe the pleasure of this welcome?"

"Magen, Chief Slayer of the Dragon Guard." He stared at Arthur, a hint of challenge flashing in his eyes. "We are here to escort you to Dragon's Hollow. The Sorcerer requests your presence."

"Well," said Arthur evenly, "it's fortunate that it is the sorcerer we are here to meet." And he gave a smile that wasn't quite a smile.

Magen raised his hand, and from out of the tunnel behind him came a huge eight-wheeled cart pulled by four large purple lizards. On the back of the cart were a number of big burly creatures covered with warts and thick green skin.

"Goblins," Woodsmoke explained to Tom.

"The dragon belongs to Arthur," Nimue said to Magen. "He has the dragonyx." She nodded to where it hung behind Woodsmoke.

If possible, Magen looked even more annoyed. "In that case, the sorcerer requests your permission to bring back the dragon body for dismemberment."

"My permission?" Arthur asked, clearly confused.

"As the dragon belongs to you and not the city, you must agree to its dismemberment. You will receive all monies as are due to you, minus the fee for transformation," Magen explained impatiently.

"In that case," Arthur said, "yes I do."

As the cart trundled past them, Magen turned. "Follow me."

The temperature dropped once they were in the tunnel, and Magen was visible only as a dark silhouette ahead. They emerged into a small square dappled in the cool purple shadows of twilight. Around it was a warren of buildings and narrow lanes. In the pale light the buildings shimmered from the dusting of gold that patterned the stone.

They continued down a long central avenue, passing beneath balconies with cascading flowers and greenery. The place looked wealthy and well cared for, the buildings ornate with detailed embellishments in metals of many colours. This was a very different place from the Meet. Occasionally they passed locals wandering back from the town centre, dressed in fine linens with trimmings of embroidery and lace.

Dragon's Hollow was well named, as it sat encircled by the shoulders of the two peaks on either side. It had trapped the heat of the day so that as night fell, warmth poured from the golden stone around them. Tom grew sticky and tired and wondered impatiently how long it would take to get to the sorcerer. He began to daydream of cold showers and icy drinks, but when they rounded the next corner, all such thoughts left his mind rapidly. They stumbled to a halt and looked around, awestruck.

In front of them was a large perfectly round lake, from which rose an enormous dragon fountain made of coloured glass, precious metals and luminous gems. Like the dragon on the gate, its wings were spread in flight, and its head was looking down upon them. Instead of flames, water poured from its mouth.

Palatial buildings were set around the pool and against the curved bowl of the peaks. In the dusk, the buildings glittered with thousands of lights. Hundreds of faeries milled about the central space, strolling around the pool and across the bridges that spanned it. Entertainers had set up in nooks, and at the start of the bridge ahead was a group of fire-breathing faeries, shooting flames of orange, blue and green high into the sky.

The first person to find their voice was Brenna. "I had no idea of the scale of this place."

"We seek to keep its splendours to ourselves." Magen had come to stand next to them, waiting until they were ready to follow him.

"So you do," Arthur murmured.

"Some of the greatest weapons of faerie are made here," Magen said proudly.

"Is this where the Forger of Light lives?" Arthur asked.

"Not any more."

Changing the subject, Magen pointed to the far side of Dragon's Hollow, to a vast house on the mountainside, glittering with inlaid silver and rich black marble. Its many windows lay in darkness, except for the top of the house, where a solitary light burned. "That's where we are heading – The House of the Beloved."

23 House of the Beloved

Magen led the way across town to the bottom of a long drive bordered with topiary. The guards remained at the gate while the others carried on up to the sorcerer's house, stopping at the bottom of a flight of steps where Arthur carefully unloaded the dragonyx. Leaving their horses with two grooms, they followed Magen into the main building.

They were obviously expected. The doors stood wide, allowing what little breeze there was to flow down the hall. Hundreds of candles flickered, reflecting off the marble floors. They followed Magen up a staircase and along a corridor, eventually coming out onto a broad covered balcony overlooking the city. A long table was set for dinner, and at the far end was a smaller table of drinks.

"Raghnall will join you soon. In the meantime, help yourself to drinks," said Magen, gesturing to the table.

"You're not staying?" said Arthur.

"My father and I don't exactly see eye to eye," Magen replied, and left abruptly.

"His father! Interesting," Woodsmoke said, heading to the drinks table.

"I'd forgotten he had children," Nimue said. "I've never met them. It doesn't surprise me they don't get on, though."

"Why's that?" asked Woodsmoke, passing her a glass of wine.

"Because he's a pompous ass," she hissed before taking a healthy swig of wine.

"Needed that did you, Nimue?" Brenna observed.

"Yes, it's been quite a day. And it's going to get worse," Nimue grumbled.

They took their drinks over to the balustrade and stood looking out across the city below. Darkness had fallen and stars glittered above them, mirroring the hundreds of flickering lamps below. The night air was silky smooth across their skin.

"This place looks too good to be true," Brenna observed.

"I had no idea how much dragon's gold there was here," said Woodsmoke.

"I have heard tales about it, but I never envisioned it could be this …" Brenna struggled for words.

Arthur finished her sentence. "Magnificent?"

"I knew you'd like this place," Nimue said, from where she had taken a seat in the shadows.

"It reminds me of Camelot."

"Camelot looked like this?" Beansprout said.

Nimue replied, "I don't think it was quite as big as the Hollow."

"Maybe not," Arthur said testily. "But it was beautiful, especially after Merlin embellished it a little."

"I loved Camelot, but I don't love the Hollow," Nimue said.

"Why not?" asked Tom.

"There's just too much of it. It exhausts me."

"Sometimes," Woodsmoke said, "the fey like to put on a display of wealth to dazzle and impress. You saw that, Tom, in Finnlugh's Under-Palace."

Tom nodded, thinking of the ballroom and the ornate library he had seen. "It's true, everything about The House of Evernight was extravagant. Finnlugh was extravagant. The Duchess of Cloy was extravagant!"

"As King of the Britons," Arthur said, "I can assure you I was …" he paused, "extravagant. Camelot was a vision of silver towers, thick walls, flags, might and wealth. It was necessary. It was meant to terrify and awe everyone who saw it."

A deep voice interrupted their conversation. "I hope the richness of your surroundings isn't upsetting you?"

They turned abruptly and saw a tall man standing in the doorway to the balcony. It was difficult to see him clearly in the low lighting, and Tom wondered how long he'd been standing there listening to their conversation. He also wondered how rude they had sounded.

"Only me," Nimue called out, "but you already know that, Raghnall."

Ignoring Nimue, Arthur answered, "Not at all. It is very pleasant after being on the road for so many weeks, and we appreciate your hospitality. I am Arthur." He held out his hand.

Raghnall stepped forward to shake his hand, and the lights on the balcony flared brightly, allowing them to see him clearly for the first time. He had thick black hair, streaked with grey, lightly oiled and swept back into a long plait. Keeping it neatly in place was a thinly beaten silver band that rested on his forehead, like a crown. He had a small, neat, triangular beard, and intense dark eyes that swept across them all imperiously before briefly resting on Nimue. His regal appearance was enhanced by his clothing. He wore a three-quarter-length coat of shimmering dark blue velvet over a shirt of fine embroidered linen, and knee-length soft leather boots. Rings adorned his fingers, and as Raghnall shook their hands Tom watched them twinkle in the lamplight.

"I am pleased you like it here. Every effort is made to provide comfort and pleasure. Not many are as immune as Nimue," he said, looking at her pointedly.

"I'm not immune, just overwhelmed," she said, rising to kiss his cheek.

"Anyone would think you starved yourself of beauty on Avalon. And I know that's not true," Raghnall said.

"Now now, Raghnall, let's not do that again," Nimue said.

"Of course not."

Tom wondered what they were referring to.

"There is food prepared for you all. I presume you are hungry – after all, dragon slaying is tiring work," Raghnall said, his eyes glittering.

"And how is it you know we slayed a dragon, Raghnall?" Arthur leaned back against the balustrade as if he owned the place.

"The lookouts along the wall." Raghnall walked over to the table and poured himself a small drink of something black and viscous. "Vivian had informed me of your arrival, so we were keeping an especially close watch." He turned, "And naturally I am more than happy to help you recover, Nimue. You will of course stay here. I have prepared a room for you – for all of you, actually," he said, his gaze sweeping across them.

"We couldn't impose," Woodsmoke said. "Just direct us to the nearest inn."

"No! It's far too late. I insist." His hand flew up, palm outwards, as if to stop further discussion. "And besides, I have a large house as you can see."

For some reason, despite their opulent surroundings, Tom wasn't entirely sure he wanted to stay at the House of the Beloved, and he sensed the others felt the same – Woodsmoke's protestations weren't just from politeness. Ever since they had entered Raghnall's house, Tom had felt uncomfortable, and the fact that Vivian seemed to be an old friend didn't reassure him. Maybe he was picking up on Nimue's mood. And he was tired and sweaty and wanted a bath and clean clothes.

As if reading Tom's thoughts, Raghnall said, "But I am so thoughtless. You must want to wash and change."

As he finished speaking a bell rang throughout the house, and in seconds a small dark-haired faery materialised in the doorway. He bowed deeply. "My lord?"

"Please escort our guests to their rooms." Raghnall nodded to them. "Dinner will be in an hour. Nimue, I will come and see to your shoulder and arm." He then strolled to the edge of the balcony and gazed across the vista below, and with that they were dismissed.

Tom had never stayed in a five-star hotel, but imagined this would be a very similar experience. His room was enormous, and it contained the biggest bed he had ever seen, covered in sheets of silk and linen, and the most enormous puffy pillows. The furnishings were as bright as the marble was dark. Thick rugs covered the floor and paintings hung from the walls. A door led to an ensuite bathroom where the bath was filled with hot steaming water smelling of cedar. Thick towels hung on a stand to the side. His bags were in his room, unpacked, and his clothes were clean and fresh. Tom doubted even a five-star hotel could do that so quickly.

Tom soaked in the tub wishing he could stay there for hours. Whatever was in the water was soothing his aching muscles, and he scrubbed himself clean with an energy he hadn't felt in days.

Feeling refreshed, Tom met the others in the hall outside his room. "How long are we staying here?" he asked.

"Considering our long days on the road and the journey ahead, I think we should stay a few nights," Arthur said. "If Raghnall has no objections."

"I agree," Brenna said. "We could use the rest. You can put up with us for a few more days, Nimue?"

Nimue looked better than she had done in days. Her eyes were bright, and she was no longer hunched over from her injured shoulder. "It's fine with me – anything to put off being alone here with Raghnall."

Arthur rolled his eyes. "I doubt you'll be alone, Nimue. Besides, he's not that bad."

"You wait. You haven't spent an evening with him yet. Anyway, the longer you're here the better I get. I may be able to come with you!"

"I think you jest, Nimue. I doubt you wish to see Merlin so soon, especially with the sylphs. And he certainly won't want to see you."

She smirked. "You may be right. But will you at least release my binding?"

"Only once we've left."

"Why not now?" Nimue glared at Arthur.

"Because I said so," he said, sounding like he was talking to a child.

"Perhaps," intervened Woodsmoke, "we should discuss this later. I'm starving." And with that he led the way downstairs, the others quickly following.

Dinner was elaborate, delicious and uncomfortable. As good as the food tasted, Tom couldn't wait for it to be over. Nimue was right. Raghnall was an insufferable show-off, a tedious bore. The conversation flowed, but only because Arthur, Beansprout and Brenna worked hard to be sociable; the rest of them struggled.

The longer the evening went on, and the more Raghnall showed off, the more competitive Arthur became. And unfortunately for Raghnall, when Arthur put his mind to it, he was very good at storytelling. Arthur didn't usually boast, so Tom could tell Raghnall was annoying him. The sorcerer relayed a long tale about a large party he had thrown for the visiting sylphs. He described the food, the decorations, the lights, the clothes, and then the music. Tom stifled a yawn.

And then Arthur started. "The week of my coronation was idyllic! Merlin surpassed himself. I have never seen Camelot look more beautiful, its towers more gilded, or the decorations so sumptuous. The visiting princes and their wives were a vision, and the feasting and hunting were unmatched in their success."

Tom caught Raghnall's expression across the table and quickly glanced away for fear he should laugh. He decided to concentrate on his food. Woodsmoke was watchful and monosyllabic, and Nimue was amused.

Raghnall asked them about their travels, but already seemed to know exactly what they had been up to. "So Nimue, Vivian tells me you had a problem with Merlin?"

"Yes, Raghnall, I did. What of it?" she challenged.

"Being trapped in a spell for centuries seems a harsh punishment," he said, "for love."

"Oh! That's what you call it? Strange, it didn't feel like that to me," she said, artfully spearing a piece of beef.

"But a highly impressive spell, nevertheless." He raised his glass to her before taking a sip.

"Not so impressive when you're trapped in it," Arthur said with a sidelong glance at Nimue.

Nimue dropped her head and looked at the table.

"Vivian gave me little information," said Raghnall, "so–"

"No surprise there," Arthur interrupted.

"I'm curious. How did you get out of it?" Raghnall continued, ignoring Arthur's tone.

"Tom prepared the ingredients to break the spell, and Herne finished it off," Arthur said airily, as if it had been the easiest thing in the world.

Tom felt Raghnall's piercing gaze fall on him, and his languid polite air seemed to disappear. "Really, Tom? There's a lot more to you than meets the eye."

Tom wasn't sure whether to be insulted or flattered. Insulted, probably. Did he look like an idiot?

Before he could respond, Woodsmoke said, "Don't we all have hidden depths, Raghnall? Even you, I'm sure."

Tom suppressed a smirk by taking a big mouthful of food, watching Raghnall's response out of the corner of his eye.

Raghnall looked at Woodsmoke, a slow smile spreading across his face. "Indeed I do. It is possible, though, to eat well, sleep well, and generally live well, even with hidden depths, don't you think?"

"Absolutely," Woodsmoke said, raising his glass. "Here's to your excellent wine."

An unpleasant undercurrent seemed to have risen to the surface, and in an effort to submerge it again, Beansprout spoke. "Excuse me, Raghnall, but could you recommend a weapon maker tomorrow? I have a piece of dragon scale I would like making into something."

Raghnall held Woodsmoke's gaze for a second longer, then turned to Beansprout. "It would be a pleasure, my dear. And of course, Arthur will need a gem-maker."

"Ah, yes. My dragonyx. Your help would be much appreciated," Arthur said smoothly.

"It's quite a feat to kill a dragon."

Arthur must have decided that Raghnall had been baited enough. "And to enchant them too, I'm sure."

"I must admit the spell requires a lot of maintenance. It is not something every sorcerer could manage for so long, or so successfully. It both repels the dragons and provides a force of protection over the city and passes."

Raghnall's humour seemed to have returned, and he called for the last course. His servant appeared and disappeared in seconds, clearing the plates and returning with dessert. Raghnall continued, "Even you, Nimue, with your great powers, could not maintain this spell. Although I gather your powers are currently bound."

"Yes, courtesy of the Cervini shaman. He seemed to take exception to my putting their leader in a spell. And Nerian still carries my poppet," Nimue said before Arthur could explain, "and refuses to restore my powers. It seems I must wait for a while."

Why, thought Tom, did she just lie to Raghnall? Why wouldn't she want him to know Arthur carried her poppet? However, despite discrete glances across the table, no one corrected her lie, and she picked up her glass and took a delicate sip. "And yet," she continued, "a dragon did attack us today, despite your spell. I have a theory."

"Please, I would like to hear your thoughts on it," Raghnall said magnanimously, his tone of voice suggesting her opinion was the last thing he wanted.

"I think Excalibur called the dragon."

"Really?" He tapped his glass thoughtfully. "I have heard of your Excalibur, Arthur. May I see it?"

Arthur pulled Excalibur free of its scabbard and handed it, hilt first, to Raghnall. The light slid across the polished blade and Tom was sure he heard it whisper, like silk across a polished surface. Raghnall handled it gently and reverently, but his eyes were greedy, and he held it inches from his face, following its smooth lines and intricate engravings. "Take me up, and cast me away," he murmured before falling silent in contemplation.

"What?" asked Tom.

"It's what the writing on the sword says," Arthur explained, watching Raghnall.

"I hear it," Raghnall whispered. "It speaks of many things: its birth in the fires of the Forger of Light, snatches of song, of victory, death, blood, strange lands, broken promises, of belonging." Raghnall's eyes were now closed, and it seemed he barely breathed, so intense were his thoughts. Nimue leaned forward, listening closely. She glanced at Arthur and then back to Raghnall, her expression concerned. Finally, Raghnall opened his eyes, looking dazed, and his gaze moved around the table, finally settling on Arthur. "I think it is one of the most incredible weapons I have heard."

"I thought only dragons could hear that. How can you hear it?" Nimue asked, watching him intently.

Raghnall made an effort to shake off his otherworldly state. "The old royal houses of the fey have many diverse and special skills. And this is my skill, Nimue, didn't you know?"

"No, actually I didn't."

"It is why I collect such weapons. It is why I live here. I love their songs." Again he appeared distracted. As if he had said too much, he handed back Excalibur to Arthur. "Yes, it most certainly called the dragon. It is very powerful."

Arthur looked with renewed admiration at Excalibur and asked, "But you couldn't hear it before? Before you tried?"

"No," Raghnall admitted, "but it is a skill I have to switch on. Living here, surrounded by such things, I would go mad if I heard these songs all the time."

"Are we in danger here? Will Excalibur call the dragons into the Hollow?" Arthur asked, concerned.

"No. The spells around the city are much more powerful than on the mountain. You can sleep easy tonight." Raghnall's gaze fell to the sword again and there was a greed in it he couldn't quite hide. "But just to be sure, I can cast a spell of protection on your scabbard, if you wish?"

Arthur looked uncertain, and Raghnall added, "It would make your journey out of the Hollow much safer."

Arthur nodded. "All right."

Raghnall nodded to Nimue. "It is a spell you are familiar with." He took Arthur's scabbard and for a few minutes held his hand over it, muttering words unknown to Tom, until a blue light passed over the scabbard. "There, as long Excalibur is sheathed the dragons will not hear it."

Nimue nodded. "It's a good spell, Arthur."

As Arthur sheathed Excalibur, Woodsmoke said, "So you collect weapons, Raghnall?"

"Yes, I have a special room I keep them in. I will show you tomorrow if you like?"

Woodsmoke nodded. "I would like that."

"But perhaps before it becomes too late we should examine your dragonyx, Arthur?" Raghnall said, looking towards the wrapped jewel on the divan where it now lay. "Not many outside the Hollow know to take the heart."

"I would imagine it's not something you advertise, Raghnall?" Arthur said softly.

Raghnall didn't answer, and instead a ghost of a smile crossed his face.

Arthur picked up the dragonyx and put it on the table, gently removing its wrappings. It glowed in the soft candlelight, and just visible through the milky opacity of the jewel's outer shell they could see the ruby luminescence, the veins of gold and the black knot at its centre. It was hard to believe Arthur had cut it out of a dragon earlier, and that it had once been a living beating heart pulsing with blood.

Raghnall rose from his seat and stood over the dragonyx, staring at it intently. He examined it from every angle, before finally putting his hand on the stone and listening.

"One of the older dragons, I think," Raghnall murmured. "What colour was it?"

"Blue and green," Nimue said.

"And it was very big," Tom added.

"Mmm, maybe it was Viridain," Raghnall said thoughtfully. "Ah well, we shall soon see tomorrow, when we visit the Chamber of Transformation."

"The what?" Beansprout said.

"The place where the dragon is taken apart for its gold and jewels. I can assure you, it's fascinating. And then we will visit the gem-makers, where you will find, Arthur, that you will get a good price for your dragonyx."

24 The Price of Dragons

The Chamber of Transformation was carved out of the rock deep beneath the left peak, and was accessed by a long tunnel that started in the town. It was rough hewn, long, low roofed and stiflingly hot. A central pit filled with flames lit up the cavern with a lurid glow, casting the faces of the goblins, trolls and fey who worked there into strange contorted shapes. The air rang with the sound of saws and hammers and the zing of metal on metal.

The dragon Arthur had slayed was spread on a large flat area of stone, where half a dozen goblins had already started to peel away its scaly skin and strip its veins and arteries of gold. Tom was forced to agree with Raghnall. As gory as it was, this was fascinating.

"I was right," Raghnall said, self-importantly. "This is Viridain. Or was."

"Do you name them all?" Tom asked.

"Only the ones we see most often. Although there are bigger dragons, this one was bold and caused many deaths over his long life. His hoard will be huge." Raghnall looked excited at the prospect of new gold. "And," he added quickly, "his hoard is not yours, Arthur. It belongs to the city."

"Don't worry," Arthur said. "I think I'll have enough gold."

"Do you know where his hoard is?" Beansprout asked.

"Not exactly, but I have a good idea." There was a speculative glint in Raghnall's eye.

"Of course you do," Nimue muttered.

Above the dragon's body was a series of wooden walkways, ropes and pulleys, and large buckets. Next to the body, running along the floor to the fire pit and other areas of the cave, were tracks carrying wheeled containers into which various parts of the dragon were placed.

The goblins had already made a lot of progress. Shiny gold sinews and what were once veins and arteries were already overflowing one container. With a shout and a mighty push, a goblin leapt onto the flat-bottomed trolley the container was on, escorting it to the edge of the fire pit. He leant on a bar which applied the brakes, and then, manipulating another switch, the cart tipped, sending the gold sliding over the edge.

Another goblin had started to fill a cart with the dragon's glittering scales, and yet another was loading what appeared to be the organs and viscera into a trolley destined for a different part of the cave. It was such a clinical operation that Tom felt repulsed.

"The process of transformation starts with the death of the dragon," Raghnall said. "The organs start to change from flesh to jewels, but we have found that the application of heat speeds up the process and improves the quality of the gems."

"So the whole dragon turns into gems?" Beansprout said.

"No. Not at all. There are parts that are quite unusable! But we are adept at getting the most out of them," Raghnall said smugly. "Of course, it has been quite some time since we have had a dragon to transform. They are notoriously difficult to kill." He looked at Arthur with begrudging admiration.

Tom stepped away from Raghnall and followed one of the tracks to the fire pit, curious to see where the gold went.

The pit descended into the rock far deeper than he'd imagined. Huge cauldrons were suspended over the fire, surrounded by metal walkways on which stood more goblins, stirring the pots with huge wooden paddles. They must be immune to the heat, thought Tom. And surely the metal walkways should burn and melt? More tracks led to another area, where the molten metals were being poured into moulds to create small ingots.

The others appeared next to him. "I have cast a protective spell over the walkways," said Raghnall, "to prevent the conduction of heat. As for the goblins, they enjoy it!"

"So all this is for one dragon?" Woodsmoke asked.

"Oh no. The melting of precious metals is a continual process here. We process gold from dragon hoards, and from the rich seams of metal found beneath the mountain. At the moment, though, this is all for Viridain, so we can calculate Arthur's bounty." He looked a little annoyed at the prospect of wealth going somewhere other than the city.

"I think I need fresh air," Brenna said suddenly, a look of distaste flashing across her face.

"Yes, me too," Beansprout agreed. "I'm hot."

The pair turned and headed towards the cave entrance.

"But I was going to show you the gem preparation!" Raghnall called, a look of anguish on his face.

"I think the heat is getting to us," said Woodsmoke, also turning to leave. "We'll see you back at the entrance." He slapped Raghnall unceremoniously on the shoulder before following Brenna and Beansprout.

"It's just me, Nimue and Tom, then," Arthur said. Tom half wished he could leave too, but Arthur gave him a quick look that compelled him to stay.

"Excellent. I'm so glad you're not squeamish," Raghnall said. He turned with a flourish and headed to the rear of the cave.

"I feel we should humour him, Tom," Arthur whispered with a wink and a smirk, and then set off after Raghnall.

Arthur rarely humoured anyone, Tom thought. What was he up to?

An hour later they found the others enjoying a cool drink on the terrace of a restaurant close to the entrance. Beansprout waved to draw their attention, and they weaved through the crowds to join them.

"Would you at least like to see the gem-makers' workshops?" Raghnall asked. He gestured across the green open space in front of them to a row of glittering shop fronts.

"Is that where I can get Viridain's scale polished up?" Beansprout said.

"Of course. And where the dragonyx can be weighed, polished and priced," he said with a nod to Arthur.

Raghnall was enjoying this, Tom thought, showing off the city and its citizens' skills. And why not? The city was beautiful, gilded and sleek. The whole place gleamed, the food was sumptuous, and the drinks were delicious. He felt pampered and rested, especially after weeks on the road. The atmosphere of success and satisfaction was addictive. He just wished he felt more relaxed here. This wasn't something he was used to, unlike Arthur. It was a strange thing to say, but Tom thought Arthur looked bigger. He seemed to have grown into himself. He was more self-assured – the promise of wealth seemed to invigorate him.

"Come on then," Arthur said after they'd finished their drinks. "Let's head to the gem-makers."

They stopped first at a small shop with a glittering array of polished scales in its window. The scales had been skilfully turned into jewellery, sword and dagger hilts, scabbards, and items Tom didn't even recognise. Inside the shop were gleaming metal cabinets displaying more polished scales. A fey bustled out of the door from the rear of the shop and was about to launch into his sales pitch when he saw Raghnall. His face froze for a fraction of a second, his eyes wide. Quickly recovering, he beamed ingratiatingly. "What a pleasure, Raghnall, it's been too long."

After a brief exchange of pleasantries, Raghnall introduced them, and then said, "Beansprout, please show him your scale."

She handed it over, and the conversation turned to business. The fey narrowed his eyes, pulled out a small magnifying glass and proceeded to examine the scale minutely. He then started on requirements, design, practicalities, time, and finally price – which was exorbitant. Clearly, whatever issues he had with Raghnall did not interrupt business. Raghnall bartered, Beansprout looked pale, Nimue questioned, but Arthur finished it all by naming a final price and declaring he would pay as a gift for Beansprout.

With a sigh of relief, Tom trailed out of the shop after them, to where Brenna and Woodsmoke waited in the sun, having long run out of patience during bargaining.

"Pleased, Beansprout?" Arthur asked, smiling.

"Well yes, but Arthur – I didn't expect you to pay!"

"My treat," he announced magnanimously. "And besides, at those prices it would have sat in your pack forever."

"True," Beansprout said, embarrassed ."It was very expensive!"

They followed Raghnall further along the row of expensive shops until they came to the largest and most ostentatious. It was a blaze of gold and glittering gems. Even Woodsmoke looked impressed.

Raghnall only had to mention dragonyx and a small silence fell across the handful of fey in the shop, both sellers and buyers. With hushed ceremony, the oldest and most imperious fey, who had a shock of rich purple hair and wore a black silk jacket, stepped from behind the long bronze-topped counter and said, "I have heard of the slaying of Viridain. Who has slain the dragon?"

Arthur stepped forward introducing himself, and the shop owner shook his hand vigorously. "Arshok. I am honoured to meet you. Please follow me to our salon, where I will offer refreshments while we negotiate." He glanced at Raghnall and added, "Perhaps just you and Arthur?"

Standing next to Nimue, Tom heard her whisper to Arthur, "Have you any idea of what it's worth?"

Arthur shook his head. "Not really."

"Then I suggest you let me come too," she said, raising an eyebrow.

Arthur turned to where the owner and Raghnall waited expectantly and said, "Nimue will join us." Raghnall flashed a brief discomforted smile as

Arshok opened a richly embellished gold door.

Woodsmoke called to Arthur, "We won't wait, see you later."

Arthur nodded his agreement and stepped into the room beyond. Tom caught a glimpse of silks and brocades, and then the door thudded shut.

"Come on," Woodsmoke said. "Let's see what else there is, other than jewellery shops. If this is where they make weapons, I want to see some." He gave the others a broad grin. "Besides, I need a break from Raghnall."

Woodsmoke led the way across the city, along broad boulevards and down tiny passageways, taking a circuitous route so they could see the city better. The beautiful buildings they passed were all manner of shapes and sizes, and while some were clearly for the town merchants, there appeared to be no poorer rundown areas at all. Eventually they came to an indoor market beside the lake. It was sprawled across a large area, with several entrances. Woodsmoke headed for the nearest one, and they plunged into the warren of stalls.

They were immediately surrounded by the loud hum of voices and jostling crowds that packed the small lanes between the shops. The bright glare of the day was shut out, replaced by the airless glitter of candles and lanterns, and the occasional chink of sunlight filtering in through the open entrances. The stall owners called to them constantly.

"Come and see the best silks this side of the Sky Meadows!"

"Come, madam, come taste the best spices in the market!"

"Sir, sir, this way for the best knives and best deals!"

The choice of wares and the dazzling displays mesmerised Tom. He had never been in such a place before; the markets of Holloway's Meet were pedestrian and grey in comparison. And Beansprout agreed. "Tom, this place is brilliant! So much stuff!"

Brenna laughed. "Take your time, and if you buy anything, make sure to haggle. We'll see you in the weapons section." And she hurried into the sea of bodies to catch up with Woodsmoke.

As Tom and Beansprout drifted down the alleys, they realised the market was divided into distinct areas. There was a section of clothing, silks, scarves and cloaks, then silverware, home wares, food, jewellery, shoes, travel supplies, magic amulets, glassware, lamps, rugs, books, and weapons. The choice was endless and the prices much cheaper than in the shops they had passed. They quickly lost track of time, meandering through the tiny lanes and buying all manner of trinkets, clothes and books.

"I think we should get a move on, Tom," Beansprout said at last, "before Woodsmoke runs out of patience."

"He's looking at weapons, he could be there all day!" Tom said.

They eventually stumbled upon the weapons quarter. The choice of weapons was vast. There were spears, axes, longbows, arrows, shields, helmets, armour, and all manner of swords and knives. The stalls spread into a central courtyard where a series of targets had been set up to test the weapons. They found Woodsmoke and Brenna by the stalls selling daggers, throwing-knives and swords. Brenna was testing the balance of a pack of throwing-knives, carefully hefting each one in her hands.

"New weapons, Brenna?" Tom asked, looking at the knives she was examining.

"I used to have a set of knives many years ago," she said, smiling at the memory. "And then I lost them, one after another. I have no idea how. I was thinking of getting some more."

"And these," Woodsmoke said, picking one up, "are very nice." He raised it to eye level, admiring its shape.

"The finest dragon metals have been combined to maximise weight, strength and longevity," the stall owner, a broad squat dwarf, explained. "Platinum, gold and dragonium. And the inlaid gems on the handles are black opals and pearls."

"Wow," Beansprout said, extending her hand. "May I?"

Brenna passed her a knife to examine, and said to the dwarf, "I like the metals, but not the jewels."

The dwarf immediately produced another knife, virtually identical but with a carved bone handle. "Dragon bone, hardened in the fires of the Djinn," he grunted.

"Better," Brenna said, examining it closely. She turned, eyed up the targets and threw the knife. The wooden targets were fashioned into a variety of creatures, including boar, dragons, trolls, and sprites. The knife sank deep into the eye of a sprite, and Tom was immediately reminded of their encounter with them in Finnlugh's Under-Palace and the Aerie.

"You seem to have kept your aim, Brenna," Tom said, impressed.

She smiled. "Not bad – I was aiming for his forehead." She went to retrieve the knife.

"He'd still be dead," Tom said. "Is it hard to learn?" Another skill to add to his growing sword skills would be good.

"Not really, you just need lots of practice," Brenna said. "I'll teach you."

"Can you throw knives, Woodsmoke?" Tom asked.

"Of course I can!" he snorted while Brenna rolled her eyes. "But I prefer my bow and sword. It's a good skill for you to learn, though. I'm sure this good dwarf has plenty of cheaper knives for you to practise with."

While Brenna negotiated a price for her set of knives, Woodsmoke helped Tom choose.

"Have you bought anything, Woodsmoke?" Beansprout asked.

"New arrows, fletches, and a sharpening stone. Speaking of which, we should get you some more arrows," he said, pointing to the stalls on the far side of the courtyard.

After Tom and Brenna paid, they made their way over to the arrow stalls. Choosing one at random, they entered the dim interior. Concentrating on making their choice, Tom suddenly became aware of someone looming close beside Woodsmoke. The faerie was tall, with fine features and high cheekbones, his hair long and fair with plaits and beads running through it. He leant in and said something in Woodsmoke's ear. Woodsmoke whipped round, his hand moving to his dagger. Subconsciously, Tom reached for his sword too, wondering briefly where Brenna was. But then Woodsmoke laughed, relief etched across his face.

"Bloodmoon, you nearly had my dagger in your stomach! What brings you to the Hollow?"

"Hunting, my friend," Bloodmoon said.

"Hunting what?" Woodsmoke asked.

"That should be discussed over a drink," he said, grinning. "And what are you doing so far from home?"

"Also hunting, of a sort."

"Indeed?" He caught sight of Tom and Beansprout looking on curiously. "Humans. Are they with you?"

"They are. And a lot of trouble they cause too. Tom, Beansprout – Bloodmoon," he said. "Many things have happened since I last saw you."

Bloodmoon shook their hands. "No Brenna?"

"Oh, she's here, somewhere. Give us half an hour and we'll see you at the Dragon's Tale, if you've time?" Woodsmoke said.

"Always. Soon, then," Bloodmoon said, and he disappeared back into the crowd.

"Who's he?" Tom asked.

"My cousin. Come, Beansprout, let's get your arrows. And then we'll find Brenna, and see what Bloodmoon is hunting."

25 Objects of Desire

The Dragon's Tale was a very old inn, lacking the ostentatious decorations of the rest of the city, although its wooden structure was decorated with the finest carvings. Its customers were mainly those visiting the market, and the stall owners, and it served cheap hearty fare.

Bloodmoon joined them shortly after they sat down in a quiet corner. He greeted Brenna with an enormous kiss that had her blushing. "Bloodmoon!" she exclaimed breathlessly. "What was that for?"

"I haven't seen you in a long time," he said, grinning. "And when you're the Queen of Aeriken I won't be able to get away with that."

"You're such a show-off," Woodsmoke said. "Just sit down and tell us what you're up to. Nothing good, I presume?

Bloodmoon sat down, placing an enormous tankard of frothing beer on the table next to his parcel. He took a long sip while the others watched him expectantly, and then said, "I'm tracking a lamia."

"What on earth for?" Woodsmoke asked. And then, looking alarmed, said, "Is there one in Dragon's Hollow?"

"Not in the city. But I think she's on the mountain. I've been following her for weeks. She moves very quickly."

"Why follow her though?" Brenna asked.

"A few weeks ago she attacked and killed the daughter of the Lady of the Four Hills. She has employed me to kill the lamia." He shrugged at their puzzled faces. "I was at a loose end. And she's paying me in tear-diamonds."

"Oh, that explains it," Woodsmoke said.

"At the risk of sounding stupid," Beansprout said, "what's a lamia, and what's a tear-diamond?"

"A lamia is a blood-sucking snake that takes the guise of a beautiful lady. They usually feed on the blood of children, but when they're hungry they'll eat anything," Bloodmoon explained. "And tear-diamonds are the most beautiful diamonds anywhere, formed from the tears of Djinn. And as anyone knows, Djinn rarely cry. I have had an advance." He pulled a small leather pouch from around his neck and took out two small tear-shaped diamonds that dazzled, even in the dim light of the tavern.

"But they're blue!" Tom said.

"Not all diamonds are white, and these will fetch me a good price, which is good because I need to buy a sword of pure dragonium." Before they could ask why, he said, "Because that's the only metal known to kill a lamia. And I only know that," he added, "because I thought I'd killed her. And then her head grew back and I had to make a tactical retreat. Fortunately a very nice satyr in the Meet told me the trick. So here I am, in the best place to get a pure dragonium sword. I've spent the morning bargaining. Your turn." And he sipped his beer while Woodsmoke told him of their hunt.

As he listened, Tom compared Bloodmoon to Woodsmoke and decided they were very different. Woodsmoke had a quiet watchfulness about him, but Bloodmoon was all words. And then he found his thoughts drifting to Arthur, and wondered if he'd got a good price for his dragonyx.

When Woodsmoke reached the end of his tale, Bloodmoon said, "So you're travelling with Arturus! And searching for Merlin! You keep interesting company these days."

"You've heard the name?" Tom asked, suddenly paying attention. "Nimue called him that."

"One of Arthur's old names, I believe. The name some of the older fey call him. That or Artaius, The Bear King of Kernow."

"Where's Kernow?" Tom said, even more confused.

"I believe it is the name of an old kingdom in Britain."

Tom thought of the stories he'd read, and the name Arthur had called himself only the other day.

"He called himself the Boar of Cornwall, not bear," Tom said, puzzled.

"I have no idea where the name came from, I just know it exists." Bloodmoon shrugged, giving Tom a wry smile.

"I forgot you had Fahey's ear for tales," Woodsmoke said.

"Does Arthur still carry Excalibur?" Bloodmoon asked.

"Of course."

"And you're staying with Raghnall?"

"Yes, why?"

"I have heard many things about Raghnall. Particularly regarding his collection of ancient magical weapons. Be careful while you stay with him."

"Don't worry, we will," Brenna said. "Arthur should have finished his business today, so hopefully we leave soon."

"Ah! The dragonyx?"

"News does travel quickly here," Woodsmoke said.

"I must go," Bloodmoon said, finishing his drink. "I have a sword to buy and a lamia to track. Safe travels." And after a flurry of handshakes and hugs, he left.

When they arrived at the House of the Beloved late that afternoon, they found Arthur on the balcony with Nimue.

"How did you get on, Arthur?" Tom asked, helping himself to a drink.

"Very well! The dragonyx has gone and instead I am rich. I've kept some money, the rest is in The Lair, as they call their banking house. And it's all thanks to Nimue."

"It was the least I could do." She was sitting on the divan again, her green eyes glinting.

"Making amends for your evil deeds?" Woodsmoke said, flinging himself in a chair.

Nimue glared at him. "You could say that. Or you could say I'm happy to help an old friend."

"Whatever you call it," Arthur said, lowering his voice, "I would have got far less without Nimue. I hate to say it, but I think Raghnall was working with Arshok to give me less money, no doubt for his own cut of the future profits. I'm beginning to hate the man."

"If you've finished business, maybe we should leave sooner rather than later, Arthur," Brenna said. "I don't trust Raghnall."

"No, nor I. But I don't want to upset him either. I suggested we might leave tomorrow and he looked very offended. He wants to show us the weapons room, was quite insistent in fact. Tomorrow he has to attend an important business meeting with the city leaders. He says he can't miss it – something about trade rights with the sylphs. He'll show us his collection when he returns, so I've agreed we'll stay one more day. At first I was hoping to stay longer, but as much as I like the city I do not wish to stay here," he said, gesturing to Raghnall's house. "And I want to see Merlin. I'm worried about him."

"Why can't we see the weapons room tonight?" Brenna asked. She had taken her new knives out and examined them in the light as she spoke.

Nimue laughed dryly, and broke into an impression of Raghnall. "Oh no, tonight I must ensure it is ready for you. I couldn't bear for you to see it other than perfect."

Brenna narrowed her eyes. "Really?"

Nimue's criticism of Raghnall reminded Tom of their conversation the previous night. "Why didn't you want Raghnall to know Arthur has your poppet, Nimue?"

"Because I don't like being too honest with him, Tom." She smiled coyly.

"But what was your old argument about Avalon?" said Tom.

"You do pay attention, don't you?" she said, narrowing her eyes at him. "He doesn't like that Avalon has restricted access. It is a powerful place, and he thinks its powers should be available to all. He's wrong." And with that she sipped her drink and fell quiet.

Realising this was the only answer he would get, Tom turned to Beansprout. "And what about your dragon scale?"

"Raghnall has influence," she said, "so it will be ready tomorrow. We can collect it when I do more shopping." She grinned. "At least we'll have time for that."

They headed back to their rooms. Tom was so tired he dozed for a while on his bed. When he woke the bath was again ready, the water scented and steaming with towels ready at the side. He could easily grow used to this, and wished they were staying longer. But, like the others, he found it hard to feel comfortable with Raghnall. And he wanted to see Merlin again. With the excitement of the past few days, he'd pushed him to the back of his mind, but now he wondered how Merlin would be. Or whether he would even agree to see them at all.

The next morning, while the others headed into the city, Tom and Woodsmoke went to check on the horses. As they crossed the large walled courtyard where the stables were located, Woodsmoke glanced over to an archway, through which they could see a track leading behind the stables and on towards the mountain.

"Interesting. I wonder where that goes?" Woodsmoke murmured.

They found the horses well fed and groomed, although there were no servants in sight.

"At least the horses are being looked after," said Woodsmoke. "But this place is creepier than Enisled. There, there, Farlight," he whispered to his horse as she nudged him. "I think you need some exercise." He started to saddle her.

"Where are you going?" Tom asked.

"I think you mean 'we'. We're going to check out that path. I think Midnight needs a run too," he said, tossing over Tom's saddle.

Tom quickly prepared his horse, fumbling with the straps, and followed Woodsmoke onto the track. He stood awkwardly for a few seconds, conscious of all the windows looking down on him, and wondered who might be watching, before following after Woodsmoke.

"Should we be on this?" Tom said, worried, as they rode behind the house. "We could get into trouble."

"It's just a road, Tom. I'm sure Raghnall won't mind."

Very quickly the road became rutted and muddy, and then there was a tangle of branches blocking the way forward. "It's a dead end," Tom said, frustrated, about to turn around.

"Wait." Woodsmoke slipped off his horse, pushed through the undergrowth and disappeared. For a few seconds Tom waited alone, listening to cracking branches and the call of a bird, and then Woodsmoke was back, grinning broadly.

"It's just a ruse, Tom." He grabbed Farlight's reins and pushed back through the undergrowth.

Tom quickly followed, pulling a reluctant Midnight behind him. For a few minutes he battled through the vegetation, and then he was through to the other side. Ahead of him a smooth, well-maintained road ran through a densely wooded area, snaking away from the house and the city and up the slopes of the mountain.

"I'm pretty sure Raghnall wouldn't like us being here," Tom said, looking around him. The forest pressed in close on both sides, and it was virtually impossible to see through the thick interlocked branches.

"Well we must make sure he doesn't know."

The road rose in a gentle incline until eventually the trees thinned and they could see the city glittering on the valley floor. After a few more minutes the path turned to follow the contours of the mountain, clinging tightly to its side, but before long they came to a halt. The road was again blocked, this time by a massive landslide.

"I think this has been blocked by magic, Tom. It seems to me the path is too well maintained to end here. But there's nothing we can do about it now. We'd better head back."

26 Under Seven Moons

They stood in front of the weapons room, gathered together in anticipation. The room was sealed by a door covered in runes and sigils, and Raghnall stood before it, murmuring incantations. Suddenly a seam appeared down the centre and the large door split into two. It opened with a quiet hiss, swinging back into blackness. Raghnall stepped inside, closely followed by the others.

Immediately a soft low light illuminated the room. It came from seven silvery moons hanging beneath a vaulted ceiling – moons that ranged from a tiny sliver of a crescent, to full and then waxing. The room had been transformed into a forest glade. Objects were displayed around the glade on pedestals, and as Raghnall approached the closest, a broad ray of moonlight illuminated it clearly and writing appeared in the air: *Brionac*. The weapon was a large spear, cradled in a silver hand on top of wooden pedestal, the moonlight glinting off its sharp tip.

"Behold," Raghnall said portentously, "Brionac, the spear of Lugh."

"One of the ancient fey kings of Ireland," Arthur said. "He was myth in my time. How do you have this?"

"I have my ways," Raghnall said.

"Brionac is supposedly impossible to overcome," said Arthur.

"All of the weapons here have true magical properties," Raghnall said. "They may belong to history, but their powers are real."

Woodsmoke stepped forward to look at it closely. "May I?" he said, indicating he wanted to pick it up.

Raghnall hesitated for a second, then said, "Of course."

Woodsmoke reached forward to take the spear as the silver hand released it. He hefted it as if to throw it. "It's perfect," he said.

Arthur had already turned away to the rest of the objects, and the others split up and drifted around the glade. Tom headed to a sword lying lengthways, cradled in two hands on a long pedestal. He grasped the hilt and pulled it from the scabbard. Immediately a deep voice started speaking words he could not understand.

Tom looked around, confused, wondering where the voice was coming from, before realising it was coming from the sword. He lifted the sword to his ear, as if that would help him translate it.

"It is called Orna. It's the sword of King Tethra," said Raghnall from behind him. "Once unsheathed it recounts all its deeds."

"Why can't I understand it?" Tom asked.

"Because it speaks in an old language not used for many years."

Raghnall turned away to where Beansprout stood in front of armour magically suspended, as if over an invisible body. "The armour of the Elven King Sorcha, Wolf Lord of the North," he called. "It repels all blades. None can pierce it."

Tom replaced Orna in its scabbard and joined Brenna, who was picking up a bow. It seemed to be made of the flimsiest material, the wood delicate and the bow string so fine as to be almost invisible.

"Artemis's Bow!" she exclaimed. She turned to Tom. "Do you think all this is real? I wouldn't put it past him to do this just to impress us."

"I don't think the lock would be so elaborate if they weren't real," he replied.

Tom continued to wander around the glade, sometimes losing sight of the others behind the trees. Raghnall's collection contained bows, spears, swords, helmets, rings of enchantment, gemstones, and even a silver saddle. Then he heard Arthur shout, "Raghnall! Is this a joke?"

Arthur stood before a collection of weapons in a clearing. On a large flat rock were a dagger, a helmet, a spear and a shield, and placed within the rock, the blade buried half way, was a sword.

Raghnall joined Arthur, smiling slyly. "No. Not a joke. I thought you'd be pleased?"

"How could I be pleased to see my own weapons displayed? And that!" Arthur pointed at the sword.

"What do you mean, your weapons?" Tom asked, going over. The others joined them, concern on their faces.

It was Nimue who spoke first. "Clarent – The Sword of Peace." She turned to Raghnall, frowning. "What incredibly bad taste, Raghnall."

Raghnall's eyes flashed. "It is a sword of great beauty, whatever it may have done."

"It almost killed me!" Arthur exclaimed angrily.

"What?" Beansprout said.

"Clarent was my ceremonial sword, never meant for combat," Arthur explained. "Morgan stole it and gave it to Mordred. It was the sword he used in the Battle of Camlann."

They fell silent, an air of unease now rising.

"And the other weapons?" Woodsmoke asked.

"Priwen, my shield; Goswhit, my helmet; Carnwennan, my dagger; and Rhongomiant, my spear. Are you planning to return them to me?" Arthur asked angrily.

"No. They are mine now," said Raghnall. "I obtained them lawfully, presuming you dead." He faced Arthur, implacable, his eyes drifting now and again to Excalibur, Arthur's hand now clutching the hilt.

"You knew I wasn't dead, Raghnall. And as I am now standing before you, very much alive, I'd like my weapons back. Or are you wanting to add Excalibur to your collection?" A dangerous icy tone had entered his voice.

"Well, it would enhance my collection," he said, with smile that didn't quite reach his eyes. "Would you like to sell it?"

"No, I would not!" Arthur yelled, pulling Excalibur out of its scabbard.

"A shame then. I had hoped not to do this, you have been such interesting guests." Raghnall made the briefest of gestures and stepped back half a pace. A flash of light enveloped him, just as Arthur swung Excalibur at his head, so swiftly that Tom barely saw it. At the same time, Woodsmoke lifted Brionac and hurled it at Raghnall.

There was a thunk as Raghnall's head hit the floor and rolled to Arthur's feet. His body had disappeared, along with Brionac.

A sharp intake of breath was followed by a stunned silence as everybody looked at Raghnall's head and then at Arthur. Within seconds the forest glade and the seven moons began to fade, and through the vanishing illusion they saw the walls start to appear.

Nimue was the first to speak, looking quizzically at Arthur. "I'm not sure that was a good idea."

"I think it was. He was about to do something treacherous, and I've had enough of him. Woodsmoke obviously agreed. I will not be threatened by a pompous idiot, who for the second time today has tried to steal from me."

They stood in a circle and, still dumbfounded, stared at Arthur while Raghnall's grinning rictus stared up at them. Tom felt a wave of nausea wash over him. Killing a dragon was one thing, but this ... He looked at Beansprout and was relieved to find she looked as bad as he felt.

"Yes, but Arthur," Nimue continued, "Raghnall was the only one keeping the dragons away from the city."

Arthur stuttered as understanding dawned. "O-Oh, I'd forgotten that ..."

"How long have we got?" Woodsmoke asked, also looking a little sheepish.

"I have no idea, but it won't be long. Arthur, I think it's time you unbound my poppet."

"Can you continue the spell?" Beansprout asked.

"I can't continue it. With his death the spell has broken. But I can make a new one. I think."

"You *think*?" Woodsmoke said.

"As he boasted, it is a powerful spell, and I don't know it."

Arthur thrust Excalibur at Tom and started searching his pockets furiously. "I thought I'd put it in my inside pocket." His earlier composure had disappeared.

"I'll go and see what's happening." Brenna swiftly changed form and flew out of the room.

"They can't possibly be here already!" Tom said, desperately hoping he was right. How could they fight half a dozen dragons or more?

"Arthur?" pressed Nimue.

"I've got it!" He produced the poppet with a flourish and thrust it at Nimue. "Here, do whatever you have to!"

As it touched her hands it immediately sizzled. Nimue cursed and dropped the poppet on to the floor. "Nerian didn't trust me to even hold it! You will have to do it, Arthur."

Arthur snatched it up, annoyed. "What do I do?"

"Unwind the cord that wraps it. Gently."

He hesitated for a second and looked at her questioningly.

"You can trust me, Arthur. And besides, what choice do you have?"

"That's what worries me," he said.

In a few seconds the cord came free, and Nimue took it from him. She clicked her fingers and the cord turned to ash. "Excellent. Now we have to find where Raghnall performed the spell."

"Why does that matter?" Beansprout asked.

"Because you can guarantee that wherever he did it will be the best place."

"We'd better start looking then," Arthur said. He retrieved Excalibur from Tom and said to Woodsmoke, "Grab weapons! Anything you think will be useful. I will take what is rightfully mine." He turned and put his dagger in his belt, his shield over his arm, his helmet on his head, and then grabbed his spear.

Tom looked at him, slightly stunned.

"What's the matter, Tom?"

"You look very ..." he struggled for words, "kingly, I suppose. You don't want the sword then?"

"No," he said, narrowing his eyes at Clarent. "That can stay here. But I saw something for you, Tom. He strode across to another sword. "Galatine."

"What?" Tom asked, confused.

"Take it. It was Sir Gawain's sword, given to him by Vivian." He smiled. "It is the sister sword to Excalibur, and Gawain was my nephew, and one of my bravest and most loyal knights. He also died because of Mordred."

"Arthur, I can't take it," Tom stuttered, overawed as another piece of the ancient past appeared before him.

"Yes you can. You're my family and I want you to have it."

Tom gazed at Galatine, speechless. "Tom, take it. We haven't got all day," Arthur said softly.

Tom felt a sudden tightness in his chest that had nothing to do with dragons, and he took the sword from Arthur, his arms dropping beneath its weight. "Thank you."

"And for you–" Woodsmoke hurried over to Beansprout, carrying a bow. "The Fail-not. Tristan's bow, I believe. This should help your aim."

Beansprout took the bow from Woodsmoke. "Thanks, but who's Tristan?"

"Another of my contemporaries," Arthur said. "I think Raghnall had a slight obsession with me. Something else I must discuss with Vivian."

As he finished speaking, Brenna flew into the room.

"How bad is it?" Nimue asked.

"At the moment, nothing seems to be happening. I can't see any dragons, but it won't be long before they realise they can access the city. And once the dragons attack, Magen and the guard will realise something has happened to the spell. And to Magen's father."

Arthur groaned. "I'd forgotten about Magen too."

"I've found the rest of Raghnall's body," Brenna continued. "He didn't go far – just outside the doors. Brionac is embedded in his chest. And to make matters worse, it will be dark soon."

"So what are we going to do about leaving?" Woodsmoke asked. "We're running out of time. If we don't leave soon we could be stuck here for days, if the pass is blocked by dragons. Or if they attack the city. Unless we move tonight." He quickly explained about the route that seemed to lead up higher over the mountain, bypassing the lower road. "And now Raghnall is dead, whatever magic was blocking his private road will have gone."

"*If* it was magic," Tom said.

"But we can't abandon the city," Brenna said. "Everyone will die!"

"I'm not suggesting we abandon it," Woodsmoke said. "You can help Nimue start the spell. If we can only protect the city, that's better than nothing. The dragons can squat on the pass all they want as long as the city is safe."

"I agree," Nimue said. "As long as I *can* protect the city. So you need to go, quickly, before the mountains are full of dragons. Unless of course you want to stay, Arthur?"

Arthur looked at the floor and then at Nimue. "I need to see Merlin. But Woodsmoke's right. If we miss our chance today, we may be stuck here for days. Or even weeks. But," he added, "I don't want to see the city fall and people die. Or you. Will you be all right if we go?"

"I'm sure I can do the spell," she reassured him, "but I need to find where Raghnall performed it."

"I noticed something on the flat roof," Brenna said. "There seemed to be some kind of apparatus up there, and markings I couldn't decipher."

"That must be it," Nimue said, and she whirled around and ran for the door.

"I'll lead the way," Brenna said, and returning to bird form she flew ahead. Beansprout ran after her, Fail-not under her arm.

Arthur turned to Woodsmoke and Tom. "I suppose that leaves us with saddling the horses."

27 Flight from the Hollow

Tom hurriedly finished packing. Hoisting the pack over his shoulder, he took a last long glance at the bed. He would miss that. He then headed to Beansprout's room and packed up her gear, hoping he hadn't missed anything.

Woodsmoke had already grabbed his own bags, and Brenna's, and had gone to saddle the horses with Arthur. Tom wandered to the window and looked out over the city below. It shone with lights, and Tom wondered if the fey had any idea that the spell had gone. Should they warn them? And if so, how? He looked up and thought he could just make out movement. A darker blackness on the night sky. Was that a dragon?

A movement closer to the house caught his eye. Magen and several dragon guards were heading towards them. He needed to warn the others.

Swinging a pack around each shoulder he headed onto the shadowy landing, partially lit from the city lights. The house felt eerily quiet. Just before he reached the back stairs, a figure stepped out of the shadows in front of him. He stopped and pulled Galatine free of its scabbard as the servant's voice spoke out of the darkness. "What have you done to Raghnall?"

"I haven't done anything!"

Tom's breath was knocked out of him as the servant jumped on him, wrestling him to the ground. Tom's right arm, holding Galatine, was pinned on the floor as the fey straddled his chest, his face inches from Tom's.

"Is he dead?" the servant said, his voice a low hiss.

Gripping the sword tightly, Tom said, "Yes. Arthur killed him. But he was trying to–"

"Do you know what you've done?" the servant howled, spittle flying into Tom's face. "You have killed us all! The dragons are coming!"

The pale light showed the servant's face twisted in anger, his eyes as black as coal.

"But Nimue is–" Tom gasped. But he couldn't finish because the servant's strong hands closed around his throat and squeezed tightly.

Rather than release his sword, Tom desperately tried to get his left hand under the servant's, but he was gripping so tightly it was impossible. Instinctively he did the next best thing and punched him hard, again and again in the side of his head. The servant sprawled across the floor, and Tom rolled awkwardly, impeded by the packs on his shoulders. Still unable to free his right arm, Tom raised his right knee as high as he could and kicked the servant hard in the chest, pulling his sword free. Before Tom could get to his feet the servant launched himself again and Tom raised Galatine and jabbed forward, immediately finding flesh as the momentum of the servant pushed him down the blade, pinning Tom to the ground again.

For a few seconds Tom could hear nothing except the gurgle of blood in the servant's throat, and then he fell silent, his body limp and heavy. Tom wriggled and pushed until he could lever the servant off him, and then dragged himself to his feet.

He had killed someone. Again. Like when he was helping Arthur back in Aeriken. But, he reminded himself, the servant had been trying to kill him. He shook himself and bending down, wiped the blade clean of blood on the servant's clothes. He then ran down the stairs to the courtyard.

Tom found Arthur and Woodsmoke in the stables, talking quietly in the lamplight.

"A servant just attacked me," he announced, as he stepped through the door.

"What?" Woodsmoke pulled Tom into the light. "Are you all right?" He looked him up and down, searching for wounds.

"I'm fine, apart from a sore throat." He showed them his bruised neck. "But I've killed him."

"What happened?" Arthur asked.

"He ambushed me in the corridor. He was furious that Raghnall was dead, and then announced the dragons were coming. Like I didn't know!"

A proud look crossed Arthur's face. "Well done, Tom. I knew your fighting skills were improving."

Tom hadn't the heart to tell him it was more by accident than design. "Arthur, I think a dragon is already overhead, and Magen and the Dragon Guards are close. They're coming here."

"Just what I need," grumbled Arthur. "How many guards?"

Tom shrugged. "Five or six."

"Magen wasn't fond of his father," Woodsmoke reminded Arthur.

"No, but he was still his father. Tom, go and tell Beansprout and

Brenna to get a move on. Woodsmoke, let's meet Magen at the gates to the house."

Nimue and the others were on a large flat area of the roof, set in the middle of several different-sized domes. It had taken Tom a few minutes to find them in the vast space, especially as he had to navigate around what appeared to be very large crossbows, aiming into the skies.

Nimue was pacing around a large intricate diagram inlaid on the roof in marble, gold and gems. Three small braziers flickering with firelight faintly illuminated the space. Beansprout watched Nimue, and Brenna leant against one of the giant crossbows, watching the skies.

Now that Tom was on the roof, it was much easier to see the dragon circling overhead.

"How long's that been there?" he asked Brenna.

"It arrived just after we got up here. And," she turned and pointed, "there's another one. Any minute now they'll realise they can reach the city."

"Should we try and shoot it?" He nodded at the crossbow.

"I *really* don't want to draw attention to ourselves."

"Oh. Yes. You're probably right." He turned to Beansprout. "Are you nearly ready? Arthur said we have to go."

"No! We're not even close," Beansprout shot back impatiently. "We need to work out what this diagram means."

"I can understand most of it," Nimue said. "Maybe we could ask the servant, he must know." She looked up briefly. "Tom, can you go and find him?"

Tom swallowed. "Unfortunately not. He's dead."

"How?" Beansprout asked.

"He attacked me and I accidentally killed him."

Beansprout fell silent and looked at him with an expression that made him feel very uncomfortable, but Nimue glanced up once more towards the dragons and went back to pacing around the circle.

"Well in that case let's hope I can work it out without him," Nimue said.

Tom turned back to Beansprout. "So, are you coming?"

"Are you insane? You heard Nimue. The spell isn't done yet!"

"But Arthur said–"

"I don't care what Arthur said. We're not ready!"

"We can't leave Nimue alone, Tom," Brenna agreed.

Before Tom had a chance to respond, Nimue shouted, "Yes! Oh that's clever." She looked up to find the others looking at her expectantly. "It *is* clever. But I don't think I can do it alone. Not yet, anyway. And it's going to take a while."

"What do you mean?" Tom asked, confused.

"It's complicated. I'll need help."

"I'll stay," Beansprout said immediately.

"So will I," Brenna added.

Now Tom was even more confused. "What do you mean, you'll stay."

Beansprout looked at him as if he was child, and repeated slowly, "I will stay to help Nimue. So will Brenna. Do you understand?"

"Thank you for your sarcasm, Beansprout," Tom said, eyes narrowing. "So, you're not coming? At all? I thought you wanted to meet Merlin?"

"This is more important than Merlin."

"That's if you want a city to come back to," Nimue said. "And Tom, tell Arthur I will be able to protect the passes eventually, but not for the next few days."

Tom pulled Beansprout aside. "Are you sure you want to do this?" He nodded at Nimue. "Do you trust her?"

"Yes. Completely." Beansprout hugged him. "Now go, Tom. Find Merlin, but be safe. And tell Arthur and Woodsmoke not to worry." She turned back to Nimue. "Tell me what you want me to do."

Half an hour later, Tom, Woodsmoke and Arthur were on Raghnall's path heading higher on the mountain. It had been difficult for Tom to persuade them to leave, but finally they had set off.

"Are you sure they want to stay, Tom?" Woodsmoke had asked, puzzled. "I don't trust Nimue."

"Well *they* do. And she needs them. And we need Nimue, so …" He'd shrugged.

Arthur had headed into the house, but Tom had stopped him at the back door, shouting, "Arthur, do you want to find Merlin or not? We can't do both."

Arthur had returned to his horse, saying, "I feel I'm abandoning them."

"They're all very capable Arthur," Woodsmoke said. "We have to respect their decision. Well, I have to, I live with two of them," he'd added with a wry grin.

"If anything happens to them ..." Arthur said.

"Then we'll all be to blame," Tom answered. "How was Magen?"

"Furious. But he thought better of arguing and went up on the city walls with the rest of his guards. I'm not sure I'll be welcomed back to the city, but–" Arthur shrugged and sighed. "We'd better go."

They'd headed up the path behind Raghnall's house and found that Woodsmoke was right. The landslide had disappeared and the way was clear. But it was now pitch black and the path ahead was almost invisible.

"I'll lead," Arthur said dismounting. "We'll take it slowly."

"Arthur, this seems like suicide," Tom said, as loose rock slipped beneath his feet and he tried to steady himself against Midnight. It was surprising how much he'd got used to his horse, he thought, as he struggled up the hill. She'd become a reassuring presence.

"Just keep going, Tom," Woodsmoke said from behind him. "I can't see Raghnall risking his life on a poorly made path, it must be pretty safe."

"In the light, maybe," Tom muttered.

After a short while they crested a ridge and looked back to see the city, and the House of the Beloved, below them in the hollow of the mountain. Magen must have warned the fey of imminent attack – either that or they had seen the dragons, because half the city was now in darkness and they could just make out the faint glow of the braziers on the roof of Raghnall's house. The city walls were well lit with torches, and the firelight glinted on the crossbows that sat atop the wall.

Suddenly, one of the dragons dived straight at the city, but before it could get close a flurry of huge arrows was released and the dragon withdrew with a roar, belching flames onto the roof of one of the highest buildings. It immediately burst into flames which, within seconds, were reaching high into the night sky.

"The city's burning!" Tom exclaimed.

"Not yet, Tom," Woodsmoke said, trying to reassure him. "I'm sure they must have plans for this."

"I knew we shouldn't have left," Arthur said.

"But we couldn't have stopped this," Woodsmoke said. "Come on, we have to get as far as we can by daybreak. At least the dragons will be preoccupied. Too preoccupied to hear your sword, I hope, Arthur, because now Raghnall's dead the spell he put on the scabbard is gone."

A skittering of rocks caused them to spin away from the city back towards the high pass.

"What was that?" Tom asked, his right hand moving to Galatine.

They stood listening for a few seconds, but heard nothing else.

"Just rock fall," Arthur said. "Certainly not a dragon."

They moved slowly over the rock-strewn ground, lit faintly by a half moon above them. The path here was easier to follow and they picked up their pace, all the time moving higher and higher up the mountain, until the path met another and they found themselves on the broad main pass. They heaved a sigh of relief, but it was short lived. Something reared up beneath Farlight, and Woodsmoke fell from his horse, crashing to the ground. Within seconds a large writhing serpent was upon him, and with a scream of terror, Farlight raced away.

Tom and Arthur dropped to the ground, weapons drawn, and ran across to Woodsmoke, only then realising that the snake had the head and body of a woman. It was the lamia that Bloodmoon had been tracking. She snapped and bit at Woodsmoke's face, trying to sink her long teeth into his neck, her hands pushing his shoulders against the ground. His left arm was pinned against his body, but with his right hand he pushed her head back, keeping it inches from his own. Her strong muscular body continued to wrap tightly around his chest, and Woodsmoke struggled for breath as her teeth inched nearer and nearer.

Scared of using their swords in case they stabbed Woodsmoke, Arthur and Tom used their combined strength to pull the serpent off him, throwing her across the ground. She reared up and lunged at Arthur. He swung Excalibur, but she reared back before striking again.

Woodsmoke struggled to his feet, clutching his ribs, as Tom and Arthur advanced on the lamia. Her tail flicked out beneath Tom's feet and he stumbled backwards, rolling to his feet again. She was frighteningly quick, and she leapt on Arthur, wrapping her tail around his legs and pinning him to the ground.

Just as Tom was thinking he could never pull her from Arthur on his own, another figure ran to his side. Bloodmoon. "Tom!" he yelled. "Pull her head back. Just grab her hair."

Tom got as close as he could, stepping across Arthur's and the lamia's prone bodies, and grabbed a handful of her hair, pulling her head up with all his strength.

"Arthur, keep your head down!" Bloodmoon yelled, and he stood behind Arthur, his sword ready to strike. "Tom, pull higher!"

The lamia was incredibly strong, but as she realised what was happening she loosened her grip on Arthur, allowing Tom to pull her head high above Arthur's chest. Without hesitating, Bloodmoon attacked, his sword passing within inches of Tom's chest, swiping her head off and leaving it swinging from Tom's hands. Hot blood spat from her neck, and her body slumped across Arthur's, convulsing in its death throes.

Tom yelled in horror and threw her head away, watching it roll across the ground, the jaw wide and the long teeth glinting.

"Can somebody get this thing off me?" Arthur groaned, and he pushed against the lamia's body. Bloodmoon and Tom pulled the still-twitching body off Arthur and then stood trying to catch their breath.

Woodsmoke had sank to the floor again, and Arthur lay breathing heavily, covered in blood. Bloodmoon grinned at Tom. "I timed that well!"

"You call that good timing? Five minutes earlier would have been better."

"Not as much fun, though," Bloodmoon said, striding over and picking up the lamia's head. He examined it in the moonlight, saying, "I lost her earlier, but only briefly. She's been very tricky."

"So now you can claim your reward, cousin," Woodsmoke said. "You should give us a share. I think she's broken my ribs."

Bloodmoon laughed. "Good try, but I don't think so." He strode across to his pack and, pulling a large sack free, lowered the Lamia's head into it. "I'll take this with me for proof. And now I think it's time for a drink." He took a large bottle from his bag, pulled the cork out with his teeth and drank deeply. "Anyone else?"

Three hands shot out as, in unison, they said, "Yes please."

28 The House of Smoke and Glass

They reached the pass into the Sky Meadows at dawn. It was an unassuming break in the rock, and on the other side an expanse of fields stretched ahead of them, encompassed by a ring of rock. Drifts of mist rose from the ground, mingling with the scent of wild flowers and grass.

High above them was a city in the air, its buildings shimmering in the pale dawn light, and in the centre of the meadows was a beam of light leading to the city above. The sound of water drew them to their left, and they found a stream running into a shallow pool.

"Thank the gods," Arthur said. "I stink of lamia blood."

"Is it worse than dragon blood?" Woodsmoke asked.

"Actually I think it is. There's more of it on me, anyway." And he was right. The entire front of his body was covered in blood that was now drying in thick crusty clots. It was even in his hair.

Tom glanced down at his shirt where a broad splatter of blood from the lamia's beheading had landed across his chest. "The sylphs will wonder what's going on if we turn up like this. Honestly, Arthur. Two beheadings in one day." He tried to push the memory of killing the servant to the back of his mind.

"I am not responsible for the second one!" Arthur exclaimed.

"Three beheadings in a week!" Woodsmoke reminded them. "You are responsible for the dragon, though, Arthur."

Throwing off their clothes they waded into the pool, washing away the blood and dust.

"Does anyone need to rest?" Arthur asked.

"No, let's just get on with it," Woodsmoke said, wincing as he explored his bruised ribs. "But I should warn you, if the sylphs choose to attack, we will have no chance."

"Why not?" Tom asked.

"They're a warrior race, much stronger than we are, and our weapons will be of little use against them. Even Excalibur. There's a reason the other realms let them be."

With Woodsmoke's warning ringing in their ears, they tied the horses up next to the pool and set off on foot, striding through the waist-high grasses. It reminded Tom of the meadows outside Finnlugh's Under-Palace.

The Sky Meadows seemed eerily devoid of life. There were no other fey or sylphs, and they crossed in silence. Soon they reached the beam of light which, close up, was much larger than Tom expected.

"What are we supposed to do now?" he asked.

"There's only one way to find out," Arthur said, and stepped into it.

"Arthur, wait," Woodsmoke said.

But he'd gone, disappearing in a split second.

"Where's he gone?" Tom asked, alarmed.

Woodsmoke sighed. "Up there, I hope. Come on, let's follow, and hope it's not going to kill us."

They stepped through together, and instantly Tom felt a sensation similar to that he'd experienced in the portals, although it was over more quickly. The feeling had barely registered before he found himself on a large platform facing a walled city. Arthur and Woodsmoke stood next to him.

Tom looked down and let out an involuntary yelp. "I can see through the floor!"

Far below were the Sky Meadows, a small patch of green amongst the mountain ridges. He clutched his stomach. "I feel sick. Is the floor safe?" he asked, tentatively stretching out a toe.

Woodsmoke took a few paces and looked back at Tom, grinning. "I think we're good, Tom."

"So this is the Realm of Air," Arthur said, looking impressed.

The city was a white-walled vision. It stretched ahead of them, the curve of its walls disappearing into drifting clouds at either side. But more impressive was its height. A multitude of buildings soared high above them, disappearing into the clouds. Every now and then the clouds drifted away, and Tom could see towers glittering in rays of sunshine.

They headed to the city gates and were met by a sylph carrying a long silver spear. He was far taller than them, and his body-length wings were tucked behind him. Unnervingly he was dressed for combat, wearing a breastplate and armguards, and he had the hardened face of the battle-ready. He was pale and blonde, and Tom felt he was in the presence of an angel.

"Welcome to the Realm of Air. What do you seek here?"

"We seek Merlin," Arthur said. "We believe he was brought here."

"And you are?"

Arthur introduced them all. "We were with him at Ceridwen's Cauldron."

The sylph looked at them thoughtfully. "Yes, we who guard the city have been warned to expect you."

"Warned?" Arthur asked cautiously. "We are his friends. We helped resurrect him. Can you take us to him?"

"No. You are to go to Adalyn, Commander of the City Guard. She wishes to see you first. Follow me."

He led them up a series of stairs built into the walls, until finally they emerged into a circular tower looking out across the city. The broad windows were open and a chill breeze drifted into the room. Seated at a central table was an older white-haired sylph. She lifted her head from the papers in front of her as they entered, and Tom was shocked to see a large scar that began on her right cheek and continued across where her right eye should have been. It was rare to see disfigurement in the fey.

"Adalyn. Merlin's companions from the Cauldron are here."

She sighed. "So you have come. We weren't sure you would." She turned to the sylph. "You may go."

"Why wouldn't I?" Arthur asked, bristling with annoyance as the door shut behind them. "My reunion with Merlin was interrupted. I thought I'd try again."

She stood up, towering over all of them. "I do not apologise for rescuing Merlin when he summoned us. He felt vulnerable with the witch Nimue in your company."

"Nimue was not with us," Arthur retorted angrily.

Adalyn held her hand up to stop Arthur. "I do not accuse you of betraying him," she said softly. "All those who are twice born feel weak on awakening. Her presence was an unpleasant reminder of his imprisonment."

Tom took a deep breath of relief as the tension in the room seemed to dissipate, and sensed Arthur also taking a moment to gather himself.

"So we can see him?" he continued. "We have travelled a long way."

"And what is your intent?" she asked, moving around the table. They all had to look up to meet her gaze.

"Just to see him. I want to make sure he is all right, and then we leave. That's all."

"You are?"

"Arthur, King of the Britons. Merlin's very old friend," he added, a little defiantly.

"Yes, of course." She smiled, looking far less severe. "He has talked of you recently. And where is the witch now?"

They shuffled and looked uncomfortable again as Arthur answered, "In Dragons' Hollow, defending the city and rebuilding the spell."

Adalyn looked confused. "Why does she need to rebuild the spell?"

"Because Raghnall has died, and therefore the spell has ceased to work," Arthur said vaguely.

Arthur looked the most uncomfortable Tom had ever seen him. Icy fingers were clutching his own stomach, for the same reason, he was sure. How well did the sylphs get on with Raghnall? Would they be upset at his death? And how much trouble would they be in if they knew Arthur had killed him?

But all Adalyn said was, "So the passage to the Sky Meadows may close again." She shrugged. "It does not concern us. I shall escort you to Merlin's house."

They followed her to the top of the city walls, the winds up here strong and cold, Tom sensing her shrug of indifference was not quite what it seemed.

"Merlin's house is on the edge of the city, where there are roads. For those without wings, the inner city is impossible to access."

They looked over to where towers pinnacled into the sky and the sylphs flew, their wings catching the light. Tom couldn't see a single road or staircase.

Adalyn led them down the length of the wall to where a bridge, which seemed to made of gossamer-thin glass, spanned the drop below. Crossing it, they came to a tower of smoky white glass. She led them up another spiral staircase until they reached an arched doorway.

"I'll leave you here," she said. "I presume you can make your own way back." Without waiting for an answer, she went over to an archway in the wall and stepped out, expanding her wings as she dropped, before soaring not to the city walls, Tom noticed, but over them to the Sky Meadows below.

Arthur was already knocking on the door, but Tom looked at Woodsmoke. "Did you see that?"

"No, what?"

"She flew down to the Sky Meadows. I think we're in trouble."

Before he could explain further, the door flew open and an irate Merlin stood before them. "Why are you disturbing me?" He fell silent as he registered who they were, and then said in shock, "Arthur, I didn't think you'd come." He stepped forward and grabbed him tightly.

Merlin ushered them into his room, and Tom immediately noticed its resemblance to the tower in the spell. It was full of tables and books, rocks, herbs, and gemstones, and on the far side was a large messy bed. But this room was much bigger, and its walls and ceiling were made of smoky glass that dimmed the dazzling light from outside, casting strange shadows in the room.

Merlin was as Tom remembered him. His hair was long, grey and tangled, and his beard grew thick and strong, halfway down his chest. But now his face was full of life and vigour, and he seemed none the worse for his long imprisonment and death.

He turned to Tom and Woodsmoke. "And who are these?" he asked.

"Woodsmoke is a good friend from the Realm of Earth," Arthur said, squeezing Woodsmoke's shoulder. Woodsmoke nodded and shook Merlin's hand, and Tom felt relieved that his anger with Arthur seemed long forgotten.

Then Arthur turned to Tom. "And Tom is a long-distance descendant of mine. He woke me from my long sleep. I'm sure you remember that bargain, Merlin?"

Merlin's piercing blue eyes fixed on Tom like a bird of prey, and Tom almost stuttered as he said hello.

"It seems Tom has a knack for breaking long sleeps," Arthur added. "He helped break Nimue's spell, too."

"I really didn't," Tom repeated, for what felt like the millionth time. "Herne broke the spell, not me."

"But you helped! The shaman said so," Arthur insisted.

"Herne was involved? How?" Merlin asked.

"The Cervini summoned him."

"Herne," Merlin repeated, "and the Cervini. Names I have not heard in a long time. The Cervini were there when Nimue's spell was broken?"

Arthur nodded. For a few seconds, Merlin was lost in thought, then he turned to Tom. "And how did you help?"

"I used your spell books, actually." He shrugged. "I was desperate."

"And Vivian still lives? She summoned you here to wake Arthur?"

"Sort of, in a very indirect way," Tom said, remembering how he'd arrived in the Other.

Merlin took a deep breath. "And Nimue, where is she now?"

"In Dragon's Hollow. She will not harm you further, Merlin," Arthur reassured him.

"I do not fear Nimue – except for those few seconds when I awoke. I was so confused," he said. "So much noise, so much light. It was too much. I cast the first spell I could think of to take me to the securest place I knew." He gestured around him. "As for Nimue, everything she did, I let her do. Even while I was teaching her the spell, I knew she would turn it against me. I almost welcomed it." His eyes lost their intensity for a moment as he stared back into the past.

"Do you remember it all? The imprisonment, I mean?" Tom asked.

"It was like a beautiful dream," Merlin said softly.

"Come," Arthur insisted, "I want to hear about everything that's happened."

They sat before the fireplace, and while they talked Tom drifted over to the smoked glass walls, peering through to the city beyond. Of all the places he'd been so far, this felt the most alien. The sylphs were very different to the other fey, both in appearance and demeanour. Their appearance at the Cauldron had been swift, aggressive and unnerving. That night they had seemed so pale they shimmered, and there had been other creatures with them, things with sharp teeth and clawed fingers. Where were they? Now he was here he had a feeling they shouldn't have come.

Woodsmoke joined him. "Why do you think we're in trouble, Tom?"

"Arthur killed Raghnall," Tom said quietly. "What if this breaks some sort of deal they had with him? You said it yourself, they are a warrior race. Warriors need weapons. What better place to get them than from the Hollow?"

Woodsmoke looked thoughtful. "Didn't Raghnall say the meeting he was going to was something to do with trade agreements with the sylphs? Trade with them would be very lucrative, even if the sylphs got their weapons for better prices than everyone else."

"So if the city falls, the sylphs' main source of weapons will be gone. They'll be very angry," Tom said.

"But now Nimue is the key to protecting the city, and Arthur is surely protected by Merlin."

They talked quietly for a while, discussing the possibilities, and then Merlin called them over. "Come, you must join us."

Merlin had placed food and drink on the table in front of the fire, and

Tom realised he hadn't eaten for hours.

"If you're sure we aren't interrupting you," Tom said, lowering himself into a chair and reaching for a glass.

They talked for hours, Merlin asking them all sorts of questions about the other realms and the other Earth. They were finally interrupted when long shadows flashed across the room, and then the door flew open.

Merlin stood. "What's going on, Adalyn?" he asked, as she stepped into the room with three sylphs behind her.

"Arthur and Woodsmoke, you are under arrest for the murder of Raghnall, Sorcerer of Dragon's Hollow. Tom, you are arrested for the death of Grindan, Raghnall's servant."

Tom and Woodsmoke sat momentarily stunned, while Arthur leapt to his feet and unsheathed Excalibur. But Merlin stepped in front of him, his face thunderous. "How dare you arrest Arthur! And here, in my home!"

Adalyn stepped forward, her face rigid with anger. "Raghnall is dead, Merlin. Killed by Arthur."

Arthur stepped round Merlin, equally furious. "Because he was trying to kill all of us! For this," he said, brandishing Excalibur. "Do you think I would stand there and let him?"

Adalyn briefly looked at Excalibur, then said icily, "And Nimue stands in his place to protect the city! It seems you have divided loyalties, Arthur. She is currently under guard while she completes the spell, and then she will come here to answer to us. In the meantime you will be locked away until the trial."

29 Tower of Winds

"You are making a mistake Adalyn. You don't need to lock them up, let them stay here while you investigate," Merlin said.

"So that you can engineer their escape? I don't think so."

"Then don't make it worse by using the tower in the city. I would like to visit them; they are entitled to support. Or are you so eager for a conviction that you don't respect your own laws any more?" he said scornfully.

"How quickly you insult us, Merlin," Adalyn sneered. "Do not presume too much on our hospitality. Whilst some are happy to have you returned to us, there are others for whom you are only a memory and a story. Since then many new alliances have been forged which surpass your importance to the Realm of Air."

"See it as a request from an old man who pleads for his friends," he said, clearly trying to control his temper. "If I can remind you, I am here because they rescued me. That deserves some leniency, surely. I think Galen would see it that way."

She narrowed her eyes at the mention of that name. "Use the Tower of Winds," she said to those behind her.

"And I will speak to the city elders," Merlin said. He turned to Arthur. "Trust me, Arthur, I will get you out of this. Have patience." He pressed Arthur's hand.

Woodsmoke nodded in agreement, and Arthur reluctantly sheathed Excalibur. Woodsmoke then said quietly to Tom, "This is not the time to pick a fight, Tom. Our chance will come."

They were unceremoniously escorted to a high tower at a place far along the city walls, and an hour later they sat looking out over clouds. Their prison was a series of small rooms with hard beds, plain chairs and one big table. On their way to the top floor they had passed at least five other levels with secure doors. But all the doors stood wide, and the prison tower was clearly empty except for them.

"What now?" Tom asked when they were alone.

"We wait," Arthur said. "We'll see what Merlin can do, but if he doesn't succeed …" he shrugged, "we may have to fight our way out."

"I wonder if Brenna and Beansprout will be arrested," Woodsmoke said.

"They haven't done anything. I'm more worried about Nimue and what she may do," Arthur said.

Tom was thoughtful. "Nimue said she always liked to be underestimated. I think that will work in our favour."

Night was falling when they were disturbed by a large black bird rapping its beak on the windows.

Woodsmoke grinned. "Brenna!" He opened the window and she flew in and changed form, scanning the room.

"So you couldn't go five minutes without getting into trouble!" she said, exasperated.

"We didn't do anything! Except kill Raghnall and his servant," Arthur said sheepishly. "I must admit I didn't consider this might happen."

"It took some time to track you down. I checked out the highest, most-isolated towers. There's a lot of them."

"What's happening in Dragon's Hollow?" Woodsmoke asked. "Has Nimue worked the spell?"

"Not quite. The sylphs' arrival has delayed things. As soon as they arrived I knew we were in trouble. They searched the house and interrogated us. I thought they were going to arrest all of us," she said, looking tired and frustrated. "We tried to explain what had happened but they didn't want explanations. They were going to arrest Nimue as soon as they arrived, but then realised that would be incredibly stupid. They were attacked by dragons as they flew in."

"Is the city burning?" Tom asked. "We saw the dragon attack from the ridge."

"A couple of buildings were partially destroyed, but some of the fey have magic strong enough to slow fire." She sighed. "But they keep attacking. Only the dragon guard and the crossbows are slowing them down. They're ripping away all the gold and jewels from the highest buildings. And with each success they grow bolder."

"Is Beansprout all right?" Arthur asked. "Have they threatened to arrest her?"

"No they haven't – or me. She's helping Nimue, and is doing very well.

She seems quite interested in magic."

Tom wondered whether to say anything about their previous argument, but decided not to. Beansprout might be right about Nimue. He did think of something else though. "Do you think Nimue might resist arrest, like she did with the Cervini?"

"Oh no. In fact she's looking forward to coming here. I think she has a plan."

Brenna stayed with them a while longer before swooping back to the Hollow, promising to return with more news.

Their next visitor was Merlin, who arrived breathless and grumpy.

"Galen is not as sympathetic as I thought. He insists you be tried before the high court. All of you."

"Who is this Galen?" Arthur asked.

"A very old friend. One of the few who was alive in my time. He sits at the head of the Council of Judgement. There are six of them, and the others are younger. They don't know me at all. Galen is under pressure to serve justice. There aren't any kings, queens, princes or princesses here. The Council rules on everything and their power is absolute."

"And what could the consequences be?" Woodsmoke asked, his usual relaxed demeanour replaced with an alert watchfulness.

"A guilty charge could be anything from banishment or imprisonment to death."

"Death?" Tom said, alarmed. "Don't we get a lawyer or something?" he asked, thinking of how justice worked at home.

"I have no idea what one of those is, Tom," Merlin said, "so no. Friends may plead on your behalf, but that's all. However," he added, in an effort to reassure them, "I am one of the most powerful wizards ever, and I am pleased to say that after my long period of imprisonment my powers remain as strong as ever. That said, I cannot take on the entire Realm of Air. Therefore, if things go badly in court, I will ensure you get away, but you'd be fugitives. Forever. We *must* resolve this legally, with no repercussions."

"And when will we be seen?" Arthur asked. He looked pale, but his voice held a steely determination.

"The day after tomorrow, at dawn, at the Palace of Reckoning, in front of the seven who sit on the Reckoning Panel."

"So soon!" Tom said, not sure if this was a good thing or not.

"The issue is not just about you, it's also about the spell and the repercussions. They want to settle this quickly. It's a public trial, so others will be there." He paused and sighed softly. "I must confess, I think my long imprisonment has addled my brain a little." Merlin rested his gaze on Arthur. "I had almost forgotten about the dragon wars, it was so long ago."

"The dragon wars?" Tom asked, intrigued.

Woodsmoke nodded. "That *was* a long time ago, even in our long lifetimes."

"For years," Merlin explained, "the Realm of Air waged an intermittent, long and bloody war with the dragons. At first, Dragon Skin Mountain was home to only a handful of dragons. Most of them lived in the deserts of the Djinn – the Realm of Fire. But as the Djinn claimed more land, the dragons came here, drawn to the rich reserves of the mountain, and they ravaged the lands and attacked the sylphs. Until Raghnall came along to contain them. His spell allowed access to the dragon gold, the small village grew into the city it is now, and he gave peace to the sylphs. Raghnall's death has far-reaching consequences."

"Raghnall must have been really old!" Tom said, trying to work it out.

"Very old. I met him once, briefly. I never liked him so avoided him after that."

"And his spell extended here?" Tom tried to get his head around the size of the spell Raghnall had made.

"The dragons could attack again; the sylphs would be at war," Arthur said, as understanding dawned.

"Adalyn was right. I have no influence here. Not any more. I am a man out of my time." Suddenly Merlin's defiance crumbled, and his shoulders sagged as he looked into some indeterminate future. "Maybe you shouldn't have woken me. I realise now this is not my home, and whatever happens I cannot continue to live here." He looked at Arthur in panic. "Where will I go?"

"We *will* get out of here, and you will live with me, close to the Cervini. You do have friends here Merlin, as do I," Arthur said, smiling at the others. "I am also a man out of time, but we will walk new paths, old friend."

Merlin didn't seem convinced, but he stood and nodded to them all.

"I will see you tomorrow with any news." And he swept from the room, his worn grey cloak swinging behind him.

The reality of their situation was now clear to Tom, and he felt a horrible tightness in the pit of his stomach. He hadn't come back here only to be on the run. But he had killed someone, he thought, feeling sick at the memory. And then, with a sudden pang, he thought of his granddad. He hadn't even seen him yet. What if he never did? And Fahey and Finnlugh? Tom had taken it for granted he'd see them all again, but now he might never be able to. Perhaps he'd never see Beansprout again!

And then he tried to be positive. "They aren't going to kill us. I think the worst that might happen is banishment. And I really don't ever want to come here again anyway."

"Maybe," Woodsmoke said, leaning back into his chair, his long legs resting on the table top. "But I'm not sure I share your confidence. I hate feeling we're relying on Nimue."

Tom slept badly. Only the fact that he'd been up for more than twenty-four hours meant he slept at all. The bed was hard and lumpy, the blankets too thin, and his mind raced with horrible possibilities. It was only with the dawn that he managed to sleep deeply for a few hours.

He was woken by voices in the main room, and he blearily stumbled through to find Brenna was back. "Nimue is here, in another tower. Her trial's the same time as yours."

"How do you know?" Arthur asked.

She grinned. "I eavesdropped. Anyway, the spell is complete, sort of, and the city is safe, but very damaged."

"But how long will the spell last if she's here?" Tom asked, worried about Beansprout.

"Long enough. Nimue has plans, I'm not sure what. She's very good at secrets. I'd better get back to check on Beansprout. If I can't return, good luck for tomorrow." Her expression became serious. "One way or another, we'll get you out of here."

After Brenna left, they spent the day pacing around the narrow confines of the tower rooms. Merlin visited, looking drawn and anxious, bringing news that a representative from Dragon's Hollow was going to be at the trial as well. It was a long, horrible day of waiting.

30 Excalibur's Song

On the morning of the trial they were woken early, while the sky was still dark. A heavily armed sylph with eyes so pale as to be almost colourless, entered with a tray of food, which he left on the table.

Tom felt shattered. He had barely slept with worry, and the sound of the wind blowing relentlessly around the tower intruded into his dreams. He forced down some food in an effort to fortify himself for the trial.

They were all quiet, locked within their own thoughts. Half an hour later the sylph returned with another, and they were escorted down the long winding stairs.

Outside on the broad walls, the freezing wind sliced through Tom's cloak, and he started shivering. Half a dozen sylphs surrounded a large metal basket into which they were hustled, its door firmly locked behind them.

The sylphs then took hold of short chains attached to the top and sides, and they were lifted into the air and carried across the city towards the Palace of Reckoning. Tom had never been so cold in his life. Or so scared. Or so breathless, he realised, as he struggled to get a full lungful of air – they were incredibly high. Below them, the city was beautiful, in a stark and unforgiving way. In the dawn pallor it was all shades of grey, with pockets of blackness imposed by hard angles and high towers. Flashes of gold and silver decorated the walls and the tips of towers, the glinting metals making the place seem even colder. He hugged his cloak around him and thought longingly of Dragon's Hollow, the House of the Beloved, and the bed he'd slept in there.

The sun was just emerging over the far horizon when the palace came into view. Tom caught a glimpse of a broad terrace along one side, before they were lowered into the palace courtyard. Nothing here was small, Tom thought, feeling tiny and insignificant as he gazed up at the walls, their lofty heights disappearing into the grey haze of dawn.

When the cage door was unlocked, Tom, Arthur and Woodsmoke walked around the shadowy courtyard, stamping vigorously to keep warm.

The sylphs watched them, clearly impervious to the cold.

Nimue arrived alone, in a smaller cage, escorted by two sylphs. She looked tiny and defenceless, barely half the height of the sylphs towering over her, but she moved with a steady, almost stately grace, as the sylphs ushered her to the far side of the courtyard. Clearly she was being kept apart from Tom and the others before the trial. She glanced over at them, giving a barely perceptible smile and nod, before turning away.

Within minutes, Merlin arrived in another single cage. Tom glanced anxiously at Nimue, but she ignored him, deep in thought.

Merlin didn't waste time on greetings. "The terrace is almost full already."

"Full of what?" Tom asked, distracted by Nimue in the distance.

Merlin looked at him impatiently. "Sylphs! Come to watch your trial!"

"Oh, of course," Tom said, embarrassed.

Woodsmoke gave him a sidelong look full of amusement. "Keep your mind on the moment, Tom," he said softly.

"Bringing you here means they want to make an example of you," Merlin continued, his face full of worry. "There are smaller places where they hold trials, but none of them has the pomp of this place." He looked around distastefully.

They were interrupted by an ancient sylph, his face creased with age, his wings a dark grizzled grey.

"Galen," Merlin said. "Are you sure you want to do this?"

"Justice must be served," the sylph muttered angrily. He glared at the three of them, his gaze finally settling on Arthur. "Arthur, I presume?"

Arthur nodded and tried to shake his hand, but Galen ignored him, saying only, "You will be tried first," before stalking off into the palace.

"I have a feeling this morning is not going to go well," Arthur said.

The terrace was a windswept place stretching away from the palace. Immediately beyond the main building was a row of pillars supporting a deep roofed walkway. Four seats had been placed in front of the pillared walk, and Tom and the others stood before them, gazing out at the crowd gathered in tiered seats that rose like an amphitheatre.

The sylphs were silent. There were no hushed conversations or debates; instead they sat like statues. Even more unnerving was the row of women-headed bird creatures perched along the highest row of the terrace.

He whispered, "Woodsmoke, those creatures were at Ceridwen's Cauldron. What are they?" Their beady eyes, sharp teeth and cruel shrieks were etched on his memory.

"Harpies, the constant companions of the sylphs," Woodsmoke said. "They'll steal food from your plate and leave you to starve to death. And then feed on your body."

Tom wished he hadn't asked.

Between them and the crowd was a long stone table with seven sylphs seated behind it, facing them, their backs to the audience. They were a range of ages, with different wings, from white, to tawny greys, dark browns and silvers – but they all looked serious. In the centre was Galen. Seated to the side was one of the fey from Dragon's Hollow.

Tom turned to his right and looked at Nimue, who was now standing next to him. Feeling his gaze upon her, she gave him the ghost of a smile before turning back to the crowd.

Galen stood, and his voice boomed across the space as if he had a microphone. "The four who stand before us are all accused of murder. The repercussions of their actions will impact on the safety of this realm, and their punishment will fit their crimes accordingly. Arthur, once King of Britain, will be tried first. Woodsmoke, Tom and Nimue, you may sit until called."

Tom sat pondering Galen's description of Arthur as "Once King of Britain." It was as if he wanted to remind them that Arthur wasn't powerful any more. He looked at Arthur, who stood rigid, facing Galen and the others. Tom had no idea what he might be feeling.

None of them had been allowed their weapons. Arthur's reclaimed weapons and armour sat on the table in front of the panel, along with Excalibur, Galatine, Woodsmoke's bow, sword, and hunting knife, and Brionac.

"Arthur," Galen began, "you face the most serious charge of all, as you instigated the attack on Raghnall. We found his head lying in the weapons room of the House of the Beloved. His body lay outside the room, a deep wound in the chest made from this spear here," he gestured to Brionac, "which we know to have been thrown by Woodsmoke, a fey of the Realm of Earth. Do you admit your guilt?"

"Yes, I do," Arthur said, his voice also booming out across the terrace. "But as he was trying to kill my friends and me, I feel justified." His voice held no trace of regret.

"We have no evidence of his attack on you," Galen said stiffly, "only the wounds of two weapons suggesting an unequal attack."

Woodsmoke stood and shouted, "You have the word of the three people sitting here with Arthur!"

"Sit down!" Galen said. "You are all conspirators. Of course you will support each other."

"You have evidence to the contrary? That he *wasn't* attacking Arthur?" Nimue said. Unlike Woodsmoke, she remained seated, her hands resting in her lap.

Galen looked angry. "No! And I do not need any. We of the Panel of Reckoning know Raghnall. He would not attempt to kill anyone. Sit down!"

The city guards grabbed Woodsmoke across the shoulders and forced him to sit. Tom felt sick. This was not a trial. There was no evidence in their favour. Merlin was right. They were going to make an example of them.

Galen continued. "There are weapons here that have been taken from Raghnall's collection. So you are all thieves as well?"

"No. I claim what is mine," Arthur explained. "Many of those weapons were mine in my lifetime. Raghnall was the thief, he tried to take Excalibur. By force."

Galen picked up Excalibur. "This is Excalibur?"

"It is."

Galen drew Excalibur from its scabbard, and the rising sun glittered along its length, throwing beams of light across the terrace. Tom glanced again at Nimue, and although she didn't look at him, she smiled her shy soft smile again.

"It is fine workmanship," Galen said admiringly.

"Made by the Forger of Light," Merlin said, from where he stood on the other side of Arthur.

A ripple of unease passed across the watching crowd, prompting some sign of life at last.

Galen looked up quickly and crashed Excalibur back onto the table. "Do not mention his name here!" he said furiously. Tom felt a stir of curiosity at what the Forger of Light had done.

"That is irrelevant. Arthur, you have murdered Raghnall, and by doing so have placed us at risk of attack from dragons. Your sentence is death. At the end of these proceedings you shall be dropped from the terrace. The fall will be long enough for you to consider your actions."

Tom drew his breath in sharply and looked in horror at Galen and Arthur. Involuntarily he rose to feet, as Woodsmoke shouted, "No! It's not fair!"

Arthur didn't speak, but he glared at Galen as he sat slowly on the chair behind him. He then glanced around the terrace, and Tom realised he was assessing their chance of escape. Arthur wouldn't give up without a fight.

Galen sought to wrestle back control. "Tom, a human interloper in the affairs of the Realm of Air, and Woodsmoke, will also be put to death."

Tom felt faint. He could barely believe his ears.

"Woodsmoke, the spear you carried here is from Raghnall's weapons room and is the weapon that pierced Raghnall's chest. Do you deny it?"

"No," Woodsmoke said. "I sought to protect my friends and would do it again."

"And Tom, you are responsible for the death of Grindan. The death of a harmless servant will not be tolerated."

"He was not harmless!" Tom exclaimed. "He tried to kill me! Look at the marks on my neck." And he pulled his cloak down, showing the bruising on his throat.

Galen refused to engage in conversation, instead looking at Nimue. "And so, we come to Nimue, the witch."

Merlin stepped forward, shouting, "Galen, they all helped to rescue me and are responsible for my resurrection. I beg you to take that into consideration."

"We have Merlin. And while their actions to rescue you were admirable, their other actions far outweigh them. The sentence remains." Galen's tone was firm, and he turned away from Merlin and back to Nimue.

Tom felt as if the air had been ripped from his lungs and the bones ripped from his legs. He collapsed onto his chair and looked at Woodsmoke, but Woodsmoke was glaring at Galen, his fists clenched, unable to offer Tom any reassurance. Beyond him, Arthur sat stony faced.

How could they hope to escape? They really were going to die.

"Nimue, please stand before the panel."

Nimue rose slowly to her feet, brushing off her gown as she stood, the only one who now looked composed.

"Your crime is that of imprisoning Merlin, lifelong friend of the Realm of Air, resulting in his eventual death. On his resurrection you then attempted to injure him once again, and were stopped only by our arrival."

Merlin again intervened. "I do not wish you to try Nimue. It is not your business."

"I decide what is tried here, Merlin, not you," Galen said. "Nimue, have you anything to say?"

"I have much to say on these charges, Galen, but what would be the point?" She shrugged.

Galen didn't seem to appreciate her tone, but continued. "Your casting of the spell of protection over Dragon's Hollow and the Realm of Air following Raghnall's death is much appreciated, and we will therefore commute your sentence from death to banishment from the Realm of Air, as long as you agree to maintain the spell in Dragon's Hollow."

"So you seek not to kill me, but to imprison me for life in the Hollow?" she asked, amused.

"You will keep your life." Galen glared at her.

"I am a witch of Avalon. Do you really think you could kill me or imprison me without magical help?" Her words fell into endless silence, and the panel twitched uncomfortably. Satisfied she had their full attention, she asked, "Who told you I have protected the Realm of Air?"

"Adalyn said you had finished the spell and extended protection to us." He looked to where Adalyn stood in the shadows of the pillared walkway.

"I have cast the spell to protect the city, but such was the speed of my arrest, I could not complete the circle of protection."

Adalyn stepped into the weak sunshine. "That is not true. We ascertained the spell has been completed."

Nimue sighed. "How careless of me. Was I not clear? What I should have said was that the spell to protect the Realm of Air *had* been completed, but was only temporary. It is now broken." She stood as if deep in thought. "In fact it probably finished at dawn. How long do you think it would take dragons to get here?"

As the full implications of her news sank in, she added, almost apologetically, "I did tell Adalyn that I *really* needed more time."

Adalyn glared at Nimue, but Tom felt a little bubble of hope starting to form inside him. And then there was a sound that chilled his blood – the far-off roar of dragons. Adalyn nodded to the guards standing behind them. All but two ran to the edge of the terrace and dived over, their wings spreading majestically before they dropped from sight. The other sylphs in the crowd rose restlessly, trying to see beyond the terrace, while the harpies cried out raucously for the blood of Tom, Woodsmoke and Arthur.

Galen looked furious. "I demand you complete the spell at once."

"I don't think so," Nimue said, her voice carrying clearly across the terrace, despite the increasing noise. "The Realm of Air can burn for all I care."

"You will complete the spell or we will bring your other friends here as well."

"No you won't. You'll find you cannot enter Dragon's Hollow at the moment," she said, her eyes bright with malice. "So what will you threaten to do now? You have already sentenced my friends to death."

"What do you mean, we cannot enter Dragon's Hollow?" Galen asked, incensed.

"I mean that once we left the city, I set a spell to prevent you entering it. Do you think I'm stupid?" Nimue asked, clearly enjoying herself.

Galen stood silent, the other sylphs sitting helplessly by his side as Adalyn strode over to Nimue and put the long blade of her sword to Nimue's throat. "Fix this now," Adalyn said, almost spitting in her face.

"No. If you kill me everything will fall. I'll tell you what I'm prepared to do. Please remove your sword."

Adalyn glanced at Galen, and at his nod reluctantly withdrew her sword.

Tom sat, his heart pounding as he heard the dragons coming closer. The terraces were emptying as sylphs dived over the edge, spears extended, to join the fight.

"What?" yelled Galen, frustrated at Nimue's endless calm.

"You will release Arthur, Tom and Woodsmoke, and drop all charges against them. You will escort us from here to Dragon's Hollow. Or," she smirked, "as close as you can get. In exchange I will extend my protection to the Realm of Air."

She turned to the fey from the City Council. "I have decided I would like to stay in Dragon's Hollow. It will be my pleasure to live at the House of the Beloved and protect the city. If it pleases you?" she asked graciously. "Of course, I would like my friends to be able to visit me as often as they wish."

As she finished speaking, a large red and black dragon soared up from below the terrace and released a stream of fire above their heads, before sylphs attacked it from all angles, drawing it out beyond the city. Tom watched as the bright white bodies of the sylphs turned and dived in the air, their spears flashing in the sun as the dragon whipped around, almost impervious to their attempts to wound it.

The fey paled and stuttered. "Y-You're welcome to live at Dragon's Hollow as long as you wish."

"Excellent. So, should we be going?" Nimue turned to smile at Adalyn.

"Remember, I need to be in the Hollow to complete the spell."

Tom and the others were now on their feet, stunned at the turn the morning had taken. Merlin gazed at Nimue, unable to hide the admiration and pride he felt. And Tom couldn't blame him. No wonder he'd been infatuated.

Adalyn looked to Galen for advice. He had fled from the table and now towered over Nimue. "You will never be welcome here again," he hissed.

"Fortunately, I am far more understanding. I look forward to seeing you in Dragon's Hollow."

Galen turned to the others. "Your sentences are reduced to banishment."

Tom felt his knees weaken with the relief of it all, but stood his ground next to Woodsmoke and Arthur, as if he'd never doubted the outcome in the first place.

Merlin interrupted. "I'm going with them, Galen. I really don't feel welcome here any more." He looked around at the view, and a shadow of regret crossed his face. "I'll send for my things later."

"As you wish," Galen said, making no attempt to dissuade him. To Adalyn he said, "Take them now."

As he finished speaking, more dragons burst into view, breathing long plumes of flames and pursued by sylphs. One, the colour of sulphurous yellow, flew low across the terrace, its claws extended, heading for the weapons on the table. Propelled into action, Tom, Arthur and Woodsmoke ran to grab their weapons, dodging and weaving amongst the flashing spears, flames and talons. Tom felt the searing heat of the flames pass over his head, and instinctively dropped and rolled. Regaining his feet, he grabbed Galatine and Arthur's shield before taking cover under the stone table. Looking out, all he could see were running feet and flames, and he heard roars as more dragons flew low over the terrace. Woodsmoke rolled next to him, preparing his bow, and Arthur joined him on his other side.

"I hope you're not planning to sit here all day?" Arthur shouted over the din.

"Of course not!" Tom said, wishing he could.

The thump of large clawed feet made them turn towards the far end of the table, where a dragon was trying his best to peer underneath. There was an enormous shudder as the heavy table started to move, and flames licked around them.

"Now!" shouted Woodsmoke, and before Tom could think they ran headlong towards the palace doors and temporary safety.

As Tom entered the broad echoing room behind the terrace, he almost collided with Nimue, who stood looking up at Merlin. They were both subdued, as if a full-scale battle wasn't going on outside at all.

"We could intervene now, drive back the dragons a little," said Merlin.

"No, they deserve this," Nimue replied, looking out with satisfaction on the results of her work. "I want them to remember this day, Merlin."

31 Decisions and Deal Making

Nimue again subdued Excalibur's call, and after a hazardous descent beneath the city, Tom, Arthur and Merlin set off on the long ride back down the ridge.

The sylphs took Nimue as far down the ridge as they were able. From a distance she looked like a bird in a gilded cage.

Fortunately, they didn't encounter any dragons, and those they saw flew high overhead, as if drawn to the Realm of Air. Tom wondered if Nimue had cast some sort of spell that kept them attacking the sylphs. Every now and then he looked back to the city high above, and saw flashes of flame and glinting light and the swirl of sylphs. He tried to feel sorry for them, but couldn't. Even now, the thought of being sentenced to death seemed like a nightmare, and he kept wondering if, once the spell was resurrected, they would come back for him.

Woodsmoke tried to reassure him. "It's over, Tom. We have their word. And besides, Nimue would drop the spell like a thunderbolt if they ever threatened us again. They have too much to lose."

"What do you think about Nimue?" Tom asked, knowing Woodsmoke had been suspicious of her.

"There's a lot more to Nimue than meets the eye," he said. Then he glanced at Tom and smiled. "I think she's too old for you, Tom!"

Tom felt himself blushing, and laughed. "I know! But I can look, can't I?"

"As long as that's all it is!" Woodsmoke said, teasing him. "I think she'd turn you into a toad if you tried anything."

The courtyard of Raghnall's House was dark when they arrived, the only light coming from a lantern that burned with a small golden flame over the door to the stables.

Tom slipped off his horse, bone weary, his eyes struggling to stay open, but the sudden change of scene and the unsaddling of the horses woke him up again.

"So this is Raghnall's place?" Merlin said.

"Was," reminded Arthur. "I thought you'd met him."

"I did, but only in the city, so I never came here." He looked up and around. "He did quite well for himself, didn't he?"

"Wait till you see inside," Tom said, thinking longingly of his bed and hot bath.

Although they tried to be quiet, the clatter of hooves must have reached into the house, because it wasn't long before the back door flew open and Beansprout appeared, exclaiming, "Could you be any louder?"

"Thanks, Beansprout. Nice to see you too, after my brush with death," Tom said.

She strolled over to them, leaning on the open stable door. Her hair was loose, and she was wearing a long floaty dress he'd never seen before.

"What are you wearing?" Tom asked.

"It's called a dress, Tom. You know, not trousers."

"Ha, so funny. But why?"

"I think," Woodsmoke said, interrupting, "it's called the Nimue effect."

"Nice to see you too, Woodsmoke," she said, and poked out her tongue.

Arthur hugged her tightly. "I'm glad you're safe. You're becoming quite the warrior maiden, Beansprout."

She looked embarrassed. "Not really, Arthur! I just helped Nimue and Brenna."

"You stayed when you could have run," he said. "That's very brave."

"Yes it is. A quality not be underestimated," Merlin said, stepping out of the shadows. "My pleasure, my lady," he said, kissing her extended hand. "Merlin, at your service."

"Beansprout, at yours," she said. "I've come to show you to your room, Merlin."

A look of concern crossed Merlin's face. "Are you sure I can stay here?"

"Of course. She told you so, didn't she?" Beansprout asked.

Tom recalled the brief conversation Nimue had had earlier with Merlin. It had been awkward. Nimue had been defiantly polite, as if she hadn't trapped him in a spell hundreds of years earlier, and Merlin had seemed almost meek and apologetic, as if he was responsible for everything in the first place.

"Well, yes," Merlin said hesitantly.

Arthur interrupted. "Are you sure you want to stay here?"

"Just for tonight. I'll find somewhere else tomorrow. In the meantime," he said, "can I help to complete the spell to protect the Realm of Air?"

"It's done. Finally," said Beansprout.

Tom knew Beansprout wouldn't openly criticise Nimue, but she did look concerned. "Nimue didn't want to rush."

"She has a stubborn streak," Merlin said. "You'll get used to that."

The next morning, Tom woke to pale bands of sunshine streaking in round the edges of the heavy silk curtains. He was back in his old room, as he now thought of it. Sitting up, he looked hopefully to where he'd left his clothes strewn across the floor, but they were still there, wrinkled and dirty. He flopped back on his pillows, huffing with disappointment. Then his stomach rumbled and he realised he was starving, so after dressing he made his way downstairs to the main balcony, where they had always eaten. But that too was empty. Wondering if he was completely alone, he shouted, "Hello? Anybody here?"

Silence.

Tom headed down the long corridor to the back of the house. This was where he'd been attacked. He was relieved to see the body of the servant had been removed, the place they'd fought marked only by a small patch of dried blood.

He carried on down to the cavernous kitchen, and that's where he found everyone. Arthur was standing over a flaming grill, cooking sausages, bacon and eggs, assisted by Merlin, who wore a long apron wrapped around his long flowing clothes. A slight odour of burning drifted around the room.

"Are you sure you know what you're doing?" Brenna asked, amused. She sat at a long wooden table, cradling a cup in her right hand, her chin on her left as she watched the activity across the room. Her long dark hair was bound at the nape of her neck, making the feathers that edged her hairline more obvious.

"Of course I do," Arthur said cheerily. "A little bit of burnt bacon makes it taste better."

Beansprout sat next to Nimue, and they were talking quietly. She gave Tom a guilty look as he sat down opposite them. Tom sensed a plan. "What's up, Beansprout?"

"Nothing," she said, wide-eyed with feigned surprise. "We're just discussing my future."

They gazed at him placidly across the table, and he felt his heart sink a little. "You're staying here, aren't you?"

After a second's hesitation, Beansprout nodded. "Nimue said she will teach me magic." She rushed on, "Don't look like that! Please be happy for me, Tom."

He sat not knowing what to say, and not even sure what he thought. He turned to Woodsmoke who had sat down next to him with a steaming cup of coffee. "What do you think?"

"I think Beansprout will be just fine," he said, looking at her a little sadly. "But we'll miss her at Vanishing Hall."

She met Woodsmoke's gaze and then looked quickly at the table, blinking back tears. "I won't be here forever, I'll come and visit."

"You'd better. What about you, Tom? Are you coming back with me?"

They were interrupted by Arthur and Merlin placing steaming plates of food in front of them.

"I thought you were coming with me to New Camelot?" Arthur said, looking between them.

Now Woodsmoke sighed and looked at the table.

"New Camelot?" Tom asked, confused. "Where's that?"

"Ceridwen's old castle, of course," Arthur said, through a mouthful of bacon. "Merlin's coming too. We're going to clean the place up, find some servants. What do you think?" he asked, looking excited.

Tom felt his heart sink even more. Everyone was splitting up. He turned to Brenna. "Are you going back to Aeriken?"

She nodded. "I'll spend a few days at Vanishing Hall, and then I'll go." She looked at her friends around the table. "I have some decisions to make."

Tom must have looked a little lost, because Woodsmoke said, "You're welcome to stay, you know that. But you don't have to make your mind up now."

Tom had that sense of doubt again. Doubt about what he was going to do with himself and his life. Everyone seemed to have a purpose, except him.

And then he realised what he did want to do.

"I've missed granddad," he said. "I'll come with you, Woodsmoke, spend some time with him, and then," he looked at Arthur's expectant face and laughed. "And then I'll come and live with you for a while, Arthur."

"Good choice, Tom." Woodsmoke grinned, and slapped him across the shoulder so hard it made Tom wince. "Anyway, we'd better eat up and get dressed. We have a funeral to go to."

"Whose?" Tom asked, confused again.

"Raghnall's, of course. His servant was buried yesterday."

"But surely we're not welcome." Tom looked around the table, wondering what he'd missed, and whether they might be arrested again.

Nimue had been quiet, but now she finally spoke. "We have made a deal with the Council. In order that you are always welcome here, that I can live here, and that Raghnall's memory is preserved, we have manufactured a lie. Raghnall and his servant got into a fight and killed each other. We found their dead bodies and raced to protect the city from dragons. I have agreed to stay and defend the city. Magen, partly because he hated his father, and partly because he doesn't want a long bloody war with dragons, is supporting the lie and has agreed to let me stay. So now we go to the funeral and mourn Raghnall with the rest of city."

It was a week later, and the city had almost returned to normal. The streets had been cleared of the rich purple banners hung in honour of Raghnall. The debris left after the dragon attacks had also been cleared, and only the blackened parts of the damaged buildings remained as evidence. The town was working quickly to repair and replace the missing gilding and jewels.

Tom, Arthur, Merlin, Brenna and Woodsmoke wound their way through the city to the tunnel and the gate. They had said their goodbyes to Nimue and Beansprout at the House of the Beloved, and although Tom was sad to leave Beansprout, she had looked so happy he had to feel pleased for her.

In the end, Merlin had stayed with them at Nimue's. Nimue had refused to hear of him leaving, which Tom thought was weird. He couldn't quite get his head round the nature of their relationship. She had imprisoned him in a spell which had killed him, and yet seemed sorry for it, and Merlin didn't seem to want to revenge. It was all inexplicable. When he voiced his confusion to Woodsmoke, all he said was, "Old friends do strange things, Tom. Life's like that sometimes. I wouldn't worry about it."

They travelled down the long dark tunnel, leaving Dragon's Hollow behind them, and passed through the rose-gold gate into the bright hot sunshine of the mountainside. They stood for a few seconds, dazzled and blinking, and then looked down the mountain to where the road led to the moors and streams and then the Cervini, in a rolling tide of green. Beyond them, Tom imagined the plains and Holloways and woods stretching out all the way to Aeriken, and then to the lake and Avalon. He felt he had travelled a long way.

Arthur shouted, jolting him back into the present, and he found he was sitting alone, the others disappearing down the path ahead. Arthur turned back to look at him. "Come on Tom, new beginnings call!"

Tom laughed and nudged Midnight into a trot. Yes, new beginnings were calling. Whatever they may be.

T. J. GREEN

YOUNG ADULT ARTHURIAN FANTASY

GALATINE'S CURSE

TOM'S ARTHURIAN LEGACY BOOK THREE

And so to bed; where yet in sleep I seem'd
To sail with Arthur under looming shores,
Point after point; till on to dawn when dreams
Begin to feel the truth and stir of day

– Alfred, Lord Tennyson (1809–92)

1 The White Wolves of Inglewood

Deep in the tangled centre of Inglewood, Tom eased his horse to a stop. In the silence that followed he listened for movement – the crack of a branch, the rustle of leaves, the skitter of footfall. Thick mist oozed around him, muffling sight and sound, and he admitted to himself he'd lost the hunt.

And now something was following him.

Tom heard the low throaty growl of the wolf moments before it leapt at him. He pulled Galatine free of its scabbard and lashed out, knowing he had only seconds before the wolf ripped his throat out. He felt its hot breath and thick matted fur, saw a flash of its wild yellow eyes, before feeling the sword cut deep into its side. It fell back into the trees, yelping.

Midnight bolted, and Tom grabbed the reins and held on, trying to calm her down. As they pounded through the wood, a branch whipped across his chest, knocking him to the ground. Midnight disappeared into the mist. Winded, Tom lay on the damp forest floor, wincing as he felt his ribs aching. He hoped Midnight hadn't gone far. Enisled was a long walk away.

He rolled to his feet and immediately froze as he again heard the low cunning rumble of the wolf, followed by a spine-tingling howl, repeated again and again as the pack arrived.

He was surrounded.

Pale yellow eyes glimmered through the mist. As the wolves crept closer, their white fur and sharp snouts inched into view, until Tom could see the whole length of their low crouching forms ready to spring at him. Now he hoped Midnight *was* a long way away. They would rip her to shreds, and him too if he didn't do something.

He couldn't possibly fight them all off. The nearest tree was only a few paces away. He inched backwards until he felt the rough bark pressing into his back, and then turned and scrambled upwards, grasping at small holes and irregularities in the trunk until he reached the first branch. He heard the wolves snapping and jumping for his feet, and swung himself up, higher and higher. By the time he reached a fork he could comfortably wedge himself into, his hands were scratched and bleeding, and sweat trickled down his neck.

Gripping a branch, Tom peered down. These wolves were lean, strong, and battle-scarred, and they gazed up at him with avid hunger, settling back on their haunches, preparing to wait him out. How long could he stay here? Already the chill mist was reaching into his bones.

If he could take out a couple, the rest might flee. From his precarious position, he pulled his bow round in front of him and aimed for the largest wolf in the centre of the pack. The arrow fell short. He knew he should have paid better attention to his lessons. He aimed again. This time the arrow streamed through the air, heading straight for the wolf ... then it veered off, missing it completely.

A cloaked, deeply-hooded figure emerged from the mist and raised an arm towards Tom. Not knowing if the person was threatening him or protecting the wolves, Tom lifted his bow, preparing to fire. He felt a sharp tug at his waist and looked down to see Galatine moving, struggling out of its scabbard. His hand flew to the hilt and he gripped it tightly, securing it under his jacket and cloak. The figure continued to point and Galatine continued to wiggle, and Tom quickly took aim and fired at his unknown attacker who, with a quick flick of the hand, turned the arrow. It thudded into the nearest tree.

Tom was preparing to shoot again when he heard the sound of horses approaching, and voices shouting his name. The figure turned and ran, and the wolves fled too, disappearing into the trees.

Woodsmoke, Arthur, Merlin and Rek cantered into view. Tom smiled when he saw them, feeling relieved. They were all close friends now, particularly Woodsmoke and Arthur. Woodsmoke had been the first fey Tom had met, and was now a brother as much as a friend. And of course Arthur, who had been King Arthur, sitting astride his horse, looking fully in command. Tom's relationship with him changed constantly. Sometimes Arthur was a friend, sometimes a father figure, sometimes reckless, sometimes protective.

Orlas and Rek were in their stag form, the two shape-shifting fey standing as high as the horses. The pair had been a great help when it came to finding Merlin.

And of course there was Merlin himself, whom Tom could never categorise. Old, wise and powerful, he was completely changeable, his whims and fancies unpredictable. But a good friend regardless. Merlin had also shape-shifted into a stag, one of the wizard's favourite animals.

Tom shouted down, "I'm up here!"

As they halted and looked up, the stags changed into human form, Rek and Orlas's skin dappled in browns and creams, like deer markings.

"What you doing up there, Tom?" Rek called.

"Escaping from wolves," Tom shouted to the old grey-haired Cervini, as he climbed down to join them.

"I thought maybe you were trying to turn into a bird?" Merlin said, raising his eyebrows.

Tom landed with a thump. "Funny, Merlin."

"We've been following your trail," Woodsmoke said, sliding off his horse. He looked the same age as Tom, but was in fact several hundred years older. "We saw the wolves' footprints. Are you all right?"

"I'm fine, but Midnight has bolted. She headed that way," he said, pointing into the trees. "But someone is out there, with the wolves."

"What do you mean, someone?" Arthur asked, immediately on his guard. He scanned the surrounding area.

"I don't know who – I couldn't see their face, but they had magical powers, because they could deflect my arrows. And I think they were trying to steal my sword, sort of summon it with magic."

"Show us where," Arthur said.

Tom led them to the spot where the figure had stood. "Here. As soon as you arrived, they disappeared."

Woodsmoke examined the ground. "Strange. I can't see any tracks, not even the wolves'. I can't smell anything, either."

Orlas agreed. "Nor I. But here's your arrow." The Cervinis' leader was tall and muscular, with long dark hair. He plucked the arrow from the tree and handed it back to Tom.

"I wonder who wants to hide their tracks," Merlin said, deep in thought.

Arthur shook his head. "Well there's not much we can do about it now. At least you're not hurt, Tom."

Tom grinned. "No, I'm fine. Sorry I lost you," he said referring to the hunt. "I thought I was behind you, and then I hit a thick patch of mist and the next thing, you were gone. Did you find the boar?"

"We found *some* boars, and killed a few, but didn't find *the* boar," said

Arthur. "For such a huge beast, the damn thing is able to disappear pretty quickly."

Arthur had organised the hunt for the Black Boar of Inglewood, as they had named it. The forest began a few miles beyond Enisled, in a deep valley on the edge of the moors. It was dark and damp, and prone to pooling mists that hung around for days. However, it was full of wild deer, pheasants, and boar (and wolves, unfortunately) and had become Arthur's favourite hunting ground. Since moving in to Ceridwen's old castle at Enisled, he'd established some of his old routines, one of which was hunting. Slaying the Black Boar was becoming an obsession. The animal had first appeared a few weeks ago, its size making it an obvious target. But it was quick. Tom half wondered if it was enchanted.

"Anyway," continued Arthur, "the rest of the group have taken back the spoils, and we came looking for you." He held his hand out to Tom and pulled him up to sit behind him on his horse, Cafal. "Come on. We'll help you find Midnight."

They found the horse's trail, and eventually spotted her grazing a few miles on from where Tom had fallen.

A few hours later they crested a low rise, and Enisled's castle appeared in the distance. It was early evening and lights shone from the towers, the rest of the building melting into the twilight.

The castle looked very different to when they had first seen it. Then it had been sealed up, access forbidden by Herne, due to the life-giving Ceridwen's Cauldron inside. Tom and the others had been allowed to enter because Herne wanted Merlin to be resurrected.

Now that the cauldron had been destroyed by the sylphs, there was no further need for the castle to be sealed.

Up ahead, Orlas stopped to look at the view, changing to human form. "I still can't believe how different this looks, Arthur," he said, when the others drew level. "It was in a pitiful state when you bought it from me. And look at it now!"

Arthur laughed. "I have Merlin to thank for some of that. And of course the Cervini and my new employees."

"Are you really going to call it New Camelot?" Tom asked.

"Why not? I loved Camelot; it seems appropriate." Arthur seemed slightly put out that Tom should question his decision.

Merlin agreed. "It feels like home."

"But it's not very original!" Tom said.

"Isn't she beautiful?" Arthur said, gazing fondly at the castle and ignoring Tom's protests.

"Very," Woodsmoke said, rolling his eyes. He was used to Arthur extolling the virtues of his castle. "You stay and admire it, I'm heading back." He spurred Farlight on, racing across the moor, quickly followed by Rek and Orlas.

As if reminding him of the late hour, Tom's stomach rumbled. "Come on, Arthur, you're the host. No-one eats until you do. Get a move on!" And he raced away, leaving Arthur and Merlin to catch up.

As Tom strode through the door into his large second-floor bedroom, Beansprout flew from the seat in front of the fire and launched herself at him, hugging him fiercely. With the wind knocked out of him it took him a few seconds to speak.

"Beansprout!" he eventually spluttered. "Are you trying to kill me?"

"I'm just saying hello, Tom! It's been so long." She stepped back to look at him. "You've grown! And look at those shoulders! You've got all muscular, Tom."

"It's all the fighting practice Arthur and Woodsmoke make me do!" he said, feeling secretly flattered. "And it hasn't been that long – only a few months."

She smiled, and Tom couldn't help smiling back. Beansprout was his cousin, always happy and positive about everything, and she looked particularly relaxed at the moment. Her pale red hair was tied in a loose plait, and she wore a long vivid-green dress.

He gestured vaguely. "I think magic is suiting you, you look all smiley."

"It *does* suit me! Nimue says I'm a natural." Nimue was the priestess of Avalon who had now become the Dragon Sorcerer of Dragon's Hollow. She had replaced Raghnall, who'd been killed by Arthur and Woodsmoke after he tried to trap them in his weapons room. Without Nimue's protection spell, Dragon's Hollow would be a ruin inhabited only by dragons.

"Show us some magic, then," Tom said, curious to see what Beansprout could do.

"It's not a parlour trick, Tom," she said indignantly. And then she winked. "Maybe later."

"So Nimue was happy to let you leave?" Tom dropped his cloak on to the floor, before sinking into a chair and pulling off his boots.

"Not really. She said it's too soon, and I should have a full year of practice before leaving, just to learn the basics. But I drove her mad asking, and in the end she said yes. I promised I wouldn't be long, but I *had* to come for the tournament." She grinned at her small victory, and sat in the chair opposite him.

Arthur had decided to hold a tournament in which his new friends and the local fey would compete in sword fighting, archery, knife throwing, wrestling, and horsemanship. So many wanted to take part or spectate that it had turned into a much bigger event than originally planned, and was now being held over three days. Arthur had asked friends to adjudicate, as well as compete. The competition would begin in two days' time in the castle grounds.

"By the way, Nimue says hello." Beansprout wrinkled her nose. "Tom, you stink."

"I've been hunting all day – I was nearly eaten by wolves! Of course I stink! How is Nimue?" Tom tried to sound offhand. Nimue was probably the prettiest, cleverest woman he'd ever met, and her green eyes haunted him.

"She's amazing, of course. She teaches me so much! One day maybe I'll know half of what she does." Beansprout leaned back with a sigh. And then she added, as offhand as Tom had been, "And how's Woodsmoke?"

"Woodsmoke's … you know, like Woodsmoke. All Zen, except when Arthur goes a bit control-ish." He frowned. "Did you travel on your own?"

"No! Granddad and Fahey are here too. You've got a terrible memory, Tom."

"Oh, yeah," Tom said, as comprehension slowly dawned. "So they made it to Dragon's Hollow, then?"

"And loved it! They loved Nimue too." She smirked. "I think it's because she just let them get on with things. Unlike Fahey's sister …"

Tom looked puzzled. "Fahey's sister? Who's that?"

"Driselda. Apparently she's been living with another sister for years, but they had an argument and she arrived just after you left with Woodsmoke, with her two daughters and three sons. I think. If I'm honest, I lost track," she said, looking sheepish. "In the space of one week she succeeded in turning their routine upside down." She giggled. "It sounds quite funny really."

Tom laughed. "I bet they didn't think so. So they've moved out?"

"Sort of. It coincided with their trip, but I think they're going to see how much they like living here."

Tom looked surprised. "Here? Jack and Fahey might move in?"

"Why, will they cramp your style, Tom?" Beansprout asked with silky sarcasm.

"No! Yes, maybe." At least the castle had lots of room. As much as he loved his grandfather, he wasn't sure he wanted to live with him all the time.

"Arthur wouldn't mind, surely. He has to put up with you," she said, grinning.

"Funny." And then he had a thought. "I presume you didn't encounter any dragons on the way?"

"No! Nimue has things well under control. You should come and visit – I'll be heading straight back after the tournament."

"Maybe, but I feel like I've only just got here." He was enjoying living in the Other and didn't want to go home, but every now and again he wondered what on earth he was doing, and now he just wanted to stay at Arthur's for a while.

"Anyway, Tom, I'm starving and you stink, remember? Get in that bath or no-one will speak to you all night."

2 New Camelot

Tom and Beansprout entered what Arthur referred to as his small dining room, on the first floor of the castle. Arthur was standing in front of the fire, resplendent in his black velvet tunic, holding a glass of his favourite beer. It was the Red Earth Ale from Holloways Meet – Arthur kept the cellars stocked with it.

Other guests stood around, chatting and catching up on news. Tonight there were just ten of them, including Jack, Fahey, Rek, Orlas and his wife Aislin, Woodsmoke and Merlin. Tomorrow the rest of the guests would arrive for the tournament, and Arthur had planned a banquet in the main hall of the castle.

Tom realised he and Beansprout were the last to arrive. He shuffled in quietly, looking sheepish, while Beansprout bounded in announcing, "Sorry we're late, Tom took forever to get clean."

"I was trying to have a relaxing soak in the bath, but someone kept yelling through the door at me!" he said, glaring at Beansprout. He headed to the long sideboard and poured himself a glass of beer.

"I don't blame you, Tom," Jack said, heading over to hug him. "We've had a long journey today. I could go to bed."

Tom grinned. "Hi, Granddad," he said, returning his hug, realising he should have greeted him properly. "You look pretty good all things considered. I bet *you* weren't attacked by wolves." He caught Fahey's eye across the room and waved.

"No, I was not. Nor dragons, either. But it's a long way." He glanced round at Beansprout. "She's stronger than she looks. It was hard to keep up. And you've grown too."

"I know, Beansprout told me."

Arthur clinked his glass for attention. "Come everyone, let us sit, eat and make merry." He headed to the long candlelit table, the soft light showing Arthur at his most handsome and charismatic.

As they took their seats Arthur raised his glass. "To old friends–" he nodded towards Merlin sitting on his right, "and all my new ones, many of whom are very dear to me already."

They all clinked glasses with their neighbours, Orlas repeating, "To old friends and new!"

Tom sat next to Rek who smirked at him. "You're still getting used to all this, aren't you?" He gestured around him to the room, food and wine.

Tom nodded. "Is it that obvious?"

"Not really. I just pay more attention than most." He took a bite of bread. "Arthur's quite a force to be reckoned with, isn't he." It wasn't a question.

Tom nodded, a wry smile escaping. "When he has a plan, he sticks at it. First there was finding Merlin. I think you know how that went." He glanced over to where Merlin sat laughing with Aislin. "Being trapped in a spell and then almost being killed by dragons was ... interesting. And then this castle and the tournament have been plans number two and three."

"And are you number four?" Rek fixed his dark eyes on him intently.

"What do you mean?" Tom asked, startled, but knowing exactly what he meant.

"Sword training, archery, knife throwing, horse-riding. It's quite the education he's got lined up."

Tom swallowed a large chunk of chicken. "He says I need those skills to survive here. He's probably right."

"Well, it will help, but I think you were doing all right anyway." Rek looked across to where Woodsmoke sat talking with Beansprout. They hadn't seen each other in months, and had lots to catch up on. "What does Woodsmoke think?"

"He says it's a good idea. He's teaching me archery."

"You've got two good teachers," Rek said, reaching for a leg of chicken.

Tom laughed. "I have. I'm lucky. And you, of course – you've taught me lots." Ever since Rek had arrived he'd been assessing Tom's skills and sparring with him.

"It's good to practise with different people, my friend. I shall enjoy watching you in the tournament."

"Aren't you competing?" Tom asked, surprised.

"Only with the sword. My eyes aren't what they used to be."

Tom grinned at him. Rek may have been old and grey-haired, but he remained lean and fast, and he knew Orlas trusted his judgement completely.

"I don't believe that for a second!"

Rek smiled back. "I figure I should give the young ones a chance." He nodded at Woodsmoke. "Besides, I think Woodsmoke's got the edge on archery. So who else is coming?"

Tom thought over the list of guests. "Arthur's invited Prince Finnlugh and some of his friends and family. It will be good to see him again."

"One of the royal tribes of the fey, I presume, with a name like that?"

"He lives in this huge Under-Palace not far from Woodsmoke," he said, remembering the labyrinth of rooms under the hill. "And Brenna arrives tomorrow, with some of the Aerikeen."

"Now that is good news," Rek said, raising his glass to celebrate. "Is she queen yet?"

"She'd better not be! I'm hoping for an invite. Any more Cervini coming?"

"Oh yes – Nerian, our shaman's arriving tomorrow. Remember him?"

"Of course! I'm not likely to forget the man who summoned Herne." Although, strictly speaking, all Tom could remember was a split-second image of the immense striding figure of Herne crossing the fire and breaking Nimue's spell, before Tom fell unconscious for days.

"Well he's coming with some of our best fighters. It will be quite the party, Tom," Rek said, winking.

At the end of the night Tom staggered to his room, full of food, and reflected on what a very interesting life he now led. There was no more school, housing estates, cars, traffic lights, computers, phones or TVs. Instead, here he was in the Other with King Arthur, his living-legend ancestor, in a castle on the soft green moors of Enisled. His best friends were a fey who was skilled in hunting, a shape-shifting bird who was heir to Aeriken, and his cousin, who lived with one of the most powerful witches in history (or legend, depending on your point of view), and who was now becoming one herself. His grandfather, a sort of bard in training, was best friends with Fahey, a skilled bard who conjured magic with words. Tom's newest friends were shape-shifting deer. And of course, there was Merlin, who now lived with them at New Camelot – the most famous sorcerer in the most famous castle of all.

Life was good.

Hours later he woke up, and couldn't work out why. He had heard something, but what?

He got out of bed and walked across to the window, pulling back the heavy brocade curtains. His room looked out across the grounds at the rear of the castle. The shadows were thick and velvety, and trees shimmered in the breeze. Far below, in the formal gardens, Tom saw a man-shaped shadow flit across an expanse of lawn. As if it knew it was being watched, the figure stopped and looked up at him, and then fled into the grounds. The howl of wolves started, piercing the silence of night. Tom shivered. It was unusual to hear wolves so close to the castle, and why was someone running in the grounds? It must have been a guard. Tom shrugged and went back to bed.

3 An Intruder

The next day the sun was high, the sky was a cloudless blue, and it was hot. Tom strode across the gardens with Arthur and Merlin, heading towards the area set aside for the tournament.

Servants were constructing two large pavilions on Arthur's fine green lawns. One was for food and drink, to keep the competitors fed and watered all day, and the other would store the weapons used for the events. Close to the pavilions were the areas marked out for the competitions. One area was for archery, and a fey dressed in dark green was pacing out the distance to the targets. The other area was for knife throwing, and had a similar set up to the weapons market in Dragon's Hollow. The targets were large wooden carvings of wolves, a wood sprite, boar, and trolls, plus some creatures Tom didn't recognise but which had a lot of claws and teeth. There was also an arena for sword fighting and wrestling, and a large enclosure filled with trees, bushes and obstacles, for displays of horsemanship.

Arthur's standards were very high. They stood before the food pavilion admiring the fine embroideries of dragons, woods and boars, the gold and silver thread glinting in the sun.

"I'm not sure these pavilions have enough gilding on them, Merlin," he said. "I really want them to catch the eye as the guests arrive."

It would be impossible to miss them, thought Tom. They were huge.

"Don't worry," Merlin reassured him. "I can burnish them if needed, I have just the spell for it."

"And Merlin, you *are* going to change into something a little more respectable, aren't you?"

Tom grinned as Merlin's face fell. Merlin maintained a look of constant distraction and disorder. His beard was unkempt, his hair long and messy, and he still wore the old threadbare grey cloak they had found him in, in Nimue's silver tower.

"I don't see why I should change," he muttered.

"Because you look scruffy," Arthur retorted. "It would be nice if you could make an effort."

Only Arthur could get away with saying that.

Before an argument could start, Tom decided this would be a good time to mention what he'd seen the night before. "I think I saw someone run across the lawns last night."

"What do you mean, Tom?" said Arthur. "When?"

"In the middle of the night. I saw someone run from over there." He pointed towards the edge of the lawns next to the gardens. "He, or she, seemed to look right at me, and then ran to the trees over there." He gestured to where the orchards began.

"Well I doubt it was an intruder, Tom. The walls are too high and strongly built for anyone to get in. And how could they possibly see you? You're three floors up."

"I know, but it seemed that way."

Merlin frowned. "I have put spells of protection across the walls. Only someone with magical abilities could get through."

That seemed to make Arthur's mind up. "Must have been a guard, Tom. Let's just finish the inspection."

"I'll leave you to it, Arthur," said Tom, unconvinced. "I'm going for a wander."

Arthur and Merlin waved after him distractedly as he headed to the orchards.

Within a short distance, the hum of noise from the activities dulled, and once he entered the orchard it disappeared completely. The trees around him were old and gnarled, their trunks a pale silver-grey. Branches twisted and knotted together, and the rub of their intertwined branches produced a slippery whispering noise that was disorientating. The orchard had clearly been here a long time, planted back in Ceridwen's day. Some of the trees had grown to huge proportions, particularly the walnut trees, but despite the long years of neglect they were still vigorous and covered with buds. Underfoot the grass was long, so evidence of an intruder should be easy to see.

It took a good while, but eventually Tom saw a patch of flattened grass, and followed a trail to the base of the wall. He examined the pitted stone blocks. It was possible to climb it; gaps in the stone provided small hand and footholds. But it would be tricky, and it was high. A fall could kill you. At his feet, something glinted in the sunlight, half buried in the soil. Pulling it free he brushed it off and held it to the light. It was a round silver disc, probably a brooch, with a pin and clasp on the back. In its centre was a wolf's head, carved in immaculate detail, and around the edge of the silver disk was a ring of paw prints.

Someone *had* been here. Tom wondered if it was the cloaked figure from the Inglewood. Whoever it was had possessed magical abilities, and they wanted Galatine.

Tom found Merlin in his tower. It rose from the centre of the castle, its windows looking out across the castle's grounds and walls to the moors beyond. The east window gave a view of the octagonal courtyard on the roof below, where Ceridwen's cauldron had been before the sylphs had blasted it to pieces. Merlin's was the only window that looked out on it. The other walls enclosing the octagonal space were windowless, making it completely private. Merlin said it reminded him of his own mortality – which Tom found odd, as the cauldron had been responsible for his rebirth.

The tower was square instead of round, but otherwise reminded Tom of the tower in the Realm of Air. Merlin had filled it with the things he had finally brought back from there. A long wooden bench ran down the centre of the room, the walls were lined with books, jars and pots, and the floor was made of solid stone slabs. Above him the thick wooden rafters were hung with dried herbs.

Merlin sat at the centre table reading a large, black, leather-bound spell book. His finger ran across the page and he muttered to himself softly. He jumped when Tom spoke.

"Merlin, I found something at the base of the walls by the orchard. I think our visitor left it."

Merlin's sharp blue eyes narrowed. "So you really think we have had a visitor?" He took the disc that Tom offered. "It looks a bit dirty, Tom. It could have lain there for years."

"But the ground was trampled, and there was a trail through the grasses," Tom insisted.

Merlin rummaged amongst the myriad objects on his table and finally pulled free a magnifying glass. "The detail is good," he said, examining the disc. "The eyes are obsidian."

"They're what?"

"Obsidian. It's volcanic rock from the Realm of Fire. And the pawprints have flecks of ruby in them. Tiny. Ingenious."

He handed the magnifying glass and disc to Tom, who was surprised to see Merlin was right. There was so much detail, it was incredible. He could see tiny blades of grass beneath the pawprints, and the fur on the wolf was so fine he could have sworn it moved.

"What does it mean, Merlin?"

He sighed. "I'm not sure it means anything." Taking it back he turned it over and examined the other side. "Probably an old brooch someone dropped."

"But who does it belong to?"

"I don't know, but leave it with me, Tom. I'll consult my books."

Leaving the tower, Tom found quite a commotion outside. Two-dozen riders on huge black stallions had filled the courtyard, their silver standards shining, dazzling everyone. Tom grinned, recognising them immediately. "Finnlugh! Over here."

A tall slim faery with shining white-blond hair turned and waved, then jumped from his horse and in seconds was at Tom's side, hugging him with surprising strength. "It's been too long, Tom! I *knew* you'd come back."

"Then you knew more than I did. I thought they'd abandoned me forever."

The last time he'd seen Finnlugh – Prince Finnlugh, Bringer of Starfall and Chaos, and Head of the House of Evernight – had been when Tom was returning to Earth and his granddad's cottage. Finnlugh hadn't changed; pale skinned, with sharp precise features and dark blue eyes, and the slight point to his ears that all royal fey had. His long hair was loose and he wore a midnight-blue tunic. Around his neck was a thick silver chain, the end tucked into his jacket. His clothes were immaculate, and of the finest cut and quality, and he emanated an aura of power and wealth. But for all that, he was friendly and genuinely pleased to see Tom. "You know they would never have done that," he said, shaking his head.

Tom shrugged. "I know, but I was starting to panic. I thought maybe they couldn't get back."

"Well, you're here now, and I hear you've been busy resurrecting Merlin and fighting dragons!"

Tom grinned. "It isn't something I'd have done back home."

"Home sounds like a very boring place – much better to have come back here. I presume you'll be in the tournament tomorrow?"

"Of course, but I'm not sure I'll be any good."

"There's nothing like competition to increase your skills, Tom."

"I know, but everyone else will be so much better."

"You don't know that. It's also meant to be fun."

They were interrupted by Arthur, who appeared from the hall behind them. "Good to see you, Finnlugh," he said, shaking his hand.

"Arthur – good to see you too. Impressive castle."

Arthur swelled with pride. "Come, I'll show you the grounds. You can pick your favourite spot. I presume you still want to stay in your tents?"

"Absolutely. We will appreciate being under the stars. Besides, there are rather a lot of us!" Finnlugh said, glancing behind him.

Finnlugh's companions had now dismounted and their horses were being led away by the grooms. They were a mixture of men and women, all tall, some with the same white-blond hair as Finnlugh, others with hair the colour of sunsets, forests, and blue skies. Tom had forgotten Finnlugh's royal family looked a little more otherworldly than other fey.

Finnlugh called to him. "I'll see you later, Tom. We have much to speak of." And with a theatrical wave he fell into step beside Arthur.

Tom watched them cross the main hall, wondering which events they would be competing in. His attention was quickly distracted by more noise, as a flock of birds wheeled overhead and then flew into the courtyard, swiftly changing form as they landed. Brenna and the Aerikeen had arrived.

Brenna was looking more like a bird, even in her human form. Her long black hair still fell to her waist, but the feathers along her hairline seemed thicker and they ran through her hair like down. The dark leather trousers and jacket she always wore also now seemed to be covered in tiny fine feathers, and her eyes were dark with almost no whites showing.

Her smile was so warm and friendly Tom felt a rush of affection. He had missed her, and wished she would come to live at New Camelot too. He gave her such a hug she protested. "Tom, you're crushing me!" She held him at arm's length. "You've grown. How dare things change when I haven't seen you!"

He smiled. "Well, you should visit more often then."

"Yes, I should," she agreed. "But unfortunately I've been kept pretty busy."

"But not busy enough to miss a tournament?" he teased.

"There's always time for one of those." She glanced behind her. "I'm being rude, let me introduce you."

A young Aerikeen with soft, brown, shoulder-length hair and feathers along her hairline and down her neck stepped forward. Her eyes were hazel brown, and like Brenna, there was almost no whites to her eyes. She was also very pretty.

"This is Adil, my cousin."

Adil nodded in greeting. "I've heard so much about you, Tom."

"You have?" he asked, puzzled.

"Of course, Tom. You helped save us." She blushed slightly, before stepping back.

Brenna introduced the others, and Tom knew he would never remember all their names. These Aerikeen were young, bright-eyed and eager to be involved in the tournament. "These are all survivors of Morgan," Brenna said, referring to Morgan Le Fay who had tried to kill them all at the Aerie in Aeriken. "They are helping to rebuild our way of life. I thought they should have some fun over the next few days."

Tom welcomed them, feeling it was his responsibility while Arthur was with Finnlugh.

"I take it Arthur has invited people to watch the tournament?" Adil asked. "There's a crowd of people on the moors outside the walls; a small tented city seems to have sprung up."

"He has, but I'm not sure how many," Tom said, slightly alarmed. "I think the competitors have brought their own supporters." He had a gnawing worry that Arthur wasn't in fact expecting this many at all. "I think everyone's excited apart from me – I'm just nervous."

Brenna laughed. "You'll be fine, Tom." She gave him another hug and big smile. "It's so good to see you." She lowered her voice and put her mouth to his ear. "I told you I'd miss our adventures."

He grinned. "Come on, I want to show you something." He led them into the main hall and heard Brenna's intake of breath.

"Arthur *has* been busy! Look at this place." She gazed at the tapestries, the rugs, the chandeliers, and the wooden table filled with trays of delicacies for the visitors.

"His small army of servants have been busy," Tom said wryly.

"I'm glad to see the profits from the dragonyx haven't gone to waste," she said laughing, and reached for a sweet cake on a gilded platter.

"Wait until you see the banquet he's prepared for later. Come on," he said, "I'll show you to your rooms. You're next to Beansprout."

4 The Incomplete Tale

After leaving Brenna, Tom headed back up to Merlin's workshop. Beansprout was there too, and they were examining the disc in front of the fire.

"Why have you got a fire going? It's really hot out."

"Some spells require fire, Tom," Beansprout said, distracted by the disc in her hands.

"Oh, so you're doing spells?" Tom was starting to sweat already. "Will I get in the way?"

"Not at all." Merlin beckoned him over. "We thought if we applied heat it might change the metal in some way, maybe revealing another image or message."

"Why? I thought it was just a brooch." Tom watched as Beansprout gripped the disc with forceps and held it in the flame.

"We're going to try it without a spell first, and see what happens," Merlin said.

The disc started to glow, and after a few minutes Beansprout took it out of the flame and placed it on a small table next to the fire.

After examining both sides carefully through his magnifying glass, Merlin let out a deep sigh. "Nothing. But that doesn't surprise me. Let's try a reveal spell. We'll start with the simple ones."

He held the disc in the flames, muttering softly under his breath. It seemed to Tom that the image of the wolf blinked, in response to whatever it was Merlin said. But Merlin sighed again and placed the disc back on the table. "No."

Tom felt a surge of disappointment and realised he'd been holding his breath. What had he expected to happen? All he'd found was some old brooch.

For the next hour he watched as Merlin tried spell after spell. Now and again he would stop to explain to Beansprout what he was doing, and to ask her questions. "Has Nimue explained the principals of fire to you?"

Beansprout nodded. "Yes, she covered all four elements."

"Good. In that case, show me how you would create fire in your hand."

Tom was alarmed, but Beansprout didn't look worried. She sat for moment in quiet concentration, holding her hand out in front of her. A small blue flame appeared, growing bigger as she concentrated. As Merlin nodded encouragement her confidence grew, and soon a small pulsing ball of flame hovered over her hand before she threw it in the fire. Tom was impressed, and started to see Beansprout as someone far more interesting than just his younger cousin.

Merlin clapped. "Well done, I see Nimue has done a very good job. But if I'm honest I expected nothing less. Now, back to this brooch."

He pulled the spell book towards him and flicked its pages absently. "Mmm, perhaps we should try a spell of awakening." He held the disc tightly in his hands and whispered over it, before blowing softly into his hands. When he opened them, nothing had happened. This was going to be a waste of time.

"Maybe it really is just a brooch and it does nothing?" said Tom.

"And maybe," Merlin said, raising his right eyebrow, the left staying firmly in place, "we haven't found the right spell yet."

"Spells can take time, Tom," Beansprout explained. "You have no patience."

"You're right. I'm going. I'll see you in the Great Hall."

They immediately turned their attention back to the brooch.

"Don't be late, you have two hours! And bring the brooch with you. I want to show it to Nerian."

The last two days had turned into a chore of fancy clothes and grooming. Tom returned to his room to find his clothes laid out for the evening. There was a fine linen tunic and trousers, and polished black leather boots. The bath was run, and a small tray of food had been left on a side table. While his room might not have had the opulence of the one he'd stayed in at Raghnall's, in the House of the Beloved, it was pretty close. He grinned. He wouldn't get this at home.

Two hours later he was standing at Arthur's side, greeting the guests as they came through the polished ebony doors that led into the Great Hall. This was not to be confused with the Main Hall, which was the main entrance hall of the castle. The Great Hall was on the first floor and overlooked the gardens at the back of the house. It had a high carved ceiling with a series of chandeliers down the centre. At the far end, tucked into a corner, was a dais for the musicians, and later for Fahey, who was going to enthral them with his stories. Long tables were set up down the centre of the hall and the room dazzled with silver and glassware, laid out on snowy linen cloths.

Out of the corner of his eye, Tom could see his grandfather and Fahey chatting quietly together. He felt a rush of guilt as he hadn't spent time with them today – but thinking about it, he hadn't seen them. They hadn't even been at breakfast. That was unheard of. They must have been preparing.

Finnlugh arrived and cornered Tom. "Tom, I absolutely insist that we speak later. It's been too long. And I have questions to ask about a certain sword I hear you have acquired from my recently deceased great-great uncle, second removed on my mother's side."

Tom was immediately baffled. "What are you talking about, Finnlugh?"

"Raghnall," he said, raising his head quizzically. "Remember him?"

Tom gasped, horrified. "He was your relative?"

"Don't worry, Tom. All of the royal tribes are related. It's down to years of intermarriage. I'm not grieving, it's all right." He smiled at Tom's discomfort, and Tom hoped Arthur couldn't hear. He was currently distracted with Finnlugh's cousin, Duke Ironroot.

"We didn't know! But ..." Tom felt he should explain, "he did try to kill us."

Finnlugh patted his shoulder. "Later, Tom." And he moved off enigmatically into the mingling guests, a glass of Arthur's sparkling elderberry wine in hand.

The next person Tom wanted to talk to was Nerian, the Cervini shaman. He'd arrived that afternoon, with another dozen Cervini. Nerian hadn't changed either. His long hair was still matted into dreadlocks and plaited with beads and feathers. He wore a necklace of small interlinked animal bones, and tonight his ceremonial stag horns.

"Nerian, I haven't seen you for ages," Tom said, excited. "I've found something I want to show you."

Nerian narrowed his eyes. "It sounds intriguing. Something magical?" Then he paused. "Are you in trouble again?"

"I hope not! Can I show you later?"

He nodded. "Of course."

As he moved into the crowd, Tom wondered when he was going to have time to speak to everyone.

After another half hour of hand shaking, Tom was ready to sit down and eat. As enjoyable as it was to meet old friends and new, he was ready for food. Fortunately, so was Arthur. He stood next to Tom, taller and broader, his long dark hair falling to his shoulders. He wore a grey silk tunic and looked very regal, even without a crown.

Much like the previous night, Arthur had a speech of welcome prepared, but tonight it was about the tournament. "It will commence tomorrow morning at ten, and will run for three days. We begin with novice sword fighting, which will run at the same time as the knife throwing. On the second day there will be archery and advanced sword fighting, and on the last day, wrestling and horsemanship." He smiled magnanimously. "This will be a fine event that will prove our skills, and I hope to repeat it every year!" He raised his glass. "To new friends and new beginnings!" A cheer erupted and glasses chinked, and the banquet was underway.

It wasn't until much later in the evening that Tom was able to speak to Nerian again. On the far dais a small band was playing; the tables had been cleared and the dancing had started. Couples drifted around the room, cheek to cheek, or twirling around as the music demanded. Tom could see Woodsmoke dancing with Beansprout, and Brenna was dancing with Fahey. Tom grinned as he saw his grandfather dancing with a stately Cervini elder. A few card tables had sprung up in an adjoining room, and he noticed Rek heading there, a look of serious intent on his face.

The fireplaces at either end of the room were filled with candles and flowers, and more candles burned in niches and sconces. Nerian sat with Tom in a quiet corner close to one of the fireplaces, his antlers shadow-fighting on the walls. Within seconds Finnlugh joined them, pulling up a free chair. "May I? I fear if I don't speak to you now, Tom, I might not get the chance tomorrow."

"Of course. Do you know Nerian?"

"We had the pleasure earlier." Nerian nodded to Finnlugh.

"I'm glad you're here, I wanted to show this to both of you." Tom pulled the brooch from his pocket. Beansprout had returned it to him, telling him that magic had revealed nothing.

Nerian looked at it thoughtfully, running his fingers over the design. "A wolf's head? I wonder …" He trailed off, gazing into the middle distance.

"What?" Tom prompted.

But Nerian was thinking and he fell silent, handing it over to Finnlugh's outstretched hand.

Finnlugh turned it over, examining the details. "I remember hearing about a Wolf Mage when I was young. I wonder if this has anything to do with him."

"Who's the Wolf Mage?" Tom asked.

"That's it," Nerian said, nodding. "The Wolf Mage. I was told his story as a young fawn. Where did you find it?" His pupils had rapidly dilated, and in that second Tom had a vision of him as Herne the Hunter, and almost forgot what they were talking about.

Shaking off his nervousness, Tom said, "I found it in the orchard, under the wall. I thought I'd seen an intruder so I went to check it out. The ground was trampled, and I found this in the dirt." He asked again, "Who's the Wolf Mage?"

Nerian stirred from his reverie. "If I remember correctly, he's the brother of the Forger of Light, who made Excalibur and Galatine, the sword I believe you now have?"

"How did you know I had Galatine?"

"Word gets around, Tom," Finnlugh said. "Did *you* know the Forger of Light had forged Galatine?"

"I suppose I did," Tom said, trying to remember what Arthur had told him. "I think Arthur called it the sister sword to Excalibur. It was made for Gawain, his nephew. Why, does that matter?"

"Galatine was indeed given to Gawain by Vivian, as a reward for his loyalty to Arthur," Finnlugh explained. "However, according to the myths of the fey – if I remember correctly – the sword was not made for him, and isn't really a sister sword. It predates Excalibur, and was made for the Forger of Light's brother, the Wolf Mage." He sighed, looking puzzled. "I am not entirely sure why it was given to Gawain. The roots, the details of the story are lost, at least to me. It was a very long time ago."

Tom was shocked. "It was made for someone else? I didn't know that. I don't think Arthur or Merlin do either."

"Why would you?" Nerian asked. "It's an old story, almost forgotten. But I believe this is his image, so someone knows of him."

"Are you saying the intruder is something to do with the Wolf Mage?" Tom asked, still confused. He looked around the room as if someone might suddenly reveal themselves.

"Maybe, or why is his brooch here?" Finnlugh said. "It's too much of a coincidence otherwise."

"The intruder must have been the same person I saw in the wood,"

Tom said, the events now starting to make sense. Finnlugh and Nerian looked confused, so he continued. "I was separated from the others in the Inglewood, and someone wearing a hooded cloak tried to summon my sword with magic."

"And was that cloak pinned by this brooch?" Nerian asked.

"They were too far away for me to see. Tell me more about the Wolf Mage." Tom's curiosity was now piqued.

"His name was Filtiarn," Nerian said. "He had the rare ability of being able to communicate with beasts, and was particularly fond of wolves. He ran with them, lived with them, almost was one. Years ago he was very powerful, as was the Forger of Light, but neither of them has been seen for many years. By now they must be dead. That's all I know."

"Are they part of the royal tribes – like you?" he asked Finnlugh.

He shook his head. "No. They were of different tribes, possessing different magic – such as skills in metal forging."

"But they were good?" Tom asked, trying to assess how far someone would go to get the sword back. "I mean, we should have nothing to fear from anyone who might know them? Surely the Forger of Light was good if he made such powerful weapons."

Finnlugh looked thoughtful. "It depends how you define good. Each weapon or object he made was for a purpose. Excalibur helps Arthur cheat death, and consolidate power. It is a weapon that bestows righteous kingship, or leadership. Where Arthur walks, others follow, yes?" Then he shrugged. "But nevertheless, such weapons can almost be curses."

Tom was shocked. "And Galatine? Is that cursed?"

Nerian corrected him. "The swords are not cursed, Tom, they are powerful, made by magic to give the bearer greater power. All magical weapons do so. I have no idea what powers Galatine may have. Unfortunately power can be a curse. It is much envied by the stupid and the greedy."

"You remember the weapons in Raghnall's weapons room?" Finnlugh asked. "They were all full of strange powers, but of course not all were forged by the Forger of Light. They were coveted by many and have passed through numerous owners, and will again. And if you recall," – his hand flew to his chest where he kept the Starlight Jewel – "I have had problems of my own regarding this." Tom caught a chink of blue in the candlelight.

"I couldn't possibly forget the weapons room or your jewel," Tom said. "Both nearly got us killed." He sighed, feeling suddenly out of his depth. "But Galatine doesn't seem to have great powers. I've had it for months and it's fine. I'm fine. I can't believe anyone would want it, especially after so long. Surely they must be dead?"

Nerian eyes dark were unfathomable. "Well, if this brooch has only been recently left here – and it seems it has, considering the disturbance of the ground – then the two brothers would be the most immediate suspects."

"Or someone who wants to help them," Finnlugh pointed out. "Wait, why don't we call Fahey? He has a rich store of tales." He stood, looking around the room, and then darted away, returning in seconds with Fahey.

"Good evening, gentlemen," Fahey said, grinning and pulling up a stool. He was looking very dapper tonight. His long hair was pulled back into a tight ponytail, and he was wearing a well-tailored jacket, and trousers of the finest dark green linen. "I gather you want me?"

"Yes, we want to know if you've heard of the Wolf Mage," Tom said.

"The Wolf Mage! Why are you asking about him?" Fahey asked, intrigued.

"So you've heard of him?" Tom said, leaning forward in anticipation.

"Of course I've heard of him. It's my job to know," he said, preening slightly. "He was the original owner of your beautiful sword, Tom."

"Why didn't you tell me before?" Tom asked, thinking of the weeks he'd spent at Vanishing Hall.

Fahey shrugged. "I presumed you knew."

Tom rolled his eyes. "So what else do you know about him and the Forger of Light?"

"Well, the intriguing thing is," Fahey said, looking at them one by one, "that neither of them has a completed tale."

"All right, I'll bite," Nerian said, laughing. "What do you mean by that?"

"Well, they just disappeared. Filtiarn first, back around the time of the dragon wars, and then Giolladhe – the Forger of Light – not long after he made Excalibur. And nobody knows where they went or what happened to them."

"We found this," Finnlugh said, handing him the brooch.

Fahey held it up to the light. "The Wolf Mage! I have seen this image before. Where did you find it?"

"In the orchard," Tom said, "under the wall."

"How exciting," Fahey said, his eyes shining. "This means the tale is not yet over – and we will be part of it!" He leapt to his feet, handing the brooch back. "No time to talk. The dancing is over, and it's time for your tale

Tom, and how you resurrected Merlin. We will speak later." And with a swirl of his coat tails, he headed to the dais.

5 When the Wolf Moon Rises

At one point it felt like the party would go all night, but eventually the competitors decided they wanted to be at their best for the next day and began to head off to bed. Finally only a few remained: Arthur, Woodsmoke, Beansprout, Brenna, Tom, Finnlugh, Nerian, Jack and Fahey. They sat in front of the fire, having a nightcap and winding down.

"I had such a great time," Beansprout said, leaning back in her chair and kicking her shoes off. "I haven't seen so many people for ages."

"You certainly know how to throw a good party," Jack agreed. "I think your story went well, Fahey."

Woodsmoke laughed. "Well, you can't go wrong with a tale about the return of Merlin, and all set in this castle!"

Fahey smiled and sipped his mead. "The trick is to know one's audience."

"You know that brooch I found, Merlin?" said Tom. "We think it belongs to the Wolf Mage."

"No," corrected Nerian, holding up a finger. "I said it symbolised him."

"What brooch?" Arthur asked, looking between them.

"Sorry, Arthur," Tom said. "I found this earlier." He pulled the brooch out of his pocket and gave it to Arthur. "It was at the bottom of the orchard wall. I showed it to Merlin, and then Nerian, Finnlugh and Fahey."

"Oh, leave me till last," Arthur complained.

"You were busy," Tom pointed out.

Merlin ignored them both. "Well I have never heard of the Wolf Mage. Who is he?"

Finnlugh explained the connection to the Forger of Light. "It's no wonder you haven't heard of him."

"But," Tom interrupted, "it seems Galatine was made for the Wolf Mage. We think someone wants it back."

Arthur now looked exasperated. "No, Galatine belonged to Gawain."

"But it wasn't made for him, Arthur," Nerian explained softly. "Vivian appropriated it."

Arthur shot to his feet and starting pacing up and down. "That woman always interferes!"

"Arthur," Merlin remonstrated, "she acts for the best."

He snorted. "Whose best, though?"

"Yours, usually," Merlin said, scratching his chin.

That seemed to deflate Arthur's anger, and he sat with a huff. "Do we need to worry? I mean, are they dangerous?"

"Maybe," said Finnlugh. "It depends who's after it, and how badly they want it. And …" he paused thoughtfully, "what they want it for."

"Where is Galatine now?" Woodsmoke asked.

"In the armoury, of course," Tom said.

With unspoken agreement everyone got to their feet and set off, through dark corridors and down shadowy stairways to the basement, where the armoury was kept. They came to a halt in front of a large solid wooden door with two locks, and two iron bars across it. Standing to attention was a huge Cervini, who Tom recognised as Dargus, one of the Cervini who'd been eager to help Arthur on his return.

"Evening, Dargus," said Arthur. "Has anything unusual happened here tonight? Have you seen or heard *anything*?"

"No, Sir," he said. "Everything is quiet as usual. The last activity was about six hours ago when the Cervini locked their weapons away for the night, after final practice this afternoon."

"Good. Open the door so we can check a few things, please."

Dargus looked confused, but did as he was asked.

The weapons room was windowless, made of solid stone with a paved floor. There were racks and racks of weapons, most of them belonging to visitors who were here for the tournament. They were grouped together into swords, knives, shields, lances, and others. Adjoining the weapons room was a smithy for making repairs to the weapons.

After lighting the lamps, Tom led the way to the far side of the room where the swords were housed. Excalibur was mounted on a rack in pride of place, and next to it was Galatine. Despite knowing it was securely locked and guarded, Tom felt relief wash over him. "It's here."

"May I?" Finnlugh asked. He lifted the sword and held it under the nearest lamp.

Galatine's hilt had a simple design of curving interlocked symbols, and on both sides, embedded at the cross, was a yellow gemstone with a swirl of black. Fine engravings ran down its blade. Tom had often puzzled at these – they looked like writing, but he couldn't read it, unlike Arthur's which clearly read, "Take me Up" and "Cast me away."

"Have you ever wondered what the gemstone is, Tom, and why it is yellow?" Finnlugh asked.

"Not really," Tom said, feeling a little embarrassed.

"It's a fire opal. And I believe the yellow represents a wolf's eyes. Or rather, Filtiarn's wolves' eyes; their eyes were only ever yellow."

Tom thought back to the wolves he'd been surrounded by the other day. They'd all had yellow eyes.

Finnlugh continued, "There's something written here in ancient fey script. I must admit, I can't read it. Nerian?"

Nerian examined it carefully. "That's because it's magical script, very old now, and not commonly used. There are two lines – one on each side."

"What does it say?" Tom said.

"When the Wolf Moon rises," he turned the blade over, "so shall the Wolf Mage."

"What does that mean?" Arthur asked, sounding annoyed. Arthur hated not knowing everything.

"That makes things a little more worrying," Nerian said. "The Wolf Moon rises next month."

"What's the Wolf Moon?" Beansprout asked. "It sounds romantic!"

"It occurs once every thousand years. Everyone will celebrate it," Nerian said.

Woodsmoke agreed. "Yes, there's nothing sinister about it, it just doesn't happen that often."

"Well there may not be anything sinister about it normally, but it says here the Wolf Mage rises on the Wolf Moon! Is he some kind of werewolf?" Jack said, casting a worried glance at Tom and Beansprout.

Fahey sighed. "No, he is not a Werewolf. What a vivid imagination you have, Jack."

"Can I suggest we continue this elsewhere?" Beansprout had started to shiver, and she shuffled on her feet, trying to keep warm.

Woodsmoke immediately threw his jacket around her, and Arthur came to a decision.

"This can stay with me overnight, and I'll double the guard on the armoury." He picked up Excalibur as well. Woodsmoke grabbed his bow and arrow and hunting knife, and Brenna reached for her sword.

Arthur tried to reassure them all as they walked up to bed. "The castle is full of the finest warriors. I think whoever came here is just looking. He won't be fool enough to attack. You should all go and sleep. Tomorrow will be a long day."

6 The Tournament Begins

When Tom walked out to the pavilions the next morning, a large group of fey were already mingling and chatting to each other, clearly excited at the coming day. Breakfast was set out on long trestle tables, and most of the food had already been eaten. Small bets were being wagered, and Tom could see the steady passing of cash into the hands of two satyrs. A stream of people were going in and out of the weapons pavilion.

It was going to be another hot day. Benches had been set up for spectators, who were saving seats with hats and flags. Tom tingled with anticipation – once his event was over he could really enjoy the tournament. He'd only entered the sword fighting competition, as he wasn't confident about his archery skills – or his sword-fighting if he was honest. But at least he was in the beginners' category.

All of his friends were entering several events. Arthur was of course competing in the expert category in sword fighting, and Tom couldn't imagine anyone beating him. Arthur was also in horse showmanship, but Tom was pretty sure Finnlugh would win that.

The opening rounds were on at the same time, so the crowd would be moving around. As Tom strolled between the pavilions, he scanned the crowds for anyone who looked out of place or suspicious – but he knew trying to spot the intruder would be almost impossible. When Arthur had learned about the tented village that had sprung up outside, he'd opened up the castle grounds to the visitors and they had flooded in, many setting up small stores and cooking areas.

"You look miles away, Tom."

Tom looked around, at first not recognising the voice, and then he grinned. "Bloodmoon! I didn't know you were coming."

Woodsmoke's cousin was as blond as Woodsmoke was dark. Tom shook his hand, pleased to see him. "The last time I saw you, you beheaded the lamia and covered me in blood!"

Bloodmoon laughed. "But I saved your life! Don't worry, no lamias on my agenda today, just healthy competition."

"Does Woodsmoke know you're here?"

"Not yet, I've just arrived." He became serious. "So what were you looking for Tom? Or who?"

Tom filled him in on the intruder and the attack in Inglewood. Bloodmoon narrowed his eyes. "I saw many wolves coming through Inglewood, more than I'd normally expect. It made getting through there without losing blood a little more complicated than usual." He thought for a moment. "I'm not sure if they all had yellow eyes, though. On the day you were attacked, did you think the mist was unnatural?"

"I don't think so. You know Inglewood, it's always murky and misty. I just happened to have got separated from the others."

"Well it seems to me, Tom, that an attack in the woods and an intruder here is not a coincidence. I think you should be careful." Bloodmoon was clearly concerned and seemed oblivious to the party atmosphere around him. "Are you using Galatine today?"

"No, I'm using my old sword. We're not allowed to use magical weapons in the competition."

Woodsmoke appeared out of the crowd with Brenna and Beansprout, their faces breaking into smiles when they spotted Bloodmoon. Woodsmoke looked relieved to see Tom. "I've been looking for you everywhere. You shouldn't wander around on your own, you might be in danger."

Bloodmoon nodded. "I agree. Tom's filled me in on the news."

"I'll be fine! Stop worrying." Although Tom wasn't convinced. He couldn't shake off the feeling of being watched.

Woodsmoke just nodded. "The beginners' sword fighting is the first event – shouldn't you be getting ready?"

"I know, I know. I'll head there now."

Tom set off for the weapons tent, wishing he didn't feel so nervous and annoyed. He couldn't believe he was in danger – not here, not now. It was unlikely anything would happen, it was just a lot of worry over nothing.

The young fey and Cervini who had registered for the beginners', headed out behind the tent for some last-minute practice. They were joined by those competing in the knife-throwing event, which was on at the same time. At least the crowd would be divided between the two, Tom thought, relieved. He collected his sword and shield and started loosening up. He missed Galatine; it was so well balanced that although it was heavy, he found it easy to handle. Consequently, going back to his old sword was difficult and he felt at a disadvantage. And he still found using a shield difficult. It covered a good third of his body, and was of plain design, made of a metal the fey called Arterium, that was light but very strong. And of course it had been made in Dragon's Hollow, like most weapons.

Now it was nearly time, Tom started to feel nervous about all the people who would be watching him. His thoughts were interrupted by a loud bell reverberating through the grounds, summoning them to the draw that was to take place at the edge of the designated areas.

As they left the tent, the two groups separated. The raised benches were now full, and Orlas stood waiting, looking imposing. His tanned skin and deer markings glowed in the sun, and the gold torcs around the tops of his muscled arms reflected the light. Next to him was Duke Ironroot, a relative of Finnlugh and an expert swordsman, who'd been chosen to adjudicate. Ironroot was a huge dark-haired fey with thick eyebrows and eyes the colour of flint. His beard was flecked with purple and his expression was permanently grim. Few argued with him.

When the sixteen competitors were ready, Orlas dipped his hand into a silver helmet and randomly selected two names. There were to be eight fights, and those who lost would be eliminated, the fights progressing down to the final two.

The first two opponents stepped forward – a fey who had arrived with Finnlugh, and a Cervini. The other competitors watched, Tom wondering how good they would be. As the pair entered the ring, the crowd fell silent.

They started slowly, circling, weighing up each other's strengths and weaknesses. The aim was to either cause their opponent to lose their sword, or break through their defences with a move that would cause injury – but stopping short, of course.

The first match didn't last long. It started slowly, but within a couple of minutes both swordsmen lost their nervousness and forgot the watching crowd, advancing on each other, thrusting and parrying quickly. The crowd got behind them, and cheers and groans filled the air.

The fey was quick, but the Cervini was strong. Several times they rolled across the ground to avoid the other's advance, shields rising quickly as they regained their feet.

Tom started to worry. They were really good. He couldn't possibly hope to beat either of them.

And then it was over. The Cervini's strength had prevailed and he had brought his sword up under the fey's and, without Tom seeing how it happened, the fey was barehanded and the Cevini's sword was at his throat.

They stepped apart, breathing heavily as they bowed to each other. The fey grimaced, barely polite, but the Cervini beamed and bowed to the crowd as he accepted their cheers.

As they left the ring, Orlas drew two more names from the helmet. Again Tom had to wait. The next fight was between a Cervini and a satyr, well matched in size and strength. This bout was longer, and by the time the satyr had won, both competitors were sweating and panting heavily. The crowd were on their feet, cheering and yelling.

As Orlas stepped forward again they fell quiet, then resumed cheering as the next two names were called. Tom's was one of them. His opponent was Adil, Brenna's Aerikeen cousin, who grinned at him with what Tom thought an overly confident swagger, her shyness from the other day gone. If she fought anywhere near as well as Brenna, he was in trouble, and his stomach churned as he entered the ring. He heard a shout of encouragement from a voice he vaguely recognised as Beansprout's.

They started pacing around, testing each other's speed. As Tom challenged her, Adil responded quickly, blocking him then attacking his left side, forcing him to bring up his shield before he struck back. He forgot the crowd, concentrating only on her next moves, trying to stay one step ahead. The sun was now high overhead and he blinked, trying to get the sweat from his eyes. Adil seemed to be coping better with the heat than he was, and she was really quick. At one point she almost got beyond Tom's shield and he stepped and rolled, using his shield as a springboard. Surprised by his move she hesitated, giving him the upper hand, allowing him to get in close and finally flick her sword out her grasp.

Adil's eyes hardened, but she managed to control her anger, nodding to Tom as he realised he had won. After bowing to her, he turned to the crowd, grinning. Adrenalin surged through him, and he almost ran out of the ring. Now he couldn't wait to fight again. Buoyed by success, he started to relax.

Over the next half hour they watched three more fights, and Tom paid attention to the competitors' fighting styles, weighing up his chance of future success. Adil stood next to him, looking him up and down. "You fought well, Tom. Who taught you?"

"Arthur mainly, but also my friends Woodsmoke, Rek, and Brenna of course."

"She speaks highly of you and your friends, for what you did for us. And you saved Merlin. You're quite the hero," she said, with a cheeky grin.

He shook his head, embarrassed. "No I'm not. I just helped a little."

She smiled. "If you say so." She looked at their group of competitors, all watching the current fight. "Have you noticed the odd one out?"

"What?" Tom looked at her, wondering what she meant.

"The fey with the dark hair, over there, standing at the edge of the group. He watches you, very discreetly."

Tom's attention slid from the fight as he stared at the fey she had pointed out.

"Not so obvious, Tom, he'll know you're onto him."

"How long has he been watching me?"

"Ever since our fight, but he's careful not to be obvious."

"Maybe he's watching everyone. I have been too, you know, checking out the competition."

"No," she said. "He only watches you."

"Who is he?" Tom felt a stir of discomfort as he wondered if this was the intruder. But surely this fey was too young to be one of the brothers?

"I have no idea. He doesn't seem to mix with the other fey."

They looked away from him as they talked, Tom occasionally risking a glance whilst pretending to scan the crowd.

The fight finished and Orlas called the last two competitors. "Elan and Gelas."

The dark-haired fey glanced briefly at Tom as he passed.

He fought with a quiet intensity that was mesmerising to watch. His movements were precise and deft, and Tom had the feeling he was far more skilled than he was letting on. The fight was over in little more than a minute, the Cervini he fought startled by the speed of his defeat. The crowd seemed to feel cheated too, and gave a slow applause as the competitors left the field. Duke Ironroot turned to watch him pass, a slight frown on his face, as if he were trying to place him.

Orlas announced a short break before the second round, and the benches emptied rapidly as people left to find drinks.

"Well, that's me finished," Adil said. "I'm going to practise for the archery – let's hope I do better in that. I'll make some enquiries about Elan, but in the meantime, be careful."

Tom looked around for Elan, but he had disappeared. He headed for the food pavilion where, glad to be out of the sun, he grabbed a long cold drink and large slab of cake and went in search of his friends. He spotted Woodsmoke, who was carrying a tray of glasses filled with ale.

"Good work, Tom!" he said, slapping him across the shoulders with remarkable dexterity, the drinks not wobbling at all. "I knew you'd rise to the occasion. Excellent footwork, and a very impressive roll. Just remember to keep your sword raised at all times. Follow me, we're out here," he said, before Tom could get a word in.

Woodsmoke led him to Brenna, Bloodmoon, Beansprout and Arthur.

"Excellent start, Tom," said Arthur, beaming. "Just remember to keep your sword up." He raised his glass to Tom before taking a healthy gulp.

"I'm almost hoarse with shouting," Beansprout said, her shoulders shrugging up and down with excitement. "Brenna said you beat one of her best!"

"Yes, you did. But I'm secretly pleased you won, Tom." Brenna held her finger to her lips and Tom laughed. "I'm in the knife-throwing event next, so I won't see you fight – good luck!"

Tom had been about to tell them his suspicions of being watched, but in the light of all this excitement it seemed stupid, like he was imagining it. And he didn't want to worry the others while they were having so much fun. "So you're enjoying it, then?"

"Best idea I've had all year, Tom," Arthur said. "I've already decided I'm doing it again next year. Maybe make it five days rather than three."

He continued to describe his plan, but Tom switched off as he saw Elan out of the corner of his eye. It looked as if he was returning from the orchards. As he disappeared into the crowds, the bell sounded for the next round.

"Better go," Tom said, and he headed back to the fighting area, good luck wishes ringing in his ears.

7 The Enemy Within

Now there were only eight competitors assembled around the fighting circle. They stood nervously, trying to avoid each other's eyes while the crowds settled like a flock of birds onto the benches. Elan was standing close to Tom, and was at least a head taller.

Orlas announced the second round and pulled two more names from the helmet. The satyr was called to fight the Cervini from the first fight. The contest was close and hard fought, both of them muscular, tall and broad shouldered. The Cervini's skin with its dappled markings seemed to ripple in the sun, and the satyr's deer feet moved nimbly, his horns and yellow eyes making him look malevolent. But as Tom now knew, their appearance was deceptive – satyrs were in fact the most social and even-tempered creatures in the Realm of Earth. Tom watched them both, admiring their skill and strength, but once more he was distracted by Elan, which annoyed him. Again the satyr won and Tom thought he would probably win their section; he seemed too good.

He was jolted out of his reverie by Orlas, who called his name with Elan's. Inwardly his heart sank, but he headed into the ring, head held high, buoyed by his earlier success. They bowed to each other and Elan looked him in the eyes, showing only contempt. Tom had the feeling this wasn't going to be a normal fight.

Elan started quickly, testing Tom's reflexes with quick jabbing movements and sweeping attacks, and Tom had to keep defending, finding no gap in which to retaliate. But then Elan seemed to falter, almost stumbling, and Tom took his chance to attack before realising Elan's move was a feint, designed to lure him in and then throw him off balance. Elan struck and Tom retreated rapidly, only just able to defend himself and hold on to his sword. He heard the crowd's sharp intake of breath. His heart pounded and sweat streamed down his face, and he chided himself for his stupidity. He took a deep breath to calm himself, and heard Arthur's words of advice from the many sessions they had fought together: *Sometimes, Tom, you just need to let your opponent wear themselves out.*

Rather than attack, he just kept defending. The crowd's cheers turned to jeers, but Tom ignored them, pleased when Elan became frustrated, his attacks becoming more wayward as he grew angrier. It was time for Tom to seize the advantage. As Elan finished a flurry of attacks that saw Tom bringing up his shield and side-stepping furiously, Elan fell back, out of breath, and Tom ran forward, mercilessly attacking. Finally he swiped at Elan's legs, and he fell. Before he could roll away, Tom stood over him, holding his sword to his opponent's neck, exerting just enough pressure to make him uncomfortable.

Tom had won. He stared Elan down, as Elan scowled back at him, furious.

Tom withdrew his sword and stepped back, then bowed to the roaring crowd who had clearly enjoyed the fight. Then, suddenly, there was a collective intake of breath, and shouts of warning. Out of the corner of his eye he was aware of movement, and he ducked and rolled quickly, narrowly avoiding Elan's sword.

This was no longer a contest, it was a proper fight.

He barely registered Orlas and Duke Ironroot stepping forward before he ran full charge at Elan. He was furious – what was Elan thinking? The air rang with the clash of swords, and Tom felt a sting across his arm as Elan cut him. He retaliated and slashed Elan across the cheek, a line of blood immediately welling up. But before they could continue, Orlas and Ironroot intervened and Elan ran for a gap between the benches and the competitors' area. He was fast, and his run was so unexpected that he was gone before anyone could catch him.

Woodsmoke vaulted over half a dozen benches, closely followed by Bloodmoon, and the pair gave chase.

Arthur joined Tom, Orlas and Ironroot in the ring. "What in Herne's name is going on?" he said.

"I have no idea – he attacked me! Although I gather he's been watching me."

"How do you know that?" Orlas said, looking worried and examining Tom's arm. "I didn't see anything."

"Adil, the Aerikeen I fought, noticed him." He shook his arm free from Orlas. "Don't worry, it's just a flesh wound."

Ironroot hustled them all to the side of the ring as the crowd started to murmur. He pulled them aside, his arm muscles flexing impressively. "Let's get on with the last fight, Orlas," he said.

Orlas nodded his agreement and raised a hand to still the restless spectators. He announced the next fight while Ironroot stood impassive, carefully watching the crowd. He had a stark warning for the last two competitors. "No funny business, or you fight me." The pair glanced at each other nervously and then stepped into the circle.

While they fought, Arthur said, "Why didn't you tell me?"

"Because I thought it was nothing, or that maybe he had a grudge for some reason." He shrugged, not wanting to worry Arthur. He already had enough on his plate today.

"Tom," he sighed. "I know you're lying." His tone was hurt, but trying to be patient. That of a worried older brother rather than a father figure.

Tom rolled his eyes. "Arthur! I'm fine, so stop fussing. He's gone now, and I have another fight. Go!"

With Elan gone Tom felt able to relax a little, and even enjoy the final fights. All too soon they were down to the final four and he was called to fight Clia, a female Cervini. Orlas proudly introduced her, but gave Tom an encouraging grin too.

As Tom started the fight he realised he'd found a rhythm he hadn't had before, even when he'd been practising for hours. In the short time of the competition he'd actually learnt a lot. Arthur and Woodsmoke had been right, as usual. Although he was hot and sweaty, and his muscles ached, a thrill of adrenalin kept him alert and strong. Clia was a good opponent, but he found he could anticipate her moves. Before he knew it he had disarmed her and won. They bowed respectfully to each other and then to the crowd, and left the ring. Tom was in the final.

The crowd hushed in anticipation. Tom stood in the ring looking up at the satyr, Satini, thinking his luck might have run out. The sun was now falling towards the horizon, and shadows were stretching across the grass. The grounds, however, held the heat, and a trickle of perspiration fell between Tom's shoulder blades.

They bowed and the fight began.

The arena rang with the clash of steel and Satini's and Tom's grunts. Both advanced and fell back, testing the other's strengths and weaknesses. Every time Tom defended a blow he staggered back. Satini was strong. Tom blinked the sweat from his eyes and tried not be intimidated by Satini's size, or his Otherwordly appearance. He couldn't help noticing that Satini didn't seem to sweat or tire, and realised he was losing ground.

The crowd followed them step by step, blow by blow. With one final, enormous swing of his sword, Satini flicked Tom's from his grasp, and Tom sank to his knees. He had lost.

Satini bowed graciously to the crowd, then grinned and pulled Tom to his feet, engulfing his hand. "You fight well," he said in his gravelly voice. "You are a worthy adversary."

"You fight better," Tom said, breathing heavily. "But if I had to lose to anyone, it would be you." He shook Satini's hand and then both turned to Orlas and Ironroot. The crowd was bellowing and a few satyrs started singing something Tom didn't recognise. It seemed the party had begun.

8 First Blood

Tom was hot and sweaty, but he was also very happy. Arthur was waiting for him with an ice cold beer. "Congratulations, Tom!" he said, shaking his hand. "You've made me proud. Satini was an excellent opponent, you acquitted yourself well."

"Cheers, I was taught by the best." Tom took a long glug of his beer with relish. "And thanks for the beer, this is just what I needed. Shall we go and find the others?"

"I've got to head off Tom – I have host obligations, but I'll see you later." He gave Tom a final powerful squeeze of his shoulder before disappearing into the crowds.

Tom turned to find Adil behind him, appraising him with a slow smile. "Well done, Tom. I'm quite impressed."

He felt himself blushing. "Ch-cheers," he stammered. "You were watching, then?" He inwardly smacked himself. *Obviously* she was watching.

"Of course. Are you going to be around tonight?"

"Around?"

"You know, around the campfires, celebrating?"

"I guess so."

"Good, I'll see you later." And with a long last look at him, she headed into the crowds, leaving Tom wondering if his heart was beating faster because of the fight, or something else.

The awards would be held on the final day, so Tom waved to the crowd then headed to the food tent. He grabbed some kind of faery meat pasty and headed to the knife-throwing. A few people patted him on the back as he passed, which was embarrassing but nice, and he found Beansprout standing on the edge of the enclosure, a look of concentration on her face. Following her gaze, Tom realised she was watching Brenna.

"How's she doing?" he asked.

She turned to him, shocked. "Sorry, Tom, miles away. Very well. You?"

"Came second." He shrugged. "I was beaten by the best. Satini is amazing."

"Awesome! Really sorry I missed your final match, but I saw you in every other round. You're really good! I always tell you to trust yourself more."

He grinned, pleased Beansprout had watched many of his fights. "Cheers, I surprised myself if I'm honest."

"Well done." She leaned over and kissed him on the cheek. "Now shut up, I'm watching Brenna."

Before he could say anything else, Woodsmoke appeared. "I've been looking for you."

They stepped out of the crowd's hearing.

"Did you find Elan?" Tom asked, suddenly anxious.

"No. But we found his trail. We followed him over the wall and tracked him to Inglewood. Unfortunately his trail disappeared quite quickly."

"You went to Inglewood! But that's miles away."

"We travel quickly when we need to, Tom. Besides, he disappeared hours ago. You've just been sidetracked."

"Where's Bloodmoon?"

"Investigating, he's good at that. And congratulations on coming second."

"Thanks. I had fun." Tom rolled his shoulders and winced. "But I think I'm going to ache tomorrow."

"You'll live. So, who's Elan?" Woodsmoke wasn't going to let this drop.

"I don't know," Tom said, exasperated. "He just appeared in the event. Maybe the officials will know more? He must have registered with someone. Although no-one seemed to know him, and I didn't see him talking to anyone."

"Well he seemed to know you. I just can't work out what he was doing. I mean, was he trying to kill you, beat you, humiliate you? It's not like he could have done much with everyone watching," Woodsmoke said thoughtfully.

"He tried very hard to hurt me!"

"Come on," Woodsmoke said, pulling him along. "Let's ask Finnlugh or Ironroot."

They found both in the weapons pavilion, already talking about Elan.

"Ah, there you are Tom," Finnlugh said. "I've just been hearing about the attack from the mysterious Elan."

"So you don't know him either?"

"No," Ironroot said. "But I suspect he may be from the fey lands beyond Inglewood, close to the shore and the string of islands they call the Serpent's Tail. You probably noticed he had dark hair and suntanned skin."

"Is that in any way related to the Forger of Light and the Wolf Mage?" Woodsmoke asked.

"No idea, but I'll find out what I can," Finnlugh reassured them. "In the meantime, enjoy the tournament. There's nothing else we can do at the moment."

Tom left for his room – he really needed a bath – after which he'd come back for the evening's entertainment. He wandered through the crowds, glad to be alone with his thoughts. The day had been busy, hot and exhausting, and his head was buzzing with all sorts of things.

Closer to the castle the grounds became emptier, and he strolled down the garden paths wondering why he hadn't seen his granddad or Fahey during the day. He presumed they'd been lost in the crowds. He passed the guards at the big back entrance of the castle, and made his way down empty corridors, hearing the occasional muted shout from outside.

He trudged up the stairs and into his room, and at once all thoughts of exhaustion left him. His room had been ransacked, and Jack and Fahey were lying motionless on the floor, both with bleeding head wounds. Jack lay face down on the rug outside the bathroom, and Fahey was halfway to the door. His heart skipped a beat and he felt suddenly sick. He stuck his head into the corridor shouting, "Help, Help! Come quickly!" He then ran over to Fahey and Jack. "Granddad, Fahey!" He reached Fahey first and shook him, pleased to see his eyelids flutter. He then ran to his granddad who also stirred slightly as Tom shook his shoulder. "Granddad, can you hear me?" he said urgently. A pool of blood was soaking into the floor, and there was a thick matted clot on the back of his head.

Jack didn't respond.

Turning back to Fahey, he shook him again, then gently checked his head. There was a large gash on the side of his head too. Someone had struck them both and just left them here. And for what? Panic rose as he realised they could die if they didn't get help soon.

He looked up to yell again as Merlin appeared at the door, a twinkle in his blue eyes. "Did I hear...?" His voice trailed off as he took in the scene, then hastened over to Fahey and Jack.

"Any idea when this happened?" Merlin asked as he examined them.

"No. I just got back. But why are they in my room, Merlin?"

"At this stage, Tom, we have far more questions than answers. Before we do anything else we need to move them. It's a good job I told Arthur to set up an infirmary." He looked up from where he was crouched on the floor next to Jack, calm and resolute. "They'll be all right, Tom, but I need you to go and find Nerian. Bring him to the infirmary. Now!"

As Tom ran from his room he heard Merlin shout, "And send the servants to help!"

Fifteen or so frantic minutes later, Tom finally found Nerian in conversation with a grizzled satyr – they appeared to be discussing stages of the moon and old prophecies. With muttered apologies he dragged Nerian away, breathlessly trying to explain what had happened.

The infirmary was on the ground floor, next to the kitchen and stores and overlooking the walled herb and vegetable gardens. It had been chosen because of its big windows and the natural light that flooded in. Merlin had started cleaning Jack's and Fahey's wounds. A young female fey stood at his side, handing him strips of linen, and helping him staunch the bleeding.

Jack now looked ashen.

Nerian immediately assessed the situation. "Run to my room and bring me my large leather bag, Tom." He turned his attention to Jack's wound.

"And bring my large spell book, you know the one," Merlin added.

Dusk had fallen, and the candlelit sick room was filled with the pleasant smell of burning oils and the spicy rich aroma of incense. Tom sat by the open window, letting the warm evening breeze wash over him, breathing in the soothing scent of the lavender oil. He was exhausted, but his mind raced with the events of the day.

A servant had been sent to fetch Arthur, Woodsmoke, Brenna, and Beansprout, who had joined them now that the final knife throwing event had finished. The rest of the guests were celebrating in the pavilions outside. Three boars had been roasting all afternoon, and the party promised to be a long one.

Finnlugh had also stayed a while, using the Starlight Jewel to aid the healing process, before leaving at Arthur's request to help keep an eye on the crowds.

Arthur was standing by the fire, looking grave. "I think I should cancel the rest of the tournament. It's clear someone is using it as cover to attack us." His voice shook with anger.

"There's no point now, Arthur," Merlin said. He was sitting by Fahey's bed, watching the slow rise and fall of his chest. Fahey's head was wrapped in bandages, but his colour was good and his breathing steady. "Just double the guards on the castle and lock all the doors except for the ones at the rear and the main hall."

"How can you say that after what's happened?" Arthur said. "I feel guilty about all of this. And I presume it's to find Galatine."

"And *have* they found it?" Tom asked, having forgotten all about his sword.

"No. It's very well hidden and protected, exactly where I put it earlier."

Tom had another thought. "Have they attacked the armoury? Surely that's one of the first places they'd have looked?"

Leaving Nerian and Merlin in the sick bay, the others raced to the armoury, where Dargus had been on guard the previous night. As they ran down the long corridor they saw the door hanging open. There was no-one in sight.

Tom's heart was pounding. *Please*, he thought, *let the guard be OK.*

As they entered the room they heard a hammering on the door of the inner forge, and a voice shouting, "Help, I'm locked in!"

Arthur unlocked the door and flung it open. Dargus stood on the other side, covered in grime but otherwise well.

"Thank Herne you've found me," he exclaimed. "I thought I'd die in there."

Arthur looked angry but relieved. "You fared better than some," he said. "Can you remember what happened?"

Dargus frowned. "Not really. I remember letting a woman into the weapons room, but I didn't know why I was doing as she asked. And the more I thought about it the more my head hurt. Then she suggested I should be in the forge, so I walked in and the door slammed behind me. That's all I remember, until I woke up in here."

"A woman? Who?" Arthur asked.

"I don't know, I've never seen her before. And for the life of me, I can't remember what she looked like." He clutched his head. "Ow, the more I try the more my head hurts."

Arthur sighed. "You'd better head up to the infirmary too." He nodded to the floor above. "Go on, I'll arrange a new guard. And Dargus," he added, as he watched him go. "Keep this quiet."

Brenna placed a hand on Arthur's arm. "This isn't your fault. None of us could have had any idea this would happen."

"I still think I should cancel the tournament," Arthur said.

"No." Brenna shook her head. "Woodsmoke's right. You've spent months planning this and it would be harder to stop it."

"I agree, and we can watch the crowds, see if anything unusual happens," Beansprout added. She leant against the wall, looking pale and tired.

Arthur paced up and down and ran a hand across his face. "This reminds me of a time when my other castle, Caerleon, was attacked." He said it so casually, like everyone had other castles. "It was during a visit by the neighbouring princes of Ireland, who had come to discuss trade. Someone tried to sabotage the deal by attacking the delegation, so Lancelot, Gawain, Galahad and I set a trap, and it worked well."

"A trap?" Tom said, feeling alert for the first time in hours.

Arthur continued to pace up and down, his usual activity when he had a lot on his mind. "I need to think on it, but for now we say nothing, and I'll cover this place in guards. Whoever it was may return, because they haven't found what they were looking for."

"We presume they're looking for Galatine? They might not be," Woodsmoke said.

"No, maybe not," Arthur said thoughtfully. "But then, what else is going on?" He shook his head, frustrated by the events. "I'm returning to the party. I want everything to look normal, and we act as if nothing's happened. Come on everyone, let's go."

"Everyone?" Beansprout said, reluctance written all over her face.

Arthur winked. "Just a few hours, my lady," and he held out his hand. "We are to look carefree."

Beansprout grudgingly took his hand and he led her from the room, followed by the others. Locking the armoury door, they left to find a new guard and then headed to the party.

They strolled across the grounds, past stalls selling all manner of wares — jewellery, clothes, food, amulets, weapons, charms and more. Laughter and singing were everywhere. Tom had never experienced anything like it, and he found his energy returning with the excitement of it all.

A large fire was burning in front of the colourful tents belonging to the royal tribes of fey, and another half a dozen smaller fires were scattered around the grounds, where other visitors had set up camp for the night. The tents of the royal tribes were distinct from the others, partly because of their size – they were like mansions – and partly because of their unique design. Trees and bushes had sprung up where before there were none, weaving together tightly to make organic tents, with small lights sprinkled in the branches. The insides were lined with silks and velvets, and carpets were rolled out across the floors.

They found Bloodmoon, Orlas, Aislin, Rek and Finnlugh sitting around a small fire in front of Finnlugh's tent, deep in conversation. They stood to greet them as they arrived, but Arthur spoke first. "I don't want anyone to know of what happened," he said quietly. "We keep it between us."

"I've heard about the attack," Bloodmoon said. "Unfortunately I have been able to find out very little. Elan kept to himself. He wasn't witnessed talking to anyone. However, he was outside the grounds this afternoon, we know that. That means someone else attacked Jack and Fahey."

Arthur groaned. "You're right, Bloodmoon. Now we have two to worry about. Dargus was attacked by a woman, she must have attacked the other two as well."

"What are you planning Arthur?" Orlas asked.

"I'm not entirely sure yet, but someone here is intent on causing trouble and I intend to find out who."

"And how are Jack and Fahey?" Aislin asked, concerned, her large brown eyes looking molten in the firelight.

"Recovering slowly," Woodsmoke said. "I'm tempted to head back to Inglewood to search for Elan; that's where he disappeared to earlier."

"If you go, I'll come. I can't wait to get my hands on him," Rek said, looking grim.

Finnlugh shook his head. "That would be madness, although I understand your reasoning." He gestured to the stools set around the fire. "Come, there is nothing else we can do tonight. Sit, eat, drink." As everyone found a seat, he said, "You know, I have been thinking about this Wolf Mage, and I think it may well be worth me visiting my cousin's Under-Palace – it's not far from here. One of our ancestors, who lived there years before, wrote books about famous fey; I wonder if that's where I've seen the name."

Aislin protested. "But you'll miss the tournament!"

"No, I'll be there and back in a day," Finnlugh said, looking excited at the prospect of action. "I shall leave at dawn, and I'll be back for the horsemanship event, you can be sure!" He turned to Brenna and Tom. "And now there's nothing to do except celebrate your third position with the knives today, and Tom's second in the sword fighting!"

Brenna grinned as she accepted a drink. "I had stiff competition."

"Sorry! I forgot to ask," Tom exclaimed. He'd been so caught up in other events he'd completely forgotten about the competition.

"Don't worry, Tom, you had a busy afternoon." She held up her glass. "Here's to your success too."

By the time Tom got to bed that night it was very late, and the moon was high overhead. He realised with a feeling of guilt that he hadn't seen Adil at all. He promised himself he'd try to find her tomorrow. At least no-one would be creeping across the grounds tonight, he thought, as his head hit the pillow. He slept like the dead.

9 The Clash of Steel

Early the next day Tom headed to the infirmary. Nerian was there, his matted hair bound back, his necklace of bones and feathers more clearly visible as a result. Like the other Cervini, he wore a sleeveless animal-skin jacket and trousers, and was barefoot. He was bent over a small pot hanging from a chain over the fire, stirring a viscous dark green liquid, the heat already making the room warm. An unmade bed indicated where Nerian had slept, and he looked up as Tom entered.

"How are you, Tom?" He looked tired, his eyes heavy.

"Better than these two, I think."

Jack and Fahey were still unconscious, but both looked better, particularly his granddad, his colour looking brighter.

"And you? Long night?"

"Not so bad," he said, with a small smile. "I've slept a little. They are recovering well, I'm not sure how good their memory will be, though."

"At this point I'm just glad they survived." Tom stood looking at Jack and Fahey, feeling terrible he hadn't been around to stop this.

As if he'd read his thoughts, Nerian said, "Tom, this is not your fault."

"I still can't work out why they were in my room," he said, frustrated. He sat down next to Nerian, watching him absently.

"I'm wondering if they were under some sort of spell."

"A spell? Why do you think that?"

"Your granddad and Fahey wouldn't willingly have led someone to your room, unless of course they knew them, but that's unlikely. And they knew someone may be after Galatine, or something else. It just makes me think they didn't know what they were doing, and therefore won't remember anything about who it was or what they wanted. And if you recall, Dargus was also enchanted." He finished stirring the pot and took it off the heat, adding in one final herb. "I fear we are dealing with someone very dangerous."

"How *is* Dargus?" Tom looked around the room. "Where is he?"

"He left earlier – he was fine."

"This could happen again, but how can we stop them if we don't know anything!"

"Do you remember the satyr I was talking to last night?"

"Yes, he looked very old." Tom remembered he had a white beard, flecked with red, and his horns were gnarled and very long.

"He is an elder of their tribe, well versed in ancient lore and the ways of the land." Nerian again stirred the liquid and Tom did a double take. It was now a pale golden colour and smelt of a rich spicy pepper that made him want to sneeze.

"What did you do to that?"

"I added a herb called clarian. This brew helps heal the mind." He started to pour the thick liquid into two cups. "I asked him about Filtiarn and Giolladhe. He remembers a saying in their lore that says when the moon waxes yellow in the lupine sign, the wolf mage will rise and shed his skin until the moon falls for another thousand years, unless he can draw down the moon."

"Waxes yellow in the lupine sign? He'll shed his skin? That sounds disgusting. I don't understand that at all," Tom said, exasperated.

"It refers to the engravings on Galatine, Tom, remember? The moon waxing yellow in the lupine sign refers to the moon cycle of the wolf, or Wolf Moon, which starts in a few days."

Tom sighed. "I'm still confused about this moon cycle of the wolf stuff."

"All moon cycles here belong to different animals or spirits. Some recur frequently, others not so. The wolf cycle comes every thousand years, and usually brings a deep yellow moon. It is a time of great celebration – the fey wear masks and throw parties."

They were disturbed by Merlin who swept in, wearing his usual long grey robes, closely followed by Arthur.

"Morning, any news?" Arthur asked immediately. His hair was tied back and he had trimmed his beard, probably because today he was competing in the sword fighting.

Nerian filled him in on what he had been telling Tom.

"The wolf moon cycle?" said Merlin. "I must confess this is unfamiliar to me. I am far more familiar with the lores of Britain. What does 'shed his skin' mean?"

"Unfortunately, he doesn't know. It's an old saying, its origin lost in time," Nerian said.

"We need to know more about Giolladhe and Filtiarn," said Arthur. "Until then we can do nothing. The root of everything lies with them." He turned to look at Fahey and Jack, full of concern and frustration. "We *will* get our revenge. But in the meantime I'm going to go and win the sword fighting." He looked so determined, and his skills were so good, that Tom didn't doubt it for a second.

Tom stayed with Nerian and watched him and the female fey try to wake Jack and Fahey, until Nerian looked at him. "Go Tom," he said. "There's nothing else you can do. We'll send a message when they're awake."

Tom found Beansprout at breakfast, and after reassuring her about Jack and Fahey, they wandered out to the grounds. For the next few hours they meandered amongst the stalls, catching up with friends and watching the events. They visited Finnlugh's tent and found he'd left before dawn on his big black stallion. They hoped he would bring back news. The archery was on at the same time as the sword fighting, so they divided their time between watching Woodsmoke in the target area, and Arthur, Bloodmoon, Orlas, Rek, and Ironroot, who were competing in the sword fighting. There were new judges who Tom didn't know at all, and they were very strict.

The day flew by in a blur of sunshine, tension, food, and cheering. The competition in both events was intense, and Tom was enthralled with the sword fighting, which he watched avidly, trying to pick up skills. The competitors moved swiftly, almost a blur at times, rolling and jabbing and circling each other, until he was exhausted just spectating. The crowd was equal parts cheering, and silent with suspense.

The fey were quick, lithe, and strong, but of course this raised Arthur's competitive spirit even further. Tom often forgot that under Arthur's debonair attitude and easy-going manner lay a core of steel. Weapons of power had been banned as they offered an unfair advantage, but even so, Arthur's skills surpassed all, including those with a certain natural magic and enhanced skills at their disposal. Watching him again, Tom experienced a jolt of the unfamiliar as he remembered who he was watching and where he was.

In one of the earlier rounds he watched Arthur and Bloodmoon compete against each other. Bloodmoon never said much about where he'd been or what he'd been up to, but Tom got the impression it was always slightly shady. His fighting skills were good, and the crowd were on their feet watching them. Tom liked Bloodmoon, but he wanted Arthur to win, so he was relieved when Arthur finally flicked Bloodmoon's sword from his hand.

After many rounds, some fights lasting a long time, Arthur ended up in the final against Ironroot.

Meanwhile, Woodsmoke was battling a highly skilled female fey from north of Dragon Skin Mountain. The archery competition comprised three distances, as well as shooting several targets at the same time, and finally, moving targets.

The fey seemed to have taken a shine to him, and was a little flirty. Tom watched with amusement as Woodsmoke first tried to ignore it and then accepted her attentions with discomfort.

He turned to Beansprout. "Why aren't you competing? I thought you were getting pretty good with your archery?"

"I haven't really practised lately, I've been so busy with magic. Any sign of Elan today?"

"No." Tom sighed. "I've been checking the crowds, but I guess he won't dare return now."

"Woodsmoke is so skilled – they all are," Beansprout said, distracted. "I wouldn't stand a chance anyway." And then she leapt to her feet, cheering Woodsmoke's latest shot.

Tom headed back to watch Arthur and Ironroot. The crowd was silent as the pair walked into the centre and faced each other. They bowed, and then the clash of swords shattered the silence. The crowds cheered and they were off, fighting furiously, their concentration intense. Neither would give an inch, and they were well-matched, both quick and strong with extraordinary skills. Tom could barely keep track of their movements, and wondered if he would ever be as good. The match was prolonged, but the crowd's attention never wavered. Arthur finally won, after somehow managing to throw Ironroot to the ground and pin him there with his sword at his throat. Ironroot was clearly furious at himself, but stood and shook Arthur's hand. Arthur raised his sword, grinning at the crowd. Tom laughed; he had never seen Arthur look so happy.

Tom found Beansprout heading away from the archery. "How did Woodsmoke do?"

She grinned. "He won, of course. Beat *that woman* easily!"

"Great, so did Arthur. Let's grab some food." He shepherded her across to the pavilions.

As the light faded and long shadows spread across the ground, they celebrated around the campfires with the others for a while, finding Arthur,

Woodsmoke, Bloodmoon and Brenna with the Aeriken.

Adil smiled as they approached. "Tom, what happened to you yesterday?"

"Oh, you know, stuff. Sorry." She looked very pretty, he thought, in the evening light, the flames throwing shadows everywhere.

She patted an empty seat next to her. "That's OK. Come and tell me what you've been up to."

Beansprout raised an eyebrow, but Tom ignored her with a lofty look, and sat down, smiling at Adil. However, it wasn't long before they received word that Jack and Fahey were awake, and so they headed back to the infirmary.

10 Hidden Histories

Jack and Fahey were sitting up, sipping soup and the golden restorative drink. Both smiled weakly as their visitors arrived.

"It's about time," Woodsmoke said, relief washing over his face.

"Fahey awoke first, a few hours ago, then Jack, but we thought we'd let them have a few hours of peace," Merlin said softly, his blue eyes solemn.

"I've got a pounding headache," Jack said, grimacing.

Beansprout sat next to him, kissing him gently on the cheek. "You had us worried. That was quite a thump you had."

"You don't have to tell me!" Jack said. "This drink's working wonders, though."

"I think I got off lightly," Fahey said.

"Your injury's still bad enough," Brenna said, settling in the chair next to him. "Can you remember anything?"

"Nothing at all. The last thing I remember is heading down the corridor with Jack to see the games."

"Same here," Jack said.

"I doubt you'll recall anything more," Nerian said, looking exhausted as he sat by the embers of the fire, the shadows making his eyes enormous.

The windows were wide open and warm summer air drifted gently through the room. From outside they could hear muted shouts, laughter and music drifting across the grounds. A feeling of peace washed over the infirmary as relief at Jack's and Fahey's recovery sank in.

The kitchen staff brought platters of food and drink, and they sat and chatted about the events of the day. Despite their ordeal, Jack and Fahey were keen to know what they had missed.

About an hour later, Finnlugh swept into the room, his bright white hair shining in the candlelight. He looked none the worse for his long journey.

"You have news?" Arthur paused expectantly, a drink halfway to his mouth.

"I do indeed, very enlightening news! My cousin has an excellent library," Finnlugh said, as he sat on the edge of an empty bed.

From a pocket deep in his cloak, Finnlugh pulled out a small leather book. "I have found the diaries of the ancestor I mentioned, who we called the Gatherer – he was forever searching for scraps of knowledge about this and that. He wrote books, some good, some bad. There are a few very interesting entries I would like to read you. Unless …" He looked to Fahey. "Would you like to do the honours?"

"Great Herne, no," Fahey protested from the depths of his pillows. "You go ahead."

Finnlugh opened the book, pulled a candle close, coughed gently to clear his throat and began.

"The Waning Hawk Moon

"I arrived in Dragon's Hollow over a week ago, travelling the blackened land over Dragon Skin Mountain. Despite the protection cast by Raghnall, the dragon tamer, I found it a perilous journey, and hardly slept. I have been staying in Raghnall's house, which he has called, quite precociously, the House of the Beloved. It is a small affair of black marble at the moment, but he assures me it will get bigger. If he wasn't a relative I would have nothing to do with him. I find him insufferable, even more so now he has ensorcelled the dragons. The Hollow is becoming quite the place to be, houses are springing up everywhere, and Raghnall has become a bit of a dandy.

"I am in Dragon's Hollow to meet Giolladhe and Filtiarn, the two brothers who have great

powers – two more additions to my book. A couple of days ago Raghnall finally introduced me to Giolladhe, or the Forger of Light, as everyone calls him. He is a peculiar man. Very skilled, generous with his powers – although he charges exorbitant fees – and full of knowledge of things dark and light, and things that should remain hidden. Giolladhe's abilities have called him far and wide across the Realm of Earth, making objects of skill and power. He has made rings of beauty, lockets of wisdom, chains of servitude, shields of strength, lances of purity and swords of power. He supplies the djinns of the desert and fire, the sylphs in their airy palaces, the water sprites in their cities far beneath the rolling waves, and the fey who roam across meadows and forests.

"He arrived here during the Dragon Wars. The mountains are rich with dragon gold and seamed with thick deposits of metals and gems. The Hollow speaks of him reverently. But, like Raghnall, he is full of pomp. I told him I was documenting great works for my book on skilled fey and he was only too pleased to show me his forge. I went there today.

"It is a large place – a cave, in fact – underneath the right shoulder of the mountain. There is a small winding passage cut into the rock that leads to it, sealed by a heavy copper door, covered in filigree and runes. The way it is constructed you would think it is meant to be a secret, but everyone knows its whereabouts, although anyone infirm would have trouble reaching it along the narrow path up the craggy mountain side. Fortunately I am relatively fit.

"The passageway winds to and fro, eventually reaching the main room, from which several doors lead off. The forge itself is huge. The fire glowing within makes the place stiflingly hot, but along the workbenches and wall are articles of great beauty. He showed me the objects he had been commissioned to make, as well as those he designed for general sale.

"He was at that stage working on a sword called Galatine, quite beautiful, with two fire opals set one on either side of the hilt. He said he was making adjustments for his brother, Filtiarn, the person I am planning to interview for my book, whose skills lie not with metals, but with the power to speak and understand any creature. He arrived in Dragon's Hollow just before Giolladhe. His skills have also brought him fame and wealth, as he is used by the many realms to help them communicate with creatures and resolve disputes. He had endeavoured to communicate with the dragons in their harsh guttural language, trying to broker peace, which brought him great respect amongst the sylphs – who of course have battled with the dragons for years. However the language barrier proved too difficult, and common ground could not be established, the dragons unwilling to relinquish their gains. In truth, I believe Filtiarn's sympathies lay more with the dragons, they had been there first. But their destructive powers were such that he stood aside when Raghnall cast his spells.

"According to Giolladhe, Filtiarn has decided that in order to avoid future miscommunications he wants his sword enhanced to improve his power of communication – I believe he wishes to re-open negotiations with the dragons, so there is no need for Raghnall's spell. In addition, such is his affinity with wolves (the reason he is called the Wolf Mage), he also wants to run with them, especially the white wolves who howl his name and follow him across the forests of the realm. He has asked Giolladhe to give his sword the power to turn him into a wolf at will – I find that astonishing.

"All afternoon I have listened to Giolladhe boast that it will be one of his greatest achievements. He has drawn down the power of the moon, specifically the Wolf Moon, and I wondered why he chose the Wolf Moon when it only came every thousand years. He assured me, however, that it could be used on any full moon, although the Wolf Moon will be the most potent. He says there are limitations on the transformation. It will only last one month, and to reactivate the spell, the ceremony of transformation must be performed again. This of course makes sense, for a wolf can hardly carry a sword! The enhancements are nearly finished, and the additional engravings are quite exceptional. He has also manufactured a receptacle for Galatine, a magnificent moonstone, into which the sword fits, and which will be embellished with some precious metals. He is to show his brother soon, and he says I may come too. It will be an excellent chance to meet him.

"The Waxing Wolf Moon
"This afternoon I again went to the forge. Filtiarn was already there. Unlike Giolladhe, who is blond and green eyed, Filtiarn is dark – his hair almost black – and he has dark blue eyes. He was accompanied by a young wolf, which followed him around the room. It was quite unnerving. I found I liked Filtiarn better. He had a warm gentle smile, and a patient understanding. He was very solicitous to my health.
"Giolladhe performed a spell which bound the sword to Filtiarn, explaining that he could not

perform the rest of the actions until the full moon. I confess, I do not know why the sword is bound to Filtiarn, I have never heard of that before, and neither had Filtiarn, but Giolladhe explained it was necessary for the rest of the spell to work effectively. Filtiarn was very cross and wondered why Giolladhe had bound the power of transformation to such a slow and restrictive cycle. Giolladhe explained – quite patronisingly – that transformation was difficult, and required a lot of power. The most effective way to do this was to draw on the moon, and the full moon was the most potent. At this point the arguing became angry and Giolladhe said he was lucky to be able to transform at all. I think they had forgotten I was there. In fact I tried to make it that way – I hid at the back, pretending to admire Giolladhe's other work, whilst making notes for my book.

"Finally Filtiarn stormed off, without Galatine as Giolladhe was still perfecting it, and they made arrangements to meet in the glade in the forests of the shoulders of the mountain, to perform the ceremony under the Wolf Moon. I asked if I could attend, but Giolladhe was now in a foul mood and refused, and after that I left. However I have no intention of being denied the ceremony, and so I intend to find the grove.

"The Morning after the Full Wolf Moon

"I am in quite a state and I know not what to do. Last night I witnessed Filtiarn's transformation. I had spent several days trotting around the forest, becoming covered in twigs, dirt and dust, until I found a grove, not far from Giolladhe's, with a large flattened rock, which I deemed to be the outside area designated for magical happenings. Obviously I could not ask anybody, it would have given away my intent, but I was right.

"Last night I lay hidden for hours until they both arrived. Neither, it seemed, had quite forgiven the other, but they pressed on with the ceremony. I am obviously familiar with magic, but do not practise it myself. My own natural talents are eloquence, written and verbal, and other abilities do not interest me. However, this was fascinating. The moon fell full upon the clearing, the yellow light bathing the spot in luminescent beauty. As Giolladhe performed the spell, the light seemed to grow brighter, stronger, until the grove dazzled. It seemed as if the moon had lowered herself directly over us. The sword was placed in the moonstone, and as the light hit, it glowed as if it were on fire. Filtiarn was kneeling in front of it, and it struck him clearly in the chest. I almost cried out at this point, because his whole body was consumed with light, and he screamed and fell to the floor writhing. And then the most monstrous thing happened. He turned into a great black boar. Not a wolf. And Giolladhe laughed and laughed until tears ran down his cheeks, and I could do nothing. Nothing. The young wolf howled and ran round and round the boar whimpering, and the boar seemed to lie as if dead. Giolladhe grabbed Galatine and ran, leaving the moonstone in the clearing.

"For what seemed like an age, I sat and wondered what to do, but because the boar lay still, I crept to his side and sat there, stroking him, and saying soothing things, which of course I'm sure he couldn't understand. Or maybe he could. Could Filtiarn understand human speech? The wolf, sensing I was no danger, lay close to me, and I comforted it too. I realised there was nothing I could do. To tell anyone what had happened would mean admitting that I was there. I fear what Giolladhe would do. As time passed the boar seemed to recover and staggered to its feet, and at this point I fled the forest. Boar can be killers.

"And all today I have debated my actions, and have again decided there is nothing I can do. Clearly Giolladhe has betrayed his brother. I can only hope that in a month Filtiarn will return to his human form. In a few days I will visit Giolladhe and ask his *progress. I confess I cannot bring myself to go*

before. It will be interesting to see his response.

"*The Waning Wolf Moon*

I saw Giolladhe today. He said the ceremony

went well, and his brother bounded into the forest

with his wolf. I asked him if he will return to human

form in a month and he said, of course, just as

agreed. But his smile did not reach his eyes, and I

fear what will become of Filtiarn. I have decided to

stay in the Hollow for another month, and continue

to write my book, whilst waiting for Filtiarn to

return."

Finnlugh looked up to a spellbound room, all eyes fixed on him. Even Jack and Fahey had roused slightly. "I shall flick forward a few pages to a later entry." He skimmed through some pages and then read again.

"*The Morning after the Hare Full Moon*

"*Last night I did something quite rash. I went to the*

clearing where Giolladhe performed the spell and

waited to see if Filtiarn would return. I again hid in

deep shadows, squashed beneath some bushes. It

was a good job I did, as Giolladhe also returned,

sitting on the flat rock which served as the altar, his

feet propped on the moonstone which was still

there. I confess I was quite surprised, I would have thought he'd remove it.

"After waiting for some hours Filtiarn returned, in his guise as a great black boar. His eyes glowed a dangerous yellow, and this time he was alone; the young wolf was nowhere to be seen. He walked right up to the altar stone and sat in front of Giolladhe, waiting. And Giolladhe just sat and looked at him as the bright white light from the Hare Moon fell upon them. I feared nothing would be said at all, but eventually Giolladhe laughed. 'You can wait here all night, dear brother, there will be no transformation.' The boar grunted and snuffled and pawed the ground. Giolladhe laughed and said, 'What was that? I can't understand you. I locked you into the thousand-year Wolf Moon cycle, dear brother. Isn't that funny? You must wait a full thousand years until you transform back into fey. But you will only remain in that form for one month, unless you have the sword and the moonstone, and the knowledge to perform the ritual and break the spell. At the end of that month you shall again become a boar, and thus shall the cycle continue for another thousand years.' The boar howled and howled; I thought my heart would break. And Giolladhe just laughed. 'Good luck with that, because I won't help you, you ungrateful cur.' And *then he stood and shouted, 'This is what you get for*

questioning my skills!' And he turned and left, and

Filtiarn just collapsed. It was obvious to me that he

had understand everything and had retained his

human intellect.

  "I waited sometime, and when it was safe I

crept out from hiding place and fled the forest. And I

am now leaving the Hollow. I cannot bear to be here

any more, and I fear to see Giolladhe again as I may

say something I regret and find myself in great

harm."

Finnlugh took a deep breath as he looked up, and held his hand up to still any questions. "One more passage," he said, as he pulled another leather-bound book from his cloak and rifled through the pages. "This features Giolladhe's great deeds. One of many stories about fey heroes.

  "The Forger of Light's reputation had spread

far and wide. He was asked to create a sword for

the Earth beyond the bright realms, in the shadows

of the Otherworld; a sword to unite and lead, to

deflect loss, to add glamour. The price was high, but

willingly paid, and the sword Excalibur passed to the

Lady of the Lake and then beyond the shores of

Avalon. She returned to him seeking a second sword

to give to a knight of this great king, but specified

no attributes other than that it should be of fine

workmanship, and be possessed of fey engravings

and glamour, so that all who should see it would

never question the righteousness of the owner.

Giolladhe declared that his brother must be dead,

and that it would be a shame for such a fine sword

to languish unused and underappreciated, and so he

gave Galatine to the Lady and it passed beyond the

Realms."

The room was quiet as Finnlugh finished.

"I know many tales," Fahey said, "but I have never heard of Filtiarn and Galatine and the transformation. Is your relative the only one to have known?" He looked puzzled, and a little annoyed.

"I think he must be, or him and maybe only a few others. He was obviously far too terrified to tell anyone," Finnlugh reasoned.

Bloodmoon spoke from where he sat by the fire, listening intently. "But Filtiarn transformed for one month every thousand years. If he had retained his wits he would have gone searching for the sword and his brother. He would have told someone. Family members. Friends."

"Well clearly the satyrs knew something at some point," Nerian said, "although they have forgotten how."

Tom nodded. "Maybe this is why Giolladhe eventually left Dragon's Hollow. He had to hide from Filtiarn."

"How did Vivian find him?" Arthur asked.

"I would imagine he'd disappear for just that month, and when the danger had passed he could return again, to continue his business," Merlin said thoughtfully.

"Until he upset the sylphs," Tom reminded them, thinking of their time at the Palace of Reckoning. "They didn't want to talk about him at all."

"By Herne! Is that great beast, the black boar in Inglewood, the one from the tale? Is it Filtiarn?" Arthur spluttered.

"What boar?" Finnlugh asked, amused to be the centre of so much curiosity.

"There's an enormous bloody great boar trampling around Inglewood, and I can't catch it," Arthur explained. "And it's always surrounded by wolves."

"But that's not the point!" Beansprout erupted from her chair next to

Jack, who despite all the excitement was now dozing again, his head lolling on the pillow. "If that *is* Filtiarn, he's been trapped in that form for over a thousand years!"

"Closer to five thousand – the dragon wars were a long time ago," Nerian said. "The sword has been in your Earth for fifteen-hundred of your Earth years."

A collective gasp echoed across the room as the enormity of the spell and the injustice registered.

"We must help him," Brenna said, "not hinder him."

"We can't forget what someone's done to Jack and Fahey," Arthur said.

"Of course not, but how desperate would *you* be if you found the sword to set you free was within your reach?" Brenna said, looking at all of them.

"And a Wolf Moon was about to occur," Nerian said softly, from his place next to the fire.

Arthur whirled round. "Is it? I didn't know that."

"Yes, the full moon will be in about two weeks. I would imagine that wherever he is, he'll be turning any day now."

"So someone is helping him," Bloodmoon said. "A boar could not have knocked out these two and put them under a spell."

"Are we going to give them Galatine?" Beansprout asked, slightly confused.

"No!" Arthur said indignantly. "I will *loan* them Galatine to release the spell, and then I wish it to be returned. It was Gawain's, and it's now Tom's. It has value to me." He looked a little sad. "I've lost too much and don't want to lose any more. However, I want to know what's going on before I give the sword to anybody."

"But Arthur–" Beansprout started.

Arthur interrupted. "For all we know it could be used as a weapon against us. I won't let that happen."

Silence fell for a few seconds as they considered Arthur's words and realised he was right. They had no idea what the sword might be used to do.

"Elan." Woodsmoke sat deep in thought. "He fled to the wood. He must be a grandson, or great grandson, or something. And he's clearly been watching you, Tom." Woodsmoke looked at him, and a smile started to spread. "I think you need to carry Galatine again."

"You want me to be bait!" Tom was indignant and a little resentful.

"What if he puts a spell on me, whacks me over the head and steals Galatine?"

Arthur was equally indignant. "Woodsmoke, that is underhand, dangerous, and ..." a note of admiration crept into his voice, "quite brilliant!"

"Will everyone please stop rejoicing in me as bait!"

Merlin held up a hand for peace. "May I suggest an alternative. I will glamour your old sword, so it looks like Galatine, and add a little extra protection to your bough. You still carry your talisman, Tom?"

"Yes, but ..." Tom couldn't believe his ears. No-one seemed to be saying this was a bad idea. And then he realised he could get even with Elan. He grinned. "Oh, all right then."

11 To Catch a Spy

The next morning Tom, Beansprout and Woodsmoke were sitting on the top row of the wooden benches around the horse-riding skills arena, looking out across the racing tracks, jumps, ditches, and pools of water. Overhanging trees and bushes provided further obstacles, and the taller trees had viewing platforms in them, like miniature tree houses. A few fey were already making their way up their ladders.

To Tom, the competition ground looked like a death trap.

"This event is going to be so much fun!" Beansprout said.

"If you like risking life and limb," Tom said.

Woodsmoke surveyed the ground. "I must admit, I was tempted to enter, but it looks very tricky. Did Merlin help with this?"

"I think so, I saw him heading over this way yesterday afternoon. I believe there's a few surprises in there."

"He's had a busy few days, then," Woodsmoke said, nodding at Tom's sword where it lay in its scabbard.

Tom pulled it free and laid it on his lap, turning it over so that it flashed in the sunlight. It was his old sword, but it looked just like Galatine.

"That is such a cool spell," Beansprout said. "I can't tell the difference at all."

"Neither can I, and it's my sword!" Tom looked at its fine engravings and the large pair of yellow fire opals on either side of the hilt.

"And have you got the bough?" Beansprout asked.

Tom pulled it from an inner pocket. Vivian had given him the small silver bough when he'd first arrived in the Realm of Earth. It gave him a level of magical protection that had enabled him to wake Arthur, and had also saved him from becoming trapped in Nimue's spell. It was the length of his hand span, and fashioned into the shape of a twig, with buds along it, as if it was ready to break into leaf. In fact, when Vivian had given it to him it had been a living branch that quickly turned to silver in his hands.

"Merlin's enhanced its protection," he said. "Don't ask me how. He just muttered something over it."

Woodsmoke grinned. "I'm sure it was more than a mutter, Tom."

"Well let's hope the sword draws some attention so we can catch whoever attacked us." He put the bough back in his pocket, reassured by its presence.

From their vantage point they watched as fey wandered over and found spots on the wide benches. The only other event on today was the wrestling, which was taking place in what had been the sword-fighting area.

"What exactly are we looking for?" Beansprout asked, scanning their surroundings.

"Anyone who looks like Elan, or who just looks suspicious," Tom said, taking a big bite of the wood-smoked pork sandwich he was having for breakfast.

"Just make sure you flash that sword about regularly," Woodsmoke said. "No-one can steal it if they don't know you've got it. We'll move around the different sections so that everyone can get a good look."

Slowly the benches filled up around them, a mixture of young and old – Aerikeen, Cervini, satyrs, fey, dryads, pixies, and even a few goblins. And then half a dozen judges arrived, a mixture of the different races, Merlin amongst them, and headed to their posts around the ground and on the tree platforms.

"Who's competing in this?" Tom asked.

"Bloodmoon, most of Finnlugh's crowd, and Brenna and a few Aerikeen," Beansprout said.

An enormous blast from a trumpet resounded through the trees and the first competitor approached the start of the course, marked by a flag with a dragon on it. The rider was a fey on a large black horse, and after another short sharp blast of the horn he was off, galloping through the trees at a blistering pace. Within seconds he disappeared from view, reappearing seconds later, weaving effortlessly through the trees, over the obstacles and through the water. There were unexpected hazards too, like obstacles that moved, water that rose up, and mist that rolled suddenly across the ground. All things considered, Tom thought it was a miracle that the rider made it through the course at all.

As rider after rider competed, with varying success depending on which obstacles arose, Tom found he was forgetting all about his sword, until Woodsmoke prodded him. "Come on, time for a walk."

"Suppose so," Tom said, and he and Beansprout clambered down after him, through the crowded benches. There were lots of ooh and aahs, and a thud as a rider fell from his horse, and then the arena was behind them as they walked to the refreshments tent.

They found Rek sitting with Orlas at a long table, drinking a pint of Dryad's Pride.

"You should try one of these," Rek said by way of greeting, indicating the dark brew. "It'll put hairs on your chest."

"I don't want hair on my chest, thank you," Beansprout said archly.

Rek grinned. "Only for the men, my lady."

"Don't worry, I'll risk it," Beansprout said, as Woodsmoke brought three pints over from the bar.

"Where's Arthur?" Orlas asked.

"As it's the final day, he's taking part in the judging and getting ready for the awards," Tom said. "And watching out for more unexpected visitors, probably."

Orlas nodded and extended his hand. "So, I think you should show me this amazing sword of yours, Tom. I haven't had a chance to examine it properly yet."

Tom handed it over, and Orlas made a show of examining it minutely and then held it up to the light. He even got to his feet and swished it around a few times so everyone got a good look.

"Nicely done," Woodsmoke said, as Orlas sat down again.

"Thank you, I aim to please. And," he nodded discreetly across the tent, "quite a few are looking."

"Not surprising after all that," Rek said, rolling his eyes.

Orlas ignored him. "How are Jack and Fahey?"

"Not too bad, really," Tom said. "I just want to catch whoever did it."

"We all do," Rek said. "When you've finished your drink, we'll follow at a distance."

After chatting for a few more minutes Tom, Woodsmoke and Beansprout set off, keeping to the edges of the crowds and scanning for familiar faces.

The next couple of hours were spent sitting, walking and watching. By early afternoon Tom decided the plan wasn't working. "I need to be on my own."

"It's too dangerous!" Woodsmoke said immediately.

"Whoever it is isn't going to attack when I have bodyguards."

"You're right. Tom, I think we need to have an argument and then you need to walk off in a strop." Beansprout looked very pleased with herself. "If you head to the orchards, keeping in the open for safety, it also means you can be seen on your own. Enter by the massive old plum tree and head for the walnut. We'll circle round and meet you there."

"What do you mean, pick a fight?" But instead of replying, Beansprout started having a go at him about something to do with cheating and bad sportsmanship, and then Woodsmoke rounded on him, and for a few seconds he felt anger mounting before realising it was a ruse.

"I'm not sticking around to listen to this!" he yelled. "You can both go stuff yourselves." And he marched off across the grounds, trying not to smile.

He pushed through the crowds and past the stalls, scowling, people stepping aside to let him through. When he reached open ground he slowed to give the others a chance to get in position, and strolled across the manicured lawns until he reached the meadows bordering the orchards. As he walked he swung his sword, swishing it through the long grass, looking mutinous, as if to challenge anyone who crossed his path, watching out of the corner of his eye to see if anyone was following him. Once or twice he thought someone was, but when he turned he saw nothing except grass and trees and the pavilions in the distance.

He slowed further as he reached the orchards. Finding the gnarled old plum he plunged into the trees, singing loudly to advertise his presence. The sunlight fell through the leaves in dappled waves, and as he advanced towards the walnut tree he stopped singing and walked in silence, listening for the sounds of anyone following him, accompanied only by the murmur of the bees.

In fact the bees' hum almost caused him to miss it – a low whispering drone.

He whirled around to see a figure in a long, hooded cloak, camouflaged by the shadows. He couldn't see a face, but he could hear a voice, and it sounded like a spell.

"Why don't you come a little closer and say that?" Tom raised his sword and stepped closer.

The figure held its ground and raised its voice, at the same time as its hands started to weave strange shapes.

Tom advanced on the intruder. "Spell not working?" He waved the fake Galatine. "If you want this, you'll have to come and get it."

The figure turned and ran, and Tom followed, yelling, "You'll have to find more than spells to stop me."

The cloaked figure raced through the high grasses, and then turned swiftly towards the high boundary wall, the hood falling back to reveal long red hair falling across slim shoulders – it was enough to show Tom his attacker was a young woman.

He changed direction to intercept. "Come back and fight, you coward!"

Two stags, Orlas and Rek, thundered into view, cutting off the boundary wall, and Woodsmoke stepped out of the trees, bow raised. As the woman turned again, Beansprout appeared in front of her and she hesitated for a second, giving Tom time to catch up. He leapt on her from behind, and they fell heavily to the floor.

She fought like a wild cat, throwing Tom off with surprising strength and leaping back onto her feet, her head held high and her eyes flashing with malice – but also with panic. She wasn't as confident as she appeared. And she was young, maybe the same age as Elan. Again she started to whisper spells, and as the others advanced she threw her arms wide and they all flew backwards, crashing into trees and branches and the wall. Tom felt the wave of power pass through him as he too flew backwards, hitting the ground behind him with a resounding thud. He lay winded, trying to catch his breath.

The woman glanced at Tom's sword, still clutched in his hand, as if weighing up whether to try and grab it. Then she thought better of it and fled over the wall in one mad scramble.

Groaning, they rose to their feet, clutching heads, shoulders, and backs.

"What the hell happened?" Rek yelled angrily.

"And who was she?" Woodsmoke asked.

"Did she take the sword?" Orlas asked, clutching his ribs.

"Please stop asking questions! And no," Tom said, standing on unsteady legs, looking at the patch of Tom-shaped grass beneath him.

"I think her knowledge of magic is very poor," Beansprout said, grimacing. "When she couldn't bewitch you she was stuck, and had to use that other spell. It was pretty crude."

"But effective," Tom said sarcastically.

"At least she didn't smack you across the back of the head, Tom," Woodsmoke said grimly.

Orlas sighed. "Well, so much for our trap."

"But at least we know who attacked Fahey and Jack," said Tom, turning back to the castle. "That's kind of a win."

12 The Wolf Moon Waxes

Entering through the side doors of the castle, they limped into the infirmary to report on the attack.

Nerian was sitting with Jack and Fahey in a patch of sunshine by the open window. He looked at their dejected forms and immediately said, "So I take it your plan failed?"

"You might say that," Rek said sarcastically, slumping into a chair.

"Have you got anything for a sore back?" Tom said. "I hit a tree root particularly heavily."

"I'm sure I have a salve here somewhere." As he reached into his bag, Nerian was unable to repress a grin at Tom's discomfort. "How did that happen?"

"We were attacked in the orchard by a witch," Orlas explained. He turned to the young fey who was helping Nerian. She had just finished redressing Jack's head wound. "I would be most grateful if you could bring us some refreshments," he said politely. She nodded and left, returning with jugs of water and beer, and a platter of finger food which she set on the table by the fireplace.

Jack came over to Tom and examined his back, where a large bruise was now blooming a rich purple. "I knew that was a risky plan, Tom. You shouldn't have done it."

"At least we know who attacked you, though," Tom said, smiling ruefully. Jack still had a dazed look about him from the assault, compounded by the bandage wound around his head. Tom was amazed he was even walking about.

"Had you seen her in the grounds before?" Nerian asked.

They all shook their heads. "No, but she was young, with long red hair," Beansprout said. "And she looked really worried."

"Worried enough not to attack again?" Nerian said.

"Yes, maybe," Orlas said, as he helped himself to some food.

"So what happens about Galatine now?" said Fahey.

"It depends. How long did you say until the Wolf Moon?" Beansprout asked, watching Nerian as he examined Rek's injuries.

"I believe it starts tonight," he said straightening up. "But it will be two weeks until it becomes full, and then wanes again. It depends if he turns at the very beginning of the month, or only on the full moon."

"It sounds like a werewolf," Tom said, brightening.

Jack laughed nervously. "Fahey tells me werewolves don't exist, Tom. This is different, isn't it?" He looked at Nerian, who chuckled.

"Yes, werewolves are different. They do exist, but Filtiarn isn't one. And besides, he's a boar."

"OK," Tom muttered, wondering what else lived here in the Other that he'd thought only existed in myths and legends. He guessed if there were dragons, werewolves and witches, then pretty much everything weird and wonderful must be here. And yet it always surprised him.

"When Finnlugh read from the Gatherer's diary," Beansprout said, "it seemed to suggest the full month, but maybe we should read it again." She turned to Tom. "Finnlugh gave you the book, didn't he?"

Tom nodded. "It's in my room."

"Good, check it again. But be careful where you put it, Tom. We don't want that to go missing too." She smiled and looked at Jack, Fahey and Nerian. "Well, seeing as you two look so much better, and Nerian hasn't had any fun at all, I think we should go and watch the end of the tournament."

Promising to catch up with them later, Tom returned to his room, deep in thought, while the others headed back to the finals. He was relieved to find the diary where he left it, on a burnished copper table next to his bed, along with two more books Finnlugh had suggested might offer further insights into the two brothers.

He picked up the diary and stroked the worn and stained leather cover. In places it was cracked, but considering its age that wasn't surprising. It was curious that so few knew of Filtiarn's story, but it was long ago, and maybe Filtiarn hadn't wanted anyone other than his own family to know of the curse. It would make sense. Wouldn't it be embarrassing to be cursed and duped by your own brother?

He thumbed through the pages, wondering what else the Gatherer had been up to, then settled back on his bed to read. It was only later, flicking through the back pages, that he discovered a pocket in the leather back cover.

Inside were some old drawings and maps — and one of them looked like Dragon's Hollow.

The tournament was nearly over. The wrestling had finished and a winner was announced — a satyr from the woods around Aeriken. The final rounds of the horse riding skills were finishing; the stands were full, the crowds on their feet, cheering and shouting.

In front of the pavilions a podium had been set up for the awards presentation, and Tom found everyone lounging on blankets on the grass in front of it, soaking up the late afternoon sunshine. Arthur stood to the right of the podium, regal in a fine linen shirt, trousers and boots. Next to him stood Orlas and Ironroot, there to help with the prize giving, and a straggle of visitors who'd been involved with the judging. On a long table behind the podium was a row of cups, shields and plaques, ready to be given out.

Tom waved at the others and headed towards Arthur, who looked relieved to see him.

"I've been worried about you," said Arthur. "I haven't seen you for hours!"

"I've been reading, and I've found out some interesting things."

"I heard all about the incident earlier. Are you all right?"

"I'm fine, but after this I need to show you what I've discovered."

A long loud blast from a horn interrupted them.

"That sounds like the end of horse riding, Tom. We're nearly finished now. Don't go anywhere, you have a prize to collect." He grinned before turning to Orlas.

Tom groaned and joined the others on the grass, sitting next to Brenna.

"I thought you were competing," Tom asked, curious. "Shouldn't you be over there?"

Brenna laughed. "I was out in the early rounds — there's stiff competition in the horse riding." As she spoke the crowd erupted again, cheering and clapping, before slowly starting to disperse from the benches.

The grassed area started to fill up and eventually, as everyone finally settled with drinks and food, Arthur started the prize giving. Tom generally hated these things, but had to admit that Arthur did it with a certain panache. He was glad that his granddad was there to see him collect his award, and that he and Fahey could enjoy at least some of the tournament.

Tom found his mind returning again and again to the woman in the orchard. Who was she, and how was Elan linked to it all?

But Beansprout had decided the night was all about celebrating. "There's plenty of time to worry about Filtiarn, Tom," she said, noticing him brooding, "and this isn't it." She grinned. "Tonight is about celebrating friendships. Later ..." she pointed to where Merlin was walking out to the edge of the field, "there'll be fireworks."

Tom laughed. "In that case, Beansprout, I'll enjoy the party."

And then Adil, the young Aeriken from the sword fighting round, sat next to him with a smile, and he thought the night might become even more interesting.

13 Planning the Hunt

By mid-morning, the sprawl of tents and stalls had been packed up, leaving in their place flattened grass and furrowed land. A team of servants was already at work on clearing the grounds and dismantling the pavilions. People dawdled out of the gates and on to the moors, back to their villages and homes, carrying tales of daring and courage.

Arthur had mingled amongst them, shaking hands and promising to put on the event again. Tom had watched, curious, wondering if this was how it had been in Arthur's time, with pageants and contests, and knights setting off on their quests and adventures. He had a sudden pang for what had once been. He liked Arthur's quiet informality, his ability to treat everyone equally. No wonder he had been a good king.

Finnlugh and the royal household were mounted on stamping horses that snorted with excitement, ready to be off. Finnlugh slipped to the ground as he saw Arthur and Tom.

"Well done, Arthur!" he said, shaking his hand. "Excellent event. I shall look forward to the next. Do you need me to help with the witch?" He grinned rakishly. "You know I always enjoy a challenge."

"Thank you, but no," Arthur said, smiling. "I think small numbers will be advantageous in this case."

"Well, you know where I am if you need me." Finnlugh turned to Tom and shook his hand. "Good to see you back. Make sure you stay this time."

"I'm not going anywhere!" Tom said, his heart skipping a beat at the thought.

Finnlugh swung himself up onto his horse. "Look after the books – it'll be a good excuse to come and see me when you've finished with them. I'll keep looking too; if I find out more, I'll let you know." And with a flash of white-blond hair and the gleam of sun on silver lances, bridles and stirrups, the royal household disappeared.

Tom felt a stab of sadness as Finnlugh left. He would miss him. But as he and Arthur headed back to the castle, he was cheered by the thought of the conversation they'd had with Brenna earlier, at breakfast. She had sent the other Aerikeen home, while opting herself to stay and help. Tom had teased her, saying, "I'm sure we could manage without you, Brenna. You must have lots to do."

With a glint in her eye, she'd said, "Thank you, Tom. When I need your advice I'll ask for it."

He'd scooted out of the way as she tried to cuff him on the shoulder.

Also at breakfast, Orlas and his wife had announced their intention of returning to the White Woods with the rest of the Cervini. "I'm sure you'll be happy to get your home back, Arthur," Orlas had said. "Rek wanted to stay, but I need him. I'm not sure he'll forgive me." He'd turned to the grizzled older warrior. "I'm sure they'll manage without you."

"I'm sure they will, but I'll miss out on all the fun!" Rek had moaned, his mouth full of sausage.

Tom smiled. They had got to know the Cervini well since moving into the castle, and had become good friends, especially with Rek. "We'll miss you," he'd said. "But Brenna can come get you if we need support."

Tom's thoughts returned to the present as he and Arthur entered the infirmary, where they had arranged to meet the others. Tom immediately felt soothed by its calm atmosphere. The windows were open and a warm breeze flowed through the room. The gardens outside were a vigorous green, and the walls blocked out the noise of the departing guests.

Nerian was standing by an open window, talking with Jack and Fahey, his bag in his hands. He turned as they entered. "I'm glad to see you before I go. These two have made a good recovery. I've left some of the healing brew, but otherwise there's nothing further I can do."

"Give me a few more years of that stuff, and I might feel young again," Jack said, grinning.

Fahey laughed. "I don't think even Nerian's that good."

"Good luck finding Filtiarn," Nerian added. "I'm glad Merlin's going with you. I have a feeling you'll need him." With a swing of his dreadlocks he left.

"You know you two can't come with us," Arthur said, "so don't even try to argue."

Jack nodded. "Don't worry, I know my limitations. And besides, my head still hurts."

"I think that may have been the beer last night," Fahey said with a grimace. "But it's all right, Arthur. We have no intention of coming."

Arthur nodded. "Good. It's only that I think we'll have enough to worry about."

They were interrupted by the arrival of Brenna, Woodsmoke and Bloodmoon, and then Beansprout arrived with Merlin.

Merlin had brought the real Galatine. "I cannot find anything else on this sword that gives a clue to reversing the spell. I presume all will become clear on the night of the Wolf Moon."

"And what if it doesn't?" Woodsmoke asked. "How do we break the spell?"

"I think the first thing we need to do is find Filtiarn," Arthur said. "Soon he'll be in human form, hopefully, and will be able to speak to us. He must know how the spell works."

"If he lets us help him," Woodsmoke said.

"If we can even get near him," Bloodmoon added.

"If Elan and the woman are helping him," Tom said, "I don't understand why they wouldn't just tell us what's going on."

"When you've been betrayed before," Merlin said, "it can be hard to trust again."

Merlin's tone was measured, but Tom wondered if that applied to him too, after all Nimue had done. But something else was tickling his brain.

"I found some maps in the back of that old diary Finnlugh found," he said.

"Maps of what?" Beansprout asked, intrigued.

"One looked like Dragon's Hollow, although it appeared much smaller on the map. And a few other places I didn't recognise."

"Dragon's Hollow?" Beansprout said, excited. "Was there anything about the Forger of Light?"

Tom shrugged. "I don't think so."

Bloodmoon grinned. "Old maps, Tom! Hidden treasure?"

"Is that all you think about?" Woodsmoke asked, looking at his cousin sceptically. "Are you sure you haven't got anything better to do?"

"No. And you know I can be very useful," Bloodmoon said, smiling at Woodsmoke's discomfort. He tapped his sword where it hung in its scabbard, "And I've still got my dragonium sword. It may come in handy."

Tom shuddered slightly, remembering their encounter with the lamia.

Arthur nodded thoughtfully. "Yes, it may! I think we should get moving. Let's head for Inglewood. And bring those books with you, Tom."

14 Back to Inglewood

Within the hour they had left to search for Elan, Filtiarn, and the mysterious woman. There were seven of them: Arthur, Tom, Merlin, Beansprout, Woodsmoke, Brenna and Bloodmoon, racing on horseback across the moors to Inglewood. They had no idea what to expect so were all heavily armed, and supplied with food, water and bedding.

The day was again hot, and they were relieved to enter Inglewood. As they descended into the valley the temperature dropped, and the black shadows beneath the trees hijacked the sunlight. Arthur rode ahead with Woodsmoke, while Tom kept to the rear with Bloodmoon. The trees thickened and they slowed their pace. Even though Tom hunted here regularly, he still found it a bewildering place. Large rocks and misshapen trees provided landmarks, but he still felt he could easily get lost in here.

Arthur was aiming for the place where they normally saw the boar. Elusive though it was, it seemed to favour a certain part of the wood. And it was close to where Tom had been surrounded by the wolves.

"I recognise this place," Arthur said. "But there's a path I don't remember seeing before." He pointed to where a barely-there path snaked into the undergrowth.

"It could be a trap," Brenna said, drawing her horse to a halt.

The others did the same, and Merlin moved next to Arthur, holding a hand up for silence. He sat silently, his head bowed, his hair covering his face. For a few moments he listened intently and then said, "Let me lead."

Woodsmoke was about to protest but Merlin fixed him with a piercing glare, and he fell into step behind him with a nod and a sigh.

They followed in single file, as the path eventually led to a clearing in which was a stagnant pool. Beyond it was a rocky mound with a cave in it, the entrance dark and overgrown with bushes.

"I don't recognise this place," Arthur murmured.

As they entered the clearing a strange green smoke started to rise from the ground, eddying across the rocks and bushes and the surface of the pool, reaching out towards their horses. In response Merlin raised his hands and started an incantation, his voice soft and seductive. Immediately the smoke stopped, as if it had hit an invisible wall. Beyond this, it thickened.

Instinctively they started to retreat, but after only a few paces the white wolves emerged from the trees behind them, bellies low and teeth barred. Goosebumps rose up Tom's neck as they were forced back towards the pool, weapons ready, bunching up behind Merlin.

Arthur turned to Merlin. "What's that smoke? Can we get through it?"

"No. And stop asking questions," Merlin muttered. He continued to chant, his hands raised, and the invisible wall moved away from them, pushing the murky green smoke back, allowing them to edge forward uncertainly.

A young woman emerged from the cave. Her long silky red hair snaked down her back, almost to the floor, and she wore a black velvet gown edged with sable. It was the woman from the orchard. Elan stepped out behind her.

"Who are you that brings such powerful magic to my grove?" she said, her voice loud and clear.

"I am Merlin; prophet, sorcerer and advisor to the court of Arthur Pendragon, Boar of Cornwall, Dragon Slayer, bearer of Excalibur." Although his eyes never left her face, his hands continued to weave his magic. "But I think you know that. And you are?"

"I am Rahal, Guardian of the Wolf Mage," she said. "You must be the one responsible for protecting the boy over there. There are faces I recognise from our encounter in your grounds."

"The Wolf Mage," Arthur repeated, nodding as their assumptions were proved correct. "So it *is* about him. I do not appreciate the games, Rahal. You have attacked us, grievously. What do you want?"

"Galatine. It belongs to us." She lifted her head, her eyes flashing.

"Why didn't you come and ask for it?"

"I shouldn't need to ask for it. It is Filtiarn's to take. And I will take it for him."

She again raised her hands as if to strike with magic, but in a flash Merlin launched a flaming arrow straight through the invisible wall towards her, dispelling the green smoke and causing Rahal to shriek curses at them.

The wolves hurtled towards them in a flash of fur and teeth. Tom swiped at the first one as it leapt at his throat, and sent it whirling backward. The others were also fighting frantically, arrow after arrow flying into the wolves, a few falling dead around them. Furiously fighting and trying to control Midnight, who was bucking with fear, Tom didn't at first realise he was getting cut off from the group. He tried to make his way back as Bloodmoon fought his way over, Woodsmoke next to him, yelling, "Tom, get behind us. They want your sword."

Tom heard a scream, and Elan shouting, "Stop, stop!"

He glanced round and saw Merlin standing over Rahal's unconscious body, Elan at her side.

"What have you done?" Elan cried.

Merlin was furious. "She was trying to kill us!"

"She was trying to protect Filtiarn," he said, leaping to his feet, sword drawn.

"No – she was trying to steal Galatine! Call the wolves off, Elan," Arthur said, his sword at Rahal's throat, "or I'll kill her right now."

Elan glared at Arthur, and then yelled something at the wolves in a language Tom didn't understand. Immediately the wolves withdrew, growling and snarling in a semi-circle in front of them. Elan continued Rahal's argument. "It's our sword; we have a right to it."

"You do not have a right to knock people unconscious for it!" Arthur said, towering over Elan. "Did you not think of asking, of telling us of your plight and the curse upon Filtiarn?"

Elan faltered, "You know of the curse? No-one should know that, it's a family secret."

"Well *we* know. Repeated attacks upon us made us look into Galatine's past. You should know right now, that I do not tolerate attacks upon my friends or household, and you should be very careful what you do in the future."

Elan stepped back a pace, but his expression remained mutinous.

Arthur turned to Woodsmoke and Bloodmoon. "Check around the back of this rocky mound, I want to make sure there are no more surprises."

They nodded and set off, swords drawn.

Arthur turned to Elan. "Where's Filtiarn?"

Elan nodded behind him. "He's in the cave." Looking nervous he raised his sword as if prepared to fight. "Do you mean to attack him?"

Arthur snorted. "Great Herne, no! We are here to help, you stupid boy. Although," he looked at Elan's sword, "if you keep pointing that at me I might change my mind."

Elan nervously re-sheathed his sword. He didn't look keen for a fight, and Tom didn't blame him. No-one in their right mind should want to fight

Arthur.

"When will Filtiarn change form?" Arthur asked, returning Excalibur to its scabbard.

"Tonight, midnight as the Wolf Moon begins." Elan hesitated. "We think so, anyway. Neither of us was around the last time he changed form."

Merlin straightened and peered at Elan, Rahal still unconscious at his feet. "So you have no idea what to expect?"

Elan shook his head looking suddenly young and vulnerable.

"Show me to him," Merlin said, and Elan led him into the cave.

Arthur turned to Tom. "Go with him, I'll watch Rahal."

The cave was dark, and a small fire smouldered to the rear. The smoke wound its way up to a narrow vent in the roof, but eddies of it drifted around, and Tom's eyes started to smart.

Filtiarn wasn't far from the entrance. He lay on his side, his huge mass stretched out across the floor, an earthy musky smell emanating from him, adding to the stink of the cave.

"Have you been living here?" Merlin asked Elan, kneeling at Filtiarn's side.

He nodded. "For a few months, ever since we heard about Galatine." He looked at Tom and then the sword at his side. "Is that Galatine?"

"Yes."

"May I look at it?"

Tom glanced at Merlin. At his nod, he took it from its scabbard and handed it to Elan, who turned it over, examining it minutely in the dim light.

"Have you any idea how long we've been looking for this?" he asked, relief evident in his face.

"We have a rough idea," Tom said. "We're thinking close to four thousand years."

"Close enough. Long enough that we need to break the curse or he may not live another thousand years." He sighed. "My family history says that the last time he returned to human form he was wild, almost inhuman, and mad with grief." He looked at Tom. "Do I have to give it back?"

"For now." Tom took Galatine and returned it to its scabbard. "And why are *you* helping Filtiarn?"

"Every new generation, two guardians are assigned to Filtiarn. I'm one of them."

Tom couldn't help but notice he didn't look pleased with the job. "And who's Rahal?"

"My cousin. She was chosen for her knowledge of magic, and I was chosen for my skills with the sword. The old guardians died, and the new ones are always young. Rahal, however, is senior to me."

As much as Tom was mad at Elan for attacking him during the tournament, he felt sorry for him. "It must be a hard job."

"It's a thankless task," he agreed, annoyed and sulky.

"Do you know how to break the spell?" asked Merlin.

"Not really. Only that we need the sword. We hoped it would become clear when we had it."

Tom felt his heart sink. No-one seemed to know how to break the curse.

Merlin groaned, looking incredulous. "Haven't you any books or histories to refer to?"

"No!" Elan's voice rose in alarm and distress. "When it first happened, Filtiarn just disappeared. Of course no-one knew where he had gone. And then when he did return, after that first thousand years, he was so mad at his brother's deception that he didn't want to share anything. Apparently."

Filtiarn stirred and rolled in his sleep, and then his eyes fluttered open.

"I'm going to try something," Merlin said. In a flash he changed form, and now two boars were lying on the floor of the cave, snorting softly to each other.

Tom tried to reassure Elan, who if anything looked more alarmed than before. "It's what he does," Tom said, shrugging. "He shape-shifts. Tell me more."

"I don't know what more I can say. He lives in and around our family castle, roaming the woods and grounds, along with a pack of wolves. Every thousand years he changes form, returning only briefly to our home, and then he searches, endlessly, for Giolladhe. Guardians were assigned to watch over him, to help search for the sword with him, and to continue the search when he is in animal form. When he found out Giolladhe had given Galatine to the Lady of the Lake, he thought everything was lost. *We* thought everything was lost. But now it's back, you understand why we had to come for it ..." Elan's voice trailed off.

"You should have come to us," Tom repeated.

Elan's voice dropped and he couldn't look at Tom. "To speak of the curse outside the family is to risk death. Both for us and you."

"Why?"

"Our family is proud. To admit that one brother double-crossed another is too embarrassing. Especially two very famous brothers whose deeds are well known across the Realms."

Tom gasped, trying to ignore the snorting and snuffling coming from Merlin and Filtiarn. "Are you kidding me? That's the stupidest thing I've ever heard. It was forever ago!"

"My father doesn't think so. Our family may have fallen on hard times, but the family pride remains. Things will change now we have the sword. We can pretend you don't know anything, and that we managed to steal it."

"But you don't know the spell. And neither does he by the sound of it. And there's nothing inscribed on the sword that will help break it."

"At least we have the sword!"

Tom felt his frustration growing. "Elan, I don't think you can do this without us. It may not look like it, but Merlin is one of the greatest sorcerers ever." They turned to look at Merlin and Filtiarn, as they shuffled to their feet and waddled out of the cave.

"Really?"

"Yes! You need him to undo the spell. Especially if Rahal can't do it."

"My father will kill us."

"I think he'd be angrier still if you let this opportunity pass. You said it yourself. Filtiarn may not survive to see another Wolf Moon."

Elan looked out of the cave, clearly wondering what he should do.

Tom patted him on the shoulder. "Come on, let's see what the others are up to."

15 Brother's Betrayal

Night was falling as Tom and Elan left the cave. Someone had started a fire in the centre of the clearing, and branches were stacked in a pile next to it. In the shadows at the far edges, the wolves sat and watched them, their yellow eyes glinting in the firelight.

A few logs had been pulled around the fire, and Beansprout and Brenna were sitting warming their hands, their cloaks pulled close. Lying next to them, where they could easily watch her for signs of movement, was the prostrate form of Rahal, wrapped in a blanket. After a warm day, the air was now chilly, and a few stars had started to spark in the night sky.

Tom and Elan joined Arthur where he stood talking to Merlin, no longer in boar form.

"How is he?" Arthur asked, looking in concern at Filtiarn snuffling in the edges of the fire.

"Confused," said Merlin. "There were flashes of comprehension, but mostly all he could say was that he was hungry and tired."

"Hungry?"

"It's a primal urge in animals as well as humans. I'm not sure if we'll get any more sense out of him once he changes."

"So his mind might have gone forever?" said Tom.

A sad smile flickered across Merlin's face. "Maybe. But perhaps not being able to reason with a human mind is a way of preserving his sanity, Tom."

"But you can think clearly as an animal?" Elan asked.

"Yes, but I only turn for a short period, and shapeshifters such as Brenna are meant to change. Filtiarn has lived as a boar for a thousand years, and more."

Arthur shivered. "I only turned for a short time in Nimue's spell, and all I can remember is trees and more trees. I don't think I had one logical human thought in my head."

Merlin nodded thoughtfully. "All being well, he will change form later and his human reasoning will return. Until then, we wait."

Bloodmoon and Woodsmoke had returned with news that they could find nothing else of danger in the surrounding area. They had shot rabbits and a pheasant for supper, and sat side by side, expertly skinning, de-feathering and gutting the carcasses, before chopping them into chunks and placing them in a large pot over the fire, along with water and herbs. The smell of cooking reminded Tom how hungry he was.

He left Elan talking with Arthur and Merlin, and sat next to Beansprout, nibbling on a piece of cheese. It was strange seeing her out of her long dresses. She was now wearing dark leather trousers, a shirt, and a leather tunic that doubled as some kind of body armour. "How're you, Beansprout?" he mumbled.

"OK, Tom. Just realising this is going to be harder than we thought." She turned her gaze from the fire to look at him. "I mean – we don't know anything! Just a few old stories. It would seem like a story if we didn't actually have proof in front of us." She glanced at Filtiarn.

Brenna leaned across. "Didn't you say you'd found some old maps?"

"Ooh yes!" Beansprout said, brightening. "Let's have a look, Tom."

He pulled the book out of his pack, carefully extracting the maps at the back. "This is the one that looked like Dragon's Hollow."

They stared at the map in the firelight, following the lines and contours. "Looks like it to me, but it's smaller," Beansprout said. "Look, he's marked a few places. That could be Raghnall's place, and there's the mines, and there's a mark on the hill behind Raghnall's."

Woodsmoke joined them, leaning over Beansprout. "I knew that path led somewhere!"

Tom looked up at him, confused. "You mean the one that leads up the mountain? We know where it goes. To the top."

Woodsmoke shook his head. "Tom, Tom, Tom. Subterfuge only! Convenient, yes. But I bet that's Giolladhe's place. The route to it must be off that main path."

Now Brenna looked confused. "But why would he hide it? What does it matter?"

"If Raghnall hid it, it's because there's something valuable there he didn't want anyone to know about," Woodsmoke reasoned. "He was a sneaky rat, remember?"

"Maybe," Beansprout said.

Tom had pulled some of the other drawings out and was examining them too. "He's drawn some people. Must be some of his famous fey." Underneath the drawings were names of fey he didn't recognise, but then he gasped. "Look! Giolladhe and Filtiarn."

On one page, tattered and worn like all the others, were pen and ink drawings of two men, one with light hair (or so Tom presumed – it had less ink than the other), and one dark. The blond one had short hair, thick and wavy, and a sharp chin and narrowed eyes, and underneath was written *Giolladhe*. The dark-haired one had longer hair, and a slight beard, and under him it said *Filtiarn*. Next to both was written, *The famous brothers*.

"How amazing," Beansprout said. "To see a picture of the Forger of Light! And Filtiarn, who's right here! He looks so young and handsome," she said with a wistful sigh.

By now Elan had joined them. Beansprout looked at him, comparing him to the picture. "He looks a bit like you, Elan."

Tom thought he detected a snort from Woodsmoke, who didn't seem too pleased at Beansprout comparing handsome men.

"I bet he doesn't look like that any more," Tom said, wondering what was going on with Woodsmoke. "And look, a drawing of Galatine." He pulled his sword free. "It's incredibly detailed. The Gatherer was a very skilled artist as well."

"Where did you get those from?" Elan asked, looking at the drawings with interest.

"A friend of ours found them, they were in a diary. Someone watched Filtiarn get cursed."

Elan looked shocked. "And they didn't help him?"

"He couldn't help him," Tom explained. "He was scared."

"What else is in there, Tom?" Brenna said.

Tom passed her some more papers, and she opened one and looked puzzled. "Galatine's moonstone." She looked up, startled. "What's this?"

Before anyone could answer, Rahal stirred and her eyes flickered open. Brenna pulled her dagger free and placed it under Rahal's chin, calling sharply, "Arthur, Rahal's awake."

"Don't hurt her!" Elan shouted. "She was only doing what she thought was best."

"So am I," Brenna warned with a sidelong glance.

Elan ran to Rahal's side. "Rahal, it's all right. You're safe."

Arthur stood over her, putting her in shadow, and she recoiled nervously. "Rahal, if you promise not to try anything stupid, Brenna will put away the dagger."

She glanced nervously at Elan, who nodded and said, "Honestly, we're fine. They want to help."

"All right, no magic, no tricks." She rested back against the log and put a hand to her head. "What did he do to me?"

"Only a little spell," Merlin called over from where he sat next to Filtiarn.

Tom reminded himself never to underestimate Merlin's hearing.

Arthur smiled before continuing. "As I said earlier, Rahal, we are here to help you break the spell. In a few hours Filtiarn will change form. We need you to tell us what you know of the spell, if we are to break it forever."

"It's our family secret," she said quietly. "It is not for others to know."

"That time has gone," Elan said. "They're right. In all these years no-one has come close to breaking the spell. In another month we may not have another chance." He grabbed her hand. "I've told them what I know, but it's not much. Do you know any more?"

For a few seconds she sat in silence and then came to a decision. Looking at Arthur she said, "I know where we've searched, and I know we found nothing in years. The old guardians had given up hope. They were old and I know they stopped looking, and if I'm honest we didn't know where to start.

"All the guardians keep records and I've read them all. When Filtiarn originally went missing no-one knew what had happened, and all Giolladhe said was that he had set off with his wolves to explore his new abilities."

"Who did he tell that to?" Arthur asked.

"Their family, and his wife and children, when they wondered where Filtiarn was. They knew Giolladhe was helping him to shape-shift, so that wasn't a surprise. What was puzzling was the fact that he never returned. Giolladhe denied having any knowledge of what he was doing."

"Fancy lying to everyone. About your own brother!" Beansprout said.

"Not everyone has your scruples," Woodsmoke said, squashing in next to her on the log. "Go on," he said, to Rahal.

"Many years later, after endless searches and speculation, the boar arrived on our land and wouldn't leave. He brought with him a pack of wolves, and his wife had a flash of insight or something. Everyone thought it was a fancy at first. But she was convinced from the start that it was Filtiarn. She forbade anyone to hunt the boar, on pain of death. And eventually, after a thousand years, he turned back to his human form and revealed the story.

His father was furious."

"So when he first turned he was himself again?"

"That's what I understand," she said. "Well, after a few hours of confusion at most. I think a burning anger kept him sane. From what I can gather, his father really didn't understand the deliberateness of the betrayal at first, and he joined Filtiarn on his search. Insisted in fact."

"When did he find out?" Arthur asked.

"When they found Giolladhe had fled, and no-one knew where to. Of course Filtiarn had to explain their argument – he'd kept quiet about it up to that point, probably hoping he was wrong, or that Giolladhe was exaggerating. His family was devastated. And then Filtiarn changed form. For years they kept searching for Giolladhe, but he kept a low profile, and then his father died, and his mother, and then his wife, and the hunt was forgotten, and then, finally, Giolladhe returned to Dragon's Hollow."

"Why didn't Filtiarn's children find him there?" Arthur sounded incredulous, and Tom knew that if it had been Arthur, he would never have stopped looking.

"Because no-one told the family he was back, and no-one knew about the curse. And by then I think the guardian who had been appointed was probably terrified of Giolladhe." Rahal dropped her eyes to her hands, which fidgeted nervously in her lap. "If I'm honest, I'm scared of him too."

Tom saw Arthur deflate a little, as he considered her words.

"Anyway," she continued, "we knew we needed Galatine. Filtiarn had told us that much, but we never found it. The next time he turned, the Guardians searched with him, but found nothing. And so it went on, until eventually Galatine passed to you, Arthur."

"I had no idea—"

"I know," she interrupted. "It's not your fault. But we have it now, and I still don't know what to do other than perform a spell we don't know on the night of the full moon."

"And you've never found the spell?"

"Never," she said, her face filled with regret. "Not one scrap of paper, whisper of a spell, a hint or a clue. Nothing. However, we have gathered a large store of knowledge about spells during the Wolf Moon, not specifically shape-shifting, but it's something."

"We need something else too," Brenna said, holding a piece of paper in her hands.

"Like what?" Arthur said, a hint of impatience in his voice.

"The moonstone. Don't you remember the story Finnlugh told? The moonstone the sword sat in, that was in the clearing on the night of the spell?"

Tom groaned. "Yes, I remember. It was at Giolladhe's feet during the spell."

"He's drawn it, right here. It must play a part in the ritual." She passed the drawing to Tom.

Arthur rubbed his face with his hands and took a deep breath before looking at Elan and Rahal. "Have you any idea what this could be? Or where it is?"

They looked at each other, and then at Arthur, shaking their heads. "I've never heard of it before," Elan admitted.

Arthur jumped to his feet and began pacing up and down. "This just keeps getting worse."

Bloodmoon interrupted from where he sat tending the food and watching the events unfold. "Come on everyone, eat. It fuels the brain."

They were glad of the interruption, and for a few minutes sat eating and thinking about their dilemma, until one by one they wrapped themselves in blankets to get some sleep. As Merlin said, they would all be awake soon enough if Filtiarn changed.

16 The Wolf Mage Rises

A long groan, grunts, and a painfilled howl shocked them from their sleep. They were awake in seconds, weapons drawn.

Merlin called out, "Stand back, it's started!"

Tom's tiredness vanished in seconds and he rolled free of his blankets, retreating with the others behind the fire.

The wolves crept closer, sniffing the air and whining, sensing that Filtiarn was changing. Everyone was transfixed. Filtiarn's large solid form now became fluid, his body rippling as he began to change shape. His hairy coat began to melt and morph into white skin, and his huge head shrank. The dull glow of the fire exaggerated the unreal aspect of the scene, as Filtiarn's body cast grotesque shadows. Tom couldn't quite work out what was happening, but it was clear from Filtiarn's unearthly howls that it was a painful and brutal process.

And then it was over, and the long skinny form of a man lay motionless by the fire, his limbs looking almost wasted. Tom couldn't believe that the huge form of the boar could produce such an emaciated figure.

Arthur grabbed a blanket and threw it over Filtiarn's body, as Rahal and Elan rushed to his side.

"Filtiarn, can you hear me?" Rahal said softly.

He groaned, and moved slowly until he was sitting up, Elan supporting him. Filtiarn's face turned to them, shocking Tom with its intensity. His dark eyes looked hollowed out and full of fear.

"It's all right," Rahal said, trying to reassure him. "I'm your guardian, you're with friends."

He looked at her, and the wildness in his eyes ebbed for a second.

Merlin intervened. "He needs quiet. Come on, let's get him to the cave until he's stronger. I'll start another fire there."

Arthur bent to help him to his feet, and Elan supported his other arm. Slowly, on shaking legs, Filtiarn made his way to the cave.

Beansprout looked at Tom. "It's a miracle he's still alive. I mean ... he looks terrible."

"A cruel fate indeed," Woodsmoke said, heading back to the logs by the fire, the others following.

Within minutes Arthur joined them, his face grave. "He won't survive another change, I'm sure of it. Come on, Tom, let's have a look at the rest of those pictures."

Tom handed the drawings round, and Arthur examined the one of the moonstone. "So, we need to find this, in order for the spell to work."

"Maybe it's in the weapon's room in the House of the Beloved?" Bloodmoon said.

"No, I'm pretty sure I'd remember that," Beansprout said, peering at the drawing over Arthur's shoulder.

"Is the room still locked?" Woodsmoke asked from where he sat on the ground, leaning back against the log, his long legs stretched out so that his feet were almost in the fire.

"Oh yes," Beansprout said, joining him, her blanket pulled close around her shoulders. "There's still all sorts of amazing, dangerous and valuable weapons in there."

Woodsmoke teased her. "Ever tempted?"

"Plenty of times, but I'll stick with Fail-not, thanks," she said, grinning. Fail-not was Tristan's bow, given to her by Woodsmoke. "Nimue is very protective of them, says they're a rich legacy of magical knowledge that must be kept safe."

Arthur snorted. "Yes, I'm sure that's why she keeps them locked up."

"It doesn't help us though, does it?" Brenna said.

"I think we need to go back to Dragon's Hollow, that's where it all began," Arthur said thoughtfully. "We need to find his old workshop and see if there're any clues in there."

"And see what's in Raghnall's library," Brenna added. "He must have one, and he'd have known Giolladhe."

Beansprout nodded, "The library's huge, full of arcane materials. I'm happy to do that."

"One thing's certain," Bloodmoon said. "Filtiarn won't be able to travel with us, he's far too weak."

"And it will take at least a week to get to Dragon's Hollow," Woodsmoke pointed out.

"But he could follow, at his own pace," Beansprout said. "Hopefully arriving in time for the full moon."

Merlin appeared out of the darkness and sat next to Tom.

"How is he?" Tom asked.

"Confused," Merlin said. "I'm hoping we get more sense out of him in the morning."

"Merlin," Beansprout said, "do we need to perform the spell on the full moon?"

"For the best possible chance, yes. In the Gatherer's story, he talks of drawing down the power of the moon for the spell – that means a full moon."

"So we have to find the moonstone and the spell, all within a few days?" Tom said. This was going to be almost impossible. "Presuming it's all hidden at Dragon's Hollow."

A collective groan sounded as they realised the seriousness of their position.

"We need to sleep," Arthur said. "Tomorrow's going to be a long day."

After a poor night's sleep, Tom woke with a groggy head to a mist-filled dawn.

He sat pulling his blankets around his shoulders, and moved closer to the fire, prodding it into life. And then he got a shock as he saw the wolves had surrounded them, or rather Filtiarn, whose hunched figure sat gazing into the fire. Wolves lay at his feet, nuzzled his hands, or lay with their heads on crossed paws, watching him. Tom studied him for a few seconds. His hair was still long, and it hung lank around his shoulders, matted in places, but it was no longer dark. Instead, streaks of grey ran through it. His skin was a deathly white, his face drawn, and his limbs were painfully thin. Tom recognised some of Woodsmoke's and Bloodmoon's clothes. He smiled; they must have loaned them to him in the night.

Tom looked around nervously, and then decided there was nothing to worry about. The wolves weren't interested in him at all. He built the fire up and put some water on to boil, falling back into the familiar routines of camping. Filtiarn glanced up at him and Tom smiled nervously, but Filtiarn dropped his gaze back to the fire, mute, apart from a hacking cough that made him shake uncontrollably.

It wasn't long before everyone was up, and the smell of bacon and eggs was drifting across the camp. Rahal put a plate of food in front of Filtiarn, and he ate ravenously. He looked old and fragile, but clearly his appetite was healthy. Tom couldn't help but wonder why they had brought bacon, when Filtiarn had been a boar, but as it didn't seem to bother him, he tucked into his own food with relish.

Rahal addressed them from where she sat amidst the wolves, petting them absently. "I've explained to Filtiarn who you are and how you want to help." She glanced at Filtiarn, who ignored her, and continued nervously. "He refuses your request, but asks to see Galatine."

Arthur nodded to Tom, and Tom passed it to Rahal who placed it on the floor at Filtiarn's feet. He put his plate down and picked Galatine up. His voice was barely more than a croak. "I didn't think I'd ever see this again," he said, turning it over in his hands. He looked up at Tom as if to challenge him. "I'll need to take this with me, to break the spell."

"And how are you going to find the moonstone?" Tom asked, incredulous that Filtiarn wanted to go on alone.

Arthur snorted in a very unkingly manner. "That's an excellent question, Tom, seeing as Filtiarn can barely walk!"

Filtiarn glared at Arthur. "I'll manage just fine."

"Yes, of course, that's gone so well for you over the last few thousand years," Arthur said dryly.

Filtiarn dragged himself to his feet, clutching Galatine, and the wolves started to growl softly. He was tall; he'd have been a handsome and imposing figure once. The tension around the camp shot up and everyone now paid full attention. "This is my business and I will deal with it."

Arthur refused to be baited, continuing to eat as he watched him. "How?"

"I have two weeks until the full moon, I'm sure I'll cope." But he looked unconvinced, and Rahal and Elan exchanged worried looks.

"Bravo," Arthur said. "Two weeks, fantastic. What's your plan? Or don't you have one?"

He glared again at Arthur. "I'm going to search Dragon's Hollow for the moonstone, and go back to my brother's workshop." His voice was resolute, but he swayed on his feet and Tom could tell it took a lot of effort to stay upright.

"You remember where it is, then?" Arthur asked.

"No, but I'll find it."

"Just like you found Giolladhe?"

"It is *not* your business."

"So you're happy to die as a boar," Arthur continued. "That's fine.

We'll pack and leave you to it." He looked at the others as they stared back, wondering what was happening. "You heard him, start packing!"

Woodsmoke got to his feet. "It's OK, Filtiarn, you can keep my clothes." He looked at Tom and as he turned away, gave him a wink. "Come on, Tom, you heard Arthur."

Filtiarn started coughing and dropped to his knees, unable to stop. Galatine fell to the floor. Rahal rushed to his side and he shooed her away. "I'm fine."

"No, you are not!" she shouted. "How dare you let your pride get in the way of us finally breaking your curse!"

"My dear lady," Arthur said, in his most infuriating tone. "It won't be you who dies. Just think, your responsibilities will be over. You can do whatever it is you do, and I can go back to my castle and start planning my next tournament."

Tom was disappointed. If Rahal and Elan had seen sense, why couldn't Filtiarn?

Merlin finally broke his silence. He'd been staring into the fire for a long time, listening to the exchange. He looked at Filtiarn who now rose on shaky legs to sit again on the log. "That way lies death, Filtiarn. I have seen it. You will fail."

Filtiarn stared at him, fear in his eyes. "How do you know?"

"It is my gift, or my curse, whatever you choose to call it. But I have seen it. You will not survive another change, and will not find the stone alone."

"I always get stronger in the days after the change. Always."

"It won't be enough." Merlin closed his eyes regretfully, before opening them and fixing him with a piercing stare. "But it's your choice."

Elan pleaded with him. "This is the closest we've been in years! The most we have ever known! Filtiarn, please."

Filtiarn looked around at the camp as the others packed, and resolutely turned away, walking back to the cave. Rahal and Elan cast a pleading glance back towards them, and then ran after him, followed by the oldest wolf. Tom picked Galatine up, brushing the dirt from its blade.

"Keep packing," Arthur said. "We're leaving anyway, in one direction or another."

17 Return to Dragon's Hollow

While they packed up, the wolves padded around the camp, alternating between watching them and the entrance to the cave. Tom had just about got used to them, unnerving though they were. It seemed Elan and Rahal could communicate with them too, and Tom presumed they had reassured the animals about their intentions, because they were now almost friendly as they sniffed around, curious.

As they finished packing, Filtiarn returned with the wolf at his side, Elan and Rahal trailing behind, looking relieved. He stood in front of Arthur, lifting his head proudly. "I accept your help. You're right, I can't do it alone. Will you still come with me to Dragon's Hollow?" His belligerence had gone, but Tom could tell he wasn't happy about accepting help.

Arthur smiled and clasped his hand. "Of course we'll come with you."

Bloodmoon interrupted, already astride his horse. "You will slow us up, Filtiarn, and that's the brutal fact of it. You'll have to follow us there, that way we'll have a few more days to search."

The steel returned to Filtiarn's voice as he shot an angry look at Bloodmoon. "I won't, I'm a good horseman."

"I don't doubt it, but you're just not fit enough. I ride fast, and you won't keep up. And we need as much time as we can get."

"I agree," Arthur said, trying to reason with Filtiarn. He threw an appealing glance to Rahal and Elan. "You should take your time, gather your strength with your guardians, while we ride ahead. If you tell us what you remember, it will help us when we start looking."

Rahal stepped forward, putting a hand on Filtiarn's arm. "He's right, we can follow. We don't want to jeopardise this."

Filtiarn hesitated for a second and then nodded.

"Good," Arthur said. "What do you remember of that night, and Giolladhe's workshop? You need to tell us everything."

"If I'm honest, I remember very little now, it was so long ago. And the change I undergo, it strips the memories, a little every time." He looked at the ground, his shoulders dropping. "I can't even tell you with great accuracy where his workshop is. I couldn't even find it last time."

"Tell me what you can remember," Arthur said gently.

"I remember the workshop was on the right shoulder of the mountain, on the hillside above the dragon sorcerer's house. One evening as I was leaving, the sun was setting and as I opened the door, the sun dazzled me."

"That's good," said Arthur, nodding at Woodsmoke, who turned to Tom and whispered, "I knew it!"

"Go on, what else," Arthur prompted.

"The door was set back, under a slight overhang. It was made of beaten copper, I think. He knew the dragon sorcerer well, they talked often, shared ideas and spells."

"And the moonstone. Where did you last see it?"

"I suppose at the altar in the forest. When I first turned I kept my human thoughts for a while, and I kept returning to the clearing. It was just lying there on the earth. But I took little notice of it."

"Can you remember where the clearing was?"

"In the wooded slopes behind Raghnall's house. He had marked a path to it, with torches."

"Who? Raghnall?" Arthur asked confused.

"No, Giolladhe." Filtiarn closed his eyes in grief. "I was so excited at the thought I would join my brothers." He reached out a hand and stroked the head of the old wolf. "I still can't believe that he tricked me. He was ... so cruel." Filtiarn swallowed painfully.

"Why do you think he tricked you?"

Filtiarn looked confused. "I don't know. We'd had an argument about the spell being locked into the moon's cycle, but that was all. I do remember him laughing, though, and saying I should know better than to criticise him." He closed his eyes again, as if to block out the memory.

"Are you sure there wasn't something else?" Arthur asked.

Filtiarn looked up at him. "What do you mean?"

"It seems extreme. Did he want you out of the way for some reason?"

"I don't think so. And how could this help, anyway?"

Arthur paused for a second. "I don't know, but I have a feeling there's more to this. Just think about it. Try to remember what you were doing at the time."

Filtiarn started to shout, his voice breaking. "I can't think now. I'm too tired."

"It's all right," Arthur said, soothingly. "You'll have plenty of time to think on the road. We'll carry on, and will meet you at the Hollow." He pointed to Brenna. "Our friend here is Aerikeen, she can check your progress, and when you arrive we'll send someone to meet you at the gate."

Filtiarn nodded, and suddenly looked weak. "Yes, thank you."

That was Arthur's gift, Tom thought. He engendered such trust.

Arthur smiled at Filtiarn and shook his hand. "Travel safely and we'll see you again soon."

With a flurry of goodbyes, they mounted their horses and left for Dragon's Hollow.

After days of hard riding, involving long hours, short stops and little sleep, they arrived at the base of Dragon Skin Mountain. Brenna had already flown ahead and warned Nimue of their arrival.

Tom was more tired than he'd been in a long time. Arthur and the others were expert horse riders, and Tom had kept up with difficulty. He ached all over, but he smiled as they started on the path to the Hollow, feeling he was returning home, which was an odd sensation considering how little time he had spent there. Bloodmoon had been right, though. Filtiarn would never have managed the journey at their pace.

Bloodmoon and Woodsmoke had the led the way, across parts of Blind Moor that Tom had never seen before. As usual Tom rode towards the back of their group, and Beansprout rode next to him.

"You'll be pleased to know," she now said, smiling at him, "that our new housekeeper is very efficient. He fills the baths quickly, and he's an expert cook. And you can have your old room."

"Well I hope the bath is run, because I stink, and I could sleep for a week."

"We all stink, but you can't sleep, we've got a lot to do in a very short time," she pointed out.

He groaned. "I know, but just give me tonight. I'm going to be in bed early, and then I'm up and on it. I promise!"

She laughed. "Fair enough, I'm knackered as well. And I've got Raghnall's weird stuff to go through. His library is huge – can you imagine? Thousands of years of collecting books! And there's a separate spell room."

Dragon's Hollow looked as beautiful as ever. The damage caused by the dragons' attack a few months before had been repaired, and once again the fey serenely walked along the gilded paths and roads, and the enormous dragon fountain splashed water into the lake. Across the valley, the House of the Beloved gleamed in the afternoon sun, the black marble shining like a well-polished gem. As they strolled through the city Tom saw huge round golden lanterns suspended above the streets, and every so often they'd pass fey children chasing each other around wearing wolf masks. The celebration for the Wolf Moon had started.

Nimue greeted them at the door, her grin broad. She hadn't changed. Her long dark hair curled across her shoulders, her skin was pale, and her green eyes sparkled. "I knew you couldn't keep away, Arthur. Have you missed me?"

He laughed. "I'm not sure that's how I'd describe it." And then he corrected himself as he saw her indignation. "Of course, always!"

Beansprout ran to her, giving her a big hug, which shocked Tom. They'd obviously become very close. Nimue flashed a smile at the rest of them as she welcomed them into the house. She led the way up to the broad balcony overlooking the city, and Arthur introduced Bloodmoon, who she'd never met before. He swept into full charm mode, and Tom felt a little resentful of Nimue's appreciative smile. She never looked at him like that.

He noticed Merlin kept his distance from Nimue. Suddenly, all sorts of dynamics seemed to have entered their group.

As they helped themselves to drinks, Tom noticed a subtle change in the house. The furnishings were still opulent, but there seemed less formality than before. Maybe it was because it was less tidy than he remembered. Books were stacked on the table, scarves and throws were draped over chairs and the divan. Raghnall had clearly been a neat freak, and Nimue was not.

He was jolted out of his thoughts when Nimue said, "You've grown, Tom. You're a bit broader round the shoulders I think."

He felt suddenly self conscious under her gaze, and again was slightly mesmerised by her green eyes, which still crept into his dreams sometimes. He caught Woodsmoke trying to bury a smirk, and was grateful when he rescued him.

"We've been teaching him how to fight, Nimue. What you see before you is months of hard work. He came second in the beginner's sword-fighting competition."

"Well done, Tom!" She looked genuinely pleased, and Tom mumbled his thanks, relieved when she turned to Beansprout. "We need to continue with your training."

"I know, but Merlin's been helping me too."

"Good." She nodded at Merlin. "He's a good teacher." And no-one knew that better than Nimue, Tom thought uncomfortably.

Later that evening, after long baths and a rest, they met again before dinner. Nimue wanted to show them something. She led them along an upper corridor, into a room that led out onto the roof. Along one long wall was an astrological chart, embellished with gold and silver and other precious metals and gems. The lines and swirls of stars were faintly illuminated, and Tom couldn't help saying, "Wow, that's amazing!"

On another wall was a plan of the different moon cycles. There weren't any dates, but their succession was again marked out in a flowing script, in what looked like white marble on a black wall.

"It's amazing what I keep finding," Nimue said. "When Brenna told me what you were looking for, I started to search the house. It sounds ridiculous, but I've been so busy maintaining Raghnall's spells and establishing myself here, that I still haven't explored the whole place." She looked sheepish. "And the library and spell room occupy me for hours. Anyway, Beansprout's right, the moonstone is not in the weapons room. In the rooms I have searched, it's not on display, and as well as the rooms I haven't searched, there may be hidden rooms too. And then I found this."

Merlin stood absorbed in front of the star charts. "Raghnall certainly spent his time productively. The star chart moves?"

"Yes, too slowly to see, but when you come back here, there are changes. What you see now is how the stars stand at present." Nimue pointed to a line of stars that were almost aligned. "The Wolf Moon is unusual in that it occurs only once in a thousand years, aligning with certain other stars. It has long been held to be a powerful time to perform spells and rituals, and it has a certain reputation."

Bloodmoon agreed. "I have never lived through one, but certainly there are stories amongst those who have. Strange tales, weird magics. Fahey has a store of such tales."

"I can't seem to get a straight answer," Arthur said, frustrated. "Does the ritual have to be performed on the night of the full moon, or if we miss that, could it be performed at any time through the cycle?"

Nimue nodded. "In theory, yes, any time. But the full moon is always the most powerful."

"Unless the spell says otherwise," Merlin said, once again introducing confusion.

"Right," Arthur said decisively. "I suggest that Beansprout, Nimue and Merlin search the house, including the library, for signs of the moonstone and any spells, or old diaries. I will search the woods behind the house for evidence of an old altar, or clearing. Brenna, if you would join me?"

She nodded. "But after a few thousand years, Arthur, that will be hard going."

"I know." He turned to Tom, Woodsmoke and Bloodmoon. "Will you search above the house, on the mountain? We need to find the workshop."

They nodded, and once again Tom felt daunted by their task. Surely this was impossible. But then he thought of Filtiarn, and Rahal and Elan, and how he desperately didn't want to let them down.

18 Hidden Places

After an early breakfast, Woodsmoke, Tom and Bloodmoon saddled their horses and headed up the path behind the house. The last time Tom had been here was when he'd returned from the Realm of Air, after their imprisonment and near death by the sylphs.

For a while they were sheltered by the trees on either side, and then they left the woods behind and were dazzled by the sun, already warm despite the early hour. The mountainside was covered in a mix of trees, scrub and bare earth, huge stones littering the ground. Small animal tracks snaked along the slopes, and insects chirped in the undergrowth.

Woodsmoke and Bloodmoon looked very otherworldly today. Woodsmoke always became more intense when hunting; his eyes were dark with concentration as he followed the path up and across the mountain, his focus absolute. His hair was tied back, and he wore a sleeveless leather jacket rather than a cloak.

Bloodmoon sat beside him, as blond as Woodsmoke was dark. Bloodmoon had inherited the family colouring that Fahey once described in his tale about Vanishing Hall. His skin was a creamy white, and his eyes dark green. His long hair was streaked with plaits, and it snaked down his back. The huge hilt of his dragonium sword glinted as it caught the sun. Tom felt that Woodsmoke and Bloodmoon had become his brothers, and the feeling gave him strength.

Woodsmoke pulled Farlight to a halt. "Let's push up to where the path levels out," he said. "We'll tie up the horses beneath those trees and continue on foot."

Tom groaned and Bloodmoon laughed. "All the best hunting is done by stealth, Tom."

"And remember," Woodsmoke said. "The doorway faces west."

The horses secure, they split up and left the main path, with instructions to shout if they found anything.

Hours later, Tom had found nothing. He was hot, dusty and sweaty.

The paths he had followed led only to animal burrows and dead ends, some petering out to nothing. He poked under trees, around streams, and brushed overhanging branches back from near vertical stretches of mountain, feeling as if at any moment he would plunge down the side to his death.

Eventually he came across a small overhang, and shouted to the others that he was taking a break. He sat in the shade beneath it, swigging water which had become unpleasantly warm in his animal-skin bottle, and looked out over Dragon's Hollow glittering in the valley below.

A few minutes later Bloodmoon skittered to a halt beside him. His face was streaked with dirt, and he started to complain. "I could easily die of boredom doing this, Tom."

"But think of the rewards," Tom said, knowing exactly what would motivate Bloodmoon. "Who knows what Giolladhe may have left in his workshop."

They were disturbed by a shout, and a summons, coming from somewhere high above them. They scooted out of the shade and looked up to see Woodsmoke gesturing, and scrambled up to join him.

Woodsmoke was standing on a barely-there path, grinning. "I think I've found it. I heard a stream, and thought I'd find it and fill up my water bottle. There was an overgrown path, but I realised it was edged with stones, so I started to clear it." He pointed. "Look, it's paved, although covered in dirt now. Come on, there's more."

He led the way down the path, and they forced their way through bushes, getting scratched and smacked by protruding branches, until they came to a small shallow curve in the hillside. An overhang of rock cast some shade, and a stream ran over it into a small pool. Next to it was a door.

"By Herne's knobbly horns – you've found it!" Bloodmoon exclaimed. He ran his hands over the copper door, its shine dulled by the weather. In the centre was an engraving of a large flame below a sun.

"I had to clear it," Woodsmoke said, pointing to branches lying to one side.

"Well done," Tom said. He was grateful to be out of the sun, and put his head beneath the waterfall, gasping at its coldness. He shook his head like a dog. "Who's going in first?"

"I am!" Woodsmoke said, indignant. "I found it. But it's locked."

They lined up next to each other and pushed, trying to force the lock or hinges, but the door remained stubbornly shut.

"Hold on," Bloodmoon said, rummaging in his pack. "I have some tools." He pulled out a selection of skeleton keys and sharp-edged files.

"You've brought your thieving pack?" Woodsmoke said, affronted.

"I am not a thief! Sometimes I am recruited by thieves."

"Same thing," Woodsmoke said.

"Bloodmoon, you never cease to surprise me," Tom said, not sure whether to be impressed or worried.

Bloodmoon was on his knees, his eye to the keyhole. He sat upright with shock. "There's a key in it."

"How can there be?" Tom said, doubting him. Bloodmoon moved aside, allowing Tom to see a small blockage in the lock, caused by a key on the other side. "So someone's still in there?" he said, alarmed.

"No, someone's bones are in there," Woodsmoke corrected.

"Out of the way," Bloodmoon said. "I have work to do."

They stood silent for a few minutes as he wiggled his tools in the lock, and then tried a few keys, until they finally heard a click. He smiled with satisfaction. "Now, after three."

With an enormous effort they pushed the door open. Rusty hinges groaned, and there was an ear-shattering grating noise as the door caught on debris and the key that had fallen from the lock. Bloodmoon flattened himself against the floor and managed to hook the key out of the way, so they could push it open further.

Dust billowed out, followed by a musty smell. Dirt and small stones were strewn down a passageway which stretched away into darkness.

Bloodmoon stepped aside, saying, "After you," to Woodsmoke.

They each pulled a torch from their packs, and after lighting them, started down the hall. It was eerie; the air was stale, and their footsteps sounded loud in the confined space of the hill. The passageway was long, eventually leading to a door that opened into a large room, in the centre of which was a fireplace and chimney heading into the roof. Around the walls were broad work benches, shelves, and a scattering of tools, all covered in thick dust. Three doors led out of the room.

For a few seconds they were quiet, taking in their surroundings, as the dust of hundreds of years swirled around them. Tom grinned in the gloom. "We've actually found Giolladhe's workshop! Well done, Woodsmoke!"

"It was nothing," Woodsmoke said casually. "Just my skill and hunter abilities."

"Yeah, yeah. Now to find the moonstone," Bloodmoon said, lighting the lanterns that hung overhead.

Tom paused in front of one of the benches, examining the tools spread over it. He scraped his finger across the surface, clearing a thick covering of dust. "Wow, just think, we're the first people in here for hundreds of years."

"We won't find the moonstone," Woodsmoke said.

"Why not?" Tom asked.

"He's cleared the place out, or someone has," Woodsmoke pointed out. "Nothing except tools and dust."

"Maybe he was on the run from someone," Bloodmoon said, raking through the fire before moving on to the cupboards beneath the benches.

"Filtiarn?" Tom said.

"Or the sylphs," Woodsmoke reminded them. "Remember, something happened with them."

Tom drifted around the room, absently picking up tools and putting them down again. "Maybe he didn't hide the moonstone," Tom said thoughtfully. "Maybe he just lost it." He pushed open the other doors. "There's a set of stairs, and another room, so I'll start on this one."

Woodsmoke nodded. "We'll head up the stairs and search the upper floor."

The next room was smaller, lined on one side with floor-to-ceiling shelves filled with an assortment of boxes. On the other side, at the far end, was a large cupboard. Tom started on the shelves, moving methodically along, but the boxes contained only paper and packing material. Feeling despondent, he moved to the cupboard. It was large – much bigger than he was – with double doors. The door he tried was stiff, but he pulled it open and found another door in front of him, set back into the wall. Shelves had been dismantled and were stacked to the side, looking as if they had previously been in front of the door. A hidden room? Suddenly excited, he pulled the door open. There was nothing but blackness beyond. Without wondering whether to call Woodsmoke, he stepped through. Immediately he experienced a familiar sensation of floating, weightlessness and a pulling deep in his gut. He'd stepped through a portal.

19 Mountains of Fire

Tom panicked. What if he was going back to his Earth? This would be the absolute worse thing. Or what if it was the Realm of Air again? They might never let him go. Or the Realm of Water, where he might drown? As these thoughts were flashing through his mind he landed with a thump, feeling rock and sand beneath his fingers. He rocked back on his heels and sprang to his feet, pulling Galatine free. In his other hand he held his now extinguished torch.

He found himself in a shadowy room strewn with rubble and suffused with a warm orange glow. It was in fact another cave, with rough walls and stone shelves, similar to Giolladhe's workshop except that it was fiercely hot. The heat and glow were coming from a pit in the centre, and for a few seconds Tom couldn't work out what it was. Only when he stood over it did he realise it was bubbling lava.

Lava? Where the hell was he?

He thrust his torch into the pit and it flared to life. As his eyes adjusted to the light he saw that the cave was partially collapsed, a wall of rubble blocking some of it, while the floor was crunchy and blackened in places. At some point the lava must have erupted from this pit and covered some of the room, and if it had erupted once, it could do it again.

Lava could mean only one thing – he was in the Realm of Fire. His panic turned to relief. He was still in the Other.

Herne's Horns! Was he trapped here? He whirled round and saw that the portal entrance was behind him, the familiar rock archway filled with blackness. Interesting. Giolladhe had a hidden portal that led to the Realm of Fire. A fixed portal too, which suggested he had passed through frequently. Well, Tom wasn't going back yet.

He examined the wall of rubble ahead of him, and saw a small hole at the top, a faint red glow illuminating its edges. He wedged his torch upright and scrambled up. Within seconds he was filthy and scratched, but was soon able to stick his head through the gap.

On the other side was a much larger portion of the cave, and beyond that was an entrance to an underground cavern. Tom glimpsed rock archways and rivers of lava. But something else caught his eye. A glimpse of white stone on a workbench, partially covered in debris.

The moonstone.

He was so shocked he cried out and hit his head on the roof. He'd found it! Giolladhe must have hidden it here all those years ago.

He eased backwards and started to pull the rocks away to make the entrance bigger, but as he did the roof started to slip and crumble, and in seconds the hole had vanished. Tom fell backwards, landing with a thump. He held his breath as he watched the roof, but after a few seconds the slip stopped and he breathed again.

He had to find another way round – if there was a way out of here.

He leapt to his feet and grabbed the torch, and spotted a shadowy archway in the corner of the room. Passing through it he found himself at the bottom of a flight of steps that rose steeply above him, illuminated by a weak red light pouring through a hole in the smashed door and roof at the top. He rushed up the steps and pushed aside the ruined door, entering a huge cathedral-like building made of dark red sandstone. It was a ruin; a few columns stood upright, the rest had fallen and lay broken and crushed on the floor. Above him, through the fractured roof, he could see a bright sun blazing in deep blue sky.

The place was deserted, his only company the strange faces of unknown beings carved into the walls, watching him through cracked eyes.

He scrambled over the fallen rocks of masonry, taking care not to slip into the gaps between them where he could easily be crushed, and eased his way through a hole in the wall. He immediately shielded his eyes from the intense glare, squinting until his eyes adjusted, and found he was standing on a low rise of a rocky hill. In front of him, all he could see was orange sand, rising and falling in huge dunes, interspersed with rivers of blackened molten rock and the remnants of buildings.

What had happened here? Immediately Tom wondered if it was dragons. He remembered Merlin telling them about the dragon wars, and how the dragons had left the Realm of Fire because of the djinn. He paced round the edge of the massive building he'd exited, stopping in shock when he saw the range of volcanic mountains, so close that Tom was almost on the slopes. They were still belching smoke into the air. Maybe it wasn't dragons after all.

Nothing moved in this barren landscape. Could this be where

Giolladhe had disappeared to? That would have been hundreds of years before. Was that why the key was in the lock? Could he still be here somewhere, alive? If Raghnall had lived that long, maybe Giolladhe had too.

But it seemed nothing could be alive here; the destruction was too absolute. Somewhere below him was the other side of the cave, so somewhere out there was another entrance. As Tom squinted, he thought he saw a shadow on the ground, or rather a black spot, sharp against the red sand. That must be the way down.

20 The Secrets of the House of the Beloved

Beansprout stood at the entrance to the library in the House of the Beloved and sighed. It was a sigh of pleasure, but also of trepidation.

The library was a large room set into the top two floors of the building, the upper floor being a mezzanine. A stained-glass roof cast jewel-like shades of colour onto the room. Both floors were lined with bookshelves filled with conventional books, as well as rolls of scrolls and pamphlets. In the centre of the lower floor, under the square of light, was a large table.

Beansprout headed to a section tucked in the corner under the mezzanine, where it was protected from daylight. It was here that Raghnall had stored some of his oldest books and scrolls, and she presumed that if anything referred to Giolladhe and the curse of Filtiarn all those years ago, then it would be here.

Starting methodically at the bottom shelf, she worked through the texts, finding old treatises on magic; maps, and family histories. Dust rose in clouds as she pulled the books off the shelves, and she was soon smeared in dust, print and cobwebs. She put anything of interest in piles around her, only shelving things that seemed of no relevance at all. But she quickly became side-tracked, also putting things aside for examination at her leisure.

She sighed again. She had to keep focused. Filtiarn's life was at stake.

Hours later, she moved on in exasperation, using a finding spell that Nimue had taught her, tailored to find mention of Giolladhe and Filtiarn. The spell made the books wriggle and rustle on the shelves, leading her to a shelf of history books. They were all about the dragon wars and the founding of Dragon's Hollow – this was interesting, but it didn't tell her about the curse. Maybe Raghnall had known nothing about it? Maybe it was just between the brothers.

She hoped Nimue and Merlin were having better luck searching the rest of the house. Nimue was searching Raghnall's old room, which both of them had avoided following his death, and Merlin was studying the moon cycle charts.

She was distracted by books rustling in a corner where she hadn't looked before. As the rustling became more insistent, she headed over and saw a scroll wriggling in the middle of a tightly packed shelf. The shelf was labelled *Maps and Plans*. Intriguing.

She eased the scroll free and it immediately unfurled, revealing several sheets of paper – the floor plans of the House of the Beloved. One rustled free and fell at her feet. It was the plan of the lower floor. Why would Filtiarn or Giolladhe be mentioned here?

The ink was faded and difficult to read, but the paper itself was in good condition, looking as if it had been barely touched in years. She took it to the table and examined it under the daylight.

It took her a few minutes to get orientated, but then she saw a passageway leading from the lower floor to the mountain behind the house. The end of the passage was just marked *Giolladhe*.

She gasped. It must be the workshop.

21 The Citadel of Erfann

Tom scrambled down the shattered paths of the hillside, wishing he was wearing sunglasses. The Realm of Fire was hot and relentlessly bright. And eerie.

It was strange being the only one here in such a vast and empty landscape. Black lava flows ran across the desert floor, and he walked over them warily. But they were cold and hard, some covered with layers of sand.

Stopping for a look round, he was shocked to discover he was standing on what looked like a roof. These weren't the foundations of a ruined city – this was a buried city. Everything beneath him was filled with sand, which gave him another unpleasant thought. He could be swallowed up by sink holes. But how filled up with sand was it? The other side of the cave had been intact, so potentially, areas of the city were still accessible.

Trying to ignore his misgivings he was careful to walk only on solid rock, slowly making his way to the shadowy area that marked the cave entrance. Every now and again the hard edges of the city disappeared, swallowed by sand dunes, and he lost the dark shape completely as the dunes rose above him. Finally, sweating heavily, he saw the area of blackness ahead, and edged his way towards it. When he was only a few feet away, the ground gave way beneath him and he shot downwards on a chute of sand, bumping against hard angles of stone, until he landed on a platform below.

As he waited for the dust to subside, he held his breath, rolled onto his back and looked up at what appeared to be a large rectangular entrance high above him. A skylight, perhaps, long since broken by the weight of sand. There was no way he could get out through there.

Rising to his feet, he brushed sand away and tested the ground. It seemed to be made of solid slabs of stone. On the far side was a balustraded area, and he peered over to see stairs leading down into the gloom. He still carried his torch, although the flame sputtered and smoked heavily. He'd felt stupid carrying it across the sand in the burning sunshine, but was glad he had it now.

Tom made his way downstairs onto a landing, where a long passage partly blocked by stones and piles of sand led off to his left. He was tempted to explore it, but was sure the cave he wanted to access was deeper than this. He headed down another two flights of steps, passing more partially blocked passages, until he arrived on what must have been the ground floor.

A doorway led into a passageway with a cracked stone roof, flanked by a row of columns, between which were more entrances offering glimpses of dark spaces. Tom tried to orientate himself, and headed in what he hoped was the right direction. He followed the passageway until it ended at a wall of rubble, and then retraced his steps back to what had looked like the biggest opening. He stepped into another dark, half-collapsed room. His flaring torch showed the remnants of furniture and destroyed furnishings. It was a city of the dead. Nothing moved, except for the odd whisper of sand settling. He could be buried alive at any moment, but he also couldn't wait to see more. Or to find the moonstone. He was sure that was what he'd seen.

Tom plodded along through a series of linked rooms, until he came to one with a domed roof high above, pale red light filtering through what looked like areas of glass covered in a thin film of sand. The roof was supported by thick columns of red stone, and on the far side another entrance yawned.

He was halfway to it, his feet echoing on the stone, when a voice called out, "What brings a stranger from the Realm of Earth here to the edge of the desert?"

Tom whirled around, pulling Galatine out as he sought the source of the voice, but the space was empty. "I'm trying to find Giolladhe's cave, the Forger of Light," he shouted, his heart thudding painfully in his chest.

The voice laughed. "Giolladhe! You have travelled a long way to find a dead man."

Tom's heart sank. "I don't care if he's dead. All I want is to find his workshop. Will you tell me what you know? It's important. His brother's life is at stake."

Again the voice laughed. "And what's his brother's fate to me?"

"It might be nothing to you, but it means a lot to me!"

"You should leave, boy, there is nothing for you here."

Tom was exasperated. It was infuriating talking to someone he couldn't see. "At least show yourself! Or are you scared!"

The sand shifted beneath him, knocking him onto his back. He immediately rolled onto his feet, and could barely believe his eyes as the sand rose in a whirling cloud before him, filled with fire and darkness, two flame-filled eyes glaring at him from the centre of the mass. The sand reassembled into a huge, bronze-skinned, man-shaped creature, with flames instead of hair. Two black horns protruded through his flame hair, and his fingers and toes ended in long talon-like nails.

Stunned, Tom stepped back. "Are you a djinn?"

"You may call me that – I prefer it to demon."

Tom could see why the djinn might be called a demon, but swallowed his fear and asked, "Did you know Giolladhe?"

"You think I'm old?" the djinn asked, amused.

"Well, you've obviously heard of him," Tom shot back, annoyance replacing his fear.

"So have you. Did you know him?"

"No!" Tom stopped and took a breath. "No," he said, more calmly. "But I've met his brother, who he trapped in a spell for thousands of years. We want to help him break it."

The djinn didn't appear to be listening, instead looking at Tom's sword. "You have Galatine. How did you come by that?"

"You know my sword? I got it from King Arthur; it belonged to Gawain, one of his knights. Well, actually, I got it from Raghnall."

The djinn's amused tone disappeared, the flames in his eyes roaring to life. "Raghnall! And how is that old devil?"

"Dead. Killed by my friends Arthur and Woodsmoke." Tom gripped his sword tightly, wondering if the djinn was a friend of Raghnall, though from his tone he didn't think so.

"Ha! Then you are welcome here. But you risk much to venture this far into the centre," the djinn said with a grin, exposing fine white teeth with sharp points, like a shark. "Do you seek to awaken your sword?"

"Awaken my sword? What do you mean?" Tom asked, looking at Galatine in confusion.

"Its powers have been muted, probably by Giolladhe before he gave it away. It wasn't like that when he made it, I can assure you."

"But how do you know?"

"The stone here," he said, pointing with a shiny black talon. "It does not move. The centre should swirl with motion. The stone is a djinn's eye opal."

"But we thought it was a fire opal."

"You were wrong." The djinn smiled again – it wasn't a pleasant smile.

Tom was beginning to feel very uncomfortable.

"But why would he mute it?"

"Powerful swords should be wielded only by those who deserve their power. No doubt Giolladhe did not wish someone to benefit from such a great gift."

Tom wasn't sure he believed this explanation. He thought it more likely that, should Filtiarn ever find it again, Giolladhe didn't want it to work.

"Some spells and metals require great heat for their completion," the djinn continued, "and that heat must be maintained for a very long time. The best way is to use the heat of the fire mountains and their lava flow. Hence Giolladhe made another workshop here, within the city. A workshop *we* permitted him to build; he promised weapons of power in exchange for his place here."

This djinn seemed to know a lot about how Giolladhe worked. It couldn't be a coincidence that he was here. "How do you know so much about him?"

"His story is well known. It has passed through the generations, and carries the thick smell of deceit," the djinn said with a low growl.

Tom skin pricked with goosebumps. "What did he do?"

"Dark murky secrets, boy," the djinn said. "He betrayed us in many ways. His workshop was an evil seed in the heart of the city." He lowered himself until he was at eye-level with Tom, and fixed him with a piercing stare. "He betrayed many who knew him, eventually. It is rumoured that Giolladhe made the sylphs a weapon as a gift of protection, but it turned out it sent the dragons to their door. When they found out, his life was forfeit and he fled here."

Things started to fall into place for Tom; it explained the sylph's loathing of Giolladhe.

"Why are you here?" Tom asked. "Alone in a deserted city."

"Many reasons." The djinn's eyes flared with flames. "Best not to ask."

A rumble disturbed their conversation, and the city creaked around them, sand swirling down from above.

"What was that?" Tom asked, alarmed.

"The fires in the mountain. If you want to find that workshop, you'd better hurry."

"Can you take me there? I don't know where I'm going. It could take me hours."

The djinn grinned his shark's smile again. "I like you, boy. I like that your friends killed Raghnall. And I will help you wake the sword, because it is exactly against what Giolladhe would want. You want to wake it, I presume?"

Tom's thoughts whirled as he wondered what to do for the best. "I suppose so," he said finally, thinking that if they were to rescue Filtiarn, it had to be awakened. Tom wondered if the djinn knew about the sword's ability to turn Filtiarn into a boar. "But what will happen?"

"The opals will awake and the blade will sing again."

"Does that mean I'll hear animals speak?" he spluttered, not at all sure that would be a good thing.

"Maybe," the djinn said. "It will activate whatever spell Filtiarn wove into it.

Tom experienced a flash of fear as he realised he had no idea what he would awaken in the sword, or its consequences. But the djinn had turned away.

"Come then, friend of slayer of Raghnall. Once again Giolladhe's pit will ring with the magic of light."

22 Beneath Dragon's Hollow

Merlin and Nimue stood next to Beansprout, examining the plans she had spread across the central table.

"Where did you find these again?" Merlin asked.

"Over on that shelf, using a finding spell," Beansprout said with pride.

"Well done," Nimue said, smiling, before turning her attention back to the plans. "I bet there's all sorts of hidden rooms and passageways here. I can see a couple of markings in rooms I thought I knew well." She shook her head. "What else was he hiding?"

"Time enough for that, Nimue," Merlin said. "What are we going to do about this passageway? Should we wait for Arthur?"

"No," Beansprout said quickly. "We should search now. Arthur could be hours yet. And it might be nothing."

"I agree," Nimue said. "Let's go." She rolled the plan up and led them down the stairs towards the kitchen. "From the look of this map, the passageway should lead off one of the cellars."

They passed through the kitchen and into the storage room beyond. From there a small passageway led off to more rooms. Beansprout had only been in here once before, and all she remembered was stores of dried foods, and Raghnall's fine wines. Nimue led them to the middle room, lined with racks filled with plates, bowls, cooking utensils, glasses and garden lanterns.

"Anyone would think he was running a hotel," Beansprout said, pulling a plate off a pile. "This has actual gold on it!"

Nimue took a quick look. "Porcelain too, probably the best money can buy. So if that's up here, who knows what's in the passageway."

The walls were made of polished granite, solid and unyielding, and although they examined them in great detail, there wasn't the slightest hint of a break in them.

Merlin turned to the floor, made of thick timbers. "Maybe it's a trap door?"

Once again Nimue studied the map, turning it this way and that, while

Beansprout and Merlin tugged at the floor boards and tapped them, listening for a change in sound.

"Try the far corner," Nimue said.

Beansprout crouched down and ran her hand under racks loaded with heavy pans, serving platters and glasses. She gasped. "I can feel a draught!" She knocked the floor and it sounded hollow. "It's here!"

Within minutes they moved equipment off the shelves and onto the floor in teetering piles, and then pulled the rack away from the wall. The only discernible change in the flooring was that the planks looked a little shorter and made an uneven square. Grabbing a large serving spoon off a shelf, Beansprout wedged its end into the gaps and levered the planks up. As they started to lift in one solid mass, Nimue and Merlin grabbed the edges and pulled, and the entire trap door swung upwards and back, landing with a thud against the wall.

Underneath, steps led down into darkness.

They grinned at each other. "Me first," Nimue said, "then Beansprout. Merlin, you'll go last."

They each grabbed a lantern and Nimue said, "Beansprout, you can light them for us."

Beansprout concentrated her energies and repeated the short spell she had been taught. A small flame appeared in the centre of her palm, which she directed to the lanterns. Within seconds they were burning strongly.

As they made their way down the dozen or so steps, the temperature dropped and they found themselves in a low-ceilinged passageway with walls of rough rock and ancient bricks. Before long it turned a corner and started climbing upwards, and then opened into a small square space with several exits leading from it. Beansprout's heart sank. They could easily get lost down here.

"Damn it," Nimue said, pulling the map out again. "There aren't any other passages marked on here."

"I suspect the one we want must go up, if it leads to the mountain with Giolladhe's workshop," Merlin reasoned.

"But where else could the others go?" Beansprout asked, nervously looking around.

"Other buildings, maybe?" Merlin said, thoughtfully stroking his long white beard. "Or to caves. Dragon hoards?"

"Hidden spells?" Nimue added.

"Please don't suggest splitting up," Beansprout said.

"Not a chance, dear girl," Merlin said, patting her shoulder. "Let's find the workshop first." He examined the entrance to each passage. "Only one leads up, so – after you, Nimue." He gallantly stood aside as she led the way, Beansprout close behind.

23 Galatine Awakes

The djinn led the way into another series of passageways and rooms. He didn't so much walk as lope on all fours, barely marking the sand. Tom found him unnerving, and tried not to focus on his long black claws, which looked as if they could rip Tom's innards out with ease.

Tom stumbled on the uneven ground, and as he was regaining his balance a shake and a roar shattered the silence. The djinn turned and shouted, "Move boy, the mountains may erupt at any moment!"

Staggering to his feet, Tom ran after the djinn, fearing that if they didn't get there quick enough, not only would the moonstone be gone, the portal would be destroyed too.

Tom sweated as he scrambled after the djinn, stumbling into a sand dune piled across a room, and sinking up to his knees. Within minutes the djinn had disappeared ahead of him.

After a few seconds of panic, Tom pulled himself free and for the first time thought of Woodsmoke and Bloodmoon. He hoped they hadn't followed him. It was so weird here – Tom had the feeling there was more to this place than he was being told.

He stumbled after the djinn, winding around towering piles of stones and along tightly woven paths between broken buildings, the way lit by the smoky light of his torch. The city was a warren here. Occasionally, a broken wall revealed a glimpse into a courtyard, or a room, still partially furnished.

He stopped suddenly when the djinn reappeared.

"We must tread carefully now," he said. "Or rather *you* should. There are crusts of river fire here; if they are too thin …" His words hung in the air.

"I get it," Tom said, just wanting to find the moonstone. How he would get it through the fallen ceiling and rubble wall was another matter.

The djinn led Tom to a large stone archway. Beyond was a large chamber with a flat roof that had withstood tons of sand, lava, and volcanic eruptions. Broken windows leaked in rubble and sand, and through one a river of lava oozed like a living being, splitting into tributaries across the floor, bubbling and licking in the channels it had carved over hundreds of years. Beyond that, Tom recognised the other side of Giolladhe's cave.

He took a deep breath. If he got this wrong he would be burned alive, and not even his bones would remain. Was that what had happened to Giolladhe? Were his bones now ashes?

He tentatively set off, stepping gingerly on the stone floor, until he came to the lava rivers. The first few were narrow, and he stepped over them, hoping the ground beyond was firm. The djinn bounded away in front of him, leaping easily over the fiery pits, each time looking back at Tom with a vicious grin.

Ignoring his spite, Tom kept going, until he found a larger river ahead of him. He headed left to where it narrowed, enabling him to jump again. But it was getting more difficult. Thick crusty blackened lava made lumpy islands in the middle of flowing rivers, and at one point Tom was blocked, a blackened lump the only way across. He leapt with a spring, knowing he couldn't linger. As he dropped to the ground, the crust started to snap, and Tom leapt again, terrified he would fall in. He landed with a thump on the other side, his nose almost in the lava.

He stood breathing heavily. Sweat stung his eyes and he wiped it away with his shirt, blinking furiously, ready to jump again. With relief he saw he was almost there. Just as he made ready to jump again, another huge rumble ripped through the air, and lava started to bubble and ooze furiously; the smell of sulphur was suffocating. Without stopping to think, Tom leapt again and ran into Giolladhe's cave.

The djinn smirked. "Well done! I didn't think you'd make it."

"Thanks for the vote of confidence," Tom said, annoyed and exhausted.

"It's not personal. I have little faith in humans."

Ignoring him, Tom quickly found the shelf he had seen earlier, and with relief saw the white stone, covered in ash. It was bigger than he'd expected. He pulled it to the edge of the shelf and then lifted it down, staggering slightly under its weight.

The bottom was flat, but the top was domed with a slot in the centre. He placed it on the floor, brushing away the ash. Underneath the dirt, seams of gold and silver wrapped around the moonstone in an intricate pattern.

"Now I just have to get it through there," he said, gesturing to the rubble wall. "After you wake Galatine."

Another rumble followed, and Tom's stomach started to knot. "Can we hurry please!"

The djinn smiled. "Give me the sword."

Tom wondered if this was a trick – he could lose the sword and the stone. But no, the djinn could easily take it from him. And besides, what choice did he have?

Tom pulled Galatine free and handed it over.

The djinn stroked it reverently. "This was made using fire magic, and the inscription was burnt in by djinns' tear diamonds, you know."

"No, I did not know," Tom said, wishing he'd just get on with it.

"Few fey make weapons like this any more."

Another rumble made the cave tremble.

The djinn ran a long talon across his own palm, producing a stream of green blood. Holding his hand in a fist he squeezed the blood onto either side of the blade, rubbing it into the engravings. He said something Tom couldn't catch, then a flash of black flame engulfed the sword and the engravings glowed. The djinn smiled with satisfaction. "Now, put the sword in the stone."

Tom took Galatine and gently pushed it into the opening in the moonstone. It sank in, halfway up the hilt.

Immediately the moonstone started to emit a soft white light, and the silver and gold metalwork started to glow red as it heated. The glow spread up through Galatine, the blade turning white with heat, and as it reached the hilt the stones either side blinked open like eyes. The glow intensified until a blinding flash engulfed the sword and stone and a screech echoed through the cave.

Tom scrunched his eyes closed and covered his ears for a few seconds, and then tentatively peeked at Galatine. Both the sword and the moonstone had returned to normal, although the opals now swirled with an inky blackness.

"Can I touch it now?" said Tom.

But the djinn looked past him towards the door beyond, and the rivers of lava. "You'd better go, boy. We have woken the dragon."

Tom grabbed Galatine, the hilt warm to his touch. And all of a sudden he heard it. A low guttural growl that made the floors shake, and the word, "Galatine."

"Did you hear that? Did the dragon just speak?"

"It spoke to you," the djinn said, still watching the entrance. "I only heard the growl."

Tom looked at the sword in amazement. It had worked. He could hear the dragon's thoughts. And then an enormous crashing sound reverberated through the chamber, and a burst of flame erupted in the room beyond. "I have to get the moonstone out of here!"

"Make a wish, boy," the djinn said. "Quickly. Before I become too distracted."

Of course, djinns granted wishes. Tom scooped up the moonstone. "I wish to be on the other side of this wall, in front of the portal to Earth."

As he spoke a blast of flame shot across the room beyond, licking the workshop entrance. With a flick of his wrist the djinn produced a long black whip with multiple tails that flickered like smoke and flame. He cracked it into the room beyond, and with barely a glance to Tom said, "Safe travels, boy."

In a flash, Tom was on the other side of the wall, and the portal was in front of him. He could hear the now slightly dulled roar of the dragon. Hoping the djinn would be all right, he hugged the moonstone tightly, checked Galatine was safely in its scabbard, and, before anything else could happen, stepped into the portal.

24 The Door in the Dark

They travelled in silence, plodding upwards in patches of lamplight, until they arrived at a dead end.

Beansprout couldn't hide her disappointment. "It doesn't go anywhere!"

Nimue grinned. "I bet it does! A hidden door, Merlin?"

"Of course," he said. "Only an amateur wouldn't hide it."

Beansprout's hopes lifted as Nimue placed her hand on the wall and murmured a spell.

Nothing happened.

She frowned, and tried another. Again nothing happened.

"Let me," Merlin said. "What did you try?"

"The reveal spell and an invisibility spell."

Merlin snorted. "It must be something more relevant, Nimue."

Nimue raised an eyebrow. "I was starting with something simple," she said huffily and stepped back. "Your turn, Merlin."

Beansprout suppressed a smile at their banter. It was amazing, considering their history, that they could stand to be so close now – it was as if old friendships had returned. Although Nimue remained a little aloof from Merlin, Beansprout could see she cared about him, and that they respected each other. And Merlin certainly minded his manners around her, and never outstayed his welcome, often keeping to his own company. Knowing how much his attentions had smothered her in the past must have made him modify his behaviour.

"Do you remember that obsequious king who threatened Arthur, Nimue?" he asked as he examined the wall.

"Many kings threatened Arthur; you'll have to be more specific."

"That little one, from across the sea. He arrived on a black ship with gulls' wings on the side. He turned up in court one day with an ultimatum and I banished him to a room with no doors."

She looked thoughtful. "Vaguely. Why?"

"Because I think it was the same spell that Giolladhe has used. Or Raghnall." He muttered softly under his breath and a faint line started to spread from the floor upwards, until it made the shape of a door. "I thought so, just a 'say please' spell."

"And what happened to the king?" Beansprout asked.

"We found him a week later, dead. He never could find his manners, even when his life depended on it."

Before Beansprout could say anything else, Merlin pushed the door open and they all heard a yell and the distinctive whisper of swords being drawn. Then, as the door opened fully, Merlin found a sword tip under his chin.

"Woodsmoke! It's me!" Merlin shouted, as Nimue raised her hands to attack.

"That's an excellent way to get yourself killed, Merlin!" Woodsmoke said, annoyed, as Bloodmoon sighed behind him and sheathed his sword. "Welcome to Giolladhe's workshop."

"Where have you come from?" said Bloodmoon.

"The House of the Beloved, of course," Beansprout said.

"Of course!" Woodsmoke said snarkily. "That's so obvious."

She grinned at him. "Oh hush, Woodsmoke. So, we're actually here – in the workshop!"

They filed into a dimly lit room with a low roof. The only things in it were a wooden chair and a huge wooden bed that took up most of the space. In the wall opposite the hidden doorway was another door.

"Have you found anything?" Nimue asked, looking around. "I presume there's more to the place than this?"

"There's a lot of rooms here," Bloodmoon said, "all layered on top of each other. We think some are natural caves, and others were made by magic. But there's nothing here, other than old furniture and tools."

"It's odd," Woodsmoke added. "The place has been cleared as if he was ready to leave, but there was a key in the door, locking it."

A shiver ran up Beansprout's spine. "You mean it was locked from the *inside*? But there's no sign of him?" She looked around the room as if she might see his bones in the corner.

"No sign. Not even under those rotten bed covers." Woodsmoke gestured towards the pile on the unmade bed.

Merlin stalked around the room, feeling the walls. "Any suggestion of magic?"

"Not that we can tell," Woodsmoke said. "We certainly couldn't see that door you've just come through. Although seeing anything here is difficult in this dim light."

Nimue walked over to the lantern hanging from the centre of the ceiling. "Let me see if I can improve this," she said, and with a murmur the light flared brightly and the whole room emerged from the shadows.

They spent a few minutes checking there was nothing they'd missed, before Woodsmoke said, "Come on, we'll give you the tour. You might see something we haven't."

As they followed him downstairs, Beansprout said, "Where's Tom?"

"We left him searching boxes in the downstairs storeroom. I suppose we should check on him, he's been very quiet," Bloodmoon said, a note of worry in his voice.

"Better take us there now," Merlin said.

A sudden urgency drove them down the warren of steep stairs and past open doorways until they came into the main workshop. They followed Woodsmoke into the storeroom and found it empty.

"Where is he?" Nimue said, voicing everyone's concern.

"Have we passed him somewhere in another room?" Merlin asked.

"He'd have heard us, surely?" Beansprout said, her heart sinking.

"Perhaps there's another doorway?" Woodsmoke said, now looking confused. "He can't have gone far."

"Oh yes he can," Merlin said, from in front of a cupboard. "There's a portal here."

"What!" they exclaimed as one, rushing over.

Then there was chaos as they argued about what could have happened and where Tom could be. They had to physically restrain Woodsmoke from plunging in after him.

"I *must* go!" he yelled. "Tom could be in trouble!"

"But where would you end up?" Beansprout said. She agreed Woodsmoke should go, but was worried they'd lose him as well.

As they argued, the blackness in the portal swirled and Tom fell out, bringing Beansprout down with him in a tangle of legs.

Tom gasped. "Wow! I'm back! Awesome." And then he realised who he'd crashed into. "What are you doing here, Beansprout?"

"Great Goddess, Tom!" she said, the wind knocked out of her. "Where have you been? You're filthy! And you reek of sulphur."

It was twilight, and they were sitting outside enjoying the heat after the dark dampness of the caves, listening to Tom's story and examining the moonstone.

Woodsmoke was angry. "You should never have gone in alone, Tom!"

"I didn't plan to," he reasoned. "I thought it was another room." He looked at Beansprout with guilty delight. "I met a djinn – he granted me a wish!"

"Tom, you could have been killed," she said, excited and cross at the same time. "What did you wish for?"

"Gold? Jewels?" Bloodmoon asked, his eyes lighting up.

"No! I just wished to be in front of the portal."

Bloodmoon sighed. "What a wasted opportunity."

Merlin shook his head. "Arthur will not be happy at you going alone."

"Will everyone please calm down?" Tom said, beginning to look grumpy. "I'm fine, and I've found the moonstone. That's good, right?"

Bloodmoon gave a sly wink. "I'll make a fine thief of you yet, Tom."

"No, you will not," Woodsmoke said, with a glare.

Tom interrupted them. "And look at Galatine." He showed them the swirling djinns' eye opals.

"What's happened to it?" Merlin asked, examining it.

"The sword now lives … or something like that," Tom said. "The djinn said it was muted before. Inactivated by Giolladhe before he passed it to Vivian." He paused for a second. "I think it was another way of Giolladhe trying to prevent Filtiarn changing."

Woodsmoke sighed. "My head hurts and I'm starving. Let's head back. We need to talk to Arthur, see if he's found the grove." He looked at Beansprout. "Did you find anything to break the curse?"

"Not yet, but we will. There are a few more passages to search."

"I'll seal this end," Merlin said, stroking his beard, "and we'll return above ground. I think we should explore the caves later. With one hidden portal to contend with, who knows what's down there. I feel we should be properly prepared before we look again."

25 The Clock Ticks

Tom wallowed in his bath, washing away the ash and black marks left by the fire and lava, and the smell of singed hair and sulphur.

The moonstone sat on the bathroom floor, Galatine propped next to it. Both seemed to give off a faint glow, but Tom wasn't sure if he was imagining that. Ever since the sword had woken – as he called it – he felt it, reverberating through him, like a tremor.

He hadn't heard any more animals speaking to him, but he felt aware of them, like a subtle presence on the edge of his perception. It was a strange feeling. But not as strange as hearing that dragon. He was sure it had spoken. Did that mean creatures could sense the sword? All Tom could think of was Dr Doolittle, and he sank beneath the water, trying to banish it from his thoughts.

By the time he got out of the bath it was dark and late, and he was starving. He carried the moonstone down to the long balcony overlooking the city, and placed it on the edge of the table for everyone to see. He was the first to arrive, and he helped himself from the platters of cold meats and cheeses, olives, sweet dishes and soft breads laid out on the table, nibbling on food and sipping wine as he gazed at the city, wondering what had happened here so many years before. He tried to remember what the djinn had said, but his time in the Realm of Fire already felt like a dream. He just felt lucky to be back here, and not back at his grandfather's cottage.

In a short time Arthur arrived, looking disappointed. He threw himself on the divan with a large glass of Satyr's Delight and complained, "I was clearly an idiot for thinking I would find the clearing. How did everyone else …" And then he stopped as he saw the moonstone. He looked at Tom. "Is that *the moonstone?*"

"Yes it is," Tom said with a grin.

"How? Where?" Arthur leapt to his feet, his energy returned, and looked at it from every angle as if it would disappear.

Tom felt a little sheepish. "I crossed to the Realm of Fire – accidently!"

he added quickly as he saw Arthur's expression.

"Woodsmoke let you go alone?"

"Woodsmoke didn't know! And I'm fine – I'm not a child, Arthur. And I got the moonstone!"

Arthur's frown quickly turned to a grin. "Well done, Tom. That's my boy."

As Tom relayed his experience in the Realm of Fire, Arthur continued to prowl around the moonstone. "What's this slot for?" he asked, gesturing to the top.

"It's where Galatine goes." He pulled Galatine free and placed it on the table. "Look at the stones. The djinn helped me wake the sword."

"So you had to pull the sword from the stone?" Arthur asked, a smile hovering on his face as he looked fondly at Tom.

"Yes, I suppose, sort of," Tom said, and then realised what he'd done. "Oh! It's like your old legend – with Excalibur."

Arthur hugged Tom. "I think that means something, Tom." His voice sounded gruff and Tom peered at him closely. Arthur wasn't usually an emotional man.

"It does? What?"

"I don't know, but I feel we're linked, more than we were before," Arthur said, gripping him by the shoulders. "Galatine was never 'awake' with Gawain, maybe that's because it was never meant for him."

"That's because it was meant for Filtiarn!" Tom said, trying to deflect whatever Arthur was trying to say.

"But I think it's now meant to be yours, Tom."

Before Tom could comment further, the others appeared and they changed the conversation, Tom trying to cover his confusion.

"We're getting closer," Arthur said, smiling.

"You've found the grove?" Nimue asked.

"No." Arthur's face fell. "I meant the moonstone. We have more searching to do."

Brenna leaned back against the balcony, drink in hand. "I think it's impossible. Even in a hundred years a wood will grow and change, obliterating a clearing. In a few thousand it would change *everything*. But there's an area that might be worth looking at again tomorrow. I want to look closer to the mountain, closer to Giolladhe's place."

"We could create a new grove," Nimue said. "In fact, it's something I've been meaning to do. Merlin and Beansprout could help. But we still need to try and find the original spell, and that means exploring the passages between the house and the hill."

Tom was confused. "What do you mean, a new grove? Does it matter?"

"It needs to be sacred ground, Tom," Merlin explained. "A quiet space, prepared for magic. You can do magic anywhere, but big spells require a special place. It enhances the power of the spell."

"How long would that take?" Arthur asked.

"Not long, really. A day or two. But we're already short on time," Nimue said.

"Have we any idea where Filtiarn is? He should be here soon," Woodsmoke said.

"I flew out beyond the city today," Brenna said. "They're on the moors now, and should be here late tomorrow." She looked worried. "I stopped to speak to them, and Filtiarn looks exhausted. I hope he survives the spell."

News of Filtiarn seemed to energise Arthur. "So, we search again for the original grove, on the rise that Brenna saw, and if not we make a new one. We have a few more days until the full moon." He looked out, to where the moon was edging above the mountain. "Look, it's getting closer to full."

The slight curl of the moon seemed to grin down at them, bathing them in its yellow glow, and Tom felt a tug in the pit of his stomach.

"But first we search the caves, and I suggest that's something we do together," Arthur said, his voice excited. "Tonight."

26 Guardian of the Daystar Sapphires

They headed in single file down the steps into the dark stone corridor beneath the House of the Beloved, carrying smoking torches, lanterns and weapons. Arthur led the way, with Nimue and Merlin close behind.

Soon they came to the small space with three other passages leading off it, and Merlin pointed out the path to Giolladhe's.

"I wonder how often they used this?" Beansprout said.

"Depends on what terrible secrets they were trying to keep," Woodsmoke suggested with a grimace.

"Let's try this one first," said Arthur, indicating one of the other two passages. "Can we mark it so we know where we've gone? Things could get very confusing down here."

"Excellent idea," Merlin said. With a flourish of his hand, he scrawled *House of the Beloved* in shining writing on the tunnel they had come along. He marked Giolladhe's passage, and then the one they were about to take, saying, "I shall call this number 1."

"Inspired," Bloodmoon said, sarcastically. Merlin ignored him.

For some minutes the passage wound onwards, until it eventually began to widen, and a pale light seeped around them. Arthur called out, "Stop!"

"What's happened?" Woodsmoke called.

"Come forward – very slowly. We have reached an edge," Arthur said, sounding nervous.

They shuffled towards the light, and Tom gasped. The passage had opened out, and they were on a narrow shelf, looking out across a large cave that twinkled with a faint blue glow. Far below them was a lake lit from beneath, reminding Tom of Ceridwen's Cauldron.

"Where's the light coming from?" Tom asked, as he craned round to look at the cave. It was almost circular, and although the lake was a long way down, the roof seemed far above them too.

"Great Goddess!" Nimue murmured. "It must be coming from daystar sapphires." She pointed. "There are hundreds set into the cavern walls."

"What are those? I've never heard of them," Brenna said.

"Very rare stones with strong magical properties," Nimue replied. "Only those who practise magic use them, and they're very hard to get." She gazed around with wonder.

"And yet Raghnall seems to have had his own enormous supply," Arthur said.

"I wonder," Merlin said, "could they have been used in Filtiarn's spell?"

A narrow walkway ran off to their right before petering out, and Merlin felt his way along, heading towards where a smattering of stones came within reach.

"Maybe," Nimue murmured, deep in thought. "They have the ability to enhance any spell, but the power actually makes them dangerous. I have never used them, even when I had some. If they're used incorrectly, they can cause what I can only describe as a magical explosion."

"That's a long way down," Bloodmoon said, peering over the edge. He picked up a stone and dropped it. It was several seconds before they heard a faint splash. "I think there's something down there."

"Like what?" Tom said, alarmed.

Beansprout dropped to her knees, better to look over the edge. "Can you see that black shape against the blue? It looks like it's circling around."

"It's getting bigger," Woodsmoke said. "Is that because it's getting closer?" He looked at Bloodmoon, annoyed. "Have you woken something?"

"I only dropped a stone in!" he said, indignant. "Whatever it is, it's a long way down. You worry too much, Woodsmoke!"

Before anyone else could comment there was an enormous splash and the black shape emerged from the water, silhouetted against the blue. The shape kept coming, and then a spurt of fire emerged from the blackness, followed by the familiar roar of a dragon.

"It's a bloody great dragon," Arthur yelled, pulling Excalibur free with a hiss. "Run!"

But Merlin was still at the end of the ledge, examining the stones.

"Merlin, get a bloody move on!" Arthur yelled, preparing to fight as they stood mesmerised by the dragon's approach.

And suddenly Tom was aware of Galatine, trembling, its hilt warm to the touch. "How can it live in water?" he shouted as he pulled Galatine free, its opals now swirling furiously.

"Water dragon," Nimue yelled above the roar, "very vicious, and territorial."

A blinding white light emitted from her hands, held palms forward, forming a wall in front of them just as the dragon drew level and released another stream of fire.

They instinctively ducked, but the shield held, turning into a wall of flame as the fire hit it. Beyond, the dragon flapped its enormous wings and fixed them with a vicious stare before flying round to circle back, its huge wing span creating a rush of air.

"Wow!" Tom said, rising to his feet and looking with new appreciation at Nimue.

Merlin stumbled, and Arthur ran to him, helping him to his feet. Woodsmoke and Bloodmoon had already drawn their arrows in case the shield failed.

"Get a move on, Merlin," Nimue commanded icily. She turned to Beansprout. "Join your hand to mine, and hold your other hand out, like me."

Without hesitating, Beansprout did as she asked, and Tom saw her stiffen as a wave of power travelled through her, strengthening the shield.

Tom watched the dragon turn back towards them, dripping with phosphorescent water, like a sheen of blue fire racing along its wings and dripping down its jaw. It was magnificent and terrifying all at the same time.

Arthur rejoined them, Merlin with him, panting heavily. "Run, now!" Arthur said, pushing them one by one ahead of him into the passage.

The dragon attacked again, closer than before, its wide jaws showing its sharp cruel teeth, just before a powerful stream of flame poured out. Despite the shield, Tom could feel the heat licking closer, buffeted by the enormous wings. Its roar was enraged, and only when it turned again did Nimue drop her hands, grab Beansprout by the arm and run, Arthur following closely behind.

They kept running well beyond the turn in the passage, Arthur yelling, "Don't stop!"

Another roar echoed down the passage and for one horrible moment Tom thought the beast had somehow followed them. Glancing behind he saw flame coming towards them. "Duck!" he yelled, throwing himself to the ground. Beansprout landed next to him. A flash of flame passed overhead, bringing its own roaring crackle which seemed to last forever, and then it was gone.

He rolled over to see Beansprout looking at him wide-eyed in shock. He scrambled to his feet and grabbed her hand, pulling her up. Behind him, Arthur was lying on top of Nimue, shielding her from the flames. Ahead the others struggled to their feet.

"Keep going," Woodsmoke said, and they ran the rest of the way, only slowing down when they reached the other passages.

"That was close!" Bloodmoon said with a wry grin, and he sank to his knees breathing heavily.

"It's not funny!" Woodsmoke said. "We could have been killed!"

Brenna was the only one not breathless, having flown ahead of them. "You really should think things through first, Bloodmoon," she said, a note of disapproval in her tone. Tom knew she had a soft spot for Bloodmoon, and she couldn't help a small smile escaping; Bloodmoon gave her a wink which she tried to ignore.

She turned to Merlin. "Are you all right, Merlin?"

Merlin leaned against the wall, clutching his chest. "I think so. At least I'm alive."

Nimue was cross. "Bloodmoon! I didn't even get a chance to get some stones. Now I'm going to have to go back when the damn dragon has calmed down."

"Dear lady, fear not," Merlin said. He opened his hand to reveal a clutch of stones. "I prised them free before Bloodmoon nearly killed me."

Arthur smiled and patted his shoulder. "Well done, old friend." He turned to Bloodmoon. "Had enough excitement, or shall we carry on?"

"Always onwards, Arthur," he said, getting to his feet. "After you."

The next passage snaked downwards, and then split into two.

"Which way?" Tom asked.

"Left," Arthur said, decisively.

This passage was short and ended in another cave, but this one twinkled in the light of their lanterns.

"Herne's hairy hooves!" Bloodmoon said, incredulous. "It's a huge pile of gold and jewels!"

"And weapons, shields, and ornaments," Woodsmoke added, holding up a helmet. Although it was tarnished, it still reflected a gleam of torchlight.

"Dragon hoard," Nimue said. "But where's the dragon?"

She circled the pile of jewels, and called out, "There's another exit. Bigger this time."

Joining Nimue, Tom saw she was right. "I guess a dragon needs a much bigger passage than the one we came down."

"So do we explore it?" Woodsmoke asked.

They gathered around the entrance, but it was impossible to see more than a few feet ahead.

"It could go for miles," Nimue said, shaking her head.

"But what if the spell is hidden down there somewhere?" Tom said.

"Let's check out the other passage first," Arthur said. "If we have to we'll come back here."

"I could fly down, see where it heads?" Brenna suggested.

"It's too dangerous," Woodsmoke said.

Arthur nodded. "I agree. I don't want us splitting up."

"Look at this," Bloodmoon said. He stood at the edge of the hoard, where he had been pulling objects aside, rummaging in curiosity. He held up a sheet of translucent scales. "Dragon skin."

"Oh, that's disgusting," Beansprout said with a grimace.

"But useful for spells," Merlin added. He took it from Bloodmoon, carefully folded it, and put it in his cloak.

They headed back to the last passage, and it again led downwards, a mixture of winding path and rough steps, until eventually they came to a thick wooden door. Arthur tried it, but it was locked.

"Who locks a door down here?" Tom asked, exasperated.

"Someone who wants to hide something," Arthur answered.

With a flick of his wrist, Merlin unlocked the door with magic.

"Can you teach me that?" Bloodmoon asked.

"No!" Merlin said. "You cause enough trouble."

They pushed the heavy door open and their lanterns showed a small square room. All along one wall were alcoves, filled with candles, bones, artefacts and scrolls. Along another wall was a roughly hewn wooden table. Beansprout, clearly wanting to practise magic, lit the candles from a flame she produced in her hands.

"This must be it!" Arthur said. "Where else would you hide a spell you don't want anyone else to find?"

They fanned out around the room, and started to pull objects from the alcoves.

"Gently," Merlin called to the others as he extracted a scroll, "the paper's fragile."

"What animals are these from?" Tom asked, pulling down a skull with a sharp snout and huge hinged jaw.

"Marsh snakes?" Woodsmoke suggested.

"A marsh snake? It must be huge!" Tom said, turning the skull over.

"They'll eat you in one big gulp," Brenna explained.

Tom put the skull back on the shelf with a grimace.

Merlin and Nimue had pulled several scrolls out and carefully unrolled them on the table.

"These look like contracts," Nimue said, puzzled.

"Between who?" Arthur asked, looking over her shoulder.

"The sylphs and Raghnall. And this one," she said, unrolling another, "is between the sylphs and Giolladhe."

"For weapons, I presume?" Woodsmoke said.

"A design for an amulet, a large one by the look of it. To go on one of their towers, I think." She squinted in the light, and held the lantern closer. "I think it's to repel dragons."

Beansprout interrupted from the far end of the table, where she stood with Bloodmoon. "I think we've found it." In front of them on the table was a wooden box, an image of a wolf engraved on the top.

"The only thing is," Bloodmoon said, "we can't open it."

Merlin hurried over. "It could be it, I suppose," he said, turning the box over, examining it carefully. "It's either been sealed by magic, or just some clever lock."

"It's the best lead we have for now," Nimue said. "Nothing else here suggests the spell."

"But what if it isn't?" Tom said, not liking the idea of coming back down here again.

"Let's take anything of interest," Woodsmoke suggested, casting an appraising eye over the room, "including those contracts. And then let's get out of here."

27 The Wolf Mage Arrives

Tom sat with Woodsmoke at the entrance to the tunnel leading to Dragon's Hollow, looking out over the mountain below them. The rose gold gates were partially open behind them, glittering in the sun.

It was late afternoon, and they were in the shade of a towering tree, leaning back against the trunk, each sipping a bottle of Red Earth Thunder Ale.

"I really hope we don't have to go back into those tunnels," Tom said. "They were creepy."

"I felt like I was inside Raghnall's grimy little mind," Woodsmoke agreed. "All those twists and turns and hidden secrets."

"There's probably a maze of tunnels beyond the dragon hoard. It's weird to think that beneath us all sorts of things may be hidden away."

"And things we don't really want to find," Woodsmoke said. He pointed to the path, to where a pocket of dust swirled. "I think that could be Filtiarn."

Woodsmoke and Tom had volunteered to come and welcome Filtiarn, Elan and Rahal. Both were glad to leave the preparations behind. Nimue and Beansprout were out searching again for the grove, and preparing to start a new ritual place in the woods behind their house if needed, helped by Brenna and Bloodmoon, who was not good at being cooped up in the house. Merlin and Arthur were in the library, trying to open the box.

"Do you think we can do it?" Tom asked. He looked at Woodsmoke who reclined against the tree, his legs stretched out in front of him, and wondered if he would ever be as calm or composed. Woodsmoke took everything in his stride, and if he was worried about anything, he rarely showed it.

"I'm not sure, Tom," he said, his expression sombre. "It's a big ask after so many years."

"We got Merlin out of Nimue's spell."

"With Herne's help. There's no god to help us now."

Tom looked at Galatine. "I feel sort of responsible. And I know it's stupid, but I do. I mean, I have the sword that performed the curse."

"Oh come on," Woodsmoke said. "It has nothing to do with you. Neither you nor Arthur had anything to do with it. And at least the sword's *'awake'* now. Filtiarn has a better chance than he's ever had before."

As he finished speaking the three figures rounded the bend in the path, followed by a dozen wolves, and they stood to greet them. "But you know what?" he added, before the others came within hearing. "I think there'll be another twist before this is all over."

Before Tom could question him further, Woodsmoke turned and waved. "Welcome back to Dragon's Hollow!"

Filtiarn looked tired, but better than when he had become human again. The haunted look behind his eyes remained, and Tom wasn't sure if that would ever go. Filtiarn managed a slight smile. "It's good to finally be here."

Tom looked nervously at the wolves that padded around them, sniffing at their feet. Rahal reassured him. "It's OK, Tom, they accept you as friends now."

They were beautiful creatures, their fur thick and white, their eyes intense. Tom held his hand out and one sniffed it cautiously, and then nuzzled under it, allowing Tom to pat it.

Rahal and Elan slipped off their horses, Rahal saying, "I have to confess, I need a good freshen up." She ran a hand across her face. "I feel very dusty."

"You can rest and change at Nimue's," Tom said. "We have rooms for all of you."

Elan smiled with relief. "Good, the ride has been hard on Filtiarn. Have you found anything to help us? We've found the moonstone, and have activated Galatine." He pulled the sword free and pointed to the stones swirling in the hilt.

"But we haven't found the spell yet," Woodsmoke added. "We think we're close, though."

"Wow!" Elan said, impressed. "You've found more than we have in years."

"But we had your knowledge to build on," Tom said.

"And a lot of luck," Woodsmoke added.

"Even so ..." Elan said, and he looked at Filtiarn. "Good news, yes, Filtiarn?"

Filtiarn didn't respond. Instead he stared down at his horse.

Tom held Galatine out to Filtiarn. "Do you remember the stones doing this?"

Filtiarn shook his head. "It was my sword for many years, but it never had the djinns' eye opals until my brother modified it."

Woodsmoke nodded. "Let's get to Nimue's where we can talk in comfort. Will the wolves follow us? They may unnerve the fey of the Hollow."

"I'll send them around," he said. He spoke a series of what sounded like barks and growls, but the wolves seemed to understand him, and they loped off beyond the gate, heading onto the steep mountain paths.

"Have either of you been to Dragon's Hollow before?" Woodsmoke asked Rahal and Elan.

"Never," they replied together.

"Well, you're in for quite the experience. Come with me, Rahal," Woodsmoke said, courteously. "I'll tell you all about it."

He mounted his horse and waited for Rahal, then led the way back through the tunnel, leaving Tom to follow with Elan and Filtiarn.

"Does anything look familiar to you?" Tom asked Filtiarn.

"A little. I recognised the moors we crossed, they have changed very little, but I'm pretty sure the gates were not of rose gold when I was last here." He smiled wryly. "They have obviously had good fortune."

"When were you last here?"

"Two thousand years ago. I could not bring myself to come here the last time I changed. I'm not sure I want to be here now." His hands trembled slightly as he gripped the reins of his horse, and Tom tried not to show he'd noticed.

"In that case, you'll probably find it's really different inside."

Tom had got used to the splendours of Dragon's Hollow, but Elan was quiet as they rode up towards the lake, looking around at the houses and the people. Once there, he gazed up at the huge dragon fountain in the centre of the lake. "This place is amazing."

"I certainly don't remember the fountain," Filtiarn said. He looked around, taking everything in. "The city has grown, and the houses are more decorative. I don't remember them being so richly embellished."

"Do you remember that?" Tom asked, pointing towards the House of the Beloved in the distance.

Filtiarn's eyes darkened. "Yes. I remember that. Raghnall's place.

Although it wasn't as big." He looked up at the shoulder of the mountain beyond. "That's where Giolladhe's workshop was."

"We found it," Tom explained, wondering if he should mention the portal. He decided not to, things seemed complicated enough. "And we found the underground tunnels."

"What underground tunnels?" Filtiarn asked, looking puzzled.

Was it possible that Filtiarn couldn't know? It seemed Raghnall and Giolladhe had many secrets between them. "Let's keep going," Tom said, spurring his horse onwards, "and I'll explain."

Tom sat next to Beansprout at dinner, Brenna on his other side. They were again on the long balcony overlooking the city, seated around the table, chatting as they ate. Nimue and Beansprout had done their best to make their guests feel welcome, and the table glittered with silverware and candlelight. However, there was none of the Raghnall's ostentatiousness, and everyone was relaxed and laughing. Tom was oblivious to the decor, tucking into roast chicken with relish.

Beansprout watched him eating. "Where on earth do put it all, Tom?"

"What?" he said, indignant. "I'm very hungry. Hard work does that, you know?"

"Try making a sacred glade in this heat," she said sarcastically. "That's hard work."

"Is it done?" he asked, taking a breather and sipping his beer.

"We think we may have found the original," she said with a slow smile.

"Really?"

Brenna joined in. "As I thought, we were looking too close to the house yesterday. The place I saw was on a rise, and now I know where Giolladhe's workshop is, it makes sense. It's his grove, not Raghnall's. Well," she qualified, "we think it is."

Beansprout continued. "It's off the path up the mountain, the one you used to find the workshop. But you turn off it, before it becomes too high. Off to the right. But we couldn't have found it without Brenna. The path is completely overgrown."

"I had to work back, from the grove," Brenna said. "It looked less dense than the rest of the woods."

"So is that easier? Less work to do?" Tom asked, excited.

"You'd think so, but no," Beansprout said. "We've still got a good day's work ahead of us. And we need to prepare the path from the road."

"And set up lanterns to help us find the way," Brenna added. "Although the moon will be full, it will be dark beneath the trees."

"How are you clearing the trees?"

"A combination of magic and brawn," Brenna said, with a grimace. "Guess who's helping us tomorrow."

Tom looked at her suspiciously. "Do you mean me?"

"Yes," she said, "there's lots more to do."

Arthur joined in. "I am feeling more positive about this already."

"Why?" Beansprout asked. "Have you opened the box?"

"No," Merlin answered quickly, his glass halfway to his lips. "I don't want to risk it breaking. Whatever's locking it is powerful."

"It has a wolf on it, you say?" Filtiarn asked. He ate like a bird, picking at his food slowly, and pushing it around on his plate. He looked very pale.

"Yes, a wolf's head actually," Merlin explained. "I can show you later if you like."

"Maybe tomorrow," Filtiarn said. "I'm not sure I will be up too much longer."

"Yes, yes, of course," Arthur said. He looked at Filtiarn with concern. "You must rest. Tomorrow's fine. How many days until the full moon, Nimue?"

"Two."

Only two days. The table fell silent for a second as the news sank in.

"And I would like to ask you more questions about the ritual," Nimue said. She had been silent for some time, listening to the others and watching Filtiarn. "And a little about the arrangements with the sylphs at that time, if that's all right?"

Filtiarn looked startled, as did Rahal. "Why does that matter?" she asked Nimue, slightly aggressively Tom thought.

"It all matters," Nimue said sharply, her green eyes flashing. "Understanding what went wrong then may help us put things right now."

Filtiarn, Rahal and Elan soon pleaded tiredness and excused themselves, but not before the Wolf Moon appeared over the mountain. It was bigger again, and it seemed to Tom that the yellow hue was increasing as the moon grew in size, casting a sickly light over the city. As it rose, the wolves in the forest beyond the house loosed their unearthly howls and Tom felt goosebumps rise on his skin. Filtiarn stood watching the moon for a brief second, before he turned and almost fled the balcony.

28 The Altar Stone

Tom wielded the machete with brutal determination, hacking it back and forth, creating the path to the ritual place as if there were sprites attacking him. Sweat poured into his eyes and stained the front of his thin cotton shirt, and he was covered in small twigs, leaves and dirt.

Woodsmoke was next to him, and together they moved at a good pace. The path started flat, but soon rose upwards towards the grove. It was on a hill – part of the mountain shoulder. Tom wasn't entirely sure what Beansprout had been on about; there was no original path left at all.

Brenna had flown ahead of them earlier, leading Beansprout, Bloodmoon, Nimue, Arthur and Rahal to the grove. They had slipped through the trees and bushes, hacking small branches away to mark their path, leaving Tom and Woodsmoke to create the path properly. Elan and Filtiarn had remained at the house with Merlin so Filtiarn could rest.

A flurry of wings interrupted them and Brenna appeared. She laughed at their appearance. "You two look like you're having fun!"

Woodsmoke had tied back his long hair, and a strand had escaped, hanging in front of his face. He pushed it back, smearing his face with dirt. "Yes, we're having a great time! Having fun flying around watching the rest of us work?"

"Yes, actually. It's especially fun watching Bloodmoon labouring away in the grove."

That cheered Woodsmoke up. "Good. Glad to hear he's not dodging work."

"No chance. Nimue won't hear of it."

Tom laughed as well. "So much for *protecting the ladies.*"

"Yes, Nimue really needs his protection," Brenna said with a smirk. She added, "They've found the stone altar in the centre of the grove, and some of the trees around the edge – well, the original edge – are oaks, yew and elder."

"Is that important?" Tom asked.

"Apparently yes. They will add protection to the grove and enhance the spell."

Magic stuff he would never understand, Tom thought.

Brenna continued, "I'm heading back to Nimue's, to see how Filtiarn is. Do you need anything? You're heading the right way."

"No, we're fine, thanks. How far have we to go?" Woodsmoke asked.

"You're about halfway."

Woodsmoke and Tom groaned, but before they could say anything else, Brenna flew off.

When they finally arrived at the clearing, they found Nimue and Beansprout sitting on the altar stone in the middle. Arthur lay on the floor gazing up at the sky above. All three of them looked hot and bothered. Beansprout, who now usually followed Nimue's style of long dress, instead wore a cotton shirt and the loose trousers she'd travelled in, tucked into boots. Nimue remained in a dress, having announced she was far too old to change her ways now. Tom didn't believe that at all, but decided against arguing with Nimue. If he was honest, he was still a little overawed by her.

A ring of old gnarled trees edged the clearing, demarcating it from the rest of the woods, and although some of the larger trees still stood in the centre of the glade, they had managed to fell many smaller ones, and saplings lay strewn across the ground.

"What do you think of our hard work?" Beansprout asked.

"Impressive," Woodsmoke said, sitting beside them. "Almost as impressive as ours."

Beansprout laughed, and a tendril of hair escaped and brushed against her cheek. "I think we'll all need baths later."

Arthur spoke from where he lay on the floor. "So have we done now?"

"No!" Nimue said, throwing a twig at him. "We need to clear away everything and burn what we don't need."

Arthur sat up slowly, picking the twig from his hair, which fell around his shoulders looking knotty and wild. "I knew I should have stayed in the house today."

"You know you'd have gone mad."

He poked his tongue out at her playfully, reminding Tom of the fact they were old friends who were very comfortable in each other's company. Nimue laughed, looking like a teenager.

"Where's Bloodmoon and Rahal?" Tom asked, looking around.

"Trying to find a path to Giolladhe's workshop," Beansprout said. "We think it must be in that direction." She pointed to the far side of the grove, where the side of the mountain reared in the near distance.

"I suppose you want us to help here?" Tom asked with a sigh.

"No rest for the wicked, Tom," Nimue said. "You can help us gather the wood up."

"Is the fire for tomorrow?"

"Yes," Nimue answered, "and hopefully Merlin is making progress on the spell."

"So we're sure this is the grove where it happened all those years ago?" Woodsmoke asked, looking around with interest.

"Fairly sure. The trees on the perimeter are clearly ancient, and aren't native to the area," Beansprout said.

"Which means," Nimue said, "that this was planned. And this," she patted the altar stone, "was brought here for magical purposes. The stone has an unusual red vein running through it. It's not from here."

Arthur looked interested, "How do you know?"

"It's from Avalon."

"What?" All of them looked at Nimue in shock.

"I have no idea how it's here, but the stone is all over the island. It has strong conductive properties. It holds energies – of the elements, plants, growth …" She laughed at their shocked expressions. "It's why the island is so magical. It's one of the things Raghnall used to complain about." Her face fell momentarily.

Tom jolted with a memory. "You had an argument, sort of, with Raghnall, about Avalon."

"Yes. It was an old argument. He believed Avalon shouldn't be hidden. He was wrong. It is powerful, too dangerous, even for the magical place of the Realms. It was the original crossing place between the Realms and Earth. And as Tom knows, things are buried there that should never see the light of day."

Tom nodded, remembering when he woke Arthur beneath the lake. "I guess it was quite a privilege to be there."

"And for me to be *sleeping* there," Arthur said.

Nimue nodded. "It was. It healed you, Arthur. And it was a difficult decision for me to leave."

"But you can go back?" Woodsmoke asked, puzzled.

"I can never go back. Not to live. Besides, there is too much to do here."

"Why can't you go back?" Woodsmoke persisted.

"You should never go back," she said enigmatically.

"So how is the stone here?" Arthur asked. He leaned forward, all tiredness forgotten.

"Raghnall or Giolladhe must have been to Avalon. Or a priestess arranged it."

"How long have priestesses been on Avalon? It can't have been Vivian."

"No, not Vivian," Nimue agreed. "But there were others before her. We priestesses, witches, are of an old order. We serve the Goddess. She has been here forever. Like Herne. Beansprout – we really must revert to your original name," she said, looking at Beansprout with a shake of her head. "One day, you must go there to complete your training."

"I must?" she replied, clearly excited. "To Avalon?"

"Of course. Anyway. However it happened, the stone is here. It explains why Giolladhe was such a success with his skills. This stone would have enhanced them. He must have used it many times. And I presume Raghnall would have used it too, when he needed it."

"It's fortunate we've found it," Arthur said. "It is meant to be."

"Maybe," Nimue said. "Maybe."

But Tom thought she wasn't convinced.

When they finally returned to the House of the Beloved it was dusk. They all ached, were filthy, and stank of sweat. Rahal and Bloodmoon had rejoined them, having found traces of a path up to the mountain workshop.

They were accosted on the stairs by Merlin. "There you are!" he said. "You need to come to the library now." In comparison to them, he looked refreshed, clean and dry. Tom thought he had washed his robe, but his beard was still wild, as was his hair. His appearance in many ways mattered little to him. However, his bright blue eyes sparkled.

"Why, what's happened?" Nimue asked, worried.

"We've opened the box. Or rather, Filtiarn has."

He refused to say any more, instead leading them up the stairs, past their bedrooms, which Tom gazed at wistfully as he passed, and on into the library.

The setting sun cast a warm rosy light over Brenna, Elan and Filtiarn, who were gathered around the table in the centre. In front of them lay the open box, its contents spilling onto the table. Tom saw a scroll, filled with tiny writing, and items that looked like stones, bone, skin and feathers. They turned as they entered, every one of them looking serious.

"What's wrong?" Nimue asked, striding towards them.

"We've found the spell, but the curse has a kick," Brenna said.

"What sort of kick?"

"A stone from Avalon has powered the spell. How do we get one of those?" Filtiarn asked. He was agitated, his dark eyes troubled, his gaunt, hollowed cheeks exacerbated by the soft light.

Nimue broke into a broad smile. "Is that all? We have found the grove; the altar stone is from Avalon. I'd know it anywhere."

"Really?" Filtiarn was so excited he started coughing, and Elan passed him some water.

"Are you sure?" Elan said, a doubtful look on his face.

"She's sure," Arthur said. "By tomorrow night this could be all over."

Merlin shook his head. "I'm not so certain."

"Why?" Nimue turned to Merlin. "How complex is it?"

"Very. Part of it involves a potion that Filtiarn must drink – and that we must make. There are a number of items we need to gather (some common, others not), and conditions must be right in order for it to work, which they are – the stars are aligning and the Wolf Moon is waxing. But the trouble is the language. It's archaic. Some terms are clear, others aren't. Which means although I understand some things," he shrugged, "some I don't understand at all." He looked tired and frustrated.

"Surely you must understand the language, Filtiarn?" Arthur asked.

"Yes, regular words and phrases, but there's an item listed called *Arach Frasan Fuil*. I don't know what that is, and neither does Merlin."

"What? I don't know what that is either. Rahal, Nimue?" Arthur asked, perplexed.

"No. Sorry," Rahal said, flustered. "I don't feel I'm helping at all."

Nimue looked thoughtful. "I've never heard of it either, but we have plenty of old texts. We just have to check and double check everything."

Silence fell as they understood the implications. And then a troubling thought crossed Tom's mind. "You know when we were trying to break your spell, Nimue, I was told that only the witch who cast the spell could break it. Or that death could release it? So how does that affect us?"

"Because this spell was designed to be broken. It is time bound, linked to the Wolf Moon cycle. Filtiarn's change depends on it. Regardless of who is around, he changes form every thousand years for the space of one month. Once in his human form, if we perform the ritual correctly, he will remain as human."

Merlin agreed. "Part of the curse is the knowledge of the change, and its time sensitivities. What better way to extract maximum torture than to know you are so close to being human, and yet aren't." He shook his head. "It's very cruel."

"But if the curse is still going, surely that means Giolladhe must be alive, somewhere?" Tom reasoned. "Or why is Filtiarn still changing?"

29 Arach Frasan Fuil

Night had fallen, and Tom leaned on the balcony watching the city lights twinkling. The dragon fountain was lit up from below, and it glowed red, green and gold. Around the rim of the lake, Tom could see the jugglers' fire clubs being thrown high into the air, and he watched the spectacle, mesmerised. He hadn't been into the town yet, and hoped that he'd have time to visit the market tomorrow. He looked up at the Wolf Moon, now almost full. Its sickly yellow glow was getting stronger and it chilled his blood.

The table had been cleared after dinner, and the wooden box containing the spell was now sitting on it. Nimue had rolled out the scroll and was making notes on a pad next to her. She sat at one end of the table, Beansprout, Rahal and Merlin next to her, reading and asking questions, and consulting several books stacked on the table – books on herbs, gems, and metals. Tom smiled to himself. Three witches and a wizard; he certainly kept unusual company these days. Beansprout looked animated, excited to be learning more magic, but Rahal seemed worried, despite her clear regard for Nimue and Merlin. She'd been asking questions ever since she'd arrived, and particularly this evening. And they still hadn't worked out what *Arach Frasan Fuil* was.

Arthur and the others sat at the opposite end of the table. Tom was the only one standing. He had grown suddenly restless, and could only put it down to nerves. Tomorrow night they would be making their way to the sacred grove, and they had to find out what some of the words meant, or it would never work.

Bloodmoon was examining something he'd found in the box – it looked like a tusk. He held it up. "Does this belong to a boar?"

"I think so," Rahal said, taking it from him. "The spell needs something to anchor the boar, and the change." She handed it back and then reached into the box, taking out a feather. "This is a raven's, it signifies change too."

"I must admit," Nimue said, squinting at the scroll, "this is proving harder than I thought."

Arthur interrupted, addressing Filtiarn. "How *did* you open the box?"

Filtiarn lifted his shoulders and spread his hands wide. "I merely touched it."

Arthur looked shocked. "Is that all?"

"Quite clever, really," Merlin said. "Only Filtiarn or Giolladhe could open it, and most of the time Filtiarn would be in boar form anyway. It ensures no-one else could rescue him."

"I wonder where he is?" Filtiarn said, looking down at the table. It was clear he was referring to Giolladhe.

"Does it matter?" Arthur asked. "We can break the spell without him."

"Yes, it does matter. He did this to me." He looked up and glared at everyone, suddenly furious. "Me. His brother! And I have no idea why!"

"It does seem a bit overkill, just because he thought you'd insulted his spell," Beansprout said.

"He was always quick to anger," Filtiarn explained. "But yes, his response seems *unreasonable*." His eyes flashed, but Nimue intervened with another question.

"What exactly was going on here five thousand years ago, Filtiarn?" She looked at him curiously. "I mean, the city didn't exist like this. It was overrun with dragons; traders were trying to mine for the rich seams of metals and gems, and they were battling with dragons and sylphs. And the sylphs found their city under attack as well. This would have been a battle zone. I've read accounts, but they are dry and dusty and probably don't contain the real history."

Filtiarn looked uncomfortable. "Just as you've said. It was a battleground for riches. Fey were here before the dragons."

"No they weren't," Bloodmoon corrected. Tom had forgotten he had an ear for stories, like Fahey. Bloodmoon leant forward, cupping his wine glass. "Dragons have always been in the Hollow. It was named after them. Where there's gems, there's dragons. Those are the rules of the Realms. But the fey wanted their wealth."

"Well yes, true," Filtiarn said. "But they were manageable, almost. It was when the dragons started arriving from the Realm of Fire that things became dangerous."

"Yes." Merlin nodded. "It started the Dragon Wars. What led you to ask for the spell?"

"I arrived with the early fey and attempted to negotiate with the dragons – I failed. Not long after, Giolladhe arrived – it was the best place for him to get precious metals and gems for his forging. And Raghnall had arrived too. Probably for the same reason. Raghnall immediately set up his spell, but with limited success. It was clear the dragons were stronger." He shrugged. "They're dragons, after all. I left for a while, and then thought I'd try again. And I'd decided I wanted to hunt with the wolves. I've always had a bond with them, something I can't explain."

"So you can speak dragon?" Tom asked.

Filtiarn looked at him and smiled. "Of a sort. Their language is guttural and difficult, even with my skills. I was trying to broker peace – I was a bit of a diplomat," he said modestly. "I had achieved success elsewhere where animals and fey had clashed. Sometimes just for small villages on the edge of wild forests, or for the Realm of Water where they waged daily battles with some of the fierce creatures under the sea."

So far, so true, Tom thought, remembering what the Gatherer had written in his diaries, and some of the other books Finnlugh had loaned them.

"When it was clear the fey wouldn't leave the Hollow and the dragons wouldn't stop attacking, I thought I'd try again, to help prevent more bloodshed," Filtiarn continued. "That's when I asked my brother to strengthen my sword so that I could enhance my skills. Galatine was one of his early creations, and I had owned it for a while. I was proud of it, and of him for making it. As you've seen, it is a work of great beauty. I thought he could concentrate energies within it, and that those energies could have another action – one of transformation that could help me run with my wolves, my companions of old."

"But he wasn't keen, was he?" Merlin asked, narrowing his eyes speculatively.

"No, not initially. How do you know?"

"While you were all busy with the grove, I spent some time reading those contracts we found, and it seems he and Raghnall were making a lot of money from protecting the town and the sylphs. Giolladhe had made the sylphs an amulet to protect them from the dragons. They paid a lot of money for it – I saw it in a contract. My guess is that the spell could have worked a lot better, but it suited Raghnall and Giolladhe to have it fail sometimes. It gained them protection money."

"That makes sense," Nimue added. "A few months ago a contingent of fey arrived here to present me with the annual gift to Raghnall for protection of the city. The gift that of course transfers to me, now I protect the city."

Beansprout looked at her in shock. "I didn't know that!"

"I was so disgusted, I couldn't bring myself to speak of it," Nimue said, annoyed. "Of course I refused. I don't take protection money. I do this to protect the city, as anyone with a conscience would. I confess I thought this was a later arrangement. I had no idea it had been going on for millennia."

Arthur said, "So that's why everyone looked so uncomfortable around Raghnall. He was holding them hostage."

Woodsmoke agreed. "And when we killed him they thought we had condemned them to death by dragon attack, and more extortion."

"Is that why we've been getting gifts lately?" Beansprout asked. "And the occasional freebie at the market?"

"Probably," Nimue said. "They were so pleased I didn't want their money – it was a huge amount – that they've been showing their gratitude in other ways."

"Have the sylphs forgiven you?" Bloodmoon asked Nimue, referring to the time when she had outwitted them at Arthur, Woodsmoke, and Tom's trial.

"No, not really. Although they are civil," she said with a smile. "But to go back to you, Filtiarn, you were about to disrupt the flow of money. You had to go."

Filtiarn looked at her and then Merlin in shock. "He cursed me because I could have ruined their protection racket."

"I think so," Merlin agreed.

"So where is Giolladhe now?" Elan asked. He looked agitated, as if he wanted to go searching for him right then.

"He hasn't been seen since after Excalibur was made. It was one of his final works," Merlin said.

"He had to flee," Tom said, recalling his earlier conversation. "The djinn said the amulet he made for the sylphs didn't confer protection – it drew the dragons to the Realm of Air, and eventually, somehow, they found out."

Merlin nodded. "That's true. I've been looking into the history of the Hollow in one of Raghnall's many books, and it seems he disappeared at the same time the sylphs discovered his deception. I think Raghnall blamed him completely to save his own skin, and Giolladhe had to run."

Beansprout tapped the scroll. "What if whatever this thing is in the spell, doesn't exist any more? You know, like an extinct plant, or something."

Rahal had been quiet for a while, carefully reading through a large black leather-bound book, and now her head shot up. "I've found it!"

"You have?" Beansprout asked, craning to read the passage.

Rahal groaned and covered her face with her hands. "*Arach Frasan Fuil* means Dragon Blood Jasper."

Nimue looked alarmed. "Are you sure it's not just Blood Jasper?"

Rahal looked up at Nimue, her eyes wide. "No, it's definitely Dragon Blood Jasper – that's what *Arach* is."

Nimue had gone white. "I've never heard it called that before." She looked at Merlin as if he could produce one from under his robe. "I know I haven't got one. Where in the Realm can we get one from? In time for tomorrow!"

"Slow down," Arthur said. "We are surrounded by markets selling gemstones. Why can't we just buy one?"

"Because Dragon Blood Jasper is found in one place only – in the skull of a baby dragon," Rahal said. "And we need that too."

"That's disgusting! What exactly are we supposed to do with it?" Arthur asked. He was leaning over the table, gripping the edges, his knuckles white.

Rahal read from the spell: "Take *Arach Frasan Fuil* and add whole to the potion exactly four hours after the brew has started. The following line says we are to grind the anchor to powder." She looked up. "The anchor *must* be the bone."

"This just gets worse," Nimue said, leaning back in her chair.

Tom interrupted, confused. "We're in Dragon's Hollow. Dragon central in fact. Surely a baby dragon's skull is easy to find?"

"Dragons guard their young more fiercely than their gold. How easily do you think you could get one, Tom?" Nimue asked, fixing him with her piercing stare.

"I didn't think of that," he said sheepishly.

"And that potion needs cooking time," Merlin said. "We need it in the next six to eight hours. I need to start the potion tonight." He grabbed the spell from her, and pointed out the line. "This refers to a potion that needs twenty-four hours brewing. We need to start this by eleven o'clock tonight latest."

"Oh, great Goddess. I thought we had a little more time," Nimue said, her calm demeanour shattered.

"Do we need anything else?" Brenna asked.

"I'm pretty sure we have everything else we need. Maybe more

Wolfsbane?" Nimue said, checking her list.

Tom noticed Filtiarn had fallen silent, watching them debating back and forward. He had screwed his napkin up in his palm, and squeezed it again and again, wringing it out until it looked like a piece of rag.

"Maybe we need to search the passage again?" Woodsmoke suggested. "Although that could take days."

"I'm leaving you to worry about that," Merlin said, rising to his feet and rolling up the scroll in one swift movement. "We're going to the spell room up on the roof. We need to start assembling the ingredients now, and start the brew in ..." He looked at the clock ticking on the wall – it was already nine o'clock. "Two hours. We need to weigh, grind, and prepare."

"So we have until three in the morning to get the Dragon Blood Jasper – and skull," Arthur said, jumping to his feet and starting to pace up and down. "Great. Just great."

"I'll help," Brenna said to Merlin. "I'll be your runner, for anything you may need."

Bloodmoon stood suddenly. "I have an idea. I'm heading into the Hollow. Anyone coming?"

"To do what?" Arthur asked, intrigued.

"Find the stone and skull of course," he answered with a grin.

Tom realised his whirling thoughts wouldn't settle for a few hours, and the thought of walking through the city at night excited him. "I'll come."

"Well I'm not leaving you with Bloodmoon. Herne knows what you'd get up to," Woodsmoke said, his tone mildly appalled, but clearly eager to be out of the spell-making.

"Great," Bloodmoon said. "Strength in numbers. And Arthur, we need you."

Arthur looked torn between helping Merlin and going with Bloodmoon. "Why?"

"You're the money. Bring lots of cash."

"I'm coming too," Elan said. He placed his hands over Filtiarn's, stopping their constant wringing. "We are going to do this. I promise you."

30 Smuggler's Retreat

The central streets of Dragon's Hollow were crowded with all manner of fey enjoying the cool evening air and entertainment. Jugglers and acrobats were performing under the Wolf Moon on the lakeside; huge spherical lanterns made of paper and metals that imitated the Wolf Moon, hung along the streets and by the water. They glowed yellow and orange and were etched with the snarling faces of wolves. The dragon fountain loomed above everything, and water shot from its mouth, frothing across the lake.

The Wolf Moon was almost full, and it looked enormous as it hung over the city, casting a malevolent eye over the activities. Tom felt the expectations of the next night weighing on him.

Bloodmoon walked ahead with Woodsmoke and Arthur, navigating through the crowds with a certain assurance. Every now and then he nodded at someone he knew – it was clear he was well travelled. Woodsmoke and Arthur kept up an easy stride next to him, glancing back occasionally to check Tom and Elan were still behind.

Tom pointed to where the water ruffled and something moved on the surface. "What's that in the lake?"

Elan dragged himself out of his reverie. "Mermaid, probably. Although I think they prefer salt water. May be a nymph?"

"That's so cool! I can't believe you're not looking at everything – this place is amazing!"

"Sorry, I'm distracted. We have twenty-four hours, and we haven't got everything we need." He slumped against a balustrade and looked over the lake, despondent.

"We'll do it. I know we will," Tom said, wishing he was as convinced as he sounded. "I can understand why you attacked me now – you know, at the tournament."

Elan fidgeted with his leather jacket. "I'm sorry. I was feeling pretty desperate. Stupid, I know. I wasn't thinking clearly. Like that would have solved anything."

"People do stupid things when they're desperate," Tom said, thinking of Nimue and her curse on Merlin. Although Nimue's act was a very calculated one.

Elan finally looked at Tom. "I'm worried that either we can't break the curse, and that would be devastating, or that the curse will shift to me."

Tom felt a knot form in the pit of his stomach. "Why do you think it would shift to you?"

Elan shrugged. "I don't know. But I just feel it can't be that easy."

Tom spluttered. "Easy? How is this easy? It's taken thousands of years just to get this far. And we haven't even broken it yet!"

"All right, not easy. But you know what I mean? Assemble the ingredients, and break the spell."

Tom was now frustrated. "But everything was hidden! It's only through luck and hard work that we've got this far. Stumbling into the Realm of Fire wasn't easy – I was nearly destroyed in a lava flow."

Elan sighed. "I'm not explaining this very well."

"You're just worried, understandably. It's weird to think something that's been hanging over your family could be over in a day."

Elan nodded. "You're probably right. We'd better go, before we lose the others." He headed back into the crowd. Tom hurried after him, remembering what Woodsmoke had said about a twist still to come. He hoped they were both wrong.

They caught sight of Bloodmoon and the others just as Bloodmoon turned down a side-street. It was narrow and winding and led back behind the markets, past a few small shops. Then they turned to the left and disappeared under a sign that read, "Smuggler's Retreat." Tom and Elan followed them down a flight of steps and pushed open a heavy wooden door, entering a low-ceilinged room – or rather, a cave. In fact several caves, all connected, shadowy in the low light. Smoke filled the air and the sound of music drifted from another room.

Bloodmoon stood at the bar, drink already in hand, while Arthur and Woodsmoke admired the enormous range of beverages. Tom had never before seen so many different colours and styles of bottles. There was wine, beer and spirits, and half a dozen hand pumps lined up with names in front of them.

"So what's your poison, Tom?" Bloodmoon said, grinning.

One caught his eye – Nymph's Nectar. "A pint of that, please."

"Good choice," Arthur said. "I'll join you."

Nymph's Nectar turned out to be a caramel-coloured beer, rich and sweet and malty. Tom sipped it appreciatively.

"Nothing like a good beer to clear the head," Woodsmoke said, as they settled themselves onto stools around a small round table in the corner. "This was a good idea, Bloodmoon, but aren't we supposed to be finding the stone?"

Bloodmoon seemed completely at home, looking animated and relaxed at the same time. "It is possible to combine business with pleasure, you know!"

"So who are we looking for?" Arthur asked, leaning back against the wall and surveying the room. "With a name like Smuggler's Retreat, this place must be about more than a great choice of beer."

"This is *the* best place for information on interesting goods," Bloodmoon said. "Many years ago it was used to store all sorts of things – gold, gems, weapons, art – all making their way out of the Hollow by slightly underhand means."

"And it still seems to have an unsavoury atmosphere," Woodsmoke added, although he didn't seem the least bit perturbed. "It worries me that you know this place exists."

"Well –" Bloodmoon started, but Woodsmoke stopped him with a shake of the head. "I don't want to know."

Woodsmoke was right about the atmosphere. Tom glanced around the room, trying not to stare, but there were some very interesting characters. A group of satyrs were talking loudly over a table full of glasses, the discussion becoming heated, and there were numerous shifty looking fey hunched over tables, deep in conversation, avoiding eye contact with anyone else as they exchanged packages and money. There were goblins, a couple of sprites, and even some sylphs, who looked huge in the low-ceilinged cave. There was a tenseness in the air that Tom hadn't noticed when he first came in, but he noticed it now and felt increasingly uncomfortable.

"Is this safe?" Elan asked in a low voice.

"Of course," Bloodmoon said breezily. "And we're all armed, aren't we?"

"That's not really reassuring me," Tom said.

"Anyway, I had a quiet word with the barman when we came in, and the fey we need to speak to is over there." He nodded towards the next cave, linked to theirs by an archway. "He deals with rare artefacts and interesting esoteric items. Are we ready if I go and fetch him?"

"Ready for what?" Tom asked, confused.

"Negotiation." He looked directly at each of them. "Leave the talking to me."

Woodsmoke and Arthur exchanged a long glance as Bloodmoon headed off, returning a few minutes later with a small immaculately dressed fey who reminded Tom of a car salesman. He was dressed in a black velvet jacket, slim trousers, highly polished boots, and a dark blue linen shirt with embroidered cuffs and ornate cufflinks.

He took a seat and looked expectantly at the others. "Good evening. I understand you need my assistance." He placed a glass of what looked like port on the table in front of him.

Bloodmoon slid back into his seat. "Carac, your reputation precedes you. May I say how much I admire your work."

Carac nodded, looking smug. His little finger was raised as he sipped his drink. "So does yours, Bloodmoon. I have followed your career with interest."

Bloodmoon smiled and lowered his voice. "We are looking for an *Arach Frasan Fuil*, complete with its anchor, and we believe you are the man to find one for us."

Carac's feline grin disappeared. "If you know what that is, you'll know what you ask is impossible." He started to rise as if to walk off.

Bloodmoon leant forward, hand on Carac's drink, and said in a low voice, "I know what it is, and I know you can get one. Money is not a problem."

The fey narrowed his eyes at Bloodmoon and sat down again. "The object you speak of is extremely rare. And very expensive."

"But you have one?" Bloodmoon stared at him, refusing to look away.

"No. But I know someone who has." Carac stared back at Bloodmoon, ignoring everyone else at the table, and Tom felt his breath become shallow.

"Here in the Hollow?"

"Maybe. But he won't give it up."

"Who has it?"

Carac hesitated. "He would not like strangers to know."

Bloodmoon leaned forward until he was inches from Carac's face. "I. Don't. Care."

"He won't sell it to you," the fey persisted.

"That's not for you to worry about."

"And what will I get out of this?"

Bloodmoon named a sum that had Tom almost choking – Arthur too, judging by the look on his face. "And our silence of course – your name shall not be mentioned. And this conversation never happened." He raised a quizzical brow at Carac.

Carac took only seconds to decide. "Your offer is generous." He dropped his voice to a whisper. "The most royal councilman, head of the city council, Finbhar of the House of the Fireblade."

Even Tom had heard of him. Finbhar owned a palatial building on the opposite side of town to the House of the Beloved. It was a vision of white marble, pink granite, and silver inlay. He remembered meeting him at Raghnall's funeral. He had long blue hair and small neat beard.

Bloodmoon sat back in his chair, looking thoughtful. "Tricky."

Carac grinned unpleasantly. "Very. My money, please."

Arthur reached into his cloak and pulled out a small leather bag. He checked the contents under the table, and removing only a few gold coins, slid it across to Carac.

With a nod the fey grabbed the bag and tucked it into his jacket. "Have an excellent evening gentlemen," he said, leaving them.

Arthur exploded. "Great Herne! Did you have to offer so much? I haven't got enough cash to buy the damn thing now."

"Arthur," Bloodmoon said quietly. "We aren't going to buy it. We're going to steal it."

31 An Audacious Plan

They stood in the shadow of a large tree close to Finbhar's house. The mansion loomed above them, its white marble a dull yellow under the Wolf Moon. It was now midnight, and they had three hours in which to get the skull and take it to Nimue and Merlin, and for them to prepare the potion.

"We shouldn't have stayed so long in the bar," Arthur said, looking anxiously at the house. A single light burned steadily on the top floor.

"If we'd come any sooner, the whole house would have been awake," Bloodmoon said.

"It's still lit up," Tom pointed out. The paths, trees and bushes were prettily illuminated by garden lights, making their approach difficult.

"I'm not proposing we walk up the path," Bloodmoon said, a look of incredulity on his face. "Have you never broken in somewhere before?"

"No, actually! I'm not a delinquent," Tom said. "You get arrested for that sort of thing where I come from."

"You get arrested here too," Woodsmoke pointed out crossly. "I can't believe we're actually considering this."

"Have you a better suggestion?" Bloodmoon asked.

"Yes. Ask him to sell it!"

"But if he says no, which he will, we're stuck."

"You don't know he'll refuse."

"Those things are hard to come by, and he's a collector. I know the type, trust me. He won't sell," Bloodmoon insisted.

Elan interrupted. "I'll do it. It's for my relative, after all."

"No!" Bloodmoon, Woodsmoke and Arthur said at the same time.

"Obviously I will do it," Bloodmoon continued. "I'm good at this. You will be my lookouts."

"You'll need someone in the grounds," Woodsmoke said. "As much as I hate this, I'll come with you."

Arthur tried to disagree, but Woodsmoke stopped him. "I'm much quieter than you. You'll have to get us out of trouble if anything happens."

"He's right," Tom said, wishing he had Woodsmoke's skills. "He's nearly invisible when he wants to be."

"Excellent," Bloodmoon said. "Let's find a way in. If someone's coming, give three owl hoots, and make sure it's close enough to the house for us to hear once we're inside." He took a small strip of leather from around his wrist and tied his hair back with it. His cocky sureness had been replaced with serious intent. "Elan, you stay here and watch the approach from the street. Arthur, there's another large tree further along. You stay there in case someone comes from the other direction. Tom, come with us."

Woodsmoke protested. "Why is Tom coming with us?"

"We need someone just inside the grounds with a clear view of the house. And he's smaller than Arthur. Tom, if you see lights going on in the house, three short hoots too."

It was fortunate, Tom thought as they edged up the street in the shadows, that this road was so exclusive. The houses all had large grounds, so none were close to the councillor's, which meant less foot traffic.

A low stone wall enclosed a hedge of thick shrubs and trees on the garden's perimeter. Bloodmoon paused where a large tree leaned over the wall, casting the path in shadow.

"I'll try here," he said, "and if it's clear I'll whistle once."

He vaulted the wall with ease and disappeared through the hedge.

For a few seconds they heard nothing, and Tom's heart pounded in his chest. He looked up and down the street, but nothing moved except for leaves trembling in the light breeze. Then they heard a whistle.

Woodsmoke offered a last word of advice. "Don't put yourself in danger, Tom. I want you to run and leave us there if anything happens." He then disappeared over the wall, and Tom followed, fighting his way through the hedge, getting scratched and slapped by leaves and whippy branches. Feeling like he'd made huge amounts of noise, he finally broke free and stood in the grounds next to the others.

A beautifully manicured lawn stretched ahead of them to the house, broken only by flower beds and shrubs, and a large pool covered in water lilies. The house was surrounded by a deep veranda, on both the ground floor and first floor. It was idyllic and silent except for the tinkling of running water.

"It's huge," Tom whispered. "How are you going to find it?"

"I have made discreet enquiries," Bloodmoon whispered back. "His collection is on the first floor at the back of the house. I don't just sit and drink, you know. There." He pointed to the left side of the house, where a small waterfall cascaded down a bank into a shallow pool. It was in shadow, blocked from the Wolf Moon by the bulk of the house. A stream meandered from here into the larger pool.

"Woodsmoke, follow me."

Tom watched them run around the perimeter, disappear for a few seconds, then reappear on the other side of the small pool, close to an ornate bridge. In a blink they had gone again, then Tom spotted them under the veranda. If he hadn't known where to look, he would never have seen them.

He looked nervously across the grounds. Nothing stirred. He looked back and saw a shadow move on the first floor veranda, and a door open. He presumed Bloodmoon was now in the house. He couldn't see Woodsmoke at all. And then he heard three hoots. *Crap.*

His heart started racing and he repeated the hoots, wondering who was coming as he heard the signal repeated low and soft on the balcony. A few seconds later he heard the rattle of hooves on the road, and the sound of a carriage. With luck they'd be passing. They came closer and closer, and then the worst thing happened. The carriage rolled up the driveway and made its way sedately to the front of the house. A light sprang on in the entrance and the door opened, illuminating the front steps. Tom stepped further back into the hedge, wishing it would swallow him up.

A servant helped a tall fey and a woman out of the carriage. As they walked up the steps and into the light, Tom saw the blue hair of the councilman. The woman must be his wife. She turned towards Finbhar and laughed, the light illuminating her beautiful face and dark hair. They must have been to a party – both were wearing elegant evening dress. The door shut behind them and the carriage trundled around to the back of the house, where Tom presumed the stables were located.

Tom looked back to the veranda, but there was no movement. Lights appeared in one of the ground floor rooms, and then another on the second floor. Tom gave three more short hoots. They sounded shrill in his ears. Again the signal was repeated, low from the veranda. And then came three short hoots from the road, urgent this time, and another rumble of wheels as two carriages rolled into the grounds. Herne's horns! They were having a party. This couldn't be happening. The front door flew open again and laughter drifted across the grounds as the fey exited their carriages and entered the house in high spirits.

Tom's heart was now pounding in his chest and he willed Bloodmoon to get on with it. He wondered whether to leave, but didn't move – he had to make sure they were coming. Then he saw a light flare on the first floor, and hooted again, feeling conspicuous and uncomfortably hot. A stiff breeze rustled through the trees and then the entire house fell into shadow. Tom looked up. Thick black clouds had passed across the moon, and a rumble of thunder reverberated for several seconds. This at least was in their favour.

Tom watched the veranda. After a few minutes he finally saw movement, then shadows were racing across the grounds towards him. For a horrible second Tom thought they were dogs, and stepped further back into the trees, but then the shapes materialised into Woodsmoke and Bloodmoon.

"Get out, now," Bloodmoon said, pushing Tom ahead of him.

As Tom was scrambling over the wall, he heard a howl and a shout and raised voices. He almost fell onto the road, where Elan and Arthur pulled him to his feet as Bloodmoon and Woodmoke landed with enviable grace.

"This way," Arthur said, setting off at a run.

They raced down the street, fortunately now in complete darkness. Thunder rumbled again, covering up the sound of their footsteps. Arthur headed down a side street, and they didn't stop running until they reached a main street leading to the lake, where they slowed to a stroll. Here late revellers laughed and talked, and they mingled in the thinning crowds, nodding in greeting as they passed, as if they hadn't just robbed one of the most important fey in the Hollow.

Bloodmoon glanced behind. "That was close."

"Have you got it?" Elan asked

"Of course. Never doubt a master."

32 The Spell

As they reached the House of the Beloved, the wind grew stronger, buffeting their cloaks around them. They headed up the stairs until they reached the spell room that looked out onto the roof through a wall of glass windows and doors. This was Nimue's doing. Raghnall's spell room had been in the centre of the house, but Nimue had brought all his spell books, and her own, into this room that reminded Tom of a conservatory.

Lining the back wall were shelves loaded with books and the usual jars and bottles of potions, herbs, bones, feathers, skins, gems and metals. Both outside and in were pots and troughs filled with herbs and other plants, and a long table ran down the middle of the room. In a fireplace, a small cauldron hung over a brightly blazing fire. Merlin sat next to it on a stool, patiently stirring whatever was in it. An unpleasant sickly-sweet smell filled the room.

Nimue, Rahal, Beansprout and Brenna were clustered around the table, chopping and preparing various ingredients. In the centre was the scroll, pinned at each corner.

"Well?" Nimue asked as they entered, her face etched with worry.

"My dear ladies, did you ever doubt me?" Bloodmoon said, producing the skull from his cloak with a flourish.

They grinned, and then whooped with relief. "Bloodmoon, you are quite amazing," Nimue said. "Where in the Realm did you get that?"

"We stole it," he said bluntly.

"You did what?" Beansprout said, eyes wide. She looked at Tom. "Did you help?"

"We all did. I was a lookout," he said, realising he had actually quite enjoyed it.

"And I had to go into the damn place after him!" Woodsmoke said indignantly.

"Another few minutes and we'd have all been on trial again," Arthur added. "You cut it fine, Bloodmoon."

"You should have seen what he had! That place was full of relics and all sorts of precious objects. I admit, I was distracted," he said sheepishly.

Brenna grinned. "You manage to sneak anything else out?"

"Of course not," Bloodmoon said slyly.

"Well, put it on the table," Nimue said.

Bloodmoon ceremoniously placed the skull under the lamplight where they could see it clearly. It was about the size of an adult human's, but with a long snout and jaw full of sharp teeth. The bone was old and dark brown in colour, but it still looked menacing. The thing that caught the eye was the green jewel in the centre of its forehead.

"So that's what all this fuss is about? It's actually quite cool," Tom said admiringly.

"Take a good long look, because we're about to smash it to pieces," Beansprout said, a small hammer in her hands.

"All of it?" Arthur asked, admiring it from all angles.

"It does seem a shame, doesn't it?" Rahal said, looking at it sadly. "I doubt any of us will ever see one of these again."

"That explains why I've spent a small fortune on it," Arthur muttered.

"We've been doing some reading about it while you've been gone," Beansprout said. "As we know, the dragon transforms after death into all sorts of metals and gems. But for a short time, a young dragon has a stone in the centre of the forehead – the Dragon Blood Jasper. This is only present for a few months, then it changes and becomes a regular skull. To have a baby dragon's skull is a great rarity; to have it with one of these in is even rarer. The stone is one of the greatest symbols of transformation. Youth to adulthood, naivety to wisdom, weakness to strength."

Nimue deftly leaned forward and prised the stone free with a small knife. "I'll take this."

"And the other ingredients of the spell?" Tom asked, curious.

"They all have properties necessary to aid transformation. Or in this case, banish it," Nimue said. "There are two spells on this scroll. One to cast the curse, one to end it. They're almost identical, apart from the incantation. And this skull."

Brenna picked up the skull, idly examining it. "The thing I really can't work out is, why have a spell to reverse it? Why not just curse Filtiarn forever?"

Merlin looked across from the fire. "I told you before. Power. It's a taunt. To know it exists and to constantly search for it, is psychological torture."

Brenna looked unconvinced.

"Where's Filtiarn?" Tom asked, realising he wasn't in the room.

"In bed. He's too tired for these late nights. And I think it's too depressing," Beansprout said. She reached across to Brenna, taking the skull from her and placing it on a sheet of paper. She raised the hammer.

Bloodmoon turned away. "I can't watch. It's like burning money."

"My money at that," Arthur added with a glare.

Beansprout brought the hammer down on the skull with a sickening thud, and it cracked down the middle. At the same time an enormous rumble of thunder erupted overhead, shaking the room, and a flash of lightning illuminated the sky and the roof beyond the window. Within seconds heavy raindrops started to fall.

"I hope that's not a sign," Tom said, peering through the windows.

Nimue grinned at him. "Superstitious, Tom?"

"We're about to break a curse, this makes it very creepy," he reasoned. "And I happen to be carrying a cursed sword."

"The sword is not cursed, Tom," Arthur said. "It was magical aid, or something like that."

"Yes, something like that," Nimue said, with a note of impatience. "Please leave the magic to us."

Beansprout continued to smash the skull until it was in tiny pieces, and then she poured the pieces into a mortar and ground them with the pestle.

Merlin looked at his pocket watch. "Nearly time to add the skull. Measure it carefully, Nimue – we only need a thimbleful."

Bloodmoon was horrified. "Is that all? You've crushed that priceless artefact for a thimbleful?"

"All for a good cause," Beansprout said. "And besides, we'll keep it safe for other spells."

"Best it's gone, anyway," Rahal said. "The less evidence of your night-time activities the better, surely?" She looked at Bloodmoon mischievously, and Tom was suddenly aware how pretty she was. Her dark red hair, snaking down her back and across her shoulders, seemed to glow in the firelight.

Bloodmoon seemed to think so too. He winked, and said, "Well thank you, milady, for thinking of me."

Merlin interrupted. "Come on, bring me the crushed bone, the boar's tusk and a dawnstar sapphire."

Nimue placed them carefully on the small table at his side, and the room stilled as everyone watched, Tom wondering if the dawnstar sapphire would cause a magical explosion. One by one Merlin added the ingredients, swirling the potion all the time. The smell of burnt hair filled the room and everyone coughed.

"Is it supposed to smell like that?" Tom asked, in between coughing. He opened the door onto the roof, and warm, muggy air flooded in, adding to the general soupiness of the atmosphere.

Merlin tutted, rubbing his hands across his face and down his long beard. "How do I know? I've never made this before. I am following the instructions to the letter, and now the liquid needs to reduce. The final addition will be the stone."

"Don't you grind the stone?" Arthur asked, watching the preparations with interest.

Nimue answered. "Apparently not. According to the spell it will just dissolve."

Merlin looked up, the lines on his face accentuated in the firelight, adding years to his already great age. "This will go on all night. I suggest you all go to bed. By the morning it will be done, and then it needs to rest all day. We must hope I have done it correctly."

33 After the Storm

Tom lay in bed listening to the rain lashing against the windows. It was mid-morning and he had slept fitfully, interrupted by the thunder and lightning, which had continued for hours. Now there was only the odd rumble in the distance. He hoped the rain would ease by tonight or they would get soaked, and he wasn't sure if cloud covering the Wolf Moon would affect the intensity of the spell. It was going to be a weird day.

Tom sat up and read the Gatherer's account again, ensuring they had missed nothing important. Tonight they would recreate that event. He pulled Galatine free of its scabbard and examined the fine engravings. It really was a beautiful sword, and he didn't want to give it up. It was his now, bound to him once it had been reactivated. He rubbed his hands across the djinns' eye opals, feeling their warmth. He'd heard no animals speak after that first time with the dragon – all he had was a subtle awareness of other creatures nearby. It seemed Galatine's ability to enhance communication with animals had not passed to him, and he felt a bit disappointed.

Shaking off his gloomy mood he dressed and went in search of the others, first trying the spell room. Despite the full-length windows, the room was dim. The fire had gone out, and a dark green liquid that Tom presumed was the potion sat on the table in a small glass flask with a stopper. No-one was there, so shutting the door carefully behind him, Tom headed down to the kitchen where he found Beansprout, Brenna, Woodsmoke and Arthur sitting around the table, the remnants of breakfast in front of them.

"Morning," Tom said, heading over to the range, where covered dishes were being kept warm. "I'm starved."

"Morning, Tom," Arthur said, leaning back in his chair. "We're trying to decide what to do today."

Tom sat down next to him with a full plate of eggs, bacon and fried mushrooms, and a mug of coffee. "There's not much we can do, is there?" He looked around the table. "You all look very serious."

"Just worried," Beansprout said. "If it all goes wrong tonight, well …"

She shrugged. "We'll have failed, won't we?"

He nodded and swallowed a mouthful of breakfast. "I was looking at that old diary this morning, just in case we missed something, but I couldn't see anything else. Where's Filtiarn?"

"I'm here," a deep voice said from behind him.

Everyone turned as Filtiarn entered the room, Rahal and Elan by his side, and a young white wolf pattering along beside him. "I've been told I need to build my strength, so I'm here for some breakfast." He looked better than he had in days, and his eyes had lost their wildness. With a shock Tom realised it was because Filtiarn was cheerful.

Arthur obviously agreed. "You look good, Filtiarn. Are you feeling better?"

He nodded and sat down, while Elan brought him a plate of food. "Having a good bed and lots of sleep has done wonders. And good food helps too," he said, tucking into his breakfast. Now that the lines on his face had softened and he was starting to fill out, Filtiarn was looking a lot more like the picture the Gatherer had drawn. "And Rahal tells me you have made the potion."

Rahal sat next to him. "We can't thank all of you enough. The support you've given us over the last few days has meant everything." Her eyes filled, and she brushed away a tear. "The strain of the last few months has been huge."

Arthur leaned forward and took her hand. "It is our pleasure, Rahal. I couldn't stand by, it is against my nature," he said earnestly.

"But we attacked you –" She faltered, looking down at the table.

"Not your finest moment," Woodsmoke said with a frown. "If you'd killed Jack or Fahey it would have been a different matter."

Arthur shot him a look of annoyance, but Woodsmoke stared back defiantly.

Beansprout intervened, shooting a comforting smile at Rahal and Elan. "Fortunately they're all right. Although it seems like a lifetime ago now."

"I'm so glad they're well. And I'm glad we're here now." Rahal smiled at all of them and Tom found himself smiling back. It was hard not to like Rahal and Elan. He wondered what would he have done in their situation.

Rahal pressed on. "In anticipation of success, we're taking Filtiarn into town to buy some clothes."

"Yes, I feel I should return my borrowed clothes," Filtiarn said. "And I'm curious to see how the Hollow looks now. It's certainly different to how I remember it."

"I admire your positive attitude," Arthur said. "Aren't you worried we'll fail?"

Filtiarn pushed his plate aside. "I have failed since I was cursed. This is the closest I have ever got. We have Galatine, the moonstone, the spell and the potion. I have to allow myself some hope today. I'm going to pretend it is already over, and this is the start of the rest of my life. After all, by tomorrow I could be cursed forever and I shall have to end the curse another way."

He spoke with such finality that Tom and everyone else knew exactly what he was talking about.

"I can't imagine you would kill yourself," Arthur said, looking at him with incredulity. "Not after enduring what you have for so long."

"But I always had hope." Filtiarn's expression was deadly serious. "After tonight there will be no hope if we fail. I refuse to live like this. In fact I can't. I think one last change will kill me. But *I* will choose how I die. Not Giolladhe."

If anyone hadn't understood the importance of their task before, they did now.

Arthur was insistent. "We will not fail. I will not accept defeat. I never have."

"You are fortunate, then. I hope that continues. For my sake as well as yours."

Tom asked a question that had been bothering him for some time. "Do you still talk to animals? I mean, can you hear them, understand them?"

Filtiarn looked at Tom curiously, and then patted the head of the wolf sitting next to him. "No. I hear only my wolves, my constant companions. The curse affected me in other ways. I cannot hear any other animal now. Why do you ask?"

"Now I'm carrying Galatine, and it's awake, I thought maybe I would hear something, but I can't." Tom was going to explain about the dragon, but that sounded too weird, so he kept it to himself.

"I can only presume it's because it was to enhance my own powers," said Filtiarn. "You have never had them, and therefore ..." He shrugged, his meaning clear.

"So if we break the curse, your full powers will return?"

"Maybe, Tom. Maybe."

Tom was dreading asking his next question, and he knew Arthur didn't want him to. But he had to. "If you had the sword back, would that help?"

Filtiarn shook his head. "I do not want the sword. It is yours now. I do not even wish to look at it."

Tom nodded, relieved. He loved Galatine, despite its origins. After all, it had belonged to Gawain. And it made him feel closer to Arthur.

Woodsmoke gave Filtiarn the ghost of a smile. "Enjoy your day, Filtiarn. Leave the preparations to us." He turned to Tom. "You're helping me – we're going to finish the clearing and build the fire."

"I am?" Tom said, surprised. "But it's raining!"

Woodsmoke gestured towards the windows. "It's stopping. Besides, the Wolf Moon doesn't stop for the rain."

"Don't worry," Brenna said. "I'll come and help. I'd like to keep busy. It will take my mind off tonight."

"I'll be spending the day with Merlin and Nimue," Beansprout said, barely suppressing a grin. "More magic stuff."

"And then I suggest we rest," Arthur said. "It's going to be a long night."

34 Releasing the Beast

The path from the road to the sacred grove was lined with torches that spluttered and flared in the warm breeze. The rain had long since stopped, and now scudding clouds passed across the sky, occasionally blocking the Wolf Moon.

Tom looked up at the full yellow moon that blazed above them with a feral light, and again experienced a sinking in his stomach and a creep of dread he couldn't fully explain. The feeling had been growing all day, and Galatine seemed heavy at his side. He presumed the others felt the same – apart from Filtiarn, who had a bright air of anticipation.

Merlin, Nimue and Beansprout walked ahead with Filtiarn, and the rest followed. The dozen wolves that accompanied Filtiarn had gathered close, and they slipped through the trees on either side, like ghosts, their yellow eyes glinting like tiny beacons in the darkness. Tom had got used to them, and found their presence oddly comforting.

Tom was carrying the moonstone. It was awkward and heavy, and it made his arms ache. Woodsmoke and Bloodmoon had wanted to help, but Tom had refused. He had found it, and he felt he had done little since, this was his contribution. He stopped and put it down for a few seconds, shaking his arms to return the blood flow.

Woodsmoke and Bloodmoon waited with him. "Are you sure you don't want me to carry that?" Woodsmoke asked.

"No, I'm fine," Tom repeated, slightly breathless.

"It was good of you to offer to return the sword," Woodsmoke said, his expression invisible in the darkness. "I know you didn't want to."

"No, I didn't, but it seemed right. I'm quite relieved." Tom gestured up the path, towards where Arthur walked with Rahal and Elan. "And besides, Arthur wants me to have it."

"Well, Arthur can't always get his own way," Woodsmoke said. His response reminded Tom of when Woodsmoke had disagreed with Arthur when they were searching for Nimue.

"It's just Arthur's way. He means well," Tom said, wanting to defend him.

Bloodmoon agreed with Woodsmoke. "He's a good man, but he's still a king in his head. You will always need to stand your ground with him, Tom. Old habits are hard to break."

Tom sighed. "I know, but it's OK." He bent to pick up the stone, to deflect further discussion. "We should get on."

When they arrived in the clearing, torches were flickering all around the perimeter, and the fire was burning in the centre, next to the altar stone.

Nimue called, "Put the moonstone on the altar stone please, Tom."

He struggled over, and placed the stone in the centre. "What about Galatine?"

Nimue looked to Merlin. He had unrolled the scroll and was squinting to read it under a torch held by Beansprout. "Merlin?"

He nodded. "Yes, place it in now, Tom."

Tom withdrew Galatine and carefully placed it in the moonstone. He immediately felt a tingle run along his arm and through his body, and at the same time a soft glow seemed to emanate from the centre of the stone, shining up along the blade.

Tom released it quickly, and stepped back.

"Are you all right?" Arthur asked.

"Fine, just nervous," Tom said, feeling bad for lying to Arthur.

Before he could ask anything else, Merlin marshalled them into position. "I want all of you standing well back, against the tree line. Only Filtiarn needs to be in the centre, next to us." He turned to Beansprout. "Stand next to Nimue."

Arthur looked worried. "Why do you need Beansprout?"

"There is power in three. And this is a powerful curse. And there's a line in here I don't fully understand. I'm worried about what it means."

Arthur looked aghast. "Is this a joke? We're about to perform the spell and you don't know what a line means?"

Merlin met his gaze evenly. "No. No-one understands it, not even Filtiarn. But we have to go ahead."

"But why does no-one understand it?" Arthur's voice was raised and impatient.

"Because it's an ancient document, and the language is archaic, as we've explained before." Merlin pointed behind him. "This is no time for arguments, Arthur. Now step back."

Arthur stood his ground and was about to speak again when Nimue interrupted. "Arthur. Step back. We need to begin."

Arthur glared at both of them and retreated to the edge of the grove, standing alone in a brooding silence.

Tom stood next to Elan, who had been quiet all evening and now looked pale and worried. "Are you all right?" Tom asked.

"Not really," he said. "I just want this to be over." He fixed his gaze on those in the centre and refused to say anything else.

Merlin started to speak, but it was in no language Tom could understand. Nimue handed Filtiarn the potion, and when Merlin nodded he drank it down in one long gulp. A shudder ran through him and he coughed. Merlin turned to face the altar stone and Galatine. Nimue and Beansprout joined Merlin's chanting, their voices rising on the air.

The Wolf Moon cleared overhead, filling the grove with a pallid yellow light. As the chanting continued the moon seemed to grow larger and larger until it was pressed over the grove like a gigantic eye. Tom looked up and gasped, not believing what he was seeing. This had to be an illusion. He felt dizzy, and he shook his head as if to clear his vision.

At another gesture from Merlin, Filtiarn stepped forward and grasped Galatine. Immediately a ball of light engulfed Filtiarn and shot up into the sky, straight at the Wolf Moon. Nimue, Beansprout and Merlin stepped back, but continued to chant loudly. Then Filtiarn flew backwards and landed on the ground, seemingly unconscious.

The sword, the stone and the moon remained connected in one blazing beam of light, and a shape rose from Filtiarn's body. The wolves howled around the grove, and Tom's skin prickled all over. He was so tense he could barely breathe. And then the form rising from Filtiarn became clear. It was the shape of a boar, glowing red, and pulsing as if it had a life of its own. It stepped out of Filtiarn and onto the ground next to him, turning to where Tom and Elan stood.

It fixed its hollow eye sockets on them and charged across the clearing. Tom was vaguely aware of shouts all around him. He looked at Elan in shock. Was Elan right? Was the curse about to move to him?

Before Tom could do anything Elan had stepped in front of Tom as if to protect him, holding his arms wide as the boar rushed at him. But the form passed through him and on to Tom, its hollow eye sockets getting bigger and bigger, and then it was on him and in him, and he felt the strange sensation of something settling within his blood and bones and mind.

Tom fell to the floor wondering who was screaming, before realising it was him.

And then he passed out.

35 Possessed

Tom lay on his back staring at the Wolf Moon, which had now returned to its normal size. He ached all over and felt strange. People clustered at the edge of his vision, and he heard Arthur yelling, "This is your fault! I can't believe you have been so stupid!"

Merlin and Nimue replied, but he couldn't tell what they were saying.

Beansprout leaned over him. "Tom, Tom. Thank goodness. You're awake."

Woodsmoke was on his other side, leaning over him too. "Let's help you sit up, Tom."

Tom was dazed, but saw him exchange a worried look with Beansprout as he reached out to squeeze her hand. Woodsmoke put his arm under Tom's shoulders and sat him up.

Tom's vision swam for a few seconds and then everything focused. The fire still burned in the centre of the grove, and Galatine sat in the moonstone, the firelight flickering along the blade. He could even see the stones swirling lazily in the hilt. He could see Rahal sitting by Filtiarn who still lay prone, surrounded by the wolves who sat and whined, or lay next to him on the ground. But Elan sat at Tom's feet looking at him, ashen.

Arthur was standing arguing with Nimue and Merlin, Bloodmoon and Brenna either side of him, Bloodmoon with a restraining hand on Arthur's arm.

Tom looked beyond them into the trees and realised he could see further than normal. The night was less dense. He could see the shapes of leaves and bushes, the tiniest details that should be impossible for him to discern. And he could hear things in the undergrowth – the scuttle of small things, the presence of dryads who remained firmly out of sight, and birds ruffling feathers in their nests. He could smell things too. Everyone had a distinct scent. He turned to Beansprout. "You smell of blossom. It's pretty."

"Blossom?" She looked confused.

"And you smell of some sort of musk," he said to Woodsmoke. "And pine."

"Do I now?" Woodsmoke said, a worried look on his face.

"And I can smell Brenna. She smells of mountain air, with a hint of snow."

As if she'd heard her name, Brenna turned and saw him sitting up. She smiled, relief washing across her face, and prodded Arthur. "Arthur, he's awake."

Arthur broke off and raced over, dropping to his side. "Tom. How are you? Are you all right? Can you feel that ... thing inside you?"

"I'm fine Arthur, slow down." Tom felt a weird calm settle over him, despite the knowledge that some kind of supernatural boar was inside him.

"You're not fine. You are far from fine," Arthur said crossly.

Woodsmoke cut him off, "Arthur, stop it. We don't need this right now."

Arthur glared at Woodsmoke. "What do you suggest?"

"Some rational thinking. And you can stop glaring, it won't work with me." Woodsmoke turned back to Tom. "Let's get you to your feet, shall we?"

Tom nodded, and with Beansprout's help, stood up on slightly shaky legs. Elan remained with him, silently watching.

Tom shook off their help. "I'm OK. I'll stretch my legs for a few minutes."

He took a few faltering steps, and quickly felt stronger, a rush of adrenalin coursing through him. He headed to Rahal's side. "How's Filtiarn?"

"Still unconscious," she said, looking up at him, her eyes bright with tears. "But his breathing's stable. I think he'll be all right."

"We should put him by the fire," Tom said. And without thinking he picked him up as if he was as light as a feather, and carried him to the fireside, throwing his cloak over him. Rahal and the wolves followed, settling around Filtiarn again.

"How did you do that?" Woodsmoke said from behind him.

Tom turned to find everyone watching him. "I don't know. I just did."

Elan spoke. "It's the boar, of course. It's given you extra strength."

Tom looked up at the Wolf Moon. He felt it was laughing at him, and the realisation hit him. "When will I turn?"

Nimue answered, her face drawn. "Two weeks, when the cycle ends, unless we can do something."

The arguing started again.

"We'll make another potion," Arthur said angrily.

"The curse is bound to Galatine," Merlin said. "Which is bound to Tom. To make it leave Tom, Galatine must be bound to someone else. It's a never-ending curse. I think that's what this phrase must mean."

"Oh! Now you know what it means!" Arthur spat. "Well done Merlin."

Beansprout started to cry. "Please don't, Arthur. Today is bad enough. It's my fault too."

Woodsmoke wrapped Beansprout in a hug, and she buried her face in his shoulder.

Arthur looked stricken. "No, I didn't mean …"

"All of you stop. Right now," Tom said. "This isn't helping."

Bloodmoon pulled a small flask from his pocket, removed the stopper and took a long drink. He passed it to Arthur. "We need to think this through. Let's sit."

Arthur looked as if he was going to argue again, but instead raised the flask to his lips.

Tom shot Bloodmoon a grateful look and threw more wood on the fire. He pulled Galatine free from the moonstone and sat on the Avalon stone, warming his feet.

"What do you want to do, Tom?" Bloodmoon asked, sitting on the ground next to Filtiarn and Rahal.

"Find Giolladhe. It seems to me that's my only way out of this."

"I agree. Where do we start?"

Tom smiled. He liked that Bloodmoon was letting him lead rather than telling him what to do. "Good question. There are four realms to find him in, and only two weeks in which to do so." He laughed dryly. "That's not so hard, right?"

"There are places he'll be known to have favoured. We can start there," Woodsmoke suggested. He had stopped comforting Beansprout and they both sat near the fire, passing another flask back and forth. The two of them were so comfortable together, it was as if something was unspoken between them. Woodsmoke looked at Beansprout in a different way to anyone else. Tom turned away, suddenly feeling he was spying on them.

The rest of his friends, realising there was little else they could now do, joined them around the fire, except for Brenna who sat next to Tom on the Avalon stone, nudging him gently along to make room. The moon had retreated to its normal place in the sky – if it had ever moved – and a pale yellow light illuminated the grove. It was an oddly comforting scene. Looking round at them all, Tom realised how much they meant to him. They weren't just his friends, they were his family. To lose them so soon was unthinkable.

"But first we should celebrate," Tom said, desperate to cheer himself and the others up. "For Filtiarn, it's over."

As he spoke Filtiarn blinked and stretched, and Rahal sighed with relief. She eased him upright. "Welcome back," she said, giving him a shy smile.

"I feel different," he said, sounding slightly incredulous. "I can't feel the beast any more."

The joy faded from Rahal's face. "No, it has left you, but moved elsewhere …" Her voice trailed off.

Filtiarn immediately looked at Elan, but he shook his head and nodded towards Tom.

"No. It can't be," he stammered. "How can this have happened?"

"It doesn't matter how," Tom said, reluctant to have the argument start again. "Did the beast make you stronger? You said you could feel it."

Filtiarn looked bewildered. "At first, but then it just ate at me, using my strength. Now it's gone, I feel lighter." He couldn't help grinning. "I can't believe it. You've done it. But the cost –"

"Forget it," Tom said, genuinely pleased to see Filtiarn looking so happy. "You've carried the burden enough. Enjoy your freedom, Filtiarn." Suddenly he knew where he needed to be. "I should rest, I'm going to bed." He stood, and when Woodsmoke went to stand too, said, "No. I want to be alone." He squeezed Woodsmoke's shoulder as he passed. "Goodnight everyone."

And he left the clearing, leaving them talking over his fate.

36 The Forger of Light

Tom didn't waste time sleeping, or even heading to the House of the Beloved. He was going to the Realm of Fire and the dragon.

The second he'd heard the dragon say "Galatine", something had triggered a warning in his head. He could hear it for a reason. It had recognised Galatine. Why would a dragon recognise Galatine unless it had seen the sword before? Unless it had made it.

He had no idea how Giolladhe had become a dragon, but he knew beyond doubt it was him.

Tom still couldn't understand animals, even now he was possessed by a supernatural boar, but he had inherited its strength, and its ability to hear and see far beyond normal human abilities, and this gave him an advantage. He aimed to make full use of that.

He passed down the path to the main road behind Raghnall's house, and then up on to the shoulder of the mountain, avoiding the short cut they had found on the other side of the grove. He had deliberately said nothing to the others. This was his fight, and he didn't want them helping. Even his closest friends. Every single one of them would have insisted on coming, but he didn't want them to. A dragon was deadly, and no-one else should risk their life for him. He wondered if this was the bravado of the boar.

He was worried that he wouldn't find the workshop in the night, but he shouldn't have doubted himself. The Wolf Moon gave him good light, and his eyesight and sense of smell quickly identified the path to him. Soon he stood in front of the copper doorway, looking black in the shadows. Tom opened it – it hadn't been locked – and passed down the passage and into the workshop. He didn't even need to light a lamp, his ability to see in the dark was so good. He carried on past the chimney looming huge in the centre of the room, and through the door at the back, until he reached the cupboard and the hidden portal.

He paused for the briefest of seconds, wondering if the lava had swallowed the room and he would be passing into a fiery death, and then stepped through anyway, arriving with a thump in Giolladhe's other workshop.

Tom felt the beast surging within him, straining against his physical dimensions, as if it couldn't wait to burst into its natural form. He breathed deeply in an effort to subdue it, almost choking on the smell of sulphur, and took his bearings.

The lava pit still bubbled in the centre of the room, the blackened pools around it showing where it had overflowed, but the floor was otherwise undamaged and he could walk over it. He sighed with relief. So far, so good. But best of all, a huge hole had reappeared in the collapsed rock wall, high up towards the roof. The rumbling eruptions must have dislodged the rock. Either that or the djinn had made it.

He scrambled up the rock wall with ease, and looked through to find the other half of the cave deserted. He slid to the floor, kicking up dust as he went, and stood at the entrance to the cavern beyond. In front of him was a scene of chaos. The rivers of lava that had punched through the walls and windows had widened, and they fizzed and hissed as they wound sinuously around fallen lumps of stone, leaving islands of untouched floor in their wake. There was no sign of the dragon or the djinn. His heightened hearing detected a slither of movement in the city beyond, but whether it was lava or dragon, he couldn't tell.

Negotiating the path out to the city was going to be more difficult than it had been days earlier; his jumps needed to be longer and higher. It meant testing his new-found strength. Oh well, better to test it here first than wait until he met the dragon.

Finding the closest place to leap to, he took a deep breath and a running jump. His legs flexed beneath him and he covered the space with ease, shocked at how far he travelled, almost overshooting the island and landing in the lava on the other side. He stopped just in time, perfectly balanced. Wow. That was intense.

Sweat was already beading on his face and down his neck. He could clearly see his path through to the arched entrance and the city beyond, so he pushed on, leaping from island to island and stone to stone, until he landed safely on the other side. He looked back, wondering how he would ever return to the portal if he killed Giolladhe, because his super strength would have gone. He shook the thought out of his head. Too much to do before then.

The shadowy half-collapsed passageways stretched away on either side, and he listened, detecting a slither away to the right. Beneath the smell of dust and sulphur he detected something earthy, a strong musky odour.

Dragon.

He followed the sound and smell along passages he hadn't seen before. The tunnels here were bigger – this must be why the dragon was in this part of the city.

Every now and again he stopped and listened and adjusted his path, crossing collapsed rooms barely lit by smouldering trickles of lava. It was a labyrinth.

And then Tom heard the slow hiss and slither of dragon, but much closer this time. A movement to his left made him spin around and he saw a mammoth wall of flame hurtling towards him. He rolled out of the way into the nearest room, and flattened himself against a wall. A huge roar echoed down the passage, chilling his blood.

Enormous footfalls thudded down the passage, and Tom looked frantically for his best way out. His most effective form of attack would be to circle around behind it, but that was impossible from here. The only way was forward. He ran to a gap in the collapsed wall and passed through to the next room. Another jet of flame followed him, and another roar. He flattened himself along the floor, breathing heavily. He hadn't even seen it yet.

The dragon laughed and then spoke, its voice deep and gravelly. "I know you're there, boy. I sense Galatine. It has been many years since I have seen it."

Tom jumped to his feet and ran into the next room, looking for a way to circle back. He shouted, "Are you Giolladhe? Hiding here beneath the desert like a worm?"

The thump and rumble of dragon's feet stopped. "How do you know my name?"

"Because it's my business to know it," Tom yelled, trying to gauge where the dragon was. He stood at the entrance to the main passage and saw another room opposite. "Any reason you're trying to kill me? Wouldn't you like to chat first? Catch up on old news, find out why I'm carrying Galatine?"

The dragon's voice echoed around him. "If you're carrying Galatine, you're here to kill me. How did you find it?" he growled. "I sent it far from here."

Tom took advantage of the break in fire, and ran across the passage into the room beyond, cursing as another jet of flame followed him. He had to keep the dragon talking while he tried to find a way to attack.

"Your friend Raghnall had it in his weapons collection," he yelled back, running into another room.

The dragon roared, "He is no friend of mine."

"Then you'll be glad to know that we killed him. And then we met your brother!" Tom yelled back, curious to see how that would provoke Giolladhe."

The dragon fell silent, and all Tom could hear was the thumping of his own heart. "Is that a surprise? That he still lives? We've saved him from your curse."

At this Giolladhe laughed, deep and guttural. "So then *you* are cursed, boy. Now I know why you are here and not Filtiarn. You should run, for I am stronger than you."

The rumble of feet headed towards Tom and he darted through another room, finally spotting a door that would allow him to circle back. He scrambled through fallen masonry and caught a glimpse of the dragon through a gap in the wall. It was the colour of sulphur, with deep red flashes of colour along its scales and wing tips. As yet he couldn't see its head. Without hesitation he ran forward, dived through the gap and stabbed Galatine deep into its side.

The dragon howled and roared and whipped around, throwing Tom against the wall, masonry and sand falling as the dragon struggled to manoeuvre in such a small space. Tom scrambled free and ran back along the passage, diving into the first available doorway.

He waited for the sound of falling stone and sand to stop, hoping the entire city wouldn't fall on his head before he killed Giolladhe and got out. Spying a gap at the top of the wall, he scrambled up to look through to the passage beyond, planning to leap onto the dragon's back, but it had disappeared.

Tom saw a flicker of dragon tail heading into a room further along. He leapt down and ran towards it, following Giolladhe into a much larger space with a domed ceiling and beams running under it. Now he could see him fully, his nerve almost failed. Giolladhe had turned to face him, and he was huge, his head bristling with sharp spiky scales, his eyes red and burning. He flexed his wings, smacking them off the walls. Lowering his head, he opened his mouth, giving a glimpse of razor-sharp teeth before spitting a wall of flame.

Tom dived out of the way, and taking advantage of the ruptured walls, scrambled upwards, grabbing a beam above his head and pulling himself onto it. He raced along until he was above the dragon and out of his line of fire. He was just about to leap onto the dragon's spiny back when a swirl of dust and sand rose in front of him and the djinn appeared, settling on one of the beams.

"You need to stop, boy," the djinn said, looking regretful.

Beneath him, Giolladhe roared, flexing his wings as he tried to turn and look upwards.

"Why?" Tom demanded, frustrated he would miss his chance.

"Because I can't let you kill him."

"Well that's just tough, because I *have* to kill him. He's cursed my sword, and now me." Tom launched himself onto the dragon's back, bringing Galatine down with enormous force, puncturing the dragon's wing and piercing his thick scaly skin with a satisfying crunch. As it flexed and howled, Tom fell off, slithering to the ground, where the edge of a wing caught him, throwing him across the floor. He rolled to his feet and found the djinn in front of him. He picked Tom up and flung him across the room and into the wall, where he landed with a crash.

Adrenalin surged through Tom, dulling the pain. He staggered to his feet, furious. "What are you doing?"

"If you want to kill the dragon, you have to kill me first."

Tom pointed Galatine at the djinn. "Why in the Realms do you want to keep that thing alive?"

"Because it was us – the djinn – who turned him into this creature, as a punishment for many transgressions. It is my job to keep him alive so that he suffers here forever. I will not let you kill him and relieve him of that torture."

Tom couldn't believe it. "I hate to break it to you, but he seems pretty fine with being a dragon. He's not exactly letting me end his years of torture."

Giolladhe sent a blast of flame at the djinn, causing him to dissolve into sand and whirl across the floor. Tom ran headlong at the dragon and again plunged Galatine deep into his side, before ducking out of reach of his giant wings. Giolladhe's roar thundered around the room.

The djinn reappeared, lifting Tom up around the throat with his hideous long clawed hands, until he was at eye level and Tom's feet were dangling in the air. "If you don't stop, I will have to kill you."

"Then you'll have to kill me," Tom managed to say, struggling to speak. And before he knew what he was doing, Tom thrust his sword at the djinn, feeling the slight resistance of flesh, before the djinn turned into sand and dropped Tom to the floor.

Tom ran for the wall and bounded up, his feet easily finding footholds, and then leapt onto the beams overhead. He couldn't believe he was having to fight a djinn and a dragon. Fortunately it seemed the more he fought, the stronger he became, the wild power of the boar within him raging with strength.

The djinn reappeared, clutching his side, dark green blood leaking onto his clawed hands. "You struck me!" He was more puzzled than outraged.

"You won't stop me," Tom said, surprised by how calm he was feeling. He had never felt so determined. It was as if he stood in the eye of a storm. "I don't want to hurt you, but I will if you don't walk away."

For a second the djinn hesitated. "You are not what you appear. You are too quick. Too strong."

"You better believe it."

Beneath them Giolladhe turned and twisted, furious at being attacked. Then he looked up, and was about to send a burst of flame at Tom when Tom dived over his head and landed on his back. Shocked at his own agility, he again plunged his sword through the scales and between the spines that ran along the dragon's back, feeling the crunch of bone. He pushed deeper as the dragon howled in pain, and Tom felt something snap as the dragon's neck flopped downwards.

If dragons had a spinal cord, Tom was pretty sure he'd just severed it. Galatine was buried up to its hilt in the dragon's back, and he wrenched it free then slid down the side of the dragon onto the floor. He glanced up at the djinn, but strangely the djinn didn't try to stop him; he just watched, green blood dripping down his side.

Tom circled to Giolladhe's head. The dragon was struggling to keep his eyes open. "What have you done to me?" he grunted, his guttural voice becoming more difficult to understand.

"What I had to do," Tom said, feeling regret at the situation he found himself in. "Filtiarn was your brother, Giolladhe. He trusted you. How could you do that to him?"

"Because he would have ruined everything."

Tom wanted to ask so many more questions, to try and understand, but he didn't think he ever would. And Giolladhe, even now, didn't seem to have an ounce of regret. Tom looked in wonder at the huge bulk of his body, the slow heave of his chest, the wings collapsed at his side, and felt an overwhelming sadness. He readied Galatine, raising it above his head.

"I'm about to release both of us, Giolladhe. You may not deserve it, but I know I do."

He brought his sword down and sliced through sinew and bone, taking off Giolladhe's head in one clean cut.

37 The Tale is Complete

Tom staggered back and sank to the floor, leaning against the wall. He was exhausted. He felt the beast within him struggle and thrash around, and then a supernatural mist oozed out of every pore.

As it left him, he felt incredibly weak; his muscles ached and his vision dimmed, making him aware of how powerful his night vision had been. Now all he could see was the big black bulk of the dragon, lit only by the palest fiery glow of lava.

But he had done it. He had lifted the curse. He laughed into the darkness, like a madman.

Now he just had to get out.

The djinn reappeared in front of him, still clutching his side. "You were possessed?" he asked, his eyes lit by the pale flames which burnt within him.

"Yes," Tom said, staggering to his feet. His legs trembled with weakness. "Ow. That really aches." He looked warily at the djinn. "Are you going to kill me now?"

"No, why would I do that?"

"Well I did stab you and ruin your life's mission," Tom said, trying to suppress the shake in his arm as he held Galatine.

"How many beings do you think have ever injured me?"

"I don't know. The dragon must have a few times."

"No-one except you." The djinn was looking at him curiously. "I'm impressed – even if you were possessed. I have never seen my own blood spilt before in battle. I do not like it."

"Lucky you," Tom said. "I've seen mine plenty of times – including now." He looked down at his arms and legs, which were covered in scratches and cuts.

The djinn laughed, although it sounded more like a growl. "We will both live."

"Will we? Because I'm not sure I'm going to get back to the portal,"

Tom said. If he could walk back down the pathways of the underground city, it would be a miracle.

"Come, my friend. I will help."

Before Tom could protest, the djinn picked him up and bounded down the corridors with loping grace, despite his injury. He leapt across fallen walls, chunks of stone and lava with ease, depositing Tom outside the portal door once more.

Tom felt dazed, and stood swaying, looking around the room at the remnants of equipment and tools, wondering what dark and strange magic Giolladhe would once have woven down here. He looked at the djinn. "Thank you. Where will you go now this is over?"

"Azkrill, the capital of our fair realm, far to the east, in the blazing deserts of Sansarkan. I will speak of Tom, the dragon slayer; slayer of Giolladhe, the Forger of Light, saviour of Filtiarn, beast possessed, djinn-wounding warrior, bearer of Galatine."

Tom had to admit that sounded quite impressive. Maybe he should adopt it as his title. "And your name?"

"Valaal, Keeper of the Forger of Light."

Tom smiled, grateful for this crazy experience. "Good to meet you, Valaal." He gestured towards the workshop. "I guess this will be the last time I see this?"

"Yes. I will seal the portal once you have gone," Valaal said. "The whole city will collapse soon anyway, 'tis best no-one comes here again."

Tom felt strangely reluctant to go. "Maybe we will meet again one day."

"Maybe we will," Valaal said, a slow smile spreading across his face.

"Before I go, will you tell me a little bit more about Giolladhe and why he was turned into a dragon? I really want to know. Everything he did is so mysterious, and so long ago."

Valaal nodded. "All right. But my heart hurts to think of it."

And for a little while, Tom ignored the threat of death by lava, and listened to the djinn.

For a few seconds Tom thought he was stuck in the portal, the room beyond was so dark, and then he remembered he'd come here with no light to guide him. To his left a faint grey strip leaked into the room, revealing the edge of the doorway. Staggering to his feet, he stumbled through the central room and down the corridor to where the front door hung open, early morning sunshine blazing through.

He shielded his eyes, temporarily blinded by the light. He was halfway down the path when he heard a shout. "He's here!"

Woodsmoke ran towards him, closely followed by Beansprout. They both looked worried, and if Tom was honest, a bit distracted.

Woodsmoke crushed him in a hug. "Where have you been?"

"And what have you been doing?" Beansprout said, looking shocked. "You're filthy! And covered in blood. Are you hurt?" She reached out and hugged him, regardless. "Great Herne, you stink. Again. And what's that weird green stuff on you?"

"Beansprout," Tom protested, "will you stop asking questions!"

Bloodmoon and Arthur rounded a corner, Bloodmoon looking quite cavalier and not the least bit worried, whereas Arthur was frowning. Bloodmoon grinned as he saw Tom, and then looked a little put out. "I smell sulphur. Someone's been hunting dragons. Could've let me know, Tom."

Arthur ran forward, pulling Tom into a hug, and then looked at him carefully. "Dragons? Don't be ridiculous, Bloodmoon. Are you all right, Tom? We've been searching for hours. This is the *last* place we thought we'd find you. Merlin and Nimue are in the passageways beneath the house."

"Where did you think I'd go?" Tom asked, incredulous.

"I honestly thought you'd gone to sulk, you know how you do sometimes," Beansprout said, sounding slightly sheepish at her accusation.

Tom was about to complain when, with a whirr of wings, Brenna landed next to them on the path. "Tom! I've been searching the forest. I'm so relieved …" She trailed off as she took in his appearance. "What have you been doing?"

Arthur ploughed on regardless. "We've been trying to figure out a plan to get rid of this curse." His voice was grumpy, now his relief at finding Tom had worn off. "You can't just go wandering off."

Tom was tired and starting to get annoyed. Did everyone really think he was so stupid? "I have been fighting a dragon, and getting rid of this curse. What do you think I've been doing?"

"Getting rid of the curse?" Arthur said, looking startled. "What do you mean?"

"I mean I've killed Giolladhe. I thought I would take matters into my own hands."

"You killed a dragon?" Beansprout said, admiration in her eyes. "Tom!

You're amazing."

"Yes," he said smugly, "I am. And now I need a bath and a sleep."

Arthur looked put out. "You didn't tell *me* I was amazing when I killed a dragon."

"Oh, Arthur," Beansprout said. "You're always amazing, you know that."

Tom pushed through them all, trying to suppress a grin, but they followed him doggedly back to the house, asking question after question, until he reached the door of his room. "All of you, please, leave me in peace! I'll tell you later." And he shut his door with a big smile.

Hours later, after a bath and having slept most of the day, Tom headed down to the balcony and found the table glittering with candlelight, silverware and cut glass. The entire household was either gathered around the table, or reclining on chairs looking out over Dragon's Hollow.

Nimue rose to greet him. She was as dazzling as the silverware. Her dark hair cascaded over her shoulders, and she wore a deep green silk dress that matched her eyes. "Glad you're here, Tom. I gather I need to congratulate you." She stood on tiptoes and kissed his cheek. "I'm not sure whether you're crazy or brilliant."

Tom couldn't help blushing. "Brilliant, of course." He thought he'd try and cover his embarrassment through bluffing, and besides, he could see Woodsmoke smirking. Ignoring him, he said, "I'm sorry if I worried everyone. I just knew what I needed to do and got on with it. And I didn't want to risk anyone else getting hurt."

"Very noble of you," Merlin said, coming over to shake his hand. "If a little foolhardy."

Arthur frowned at Merlin, then pulled a chair out for Tom and pushed a drink into his hands. "Come, sit down, Tom. You're the guest of honour. We've cooked roast suckling pig especially for you."

"My favourite beer! And my favourite food! Wow, I am being spoiled," he said, laughing.

Brenna slid into the seat next to him. Her dark eyes looked huge in the candlelight, and the fine feathers around her hairline reflected the light, giving her a dark glow. She gave him a playful punch on his arm. "How did you know the dragon was Giolladhe?"

"Because it spoke to me, and it knew what Galatine was. Who else would know that?" He shrugged. "It bothered me when I was leaving the Realm of Fire the first time, but I was in such a rush to get back, I didn't really think about it. And then, last night, I just knew."

"So you found my brother," Filtiarn said. He looked solemn and sad, and not as relieved as Tom thought he would.

Tom met his eyes across the table, noting how old and frail he looked. After his initial jubilation at the curse being broken, he now looked like an old man again. "I did, and I'm sorry I had to kill him."

"You had to do it, Tom, or you would have suffered my fate, and I wouldn't wish that on anyone. I have lost my youth, my life, my love and my children, all for the possibility of my making peace with dragons." Filtiarn looked puzzled. "And you say he was a dragon, which seems fitting. How did that happen?"

"Valaal, the djinn, told me their magician had transformed him years ago when they found the depth of his betrayal of them. For years Giolladhe had a second workshop in the Realm of Fire. It was beneath the citadel on the edge of the city of Erfann – it's where the portal led – and he used the fire of the mountains to fuel his more complicated spells. But his experiments caused problems. The mountains of fire erupted, the dragons attacked, and eventually Erfann was destroyed – this was sometime after the dragon wars. Years later, after the sylphs found out Giolladhe had double- crossed them with his so-called gift of protection, he had to flee the Hollow, pretty much as we guessed. Raghnall had refused to stand by him and essentially blamed him for everything. The djinns offered him refuge in Azkrill, their capital city. However, Giolladhe got up to his old tricks, betrayed people, double-crossed them, and eventually ended up endangering Azkrill, so they took him to Erfann where their magician transformed him, and Valaal was appointed his keeper. I felt really sorry for the djinn, and I liked Valaal. And that's as much as I know – if I've remembered it properly."

Filtiarn was silent for a moment, and then took a long drink. "So much betrayal, so much greed. I feel like I never knew him."

"You never suspected?" Arthur asked.

"We were very different," Filtiarn admitted, "but I never suspected him of such deception. It makes me question everything. Every conversation, every interaction. But I wonder where all his wealth went? He lived in a cave. It was plain, unembellished."

"That is an excellent question," Bloodmoon said. "I must make enquiries."

Filtiarn looked at Tom with an almost pleading expression. "Did he say anything about me?"

"Not really," Tom said, "other than he did it to stop you ruining everything. I'm sorry."

Filtiarn pushed his plate away, falling silent, and Tom thought he should change the subject. He turned to Beansprout. "It was the djinn's blood on me earlier – the green stuff."

"You killed a djinn?" Beansprout said, looking both horrified and impressed.

"No! I injured it. It was trying to protect Giolladhe to prolong the punishment. Anyway, he forgave me, and now we're friends – sort of."

"You injured a djinn?" Bloodmoon asked, stopping eating in surprise.

"Yes. Accidentally."

"Not many can do that, Tom."

Tom swallowed a mouthful of delicious pork. "That's what he said, but it was only because that supernatural beast was in me. It gave me superpowers. It was very cool," he said, thoughtfully, wishing he could have kept the superpowers. "That's another reason I went there straightaway. I was strong and I knew it, and I didn't know how long it would last."

Elan interrupted. "It should have been me. Who was cursed, I mean." He had been quiet up until now, watching Tom and the others. He seemed very worried.

Tom looked at him, confused. "You mean you should have had the sword?"

"No, I mean as Filtiarn's relative. You shouldn't have had to suffer that."

"Elan, it wasn't your fault. I activated the sword, not you. It was just the way it was." Tom really loved Galatine, despite everything that had happened, and he knew Filtiarn didn't want it – but what if Elan did? What if he thought it was his birthright? "Do you want Galatine? If you do, it's yours." He pulled it free from its scabbard and placed it on the table. He had shined and polished it that afternoon, cleaning away every trace of blood and flesh.

Arthur frowned and said, "Tom!" at exactly the same time as Filtiarn said, "Elan!"

Tom stopped them both with a calm look. "It's OK."

They watched as Elan picked up the sword and ran his hands along it, the swirling opals quickening at his touch. And then he looked at Tom and smiled. "No, it yours. You've earned it. But thanks for asking."

Tom grinned. "Thanks for not having it. I *really* like that sword." And he put it back in its scabbard.

Woodsmoke gave Tom the ghost of a smile, and then turned to Filtiarn, Rahal and Elan. "So what now?"

"Now we go home," Rahal said, glancing at Filtiarn. "Our family will want to see Filtiarn. I suppose we'll have a celebration."

"And I suppose I will die very soon after that," Filtiarn said, staring into his drink.

"What?" Tom said, almost choking.

Everyone stopped eating and looked at Filtiarn.

"I am dying. I know I am. Ever since the curse has broken I feel my vast age pouring back into me. The beast has taken its toll. I want to make it home, spend my last days there overlooking the ocean, remembering better days. And then you can bury me in the family tomb, next to my love." He directed this last statement to Rahal and Elan.

"But I wanted you to have many happy years yet," Rahal said, her eyes starting to fill with tears.

He patted her hands. "My dear, you have nothing to feel sorry for." He turned to the others and raised his glass. "But tonight we celebrate, because the curse is over."

There was a resounding clinking of glass and calls of congratulations, and then Nimue turned to Arthur. "And what about you? I suppose you'll be returning to New Camelot?"

"Of course, with Merlin, Tom and Woodsmoke."

They nodded in agreement.

"What about you, Bloodmoon?"

"I'll join Filtiarn in their ride across the moors," he said, looking at Rahal rather than Filtiarn. Tom grinned and Rahal blushed. "And then, who knows? I'll go where the adventure takes me."

"As long as it's not into trouble," Woodsmoke said. "I don't want to have to break you out of prison."

"It's good to know that you would, should I ever need it," Bloodmoon said in all seriousness, leaving Woodsmoke gaping at him.

"I will journey to New Camelot with you, and then return to Aeriken," Brenna said with a sigh. "There is talk of a coronation."

"Really?" Beansprout said, excited. "You've finally agreed?"

Brenna shrugged. "Sort of. As long as you all come for the ceremony."

A chorus of agreement ran around the table, and everyone looked excited except Arthur, who seemed a little worried. "You shouldn't do it unless you're absolutely sure. It's a lot of work, you know."

"I'm already doing the work, I may as well just go ahead. It will make the Aeriken happy." She glanced around the table and wagged an admonishing finger. "But don't you dare leave me out of anything!"

"Or me!" Beansprout added. "I'm staying here, of course. I have to continue my training."

Tom looked around the table, at his friends laughing and talking, and felt excited for his future. He grabbed his drink. "I'd like to propose a toast!" He grinned at them as they raised their glasses. "To friendship!"

Author's Note

Thank you for reading my series Tom's Arthurian Legacy. I hope you enjoyed reading Tom's adventures with King Arthur.

I've always enjoyed the King Arthur stories, particularly the mix of magic and reality - that hint of the Other that exists where we can't quite see it. I decided I wanted to see what would happen if King Arthur returned to this different world. It's been a lot of fun writing it, and hopefully was fun reading it.

I am planning another book in this series, and the characters will continue to grow, and I'm sure there'll be new characters too!

All authors love reviews. They're important because they help drive sales and promotions, so please leave a review on either Amazon or Goodreads – or another retailer of your choice! Your review is much appreciated.

If you'd like to read more about Tom, you can get a free short story called *Jack's Encounter*, describing how Jack met Fahey – a longer version of the prologue in *Tom's Inheritance* – by subscribing to my newsletter. You'll also receive a short story prequel about how Excalibur was made, called *Excalibur Rises*.

By staying on my mailing list you'll receive free excerpts of my new books, as well as short stories and news of giveaways. I'll also be sharing information about other books in this genre you might enjoy.

To get your FREE short story please visit my website -
http://www.tjgreen.nz

I look forward to you joining my readers' group.

About the Author

T.J. Green grew up in England and now lives in the Hutt Valley, near Wellington, New Zealand, with her partner Jason, and her cats Sacha and Leia. When she's not writing, she enjoys reading, gardening, shopping and yoga.

In a previous life she's been a singer in a band, and has done some acting with a theatre company – both of which were lots of fun. On occasions she and a few friends make short films, which begs the question, where are the book trailers? Coming soon …

Other ongoing projects include a book set in the real world (whatever that is) – but there will be unusual things happening.

Website: http://www.tjgreen.nz

Facebook: https://www.facebook.com/tjgreenauthor/

Twitter: https://twitter.com/tjay_green

Pinterest: https://nz.pinterest.com/mount0live/my-books-and-writing/

Goodreads:
https://www.goodreads.com/author/show/15099365.T_J_Green

Instagram: https://www.instagram.com/mountolivepublishing/

Made in the USA
Lexington, KY
20 December 2018